LOVE UNDER THE STARS

"It's not often that a man gets to take a girl to watch the sky at night." Burch was speaking almost to himself. "It makes you look at things differently."

"How's that?" she managed to ask without her voice quavering.

"I can't say for sure. Sky is sky and I've spent more nights in the open than in a proper bed, but when a man has a woman to watch out for, it's not the same."

Sibyl's heart was pounding so loudly she could hardly hear his words. "I like being here," she answered. "I can't understand why, but I feel like I belong."

"It's because you were never meant to be caught in the web of staid Virginia society. You're just as wild as those cattle down there, and your spirit needs just as much space as they do."

His body was next to hers, making it hard for her to think about space, spirits, or anything else. His hands no longer held hers but were traveling hungrily over her body, exploring and setting her skin on fire. She felt helplessly carried away on a raging, uncontrollable torrent of sensation.

She tried to resist, at least she thought she did, but the heat coursing through her had changed into a desire that matched his. Burch was beyond the power of words, his aching need blotting out everything but his own overwhelming hunger. . . .

Other *Leisure* and *Love Spell* books by Leigh Greenwood:
The Cowboys Series:
JAKE
WARD
BUCK
CHET
SEAN
PETE
DREW
LUKE
MATT

The *Seven Brides* Series:
ROSE
FERN
IRIS
LAUREL
DAISY
VIOLET
LILY

Leigh Greenwood

WYOMING
Wildfire

LOVE SPELL NEW YORK CITY

To Fran, Judy, Lee, Sheri, and the CRW.

A LOVE SPELL BOOK®

November 2001

Published by

Dorchester Publishing Co., Inc.
276 Fifth Avenue
New York, NY 10001

If you purchased this book without a cover you should be aware that this book is stolen property. It was reported as "unsold and destroyed" to the publisher and neither the author nor the publisher has received any payment for this "stripped book."

Copyright © 1987 by Leigh Greenwood

All rights reserved. No part of this book may be reproduced or transmitted in any form or by any electronic or mechanical means, including photocopying, recording or by any information storage and retrieval system, without the written permission of the publisher, except where permitted by law.

ISBN 0-505-52459-7

The name "Love Spell" and its logo are trademarks of Dorchester Publishing Co., Inc.

Printed in the United States of America.

Visit us on the web at www.dorchesterpub.com.

WYOMING
Wildfire

Chapter 1

Burch Randall, in no hurry to reach his destination, allowed Old Blue to canter on a slack rein. The searing heat of the summer sun was mercifully eased by cooler, drier winds that swept down from the hills, but the season had been without rain and the range more closely resembled a desert than the lush grasslands that had drawn the first cattlemen to Wyoming in the late 1860's. Yet not even the chance of a thunderstorm could keep his mind off the problem that had bedeviled him for weeks. Everyone at the Elkhorn Ranch knew that the new heir arrived today and that Burch was as mad as a wounded grizzly that he would have to share ownership with a twenty-year-old girl from Virginia.

Grinding his teeth in helpless frustration, Burch unknowingly pulled back on the reins. Old Blue resented the unwarranted check and sidestepped in protest. Burch smothered a curse, relaxed his grip, and allowed his mount to settle into an easy stride once more.

Old Blue pricked his ears and slipped into a nervous canter as half a dozen antelope burst from a small canyon just ahead. The fleet animals glided across the plain with effortless grace, but just as the horse and rider reached the mouth of the canyon, a lone buck catapulted across their path almost on top of them. Old Blue shied abruptly at the sound of a rifle shot ricocheting down the canyon.

"You're too old to be spooked by antelope," Burch said, pulling him back on the trail just as a second bullet passed through the sleeve of his shirt, painfully grazing his arm. "Damnation!" he ejaculated furiously. Driving his spurs into his horse's sides, he galloped into the mouth of the canyon, bent on finding out who was fool enough to fire wildly after a fleeing herd. But when he reached the far end he was forced to pull up in disgust; he hadn't seen anyone and it was next to impossible to find tracks on the dry, stony ground. "Damned fool's too much of a coward to show his face," he cursed and turned Old Blue back toward home. Probably some dude from one of the ranches near Laramie, he thought. They occasionally wandered off the beaten path and became a menace until they could be rounded up again. He'd have to bring it up at the stockmen's fall meeting. It was time to do something when a man couldn't ride his own range without being shot at.

A hot stinging reminded him of his wound. He reached around the back of his arm and his fingers came away bloody. It wasn't much—no need to bother with it until he reached home—but it ruined a perfectly good shirt.

Nothing else appeared in the broad expanse of the Laramie River basin to command his attention and his thoughts soon returned to their unprofitable musings. His Uncle Wesley hadn't felt he could leave the ranch away from his only blood kin, but he had anticipated his niece would sell her half or quietly accept her share of the profits, not move out West. "She'll probably expect to get milk from a steer," Burch muttered angrily to the uninterested wind and his

8

equally indifferent horse. He could have paid her a good price, even by Eastern standards. The cattle market was booming, and though his ranch couldn't match some of the company-owned spreads above Cheyenne or in Montana, the Elkhorn was one of the largest privately owned ranches in Wyoming and certainly the best run.

Ever since he was ten years old, he had worked as hard as any paid hand to earn the position he now held. "You can't expect a man to do any job you can't do yourself" had been his uncle's favorite maxim. So it was a bitter day when the lawyer told him that not only was his cousin not going to sell, she had decided to come out West to run *her* ranch. The lawyer had listened patiently while Burch turned the air blue with curses, but when his temper cooled he knew he was helpless to prevent the unwanted arrival. Without lifting a finger, she had as much right to live at the Elkhorn as he had after close to twenty years of unremitting labor.

Damn the woman, he thought, kicking his horse into an easy gallop. If she looks anything like Uncle Wesley's brother, she has a face like a mottled cow. Not the kind of girl he wanted to marry. *That* had been the lawyer's idea, not his. His uncle had urged him to marry right after Aunt Ada's death, and for a while he stirred up hopes in the bosoms of several beauties all too ready to share his bed and wealth. Unfortunately, they didn't share his interest in the ranch and the hard work that weathered his handsome features, hardened his muscled body, or produced his wealth. Maybe it was time to settle down, but twenty-eight was still young.

"Hell," he swore with conviction, if anything happened to him now, the ranch would go to his cousin. He'd be damned if he'd see a lifetime's work turned over to some female itching to play at ranching. Most likely she'd run it into the ground in a few years and have to sell out to the first person to make her an offer. Then she'd go back East and boast for the rest of her life of having lived in the wild West. It had been his uncle's dream to see Wyoming become a state, and Burch was determined to be the owner of the Elkhorn when that day arrived.

The double yoke of oxen plodded steadily across the open plain through an enveloping silence that was punctuated only by the squeaks of protest from the overloaded wagon as it bumped over the uneven ground. The two women inside could not discern a path through the buffalo and blue grama grass, but the driver, following careful instructions received at the ranch where they had spent the previous night, was confident they would reach their destination well before sunset. He would be glad of it, too, since in all his years on the range he had seldom had a more difficult job.

A crippled ex-cowpuncher, it was difficult for Ned Wright to find any kind of work, so when he was offered the chance of a permanent position if he would drive two women and their belongings to a ranch north of Laramie, he didn't hesitate. He congratulated himself on his luck when he got his first look at the pair of them. Both were handsome women, but there was nothing in the territory that could hold a candle to that younger one.

Less than twelve hours later he was scratching his head and wondering how any girl could look so pretty and soft on the outside and still be tough as shoe leather on the inside. Pretty girls were supposed to give over to a man, not order him about like a drover on roundup. Still, he was well paid for his trouble, and if he decided not to stay, all he would have to listen to on his way back was the jingle of gold coins in his pocket.

The younger of the two women put her head through the flaps. Thick golden hair falling below her shoulders framed a complexion of creamy smoothness. "That rancher said we had to keep a good pace if we were to reach the Elkhorn before nightfall."

It was uttered as a simple statement, but Ned bridled, feeling his competence was being questioned. "This is a good pace, miss. We've still got four or five more hours of daylight, and that'll be more than enough, even if we get lost."

"We look lost now," said Sibyl Cameron, surveying the emptiness around her and shading her deep blue eyes with slim fingers. "Can't you find some shade? My aunt is suffering dreadfully from this heat."

"There's no shade to be had for anything but lizards and jackrabbits."

"My aunt is neither," the girl responded dryly.

No sense of humor either, he thought. "We're coming up to a river," he said aloud. "She can rest while I water the oxen."

"She doesn't need rest, she needs shade."

"Don't bother the poor man on my account, dear. You can't expect him to produce trees where there aren't any." The soft voice belonged to Augusta Hauxhurst, a very attractive woman barely ten years older than her niece, yet the difference in dress and character made them seem decades apart. Augusta wore her ash-blond hair in a tight bun and protected her fair complexion with a broad-brimmed straw hat. She looked very much like her niece, with the same generous mouth and delicately chiseled nose, but her blue-gray eyes and serene countenance lacked the vivacity and intensity that characterized Sibyl.

"There must be trees somewhere. This whole territory can't be covered in nothing but rocks and grass."

"The lawyer did try to warn you," her aunt ventured timidly.

"He said the climate was uncomfortable and the range-

11

lands unending. He never said the place was a virtual desert. I can't see how a camel can survive here, much less thousands of cows."

"I feel sure, dear, that if he says cows live here in great numbers, we shall soon discover that they do."

"Aunt Augusta," Sibyl said with a grunt of disgust, "why must you accept everything a man says without question?"

"They do know more about these things than we women."

"*I* know as much about farms and cows as any man," her niece asserted. Her eyes flashed in defiance while the sun reflected the myriad shades of gold in her cascading hair.

"But you've never been here before, and it does seem a rather desolate place."

Sibyl dared not admit to her aunt that she had already begun to question the wisdom of leaving Virginia. From the safety of her parlor it seemed like such a good idea, but now that she was actually face to face with the yawning wilderness, she wondered if it might not have been more prudent to accept the money and settle for a conventional existence. A mental image of her second cousin utterly routed that thought. Nothing could possibly be worse than being married to Kendrick.

Sibyl's beauty, trim figure, and old family had insured her popularity but no acceptable offers of marriage. A moderate fortune, an educated mind, independent ways, and a sharp tongue had kept all but her thick-skinned cousin at a distance. That had all changed, much to her cynical amusement, as soon as it became known she had inherited a prosperous cattle ranch. The latest aspirant to her hand was Moreton Swan of the Moreton Swan & Son Hardware and Farm Supply Company. She didn't mind hardware — one had to earn a living somehow — but she did mind Moreton Swan. No white-columned mansion on a hill was worth being mauled by that brute.

"It can't all be this bad," she said to her aunt with forced enthusiasm. "If Uncle Wesley loved it so much, there must be something about it we haven't seen yet."

"What?" asked her aunt, willing to be convinced.

"I don't know, but it has several advantages over Lexington: No one has ever heard of Moreton Swan and his wandering hands, or his mother and her beady eyes, or his father and his drooling mouth."

"Sibyl, you must not talk like that," her aunt reproved. "I know you don't like Moreton and his family, but—"

"I *loathe* Moreton and everything connected with him," she stated flatly.

She's a spirited filly all right, Ned thought, chuckling silently to himself, but with those looks it would certainly be worth the trouble to tame her. After staying a bachelor for thirty-seven years he wasn't thinking of trying himself, but he'd give a year's wages to see what happened when she met a man who could handle her.

They reached the river. The drought and blistering sun had reduced it to a tepid, slightly alkaline ribbon. Ned unhitched the oxen and the sensible beasts waded in, took a few swallows, and then waited patiently before drinking again. Sibyl climbed down to stretch her stiff legs. "I hope we get some rain before night," she remarked to her aunt, pointing to a horizon that was beginning to show red in the west. But Augusta wasn't interested in talking about the weather or exposing her tender skin to the broiling sun, and Sibyl was left to walk in silence. Meanwhile, Ned tested the river bed for a crossing, but the more he walked through the water, the more uneasy he became.

"They should have had enough to drink by now," Sibyl said, impatient to resume their journey. "My aunt can't stand much more. How much farther do we have to go?"

"No more than fifteen or twenty miles, as best I can figure.

13

We ought to make it in about three or four hours."

"Thank goodness. I can't wait to be through with this interminable journey. I've been thinking of a long hot bath for days."

Ned couldn't help staring. He had never seen a bathtub outside Laramie. Cowboys bathed in creeks or water troughs, but he couldn't imagine the proper Miss Cameron settling for anything like that. "I don't think we should cross here," he said, wading farther out into the river. "The bottom is too sandy."

"How can it be too sandy when we've seen nothing but rocks for the last hundred miles?"

"It washes down with the spring runoff," answered Ned, unsure of just where the sand did come from.

"It does that everywhere, but there's always a bed of rock underneath. How far is the next ford?"

"I don't know."

"Then how do you propose to find out?" she asked crisply.

"Follow the river until we come to one."

"But that could take hours, and my aunt's nearly exhausted now."

"If we get stuck, you'll have to unload the whole wagon," Ned warned.

"I guess we can wait while you take a few of the smaller trunks across."

"I can't, not with this leg," he said, pointing to the twisted limb that had ended his days in the saddle.

"Then we'll cross here," she decreed. "I've crossed hundreds of streams without the least bit of trouble."

"But that was in Virginia, dear," cautioned her aunt. "Maybe you should listen to Mr. Wright."

"Not if it means spending the rest of the day following this river. I want to reach the Elkhorn before midnight. If you don't want to drive the wagon, then I'll do it." Sibyl informed

14

him, climbing into the driver's seat.

Ned hitched up the team, his final protest receiving short shrift. As he waded toward midstream, the sluggish water barely up to his knees, his ever alert eyes noticed a rider in the distance. It was possible the man knew of a safe crossing, but even as the rider paused, Ned decided not to signal him. You never knew what kind of man you might meet on the range, and he didn't want to invite trouble. He waded on across.

The far bank was low enough for the oxen to pull the wagon out and Ned waved Sibyl in. She gathered up the reins and eased the wagon down the bank and into the water. At least she knows something about driving, he thought.

Sibyl angled upstream into the current until halfway across, then straightened out again. She kept the oxen at their task, never permitting the wagon to stop or the weight to mire them down. Yet she didn't hurry them or wear them out unnecessarily. She was beginning to feel rather smug when ten feet from shore she felt the ground give way under her wheels. She cracked the whip sharply, but the efforts of the straining beasts could not keep the wagon moving and she did not abuse them. "We're stuck," she acknowledged, thoroughly annoyed and somewhat chagrined. "I hope it's not quicksand."

"Quicksand!" exclaimed her aunt in wide-eyed terror. "But we can't die here, we just *can't*!"

"It's okay, Aunt Augusta, we can always walk to shore. But I'm afraid it will mean the loss of all our things." Her afflicted aunt, caught between the fear of drowning or facing strangers in no more than a soaked petticoat, looked perilously close to fainting.

"It's not quicksand," Ned reassured her. "If we throw out those heavy trunks, we can probably drive the wagon out."

"What's the use of saving the wagon if we lose everything

in it?" Sibyl asked, her temper showing signs of fraying.

"If it means having to remain in the middle of this river, I think I'd rather do without my clothes," her aunt decided. "I can't think it would be comfortable for very long."

"It won't come to that," Sibyl smiled, forcing her temper down. "We'll take a few things with us and send someone back for the rest. I suppose they will be safe enough."

They disappeared behind the canvas flaps to choose what to take with them, unaware that the distant rider had left his observation post. Ned was not unaware, however, and he watched the stranger's approach apprehensively.

Chapter 2

The rider sat in the saddle with negligent ease as his mount dodged gopher holes and leapt over the uneven ground. Even on horseback he looked extraordinarily tall. Powerful legs, bare of chaps, wrapped themselves securely about the barrel of the blue-grey gelding while the loose-fitting shirt and vest could not disguise his broad shoulders and chest. Except for the square chin and clean-shaven cheeks, his face was hidden under the low brim of his hat. His mount's steel-shod hooves sent a shower of small stones into the river as he pulled up at the water's edge. He was clearly not an ordinary cowboy, and Ned walked forward to greet him.

"Even a tenderfoot knows better than to drive an over-loaded wagon into a soft river bottom," he said, without waiting for an introduction. "Or were you planning to walk the rest of the way to Montana?" His tone was matter-of-fact, but his mockery was unmistakable.

"We're not heading for Montana."

"You don't talk like an Easterner."

"I used to ride herd above Cheyenne."

"Then you must be a fool. See that sky? A flash flood could carry you miles downstream."

"The fault was mine," Sibyl announced with rigid aloofness as she stepped through the canvas into the sunlight.

Burch turned easily toward her, but his first glimpse caused him to sit bolt upright and take a painful gulp of air. Old Blue, sensing the sudden change in his rider, caracoled nervously. Burch controlled his mount by instinct alone, his mind momentarily stunned. He was acquainted with every wealthy beauty from St. Louis to Denver, but none of them could equal this daughter of an ordinary cowboy. He blinked, cursing his sun-tired eyes for playing him false, but when he opened them again she stood before him as solidly as the rock rim in the distance. Nature's craftsmanship in flesh and bone was superior to what She had achieved in the sculpted ridge, but the girl's expression was carved from the same granite.

"Please spare my driver your abuse," she intoned haughtily.

So she was not an ordinary cowboy's daughter, Burch thought, and his interest intensified.

"If you wish to be of assistance, which I don't suppose you do, you could help us out of this river. I don't want to remain here all night, even without the threat of a flash flood."

"You can help yourself by throwing half that stuff out and handing the reins over to your driver." His bemused brain was rapidly regaining its equilibrium.

"Is that the way all men out here think, or is this just your own personal attitude?"

"I thought it up all by myself, and in less time than it took you to get stuck in that river."

Sibyl's eyes flashed and her manner became less aloof. "Our property is more important than your opinion," she said, stamping her foot angrily. "If you were a gentleman, you'd bend your wits to getting us unstuck without the loss of so much as a single petticoat."

For a moment Burch hovered on the edge of abandoning her to her fate. Then, without knowing why, his anger evaporated and a broad smile spread across his leathered features.

"You're a frisky little heifer, aren't you? Some poor homesteader is going to have his hands full."

"I'm nobody's handful," Sibyl announced indignantly, "and we are quite capable of rescuing ourselves," she said, regaining her dignity.

Augusta peeped anxiously from behind the canvas at Burch's imposing form. She looked as though she would have preferred to withdraw into the safety of the interior, but she gathered her courage and spoke to him in a calm, controlled voice.

"I do hope you will assist us. We seem to have allowed our inexperience to lead us into difficulty."

"Aunt!" exclaimed Sibyl, feeling betrayed.

"You cannot deny that we are firmly mired. It would be foolish not to permit such a strong young man to do what he can to extract us from this predicament."

"We can do without his help," Sibyl stated loftily.

"Can't we at least allow him to try?" her aunt asked reasonably. The grin of Burch's lips grew wider and wider.

"I'll do what I can, Mrs. . . . ?"

"Miss," Augusta informed him with heightened color, "Miss Augusta Hauxhurst."

"We'll have to take some of your things out first. Let me have a look."

"I don't see why you have go nosing through our wagon," Sibyl muttered, a hint of petulance in her voice.

"I'm sure we can trust him, dear," her aunt said, noticeably relieved to have his assistance.

Sibyl said no more, but from the blazing eyes and compressed lips, Burch guessed she was holding back a flood of highly unflattering observations on men in general and cowboys in particular. He clucked to his horse and splashed noisily up to the back of the wagon. His gaze was met by a wall of trunks, boxes, valises, and small pieces of furniture.

"Good Lord, I'm surprised you haven't broken an axle.

19

What can you possibly want with so much junk?"

"This is not junk," Sibyl declared, affronted. "That furniture is very valuable and the trunks contain all our clothes. Don't cowboys know anything about antiques?"

"Rather than waste time throwing your tongue at me, you might help carry some of your precious *antiques* to shore."

"I'd get soaked."

"I didn't suppose you could walk on the stuff," retorted Burch, looking at the clear, rippling water.

"It's all right, dear, the sun will soon dry us off," Augusta pointed out soothingly.

"You needn't get wet, ma'am," Burch said. "Just put your arms around my neck and I'll carry you to shore."

Augusta flamed red and trembled with alarm. "I'd prefer to wade across, but thank you for the kind offer."

Burch realized her large panic-stricken eyes were fixed, not on him, but on the huge frame of Old Blue. "He's gentle as a kitten, ma'am, and it'll only take a second." Augusta was too terrified to move, so with one powerful arm, Burch lifted her out of the wagon and into the saddle before him. Augusta turned so white Burch wondered if her heart had stopped beating, but when he lowered her carefully into Ned's waiting arms she managed a faint, "Thank you," before sinking gratefully to the ground.

Sibyl followed Burch's gallantry in high dudgeon, convinced he was laughing at her and that his exaggerated courtesy toward her aunt was a calculated attempt to annoy her. She was certain of it when he plunged back into the river, splashing noisily toward her with a broader grin than ever.

"I can walk by myself," she said with a rudeness that made her aunt flinch. She pulled off her shoes, hitched up her skirt, and slipped into the water. She reached the shore without mishap, but her pleasure in thwarting him was spoiled by knowing it was impossible to obstruct his view of her shapely legs and ankles. She climbed out on the bank

20

and dropped her skirts. "You may remove the trunks now," she said with barely controlled exasperation. "There's nothing more to distract your attention."

With a crack of laughter Burch climbed into the wagon and for the next twenty minutes he and Ned were busy with anything small enough to be carried ashore by one man. His exertions under the broiling sun caused him to become overheated and he removed his vest and shirt. The bulging muscles and sculpted torso drew Sibyl's fascinated eye. She watched spellbound as the muscles rippled and played across his back.

"Sibyl, you should be ashamed of yourself," declared her scandalized aunt.

"What for?"

"A young lady does not stare at a half-naked man."

"Why? He's not indecent."

Augusta didn't know why, precisely, but she knew she disapproved, and drew her reluctant niece away.

"If you hitch your horse to the wagon, I think we could pull it out," Sibyl suggested when the wagon's contents had been reduced by half. Burch did not answer until he had set a small bureau on the ground, but Sibyl knew she had said something that offended him.

"My horse is a highly trained cow pony. It would ruin him to hitch him to a wagon."

"How much training can it take to carry a man across open country?" she asked in an offhand manner.

"I realize you can't help your ignorance, miss, but if you talked less, people might not notice it so much. Now, if you think you can drive those oxen without overturning the wagon, get up in the seat. Ned and I will see if we can break the wheels loose."

"If I were a man, I'd teach you not to talk to me like that," raged Sibyl, hot fury flaming in her cheeks.

"Now that would be a terrible waste," Burch said, grinning, his eyes boldly traveling over her with daunting warmth. Sibyl spun on her heel and waded into the now-muddy water. But when she took up the reins, she was careful not to communicate her agitation to the oxen. Burch was amused, but did not bait her further.

"Bring them up to their yokes, but don't let them pull until I tell you."

"I know what to do," she said sulfurously as he and Ned positioned themselves, one at each front wheel.

"Pity you didn't know earlier," he shot back and was rewarded by the sounds of stifled wrath. But when he gave the signal, Sibyl concentrated on her team. Burch strained at the wheel until Augusta expected to see his muscles burst through the skin, but the wagon wouldn't budge. Twice more the men employed their combined strength against the muddy grip, but the wheel remained stuck fast.

"We'll have to unload the rest," said Ned.

"Try turning the rear wheels," Sibyl suggested. "That's where the weight is."

"If he thinks we ought to unload—" began Augusta.

"I was just about to suggest that," drawled Burch, forestalling a passionate outburst from Sibyl.

"If that's an example of Western honesty, then it's just as well Wyoming is still a territory," she said hotly.

"Sibyl, please," begged her embarrassed aunt.

"No need to worry, Miss Hauxhurst. Cowboy's hides are as thick as their heads." Augusta turned away in chagrin, but Sibyl glared at him with brimstone in her eyes.

"Ready!" Burch shouted, getting a good grip on the rear wheel as Sibyl brought the oxen up to their yokes. "Pull!" The muscles stood out along his back and shoulders as he wrestled with the wheels and the wagon rolled a few inches from the deep rut.

"I told you so," exulted Sibyl. "One more ought to do it." Once again the men and oxen strained at their task and the wagon inched forward. The air rang from Sibyl's whip and the wagon moved steadily toward the bank. Her delight was tempered only by a fear that the insolent stranger might leave her to reload the wagon by herself.

"Don't let them stop," Burch called out when the oxen found solid footing in the coarse gravel bank. Sibyl simmered with pent-up spleen but kept her attention on her work. The wagon paused when the smaller front wheels encountered the bank, but the oxen lowered their heads and with one bone-wrenching effort lifted the wheels out of the water. The rear wheels rose from the water without hesitation, and Sibyl brought the wagon to a stop next to their scattered paraphernalia.

"Thank you," Sibyl began with an effort, then stammered to a halt with Burch placed his hands on his hips, looking like a god carved out of amber stone.

"Think nothing of it. We can't have the wreckage of tenderfoot wagons littering the prairie, or their bones scaring our women."

"We won't detain you any longer." she exploded wrathfully at the galling stranger who didn't even have the courtesy to take off his hat so she could see what he looked like.

"I need to put Miss Hauxhurst's things back. If some poor cowboy was to see a lobo wolf running across the prairie in lady's undergarments, it might rattle his wits permanently."

"You are the most insulting, ill-bred, appalling, mannerless wretch I've ever met," she sputtered.

"You'd better learn to use little words if you expect anyone out here to understand you," Burch said with a deliberately broad accent. "We don't have many books nor much time to read 'em. I hope you wasn't expecting to meet a lot of educated folks."

"Not any longer," she replied, returning his volley.

Augusta picked up Burch's shirt, intending to offer it to him along with her heartfelt thanks, and discovered the bullet hole. Mildly shocked, she interrupted them. "My heavens, there's blood on your shirt."

"It's nothing, ma'am."

23

"But how could it have happened when all you did was lift some boxes?"

"It wasn't the boxes. Some careless fool was firing at a herd of antelope and nicked my arm."

"It must be very painful," said Sibyl.

"Not nearly as painful as your opinion of cowboys."

"It must be cleaned and properly bandaged," Sibyl said, ignoring his remark. "I have some medicine in one of the chests." She climbed down and began going through the drawers of a small bureau.

"It's nothing much, only a scratch."

"Sit down," she said with businesslike authority. "Next thing you know it'll be infected and your wife will have no end of worry over it and all because of your stubborn pride."

Burch gave himself up to her ministrations. "Is she always this sweet?" he asked Augusta, who was too flustered to answer. Sibyl wordlessly cleaned and bandaged the wound. "Thanks, miss, and I'm sure my wife would thank you as well." He was laughing at her again. "Now, I've got things to do at home, so if you don't mind, I'll see to the loading up. I don't have time to sit about chatting, even though it would be mighty pleasant." Sibyl could stand no more and rose to her feet to heap enough condemnation upon his head to shame ten men, but her bare feet and damp skirts made her feel at such a disadvantage that she clamped her lips together and sat down in mute anguish.

The silence of the next twenty minutes was filled by Augusta's persistent efforts to fill in the conversational void and to express her own overflowing gratitude. "I dare not think of what might have happened to us if you had not come along."

"Ned would have managed somehow," Burch said kindly. "Of course, you could have encouraged your niece to sit in the river instead of on that chest. Her temper might have boiled the water away and you could have crossed on dry land."

Augusta fell into an anxiety, expecting her temperamental niece to fly at the bait. Mercifully, Sibyl's unpredictable temper didn't explode and they prepared to resume their journey with nothing more awful than some damp clothes and lowered pride.

"You're well off the trail. Are you sure of your directions?" Burch asked as Ned took up the rains.

"We have very precise directions, thank you," Sibyl snapped.

"I suppose you're a mail-order bride for some rich California rancher," he ventured. "If he refuses to marry you, come back to Wyoming. We can always use you to scare off the wolves and rustlers."

"We're not going to California," snarled Sibyl, driven beyond the limits of restraint. "I own a ranch with my cousin less than three hours from here, and the first thing I'm going to ask him to do is finish the job that antelope-hunting fool began."

"Are you sure your wound isn't hurting you?" Augusta asked, troubled by the sudden change in Burch's expression.

"What's the name of your ranch?" he asked sharply.

"The Elkhorn, and my cousin's name is Burch Randall."

"Do you know him?" asked Augusta.

"Yes, ma'am. In fact, I'm heading in that direction myself."

"Won't you travel with us?" Augusta asked, hoping to retain the security of such a large male presence.

"I'm afraid I can't, but you'll find the ranch easy enough. Just keep about ten miles east of that ridge. There's nothing more than a few piddling creeks to cross, probably dry," he needled Sibyl, and was regarded with a molten glare. "The Elkhorn is the next stream of any size. Just follow it east for about five miles."

"I'll be sure to tell Miss Cameron's cousin how much help you've been," Augusta promised. "You must call on him soon."

25

"I most certainly will," he replied in an odd voice, and then much to their surprise, he began to laugh. It started as a queer-sounding gurgle he tried to control, but then it gathered momentum until he seemed so helplessly in its grip, Sibyl expected to see him tumble from his saddle. "I'll tell him, but it goes against the grain to be the bearer of bad news." He galloped off with another shout of laughter.

"Well!" exploded Sibyl, "I have never met anyone so incredibly rude in all my life. Not even your abominable nephew behaves that badly."

"You weren't at all civil to him, and he did rescue us from the river."

"I didn't ask for his help."

"But I did, and I'm sure we would still be in the river without it."

"I'd have figured a way out."

"You really *do* think you're the equal of any man, don't you?"

"Yes," she declared vehemently. "I'll never understand why a woman should be expected to bow before anyone's will just because he's a man."

"That's all beside the point," Augusta gently pointed out. "I still say you did not treat that young man fairly. You didn't even ask his name or thank him properly." She regarded her niece with affection. "You can't go on assuming things will be like they were in Virginia. Look around us. You must see that life here is frighteningly different. I'd be less than truthful if I said I was comfortable in my mind about the course we've taken. There is so much about this land we don't understand, I feel as though we shall have to start all over again."

"I shouldn't have let you come," Sibyl said guiltily.

"You couldn't have stopped me. How could I face my own conscience if I allowed my sister's only child to travel so far from her home alone? There's not much an old maid can do, but I can keep you from getting lonely."

Sibyl gave her aunt a hug. "I shall see that you have your own room and are waited on hand and foot. You shall have a fire every night and your dinner on a tray."

"Maybe your cousin won't want us to live with him."

"Half the house is mine."

"But what if you get married?"

"I shall never get married," she declared emphatically. "That's why I left Virginia. I did love Daddy, but I don't think I could endure a husband who thought of nothing but books and bulls."

"I don't think this is a place for a woman to live by herself. What do you really *know* about ranching?"

"My cousin can teach me all I need to know; it can't take too long. Then *he* can sell out to *me*."

"Maybe he won't *want* to sell," suggested her aunt carefully. "He probably feels that it's his home, not ours."

"It doesn't matter what he thinks," Sibyl said, summarily dismissing her unknown cousin. "I'll settle things with him in short order."

Chapter 3

Sibyl heaved a sigh of relief as the cluster of ranch buildings came into view. They had been following the creek for more than an hour, and she was completely out of patience with oxen, wagons, heat, and dust. Inside the wagon, Augusta dozed fitfully, but Sibyl was too keyed up to sleep. Before her lay the end of her journey, a raw, uncharted, and untamed country whose newness and promise kindled a feeling of excitement deep within her. She had traveled two thousand miles because she was weary of the confinement of life in genteel but exhausted Virginia. Not for her the gentle acceptance of Augusta or the unshakable belief of her mother; she refused to bow to stifling convention or narrow criticism, but in the struggle to gain her independence she had grown a tough, protective shell.

No man appeared with the generous understanding or uncritical love that would have dissolved the encrustation, and years of censoring by well-intentioned matrons and whispered innuendo from friends jealous of her beauty hardened her shell until it became a plate of armor to repel friend and foe alike. Sibyl had seized upon her inheritance as the last chance to halt this calcification of the spirit, her only chance to escape becoming an old maid or a school teacher, whose only thoughts revolved around sums and recitations. Maybe in this wild country, where men carried guns and women voted, she could find a way to turn her life into something of pleasure rather than an ordeal of endurance.

Yet the nagging doubts grew when the forests of the Mississippi valley gave way to the endless stretches of flat prairie; the haggard faces that emerged from sod huts only fueled her uncertainty. The towering mountains were a welcome relief from the crushing monotony of the grasslands, but once they left Laramie all signs of civilization vanished, and she found herself on a plain even more desolate than the first. To a person reared in the comparative hustle and bustle of a small Eastern town, the vast loneliness of the land tore at her soul.

Her most frequent answer to friends who tried to talk her out of leaving home had been, "How different can a valley in Wyoming be from a valley in Virginia?" Now she knew the answer to her question, and she could not rid her mind of the suspicion that this was but the first of many disagreeable surprises.

"Wake up, Aunt, we're almost there."

"Oh, dear, I didn't mean to doze off," Augusta said, attempting to smooth her hair and straighten her hat. "But I do feel better now that it's not so hot."

"You might know we would find trees just when we didn't need them," Sibyl said, pointing to the scattered willows and cottonwoods that grew along the creek. "It's nice to know they have something out here besides this everlasting grass. How odd! There're so many trees around the house I can't even see what it looks like."

"I must say this is a pleasant surprise," said Augusta, as the outlines of an enormous house began to take shape through the leaves. "I had begun to entertain the gravest fears as to

29

the kind of house we should be expected to occupy."

"It looks like grandfather's house," Sibyl exclaimed in surprise. A columned double porch, identical to one on the Lexington house, ran across the front, with shutters at the windows, but the brick of the Virginia home was replaced by unpainted weathered gray wood siding.

"I've never seen anything like it outside Cheyenne," Ned said in wonder. "Whatever could your uncle have wanted with a big house like that?"

"It is rather nice."

"Where you stayed last night was nice, miss. This is grand."

"Where is everyone?" her aunt asked uneasily. "You did tell your cousin we would be arriving today, didn't you?"

"Yes, I wrote him *and* sent him a telegram."

"Ranch houses are deserted most of the time," explained Ned. "The hands stay on the range, and if the owner isn't staying in Cheyenne or Laramie, he's probably out with them."

"What do they do that takes so much time?"

"Looking after cows proper takes twenty-four hours every day."

"Surely my cousin doesn't expect me to just walk in and make myself at home. Not even cowboys can be that casual."

"People out here don't usually get visitors, at least not the kind that stays," Ned said, pulling the wagon to a halt before the gate. "Most just sit for a spell and then move on."

"Come on, Aunt," Sibyl said, climbing down and looking about her. "If Cousin Burch can't be bothered to meet us, we can let ourselves in. Take the wagon around back, Ned. Maybe you can find someone to help unload it." The wagon moved off and the ladies paused outside the fence.

"You know, I believe this is the first grass I've seen," remarked Augusta.

"How can you say that when we've seen nothing else for

thousands of miles?"

"I mean *real* grass, like we have at home." She stepped inside the gate. "I don't feel quite so homesick any more."

"It needs a coat of paint," stated Sibyl critically, walking briskly toward the front steps. She had reached the first step when the front door opened and she became acutely aware of two sturdy legs encased in tan leather boots, planted squarely before her. As her eyes traveled up, the length and power of those limbs made her feel a little breathless. Over broad hips and past a powerful chest, Sibyl had to crane her neck to see the face of the tallest man she'd ever met. Cool gray eyes, set under a broad forehead and astride a long, tapering nose, watched her with the hint of a twinkle. Thick, curly sun-bleached hair peeped out from under the edges of a broad-rimmed hat; a square chin and firm mouth seemed to wait expectantly.

"You are the young man who helped us out of the river," proclaimed Augusta, delighted to meet a familiar face. "How nice to see you again. Do you live here?" she asked, moving forward to greet him.

"You might say that," answered the well-remembered, irony-laden voice.

"Then you can explain why my cousin isn't here to meet my aunt," said Sibyl, recovering quickly.

"I'm here," he replied quizzically. He was still laughing at her and that made Sibyl mad.

"He should not have sent you in his stead," she said brusquely, "but since you're here, you might as well make yourself useful. The wagon is around back."

"We can not go on meeting you without knowing your name," Augusta said, smiling kindly. "I can't think why we have not asked it before. What shall we call you?"

"Cousin Burch will do just fine," he replied, his gray eyes positively glistening with merriment.

"What!" gasped Sibyl. The shock was so unpleasant she

31

felt physically unwell.

"Are you really Ada Cameron's nephew?" asked Augusta hopefully.

"I'm afraid so," he answered, without taking his laughing eyes off Sibyl. "Aunt Ada didn't have any other nephews, so there's no chance they sent the wrong one."

"There's no need to be absurd," said Sibyl. She gathered her paralyzed wits and climbed the steps with a purposeful stride. "I'm your Cousin Sibyl, the only one on the Cameron side," she said, extending her hand.

"Looks like we're stuck with each other, there being no other cousins to swap, I mean." His eyes continued to dance merrily, but Sibyl had the unmistakable feeling that behind all this lazy humor was a mind of more than ordinary force. He certainly didn't lack the effrontery to eye her like a prize heifer. "Your aunt come to protect you from the wild cowboys?"

"I don't need protection. Aunt Augusta has always lived with me."

Burch moved down the steps to where Augusta waited uneasily. "Welcome to the Elkhorn, ma'am. I hope you don't mind if I call you Aunt Augusta, too. You're barely old enough to be my sister, but if you're to play the duenna to Cousin Sibyl, I can't call you Augusta. I wouldn't want to sound disrespectful."

Augusta swallowed hard but nodded in agreement.

"She's not my duenna, and if you wish to remain in my good graces, you'll not call her that again."

"I'll remember that, in case I want to keep on your good side, that is." Sibyl's eyes blazed, but Burch only chuckled and turned back to Augusta. "Let me take you inside."

Something close to panic came over Augusta when Burch took her tentatively extended hand in his firm grasp, but she was helpless to draw back and allowed herself to be led up the steps.

"I'm afraid you'll find this isn't the kind of house you're used to. There's been nobody to tend it except Uncle Wesley and me, and we never were too keen on cleaning."

"Men never are," Augusta agreed, dazed.

"Sanchez tried, but I don't think he knows any more than I do."

"Sanchez?"

"You can't blame him though. He's away nearly nine months of the year and doesn't have time when he's in. And Balaam won't turn his hand to anything unless he's driven to it."

"Of course," acceded Augusta, giving up any attempt to understand the conversation and meekly accompanying him into the house.

Sibyl was left standing on the porch, so angry her knuckles were white. He was fawning over Augusta just to make her mad, and he would soon find out how very well he had succeeded.

"Cousin Sibyl, aren't you coming in?"

Sibyl did not deign to reply, but the rapid staccato of her heels on the planks of the porch and hallway would have been recognized by her friends as a declaration of war. Augusta did recognize it and quaked inwardly.

The wide entrance hall extended two thirds of the way through the house, its walls lined with the mounted heads of bear, mountain sheep and goat, and antelope. At the back was a curving stairway to the second floor, and on either side were sets of sliding double doors. Sibyl opened first one and then the other. "They're empty," she announced, so surprised she hardly noticed the enormous elk head mounted above one fireplace. "Where's the furniture?"

"There isn't any," Burch disclosed. "Uncle Wesley built this house for Aunt Ada, but when she died he lost interest in it."

"But where do you sit?" She frowned as he stared at her with a blank expression. "What part of the house can you

33

use?"

"Mostly the ranch room, or the kitchen. And the bedrooms, of course."

"I mean where do you entertain visitors?"

Laughter positively danced in his eyes, and Sibyl could have bitten her tongue.

"In the kitchen."

"You can't take ladies into the kitchen," she declared flatly.

"We haven't had any ladies here since Aunt Ada died."

"Do you mean that we are the only women on this ranch?" inquired Augusta in a faint voice.

"You're just about the only women within a hundred miles of here, unless you count Indian squaws." He was watching Sibyl and nearly missed seeing Augusta stagger. "Are you all right, ma'am?" he asked, springing forward. "You shouldn't be on your feet."

Burch scooped Augusta up in his arms and strode through the door at the back of the hall into a long chamber that ran the length of the house. It, too, was filled with hunting trophies. At one end was a large kitchen; an enormous table, capable of seating more than twenty people, occupied the center of the room; and at the far end an odd collection of chairs sat grouped around an iron stove, which stood directly beneath an enormous buffalo head. Burch lowered Augusta into one of the chairs.

"I should have let you sit down earlier. You must be exhausted."

"I am a little tired," she said, almost recoiling from a cougar head just above her.

"The trip would have been much quicker on horseback."

Augusta's complexion lost the last traces of color.

"No one could expect my aunt to ride a horse two hundred miles in this heat."

"I do it all the time."

"We're accustomed to a buggy."

34

"I'll begin correcting that tomorrow."

Sibyl was about to tell him exactly what she thought of his plans, but he turned back to her aunt.

"Do you feel well enough to climb the stairs, ma'am, or shall I carry you? I wouldn't know what to do if you fainted." Augusta shook her head.

"Your rooms are at the top of the stairs on the right. I'm at the other end. All the other rooms are empty."

Augusta didn't tell him that the closest she had ever come to fainting was when he carried her from the river on horseback, his arms wrapped tightly about her, her bosom pressed against his chest.

A short, ugly, and obviously annoyed little man carrying a huge platter of meat noisily entered the room from the back of the house. "If you don't eat this food now, it ain't going to be fit for the dogs," he barked with a thick Spanish accent. "The antelope is tough as mule hide already."

"Set it on the table," Burch directed. "We'll be ready as soon as I see about the trunks." Both men disappeared, leaving Sibyl in a room smelling strongly of tobacco and sweat, facing the prospect of dining off tough antelope steak.

"He has got to be the most infuriating man I've ever met," she said, envious of her aunt's treatment in spite of herself.

"He is a bit brusque, but *so* decisive," said Augusta, who was more surprised than Sibyl to hear such words come out of her mouth. "I mean, he does take things into his own hands," she stammered, wondering why her treacherous tongue should betray her so unexpectedly.

"He most certainly does, but Cousin Burch has a few uncomfortable surprises in store for him."

"I am afraid we all do," allowed Augusta ruefully. The back door banged open, and Sanchez entered with a large pot of baked beans. They watched in dismay as he set out fried potatoes, stewed tomatoes, canned corn, and a steaming pot of virulent black coffee. Sibyl felt her appetite fade. Dinner promised to be more of an ordeal than crossing the plains.

Sibyl looked around her bedroom without enthusiasm. The bare walls were unpainted and the windows without curtains. It wasn't precisely ugly, but she could do nothing to relieve the depressing emptiness until her things arrived from Virginia. But there was plenty of space for a desk in the corner, and enough work downstairs to guarantee that she would spend no more time in her own room than it took to dress each morning. She sank to her bed, weary with an aching tiredness that was only barely dulled by the pangs of hunger. Her remembrance of the catastrophic dinner did nothing to build her optimism about the days ahead.

Sibyl couldn't understand how Burch could eat such food, but he had actually asked for seconds! Her aunt pushed her food around the plate, looking less well by the minute, and the coffee nearly took Sibyl's breath away. All the while her insensitive cousin sat stuffing his face, unable to understand why they had so little appetite.

"It must be traveling in this heat." She was too proud to tell him that she was starving but refused to eat food guaranteed to make her last hours a mortal agony.

"Does Sanchez do all your cooking?" Augusta asked cautiously.

"He cooks for the boys mostly, but he fixed this meal especially for you."

"You can send him back to the boys," Sibyl told him forthrightly. "We'll do our own cooking from now on."

Burch looked up from his plate, obviously surprised by their reaction.

"We don't want to deprive them of their cook," Augusta interposed lamely, but the damage had already been done.

"This food is not fit to eat," stated Sibyl, not mincing words. "How can you stand to put it in your mouth?"

"What's wrong with it? Sanchez runs the best chuck wagon

on the Laramie. Everyone tries to eat from our pot on roundup."

"Do you mean you *all* eat like this?"

"No, most cooks are worse." He really didn't understand why this thoughtful gesture was being rejected so emphatically.

"I'm surprised you're not sick. Where is your storeroom? Do you have a garden?"

"Ask Sanchez," he replied uncooperatively.

"How do I get fresh supplies?"

"We send a wagon to Laramie."

"I'll make up a list tonight, and you can send a wagon out first thing in the morning."

"It's not time to send the wagon. Anyway, I don't have one free or anyone to drive it."

"Ned can go."

"I'm not paying Ned to run about picking up small orders."

"*I'm* paying Ned, and he'll do what I say."

"You'll not get a cent from the ranch."

"I didn't ask you for money, but I own half of this place and that includes the wagon and the cash to pay wages. I won't have my wishes pushed aside or ignored just because it's not convenient or hasn't been done before. My aunt and I have to live here as well as you, and that's going to mean a lot of changes."

"You'll get no help from Sanchez." Burch was angry now.

"All I want from him is the key to the storerooms. He can cook for you any time you like. Tell him I want to see him after dinner."

"Tell him yourself when he comes to clean up," Burch said, rising noisily from his chair. "And don't hesitate to inform me of any other changes you'd like to make." His jaw hardened and Augusta was tempted to tug Sibyl's sleeve.

"I won't," her dauntless niece replied, "but I don't intend to

37

interfere until I'm more familiar with things. I will confine myself to *lady's work* for the present."

Burch fixed her with a glare that caused Augusta's heart to beat double time. "You'll confine yourself to *lady's work* altogether," he said harshly. "I won't tolerate meddling, nor will I stand by and watch some conceited, ignorant little girl mess up what it took my uncle twenty years of back-breaking work to put together."

He slammed out the back door. No one had ever walked out on Sibyl, and she was as surprised as her aunt when her eyes filled with tears.

"I'm afraid you may have gone a little too far, dear."

"It's my ranch just as much as it is his," she answered, angrily dashing away the tears.

"He's spent his life here. I should think it would be very difficult to accept the intrusion of strangers."

"I won't let him think I can be ignored."

"I don't imagine he means to do that."

"Then he should have sent the wagon."

"Maybe he has some other use for it."

"Then it can wait."

"Maybe it can't."

"Then I can't either," she said stormily. Augusta frowned slightly, but Sibyl was determined not to give in, even if it meant being at odds with her cousin from the start. She extracted a promise from Sanchez to show them around the cook house before he left the next day, and then spent the rest of the evening making up her list.

She went to bed exhausted, but she couldn't sleep. Her mind was racing with all the things that needed doing. How could the house look like anything but a barn with no furniture or curtains? And all those horrible animals' heads! Burch might not see anything wrong with empty rooms, bare walls, and not a speck of paint anywhere, but she didn't intend to live in squalor just because they were hundreds of miles from civilization. Something had to be done to make at least one room tolerable.

With the men away for weeks at a time, Ned would have to stay on, especially if this Balaam person was as useless as Burch said. And they would need someone to help with the housework. They couldn't be expected to rise at dawn, scrub and clean all morning, cook all afternoon, and entertain guests at night. She remembered the prematurely aged women she had seen on the plains and decided right then there were limits to what she would do. Wyoming would just have to adjust to *her* in this instance.

Chapter 4

Sibyl cornered Sanchez early the next morning. She was dismayed to learn there were no chickens and no milk cow; a flourishing kitchen garden behind one of the barns raised her hopes, but Sanchez's scornful expression informed her he wasn't responsible for it. He fetched a decrepit old man, who came toward Sibyl with great slowness, regarding her with a distrustful eye. But as soon as she could make him understand she admired his garden and intended to buy a cow, his entire appearance underwent a dramatic change. Old Balaam straightened his back, stopped dragging his foot, and his eyes glowed as one coming to the end of a long tribulation. He vanished only to reappear moments later with a half-dozen brown eggs.

"Where did these come from?" she asked, thinking of soufflé for dinner.

"Mrs. Ada's hens went wild after she died. There's some in a canyon above here, and I rob their nests."

"Can you catch some of them?"

"Sure, but you'll have to go to Laramie for a cow. There's none to be had around here, and it's worth your life to try and milk one of those wild things."

"I'll see to the cow, you just catch the chickens. I need to stock the kitchen cupboards," she said, turning back to

Sanchez. There were some intensely muttered Spanish curses, but with Balaam acting as translator—Sanchez pretended not to understand Sibyl—she selected her supplies and set them aside to be taken up to the house later.

Ned had been dispatched at first light with a long list of such items as Sibyl considered essential for their survival. "Hurry back, or you're likely to find us starved to death," she had told him.

"There's plenty of food for them that's not too particular to eat it," growled Sanchez to his horse, over the jangle of pots and pans, as he headed back to the range.

During the rest of the morning the ladies turned their efforts to the kitchen. They went through cabinets and closets, disturbing ancient webs and driving out the distant descendants of the critters who built them. "I couldn't let Ned put anything away in all this dirt," Sibyl said, sneezing at a cloud of dust.

Lunch was some hot bread and jam, with coffee from a freshly scoured pot, then it was back to work until every cupboard and closet was spotless and every can, bottle, and jar neatly arranged on its proper shelf.

"That's enough for today," Sibyl declared as she settled back with a cup of coffee.

"There is so much to be done," groaned Augusta.

"Enough for months to come, so there's no point killing ourselves today."

Her aunt looked about the room, a little overawed by its masculinity. "I don't suppose we should change this room?"

"Of course we will. You can't like these benches and tattered chairs, and something must be done about these animal heads."

"They aren't very attractive," her aunt agreed.

"I can't imagine why Burch keeps so many."

"He must be proud of them. I wonder if he shot them all himself?"

"I wouldn't be surprised," Sibyl said, looking around at the dozen or so trophies, "though I don't know when he found time to look after the ranch if he did. I wouldn't mind them half so much if they served some purpose. Hmmm, I wonder if they could be made so you could sit on them?"

Her aunt was betrayed into a giggle. "I would love to see Louisa seated on that big bear we saw in the hall." Both ladies enjoyed a laugh at the expense of the middle Hauxhurst sister, but Sibyl soon became serious again.

"There must be some furniture somewhere. I can't believe Uncle Wesley would build such a house and not buy something to put in it. If we could find some chairs for the parlor, at least we'd have somewhere to ourselves."

"We could sit here," Augusta pointed out.

"We need a room of our own," Sibyl stated firmly. "Men never seen to know how to behave unless they're told, and I think it's a great mistake to try to adjust to the rumpus they get up to. Just look at my cousin. His aunt's been dead only a few years, and already, he's worse than a field hand."

"But he's so *big* . . . "

"What has that got to do with anything?"

"I am not perfectly sure, but I doubt anyone that large will take kindly to being told what to do."

"Then he'd better improve his manners."

"Are you sure they need improving?"

"Aunt, don't you dare back down just because he's got broad shoulders and powerful thighs."

"Sibyl! You should not *see* such things."

"How can I help it when he appears on the porch looking like two oaks growing through the floorboards. I was a trifle overcome at first, but I hope I recovered quickly. Do you think he noticed?"

"No, I don't think he did," she answered, sighing regretfully.

Sibyl, covered with flour up to her elbows, was making biscuits when Burch entered the house, wearing a heavy

42

scowl. His thoughts seemed deeply involved elsewhere, but the small sounds from the kitchen drew his attention. His eyes found Sibyl and immediately the scowl disappeared; her hair was up and her dress pulled taut over her shoulders, outlining the daintiness of her waist and the tempting nape of her neck. Burch felt a nervous twinge arc through his body, and an immediate, aching tension began to build, pulsing through every nerve until he felt as though he had to reach out and touch the smooth white skin regardless of the consequences.

"I wondered if you were coming back," Sibyl said, turning around to face him. "It would be helpful to know when you intended to return for dinner." Her voice was crisp and impersonal, but there was implied criticism in her tone and Burch's eyes lost some of their warmth.

"You were asleep when I left."

"I'm afraid I overslept."

"I'm sure you were very tired."

"I was, but someone has to fix your breakfast."

Burch's eyes widened; her tone was almost friendly. "I can do without breakfast," he said, surprised Sibyl would think fixing his breakfast was part of her duty.

"You can't do a day's work on the food that Spanish person prepares," insisted Augusta, emerging from the pantry. "Just tell us when you want breakfast and we'll have it ready."

"I usually leave about five o'clock when I'm headed for the range, but not until six on other days."

"Five in the *morning*!" Augusta gasped, mistrusting her ears.

"That's when the cows get up."

"They would," grumbled Sibyl, remembering the vexatious habits of the cattle that ruled her father's life. "I never knew a cow yet with sense enough to stay in bed when she had the chance." A crack of laughter transformed Burch's whole being. He's really quite handsome when he's not frowning, thought Sibyl.

43

"Cows don't have anything to go by except the sun," Burch told Augusta with an impish grin. "When it's up, they are too."

"Then we will be up as well," she promised bravely. "Now you'd better wash up because Sibyl is about to put the biscuits in the oven."

A mouth-watering medley of aromas assailed Burch's nostrils, reminding him of long-forgotten times when, as a boy, he would be down early to breakfast or surreptitiously stick his finger in the gravy boat. He'd forgotten that food could be a pleasure instead of just something to keep a man alive. It was nice to look forward to sitting down at the table and nice to have a woman about the house again.

"I brought Jesse to meet you," he said to Sibyl, bringing his mind back to business. "He's my foreman."

"I thought that was your job."

"I'm the *owner*. Jesse, get in here." he shouted out the back door. "It takes the both of us to look after a place this size."

Sibyl stared in surprise at the man who entered the room. He was a complete stranger, but she felt sure she had seen him before.

"This is my cousin, Sibyl Cameron, and her aunt, Augusta Hauxhurst."

Jesse nodded in the direction of both ladies, but his eyes never left Sibyl. He was nearly as tall as Burch and looked to be about fifty pounds heavier, with thick limbs and a slightly stiff, muscle-bound walk. Reddish-brown hair curled thickly about his head and paled the freckles that were barely visible under the deep tan of his short nose. Piercing eyes sized her up from under thick, puckered brows; the rest of his face was covered by a coarse beard.

"All that hair makes him look like a wolf," her aunt would say later.

"Mightly pleased to meet you," Jesse said, favoring her with a friendly smile. "Burch didn't tell me I was spending the evening with two beautiful women."

"I didn't want to start a stampede."

"Save your flattery, said Sibyl, pleased with the compliment nevertheless. "There's a wash basin and towels on the stand by the door. You can hang your hats on the pegs right above them." Her words were met with blank stares from both men. "Did I say something wrong?"

"It's not our custom to take our hats off," said Burch.

"Every gentleman removes his hat in the house."

"We don't."

"Not even at the table?" Augusta asked incredulously. Burch shook his head.

"You'll take them off tonight or you'll get no dinner," Sibyl stated, facing the two men with hands on her hips.

"And you expect us to do as you say, just like that?" countered Burch.

"If it really bothers you . . . "

"No, Aunt, you're not to give in to them."

"There's no problem, ma'am," Jesse said quickly. "If you want bare heads, you'll have them."

"May we keep our boots on?" quipped Burch, looking dangerously unamused.

"Don't be provoking."

But instead of taking his hat off, Burch stood staring at her with an odd, interrogatory look that made her feel uncomfortable. She could not tell what he was thinking and was unaccountably reluctant to press him, but he surprised and confused her by walking from the room without a word.

"Sanchez's cooking never smelled anything like this," Jesse chatted easily, unruffled by Burch's abrupt departure.

Sibyl found her eyes were drawn to the door still swinging behind Burch.

"The boys will be mad as fire when they learn how you're feeding us," Jesse continued, drying his face with a towel.

"We can cook for them as well," offered Augusta uncertainly.

"I don't think Burch would approve of that."

45

"Naturally we'll discuss it with Mr. Randall, but it's only to be expected there'll be many changes now that we're living here."

"Burch doesn't like changes. He says it upsets the men and just makes for more work all around."

"Then he'll just have to accustom himself to a period of discomfort. From what I've seen, he should be thankful that Aunt Augusta and I have come to manage for him."

"If I know Burch, he'll be fit to bust with thankfulness," smiled Jesse.

Fifteen minutes later Sibyl took the golden brown biscuits from the oven. "It's time to eat," she said with a good deal of tartness. "Where's my cousin?"

Burch entered the room on the heels of her question. Both ladies stared at him in astonishment. He had completely changed his clothes, even his boots. He wore a navy suit with vest, white shirt, and tie. His hair was combed and he was freshly shaved. Yet no mere clothing could obscure the tall, muscular body underneath or diminish the aura of rough masculinity that he exuded. He was so handsome Sibyl's tongue tied itself in knots.

"I thought you might be more pleased with me if I was all duded up," he explained casually. "Can't have Wyoming dust at a lady's table."

Surprise and admiration were written large in Sibyl's eyes, but there was also a spark of anger. Jesse looked from one to the other, wondering what Burch was up to.

"You look so nice it makes me ashamed to sit down in this old dress," objected Augusta.

"Without that apron you'd be fit for the governor's table," Burch said, slipping the huge apron over Augusta's head. Startled to find herself in virtual embrace, the poor woman hemmed and hawed in utter confusion and quickly dropped into the chair he held for her. Sibyl was sorely tempted to throw the pan of biscuits at his head, but she dumped them on a plate, removed her own apron, and took the seat Jesse

46

held for her.

She was angry with Burch for putting her off balance once again, but she was upset with herself as well. She should have been thinking of his lateness and how rude it was to leave without a word, but instead she only thought of how handsome he looked and the remembrance of those powerful thighs rising from the porch floor.

"That was undoubtedly the best meal I've ever eaten," Jesse said for the tenth time. "You ladies don't know how welcome you are at Elkhorn."

"The coffee looks a little weak," Burch noted as Sibyl filled his cup.

"This is how it should look," she said, longing to pour it in his lap. He had galled her by monopolizing her aunt to such an extent that she was virtually forced to give her own attention to Jesse for the entire meal.

"I made another pot," Augusta said, getting up quickly to avoid meeting Sibyl's eyes.

"Traitor!" cried her outflanked niece.

"They work very hard and deserve to have their coffee the way they like it," Augusta explained meekly, "even if I do consider it a waste of good beans."

"If it'll please you, Aunt Augusta, I'll drink Sibyl's brown water and like it."

"It's already made. I left it on the stove through dinner. I hope it's strong enough." She poured out two cups of liquid so black it made Sibyl shudder. They both watched expectantly as Burch took the first swallow.

"Can you make a pot just like this in the morning?" he asked, sighing contentedly.

"I expect so."

"And every other morning?"

"If you like," she answered with increasing trepidation.

"If you weren't already my aunt, I'd marry you," Burch announced, planting a noisy kiss on Augusta's blushing

47

cheek.

"My aunt is not accustomed to crude attentions or over-ripe compliments," snapped Sibyl, surprised at the cutting edge in her voice.

"I like your aunt," Burch said, looking at her from hard, critical eyes. "She doesn't look down her nose or bark orders at me. She's a *real* lady."

Sibyl gasped. "You ungrateful—"

"What should I be grateful for? Being treated as though I was a savage and given orders on how to behave in my own house? You Virginians have some strange notions about how guests are supposed to behave."

"I'm not your guest; I own this house," she responded, shaking with anger.

"You may own half this ranch, but you're here only as long as I allow it. I can put you off any minute I like, so I suggest *you* learn to say please and thank you. It'll be good training for you, and it'll improve the atmosphere out of all recognition. The dinner was delicious, Aunt Augusta," he said, rising to his feet. "I'd forgotten what pleasure it could be to fill my belly."

"You'll have to thank Sibyl," Augusta said, too honest to take credit for someone else's work. "I just made the coffee."

"My compliments," Burch said, favoring Sibyl with an unyielding look. "I see the Elkhorn has at least one reason to be glad of your presence. Now, if you'll excuse me, I have some work to do before bedtime." There was an uncomfortable pause as they listened to his retreating footsteps.

"Of all the rude, offensive men, he's the worst," Sibyl proclaimed, but her condemnation lacked its usual vigor. Augusta started to open her mouth, but Sibyl forestalled her. "If you say one word to defend him, I won't speak to you," she announced with a suspicious catch in her voice. "You're supposed to be on my side." Augusta was too astonished to speak. For the second time in as many days, Sibyl's eyes sparkled with tears.

"I'm afraid Burch doesn't think too much of women," Jesse explained, getting up from the table. "We never had any about the place except Mrs. Ada. She was awful nice, but meek as a sheep. No backbone at all."

"I've got lots of backbone."

"Burch doesn't like women with backbone; he wants them like Mrs. Ada. He always expected to have this place to himself, so he's mighty put out at your being here. Seeing as how you're from the East, he didn't figure on your being interested in ranches."

"Being from the East doesn't mean I have to be completely useless," Sibyl said, smarting at the implication. "I may not know everything there is to know about running a ranch, but there's a lot your precious Mr. Randall doesn't know either."

"I wouldn't let him get you too riled, Miss Cameron. He gets like that when he's crossed. I'm sure he'll calm down by tomorrow."

"I don't care how angry he gets."

"You stick to your guns and see if old Burch doesn't come around," he advised in a brotherly way. "Now I'd better move along. I hear Burch heading out already." The front door slammed, and Sibyl flushed with mortification, knowing Burch had intentionally bypassed the most direct route to his horse to avoid having to speak to her again.

"It sure was mighty good," Jesse said again, taking his hat down from the peg.

"Will you be back for dinner tomorrow?" Augusta asked.

"I'll be here every night till roundup."

"When is that?"

"Burch hasn't decided. Maybe you can ask him tomorrow," he said with a smile as he closed the door behind him.

Augusta rose and began to clear the table, but Sibyl sat looking reflectively toward the front door, her mind burdened with too many thoughts and feelings to sort out all at once.

"Why can't he be like Jesse, instead of an argumentative,

cantankerous brute?" she asked almost wistfully.

"I don't think he's a brute."

"He an opinionated blockhead, and he was from the moment he swooped down to play the gallant knight rescuing the poor damsel. Now he'd sulking because the *poor damsel* hasn't swooned in mindless adulation." She got up with something like a snort, but her mind continued to be preoccupied by inner reflections and a look of mingled disappointment and despair settled over her lovely face. A troubled Augusta held her tongue.

Chapter 5

When Burch came down the next morning there were unmistakable sounds of activity coming from the kitchen. A little surprised, he slipped in unnoticed. Sibyl hummed a sprightly tune as she moved back and forth between stove and table, setting out sausage, Balaam's eggs, ham, biscuits, and a pot of jam. He gazed on her long slender neck and creamy white skin with an intentness that would have surprised and frightened her had she seen it. Being alone with her in the early morning solitude was akin to sharing an intimate secret, and the familiar aching returned with renewed vigor.

He had flung out of the house the night before to show her how unimportant she was to him, but two hours of aimless riding gave him plenty of time to discover the extent of his error. Her image alone had the power to cause a warmth between his thighs that was fed by a hunger so deep and vital it caused his teeth to chatter. I'm acting like a fifteen-year-old with his first saloon girl, he thought disgustedly, but he knew Sibyl had nothing to do with fifte-year-old boys or saloons. She was a beautiful, vibrant woman and the thought of her in his arms made his bones weak.

Damn Uncle Wesley! Why should he be saddled with a beautiful shrew who would devil him by day and haunt his dreams at night? He should have married that girl from Chicago; at least she wasn't as tough as buffalo hide. Now he was caged up with a tantalizing beauty who owned half his ranch, had the warmth of a she-wolf, and whose bed was strictly off limits. Damn! Damn! Damn!

His ruminations came to an abrupt halt when he saw the two coffee pots on the stove; his pulses beat a little faster. Was she really a selfish, brittle-tempered harridan set on having her way in everything, or was it possible that somewhere under that shrill armor plate was a warm, loving woman capable of making him forget the loneliness of a rancher's life?

Burch's attention was gradually drawn to the quiet repose of Sibyl's face. This was how she was meant to be, he thought, not the snapping, snarling alley cat of the last two days. He would discover some way to get past her defenses, for he had decided in that moment she must be his.

He took a deep breath and announced his presence with a cheerful, "Morning."

Sibyl nearly threw a plate of sausages into the air. "You startled me," she said crossly, and then remembered her resolution to be pleasant to him no matter what the provocation. Both of them broke into hesitant smiles.

"I'm not so foolish as to intentionally scare anyone willing to fix me this kind of breakfast. Jesse is going to wish he'd stayed."

"Doesn't he usually sleep in the bunkhouse?"

"Yes, but this summer we've had all we can do to find enough grass for the herds. He only came in to meet you." Burch scrutinized Sibyl's face but could find no indication of more than superficial interest in Jesse's whereabouts. He sat down to the table unaware of his embryonic jealousy.

"Go ahead, or everything will get cold."

Burch made rapid inroads into the pile of pancakes and sausages. "Where's your aunt?" he asked, washing down a mouthful with strong, hot coffee.

"I let her sleep," she said, rigorously repressing her own ripening jealousy. "There's a lot to do today, and she never spares herself."

"You don't either."

"I'm younger, and besides I never get tired."

He regarded her remark skeptically but let it pass. "What are you going to do today?" he asked, beginning on the ham.

"I'd like to begin with the parlor, but there's not a single chair or table to put in it."

"There might be something around here. A few things arrived after Aunt Ada died, but Uncle never bothered to unpack them."

"Where would they be?" she asked eagerly.

"I don't know. Look in the attic or the barns. We stored a lot of stuff in the sheds while the house was being built. In any case, there's not much, not like what you're used to."

"Daddy wasn't rich. He hated to spend money on clothes or the house, so we were actually poor in that way."

"What did your father do?" he asked, finding he enjoyed talking to her like this.

"He taught college, but that was only because he had to. His real interest was in developing new breeds of plants and animals that would help make Virginia farmers prosperous again."

"That was an ambitious task to take on alone."

"Daddy never considered that. He and Mama were born on plantations that never recovered after the war. He felt the cause lay in the lack of scientific agricultural methods and plain wasteful habits as much as depending on one crop."

53

"You seem to know a lot about his work."

She smiled. "It was all I heard from the time I was old enough to sit at the table. I don't think we ever had a conversation that wasn't dominated by Daddy's experiments."

"Was he successful?"

"Very much so, but that was probably his greatest misfortune, because even after years of work, the farmers showed no interest in his results. One man accepted a bushel of a new strain of oats Daddy developed, but when Daddy visited the man later to see how the crop turned out, he told Daddy he had fed it to the horses."

"Your poor father."

"That did lower his enthusiasm for a while, but Daddy never really liked people very much so, after that, he worked just to please himself and was much happier."

Burch laughed. "Did you help with his work?"

"Not the experiments." She got up to pour him another cup of coffee. "Daddy spent all his time teaching and thinking up his next project, so someone had to run the farm for him. That fell to me after mother died."

Burch began to feel uneasy. "Did you actually work the farm?"

"I didn't calve the cows if that's what you mean. We had six laborers, but I made out the orders and supervised all the work."

"Did you learn to ride?" Burch asked, turning the conversation to what he hoped was a safer topic.

"Everyone rides in Virginia, but the farm wasn't nearly as large as this and I drove a buggy."

"We don't use buggies out here. If you can't ride, you'll be confined to your own company for weeks, maybe months on end."

"Aren't there *any* women around here?"

"Only one I know of who lives closer than two days by wagon."

"And if I ride?"

"You can go all the way to Laramie in two days. Why don't I saddle two horses and we can take a ride later this morning?"

"I have too much work to do," she said, taking his empty plate.

He had the feeling work was not the reason for her refusal. "That can wait. Can you be ready by nine-thirty?"

"I can't ride in these clothes."

"No, you'd never sit a cow pony in all those skirts," he said momentarily stumped.

"We'll have to wait until I can order something from Cheyenne."

"No, we won't. Aunt Ada had trunks full of clothes. She was not nearly so well filled out as you," he said, glancing significantly at her womanly figure, "but you ought to find something to wear." Sibyl was not adverse to admiration, but his gaze almost attacked her.

"I wouldn't feel right wearing her clothes."

"Don't be foolish. You and your aunt need some proper clothes for Wyoming. Aunt Ada lost a lot of weight during her last years and she had clothes of all sizes. Uncle couldn't buy enough for her when he found out how sick she was, but she never wore most of them, just one or two to make him happy. Then she'd go back to her old gowns."

"Why can't we wear gowns if she did?"

"Because Aunt Ada never left the house. Uncle Wesley was her whole life. If he had died first, she would have died the next day. Do you want to be cooped up here for several months until I can take you to Cheyenne in the wagon?"

"Several months?" she echoed incredulously.

"I won't be free until after the fall roundup and the steers are sent to market."

"But that won't be until October or November sometime."

He patted his stomach. "If you keep feeding me like this, I'm going to be too lazy to finish before Christmas."

Sibyl looked at the lean, hard muscle of his arms and doubted he would ever be too weak to do whatever he liked.

"Remember, nine-thirty," he said, brushing her cheek with his fingers.

When she realized he had actually touched her without permission, she was so surprised she couldn't think of anything to say until he was gone. Only the empty room heard her pungent observations on men in general and a tall, impudent cousin in particular.

Once she got over feeling guilty, Sibyl enjoyed going through Ada Cameron's clothes. There was a lot that was the wrong size or would need some adjustment, but there were some lovely dresses and several items that were unlike anything she'd ever seen before.

"Do you mean to wear this?" her aunt asked, holding up a leather skirt short enough to show half her calf.

"Not if you want it," Sibyl teased.

"I don't think I *could*."

"Neither do I, but I plan to wear these boots. I don't have any shoes that can survive the winter or the kind of mud I'm persuaded must fill the yard every time it rains."

"But there's grass in the yard."

"Not around the barns and sheds." She pulled on a skirt that was only six inches off the ground. "This ought to do nicely."

"It's too short," protested Augusta.

"Not with the boots. I can't go dragging my petticoats through dust. Besides, there's no one here to stare at me except Ned and Balaam."

"What about the other men, the ones we haven't seen?"

"I won't wear it when they're around."

"Your father would never approve."

"He probably wouldn't look up from his books long enough to notice what I had on."

"Your mother would say it's quite improper," persevered Augusta, remembering her sister's very strict notions. "And I promised her I'd be responsible for you."

"I'm the only one responsible for me. You're here because I love you and couldn't think of going anywhere without you."

"Folks will say I'm older and should know better."

"According to Burch there aren't any folks about here to say anything. He informs me that I have to learn to ride if I wish to see anyone other than himself."

"What about the people we stayed with?"

"I don't think he counts people unless they live in Cheyenne or have a ranch as large as the Elkhorn. Now stop worrying about me. I've got to learn what goes on on this ranch, and I can't do it if I'm confined to the house or a wagon. I have to see things for myself instead of waiting to be told what somebody else thinks I ought to know."

"Are you sure you don't want to go home and forget all about this ranch? Your cousin will pay you generously. You could live comfortably for the rest of your life."

"I could have taken his money a month ago, but I can't leave now without admitting defeat. I didn't like running Daddy's farm at first, but eventually I learned to enjoy it. I have a feeling I'm going to learn to enjoy living out here too. I don't know why; it's certainly nothing like what I expected, but I refuse to run away. Now I've got to hurry. Burch is probably waiting for me already." She picked up some soft leather gloves and a hat she had already set aside. "How do I look?"

"I dare not say," lamented her beset aunt. "I don't think I could bear to have the words pass my lips."

Sibyl giggled and kissed her aunt. "Don't worry, I know what I'm doing."

Chapter 6

Only a slight feeling of self-consciousness betrayed Sibyl's uneasiness as she came downstairs. She had spent quite some time in choosing her clothes for this first ride, and she was unsure of Burch's reaction.

He was waiting in the ranch room when she came down, and Sibyl could tell as soon as his eyes rested on her that she had chosen well. His body tensed and any intention he had of treating her with cool detachment evaporated. His blood was up and hot.

"Am I dressed correctly?" she asked in a demure voice neither Kendrick nor Moreton would have recognized. "I've never been riding in Wyoming before, and it looked like your aunt hadn't worn any of these clothes." Sibyl was wearing a suede jacket over a red blouse, and both were cut low, revealing the whiteness of her skin. The jacket buttoned tightly over her bosom and at her waist, accenting the thrust of her young breasts.

"Aunt Ada never filled out those clothes like that," Burch said, giving voice to his thoughts rather than answering her questions. Sibyl was pleased with his admiration, but she was not yet able to admit that she would dress to please any man, even one as disturbingly handsome as her infuriating cousin. It took an effort to keep the sharpness out of her voice.

"I was dressing for utility, not for looks," she said somewhat untruthfully.

"It's a pleasure to see them so favorably combined," he replied with one of those magic smiles that transformed his face and destroyed Sibyl's composure. A barbed reproof rose to her lips as he boldly spun her around, drinking in every detail of her appearance, but his touch sent such shivers of excitement through her body that she felt hot and tongue-tied. "One look at you riding through the sagebrush and the boys won't be able to concentrate on anything less than a stampede."

"Thank you for the compliment," said Sibyl, trying to laugh, "but that's a terrible exaggeration."

"Any kind of woman can cause a ruckus out here," he said bluntly. "The pretty ones stay in Denver and St. Louis, while the others get married and turn ugly. That only leaves the *soiled doves*, and there's not a fancy house girl in all of Wyoming who can hold a candle to you."

Sibyl's jaw dropped; she hardly knew whether to thank him for his flattery or slap him for his impertinence.

"This place'll soon be full of mangy rascals just dropping by to sit a spell. If they ever get a line on your cooking and how handy you are about the house, I'll have to set some bear traps at the gate."

Sibyl's ripple of laughter sounded spontaneously. "That would be more of a hazard to me than anyone else. I couldn't cause much of a ruckus with a mangled leg."

"You'd set a man in a fever with a wooden leg," Burch said, his eyes devouring her hungrily.

Sibyl was unused to this kind of straightforward appreciation and began to feel ill at ease under Burch's heated scrutiny. Nothing about Kendrick had ever led her to suspect that the nearness of a handsome and vital man could cause such fireworks or unruly emotions. Part of her wanted to respond to the feeling of excitement his presence and touch stirred in her, but things were moving too fast and she was afraid of losing control.

"What kind of horse have you chosen for me?" she asked, moving toward the door.

"I'd rather talk about you than horses," he said, having forgotten all about their plans to ride.

"I thought cowboys worshiped their ponies," she continued, determined to change the focus of their conversation.

"Not Dusty," Burch said, giving in reluctantly and following her. "He hasn't had a saddle on his back much since Aunt Ada gave up riding. He's no good as a cow pony and I just keep him for Balaam and Sanchez."

"It doesn't sound like you have much faith in my riding."

"Easterners are usually dangerous with a horse or rifle, but I'm willing to be convinced."

"I admit I'm more used to driving, but I'll prove to you that Virginians are as good as anybody when it comes to horses."

The ranch buildings lay behind the house and stretched along the creek up toward the canyon. To reach them they had to travel a rock-strewn path that ran through the remains of a flower and herb garden. The mere existence of such neglect would normally have been an affront to Sibyl's sense of organization and would have drawn her immediate attention, but this morning she was only conscious of Burch's nearness. Nothing vegetable or mineral could compare to the vitality and magnetism of the animal at her side.

"Out here no man walks when he can ride," Burch informed her, "and a wagon isn't considered an acceptable substitute."

"I wasn't thinking of a wagon," Sibyl said, tossing her golden hair vigorously. "A smart buggy just big enough for Aunt and me, with a high-stepping horse between the shafts, would make a nice appearance."

"Just the kind of horse to stick his foot in a gopher hole or be spooked by a bull," he stated derisively.

"He wouldn't," she replied, stung.

"He would if he saw a wolf or got caught in one of our thunderstorms."

"And your cow pony keeps his head through all these terrors? How did you manage to develop this paragon in such a short time?" Really, she didn't know what there was about this man that made her put up with his conceit.

Balaam shuffled out of one of the sheds ahead, cutting off Burch's reply. "I was just coming to fetch you, Miss Cameron," he said, sending a black stream of tobacco juice into the dust beside the path. "I got you some of them hens you wanted."

"She doesn't need you going after sage hens, Balaam. The boys and I can bring her all she wants."

"It ain't that kind of hen."

"He offered to catch some of your Aunt Ada's chickens that escaped," explained Sibyl.

"And I did, too, miss. I sneaked up on them last night when they was roosting in them trees and I caught me near 'bout a dozen. Just as easy as stealing pies off a sill."

"Did you build a pen?"

"Yes, ma'am, and I cut their wing feathers just like you told me. But I don't know's you'll be getting many eggs from them, not for a while leastways. They's all spring chickens or old hens. Don't look much like laying stock to me."

"Then catch me a few more. If nothing else, we can have a good pot of chicken and dumplings. But make sure the coop is sturdy. I don't want coyotes, or whatever kind of varmints you have out here, to get them."

"Yes, ma'am," Balaam promised, and shuffled away very pleased with his renewed importance on the ranch.

"You don't let any grass grow under your feet, do you?"

"I won't make the obvious rejoinder," she said, kicking up

a cloud of dust. "I can't imagine why you were so careless with the cow and chickens. And how could you ever get along without eggs and butter?"

"I never really noticed," was his indifferent response, but he favored her with such a strange look that she was sure he was thinking of something else altogether. She lost any interest in discovering what it might be when he led a wheezing nag with a grass belly and sagging back from under the shed. It walked, with eyes nearly closed, as though it required its total concentration just to lift each foot. Sibyl didn't know whether to burst out laughing or turn on her heel.

"I didn't expect to dazzle you with my skill in the saddle," she said, rallying her sense of the ridiculous, "but then I didn't expect to have to wake the horse before I could ride him." A forced laugh failed to hide her injured pride.

Burch had chosen Dusty to tease her. "I'll saddle another horse," he grinned sheepishly.

"Don't bother. At least I know he won't run away with me. Where did you find this old sidesaddle?"

"It belonged to Aunt Ada. It's a little cracked, but it'll do until I can have one made for you." Without warning, he scooped her up in his arms.

"Put me down!" she commanded sharply, surprised out of her determined politeness.

"I can't if I'm going to lift you into the saddle," he replied with irrefutable logic.

She wanted to tell him that it was his holding her so closely she objected to, but she dared not let him know how strongly she was affected by his nearness; he was bound to think of a way to take advantage of it. His brilliant gray eyes looked deeply into hers, disconcerting her so much that she lowered her gaze.

"You'll have to relax a mite," he needled her. "If you stay this stiff, you'll slide right out of the saddle, and then I'll have to catch you again just to keep you from hitting the ground."

He was taunting her, his own excitement at her nearness attacking his reason and control. She cudgeled her brain to think of something that would show him how utterly wrong he was and at the same time undermine his momentary advantage over her. "Relax," he urged in a softer voice, "I'm not going to drop you."

"I didn't expect to be so fortunate," she replied dryly, able to ease the tension in her muscles only slightly.

"That's a little better. You can put your head on my shoulder if you like, just to keep from having to hold it up, you understand."

"Put me down and stop trying to maul my person. You should be ashamed to take advantage of me with such a shabby trick."

"It wasn't a trick."

"It was too."

"I'm not ashamed of it."

"That doesn't surprise me in the least. I don't think you could be shamed."

"But I can."

"Please don't tell me what it would take. I doubt my maidenly modesty could stand the shock."

"I think you could stand just about anything."

"I hope that's not your idea of a compliment."

"It's a Wyoming compliment."

"Then Wyoming has a lot to learn about manners."

"And Virginia has a lot to learn about having fun."

"Put me in that saddle or let me down this minute," she demanded, trying to calm her racing pulses.

"I can't talk you into staying here?"

"Certainly not!"

"I was afraid you'd feel that way."

The big lummox had the gall to look disappointed. She would have perished rather than admit she liked his arms too well for her own comfort.

"Up you go," he forewarned her and, with an expert toss, landed her comfortably in the saddle.

"I can tell you've done this before."

"Just practicing for you."

She gathered up the reins. "You have a smooth answer for everything, but don't think you've fooled me. Is there no way to get this slug moving?" she asked, getting no response from the reins or the gentle pressure of her knees.

"You've got to wake him up first," he said, giving Dusty a whacking good slap on the rump. The startled horse's eyes flew open and he bounded forward with a loud snort. Sibyl nearly lost her seat, but by the time she had regained her balance, the lazy brute had dropped out of a gallop, and it was an easy task to convince him to return to the shed.

"I'd have him run you down if I thought he was up to it," she threatened, half angry and half amused.

"There's no call to hurt the old creature's feelings."

"He's too insensate to hear a word I've said," she said, sliding from the saddle before Burch could move to help her. "I want to ride astride and I want a horse that's more alive than dead."

Burch grinned wider than ever and disappeared into the barn only to reappear a moment later with a well-favored gelding already saddled and bridled.

"You're the most deceitful, conniving man I've ever had the misfortune to be related to," Sibyl said with real feeling.

"Only by marriage," he chuckled, hugely enjoying her discomfiture but secretly pleased that she was not taken in by his tricks.

"That's the only consideration that allows me to hold up my head. Now either provide me with a mounting block or show me the nearest fence."

"I can mount you."

"And dangle me helplessly in your arms while you stand

65

about gabbing nonsense? No, thank you."

"I thought you liked my arms."

"You thought no such thing. Where is that fence?"

"I'll help you up." She regarded him skeptically. "I promise to do it right this time."

"This is your last chance to be a man of your word."

He scooped her up and for a brief moment held her tightly against his chest.

"You perfidious—" she began angrily, but he merely laughed and helped her into the saddle.

"I keep my word, even when I don't want to."

"It's good to know you have at least one redeeming trait," she countered, trying to soothe her ruffled nerves before her agitation communicated itself to her horse.

"Just one?" he quizzed her before producing a piercing whistle that made Sibyl wince.

"It's possible you have a few more," she admitted, "but you've kept them so well hidden, I can't guess what they might be."

A huge white stallion with an Arabian head and quarter horse rump charged out of the barn and up to them. He nuzzled Burch, almost knocking him down in his attempt to find the sugar he knew was hidden in the cowboy's pockets. "That's two," Sibyl told him with a merry twinkle. "You're good to your horse."

She kicked her mount into a canter and then an easy gallop. She had no idea where she was going, but she wanted to get a head start on Burch. But she underestimated the experience of a cowboy trained on the range, where mounting his horse out of a sound sleep is almost second nature. Silver Birch—the hands had given his horse that name as a joke and it had stuck—bounded forward the instant Burch's hands clasped the saddle horn. With a hop and a swing, Burch was in the saddle, thundering after Sibyl before she had gone twenty-five yards.

66

Sibyl exulted in the chase and the exhilaration of having a good horse under her and the open prairie ahead. It brought back memories of her childhood, when she rode her pony at a headlong gallop across the countryside, racing pell-mell over every hill, the wind streaming through her long golden hair and bringing tears to her eyes. Sibyl glanced over her shoulder at Burch following her, and she laughed for sheer joy. His powerful stallion covered the ground with enormous strides, but Burch weighed a hundred pounds more than Sibyl and his mount could only cut into her lead by slow inches.

Sibyl was elated with the success of her gambit. The morning was still cool, and the limitless horizon gave her a feeling of unfettered freedom; and clean, crisp air and vigorous exercise brought a blush to cheeks as soft as down. Burch drove up on her right, shouting and gesturing at something ahead, but she didn't want to listen; she felt so good she wanted to ride forever, and she swung sharply away from him. Burch yelled his warning again, but the cold fear in his voice was caught and thrown back by the onrushing wind. He set down to ride in earnest, grimly lashing Silver Birch across the shoulders with all his strength.

Sibyl rode her hardest, but Silver Birch was a magnificent animal and, under Burch's punishment, closed the gap quickly. Burch caught her bridle and swung her around in a great circle until she came to a stop facing the ranch.

"Why in hell didn't you stop when I called you?" he bellowed, his face dark with fury and his features still rigid with alarm. The laughter died in Sibyl's eyes.

"I just wanted to beat you," she answered, baffled by his rage.

"Wanted to break your neck, you mean."

"I don't need anyone to watch over me," Sibyl snapped, even more confused by his obvious relief than by his anger. Could he have been afraid she would beat him?

"What you need is someone to tan your backside when you're so headstrong."

Sibyl's anger boiled up, shattering all her resolution. "Not even my father dared strike me."

"It's not what I'd like to do myself, but by God I'll flog you if you ever pull that stunt again."

Sibyl forgot she had ever wanted to be nice to him. "If you touch me, I'll put a hole through you big enough for two weasels to run abreast."

"Anyone dumb enough to ride a strange horse at full gallop over unfamiliar ground wouldn't know which end of a gun to point."

"If you think I'm so stupid, you can have your precious horse back and I'll walk back to the ranch."

"You can break your own neck any time you like," he continued, ignoring her remark, "but I paid two hundred and fifty dollars for that horse, and I'll not see him killed just because of your childish desire to show off in front of a man."

Sibyl was so angry she wanted to cry and scream at the same time. "I don't know where you got such an exaggerated opinion of your charm and good looks," she said, spitting out the words like grape seeds after their succulent flesh has been devoured, "but I'm not that desperate. Nor am I impressed by a lot of muscles in leather britches."

"I don't allow cattle to kill themselves without cause, and I see no reason why I should make an exception in your case."

Blind rage drove Sibyl to swing at him, but he caught her arm easily. "Monster!" she cried, snatching her hand back to wipe away angry tears.

"Not monster enough to carry you back to your aunt with a broken neck."

"I wouldn't break my neck in some harmless gallop," she stormed at him. "I can ride as well as you."

"You'd need wings to cross that canyon, and I know your horse can't fly."

"I think you're crazy, or do you always get drunk after breakfast?"

"You really didn't see it, did you?"

"I don't know what you're raving about," she said, striving to hold back her tears.

Against her vigorous protests, he led her back in the direction she had been taking at a full gallop only minutes before. Scalding words of denunciation died in her throat when she found herself at the rim of a hidden canyon eight feet deep and close to twenty feet across. Had Burch been a little farther behind, she would have killed her horse and probably herself as well. Shock held her motionless.

"Tell me how you planned to cross that."

She didn't answer him; she couldn't. The full realization of what had almost happened hit her with numbing force and she slumped in the saddle, barely able to hold on to the reins.

"You didn't know it was there, did you?"

Sibyl managed to shake her head even though her whole body trembled uncontrollably. For an awful moment, she though she was going to be sick.

"It's all right," Burch reassured her in a changed voice, "it's over." He dismounted and gently helped her down.

"I didn't see it," she stammered.

"Don't think about it any more," he said, putting his arm around her and inviting her to lean on him.

"I could have been killed." The shock was so great that she clung blindly to him, seeking the comfort of his strength.

Striving to restrain urges almost too strong to be controlled, Burch held her tightly, electrified by the feeling of her body against his. He had dreamt of her in his arms but was unprepared for the storm of desire it awoke in his breast. It was incredibly wonderful to hold her close, but the fire building in his loins was agony; desire, red-hot and hungry, coursed through every vein until he felt as unsteady as she.

Her grip on him tightened until he could restrain himself no longer, and his lips descended upon hers in a crushing, devastating embrace.

Sibyl returned his kisses with ardor, clinging even more tightly to his body for the feeling of security it offered, yet drinking in the heady feeling of his burning lips on hers, feeling dazed by the sweetness of being desired by this man. She had never imagined it would be pleasant to be in the arms of a man, and the sheer magnitude of its wonderfulness made her heedless of restraint. She *wanted* him to kiss her until she was breathless.

Despite the magical sensations that overwhelmed her, Sibyl was soon unmistakably aware of Burch's hot, enflamed body against hers, calling forth an answering heat from her own quiescent, unnurtured passion. It was only gradually that she realized that her own body was responding of its own will. Her treacherous body *wanted* Burch's body as much as her lips desired his kisses. How could she possibly protect herself *from* herself?

"My God," moaned Burch, "how good you feel in my arms." His hands roamed over her body, overjoyed to realize that the reality of her outstripped his anticipation. His lips left trails of hot desire across her flesh that caused her to flush with pleasure and panic. "I want you," he whispered, pressing her hips against his swelling groin. "My God, how I want you."

Sibyl was conscious of a yearning, an escalating need to be swallowed up by the mesmerizing pleasure spreading through her limbs with lightning speed. Desire strained against reason, leaping with frantic energy to meet the fiery passion of the vigorous man nearly crushing her in his embrace. It gloried in the feeling of his lips on hers and in the hungry tongue that fed on the nectar of her mouth; it wrapped her in a euphoria she hoped would never end. Yet if it did not end soon, she would be lost.

"Stop," she managed to say, her ingrained fears and doubts shrieking insanely inside her head, but still she clung to him, unable to cast aside the feeling of indescribable pleasure his embraces gave her.

"Please let me go," she begged, but Burch, enveloped in his own red haze of desire, didn't hear her plea. He was beyond any awareness other than his own maddening needs, and he slowly lowered her to the ground. Sibyl felt herself slipping over the edge of a precipice where caution is banished and unbounded desire enthroned. She knew she must do something, or surrender completely to the passion that had already conquered her body and was striving to fasten its viselike grip on her mind as well.

Dimly, Burch knew he should not devour Sibyl here on the open prairie, but the loveliness of her, the delicious smell of her hair, the warmth of her body, the velvety feel of her skin, pushed him beyond the limits of restraint.

Unable to reach him with words, Sibyl gathered the last of her strength and dealt Burch a ringing slap, which brought him to his senses with such a savage jolt that it caused the blood to pound unmercifully in his temples. Sibyl rolled quickly out of his embrace and turned to face him, disheveled, panting, and under the sway of powerful cross currents that still threatened to immobilize her. For a moment they faced each other like protagonists frozen in time, shock and amazement holding them in its grip.

"Is this the way you treat all women?" Sibyl asked, fighting a wild desire to fling herself at him again.

"Only the ones that hug and tease a man until he can't stand it any more." Burch rolled over on his back, drained by the struggle within him.

"I didn't hug you."

"What do you call throwing your arms about a man's neck fit to choke him?" he barked, sitting up with the quickness of a rattler. Sibyl drew back instinctively.

71

"I was just holding on because I was frightened," she argued, trying to forget she had done much more.

"Then I'll have to see that you gallop toward another ravine tomorrow." He spoke more easily as the grip of passion began to loosen its hold. "The country is full of them. You might grow to like being hugged."

"Never." But her assertion lacked conviction. The delicious feeling continued to thrill her body and she could not command her voice.

"Was it so bad?"

"I could never enjoy being mauled," she said stiffly, trying to put some distance between him and her near capitulation. "I would appreciate it if you would forget this morning ever happened."

"You might as well ask me to forget I was born."

"Something like this is no more than a shameful memory for a woman," she said, sounding more like the shrill virgin of two days ago. "Mere vulgar brawling is something to be avoided in a relationship."

"I wouldn't call it brawling; more like a friendly wrestling match."

"There was nothing friendly about your intentions."

"No, ma'am, being friends was not what I had in mind."

Sibyl flushed in spite of herself. "It's time we got back," she said, getting to her feet and carefully brushing off her clothes. "Aunt Augusta will begin to wonder what's happened to us."

Burch stood up reluctantly. "You could tell her we got lost."

"I never lie to my aunt."

"Never?"

"Not even once," she stated emphatically, taking her horse's reins and heading back toward the ranch.

"Do you intend to walk back?" Burch inquired, puzzled.

"Yes."

"Why, when you've got a perfectly good horse?"

"Because I can't mount by myself, and I don't trust you to touch me again."

Without fanfare, Burch pitched her roughly into the saddle. "Hungry for you I may be," he growled, "but I'll not force any woman against her will. I can touch you without falling down in a rutting heat."

Sibyl's color rose considerably. "I didn't mean it like that."

"That's how you said it."

"I just meant I didn't trust you to control instincts you didn't really *want* to control."

"Now there you have me," he drawled, flashing his devastating grin. "I wished mighty hard we were the only two people in the world."

"I wouldn't give in even then." Unknowingly, she wanted him to try to convince her, but he only grunted in disagreement. They rode back in thoughtful silence.

"Shall we ride tomorrow?" Burch asked when they reached the barn.

"I'm not sure."

"You don't have to be afraid I'll rape you."

"I wasn't," she fired up.

"Good. I bought this horse for you to ride, not stand about eating its head off while you hide in the house."

"Oh, all right, as long as you promise to behave."

"I never said I'd behave," he retorted, leading both horses into the barn. "I just said I wouldn't force you." He cast her such a devilish grin that she was glad he couldn't see her response.

A little more encouragement, my girl, and you'll let him do anything he wants, she told herself as she started back to the house. If you don't watch it, you'll find yourself slipping into the precise trap you came out here to avoid. And there is no reason to think that those powerful legs or charming smiles are going to make him any different. Men are all alike.

But the memory of her newly discovered passion remained vivid in her mind. Now she *knew* women were possessed of the same desires and longings as men. She had enjoyed his lips, his strong arms, his lean hungry body pressed against hers. Just the memory of his greedy mouth warmed her blood and brought a foolish smile to her lips. She had been mistaken to dismiss passion as a repellant affliction of males only. A whole reality lay beyond the boundaries of her knowledge, one she knew nothing about. She could not be satisfied with just a hint of what lay beyond.

But a voice urged caution, or risk being washed away by the very tide she sought to understand.

Chapter 7

Sibyl wiped the perspiration from her forehead before opening the oven. The heavy aroma of cooking prime beef filled the kitchen; two standing rib roasts, with deep brown crinkled crusts, simmered in their own bubbling juices. Sibyl dipped out several cups of the rich brown liquid to set aside for gravy. Satisfied the roasts would be done in time, she turned her attention to getting six pans of biscuits ready to go in as soon as the meat came out.

Augusta attentively watched a large pot of green beans cooking in a thick mushroom sauce; in the cool of the pantry, a towering pile of fresh corn lay under damp towels, waiting to be popped into boiling water barely ten minutes before serving; mounds of potatoes, a deep dish filled with squash covered with cheese and bread crumbs, and steaming bowls of fresh lima beans were only part of the main fare; a nearby table held several cakes and pies, a custard, a platter of cherry tarts, and the dishes of smoked ham the women had prepared earlier; outside, large slabs of butter and pots of cream lay submerged in the well to keep them cool. The Elkhorn crew was coming to meet Sibyl this evening, and Augusta had offered to cook dinner for them.

"We almost owe it to them, when you consider the food they get from that disagreeable little Mexican," she said with unfeigned compassion. That was before she discovered that there would be two dozen hungry men seated at the table expecting to eat their fill.

"It was a very thoughtful thing to do," Sibyl assured her aunt after Augusta spent the next two days apologizing for volunteering her for such a horrendous task. "Now stop worrying about it; we won't have to do it very often. It'll be good practice for Christmas or one of the other parties Burch tells me we're supposed to give during the year. I'm just glad Ned got back with our supplies and the cow."

Ned had done more than that. "What on earth?" Sibyl exclaimed when he returned, followed by a second wagon driven by a young man and his wife. But that was nothing compared to her surprise when he pulled back the canvas flap and told her to look inside. Two dozen chickens, a boar, and a sow with a litter of well-grown pigs were crowded into the small space.

"All I wanted was a cow, not a whole farm" she protested, nearly overwhelmed.

"That's what I couldn't find, miss. Everyone was willing to part with a couple of hens, but no one would sell their cow no matter what I offered. These folk were wishing to sell up, so I bought everything. I figured you needed a churn for butter, pans for milk, and some crocks for the cheese."

Sibyl was momentarily overcome, but Augusta was delighted. "You're a splendid man, Ned. I don't know why we didn't think of it ourselves. But won't these people need them for their new place?"

"I'm Betty Crabtree, ma'am, and this is my husband, John," the young woman said, climbing down from the wagon and introducing herself to Sibyl. "We don't plan to live in the country again. In fact, I don't care if I never see another cow or pig as long as I live. John has promised to go back to his accounting job. He has a position in San Francisco if we can just get the money together to get there. Ned told us you might need some help about the place, you being new and not settled in yet."

"Well . . . " began Sibyl uncertainly.

"We don't need much more."

"There is a lot that needs doing," suggested Augusta.

"We *do* need help," agreed Sibyl, making up her mind. "Ned, show them where to put that wagon and do something about those pigs. Tell Balaam, he'll know what to do, but for goodness sakes don't let them run loose until I get a chance to talk to Mr. Randall."

It was wonderful to have milk and fresh butter again. She guessed she'd use the pigs for hams and bacon, but before she could decide where to build the smokehouse, the sow gave birth to a new litter of pigs. "You'll have to sell 'em, miss," Balaam informed her. "Mr. Burch won't have no part of running a pig farm."

The thought of Burch up to his ankles in mud and squealing pigs caused Sibyl to periodically break out into unexplained chuckles for the next two days, but her aunt was too busy to be curious about the cause. She put Betty to work scrubbing the house from top to bottom, while Ned and John spent their time building pens for the hogs and a shed for the cow. Balaam was deputized to find space for the additional chickens, some prized Rhode Island Reds. Sibyl didn't know what she was going to do with so many animals during the winter, but she decided not to worry about it until she had to.

"Why don't we eat early," Augusta suggested when they realized how long it was going to take to serve the dinner. "Then we can wait on the table."

"I'm tempted, but even if I have to get up twenty times during the meal, I'm going to sit down and eat just like I'm one of them," Sibyl decided.

"But you can't carry on a sensible conversation, much less eat your dinner properly, if you're jumping up like a jack-in-the-box the whole time."

"I know, Betty and John can serve dinner," Sibyl exclaimed, delighted to have solved her problem. "Now we can sit down and eat like we *really* belong."

Jesse was the first of the men to arrive. "Evening, Miss Cameron," he said, hanging his hat on the peg. "I scraped my boots and nearly took the skin off washing my hands," he said with a cheerful grin. "I wasn't taking any chances on being sent back to the pump and losing my place at the table. I got the boys lined up like steers at a trough. You can inspect their hands as they come through the door."

"I'll do no such thing," Sibyl said, smiling. "You'll have them thinking I'm some kind of straight-laced Puritan come to teach them manners and how to say grace."

"They'll be on their best behavior tonight, you can depend on that. They ain't seen a woman in so long they probably won't make any sound at all."

Sibyl laughed, but his comments proved prophetic. The men came through the door, self-effacing, hats in hands. They had obviously put on their best flannel shirts and jeans, the handkerchiefs tied around their necks were neat and clean, and not a single one left a trail of dirt or mud on the freshly mopped floor. They milled about at the far end of the room, barely speaking above a whisper, waiting for someone to tell them what to do.

Sibyl was pleased to see Burch had gone to the trouble of dressing himself more nicely than anyone else. He was the most handsome man there and her eyes kept straying in his direction.

"The boys would be happy to help with the food," he offered.

"We've already taken care of that. Why don't you all sit down."

"Not until you ladies are seated," Burch said.

"I still have the biscuits to go."

"We can wait." Augusta looked at Sibyl in wordless appeal. Capitulating, she took off her apron and they took their seats, one on either side of Burch.

The cowboys appeared to be extremely youthful and miserably uncomfortable; the combined shock of clean clothes and two nice-looking women embarrassed them into a bashful silence, but the smells coming from the kitchen demolished any tendency to dawdle in coming to the table. They mumbled their "Pleased to meet you" and "Pleasure, ma'am" with hung heads, and stood shifting their weight on spindly legs until Burch signaled them to take their seats.

"Just help yourself to whatever's nearest you," Augusta told them kindly.

After that, things began to take care of themselves. Burch and Jesse did most of the talking, but the men became more comfortable as their bellies grew full. Sibyl was amused to see the tension and uncertainty replaced by a luxurious contentment. When the last piece of cake had been refused and the custard eaten, Augusta rose from the table. The men scrambled quickly to their feet.

"Why don't you relax near the fireplace. You can smoke if you like," she offered.

Sibyl looked sharply at Augusta, but Burch smiled at her with grateful approval.

"Are you sure it won't bother you, ma'am? Cigars are mighty strong," Jesse said, directing his question to Sibyl.

"We can open the windows if it gets too strong, but I would appreciate it if you wouldn't use tobacco until someone can find spittoon."

Burch didn't look entirely pleased with that, but Sibyl wasn't about to have Betty spend another day scrubbing up after men too thoughtless to consider the work they made.

The men were profuse in their praise of dinner, so much so that Sibyl began to feel a little guilty about Sanchez's feelings. She wouldn't have felt so charitably toward him had she known he was pitying them for having to eat such bland, odd food and then be forced to thank her for it.

It took a long time to clean up, even with Betty's and

John's help, and when Sibyl was at last free to join the men, they were in the midst of a discussion about the roundup just ahead. Except for the pleasant fullness in their stomach, they had forgotten all about the women, and Sibyl's entering the circle produced a widespread constraint; they were still not comfortable in her presence.

"I've decided to begin the roundup early, even though it means we'll have to work the range by ourselves," Burch was saying.

"They'd bring a better price if they were fatter," Jesse pointed out.

"I've thought about that, but I think this year it'll pay us to try and beat the market."

"That could mean giving away a lot of money."

"Or saving it, if the bottom drops out. There're too many beeves for sale this year to suit me."

"What would be giving away money?" asked Sibyl.

"Burch is thinking of sending the steers to market early," Jesse explained. "I suggested we keep them on the range a few extra weeks. They don't look very good now, and they'd bring a better price with a little extra flesh on them."

"Why can't we wait?" Sibyl demanded sharply of Burch. "It seems silly to throw money away for no reason." A hush fell over the room and the crew fidgeted uneasily, but Jesse watched with apparent disinterest as Sibyl waited impatiently for an explanation Burch was not at all anxious to give.

"I doubt they'd gain any weight no matter how long we put off the roundup. There's hardly any grass left, and what there is will be needed for the winter. In fact," he said, deciding to bite the bullet, "I was planning to sell some of the breeding stock as well. All the herds are weak and I doubt if the old cows will survive a hard winter."

"But the last five have been very mild," Jesse obligingly pointed out.

"With plenty of lush grass each summer," Burch finished

for him, "but this summer was bone dry. I don't like the signs, and I don't like the condition of the herds."

"But even if it's only a few dollars a head, that would be a lot of money," argued Sibyl. "I can't agree to let you do that."

"I also think," continued Burch with deadly calm, "that every other rancher will hold his steers back, hoping they'll pick up a few pounds."

"That's because it's the sensible thing to do," snapped Sibyl. The tension in the room was so great it was almost tangible.

"If everyone takes their cattle to market at the same time, the price will drop," Burch explained with excruciating self-control. "Maybe a little, maybe a lot, it's impossible to say. All I know is that the price is the best now it's ever been; if we hit the crest of the market, even with under-fed steers, we're assured of getting a good price."

"How many will you sell this year?"

"Somewhere between twenty-five hundred and three thousand head."

"At only five dollars a head, you're talking about an extra fifteen thousand. How much can the price fluctuate?" she asked Jesse. Burch's eyes flamed dangerously; not one cowboy moved a muscle.

"I can't say, Miss Cameron," answered Jesse. "The market is a mighty changeable thing. If it stays strong, maybe two or three dollars, ten at the outside. But I think you ought to listen to Burch. He knows the market."

"This has nothing to do with markets, it's plain dollars and cents. How long can prices be depended upon to stay at this level?" Sibyl's continued referral to the second in command enraged Burch and made everyone except Jesse think of at least a dozen different things they ought to be doing; Augusta poured herself another cup of coffee after she'd already decided that any more would keep her awake.

"I can't say, Miss Cameron," responded Jesse. "You follow Burch's advice; he knows what he's doing."

"I've heard what he has to say, and I think we ought to wait as long as possible before we sell."

Burch's eyes rested on Sibyl, cold and threatening, not at all touched with the amorous heat she had come to expect. She was a trifle disconcerted by the intensity of the hostility reflected there, but she refused to back down. "It's my herd, too," she said defensively.

"I'll take your wishes into consideration," Burch said with quiet deliberation, "but we won't discuss it any more. The boys have to be off early tomorrow. We don't require breakfast, ma'am," he replied to Augusta's courageous but unenthusiastic offer to feed the men at dawn.

The tension seemed to evaporate in the hubbub created by the men's departure and their free-flowing compliments on dinner. Sibyl had almost forgotten the look on Burch's face until he closed the door behind Jesse and turned to face her with blazing eyes.

"What do you mean by trying to undermine my authority in front of the men?" he demanded, bearing down upon her as though he meant to vent his fury by attacking her bodily.

"I wasn't doing any such thing," she shot back, stung by his unfair accusation but rattled by the sheer physical force of his wrath. "I only wanted to know why you were set on giving away thousands of dollars. You should have at least told me about it. After all, I do have a right to know what goes on around here."

"And then you kept asking for Jesse's opinion."

"That's hardly significant when all he said was I should listen to you."

Burch's eyes clouded over. "Since you don't know the first thing about ranching, that advice shouldn't have been necessary."

"I don't have to have been born in Wyoming to have common sense. I see no reason to throw money away, and I have just as much right as you to make decisions around here."

"My uncle may have felt he couldn't ignore your claims on him, but he left absolute control of the ranch to me. I make all the decisions, and I say the cattle go to market as soon as we can get them to the railhead. I may even take them to Chicago myself."

"And I say they don't! I'll have my lawyers fight you over that clause, if there really is such a clause."

"I don't lie, not even to ignorant little girls without enough sense to know when to shut up."

Sibyl was nearly bereft of speech.

"Your lawyers are powerless in the territories. Before they could do anything the steers would already be in Chicago."

"That's unethical," she stormed, feeling stymied.

"I don't think so. I've let you come in here, take over this house, and do anything you want without a word of protest. I even let you saddle me with an extra hand and God only knows how many cows, pigs, and chickens, and still I haven't raised any objections. From the number of the pens and sheds you've built, we'll be taken for farmers instead of ranchers."

"But I did it so everybody would have decent food."

"I realize that. Why do you think I never interfered? Your organization is remarkable, but this is my home and it would have been nice if I had been consulted."

Sibyl squirmed at the echo of her own words.

"Be that as it may, you can have a free hand in the house and I promise not to interfere. I'll even listen to your suggestions and answer any questions you have about the management of the ranch, but there are two considerations that I absolutely insist upon: You are not to question me in front of the men, and my decisions are final."

"And if I don't agree?" she said, livid at his dictatorial stance.

"You can go back to Virginia. If you stay here and try to fight me, I'll turn you across my knee and give you the spanking your father should have given you years ago."

"You wouldn't *dare*!"

"Then I'll send you to your room until you stop behaving like a spoiled, willful brat." He slammed through the door, leaving her no means of venting her wrath. She turned to her aunt, swollen with fury wanting just the slightest touch to set it off.

"I don't think it was thoughtful of you to embarrass him in front of his men, dear," her aunt pointed out in an apologetic voice. "Men always set great store by that kind of thing."

An odd, completely unfamiliar sensation came over Sibyl, and she fled to the sanctuary of her own chamber.

"Oh dear," sighed Augusta, "I'm afraid this is going to be rather difficult."

Much to Sibyl's surprise, the threw herself on her bed and burst into tears. Deep, heartrending sobs flowed from her as a new kind of misery enslaved her whole being. Never had she felt so thoroughly wretched, not even when she thought she was going to have to choose between being a spinster and marrying Kendrick. She hated Burch Cameron; he was the most cruel and insensitive man she'd ever known, and she didn't know why she had ever thought he was handsome. No one, not even the obnoxious Moreton, and ever dared to call her ignorant or stupid. She would show him, the blind, crass beast, that she was not the empty, foolish female he thought; she would show him that she knew just as much about managing a ranch and making money as he did. One didn't have to be covered with cow dung for a decade to understand basic economics, and if he thought his strong arms or swaggering good looks were going to deflect her from pushing her ideas forward, he just didn't know her. Maybe the girls in Wyoming simpered and fell over backward when he smiled at them, but Sibyl Cameron was made of different stuff, and he would find that he had hooked a rival worthy of his rod. She'd drive him so hard he'd never think of kissing her again.

But this resolution only caused her to cry harder; victory,

even in her imagination, seemed empty and tasteless. All of a sudden she didn't know what she wanted; everything she had was useless, and everything she reached for was beyond her grasp. Wyoming wasn't turning out to be any better than Virginia. It didn't matter that he gave her complete freedom in the house; couldn't he see she had done it all for him? Why couldn't he listen to her? All she wanted was to share the ranch with him. How could he be so blind? She cried all the harder.

Chapter 8

The house was quiet when Sibyl came down the next morning; Augusta was still in her room, and she suffered from the want of some company other than her own. All at once she felt cooped up and in need of some fresh air, but she hadn't gone ten feet outside her door when she saw a small cloud of dust in the distance made by a group of approaching horsemen. Feeling unaccountably alone, she hurried back into the house, but it wasn't long before she could make out three cowboys heading toward the ranch accompanied by a huge, plodding Hereford bull and some dozen-and-a-half cows and calves. A feeling of satisfaction swept through her and set a smile on her drawn face. Her father's breeding herd was here at last! It had taken so long she had begun to worry they might have been lost or stolen. "Aunt Augusta, the herd is here," she shouted up the stairs and hurried outside.

Two of the men looked to be no more than sixteen, eighteen at the outside, and were devoting all their energies to keeping the fat and lazy animals moving, especially the huge bull. The third cowboy wasn't a boy at all but a grown man, probably about forty and of formidable size. It was immediately apparent that he had an open, outgoing personality and a curiosity about everything that happened around him.

"Hello there. I brought Burch's cows over to him. I saw these poor fellows wondering all over the hills and decided to take mercy on them."

The flow of words ceased abruptly when he got a closer look at Sibyl, and he let loose a long, slow whistle. "I heard tell Burch's Virginia cousin had come to stay, but I didn't know you looked pretty as a picture postcard. I'd'a been trampling down the sagebrush just to set and look at you for a spell."

"You can stop trying to get around me with all that flattery," smiled Sibyl, taking him to be the honest, good-natured man he seemed to be. "And just so there won't be any future misunderstanding, that herd belongs to me, not my cousin. He's not here right now, but you're welcome to come inside and wait for him if you like."

The big man got down and took off his hat in a salute. "Lasso Slaughter's the name, miss. I'm young Randall's neighbor up the creek a few miles. That's a mighty fine bull you've got there. Burch planning to use it to upgrade the herd?" He walked around the creature, who was content to stand still after his long walk. "Yes sir, a mighty fine bull. I'd like to put some of my cows to him, see what kind of steers he throws. How is he at foraging?"

"I don't know. Daddy always kept him up, but the cows were allowed out until late fall."

"Fall in Virginia's no more than midsummer out here," Lasso sniffed. "This fellow's going to have to be penned up, fed, and sheltered throughout the winter, or you'll find him a frozen carcass in some arroyo come spring."

"Of course I'll keep him up," answered Sibyl. "He's the only one of his kind. You can't expect me to let such a valuable animal wander over the range."

87

"What does Burch say about it?"

"He hasn't seen him yet, so I haven't had a chance to find out." And after last night, she was a little nervous about telling him.

"I think you're about to get your chance," Lasso said, nodding in the direction of a huge white stallion cantering easily toward the house. The bull looked up in idle curiosity, then went back to the more interesting task of trying to push his head through the fence rails to reach the more appetizing grass on the other side. "There's not much spirit in the critter, is there?"

"He's bred for beef, not spirit," retorted Sibyl, provoked into springing angrily to the defense of her father's achievement.

"If he doesn't have spirit, he won't survive."

"What's all this?" Burch asked, giving Lasso a hearty greeting. "One of the boys said he saw you heading this way with a huge bull in tow. I knew you must be up to another one of your tricks."

"That's not my trick. The little lady says it's hers."

Burch stiffened and turned mechanically toward Sibyl. She flushed slightly but stood her ground. Lasso, only casually interested at first, sensed the rapidly escalating tension and became very attentive.

"Are you responsible for all these animals being here?"

"Yes," she replied, and for the first time in her life, she felt a reluctance to explain herself. "This is my father's herd, and that is his best bull."

Burch began to study the sleepy animal. "You planned to put him to my herd?"

"Somebody's going to have to wake him up first," Lasso commented.

"It seemed such a waste to sell him when you had all these cows and father had spent so many years trying to breed one like him."

"So you had him sent out without saying a word to me."

"I didn't have time to ask you. Well, I couldn't, really, not when I had to make all the arrangements before I left Virginia."

"And you never thought to mention it to me after you got here?"

"It took them so long I guess I just forgot."

"Did it ever occur to you that he could arrive before you got here and that I might sell him?"

"Nobody would sell him once they saw him."

"If you don't mind a bull that takes a siesta every afternoon," Lasso interpolated with maddening calm. Burch's mouth twitched.

"You say it took your father twenty years to come up with this animal?"

"Burch Randall, that is the finest bull in Virginia, and if you look down your long nose at him, then you don't know anything at all about cows, no matter how stubborn you can be about markets and roundups."

"He is not the best bull in Virginia," declared Burch with a wink that caused Lasso to nearly burst his ribs trying to hold in his laughter. "He's not even the one-hundredth best bull in Virginia."

"You — you *ox!*" Sibyl finally exploded.

"He's not in Virginia, don't you see?" explained Lasso, choking. "He's in Wyoming, so he can't be the best or even the worst bull in Virginia."

Sibyl's expression became glacial when Burch laughed as hard as Lasso at the childish joke.

"He slid that past you smooth as silk," said Lasso, going off into another belly laugh.

Sibyl's feelings were still lacerated from the previous night, and she was so angry that she wouldn't have cared if the bull had lowered his head and trampled both men. She had suffered something of a shock when Burch and the bull burst upon her at the same time, but being made the butt of some stupid joke was too much.

"He's the best bull I've ever set eyes on," said Burch with a jubilant crow of laughter, "and if he doesn't make me the richest man in Wyoming, it'll only be because I don't have enough cows for him."

"You mean you like him?" Sibyl said, relieved and too confused by the rapid swing of emotions to be able to keep track of the true meaning of anything any longer.

"Of course I like him! What rancher wouldn't like a bull that could add fifty pounds to every steer he sent to market? I don't know how your father produced him, but if he puts his stamp on his offspring, he'll be the best thing to happen to the cattle industry since Crazy Horse was confined to the reservation. I've got plans for you, my man," he said, slapping the dozing bull on the shoulder. "You're the first good thing to happen to the Elkhorn since Uncle died." Burch did not see Sibyl swell with indignation. "I'm going to settle you down in some nice corner, and come next spring we're going to wear you thin doing your duty. By fall you'll be glad of a little peace and quiet."

"Miss," the young man named Gaddy spoke up, "if these are your cows, you ought to know five or six of them got run off."

"When?" asked Burch, all interest in silly jokes gone.

"When we bedded down for the night, maybe six or seven days out of Laramie. These two men came whooping and screaming down out of the hills and scattered the herd. We didn't know what to do at first—go after the men or the cows—but before we could make up our minds, they had run off close to a half dozen and disappeared. By the time we got the rest together and settled back down, there was no sign of them. We tried to follow them the next day, but the trail went into rough country, where we couldn't possibly take the herd. Since there was only two of us, it didn't make any sense to split up and take a chance on losing the rest of them."

"Do you know who they were?"

"No, but I'd recognize them again. One of them was a tiny little man, all twisted and just about the ugliest human I've ever seen. The other was about the size of that bull yonder, with several missing teeth." He reached in his vest pocket and pulled out a small piece of paper folded over twice. "Here is a likeness I made of them."

Burch recognized the pair easily. "Loomis Cutler and Ute, his half-breed pa," he stated without hesitation. "Those two have been stealing cattle in the Chalk Canyon region ever since they turned up out here. It's about time someone put a stop to it."

"You going after them?" Lasso asked.

"Just as soon as I can talk to Jesse."

"I'm coming with you. It's been too quiet here ever since the Indians went and got tame."

"We'll need some good directions."

"We'll do better'n that," Gaddy said. "We'll come with you. It goes against the grain to be trusted with something and then not deliver it. I've got just as much to complain of to this Ute fellow as you do."

"It's not likely he'll do much listening. Those two have a reputation for shooting first and skipping the questions altogether."

"Do you mean they would kill you?" Sibyl asked, unable to believe that men could be talking about death as calmly as that.

"First chance they get," answered Lasso swiftly. "Ute's mind is twisted plumb loco, and Loomis is the worst cutthroat in the territory, despite being raised a Methodist."

"Then let them have them," objected Sibyl. "It's not worth it. We have the bull. That's what counts."

"We can't do that," Burch said. "You let it be known that scabs like Ute and Loomis can run off with your cows whenever they like, and every man with a weak conscience and a wandering eye will come knocking about your place looking to fill his pockets. Pretty soon you'll be picked as clean as a week-old carcass."

"But surely nothing's worth being killed over."

"How can you say that and be from Virginia?"

"But that was different," Sibyl protested feebly.

"Not at all. You fought for what you thought was yours. We're fighting for the same thing."

"But this is cows, not people."

"It starts with cows, then moves on to people."

Sibyl began to understand something of what Burch meant and knew he wouldn't change his mind. She really couldn't see how this related to the war that had torn her beloved Virginia to shreds, but she recognized in Burch the same crusading spirit that characterized her father and her Uncle Wesley. There had been no turning either of them from an objective once it had been decided upon.

"When will you be back?"

"I don't know. I hope not more than a week."

"Is there anything I can do to help you get ready?"

"We'll make our own preparations, but one of your nice hot dinners would taste mighty good."

Sibyl hardly knew what she cooked. All she could think of what was it might be the last time she would ever see Burch alive. She had been born two years after the war ended, but no one growing up in Virginia could escape a profound knowledge of the sickening extravagance of death, the horror of mangled bodies, or the way such wanton destruction twisted the lives of those who survived. An aversion to such needless waste had been bred into the very fiber of her being, and it filled her with such a terrible foreboding that she was barely able open her mouth throughout dinner. Augusta was similarly quiet, but the prospect of facing danger seemed to have the opposite effect on the men.

Jesse and two of the more experienced hands ate with them because there was a good deal of business to be discussed. They laughed and joked about the upcoming fight, the men actually requesting that Burch allow them to come along, everyone acting like it was a treat not to be missed. Suddenly Sibyl couldn't stand it any longer, and she hurriedly left the table. Moments later Burch found her in the front parlor.

"Are you feeling okay?" he asked, completely oblivious to the cause of her worry. "You're not getting sick are you?"

"No," she said, doing her best to smile. "I just don't want anything to eat. I think my stomach is upset."

"Can I get you something?"

"No. It'll go away soon. It always does." She realized that she couldn't send him away burdened with her worries. Now she understood why wives and mothers sent their sons and husbands off to war with smiling faces, when inside they felt like all their dreams were dying.

"You will take care of yourself, won't you?"

"Are you worried about us?" he asked, incredulous.

"A little," she confessed. "You did say those men would kill you if they could."

"We might get a few bruises, but nothing more," he assured her. "Ute and Loomis are crazy, but they're not smart. It shouldn't take us more than a day, two at the most, to get those cows away from them. We'll be back before you have time to forget all the things you want to argue about with me." He lifted her chin until she was forced to look into his eyes. "I plan to take very good care of myself. I have some business I am determined to finish." He kissed her lightly on the lips. "Now we'd better go back in. Your aunt was looking mighty worried, and if we're gone any longer, she's going to have to come after us or suffer a palsy stroke."

No more was said about the expedition, and after a while Sibyl began to feel a little better; their final preparations were confined to the bunkhouse and the talk after dinner centered on other topics. But it was almost dawn before Sibyl was able to fall asleep. Every time she closed her eyes she was confronted with the vision of Burch's lifeless body being delivered to her by a pair of grinning monsters, each raucously enjoying his triumph. Even after she fell asleep, they haunted her dreams. They terrorized her aunt, wantonly shot the rest of the herd, and chased away anyone who tried to help her. It was a relief when the first streaks of dawn exploded across the night sky.

Chapter 9

"I didn't expect things to be this easy," Burch whispered, crouching low behind the large boulder.

"Don't go making plans for tomorrow just yet," Lasso warned. "They may be drunk as coots, but they're still plumb dangerous."

Traveling quickly, the four men had covered the hundred miles in a day and a half. With little difficulty, they followed tracks preserved by a rainless summer until they came upon their quarry in a run-down cabin at the head of a small canyon nestled between sparsely covered pine ridges. The only other building was a horse shed that looked about ready to fall over. A mixed collection of livestock, including Sibyl's six missing yearling beeves, were in an open corral with little food or water and no protection from the blazing sun.

"Let's get closer," Burch said. "I want to find out what those three men are talking about." The three men in question were unknown to Burch, Lasso, or the young cowboys; they sat on the corral fence, in earnest conversation, while Ute and his son guzzled straight whiskey inside the cabin. Earlier, Loomis and his pa had emerged from the cabin, brandishing nearly empty bottles, and engaged in a shouted argument no one seemed able to understand. The men looked up at the noise but resumed their deliberations when the pair staggered back to the cabin.

Burch and Lasso surreptitiously worked their way down the canyon until they were only a few hundred feet from the cabin. "You wait here until I get back."

"I'm coming with you," said Lasso. "I don't trust you not to take on the whole crowd by yourself."

"Not Loomis," Burch said rather grimly and headed down the slope, being careful to keep under cover. A few minutes later, while Lasso kept a eye on the three men on the fence, Burch reached the side of the cabin away from the corral. Being extremely careful to keep his own face out of the range of vision, he cautiously peered inside.

The interior was dark and filthy, but not nearly so unkept as its two occupants. Ute and his son appeared to be in the midst of a binge that had already gone on for several days.

"I say we throw in with Brady," growled Loomis in a sullen voice. "He promised us gold and he got us gold. Why should we stay in this stinking hole stealing just enough beeves for hides or meat? We could *buy* all the beef we wanted if we had gold."

"I don't hold with robbing trains, that's why," his pa bellowed savagely. "It's not safe. People don't care too much about a few beeves here and there, but they get real mean when you start messing about with their gold."

"We don't have to do it a lot. Another haul like the last one, and we can buy us a decent place. Nothing like this dump." He took a swipe at a broken chair with his foot before pouring half the liquor left in his bottle down his throat.

"You planning to go without me if I say no?"

"Hell, yeh," Loomis stated defiantly. The little man darted in like a snake at a slow-moving bull and caught Loomis under the chin. "Leave your old man here to rot, would you? What kind of son are you?" he asked, shattering his own empty bottle across the thick skull of his offspring.

Burch worked his way back to Lasso. "They're fighting

over joining some outlaws — the ones at the corral, I guess. Fortunately they've been too drunk to consider slaughtering any of the beeves. Let's get back to the boys." At the mouth of the canyon they held a brief council. "Wait until we're all in place," Burch told Young Ed, "then show yourself. Make sure they see you while you're still a long way off, and be sure to walk real slow. We don't want any shooting before we get close enough to jump them."

They had almost reached their positions when one of the men slid off the fence and went into the cabin, where sounds of conflict could still be heard. Burch dispatched Gaddy to follow him. A few minutes later, Young Ed appeared at the far end of the canyon; the two remaining outlaws, who noticed him almost immediately, were so intent on his approach they never heard Burch and Lasso. They were soon gagged and bound, hand and foot, and each securely tied to one of the knobby pines. Moments later, the third outlaw stepped around the corner of the cabin into Gaddy's fist and instant unconsciousness. "Now for the real renegades," Burch said.

The struggle was only sporadic now, but Ute still taunted his son with a knife. "The only way you'll leave me is dead," spat the misshapen little man. Loomis made a clumsy lunge, but he was no match for the otter-like quickness of his father and his huge arms came away empty; he had a small nick on his chest to show for his trouble.

"You too slow," hissed Ute. "Can't survive without me, big stupid." At that moment Lasso burst through the doorway and Burch vaulted in through the window.

"Kill the bastards!" screamed Ute in fury. Almost quicker than the eye could see, he hurled his knife at Burch's heart. Fortunately Ute was off balance when he took aim, or the fight might have ended right there. When the enraged half-breed realized his knife was quivering in the window frame, not Burch's heart, he darted through the doorway right into the waiting arms of Gaddy and Young Ed; they might as well have taken on a cougar. Ute's tiny body was all bone and sinew and agile as a mink; the bad whiskey hadn't diminished his strength, and he fought so viciously he might have escaped if he hadn't made the mistake of biting Young Ed. That so incensed the boy he picked up a rock and smashed it into Ute's skull. The little man subsided at last.

It took Loomis's whiskey-clouded brain several seconds to understand that the men who had entered the cabin were not his friends; then, with a bearlike roar, he charged. Lasso, nearly as big as Loomis himself, sidestepped the attack and smashed one fish into Loomis's jaw and the other into his huge stomach. About the only effect the blows had was to make Loomis even madder, but before he could charge Lasso again, Burch tripped him and sent him sprawling to the floor; both men threw themselves on him.

Loomis was slow and clumsy, but his strength and stamina were amazing. Roaring like some primeval monster, he rose from the floor, flinging Burch and Lasso from him. He staggered about the room like a giant bear, trying to trap one of the men in his crushing embrace. Burch lost his footing in some spilled whiskey when he dodged one of Loomis's clumsy attacks and fell to his knees, striking his head against the corner of one of the bunks. Lasso tried to interpose his body between Loomis and his dazed friend, but he was thrown against the wall by a forearm powerful enough to belong to a full-grown bull. Loomis picked Burch up and hugged him to his chest.

Sharp pains shot through Burch's body as the powerful arms tightened around him like bands of steel. The evil smell of Loomis's breath helped clear his head and he pushed against the powerful chest with all his strength. He couldn't break Loomis's hold, but it kept Loomis from breaking several of Burch's ribs. Using his powerful legs, Burch propelled Loomis about the room to keep him off balance. They lurched into shelves, the hot stovepipe, and the walls, but Burch was unable to break the lock on his body. All the while Lasso landed blow after blow into Loomis's back with virtually no effect. Once he tried to get a grip on Loomis's throat, but his neck was so big and powerful Loomis sent him spinning. Lasso hit his head against a beam, knocked it loose, and fell down, stunned. Loomis tightened his hold on Burch.

Burch knew he couldn't hold out much longer. If he didn't think of something soon, Loomis would crush his chest. Even now it was extremely difficult to get enough air into his lungs to keep his head clear. His own powerful arms staved off the blackness threatening him, but already the room began to lose its sharp focus. It was like being in the coils of a giant constrictor, never loosening, always tightening at every chance. Burch felt himself growing dangerously weak and, in desperation, he brought his knee up between Loomis's legs with all his remaining strength. A horrendous roar erupted from Loomis's throat and the death-dealing grip was broken at last. Burch leaned against the wall, taking huge gulps of air into his lungs. The pain in his chest was still excruciating, but gradually his gaze cleared and objects came into sharp focus.

"Look out!" Lasso warned as Loomis turned on Burch once more. Burch sidestepped deftly, and before the pain-crazed man had time to turn and charge again, Burch picked up the beam Lasso had knocked loose and brought it down on Loomis's head. The half-rotten timber broke clean in two, but Loomis sank to the floor with a grunt.

"Let's get him tied before he wakes," Burch said, panting heavily. "I never knew anyone could be so strong."

"Or so huge," Lasso added, struggling with the enormous body. "Here, grab hold of a leg and we'll drag him outside," he told Gaddy and Young Ed, who came in from tying up Ute. "And don't take any chances. Use double ropes on him."

Burch emptied the water bucket over Ute's head. "I'm burning you out," he said as Ute glared at him out of cold, reptilian eyes. "The boys are drenching the cabin with kerosene; there won't be a single stick left when we're through. I want both of you out of Wyoming." Burch struck a match and tossed it into the open doorway. With a horrendous "Whoosh!" the cabin was engulfed in flame. "Next time I come looking for you, I'll come with a gun." Ute was forced to watch as Young Ed and Gaddy tore down the shed, pulled up every post and pole in the corral, and threw them into the fire. The flames rose higher and higher with the added fuel.

"I'll see you dead," growled Ute.

"No, you won't," countered Burch. "I came into your territory and I still beat you. Next time you'll have to come into mine, and I've got two dozen men just itching to get a shot at you."

"And that doesn't even count mine," Lasso added. Ute spat at Burch.

"You lousy sonsofbitches!"

"I'm also going to file a grievance about you with the cattlemen's association, so that every rancher from here to Montana will be on the lookout for you."

"They don't know what I look like."

Burch held up the drawing that was unmistakably Ute and his son.

"This ought to make sure everybody knows your ugly face if you ever show it around here again. We don't go easy on rustlers."

"Who says I'm a rustler?"

"I do," Burch said, pointing to the six beeves slowly wandering down the canyon. "That's a hanging offense in Wyoming, and some men don't wait for the law."

"You'll pay for this," Ute threatened as the last wall of his cabin collapsed into the bed of red-hot coals. Burch didn't answer until the cabin had been reduced to a mound of ashes.

"There's nothing to keep you here any longer," he said. "Don't hang around."

They rounded up Sibyl's beeves and left.

Sibyl didn't know how she endured the long days spent waiting for Burch. She had decided against telling Augusta the real purpose behind the trip, so she had no one to share the anxiety with her. The men knew, but they went placidly on with their work, certain that their boss would outsmart two of the meanest renegades in the territory.

"It's too bad the railroad allowed the herd to be split up," said Augusta. "They should have to deliver the rest instead of Burch going after them."

"It certainly would have saved a lot of time," agreed Sibyl absently. The hours passed with painful slowness, and Sibyl drove herself to exhaustion every day to keep from thinking about what might be happening to Burch. Still she couldn't sleep, and her eyes took on a sunken, haunted look.

"You shouldn't work so hard," her aunt said on several occasions, but her wise eyes detected the presence of some secret force that compelled Sibyl to exhaust herself with tasks that could easily have been saved until later. She knew it had something to do with Burch's absence but refrained from questioning her niece.

Sibyl was in her room when she heard Balaam shouting about a cloud of dust to the south. She ran to the window and waited anxiously for the cloud to draw nearer and the beings within it to begin to take shape. When at last she was able to differentiate Old Blue's distinctive color from the surrounding haze, she uttered a cry of relief, threw herself on the bed, and broke into the tears she had been struggling to hold back for a week. Relief, joy, anger, and frustration all warred her breast, but it was joy and relief that won the day and she emerged from her room, wreathed in smiles, to welcome the returning conquerors.

She was on the porch long before the herd reached the house, but Burch broke from the group, coming ahead to meet her. Seeing him thus, with the whole plain as a backdrop, Sibyl was struck again by his rugged handsome-

101

ness. Surely there wasn't another man in all Wyoming with such powerful shoulders, such a masterful jaw, such intensely gray eyes. He exuded the same sense of power and lithe grace as his prancing stallion, and Sibyl felt prickles of pleasure run up and down her spine.

He came to her with complete disdain for the danger or difficulty of his task, expecting no praise for having so speedily accomplished it. It was part of his job, so he had done it; that was all there was to it. Sibyl's heart swelled with pride, and tears of happiness threatened to overcome her once again, but she fought them back, determined to greet Burch as casually as he came to her.

"I told you we'd bring them back," Burch called out as she came down the steps to meet him. "They're a little leaner for all this chasing about, but a little water and rest will put them to rights in no time."

"Did you have any trouble?"

"Not much," he said, but then Lasso burst into rude laughter and Sibyl knew he wasn't telling the truth. "Well, maybe a little. Old Ute wasn't too pleased to give them back, but then I didn't expect him to be."

"Not to mention the fact that Loomis nearly hugged you to death," Lasso added, and both men went off in whoops this time. Sibyl was enormously relieved to know they were safe, but for them to be laughing like boys up to tomfolery, after she'd stayed awake every night, was enough to make her remember every grievance she'd every had against Burch. She didn't know what she might have said if her aunt hadn't stepped out of the house at that moment.

"My gracious, it's just the cows. I couldn't figure out what could be the cause of so much commotion? I heard it all the way in my room." Sibyl and Burch turned toward Augusta, unaware that Lasso's laughter had ended in a strangled choke.

"Merciful Jesus," he muttered under his breath, looking at Augusta as if she were the first woman he'd ever laid eyes on.

"Now that Burch is back, maybe you can stop worrying yourself sick."

"Don't say a word to him. They actually *enjoyed* it!"

"Everybody needs a little harmless fun once in a while. Things have been a mite dull around here."

Lasso interrupted his friend without ceremony. "Is the other one married?" he demanded in a loud whisper.

"No," said Burch, diverted by the dazed look in his friend's eyes.

"Then stop jawing and introduce me."

Burch looked keenly at his friend, and a light of unholy amusement grew in his eyes. "Miss Hauxhurst, this rude lummox is a friend of mine. I'm ashamed to introduce him to you all dirty and sweaty, but I don't see any other way of getting rid of him. His name is Pinckney Slaughter, though his daddy should have been ashamed to saddle a mule with such an outlandish name. This is my cousin's aunt, Miss Augusta Hauxhurst. She's here to keep the wolves away from Sibyl, but she's a mighty fine lady just the same."

"I'm pleased to make your acquaintance, Miss Hauxhurst," Lasso said, pushing Burch aside. "I'll do my best to make you feel welcome in Wyoming. I sure hope you're planning to stay for a while."

"I'm not yet certain, Mr. Slaughter," quavered Augusta, overwhelmed by the aggressive gallantry of the huge man descending on her with such energy. "I will remain as long as Sibyl is here."

"Call me Lasso, ma'am. Mr. Slaughter seems too formal, and there ain't no man but Burch who's ever dared to call me Pinckney."

"I don't think I can, Mr. Slaughter," faltered Augusta, cringing before him. "We've only just met. I don't know you at all."

"I can take care of that quick enough, little woman," he beamed, taking her lifeless hand and tucking it into his. "You just come inside and sit while I tell you all about

103

myself."

"Mr. Slaugher . . ."

"Now don't you worry about the proprieties. Your niece is here to see that I toe the line. No one will breathe a word against you in my presence and live." He led the unresisting Augusta away. "A fine filly," he said, casting an eye over Augusta's shapely body, "a mighty fine filly."

Sibyl was stunned into immobility, but Burch had to lean on the fence to keep from sliding to the ground.

"Did you see that?" Sibyl announced, recovering her voice. "He swooped down and dragged my poor aunt away, and you didn't even try to stop him."

"Your aunt has knocked Lasso Slaughter right out of the saddle," Burch managed to gasp, sorely tried by his silent laughter. "I never would have believed it if I hadn't seen it with my own eyes. And him not this side of forty."

"Stop that useless laughing and do something. She's never even met that man, and he walked off with her like he owned her."

"Rest easy; you won't find any better man than Lasso. His spread is not as big as the Elkhorn, but it's a right good size ranch. I've never seen him get that excited about anything since his twins were born. I would say that your aunt has gotten herself a beau, and a pretty fancy one at that."

Sibyl looked blankly at the retreating figures and then back at Burch. She could not fathom the idea that her staid Aunt Augusta could attract a suitor.

"I bet that's the first time any woman has ever walked off with a man from under your nose."

"Burch Randall, you are the most contemptible man I've ever met. My aunt did not *walk off* with him from under anything; she was carried off by your marauding sidekick. He wouldn't even listen when she tried to tell him she didn't want to go. Now, you go in there and rescue her."

"Augusta can rescue herself any time she wants to. Lasso's not a brute. What I am going to do is see about corralling these yearlings. I can't wait to see Ned and Balaam square off over them."

Sibyl hesitated momentarily between following Burch and going to her aunt's rescue, deciding on the latter. Burch was taking it all as a great joke and was obviously not going to be any help. She couldn't believe that her aunt could really enjoy the company of such a loud, stalwart guest.

Inside she found Augusta sitting in stunned immobility while Lasso launched into a recital of the history of himself and his ranch in a ringing voice that soon began to beat in Sibyl's temples like the sounding of a brass bell.

"You won't have to worry about the girls pestering you, because they're hardly ever at home. The house just about runs itself, but just say the word, and I'll bring somebody in to do the heavy work."

My Lord, he acts like they're already engaged, Sibyl thought, dumbfounded.

"The Three Bars is not as big as the Elkhorn, but it's set in higher county and the air is cleaner and the view better. My herd's pretty near as good as Randall's, but that bull your niece brought in is going to give him a big leg up on everybody. I'll have to see about buying a couple of those bull calves off him. Maybe he'll give up one as a wedding present."

"That herd belongs to me," Sibyl heard herself repeating as one in a trance. Why wouldn't this obstinate man believe her? "If you want a bull calf, you'll have to talk to me."

"I reckon Burch has to indulge you now and then," Lasso said surveying her with a tolerant eye. "Anything as pretty as you is worth a mite of trouble."

"Pretty has nothing to do with it," Sibyl snapped, infuriated by his patronizing attitude. "They'd be half mine even if they belonged to the ranch."

"Well, some day you and me can sit down and discuss it, but I'd still like to talk to Burch, to be on the safe side."

"You keep talking like this, and the only safe side you're

105

going to find is the other side of that door."

"I think a cup of coffee would be nice," said Augusta, looking like she'd seen a ghost. "Would you like some, Mr. Slaughter?"

"I told you to call me Lasso. I never stand on ceremony with my friends."

"Would you like cream and sugar with your coffee, Mr. Lasso?" Augusta asked with a visible struggle.

"Don't you go mucking up good coffee with that stuff. I want it black and mean."

"That's exactly the way Burch likes it," said Sibyl.

"It's the way all cowboys drink their coffee. We don't know any other way."

"Would you like to try a cup the way we drink it?" Augusta inquired mildly.

"Don't go trying to change people as old and set in their ways as I am, little woman. It only causes a lot of friction, and everything ends up the same as before anyway."

August appeared to be quite struck by that reasonable point of view.

"Shall I fix you a cup too, dear?"

"Please."

"That's a mighty fine woman you've got there," Lasso said, rubbing his hands together as Augusta went to get the coffee. "Yep, a mighty fine woman."

"Stop talking about her like she's a heifer," Sibyl demanded, still considerably put out with him.

"I've never seen a heifer as first class as that little woman, not even those beauties you say are yours."

"They *are* mine," Sibyl almost shouted.

"If you say so," he said, humoring her.

That made her so angry she had to grip the sides of her chair to keep from attacking him. Why were men so stubborn? To listen to them talk, you'd think they were the only ones capable of doing anything at all.

"Fine lines, too," he murmured to himself, "mighty fine

106

lines."

Sibyl hovered on the verge of imprudent speech, but Burch's arrival prevented her from saying something she would probably have had to apologize for later.

"You ought to see Ned with those cows. You'd think he had been given heaven and the sky at the same time. He and Balaam are fussing about putting out hay and arguing over how big a pasture they'll need."

"Good heavens, they're only cows," said Sibyl, annoyed.

"That may be the most valuable stock in the whole of Wyoming. A man gains stature just by being associated with such a herd."

"Wait until the other ranchers hear about them. You'll have everyone from here to the boarder trying to buy them off you. How many do you have altogether?"

"They are mine," Sibyl nearly shouted. "Burch and the Elkhorn don't own as much as one unborn calf."

"That's true, they're every one Sibyl's private property. You'll have to deal with her if you want one. I'll probably have to do the same thing myself."

"Well, miss, as soon as that gets about, you're going to be mighty popular. Of course, as soon as Burch lets people get a glimpse of you, you'll be popular anyway. You ought to marry her and get her off the market before the price starts to rise."

Burch was overcome with a fit of coughing, and Augusta spilled half a cup of the coffee she was pouring. Sibyl fixed Lasso with a ferocious glare.

"The price is already too high for anyone here," she said with icy disdain. "Besides, the market has never been open."

"Now don't get yourself into a taking. You're a mighty pretty thing, and if Burch don't take to you, that's his business, but you're bound to find some man that will be happy to saddle up with you. You're not quite as well-turned out as your aunt there—a might too skinny for my taste— but there's a lot of cowboys that wouldn't mind a sharp edge or two for the chance to snuggle down with such a pretty armful."

Burch turned away with shaking shoulders; Augusta stared straight ahead, silent and immobile. Sibyl bounded to her feet quick as a startled deer.

"I'm not an armful for Burch or any other cowboy. As for finding someone who wants to snuggle up to my *sharp edges*, I wouldn't marry any man I've seen in Wyoming if I had to go to my death this very minute." She fled from the room, too angry to control herself.

"I think I spooked that filly right bad," Lasso apologized. "I hope she's not rope shy," he said to Burch.

"I don't think she likes the idea of wearing any man's brand."

"She'll probably change her mind," remarked Augusta, presenting Lasso with a cup of coffee strong enough to curl his hair. He took swallow.

"Hot damn," he uttered, "that's just the way I like it."

Chapter 10

After that, Lasso came to the ranch so often Sibyl wondered how anything ever got done at the Three Bars. "His outfit could steal him blind or spend their days in the bunkhouse, and he'd never know," she complained to Burch after one particularly irksome visit. Burch was teaching her to use a rifle. The Elkhorn crew was due to leave for roundup in a week, and he didn't want the women alone in the house with neither of them able to use firearms.

"Lasso knows he can depend on his men to do their work, or he wouldn't be here," said Burch, placing her hands on the barrel and trigger correctly.

"Do you think I could bribe them to loaf at least a little bit?" she asked, pausing in the act of aiming her weapon. "Maybe I should send over a case of whiskey."

"You don't like Lasso, do you?"

"It's not Lasso, really, it's Aunt Augusta."

"What's wrong with her? She seems fine to me."

"That's what I thought, too, but now I'm beginning to wonder. She's doing all kinds of strange things."

"Such as?"

"My aunt is scared to death of horses. She has been ever since she was a little girl. When we came out here, she would no more have thought of riding one than she would one of

109

your steers, yet all this week Mr. Slaughter has been teaching her to drive a team and buckboard. Today I heard him tell her she was doing so well he was going to buy her a sidesaddle the next time he goes to Cheyenne."

"So?"

"Aunt August didn't say a word, nothing. She didn't faint, she didn't even look scared, she just acted like she hadn't heard a word he said. And I don't think she did. Half the time when I talk to her, she doesn't even know I'm in the room, much less what I've said. I think her brain is paralyzed. That man has scared her so badly she does everything he says just like a helpless puppy."

"I don't think your aunt is helpless."

"But you don't *know* her. I do, and I've never seen her act like this. It worries me."

"Sounds like you're frustrated as well as worried. Why don't you take some of it out on that target?" Burch stood directly behind Sibyl, leaning over her shoulder, his body nearly molded to hers, his hands her on hands, helping her adjust the rifle. At first it had been impossible for Sibyl to concentrate, and every shot had missed the target by a wide margin. It was only through sheer force of willpower that she was able to master her shaking knees and pounding heart enough to occasionally hit the target.

And today was no different from any other. By dint of great effort, she ignored his unsettling presence, raised the rifle, and took careful aim; her shoulder jerked painfully at the recoil throwing her body against his, but a small hole appeared just outside the bull's-eye.

"Excellent. Been practicing?"

"No," Sibyl answered, recovering her equilibrium. "I just pretended that was Lasso's big nose. I think I hit him in the left eye."

Burch laughed and took the rifle from her to reload. "Remind me to warn him before you develop a quick draw."

"I've told you I won't touch one of those guns. It's bad

enough that I have to learn to use this rifle, like some creature in a traveling circus, but I will not let it be said that I ever wore a holster or drew a gun from my waist. My mother would turn over in her grave."

"Your mother was never in the West or she'd understand."

"That's where you're wrong," she retorted as he replaced the rifle in hands. His powerful arms held her in a virtual embrace, and Sibyl wondered if she would ever be able to concentrate long enough on that damned rifle to learn to hit something with it.

She took another shot at the target and missed. Calm down, she told herself, nothing's going to happen out here in the open. You're safe. But was she sure she wanted to be?

"That's what happens when you fire while you're worked up," Burch advised her. "Try again." She forced her mind back to the task, relaxed a little, and hit the outside of the target.

"That's better. Now tell me why I'm wrong about your mother." She tried not to think of the feel of his muscled arms against her shoulder, the heat and smell of his nearness.

"I don't think she much minded dying. Everything had changed so she could never get used to it. I don't think she wanted to. Father had his research and his teaching, but mother had lost the world she treasured, the only kind of life she understood. As soon as I was old enough to take care of myself, she just gave up."

"With your stubborn streak, I expected to hear that your mother ruled your father with an iron hand and was the terror of every erring village maid."

"You don't have to *try* to be nasty," she said, standing away from him as far as she could in the circle of his arms. "You owe my stubborn streak to the obstinate, conceited stupidity of your own sex. Every man I ever knew was convinced that he knew more than any woman ever born. You all think you know what we like, what we want, and what will be good for us. Sometimes I get the impression you think just having one of you around should be enough to make us swoon with delight." She fired without waiting for him to help her, and missed.

"Father or beaux?" he asked cryptically.

"Both," she answered succinctly and fired a shot into the center of the bull's-eye. "Moreton Swan & Company," she said triumphantly, and they both laughed, dissipating the tension.

"Do you have one for me?" he asked with a hint of more than casual interest. The tension was instantly recharged.

"I don't let myself think about that, or I'd have killed you *and* Lasso days ago."

"Am I so far beyond redemption?"

Would this man never stop torturing her? she wondered. He must be trying to drive her crazy, but she'd show him she was made of sterner stuff.

"If you're not telling me that I don't know anything about anything, and that women should stay in the kitchen and keep their mouths shut, Lasso is promising me there's still hope I can find some decent cowboy willing to snaffle me up and toss me into his saddle. Let me tell you what I'd do to anyone who dared try to throw me over his saddlebags, or anything else for that matter," she said, glaring meaningfully at him.

"I take it that includes anyone foolish enough to turn you across his knee." The wistful quality in his voice almost destroyed her resolution.

"*Especially* anyone who even threatens to turn me across his knee. It's a good thing you hadn't taught me to shoot then, or I'd be standing my trial for murder right now."

"I think you're in the proper frame of mind to see that no stray comes nosing about while we're gone. If I stay away long enough, maybe you'll forget about my knees."

"No man has ever lived that long," she replied sternly, determined to teach him a lesson, but Burch gave her such an enigmatic stare that she began to feel self-conscious.

"How long do you stay on a roundup?" she asked, changing the subject.

"It's impossible to say for sure, but several weeks at the least."

Several weeks! She'd only been thinking of a few days. Suddenly she didn't care about teaching him any lessons. What good would it do if he were going to be gone forever?

"Why does it take so long?" she asked as calmly as one could.

"After we brand all the strays we can find that we missed in the spring, we have to cut out the steers intended for market. Things are liable to take longer this year because it's especially important not to run off what little fat they have. I intend to take them to Chicago myself because I'll get a better price than selling them to some agent at the railhead."

"Does everyone go with you?" She didn't know why she asked. He was leaving, and that was all that was important.

"No. Jesse and most of the crew will stay here to look after the herds. They're in fair shape, but if we hadn't built those dams to stop the creek flooding the ranch every time we had a storm, we'd have been out of water months ago and the cattle would be too weak to look for grass."

"Where will you be if I have to find you?"

"I can't tell you, not for any particular day, but I'll leave you a map. We usually get together with several other outfits, but since we're going early this year, it's just Lasso and me."

"He agrees with you?"

"Yes." The magic evaporated. Neither had mentioned the argument since that unfortunate night, but it had been a source of constant tension between them. Since then, every sentence had had to be searched for potentially dangerous words, an extremely wearing situation on Sibyl's nerves. She had been unable to work off her anger by talking about it or to satisfy her curiosity about the roundup, so it was a relief to have it finally brought out in the open.

The defeat rankled, but Sibyl was quick to see that she could do nothing about it. She shrugged it off, determined that next time would be different.

"How can I follow a map? I don't know the countryside."

"Balaam can show you." He broke off suddenly. The fancy buggy Lasso had bought in Casper turned the corner, and they both watched fascinated as Augusta drove the horse through the gate and turned it toward the hitching post.

"See what I mean," Sibyl said, pointing to her aunt. Augusta sat rigidly upright, holding the reins correctly, but from her expression Burch guessed she expected to be flung to her death any moment. "She's scared out of her mind," Sibyl added unnecessarily.

"That's the buckle," applauded Lasso, bristling with pride. "I told you there was nothing to it for a smart gal like you. I expect you'll soon be rearing to have a go at sulky racing if I was to let you do something so foolish."

"Damn if that woman hasn't got guts," said Burch with admiration.

"Now pull back easy on the reins and bring them to a stop. That's the ticket. Isn't she the smartest thing you've ever seen at the reins?" he said, jumping down and turning to Burch.

"You've done a good job of teaching her."

"Aw, it was no problem. Gussie can learn anything. This gal's as sharp as a razor."

"*Gussie?*" repeated Sibyl, unable to believe her ears. No one, not even her own sisters, had ever dared call her anything but Augusta. By constant battering, Sibyl had become accustomed to "little woman," but when it came to referring to her straight-laced aunt as a *gal*, Sibyl's mind boggled. Burch held the horse's head while Lasso helped his inamorata down.

"She just can't seem to get enough," Lasso was saying. "First it was driving, and now it's riding. I've got to get her a saddle mare first thing tomorrow." The most thorough scrutiny of Augusta's face revealed no sign of emotion; it was devoid of color and the features set as though cast in bronze.

"Don't you think you might wait until after the roundup?" suggested Burch.

"I wouldn't dare. Gussie'd be plumb disappointed to put off throwing a leg over her first horse that long."

"*Throwing a leg over*," gasped Sibyl as Augusta blanched visibly. Burch had grown to be quite fond of Augusta, and he decided it was time someone came to her aid before Lasso killed her with his boundless admiration.

"I'd wait if I were you. We'll be going off in a few days and that'll mean you'll have to stop right in the middle of the business. And you know how things go sour when you get started and then have to quit." He led the horse to the shed, where both men began to unharness it while the ladies headed for the house. "Who knows, she might get so excited she won't wait for you to come back and finish teaching her properly."

"I guess maybe you're right," Lasso answered thoughtfully, "but I know she'll be disappointed."

"Not as disappointed as she would be if you were to have to stop before you were done. If she takes that horse out by herself, before she's really mastered the thing, there's no telling what kind of trouble she might get into."

"You're right," said Lasso, struck. "It's best to wait. I just hope it won't make her too downcast. But the first day we're back, I'm heading straight over with that mare."

"I was sure you would," smiled Burch.

"Aunt Augusta, you're crazy to let that man put you behind a horse when you know you're scared to death of them," Sibyl said to her shaken aunt as soon as they stepped inside the house.

Augusta looked as though it would be hours, maybe days before she could regain anything like a semblance of her normal demeanor, but she astounded her niece by replying in a steady voice, "I found it quite exhilarating. I begin to think that I have led a sadly humdrum existence up until now." She went away to change her clothes, leaving her niece bereft of speech.

Augusta knotted her thread and bit if off. "There," she said, draping the lace-trimmed cloth over a table in the large front parlor the ladies had taken for their own use. "How do you like it?"

"It does help, but this room is still so depressingly bare I don't think I could stand it at all if it weren't for the wallpaper." A thorough rummaging of the attics and barn lofts had turned up some miscellaneous furniture and a large assortment of wallpaper. Sibyl enjoyed deciding which pattern would look best in each room, but since Ned and Balaam had the actual job of cutting and fitting the paper and there was hardly enough furniture to make its disposition difficult, her interest soon flagged.

"I'm bored," complained Sibyl, tossing her own piece of needlework from her. "I think I'll go out of my mind if I don't *do* something."

"It is rather quiet with the men gone," agreed Augusta, who was looking more like herself after the prolonged period of inactivity.

"I'm so desperate, I'd even welcome Lasso with open arms."

"That's not very nice, dear, when you know how much he thinks of you."

"Not nearly as much as he thinks of you," said Sibyl, making another attempt to goad her aunt into talking about her suitor.

"He is a kind man, and it's very thoughtful of him to try so hard to make us feel welcome."

"What a fib, Aunt. You know Lasso doesn't have five minutes to give me. He's so anxious to get you off to himself I doubt he would know whether I was comfortable or dying of a fever."

"You have been rather rough with him. I'm persuaded if

116

you would speak kindly to him, he would be more open."

"He's already as *open* as those double doors. As for stopping his speeches, I might as well try to stop a train going downhill."

"He does have a lighthearted disposition."

"He's positively jocular. How can you endure hours of it without throwing something at him?"

"I could never be rude to anyone, especially not someone as thoughtful and pleasant as Mr. Slaughter. The poor man is lonely for adult company. It would be nice if you would try to talk to him more."

"Tired of him already?" she teased wickedly.

"I don't know what you mean," said the lady, wrapped in an invincible serenity, "but I can guess from the gleam in your eye that it is something naughty. I merely meant that it would be more mannerly than running off to shoot or ride every time he arrives. It is not exactly polite to leave me to entertain him alone."

"You don't seem to mind too much."

"I would never be so rude as to let it show if I did," said her aunt with mild reproof. Sibyl abandoned her inquisition concerning the persistent Lasso Slaughter. It was clear Augusta wasn't going to tell her anything.

"I think I shall go find the roundup." Sibyl announced suddenly. Augusta looked up quickly but answered with studied indifference.

"Do you think you should?"

"Why not? They're my cows, and I always wanted to see what they do on a roundup."

"But it's all men there, and Burch might not like it."

"Then he will just have to put a good face on it, because I don't mean to ask his permission."

"But you can't decide to go just like that," Augusta said with a wave of her hand. "What will you do? Where will you sleep?"

"I'll take the wagon and my horse. That way I'll have a

place to sleep and still be able to get about on the range with the men."

"But you can't just head off into the distance," Augusta persisted, not ready to give up. "They must be miles from here and you have never been out on your own."

"I've been studying the map Burch left. They're coming this way. They shouldn't be more than a day from us now."

"You really mean to go, don't you? You've already thought it all out."

"I'm not going just from boredom or idle curiosity," Sibyl said with unexpected heat. "If I'm ever to be a real partner in this ranch, I must know what goes on on the range. I may not be able to do the work, but I've got to know what needs to be done and how to do it. What would happen if Burch weren't here?"

"Jesse could run things for you."

"I don't want anybody to run the ranch for me; I want to do it myself. And I can't learn that here arranging furniture and baking pies."

"The men really like your pies."

"I intend to use some of them as a bribe," she confessed guiltily. "Maybe they won't be so upset at having their exclusive male society invaded if their stomachs are pleasantly full."

Chapter 11

Sibyl had a lot more than pies in her wagon when she and Ned started off before dawn a couple of days later. She hoped to reach camp in time for dinner and had brought enough food to feed the whole crew. A half dozen young cocks and two pigs had been slaughtered to add fresh meat to the menu, and a huge beef pie rested in a deep cooker. "After beans and canned ham they ought to be as hungry was a swarm of locusts," Balaam told her jealously as he saw them off.

A basket each of fresh tomatoes and late peaches rested in deep straw. "It would be a shame to can all this and never eat any of it fresh," Sibyl reasoned as she selected the most perfect fruits from each pile. Augusta kept her own counsel and relieved Sibyl's sense of guilt by assuring her that she had absolutely no curiosity to see a roundup and was perfectly comfortable being left with Balaam.

"There's a great deal of work to be done yet, and Balaam is quite handy, in spite of his complaining." So Sibyl looked forward to her expedition with a clear conscience and a sense of rising excitement.

The trip was much more enjoyable than she had expected. She had been tired, irritable, and a bit apprehensive when she first arrived at the Elkhorn and in no mood to admire the

119

very scenery that was the source of her discomfort. In the beginning, its strangeness had been sufficient to condemn it. But the past weeks had accustomed her to its contours and familiarity had bred a kind of fondness. She took great pleasure in sighting a distant herd of antelope or watching a pair of huge bald eagles soar overhead, and the crisp, clear air was exhilarating as it whipped through her streaming hair.

The once characterless prairie was now defined by ridges, bluffs, canyons, creeks, and many kinds and sizes of vegetation. Everywhere she looked there was something new to excite her but something familiar to reassure her as well. Several times she insisted upon riding to some distant point to get a better view of a spectacular canyon or butte. Ned's requests to be careful and "think of what Mr. Randall would say if I was to let you do yourself a hurt" did not deter her in the least.

"There's nothing to hurt me out here. All the Indians are gone and the cows rounded up."

"Just the market steers, miss. The bulls, cows, branded calves, and the young steers are still loose."

"Never mind about them, I'll be careful not to get hurt. I'm not a good patient. I'd worry my aunt until she abandoned me. And I'm sure Burch would make a terrible nurse." Ned thought he probably wouldn't be that good.

Sibyl's spirits remained high throughout the day, but when they came within view of the camp, she felt a little less certain of herself and resumed her seat without any prodding from Ned. She didn't know what to expect from a roundup, but what she saw staggered her. From a small rise, she could see over a plain that was literally covered with horses and cows as far as she could see. There were several herds of them spread out to graze, all being carefully controlled by the cowboys who constantly rode among them. Sanchez's chuck wagon was pulled up along a small stream and preparations for dinner had already begun. But most of the

120

men were gathered in one spot and it was this vortex of activity that drew Sibyl's attention.

"I see Sanchez's wagon," Ned said, relieved to have solved his first problem, but Sibyl had no interest in food now. She burned with curiosity about the gathering that was sending up a steady cloud of dust into the pure Wyoming air.

"You take the wagon and go help Sanchez," she said. "I'm going to find out what's going on over there."

"But what am I to do with all this food?"

"Surely Sanchez can figure out how to serve it without being told," she said impatiently. "I'll be back before supper anyway." She mounted her horse — Burch had named him Hospitality to aggravate her — and struck out through the bawling cattle and circling riders.

At first she looked for Burch or Jesse, any familiar face to make her feel more comfortable, but soon she was so caught up by the color and pageantry that she forgot everything else. One group of men was branding the calves that had been missed during the spring roundup. The bawling and the stench of burned flesh was heavy in the air. Another group was cutting out the steers meant for market. This was done carefully to avoid a stampede and to keep from running any weight off the animals. These were then held in one tightly controlled group while the rest of the herd would be driven out into the range the next day.

Sibyl drew near the circle where the men heated the irons and branded each calf with proper brand and recorded it in the book. She was fascinated by the men whose job it was to cut the desired calf from the herd, keep it from its mother, rope it, and bring it near the fire. And all of this without frightening the rest of the animals. It was tedious, demanding work, and coming at the end of the day made it all the more difficult and exhausting. But the men proceeded with high spirits and a constant flow of kidding and shouted directions that were so heavily laced with unprintable cursing Sibyl didn't know what they were saying a good bit of the time. But she found it didn't offend her ears. It somehow became an inseparable part of the men and their brutally exhausting work.

"You should have come earlier. We're just about through." The unexpected sound of Burch's voice at her elbow caught her unaware and she blushed furiously, but she was not too flustered to notice that he seemed very pleased to see her. That caused her to blush even more.

"I couldn't stand it at the ranch any longer," she confessed with an impudent smile. "After two weeks of hanging pictures and trimming table covers I was ready to do something reckless."

"Weren't you bored in Virginia?" he asked, wondering why he hadn't thought to invite her himself. This was *his* territory and the circumstance of her having to depend on him would be a welcome change.

"I didn't have time to be bored," Sibyl answered. "I had the farm to run, the house to manage, and there was always someone to visit or invite to dinner. You won't let me help with the ranch and the only person who visits is Lasso Slaughter. He only comes to see Aunt Augusta and I suspect he wouldn't even speak to me if she didn't make him."

"There's always me — and Jesse." Sibyl could not miss the invitation in his voice nor the change of inflection when he added Jesse's name.

"You don't count," she replied, trying not to show how untruthful she was being. "Jesse's nice enough, but he's always saying exactly what he thinks will please me."

"Is that why I don't count, because I don't say what pleases you?"

"I didn't mean that," she said, catching herself before she blurted out that he was the only one who *did* count. "But I didn't come here to argue. I've been wanting to see a roundup ever since I got to Wyoming and I couldn't stand it any longer. Now stop trying to goad me to say something cross and explain to me what those men are doing." Maybe if

122

he were doing all the talking she wouldn't betray herself, at least not so soon.

Burch spent the next hour taking Sibyl over the whole site, explaining what each group was doing and introducing her to the foreman of Lasso's crew. But even though they were on horseback and the noise and dust were unbelievable, she found it hard to keep her mind on the cows and not on the man riding next to her. After two weeks of seeing only Ned and Balaam, being next to Burch was like being thrown into a rapids after floating in a duck pond.

"Our cattle wander over so much territory it's easier to cover it if we work together. Everyone gets to see that his calves are properly branded and settle what to do with the mavericks. It works out well for some of the smaller ranchers, too, because they can send their steers to the railhead with ours. This way everybody knows exactly what's happening on the range and there's no questions later when a cow turns up without a calf. And mavericks don't appear with funny brands."

"What do you mean?" she asked, trying to focus her attention on the cows instead of his intoxicating nearness.

"There's always some rustling, but there's more this year than I can remember."

"Who's doing it?"

"I don't know, but I think our herd has been hit the hardest."

"Then you've got to find out who it is," she demanded, her attention on the cows at last. "What do you do with rustlers?"

Burch's eyes became very hard. "That depends, but it's not unusual for a man suspected of rustling to be found shot or even hung."

"That's horrible," shuddered Sibyl.

"We can't afford to let rustlers run loose. I figure we lost between twenty and thirty head this year."

"But to hang a man for stealing cows!"

"It's our property, our way of life. Wouldn't you shoot a

thief in your house?"

"To run him off or keep him from hurting me, but I'd never hang him."

"That's because Virginia is a state with laws to protect you. Wyoming is still a territory, and the law most often is in the hands of the cowmen."

"But you have a sheriff and judges. You can't convict a man without a jury."

"They've become so identified with the rustlers and their sympathizers it's impossible to get a conviction, no matter what the evidence." He could see that Sibyl was becoming upset and abruptly changed the subject. "This is no way for a girl who's seeing her first roundup to spend her time. Let's get some dinner and then we'll see what else we can find to do."

"Dinner!" she uttered with a start. "I told Ned to give all the food to Sanchez. If he ruins it, after I worked so hard to get it here, I'll roast him on his own spit." They arrived at the chuck wagon in the middle of a pitched argument between Ned and the red-faced cook.

"Miss Cameron will have you ground into hog food if you touch that pot," Ned warned Sanchez as he stood guard over the beef pie Sibyl had spent the better part of a day preparing.

"It ain't gonna be eaten if I don't set it out," shouted Sanchez angrily.

"You're not getting your hands on it," asserted Ned. "I never thought I'd be thankful to give up the range, but Miss Cameron's cooking makes just about anything worthwhile."

"That's a sterling tribute," grinned Burch as Sibyl rescued her pie from the combatants.

"Let me help you," Sibyl offered, hoping to soothe the ruffled sensibilities of the volatile cook. "I brought a few things to help out so you won't have to work so hard. I thought you might appreciate a little time off."

So she has learned a little diplomacy, Burch thought to

himself. I wish she could spare a little of it for me instead of abusing me every time she opens her mouth.

Burch could think of so many enjoyable things to do with that entrancing mouth. He felt his blood begin to stir, but it always heated up when he was around Sibyl, so much so it was an agony to spend nights at the ranch knowing she was just down the hall. How could a man get any sleep with a maddeningly beautiful female only a few seconds from his bed? It was better if he slept out with the men. He could ride the several hours back and forth to the ranch and still put in a full day's work easier than he could after lying awake half the night. It was much less dangerous too; sleepless nights could make you careless.

"When do the men get to eat?"

"Whenever they can," Burch answered. "They can't all stop work at the same time, so nobody waits for anybody else. We might as well start."

"But should you go first?"

"I don't usually, but I have a guest today and that gives me the right to break tradition."

"I don't want to get in the way of your work," said Sibyl, hoping he wouldn't abandon her for the entire evening.

"You won't," he replied, leaving her unsure as to what he meant.

The men began to show up for dinner, singly or in pairs. Grateful for any change in their diet yet unable to believe that anything so delicious should fall to their lot on the trail, they showered Sibyl with compliments.

"You should come by at least once a week," said one young boy who, being a member of Lasso's crew, had dropped by to sample the food of the rival cook.

"You tell anybody else the kind of victuals we got and you'll be eating nothing but dust," threatened his friend. "There's just about enough for us."

"There's more in the wagon."

"He don't have to know that, ma'am. Then he can't go

125

spreading it around that we got something better to fill our bellies than son-of-a-bitch stew." The boy realized too late that the name of the cowboy's favorite dish was not fit for a lady's ears and blushed fiery red from the tip of his hair to the bottom of his toes. "I'm sorry, ma'am, it just slipped out." Sibyl tried to keep a straight face but made the mistake of glancing at Burch. His eyes danced and his whole body shook.

"It's all right," she assured him in an unsteady voice. "You can't change its name just for my ears." The boy mumbled another apology and quickly rejoined his friend. "You devil, you almost made me laugh in that poor boy's face," she said when the boy was out of earshot.

"I couldn't help it, not when he looked at you like he expected you to cane him."

"If I beat anybody, it would be you," she said as severely as she could. Just then Jesse came hurrying up, wearing a broad grin of welcome, and dissipated the intimacy of the moment.

"I heard you had come to see a roundup. I'd be happy to show you about."

"You must have forgotten you have to supervise the holding herds tomorrow," Burch said. For a moment Sibyl thought she saw a flash of some intense emotion flare in Jesse's eyes, but it was so brief she dismissed it as imaginary.

"Then I'll be here to welcome you back when you come in ready to drop in your tracks."

"I don't tire that easily," Sibyl told him, nettled. "I'll undertake to stay in the saddle as long as anyone." The two men eyed each other with keen glances, but neither spoke.

"We'll see about that tomorrow," Burch said as he got to his feet and helped Sibyl up. "Right now I have to find a place for your wagon and get you situated for the night. We can't have you bedding down in the middle of camp. The men wouldn't get a wink of sleep."

Ned wondered whether it was the men or himself Burch

was thinking about, but of course he was careful not to wonder that out loud.

After all the food had been transferred to the chuck wagon, Ned drove the wagon a little distance to a small dip that was protected by some sagebrush on one side and a creek on the other. "We can take a little walk while Ned gets your wagon set up," Burch said, picking up a blanket and throwing it over his shoulder. They walked the short distance to the creek in silence.

"We should have brought the horses," Sibyl remarked, but her words were barely out of her mouth before Burch swept her up and waded into the stream.

"It's not deep," he pointed out unnecessarily. Sibyl's heart pounded at the emotional intensity of his words. The strength of his arms and the nearness of his body were affecting her senses in a most alarming way. Her arms were around his neck, but she felt as though they encircled the hot turbulence of a tornado. By the time he reached the other side of the narrow stream, she was so shaken she was unsteady on her legs.

"I must have turned my heel on a pebble," she said as she reached out to him, seeking support.

"Be careful, there's no doctor for miles." Even the comparative safety of the camp seemed so very far away.

"Where are you taking me?" she asked uneasily.

"Just to a rise through those cottonwoods. When the moon is full you can see the entire plain from there."

Before them spread the panorama of the open plains, thousands of cattle settled down for the night as far as the eye could see. Here and there campfires pierced the twilight but made no impression on the vast darkness that enveloped them. The voices of cowboys riding the herds and singing their bleak songs in rough voices floated to them in a mixture of entangled melodies. A distant howl caused her to turn questioning eyes to him.

"Just a wolf," Burch said, untroubled. "It's probably following an antelope herd." She walked a little closer to him. The silence was vast and menacing, but she knew the huge man walking next to her was just as dangerous. She had never felt quite so alone before and it frightened her. Sibyl felt herself slipping steadily under the spell of his physical presence. Even the smell of sweat that clung to him and the dust that covered his shirt and hat didn't bother her. At least he didn't wear jangling spurs or walk bowlegged.

"It's not often that a man gets to take a girl to watch the sky at night." Burch was speaking almost to himself. "It kinda' makes you look at things different."

"How's that?" she managed to ask without her voice quavering.

"I can't say for sure. I never gave it any thought before. Sky is sky and I've spent more nights in the open than in a proper bed, but when a man has some female to watch out for, it's not the same." Sibyl's heart was pounding so loudly she could hardly hear his words.

"Are you trying to tell me that you're in love with your cows?" she said, striving to conceal her emotional pandemonium. Burch tossed the blanket on a large rock that lay between the roots of the cottonwood trees and took her by the shoulders.

"I'm trying to tell you that you're the most beautiful girl in the world, and I've been dreaming of holding you in my arms ever since that first ride."

"You don't talk like it most of the time," she said, fiddling with the buttons on his flannel shirt. "I sometimes think you don't like me at all."

"I like you more than a sensible man lets himself like anything. I may get angry with you, but I never stay mad. One look at that pouting mouth and all my anger melts."

"I don't pout," she demurred.

"You do too. Your soft red lips push forward in the most entrancing way," he said, letting his fingers trace the lips he spoke of so lovingly, "and I just want to kiss them to take

128

away all the hurt."

"You never do," she murmured breathlessly.

"Do you want me to?"

"Not if you don't want to," she said, refusing to commit herself and all the while tilting her head back until her lips were close to his. He obliged by kissing her, gently at first, then with gathering ecstacy.

"Oh God!" he moaned, folding her tightly into his arms. "I've ached with the thought of you day in and day out. I even spend my nights out here because I can't trust myself in the same house with you."

"I didn't know," she said stupidly. "I thought you preferred it."

He kissed her again to erase any doubt. They sank down on the blanket, their arms around each other. The pervading sense of peace that lay over all the creatures below filled Sibyl with the most wonderful sense of well-being she had ever experienced. It was as though she had come home and her spirit was at rest. She involuntarily tightened her grip on Burch and he caught her in a crushing embrace.

"I like being here. I can't understand why, but I feel like I belong."

"It's because you were never meant to be caught in the web of staid Virginia society. You're just as wild as those cattle down there, and your spirit needs just as much space as they do." His body was next to hers and the heat from the contact made it hard for her to think about peace, spirits, or anything else. The only thing that seemed capable of penetrating the gathering haze was the commanding force compelling her to draw toward the man next to her. He was like a tremendous magnet, polarizing every atom of her being until every bit of her was concentrated upon him.

His hands no longer held hers but were traveling hungrily over her body, first down her side and then along her leg, hurriedly exploring and setting her skin on fire. She started to protest, to draw away, but she couldn't move or utter the objection that habit formed in her brain. His lips locked with hers and his ravaging tongue invaded her mouth. Everything was moving so fast, so quickly beyond anything she had been prepared to face, that she felt helplessly carried along by a raging, uncontrollable torrent. The feel of his leg moving between hers immobilized her. His hand, a bold and insistent hand, found one breast and began to knead it into a firming peak of mounting desire. She felt a new wave of heat spread through her belly and downward between her thighs, it was even more enslaving than the first and just as hopeless to resist. Unconsciously giving in to the waves of pleasure that grew stronger and stronger, she sank on the blanket and pulled Burch down with her. Burch took this as an open invitation, and his knee between her legs grew bolder and the hand began to unbutton her shirt. But this was going too fast for Sibyl.

"No," she said, trying to hold his hand in hers, to slow the advance of that powerful knee. But he was too strong for her; so were the demands of her own body.

"I want you," he groaned. Or was it her own voice she heard? She wasn't sure, but his hand was inside her shirt and making free with one throbbing breast.

"God, how I want you," he groaned again, and dipped his head to touch his lips to her rosy nipple.

She tried to resist, at least she thought she did, hoping to be saved from the one thing she wanted most, but the enervating heat coursing through her had changed into a desire that matched his and she was losing control of herself. Burch was beyond the power of words. His aching need blotted out everything but its own overwhelming hunger.

"Mr. Randall! Miss Cameron!" Ned's voice came from somewhere not far below them. Sibyl grew rigid with fear. They had been so overcome by their desire that they had not heard Ned cross the stream and start to climb toward the rise. He would be upon them in a few minutes. Sibyl panicked.

"Stop! It's Ned. He'll be here in a minute." Fear cleared her head and stiffened her ability to resist the inviting heat that still thundered through her veins. She pushed Burch away with all her might, but he wouldn't stop until she bit the lips trying to possess her mouth.

"What the hell! . . ." he muttered, ruthlessly snatched from the tantalizing arms of his enveloping passion.

"It's Ned, he's looking for us."

"Damn Ned," he said, reaching to bring her down beside him once more, but she scrambled to her feet and quickly buttoned her blouse.

"Don't! You can't want him to find us here like common beasts."

"I'll slit his throat," Burch growled, shaken to the core by the passion that still caused every nerve in his body to feel like it had been scalded.

"I wondered where you'd got to," Ned said as he mounted the rise of the grove of trees. "You'd better get to bed, miss, if you expect to put in a proper day tomorrow."

"Thank you, Ned. Mr. Randall was just showing me how lovely the plain looks in the moonlight."

"I expect it does, miss, but it don't look near so pretty at dawn and that'll be here before you know it."

"We're coming," Burch said, still persecuted by the desire, dreamed of so long and snatched from his grasp so agonizingly. "Where're you sleeping?"

"Under the wagon so I'll be handy in case I'm needed."

"You won't be!" Burch growled. He snatched up the blanket and preceded them down the slope.

Sibyl lay in her bed of deep straw, unable to sleep, her mind racing with what had so nearly happened. She knew she desired Burch, had known it since the day he began to teach her to ride, but she didn't know until now how deeply she felt about him; every thought was of Burch, every sound and smell, every touch under her fingertips reminded her of

131

him in some way. Deep inside her body still ached for the fulfillment it alone understood and knew she had not achieved; it was a longing for something she didn't understand, and that puzzled her. She had always known exactly what she wanted from life, and she thought the ranch was the way to get it, the way to be free in body and spirit. She had told herself she didn't want to be a wife — blind bondage she called it; she wanted to do something, to be somebody, but she wanted it on her own terms.

Now she was in danger of falling into the trap with her eyes open. A stubborn, hardheaded, gorgeous man filled her thoughts more every day. Tonight she found he could make her want to do things she didn't want to have happen to her. She wanted him, would dream of him all night, would wake tomorrow hardly able to wait to see him, and she couldn't blame anybody but herself.

Why hadn't she stayed at the ranch? Why had she been so determined to see a roundup? She wasn't kidding herself and she doubted that she fooled Aunt Augusta either. She had come to see Burch; now look what had come of it. *Fool! You love him, don't you?* She knew the answer as soon as the tears began to flow.

Burch walked restlessly about the camp, his conflict simpler but no less difficult to endure. Never had he desired any woman as he desired Sibyl, and this blinding physical need nearly drove him beyond his ability to control himself. To have aroused and then denied such a powerful passion was a punishing physical torment. He had been aware of his attraction to her from the first and had planned her downfall carefully, but his need, his hunger for her were fast becoming too great for any cool, systematic plan of action. Within a few short weeks, his emotional state was leapt beyond his control; in the beginning he had not considered marriage, but now he thought of their union as a matter of course.

He was certain they were destined to love each other, but

first he would have to break down Sibyl's barriers to love. Her mind might resist accepting their elemental attraction for each other, but her body had no such difficulty. He would use her desire for and need of him to destroy her resistance; it would be the battle within herself that would open the pathway to her citadel. It might not be the gallant way, but with Sibyl it was the only way they could be truly joined with one another.

Chapter 12

The cowboys rose before dawn. Sibyl was dragged from a deep sleep by the rattling of pans, the jingle of harnesses, and the cheerful joking of dozens of men with too much work to do and too little sleep. The cold air of early fall bit deeply into their lungs, and they crowded about camp fires to warm limbs numb from sleep and muscles stiff from strenuous exercise.

Sibyl buried her head under the covers in hopes of being able to sleep a few minutes longer but gave up when the noise grew louder rather than abated. She lay for a little while, listening to the interplay of voices, some high, others low, some joking, others clipped in morose irritation at the dawning of a new day. She smiled when she realized that with their peculiar slang, dialect, and the heavy sprinkling of profanity, she didn't have the slightest idea what they were talking about. I might as well be in a foreign country, she thought, stretching pleasurably in the coziness of her wagon. She had provided herself with a thick bed of straw and a large pile of quilts, and had passed the night in comparative luxury.

Yesterday's bracing air and exercise had made her very hungry, and when the smell of frying bacon and brewing coffee assailed Sibyl's nostrils, she threw off her covers. The

134

coldness of the morning took her breath away. With teeth chattering uncontrollably, she wasted no time getting into her clothes. Even then she was unprepared to find the sky still dark, the ground crisp with frost, and the air cold enough to penetrate her clothing. It had not occurred to her that she would need anything more than a fur-lined vest, and she had to rub her arms vigorously to keep them warm.

"You'll catch your death in that thin shirt, miss," said Ned.

"I know that now, but I didn't yesterday, and I didn't bring any heavy clothing."

"Throw one of them blankets over your shoulders."

"I'll look foolish."

"No more than anyone else. The boys wear their blankets more than they sleep in them." Sibyl thankfully wrapped herself up to her nose and followed him to the chuck wagon. Several men sat huddled in blankets like Indians, sipping scalding coffee. She longed for a cup, but her stomach rebelled at the sight of the black liquid.

"Try it; it's not as bad as it looks." Burch was at her side, wide awake and smiling.

"How can you be in such high spirits when it's still dark?" she asked with a yawn. "Not even chickens get up this early."

"I never rode herd on any chickens so I'll have to take your word for it, but it'll be light soon and the cows will start to get restless. We have to be ready before they do."

"Right now I'm not terribly fond of cows. I never realized how little time you have to sleep. And those awful songs droning in my head all night long. How can you stand it?"

"You get used to it. It becomes quite a comfort actually."

"Not until you give them singing lessons." She grimaced and accepted a cup of coffee from a hospitable young cowpuncher. "Are you *sure* I can drink this without getting sick?"

"I doubt it," Burch laughed, and she thanked the bashful fella with as much genuine warmth as she could conjure up. She took one tentative sip. It was hot enough to scald a hog, but a shudder of revulsion convulsed her whole body.

"Horrible! How *can* you put this awful stuff in your mouth?" she said, gasping for breath.

"It does wake you up," said Burch, unable to hide his amusement.

"I'd rather die than have to drink this stuff."

"Sanchez doesn't make it the way you like it. It's this or nothing."

"That's where you're wrong," she said with a satisfied smile. "No one told me I would be in danger of freezing to death, but I didn't come without making some provision for my survival. See, I brought my own," she said, pointing to Ned who had gone to fetch her coffee pot.

"How farsighted."

"Actually, Aunt Augusta thought of it," she confessed, and they both laughed. "There are some luxuries I can't give up." She settled her pot on the fire and waited impatiently for it to come to a boil. The remainder of the breakfast passed companionably until Burch asked what time she meant to start back for the ranch.

"I'm not going back. I intend to spend the whole day watching everything you do."

"You know nothing of the work. You'll only slow things down."

"I *do* know enough to be able to tell when to get out of the way." Her chin jutted out as it always did when she dug in her heels.

"Everybody will be off searching for cows most of the day, and you can't go out on the trails."

"Why not?"

"Because it's not safe. You could get hurt."

"Don't be ridiculous. I'm not going to fall off my horse, and there's nothing out there to harm me."

"I forbid you to go."

"You can't stop me."

"I won't take you with me, and Jesse won't either."

"Then I'll go by myself," she said stubbornly.

"Don't be a fool."

"You're a fool if you think you an order me about, telling me what I can and can't do, without giving me a single good reason why I should listen to you."

"I've already told you, it's not safe."

"But you haven't told me why." Sibyl's expression was fixed, and Burch knew that unless he took the time to escort her back to the ranch himself, she would be out there somewhere getting herself into God only knew what kind of trouble. As much as she infuriated him, he would never forgive himself if anything happened to her.

"I guess I'll have to take you myself," he conceded, yielding grudgingly to his fate. "It seems to be the only way to keep you from breaking your lovely neck."

"Thank you." She rewarded him with a shattering smile that caused his muscles to twitch all the way down to his toes. "You can explain everything to me as we go along."

He groaned, dreading the role of mentor to a greenhorn, even one as beautiful as Sibyl. She hurried off, and Burch resigned himself to getting nothing done that day.

Maybe it won't be so bad, he told himself. At least I'll be with her and she can't run away no matter how angry she gets. By the middle of the day, she'll be too tired to want to do anything except lie down in her wagon. That was all right with him; he wanted her rested and restless tonight. He felt his desire for her rise even now. If she kept him at arm's length for much longer, he was going to go crazy.

But the day did not unfold as he expected. Somehow Jesse managed to break away from his job and join them just before mid-morning. "You're not riding Hospitality?" he remarked after a plainly unenthusiastic greeting from Burch.

"Burch says a saddle horse doesn't make a good cow pony. He insisted I ride this one." She was on a dun pony with a rough walk but a smooth canter, sure feet, and unlimited endurance. He had already covered miles of rock-strewn ground, sandy stream beds, and eroded terrain without stumbling or putting a foot down wrong. Burch was not riding Old Blue either. He explained that each cowboy has eight to ten horses in his string, and that the outfit keeps extra horses in the remuda in case some are lamed or worked too hard.

"He's too much on the small side to be perfect," Jesse said, "but you're riding the best cow pony on the ranch."

"Whose horse is this?"

"It doesn't belong to any of the boys," Jesse assured her, "and *I* can't afford a string of ponies like that."

Turning toward Burch, Sibyl surprised a very unfriendly glare directed toward Jesse. "It's one of yours, isn't it?"

Burch didn't answer, but he couldn't repress a twinkle.

Sibyl flushed. "Go on, I dare you to deny it," she challenged.

"Okay, he's one of mine, but as Jesse pointed out, he's too small for a man of my size. He is an extra, just right for a featherweight like you, so I was telling the truth."

"Only the part you wanted me to hear. That's just like a man."

"I cry truce, or do I have to be afraid you brought your rifle?" he asked with a grin. Her spurt of anger disappeared in the face of his good humor, and Jesse seemed to be the only one disappointed that they were soon on comfortable terms again.

They had been following Elkhorn Creek for several miles, and Sibyl's attention kept wandering to the numerous hay meadows that lined its banks. She listened with only half an ear as Burch explained why he kept the crew through the winter while other ranchers paid them off.

"Any man who saves three steers pays for himself, and I get a much better price in the end from the extra care. In addition, I don't lose my hands to another outfit so I benefit from the experience and loyalty."

"But doesn't it cost more?" she asked without thinking, and was momentarily disconcerted to see a tightening about Burch's mouth.

"Uncle didn't always keep his hands on, but we found it paid. I know you won't be satisfied until you've seen the proof, so remind me to show you the books when we get home. Or maybe you'd prefer to check with Jesse?" This reading of her character rather shocked Sibyl, but it infuriated her as well.

"If you're going to be paying these men anyway," she retorted, "why don't you keep the underweight steers and fatten them up next year when we have better grass? You'd get twice as much for them as you can now."

"Not if they're dead," Burch snapped.

"Can't you feed them?"

"Everything I have will go to feed your herd. I've tried to buy hay, but no one has any extra."

She could have bitten her tongue. "What are their chances of surviving the winter?" she asked, considerably subdued.

"Not good. We're better off than most because we didn't let the cows graze our hay meadows, but the range is overcrowded and overgrazed. Everyone is facing the same problem, but the big outfits keep throwing herds on the range as fast as they come in from Oregon and Texas. Weak cattle could mean serious losses."

"Are all these hay meadows we're passing ours?" Sibyl inquired, struck with an idea.

"Yes."

"Is this all of it, or is there any more?"

"Altogether I'd say we had about five or six times what you've seen this morning."

"Then you've got your feed. That much hay ought to carry the whole herd through the winter."

"I wish it did, but it doesn't last more than a couple of months at the most."

"Do you cut and stack it?" Burch shook his head. "Then

you're wasting it. If it's left on the ground, the cows will trample a good half to two thirds of it into the mud. That's if they don't eat it before it's needed." A blank expression settled over Jesse's face, but Burch quickly grasped the potential of the idea. Sibyl hurried on. "Instead of giving the crew a month off, put them to work cutting every bit of hay they can find. You can stack it near the water so they can keep the ice open and watch the cows at the same time."

"The boys have to get their time in town," Jesse reminded Burch. "They'll quit if they don't."

"They can go a few at a time," Burch countered with dawning understanding.

"The cows won't eat anything unless they have to dig for it," Jesse warned.

"They'll learn if we have to feed them by hand," Burch insisted, grinning broadly now. "And keeping the cows together will make the men's work easier. Damn, what an idea! Did you think of that by yourself?"

"No, everybody uses haystacks back home."

"But you're the first one to think of using them here," Burch said, impressed in spite of himself. "Wait until the men hear about this!"

"Yeah, just wait," Jesse added gloomily. He left them very soon after that.

Sibyl felt like she was floating on air. Basking in the warmth of Burch's approval, it was impossible for her to grow tired. Her curiosity was inexhaustible and her will indomitable. She insisted that he not vary his work in any degree because of her presence. He didn't take his usual long looping ride, but they did range far over the plain, supervising the cowboys who were searching the arroyos and canyons for cattle.

The day was filled with much shared fun, and during its course, a feeling of closeness grew up between Sibyl and Burch. It wasn't long before she found that even as he explained some part of the roundup or they galloped toward the next rise, she was very conscious of his body next to hers, his hand occasionally on her saddle horn, his leg in the stirrup next to hers. He often rode ahead of her and she was repeatedly made aware of the broad power of his back, the massive strength of his legs. Seeing him rope a full-grown steer and effortlessly throw it to the ground did nothing to diminish her admiration. He was a man who could *do* instead of talk, and he was proving it right before her eyes.

Midday found them tired and hungry and far from camp. "When do we eat?" she asked when the rumbling in her stomach began to distract her.

"Tonight."

"I mean lunch."

"We don't. We only eat at dawn and dusk."

"Nobody eats anything?"

"Everyone's away from camp, and it wastes too much time to go back."

"But I'll starve before then."

"You mean you didn't have the foresight to pack a lunch?"

"I didn't know I needed to," she answered crossly.

"Then it's a good thing I did." He reached into his saddlebags and offered her a carefully wrapped cloth. "I thought you might get hungry." For a moment he wasn't sure she would accept it.

"Did you bring something for yourself?"

"Of course."

"Where do we stop?" she inquired, breaking into a smile. "I could eat a horse."

"There's a line cabin near here. It'll give us some shade and fresh water." The small log cabin was reached quickly.

"I've noticed these before," she said, inspecting the pitifully bare shack. "What are they used for?"

"The men use them when they get too far away to return to the bunkhouse. They're especially useful in the winter and during bad weather."

"They don't look very comfortable," she observed dubiously. The tiny cabin contained one bed and a small stove; the log walls were chinked with mud.

"Why are the walls covered with paper?"

"It gives the men something to read and also serves to insulate the cabin against the wind."

"This is out of a catalog."

"Reading wish books is a favorite way to while away a long winter afternoon." She was still reading the walls when he came back with some fresh water. She spread the food on top of the stove and they sat on the bed to eat.

"Where are the chairs?"

"*It* was probably cut up for firewood, if there was one. When a man sets a horse all day, a bed is more welcome. This cabin is too close to the ranch to be a two-man cabin, so there's no need to be prepared for company."

After lunch Sibyl felt drowsy and Burch encouraged her to stretch on the bed. It wasn't very comfortable, but then she only planned to lie down for a few minutes. Just enough to relax before climbing back in the saddle.

Sibyl opened her eyes to find Burch at her side, staring at her with an intensity that set her pulses to racing immediately. "How long have I been asleep?"

"Not long," he smiled, caressing her cheek with his fingertips.

"Have you been sitting here the whole time?"

"Just about."

"It must be boring."

"Do you know how beautiful you are when you're asleep?"

"Of course not," she laughed, pleased. "I've never watched myself sleep." When he didn't return her smile she felt a tremor of apprehension. "Don't tell me I look worse when I'm awake?"

"You're even more lovely awake." He let his finger trail along her neck. Instinctively, she took his hand and drew it to her lips. An avalanche of desire came crashing down and destroyed Burch's restraint. He wrapped Sibyl in a crushing embrace and covered her mouth with his hungry, insistent kisses. With a leaping heart, she responded to his embrace, clinging to him and welcoming his lips. A low moan escaped him and his hands began to move over her body. No protest escaped her lips when Burch eased on the bed next to her. The feel of the length of his hard, lean body against her pliant flesh caused her passion to flame like dry tinder. Without caring how it happened, she found the front of her shirt open and his hot demanding lips deserting hers for the mounding peaks of her full young breasts. "Burch!" she groaned as his teeth and tongue teased her nipples until she thought she'd go mad. A raging fire swept through her body, spreading from every point where he touched her.

But when his knee pried her legs apart and a bold hand began to caress her where she'd never been touched before, she felt a new sensation coming from deep within her, knifing out through her body, making every nerve so painfully sensitive her whole being trembled with its force. Her hands joined Burch's to free her body of the last remnants of clothing. She lay before him in her perfection, vulnerable and inviting.

Burch's lips trailed kisses along her quivering flesh while his hands touched and pressed and massaged until she thought she would scream with desire. She drew his lips to hers and with fumbling fingers began to help him out of his clothes. Her hands played through the soft hair on his chest and across the powerful muscles of his shoulders. Down the small of his back they went until they reached the swell of his buttocks. She felt the hard, pulsing of his passion against her belly and opened her legs to receive him in an act of fulfillment both her body and mind demanded.

As Burch eased himself into her, a spiral of fiery pleasure radiated through her whole body. "This might hurt a little," he whispered in her ear, but she was too deep in the toils of her need to heed any warning. She clung to him, pressing his buttocks to her, trying to draw him within her to reach her rampaging need. A sharp pain momentarily penetrated the blanket of sensual delight that enveloped her, but then she experienced the wonder of his bigness deep within her, filling her with his heat and desire, and all memory of pain was wiped from her mind. She rose to meet him, her body arching against his with fierce, demanding want. The tempo of their lovemaking increased and her grasp on reality weakened until she felt cut loose and borne aloft by the waves of pleasure that washed over, through, and around her. Hungry for more, she sought Burch's lips while her hands urged him to continue the ascent of spiraling desire that threatened to consume her very soul. Abruptly she felt his body tense and he deposited his hot seed deep within her. Her body seemed to explode and a fresh wave swept over her, leaving her breathless and incredulous.

His passion spent, Burch lay still within her as her body began a slow descent. Her eyes softened as she gazed contentedly at the handsome features that had become so dear to her. It seemed like a long time before his breathing returned to normal, but when he opened his eyes again she smiled and he gently kissed her lips. She welcomed his embrace, inviting his hands to begin their explorations again as hers sought to become familiar with him. Almost instantly she felt him begin to grow within her and the passion she thought totally spent renewed itself in an instant. They made love again. This time there was less urgency and more gentleness in their union, but to Sibyl it was the same shattering experience.

Sibyl lay contentedly within the circle of Burch's arms. He had slept briefly, but she was too keyed up, too full of wonder at what had happened to be able to close her eyes. One short hour had changed everything the experiences of a lifetime had taught her. She was honest enough to realize that she might merely have told herself what she wanted to believe was true, but none of that mattered now. It was clear she had to start again, trying to incorporate this new experience into her plans. And that wasn't going to be easy.

"Don't you have to get back to work?" she asked.

"Hmmm," replied Burch, tightening his hold on her. Sibyl was in no hurry to move. She could hardly believe that she was willing to continue lying with a man's arms about her, but the sensation was so new and so enticing that she happily snuggled deeper into his embrace.

"The boys will see to the roundup," he murmured, kissing the top of her head. "Who cares about a few old cows anyway." Sibyl was so startled she sat bolt upright, only to flush brightly when Burch's smiles proved that he had dangled the bait and she'd taken it in one bite.

"I should have known you could never trust a man," she said, trying to cover her chagrin by pulling from him, but he pulled her back down.

"I promise never to tease you again if you will promise never to pull away from me."

"That's a mighty tempting offer," Sibyl responded, on her mettle now, "but I doubt if I can trust you to keep such a promise, and I don't know if I want to."

"Shrew" he chided, pulling her back down and covering her face with kisses. "Does this make you feel more assured?"

"I don't know," she replied, unwilling to give away how thoroughly the occurrences of the afternoon had shaken her. "If I were a cow, I don't think I would trust any man with the smell of roast beef in his nostrils."

With an appreciative shout of laughter, Burch wrestled her down and proceeded to prove that not every flame turned its victims to cinders.

Sibyl was not sure how she got through the afternoon. Burch seemed to resume his work as though it had never been interrupted; for her the rest of the day was a haze of activity.

She was relieved when he asked her if she wanted to go to her wagon or watch the branding of the calves. She chose her wagon, and a period of quiet did much to restore her sense of reality. A quick bath in a secluded bend of the icy stream did even more. If she had entertained any doubts about what had happened that afternoon, the streaks of blood on her thighs confirmed that she had at last surrendered herself.

She returned to camp caught between exhilaration of her new experience and growing disgust at not having enough strength of mind to resist temptation. *After giving in to him once, how do you propose to deny him in the future?* she asked, vexed with herself. She wasn't sure she wanted to deny him, and that made her even more angry. *And don't kid yourself that he's in love with you; he's never even used the word. It was probably just animal lust. He'd feel the same about any other pretty woman.*

But what about her? Was it lust that made her encourage him? She hadn't come here intending to seduce him, but what had she come here for? She pulled her clothes on and adjusted them with short, angry movements. Her mind was in a turmoil and she needed time to sort things out. She was not fool enough to deny that she found Burch extremely attractive; in fact, he'd just proved she couldn't resist him. But what kind of love did she want from him? A physical relationship that left her mind and emotions free? Or something else?

She knew immediately that she wanted something else, something that required a union of their spirits as well as their bodies. But she didn't know how to put it into words, and she had no idea how to begin working toward it. She had spent so long avoiding all thoughts of a permanent union with a man that when she found she couldn't live without one, she didn't know how to act.

I'll ask Aunt Augusta, she thought. *Somehow she always knows the answer.* She'd go back to the ranch first thing tomorrow morning. She didn't want to run the risk of another encounter before she knew where all this was supposed to end. She admitted she was too weak to resist Burch, that she didn't want to resist him, but he couldn't be allowed to think that she was his just for the asking.

Sibyl snuggled down into her quilts. She had felt chagrined when Burch took her decision to return to the ranch with a total lack of surprise or disappointment. She had no intention of allowing herself to be talked into staying, but his not making the attempt was disturbing. There was already enough uncertainty about the nature of his feelings for her, and this did nothing to reassure her. At least their leave-taking had been more gratifying.

She had enjoyed an evening of cowboy high jinks and intended to slip away after saying good night in the presence of the other men. "You don't have to accompany me," she said when he rose to go with her. "Ned can see me to my wagon."

"I have every confidence Ned will take good care of you," he agreed, but he came anyway. She was still miffed, and inclined to be crabby.

"You don't care if I travel twenty-five miles across open prairie tomorrow, but I can't be trusted to walk fifty yards in the moonlight."

Without ceremony Burch cut through any pretense of not knowing the reason for her ill-humor. "Do you want me to beg you to stay?"

It's just like a man to reduce everything to its most unflattering essentials, she thought, feeling aggrieved. "Nothing you can say will make me change my mind."

"That's why I didn't say anything."

That was going too far. "You could at least try."

"And give you the pleasure of turning me down?"

"Not entirely, but at least I would know I meant something to you. I'm not even sure that you'll miss me."

Burch spun her around and gave her a kiss so long and passionate that she had to lean on him for support.

"Are you convinced?"

"A little."

"Would another help?"

After all, she was going to leave the first thing in the morning. What harm would one more kiss do? She clung to him a minute too long, and Burch's eyes began to gleam with desire.

"Don't," she said, backing away from him quickly.

"But you said you weren't convinced," he replied.

"I'm convinced you want me; it's the way you want me I worry about."

"On any terms." Sibyl didn't believe him, but she crawled into bed with the delicious feeling of knowing that the man of her choice plainly desired her. She fell into a deep sleep that was to be interrupted much too soon.

Chapter 13

A thunderous rumble that seemed to come from the center of the earth dragged Sibyl from her deep slumber. At first her mind was too clogged with sleep to function, but then it began to make ridiculous suggestions such as distant explosions or even an earthquake. She came wide awake when Ned climbed into the wagon, his face as white as a sheet.

"It's a stampede, miss, and they're heading right for the wagon." Scrambling to the front of the wagon, Sibyl was horrified to see a seething mass of horned heads moving toward them at top speed. She expected instant, horrible death. Why, she asked, should she lose her life just when she had found a reason to keep it? But the stampeding animals, reaching the wagon with incredible rapidity, divided as though by plan and swept by on either side of her.

Sibyl could hear the clink of their horns as they struck against each other and scraped the side of the wagon. A terrifying ripping sound brought a scream to her lips. One pair of horns after another tore into the wagon's canvas covering; in seconds it was in shreds, and only the upper two thirds of the wooden staves that arched above her head remained sheathed in canvas. Now Sibyl was able to look directly into the frightened eyes of the stampeding steers, only inches away from her. It made her sick with fear to think how easy it would be for them to overturn the wagon. She shouted to Ned, but her words were drowned out by the thunder of thousands of hooves pounding the dry, hard ground. As far as she could see there were animals in headlong flight away from the creek, back to the uplands from which they had come.

Then almost as quickly as it began, it was over. All that remained was a distant rumble and the yells of the cowboys trying to turn the leaders. "What happened?" she asked when the noise had almost died away and she was at last able to speak. "What caused them to stampede?"

"I don't know, but it doesn't take anything to stampede a herd. These cows are as wild as bedamned. Many a cowboy had lost his life because some steer ran off in the middle of the night with no better excuse than he didn't like the tune some drover was singing."

"They must have destroyed the camp," she said, starting to climb down.

"Don't leave the wagon, miss. They've been known to come back. Usually it's at a walk, but you can't ever be too sure with those ornery critters."

The tension was terrible, but she didn't have to wait very long. The weakened cows had soon slowed down and the men were able to turn them and head them back to their bedding grounds. "It'll take them the better part of tomorrow to sort them out again," Ned said as the milling cattle slowly settled into an uneasy quiet.

"You all right, Miss Cameron?" Jesse asked, riding up.

"I'm fine now, but I was never more terrified in my life."

"It was good you stayed in your wagon."

"I couldn't have gotten out if I'd wanted to."

"Make sure you don't get out. The herd is settling down now, but it won't take much to set them off again."

"What caused the stampede?"

"I don't know. Probably just a coyote or maybe even an

owl. These crazy cows don't need a reason to run."

"Where's Burch?"

"I haven't see him since he rode off on Old Blue. Most likely he's with Lasso. Things always get in a terrible mix-up after a stampede. You calm down and try to get some sleep. Everything's all right now, but I'll make sure to keep an eye on you."

But Sibyl couldn't calm down. She could only guess at the dangers posed by a stampede, but she was sure that nothing Burch had to say to Lasso would have kept him from seeing for himself that she was all right.

"Where are our horses?"

Ned looked at her without comprehension. "The ones that pull the wagon," she said, agitated. The feeling that something had happened to Burch was growing stronger all the time.

"They probably ran off during the commotion."

"Can you find Mr. Randall for me?"

"It's not safe out there."

"Please, I've got to see him. If you won't go look for him, I will." Ned tried to talk her into changing her mind, but she wouldn't listen to any of his arguments.

"If you can't find some horses to pull this wagon, I'll ride Hospitality," she insisted stubbornly.

"I'll go look," grumbled Ned. "If I was to let you go nosing about out there, knowing nothing about cows like you do, you'd probably have them on their feet again in five minutes."

It felt like he was gone for hours, and her fears ate away at her nerves dreadfully. She had almost reached the point of setting out on her own when Ned, leading the horses, came back with Jesse hard on his heels.

"You can't go looking for Burch," Jesse said. "There's no telling where he is. He'll come back when he's ready."

"I'm sure something's wrong, I just *feel* it. I can't sit here and do nothing."

"Burch never got in the way of a stampede before, and I can't see him risking his neck now."

"Are you implying that Burch is a coward?" Sibyl asked, bristling.

"Of course not. All I meant was Burch is not one to get himself into trouble if he can avoid it."

"Then why isn't he back? Everybody else is."

"I told you, he's probably talking to Lasso or some of the boys. There's hundreds of things he could be doing."

"Something's wrong, and I'm going to find out what it is."

"I can't let you go looking through those hills in the dark."

"You can't stop me." Her anger flared quickly because of her anxiety for Burch. "This is my wagon and I'll drive it myself if necessary."

Jesse's arguments were no more successful than Ned's had been.

"Stay here if you like, but I'm not afraid of a few cows," she said rudely.

"I'm coming along. I'd never forgive myself if I let anything happen to you."

It was easy to follow the trail of the stampede in the moonlight. "Burch is going to be furious when he finds out you've been running about on a wild-goose chase in the dark over this ground," Jesse scolded. "He's probably just checking with the point riders and thinks you're safe in camp." Now that they were under way, Sibyl herself began to wonder if she might not have acted too hastily, but she couldn't shake the feeling that something was dreadfully wrong. A boy came galloping after them before they had gone far.

"Have you see Mr. Randall?" he asked Jesse. "He's not in camp." If Sibyl hadn't been so terribly worried that she would find Burch lying dead before her any minute, she might have seen a look of blazing anger flash across Jesse's features.

"We're going to look for him now, Jenkins," Jesse said, with rigid control. "You go on back to camp."

"No," countermanded Sibyl, "come with us. It'll be quicker

152

if we have two people to help look. Ride on either side of the wagon and cover as much ground as you can without losing sight of us. Ned and I will stay in the center of the trail." She mounted Hospitality; now that she was certain something was wrong, it was impossible for her to depend upon someone else to find Burch while she rode in the agonizingly slow wagon.

After a few miles the tracks began to make a gradual circle and Sibyl felt better. It meant the herd was slowing down and the cowboys were getting them under control. It also meant there was less chance of an accident. The circle continued until they had almost turned back toward the camp. Sibyl took her first deep breath, feeling a little foolish but a great deal relieved. Burch was probably storming through the camp right now looking for her. She was going to have a difficult time explaining this escapade to him — and just when he was beginning to give her credit for some intelligence.

Then she saw the silhouette of Old Blue standing perfectly still in the distance, one leg dangling uselessly beneath him.

"Burch!" she screamed in pure terror. Whipping and driving Hospitality with her spurs, she galloped recklessly over the hazardous ground. As she drew closer, she saw an oddly crumpled heap lying on the churned -up earth and her heart stopped beating. "Please, don't be dead," she moaned piteously. "Please, God, don't let him be dead."

Sibyl fell rather than slid from the saddle. She had to wipe the tears from her eyes before she could see Burch. What she saw caused them to flow even faster. Burch lay sprawled on the ground, his powerful arms and legs at crazy angles with his body. His shirt and vest were shredded, revealing ugly cuts and gashes made by flying hooves when his body hit the ground and rolled to a halt. Sibyl knelt beside him, helpless, hopeless, staring out of vacant eyes at the broken body. Profound anguish welled up within her, threatening her sanity.

Jesse and Jenkins had followed her headlong flight while Ned drove the careening wagon over the ground as fast as he dared. The first to reach her, Jenkins jumped from his horse, took one brief look at Sibyl, and knelt over the still form. He felt for a heartbeat, then put his cheek to Burch's nostrils.

"He's still alive, but just barely." Sibyl could hardly believe her ears. She pulled back from the yawning abyss, hope and desperation clearing her mind and enabling her to act quickly. She realized that Burch must get immediate attention or he might still die.

"Bring Ned and the wagon," she said to Jesse, who had just ridden up.

"How is he?"

"Get the wagon!" she screamed. "There's no time to lose. Jenkins, you go for a doctor as fast as you can."

"The closest one is twenty miles away."

"Then take the fastest horse you can find, and tell him Mr. Randall has been badly hurt. Ned and I will carry him back to the ranch in the wagon."

"What about his horse?"

"What about him?" she asked, without taking her eyes off Burch.

"His leg's broken. He has to be shot."

"Somebody else can shoot him; you've got to go for the doctor." Burch looked so deathly pale it was hard to believe that he was still alive. Ned arrived with the wagon and they lifted him with infinite care onto the straw pallet. A shot and then the thud of Old Blue's body against the earth would have been too much for her if she hadn't been concentrating on Burch's broken leg. It hung at a sickening angle, and Sibyl fought back her nausea. His left arm was also broken, but that was a clean break. It was the leg that worried her.

"Head for the nearest stream," she told Ned. "Jesse, find Sanchez and bring whatever he has in his medicine bag. And make sure he gives you something to heat water in."

"How will I know where to find you?"

"If you can find a cow in this endless wasteland, it shouldn't be too hard to find a whole wagon. Now go!" She rode next to Burch, thankful for the deep straw, cursing the godforsaken land for every lurch the wagon took and cursing Ned every time he slowed down to ease through some gully or swale. The minutes passed with agonizing slowness. In the dim interior, she was barely able to make out Burch's features and was totally unable to hear him breathe. She kept touching him to make sure that he was warm. She remembered the virile strength of his lovemaking only hours earlier, and the whole nightmare seemed like a monstrous bad joke.

Now that she had found a man to love—and she finally admitted that she did love him—it seemed so unfair to lose him after only a taste of the rapture she had discovered in his arms. He was *not* going to die, not if she could do anything about it, she swore. She didn't know much about nursing, but the doctor and Aunt Augusta would help her. Somehow the three of them would pull him through. But looking at the broken, pale, deathly still man lying next to her caused cold fear to clutch at her heart. She piled more blankets over him and tried to keep her mind from thinking the unthinkable.

At last the wagon stopped, and Sibyl jumped down to find herself next to a small stream with barely any water at all. "It's the best I can find close by with all this drought," Ned apologized. "I'm afraid it's rather alkaline."

"It doesn't matter; we're not going to drink it. Light the lantern while I try to find something to hold water. The most important thing right now is to clean his wounds." A tin cup was the only container she could find.

"Where is Jesse?" she cried, but no horseman appeared out of the night.

She had to unbutton Burch's shirt and cut away the pieces before she could reach the wounds on his chest. The cleaning was difficult because of the small quantity of water that could be heated at one time and the torn character of the wounds.

She was positive several of his ribs were broken as well.

"I can't wait for Jesse any longer," she said when she had cleaned away the worst of the dirt. "We'll have to start for the ranch without him." The lantern swayed back and forth, creating ghostly shadows within the wagon, but it gave Sibyl some comfort to be able to see Burch's face.

Dawn came and first light was even more dreary than the moonlight. The ranch was still wrapped in quiet when they reached it, but the arrival of the wagon brought everyone out quickly. Balaam shuffled from the bunkhouse, and Augusta hurried down the steps to see what could have caused her niece to travel through the night.

"Burch has been hurt in a stampede," Sibyl said without preamble. "Get his bed ready. Balaam and Ned will help me carry him up. Jenkins has already gone to fetch the doctor." By the time they had fashioned a litter to carry him upstairs, Augusta had the bed turned down, a pan of warm water on the bedside table, and wads of lint and bandages ready.

"You'll have to cut his clothes off," Augusta said when she saw the broken limbs.

"There are some razors on his dressing table. Well," Sibyl spoke impatiently when the men seemed reluctant to proceed, "are you going to do it, or shall I?"

"But you're a lady, miss," Ned gulped.

"Would you want him to die because of a silly distinction such as that?" Chastised, Ned accepted the razor and began to cut the clothes away. The boots took more time. Balaam, unable to believe that any lady could bear the sight of a naked man, spread a sheet over Burch in an attempt to preserve their modesty.

"We need some splints," said Sibyl, helping her aunt treat each of the wounds with a strong solution of alcohol. "We have to set that arm."

"What about his leg?"

"I don't know. I hope the doctor gets here soon. It looks bad." The ladies had finished cleaning and bandaging the wounds by the time the men returned with the splints. "Can either of you set his arm?"

Balaam nodded, coming closer to the bed. "It don't look too bad," he said, gently testing the limb. "Hold his shoulder." Sibyl clenched her teeth before she and Ned took a firm hold on Burch. When Balaam wrenched the arm around to slip the bone into place, Burch stirred with a groan. Somehow it made Sibyl feel better to know he could feel pain. As long as he hurt, he was alive.

"I don't know about that leg," Balaam said after the splint was firmly in place on the arm. "I'm afraid to touch one that bad."

"Then there's really nothing we can do for him until the doctor arrives," Augusta said. "I suggest we leave him to rest."

Ned and Balaam had chores to do, Augusta meals to attend to, but Sibyl could not keep her mind on any task. She nearly wore herself out climbing the steps to listen quietly by Burch's bedside to assure herself that he was still breathing. She wanted no food and didn't even finish one cup of coffee. Only when Jesse finally showed up just before noon with the needed medicine did she get a chance to work off some of her spleen.

"It's about time you found your way home," she snapped, snatching the tin box from him. "If I'd known you'd get lost, I'd have kept you with me and sent Jenkins." Jesse's eyes blazed angrily, but Sibyl was too enraged, worried, and scared to care. "You've got to finish the roundup and take those steers to Chicago yourself. Lose a single one or fail to get the top price and you'd better never set foot on my ranch again. If I didn't know better, I'd swear you wanted Burch dead and that you were glad those cows nearly killed him. Now get out of here before I do something I shouldn't."

"It's not his fault Burch was hurt," remarked Augusta. "Don't you think you were a little unreasonable?"

"No," she replied emphatically and stamped back into the house. Nothing else occurred to upset her, and there was no

157

change in Burch's condition when Jenkins returned that afternoon.

"The doctor was away, miss, but I left a message with his wife he was to follow as soon as he could. Then I changed my mind and went after him. He oughta be along in a few minutes. I thought I'd come ahead just to let you know," he said apologetically.

"Thank you, Jenkins. I want you to go back to camp. I'm sending Jesse to Chicago with the steers. You will need to take over until he gets back." Jenkins started to say something but changed his mind. "How long before you're through with the roundup?"

"Not long. Mr. Randall was telling me something about haystacks and only letting a few of the men go to Casper at a time."

"I'll explain all that later. Will you stay here, I mean, not go to Casper?"

"Yes, miss. I'm not leaving Mr. Randall until he's up on his feet, able to see after himself."

Sibyl thought he spoke with more than usually grim determination, but she put it down to loyalty and left him to go tell her aunt that the doctor was coming.

It was a harrowing visit. The doctor was neither learned nor skilled in comforting fearful relatives, but he was a good, practical man and complimented the women on their work. "Not that it makes a lot of difference, but it won't do for him to develop a fever from infections on top of everything else. He's got a broken arm, a badly busted leg, half a dozen broken ribs and, unless I miss my guess, a concussion as well. He'll need all his strength to get over this. What worries me most is this leg. It's a nasty break, and if it doesn't heal properly, he won't be able use it. He might even lose the leg," the doctor continued inexorably, even though Sibyl was looking quite unwell herself. "I'll set it, but you'll have to see to the rest. I'm due thirty miles the other side of my place before nightfall. I only came because we can't afford to lose a man like Mr. Randall, not with the kind of rascals that are loose in these parts." And with that enigmatic remark, he set to work.

It took him a good while, and Sibyl was certain a better-trained man could have set the leg more quickly with less bruising, but she was thankful he'd come.

"Keep him as quiet and warm as you can. There'll be a lot of pain for a while and probably some fever as well. Just don't let him try to move about on that leg for at least a month. I'll be back before the end of the week, but it's just as well if he can be made to realize from the first that he's in for a long convalescence. It'll save us a lot of trouble later. Burch is a sensible man in most ways, but I doubt he's going to like being tied to his bed for a month."

"For a month! Are you sure?"

"More like two, but don't tell him that now. The shock will set him back. There's nothing he can do, anyway. The cattle will be gone and the men in town. The whole place is ready to close down for winter. He couldn't have chosen a better time to get laid up."

Sibyl doubted Burch would share the doctor's view of the situation, but she forebore to dispute with him.

At last the doctor had gone, Ned and Balaam were back in the bunkhouse, and Sibyl was alone with Burch and her aunt for the first time that morning. All at once the tension, the fear, and the worry was too much for her and she burst into tears. Augusta gathered Sibyl in her arms and let her sob until the stiffness left her body and she felt weak and drained.

"Do you feel better now?" her aunt asked when she sat up and began to wipe her eyes. "It always helps to have a good cry."

"But I never cry," protested Sibyl.

"Now you see what a wonderful comfort you've been wasting," smiled her aunt. "That's one thing men don't know about that we women do."

"I don't know why I broke down like that."

"Don't you?" Augusta asked quietly. Sibyl glanced up quickly, her eyes questioning.

"What do you mean?"

"You don't have to pretend with me. I know you're in love with him."

"But how did you know?" she asked, amazed. "I only realized it myself yesterday."

"I think I've known since you first saw him. That's why I decided not to go back to Virginia," she said, glancing at the figure lying so motionless before them. "I'll never have any children of my own, and I wouldn't forgive myself if I were to miss knowing yours."

Sibyl could only stare.

Chapter 14

Next day, before breakfast had been finished, Lasso was at the Elkhorn, considerably upset by the news of Burch's accident.

"This is a terrible thing," he said over and over again. "I don't know how it could happen to someone like Burch. Never knew him to take a fall before. And Old Blue! It makes me sick to think of losing a horse like that." He insisted upon visiting the sickroom, but was so overset by seeing Burch lying as one dead that Sibyl thought Augusta was going to have to make up a bed for him too. But a good slug of whiskey brought the color back to his cheeks and the robust ring to his voice.

"I was a mite put out to hear you were left here by yourself when Sibyl went gallivanting off to the roundup," he informed Augusta as she sat alone with him in the ranch room. "A gentle lady like you ought not be left with nobody to protect her."

"Balaam stayed here the whole time."

"What's *he* worth? A broken-down old gabster. What could he do if Indians came swooping down or rustlers surrounded the ranch?"

Augusta's pupils expanded until the blue almost disappeared from her eyes.

161

"I don't suppose anybody could do very much," she said in a breathless whisper.

"Nonsense! One good man could hold off a small army from this house. Why, if I had a good set of rifles, I could see that no one crossed the lane around the house all by myself."

"I was led to believe that there were no more Indians about," Augusta murmured timorously.

"That's true," admitted Lasso, regretfully relinquishing the gratifying vision of dazzling Augusta with his bravery, "but the area has become plumb filthy with rustlers. If Burch and I didn't have a natural fence in the canyon walls and plenty of men on the range year round, we would be robbed blind."

"Do people really steal cows?" Augusta asked, unable to account for such an odd habit.

"Whole herds sometimes," disclosed Lasso, warming to his subject. "Why, over near Clear Water Creek — that's near to Sheridan — one rancher had his whole herd taken in less than a month. But the worst is to the west of the Big Horns. Things are so bad there some of the ranchers are talking about selling up." Augusta listened, fascinated.

"But this is nothing for a proper lady to be troubling her mind with. A good man will give you all the protection you need in these parts. Of course a pretty gal like you probably has them coming to the door every day. Or waiting back in Virginia," he added as an afterthought. "What does Burch say to such goings-on?"

"Well, he's not really home very much," mumbled Augusta, completely incapable of imagining such an eventuality but reluctant to dispel the delightful notion Lasso had of her bountiful suitors.

"They're probably already on line trying to snap you up at the Christmas party. A thoughtful man would get in a word now if he wanted a dance." He looked inquiringly at Augusta, but she sat as though carved in stone. "How many foolhardy cowboys have you had asking to stand up with you already?" he asked with fierce energy.

"I can't say that I've been keeping track of that kind of thing," Augusta told him, barely able to think at all.

"Well, I'm speaking up right now," he proclaimed, forging ahead. "I want you to keep the best dances for me, and you can tell any cowboy with enough sass to come asking you to dance that he'd better keep his tongue soft in his head, or I'll cut it out for him."

"Oh, they wouldn't say anything unbecoming," faltered Augusta, unable to believe that her poor person could inspire any man to such spirited action.

"They'd better not. Now that Burch is feeling under the weather, I feel responsible for you. Where's Jesse? I gotta talk to him about keeping an eye on you when I'm not about."

"Jesse has taken the steers to Chicago."

"He's gone and left you alone? Burch can't be such a fool as that."

"I believe it was Sibyl's idea for him to go, but she asked Jenkins to stay. And of course Ned and Balaam are here, so you see we are really quite well protected."

"I guess that'll do," Lasso conceded, but his dissatisfaction was obvious.

Augusta seemed to grow more and more stiffly upright as she realized that concern for *her* was the cause of Lasso's wanting to instigate these extraordinary precautions.

"Well, I must be off, or no telling what the boys will get up to. Don't you let that niece of yours make you sit up with Burch day and night. He's a tough young rascal. He'll pull through no matter what that doctor does to him."

He shook Augusta's hand vigorously, just as though it were the first time he'd met her, and departed in a crescendo of good-byes loud enough to reach anyone as far away as the cattle sheds. Before the staggered woman could recover her senses, he was back again, this time to thrust a large cage into her hands.

"It's not much, just a cat, but I thought you might like to

have something to keep you company." He didn't wait for her reply, which was just as well, because Augusta was incapable of one. She stood rooted to the spot, her mind frozen, her eyes unseeing, unable to believe that any of this was happening to her. She looked at the large tabby cat in wonder, and the strangest expression appeared on her face. If *she* had been the cat, one might have accused her of having just swallowed the canary.

Sibyl sat in the shadow of the lamp, her sunken eyes fixed on Burch's ashen countenance as he moved restlessly about in the dim light. Over the last two days, his condition had grown steadily worse, and she was worried that his rising fever would become critical. For the tenth time in the last hour, she rose to check his pulse, but there was no change. After lingering helplessly by his bed for a time, she went to the window and peered intently into the night, oppressed by the inpenetrable blanket of darkness that surrounded them. The lonely hours moved with maddening slowness, and in the silence Sibyl felt more alone than she had ever felt in her life. It was as though there were no one else in the world except the two of them, and she was powerless to do anything to ease his pain or speed his recovery.

At last the first cold, gray streaks of light pierced the night, bringing the promise of dawn, and Sibyl's hopes began to rise. Dr. Clay had said he would return today, and she silently prayed it would be soon. She dreaded to touch the hot, dry skin or listen to the groans uttered whenever his feverish tossings caused him to move the leg. It was still terribly swollen and she could not look at it without a cold, clammy fear that the doctor might have to amputate. Not once in the two days had Burch regained consciousness, and she couldn't get the doctor's warning of a concussion out of her head; the glazed look in his eyes made her more fearful than ever that he might develop brain fever.

Augusta entered the room soundlessly. She was looking a

little worn down herself, but Sibyl had insisted upon taking the night vigil so that her aunt would not have to bear the brunt of Burch's illness.

"He doesn't look any better," Augusta said, pouring fresh water into the basin and beginning to bathe his forehead.

"He's been growing steadily more feverish all through the night. I wish the doctor would come. I feel so helpless, not knowing what's happening or what to do for him."

"You're doing all you can."

"But that's not enough!" she cried. The anguish was so immense, so dreadfully naked, Augusta felt more ineffectual than she had since Sibyl's mother died. She put her arm about her niece's shoulders, but Sibyl turned away to hide the tears that were streaming down her face.

"It's so horrid to have to sit here and watch him get worse," she sobbed. "I feel so *useless.*"

"He's not dying, Sibyl."

"But he might."

"No, he won't. He's very sick, but that was to be expected. He has a very strong constitution and you've taken such good care of him. You should lie down and get some sleep. You're not looking very well yourself."

"I can't. I've got to see the doctor."

"I'll call you when he comes. If you don't get some rest, you'll be sick, and then you'll be no good to either him or yourself. Do try and be sensible."

Sibyl swallowed the reproof without cavil.

"You'll call me as soon as he comes?"

"Of course. Now go stretch out for a bit. I'll fix us a big breakfast after the doctor leaves, and then you can have a good, long rest."

Sibyl went to her room, expecting to lie awake waiting for the sound of the doctor's buggy, but the nervous exhaustion of the past days had been even greater than the physical strain, and she fell into almost instant slumber.

"Sibyl, the doctor is here." Augusta's voice barely penetrated the wall of fatigue that made every part of her feel like it weighed a thousand pounds.

"Do wake up, Sibyl. I can't stand here shaking you all morning. Burch is much better."

Sibyl sat up too quickly and the room spun madly before her eyes. Slowly it stopped turning and the grotesque figure before her eyes dissolved into her aunt's kindly face.

"His temperature broke right after you went to sleep, and the doctor says he's out of danger. All he needs now is to be kept quiet until the bone can begin to knit." The sense of relief was so enormous Sibyl's brain began to reel once again, and she felt herself falling, tumbling head over heels into an endless void. A heavy black veil descended over her eyes and once again she was sound asleep.

"He actually opened his eyes for a few minutes this afternoon," Augusta told Sibyl as she ravenously devoured her first food of the day. After the news that Burch was past the crisis, she had slept till mid-afternoon. "I had a little extra of the soup I had made for my lunch and I gave it to him. I don't think he liked it very much, but it will be good for him. The doctor said he was to have clear soups for at least a week."

"It's a good thing he can't move, or he'd get up and fix his own dinner," Sibyl mumbled with her mouth full.

"Not yet. He was glad enough to have me feed it to him."

"You should have waked me. It's not fair for you to have all the work to do by yourself."

"You needed your sleep. After nearly two days and nights in that room, you were ready to fall into a fever yourself. Besides, Ned sat with him for a while this afternoon, and I was able to take a turn about the yard. Lasso came to see Burch and stayed for lunch."

"Lasso came by?"

"He's been here every day since Burch was hurt. His

concern is wonderful. You'd think Burch was his own son."

"I know Lasso wishes he had something more than those two little girls, but he's hardly old enough to have a son as old as Burch."

"You know what I mean."

"Like an uncle?" offered Sibyl skeptically. Her aunt refused the bait.

"It is very thoughtful of him. He even offered to sleep here so he could be close by in case we needed him."

"What! I hope you told him we didn't need two men to look after."

"I didn't put it like that, but I did explain that we were perfectly capable of taking care of Burch. I also promised that we would send for him at the first hint of difficulty."

"Aunt, you're a sly one."

"I disapprove of your choice of words, dear, but if you mean that I prefer to use a gentle word instead of the rude ones you favor, then you're quite right."

"That's not what I mean and you know it," Sibyl rebutted promptly, but she was nevertheless taken back by the bluntness of her aunt's reproof. Augusta was *never* blunt.

An energetic knocking sound at the back door, and Jenkins entered the room, bringing this promising discussion to a halt. His anxious concern ever since the accident had given him a special place in Sibyl's heart. "I hear tell Mr. Randall's on the mend," he said.

"Yes, finally. He's not going to be able to get out of bed for a long time, but the doctor says his wounds are no longer dangerous and the breaks are starting to heal. However, I expect they're going to continue to be painful for some time."

"If I know Mr. Randall, he'll be rearing to get up before the week's out."

"The doctor left the strictest orders for him to stay in bed for at least a month, so don't you go putting any ideas into his head," ordered Sibyl sternly. "If he gets up too soon, he might never be able to use that leg again."

"Then you'll have to tie him down, because Mr. Randall won't never stay in bed unless he's made to."

"I can make him."

"How?"

"The doctor left some laudanum," explained Augusta.

"You're gonna need a lot, enough to keep him out cold," Jenkins advised them, his beardless face breaking into a rare smile. "When he wakes up, you be sure and tell him everything's taken care of. All he has to worry about is getting himself well again."

"You still don't have any idea what might have caused him to fall?" Sibyl asked, reverting to an old, unanswered question.

"Funny you should bring that up, because I came to tell you about something I don't understand."

"Something about the accident?"

"Yes, ma'am, but I can't be sure it means anything. You see, sometimes Mr. Randall would let Old Blue roam free at night so he could graze, and at other times he put hobbles on him. Seems that it depended on how Old Blue was acting that day. When I went to put Blue down, I noticed that he had a rope burn on one fetlock just above the ankle, like a rope had been tied or wrapped about the leg and then been pulled off."

"It must have been the hobbles."

"I don't know, but it was the leg that was busted, and I can't get it out of my mind that there was a rope on this leg when Mr. Randall mounted him."

"Do you mean that Burch forgot to remove the hobbles?"

"I don't know what I mean, because that don't make any more sense than the rest of it. Mr. Randall was never careless, and nobody's fool enough to mount a horse what's got his feet tangled in some rope. Besides, Old Blue was just about the smartest horse we had. He'd never be dumb enough to try and run with hobbles on. That's not it, but I'm danged if I can tell you what it is. All I know is I keep seeing

Old Blue running with a piece of rope tied to his leg and some steer running up on that rope and bringing the both of them down."

Sibyl's mouth dropped open. "Do you mean somebody did it intentionally?"

"I don't know anybody who'd do a rotten thing like that to Mr. Burch, but there's something here that needs a deal of explaining before I'm satisfied in my mind." He noticed the frightened look on Augusta's face and immediately began to apologize. "I didn't mean to upset anybody, but I thought you ought to know."

"You were right to tell me," Sibyl said absently. "Have you told anyone else?"

"No. Just about everybody else's gone anyway."

"Then don't. I'm sure it was an accident. It *must* have been."

Chapter 15

"Be careful," Sibyl cautioned as Ned and Balaam helped Burch down the steps. "If you let him hurt that leg again, you'll have to sit up with him." Over the last few days Burch had become increasingly impatient with his confinement, so when Sibyl found him out of bed trying to hop about on his one good leg and using his broken arm as a brace, there was nothing for her to do but agree to bring him downstairs.

"But you must promise to remain in your chair," Augusta admonished firmly. "You know what the doctor has said about keeping your leg still."

"Damn the doctor," cursed Burch, too annoyed to consider Augusta's sensibilities. "If you don't let me out of this room, I'll *slide* down the banister and there's no end to the terrible things I'll do to myself then."

"Just like every other man—stubborn, pigheaded, and never willing to be the least bit cooperative," Sibyl complained with a reluctant grin, resisting the impulse to extract a promise from him to obey Augusta implicitly. She knew Burch would have agreed to any condition to get out of that room, but he had to know that a second injury to his leg could make him a cripple for life. So, much against her will, she had summoned Ned and Balaam to carry Burch downstairs.

"I refuse to be hauled about like a useless cripple," he said morosely, which would have been easier on everyone. Instead they were forced to struggle with his splints on the stairs, trying to stay out of each other's way and not lose their hold on an invalid who was doing absolutely nothing to cooperate — that is, unless you consider a stream of pungent curses being useful. If it hadn't been so serious and so exasperating, Sibyl would have laughed, but she held her tongue until Burch was seated in his favorite chair with his leg up on a stool and his broken arm resting on his chest.

In some ways it was a relief to have Burch leave his room. As long as he lay in bed he refused to wear a shirt, and the uninterrupted viewing of his powerful torso caused unruly sensations to keep up a steady assault on her nervous system. Sibyl's sense of his physical presence had weakened when he was so ill, but with his returning health her sensitivity had doubled and the memory of the incredible pleasure that magnificent body had given her had grown more poignant. Whenever she thought he might die, the remembrance of that afternoon in the line cabin caused her to redouble her vigilance. She would love him if he were never able to leave his bed again, but as long as she could look upon that virile body, feel its magnetism, she could never entirely forget its prowess.

It was good to have Burch feeling so much better, but in some ways it had been easier for them when he was too weak and ill to object to his treatment. Now that his strength was returning, he made no effort to contain his impatience and constantly complained of one thing after another. He even criticized his food.

"He must be desperate," Augusta said, "for he has always

been most complimentary whenever he mentioned your cooking."

"When can I get a breath a fresh air?" he asked the minute he was settled downstairs.

"You ungrateful man. You no sooner force us to bring you downstairs—against our better judgment, I might add—then you want to know what else you can do that you have no business doing."

"For a man used to spending his nights in the open, being closed in by walls is like being in Hell."

"It's too cold for you to be outside," Sibyl informed him, putting more coal into the stove. "It's not even November yet and there was ice in the buckets this morning."

"I could keep you warm," he said, his irritability quickly forgotten. "Just until you got used to the cold."

"Hush!" she said, trying not to giggle. "You'll shock Aunt Augusta." Yet she couldn't help but think how nice it would be to have Burch's bare skin next to hers.

"There's room enough for two in the bed."

"If you so much as hint that in front of my aunt, I'll never speak to you again," she said sternly, but her insides were feeling definitely funny.

"I hope Jesse gets back soon," he said, obligingly changing the subject as Augusta entered the room. "I heard some geese fly over yesterday. They don't usually head south until three or four weeks from now, so we must be in for a really cold winter. We've got to make some plans."

"What kind of plans?" inquired Sibyl, immediately interested, her visions of being warmed by the fire of Burch's embrace momentarily interrupted.

"For looking after the herd. I never keep all the men through the winter, just five or six to ride the lines and make sure the cattle can get through the ice to find water or don't get caught in a drift. When it gets to twenty below, they're more likely to die of thirst than of starvation. Cows are stupid. They don't know to eat the snow that's lying all around them instead of trying to find open water. Some of them don't even know you have to break the ice first."

"Why don't you keep all the men if you need them?"

"Because it costs too much money to feed them and pay their wages. I'm still not sure how I'm going to feed your herd. I can't worry about feeding two dozen men as well."

"I want to help."

"I was sure you would," Burch said sarcastically.

"This is my ranch too," Sibyl said, firing up, "and there's no reason why you should always try to keep me from having anything to do with the decisions."

"Because you don't know anything about it, that's why."

"It wouldn't hurt to listen to what I have to say, would it? Afterward, you could tell me what a little fool I was and then reject my idea." Anger made her cheeks flame and Burch thought how pretty she looked. A throbbing desire stirred his blood and he thought back to the afternoon in that line cabin. That recollection had haunted him often during his confinement, and never more than now.

But Sibyl was under the sway of a quite different emotion, all of her susceptibility to his rugged good looks and physical magnetism momentarily swept aside.

"Why can't you buy the hay and grain you need?"

"A simple matter of money: I don't have any. Until I find out what price Jesse got on the herd, I won't know whether I'm rich or nearly broke."

"How can that be?" she asked doubtfully. "You've got thousands of cows and miles of land. The lawyers told me that just last year you made over a hundred and fifty thousand dollars."

"What the lawyers apparently didn't tell you was that Uncle Wesley was deeply in debt. We've got the best

173

breeding herd and own the most land of any privately held ranch in Wyoming, but Uncle paid dearly for it. It'll take a good price for this year's herd to meet the last payment, and under the agreement it's due the first of December. It can't be put off. If we have a good calf crop next year, we'll be in a strong position to make money. As for the land, well, we still don't have all we need."

"But there's miles of it out there, and there's nobody here except you and Lasso."

"That's government land. We've been fighting a battle that grows increasingly difficult every year: We're caught between the homesteaders who want to fence everything in and the rustlers who want to steal us blind. We've been able to keep most people out up till now, but we can't keep it up for much longer."

"You mean the success of this ranch depends on land you don't even control?"

"We control it, we just don't own it."

"If you don't own it, how can you control it?"

"If you control the water, you control the rangelands around it. Uncle bought up every parcel he could along the creek. He even had the hands stake claims and sell to him. We also have land along the Clearwater where it meets the Elkhorn. As a matter of fact, there are two strategic spots I want you and Augusta to file on, and I've even got one for Ned. Along with the dams, that ought to give Lasso and me control of the creek for at least thirty miles. That ought to be enough to keep out the homesteaders for a few more years."

"Isn't that illegal?" asked Augusta.

"Not strictly, but it is outside the spirit of the law. But what else are we to do? You can't run cattle on one hundred and sixty acres when it takes twenty-five for just one head and the government won't sell you more than one allotment. Nobody knows how much land there is, where it is, or who owns it, so until the government surveyors get in here, we can keep on pretty much as we are until then."

"So the problem is cash?"

"In a nutshell."

"Then I'll buy the feed and pay the hands." The problem solved, Sibyl's thoughts wandered off again to a study of the angle of Burch's jaw.

"You'll do no such thing," Burch decreed, sitting up rigidly. "I will not have any woman paying my bills."

Sibyl's thoughts jackknifed. "They aren't *your* bills, they're *ours*," she said, her eyes sparking angrily. "I have a right to help support the ranch even if you don't like it."

"I thought you said your father was just a poor teacher."

"We weren't rich, but we weren't exactly poor either. I sold Daddy's farm and some land Mother left me. The money's sitting in the bank doing nothing."

"But you shouldn't use that money. You might want to go back to Virginia." The words were out before Burch understood the importance of what he had said. He was confounded to find that as much as he'd raged against Sibyl coming to Wyoming, he would be desolated if she should ever go back. He couldn't imagine the Elkhorn without her.

"I still have the house in Lexington and a little land in town that brings in a rental income," Sibyl stated, looking hurt and tantalizingly vulnerable at the same time. "I will not become your *pensioner*."

"And I have some money of my own to help share the expenses," added Augusta.

"In other words, you are completely independent of me for your support." Burch summed up, seeing another of the arrows in the quiver of his masculinity snatched from him.

"Of course, there's my half of the ranch," Sibyl interposed, eyes glittering. "If I were to sell, I could be quite well off, even able to live in luxury."

175

"Not luxury," contradicted Burch, feeling a spurt of anger, "but you wouldn't have to beg for your dinner."

"I don't plan to sell," Sibyl admitted, forgetting her intention to annoy him when she saw how much it would hurt him. She knew she would *give* her half to Burch before she could do anything that would wound him so deeply. One glorious afternoon in his arms had changed her forever.

Sibyl sounded so meek that Burch was emboldened to hope she had backed down from her insistence on paying for the hay, but in that he'd gone too far.

"That is already settled," she stated firmly, regarding him with a wary but determined look. "Providing for the herd is just as much my responsibility as it is yours."

"But the money for running the ranch ought to come out of operating income, not your private funds," Burch insisted.

"Don't you use your own money?"

"I don't have any money separate from the ranch. If I need something, I buy it."

"There ought to be some way to determine the total income and expenses, and then pay each of us an equal sum. Then we would know where we stand."

"Much more businesslike," he said briskly.

"Also more fair." She didn't trust the way he was looking at her.

"Then I must know the value of the breeding herd, and the furniture you're forever talking about."

"What do you need that for?" she asked, scenting danger.

"The ranch owes you for the feed, the herd, and the furnishing of the house. And that doesn't include the chickens, the pigs, and the milk cow."

"Don't be absurd," she protested, feeling cornered by her own words. "You provided the house and I intend to provide the furniture."

"No, you already own half the house."

"Then half the furniture will be in my half of the house and the rest will be a loan," she responded, vexed. "Besides, part of it belongs to Aunt Augusta."

"Okay, I'll forget the furniture and the work you do around here, but I will not forget the herd. They must be worth thousands."

"Then consider them still mine, and the feed and hay is an exchange for taking care of them this winter." She had eliminated one more debt. It was getting increasingly more difficult to keep her temper under control; she wasn't used to being left with no defense.

"Okay, they're still yours, and the ranch will pay for the bull's services." Sibyl agreed with him reluctantly.

It was a small victory for Burch. His pride had warred with his concern for the ranch, and pride came in second. Had he been able to move out of the chair by himself, he might have argued further, planning to somehow produce a solution of his own, but being unable to get about without aid had made him feel foolishly dependent and completely unmanned. Ever since the accident he had been in the position of having to receive help from Sibyl, and he couldn't accept it that easily. He had to reestablish his control, and her fighting him on every point made it more difficult.

And the fact that Sibyl was a lovely, desirable, fascinating woman he hoped to keep by his side didn't change his feelings one bit. He constantly felt torn between his desire to do anything that would keep her near him and the necessity of fighting her tooth and nail over virtually every move he made. He wasn't so full of senseless pride that he was going to throw away her offer of help, but neither was he going to knuckle under to her, no matter how much his memories of the delicious pleasure to be found in her arms tortured his dreams. He swore the ranch would pay back every cent; he couldn't stand knowing that he was beholden to some women for the well-being of *his* ranch. Good Lord, Uncle Wesley would turn in his grave!

"How do I go about buying hay?" Sibyl asked, trying to turn the conversation to less dangerous channels. "I don't imagine peddlers come by offering wagon loads for sale."

"It has to be brought in by rail," Burch replied humorlessly. "One of the boys will have to ride to Casper or Laramie and see what he can find. We may have to go as far as Cheyenne because of the drought."

"I'll send Jenkins tomorrow."

"Better still, wire Jesse to buy it in Chicago and bring it back with him. You'd best tell him to get all he can if we're to keep your herd alive as well. I've been building castles in the air ever since I saw that bull. Your father must have been a genius." The tension was gone, and once again Sibyl gave in to the enjoyment of just being in Burch's company.

"He started the herd with his own father's blood cattle, or the few animals that survived the marauding soldiers. There wasn't much those two armies didn't eat up, and it didn't matter to them if it was a priceless bull or a stray heifer."

A stentorian knocking at the door, followed by the hearty voice of Lasso Slaughter, signaled the end of the quiet morning. Burch's face broke into a smile of welcome, Sibyl frowned in disgust, and Augusta looked suspended somewhere between resignation and delirium. Sibyl was unable to see one redeeming characteristic in that loud, boisterous buffoon. It was a complete mystery to her how her aunt, who was the most gentle, well-bred woman alive, could continue to tolerate him. Not even for the endless stream of little presents could she have stood the broad hints, extravagant compliments, and low humor that at times bordered on the crude.

"I didn't think you'd stay in bed long," Lasso thundered. "Look who I brought to see you." He pointed to Burch's hunting dog, who followed at his heels. "The poor beast was lying about the steps looking lost."

Brutus, who was a mixture of several breeds, all of them very large, sighted his master and bounded forward with a joyful volley of earsplitting barks.

"Stop him!" Sibyl shrieked when she realized the hound intended to jump into Burch's lap. She had horrible visions of Burch in a tangled heap and the stupid dog licking his face as he passed out from pain.

"Sit!" Burch's incisive command halted the dog's advance, but he didn't sit. Instead he put his paws on Burch's arm—fortunately his good arm—and licked his face with gusto.

"What do you mean bringing that dog in here?" Sibyl demanded, turning on Lasso. "It's no thanks to you that he hasn't turned Burch onto the floor and broken his other arm. Take him right back outside until he learns to behave."

"The poor mutt hasn't done a bit of harm," Lasso said, grinning at Burch's efforts to keep from having his face thoroughly licked. "He's just crazy with missing Burch."

"He can look through the window. Now go on and get him out of here."

"You're cruel, Miss Sibyl. There's no heart in you."

"When you have to clean the hair off the sofa, or get down on your hands and knees to mop up his muddy tracks, you'll feel a little differently about it too."

"You'd better put him out," conceded Burch. "Even Aunt Ada wouldn't allow him in the house for more than five minutes."

"Come on, boy," Lasso called, whistling to the dog. "It seems you're just not good enough for this place any more."

Sibyl's annoyance was fanned into anger by Lasso's remark, but before she could utter the sharp retort that sprang to her mind, the dog spotted Augusta's cat spread out on the back of one of the chairs. With a joyous bark, he immedi-

179

ately gave chase.

The cat wasted no time in useless hissing and spitting. Any dog used to tangling with wolves and chasing after cougars meant business. She jumped from the back of the chair to the top of the china cabinet. Brutus leaped against the cabinet, leaving deep scars in its shiny surface with his toenails and sending several plates hurtling from the grooved shelves to shatter on the floor. Still not feeling entirely safe, the cat leapt over to the top of the curtains. Her claws dug in and held, but the weight of her body caused her to slide down, creating huge rents in the fragile material. The bottom half of the curtain was immediately shredded into ribbons by Brutus's frantic efforts to climb it to get at the cat, who remained annoyingly just out of reach.

The feline inspected her position and concluded that it could still be improved. With a beautifully athletic arching leap, she sprang from the curtains, landed on Lasso's head, and then vaulted atop the buffalo head hung high above the mantel.

Safely out of Brutus's reach at last, she proceeded to insult him by first engaging in a violent fit of hissing and spitting, then by calmly spreading herself out between the buffalo's horns and washing her paws. Brutus was properly enraged, but he was intelligent enough to realize it was futile to try to reach the cat. He sat back on his haunches and barked derisively at a foe who would sink to such unsportsmanlike conduct as to climb completely out of his reach. The whole thing had taken less than a minute.

Augusta watched the destruction of the room in stupedfied silence, but a wail like the battle cry of an untamed savage erupted from Sibyl. She grabbed a broom and brought it down on Brutus's hindquarters with all her might. The startled beast turned on his unsuspecting adversary with a savage snarl, only to be brought up short when he saw it was

Sibyl. But his brief savagery was quite enough to destroy the last shreds of Sibyl's temper. She dealt him a thumping swat that sent him scampering out of the room with his tail between his legs. Without missing a beat she turned on Lasso and belabored him about the shoulders.

"Are you crazy?" the dumbfounded man squawked. "Cut that out!"

"I wish I could break your neck, you overgrown buffoon. Anyone but a born fool would have known better than to bring a dog into a room with a cat, especially when it was you who gave Augusta the cat. What did you expect them to do, shake hands?" She whacked him over the head again, and Lasso snatched the broom from her hands, holding it above his head out of her reach.

"You shouldn't be allowed anything any more dangerous than a dishcloth," he yelped as she slapped ineffectually at his powerful arms.

"And you should be kept in the barnyard where you belong!" Sibyl paused to catch her breath and realized that Burch was laughing so hard he was in more danger of falling out of the chair than when the dog had jumped on him. Such a breach of loyalty immediately brought her unspent wrath down upon his head.

"What are you laughing for? Do you think it's funny to see the room we've worked so hard to make look decent utterly destroyed because your boneheaded friend brought an outdoors hunting dog in to visit?" Burch was too sorely tried to be capable of words.

"I hope you slide right out of that chair and your leg hurts so much you can't sleep for a week," Sibyl raged at him, but now Lasso had started to laugh, and Sibyl was so furious at both of them, she couldn't speak.

"That cat, when it leaped on your head . . ." was all Burch could get out before going off again.

"It's nothing compared to the little woman beating me like I was a dusty carpet," Lasso howled raucously.

"I hope you both choke," Sibyl cried and raced from the room to keep them from seeing the tears sparkling in her eyes.

"My, my," Augusta said to no one at all. "This will take some doing to put right."

Two days later, Sibyl had still not forgiven Burch. She scrupulously provided his meals and tended his wounds, but she refused to speak to him unless she had to, and she would not spend any time in the same room with him as soon as the work that kept her there was done.

"How long is she going to carry on like this?" Burch inquired of Augusta after a meal eaten in total silence.

"I can't say. Your laughter hurt her deeply. She spent a long time on this room and was rightfully proud of the results."

"But I wasn't laughing at *her*. I was laughing at that damned cat and her beating Lasso with a broom like he was a street vagrant."

"That's the same as laughing at her."

"No, it isn't.

"I doubt you'll be able to convince her of that, and after all, that's what matters."

"It's a damned nuisance to be stuck in a house with a female that glares at you all the time like you were the devil himself, and then does everything she's expected to do with positive Christian resignation, just like she expected to be thrown to the lions the minute I get well."

"Sibyl was greatly upset by your accident, and she almost worried herself into a fever over you. She's still worried that your leg might not heal properly. I don't know, but I think your laughing at her made her feel you didn't value anything she had done for you."

"But that's nonsense. I owe her my life. If she hadn't insisted on looking for me, I might have died out there."

"Have you told her?"

"I don't have to; she knows it."

"It's not the same to know something as it is to have someone put it into words," Augusta pointed out mildly.

"Then I'll tell her right now."

"You've waited too long. She won't accept your thanks now."

"Women, by God! It's impossible to understand them."

"It's quite easy really. All we want is a little love and to feel needed."

Burch looked at the room about him. Even with the windows stripped of the torn curtains and the cabinet scratched past repair, he acknowledged that Sibyl had made a great difference in his life. He did need her in other ways too, ways that had little to do with the physical pleasure that her body gave him, ways he was only beginning to understand, and he hadn't even been able to figure that out for himself. It took this kindly aunt, speaking softly and apologetically, to show him what should have been obvious to anyone who was as smart as he took himself to be.

But all attempts to speak to Sibyl met with polite rebuff. She simply walked out of the room if he attempted to speak to her about anything of a personal nature. Any single word that strayed from the business of the house, his illness, or the ranch was met with a raised eyebrow and a readiness to turn her back on him. The impasse might have gone on for more than one horrendous week if Sibyl's furniture hadn't arrived.

Burch had just been settled in the ranch room for the afternoon when Balaam came shuffling in to warn him that they were about to be descended upon by a caravan of squatters.

183

"I thought you'd given up drinking?" Burch taunted him. "Squatters don't come through this time of year and they would never wander this far off the Oregon Trail."

"I ain't been drinking," snorted Balaam, affronted that he would be accused of being drunk on the job. "It's a mess of wagons and they're plumb full of house things. And they's coming this way because they asked special for the Elkhorn ranch."

"Well, see what they want and get rid of them as soon as you can."

"They don't want you, they want Miss Cameron." Burch regarded him skeptically. "Yes sir, Miss Sibyl Cameron, late of Lexington, Virginia. And there's only one person here that fits that description."

"I'll see what it's about," Augusta said, rising from her chair. But she had not reached the front door before Sibyl came bounding down the stairs like a twelve-year-old late to dinner and afraid of getting no dessert.

"My furniture's come at last!" she cried, and burst through the door without waiting for Augusta. Burch could not remain in his chair, waiting for someone to tell him who stood at his front door, so with Balaam's assistance, he hopped to the porch on his one good leg. He was dismayed to find half a dozen wagons, all piled high with crates, pulled up in front of the house.

"Good God, did she empty every house in Lexington?" he exclaimed, wondering where she could possibly find a place for that much furniture, even in a house as large as the Elkhorn.

"Part of it belongs to me," confessed Augusta. "I hope you don't mind my bringing it, but I couldn't leave it with no one to care for it, especially since I had no idea when I might be returning."

"It doesn't matter, there's plenty of room," Burch relented, wondering if there would ever be an end to the upsets, discomforts, and surprises Sibyl caused. As for Sibyl herself, all traces of her anger and sulkiness were forgotten.

"It's all here, and it doesn't look like they broke anything. You won't recognize the place when we get through," she told Burch, almost dancing with excitement. "It'll look just beautiful with the paper Ned and Balaam have been putting up."

"You've got far more than for just three rooms," he said, thinking of the saloon, parlor, and dining room where Sibyl had kept the men busy with the wallpaper.

"I'm going to put furniture in every room in the house. I'm sick to death of living in a big empty shell. I feel like it's a warehouse."

"Looks like it's going to be a full warehouse."

Sibyl merely laughed and told Balaam to go fetch Ned and anybody else he could find.

"There's a lot of work to be done and these men can use some help."

Things got a mite tense after that, and Burch found it much more comfortable, as well as safer, to remain in the ranch room. So did Lasso when he came for what had become his daily visit.

"I can't get a word in with Augusta, what with Sibyl asking her where this piece ought to go or her worrying if one of them clumsy oafs will scratch some table or what not."

"Have a seat and rest a while. It's not safe for man nor beast out there."

"Especially not beast," Lasso said with a crack of laughter, but Burch was easily able to refrain from joining him. "She shoved a lamp at me with orders to put it on the table just like I was a parlor maid," continued Lasso, his dignity affronted. "If I'd stayed, it would have been doilies or framed needlepoint next." He shook his head. "I don't understand why womenfolk get so worked up over silly things like furniture. I knew Sibyl was a little peculiar, I could see that months ago"—he failed to notice the pucker that appeared between Burch's eyes—"but there's Augusta, as sensible a woman as you could want, running about acting like she's plumb distracted."

"You know women and houses."

"No, I don't. My Mary never did care for houses. As long as she had her horse and the open range, she was as happy as a June bug. She didn't care if the dinner burned or the seat of my pants was completely worn through."

"If that's the kind of woman you want, you'd better back off from Augusta before its too late." Lasso eyed his friend sharply. "It's obvious to everyone except Sibyl that you're going to ask Augusta to marry you."

"Do you think she'll disapprove?"

"She'll hate it. If she had any idea right now of what you're up to, not to mention the least suspicion that her aunt might accept, she'd whisk that poor woman off to Lexington and you'd never see her again." He laughed. "She considers you only one small step better than a savage."

"I know she doesn't like me, but I won't let her stand in my way."

"You'd better worry more about how you're going to like being chained and civilized than anything Sibyl might do. It's not Sibyl you're hoping to marry."

"You think Augusta will try and turn me into a dude?"

"I can't say what she'll do. Augusta is a kind, sensitive woman, but she's also a lady. It's the way she's been brought up, and it's the only way she knows how to live. You can teach her to ride and she may even do it to please you, but she'll always dislike and fear horses. She's going to be unhappy unless there's some order and gentleness in her life. You can't treat her like you did Mary. If you do, you'll break

186

her heart."

"I'd never do anything to hurt her. I love that little gal," Lasso declared passionately, but then fell into silent contemplation. "Do you really mean all that?" he asked at last. "She could be different."

"I don't think so. I've lived in the same house with her for nearly three months, and I know you'll never turn her into anything resembling Mary. If you want Augusta, you're going to have to accept her as she is. Otherwise, you ought to leave her alone."

"Is that what you're doing with Sibyl?" The friends' eyes met and held.

"I'm not looking to be married," Burch replied, uncomfortable at having his affairs looked into by anyone.

"Then you'd better get that leg to working again and get away from here, or you'll be calling on the parson before spring."

"I doubt that. Sibyl thinks I'm stubborn, opinionated, prone to ride roughshod over people, think women are good for nothing but cooking, or any number of other things she sees as a fault."

"That's never stopped one of them from getting married yet. She's all taken up with this furniture and stuff right now, but the next step will be to find herself a husband. You see if that gal doesn't come cozying up to you."

"She'll have to start speaking to me first."

"Like that, is it?" questioned Lasso with raised eyebrows. "You're caught for sure."

"Like hell I am." The gray eyes clouded with confusion. "Let's run away, both of us, and spend the winter hunting."

"And be found frozen to death or eaten by wolves? You *have* got it bad. You're desperate and don't even know it."

Chapter 16

For the next few days Sibyl's feverish activity kept the house in a constant turmoil, but her sulky behavior and black silences were entirely forgotten. She drove Ned, Balaam, Jenkins, and any other man unwise enough to come near the house to the point of exhaustion. Burch grew tired just watching so much activity, but Sibyl bloomed with the bustle and commotion. What with prying open crates to see what they contained, trying to decide what to put where, and then changing her mind when she found something she had forgotten, it took the better part of two days just to unload the wagons. Bountiful provisions were made for the men at mealtime and they were even allowed to rest while the dishes were cleaned up, but otherwise they were kept busy uncrating a table, lifting a sofa, or putting up a bed.

"The better part of Lexington must be eating its dinner standing up," Burch remarked as he counted twenty chairs being carried into the dining room. Behind the house the pile of broken crates and straw packing was reaching elephantine proportions.

"There's enough wood for a dozen cow sheds, and kindling for half the county," Lasso pointed out, looking at the remains of a crate that had contained a prized table the ladies determined should stand in the entrance hall. Rugs appeared on the floors and pictures on the walls. Curtains went up at the windows and the corners of every room began to fill up.

"Pretty soon there's not going to be any room left for people," complained Burch.

"Especially men," added Lasso, disgusted by the abundance of lace on curtains, table covers, and armrests. "They'll be after us to scrape our boots and dust our clothes till it'd be more of a pleasure to bed down in the badlands." But Burch was in for an even greater surprise.

By evening his leg was paining him; he was tired, irritable, and in need of a good rest when he opened his bedroom door to find that his modest bed had been replaced by a monster four-poster hung with brocade and piled high with soft feather mattresses and eiderdown pillows.

"Where in the hell did this thing come from?" he demanded of Sibyl.

"It belonged to my grandparents. They slept in it their whole married life."

"What have you done with my bed?"

"It's in one of the guest rooms."

"Then see that's it's brought back right now."

"That's impossible," she told him impatiently.

"If you got this thing in here, you can get it out again. I can't possibly sleep with two ghosts, especially not your grandparents'."

"Everybody's already gone. Besides, they would need at least two hours to take the bed down and move it."

"I'll sleep in it if you'll come protect me," he remarked, an impish light dancing in his eyes.

"Absolutely not!" Would she ever stop acting like a foolish

teenager when he smiled at her like that?

"I'll tell Augusta you tried to seduce me, and I had to sleep in the guest room to escape your improper advances."

"You wouldn't dare!" she shrieked, trying not to laugh. "After I positively violated my conscience to give you this bed, you've got to use it."

"Why?" he demanded, suspicious of the sudden merriment dancing in her face.

"Because I'll never speak to you again if you don't."

"Careful, I might take that as an inducement." Sibyl was nettled at that.

"Why was it such a struggle?" he asked. Sibyl's glare subsided and a puckish smile turned up the corners of her mouth.

"It was my grandfather Cameron's bed. He was a severe old patriarch, from what Aunt Augusta tells me, and very proud of his position and family. He didn't think much of women and even less of children."

"If you're trying to say that I—"

"He was proud, mean-spirited, sure he was right, and stubborn as an oak stump," she finished comprehensively.

"I thought you would get around to that before long."

"This bed was the symbol of his unbending power. I couldn't use it and Aunt would lie awake all night if I even suggested putting it in her room."

"So you thought that I, being as much like your grandfather as two peas in a pod, would be perfectly happy in that medieval monster," he finished for her, failing to see any humor in the situation. "And what about your conscience? You did say you had one."

"Grandfather was a very particular man, rather stiff and formal. The only thing he hated near as much as a Yankee was westerners. Not Wyoming because there wasn't any such place in his day, but everything west of the Blue Ridge. He considered them next door to barbarians. I think he would have moved to New York before he would have lived on a

190

cattle ranch." Her eyes were alive with mischief. "But I never knew grandfather, so it really wasn't much of a struggle."

"I can believe that," barked Burch. His leg was throbbing painfully and his house turned inside out by a shrew that hadn't spoken to him for a week but was still coming up with ways to make his life miserable. To top it off, she was looking absolutely adorable and his starved body ached relentlessly for the release he could find only in her arms. The combination of irritants was too much, and his temper snapped. "The only thing that does cause you a struggle is to believe that I might know more about something than you do."

"That's not true," Sibyl objected, her own temper flaring up immediately. "You determination to think that I don't know anything at all is what makes me so furious."

"You may know enough to run a small farm in Virginia, but that's not sufficient to set your opinion against mine when it comes to this ranch."

"Whose opinion can you expect me to set against yours if not mine?" she interrupted him, exasperated.

"Nobody's. I know more than you on almost everything."

"Oh, bother your generous *almost*," Sibyl flung at him. "What you mean is that you know *everything*, and you'd like nothing better than for me to shut my mouth and stay in the kitchen."

"The kitchen's not the only room . . ." he began, his gaze growing hot as it caressed her body.

"Don't you dare say it, or I'll break your other leg." The memory of that afternoon in the line cabin changed swiftly from a wondrous awakening to a galling humiliation. "I thought you might change, but I can see that you're never going to be anything more than the narrow-minded bigot you are right now."

Burch's mild anger turned into snarling fury. "Don't you ever call me that again."

"What will you do?" she taunted, taking care to move out of his reach.

"Give you that spanking I promised."

"Do you always beat people who disagree with you?" she flashed back at him.

"Not when they're adults."

The Devil flew all over Sibyl. "You're nothing but an ill-bred saddle bum," she raged. "Is your brain so limited that it can't see more than one possible solution to any problem?"

"The only *limit* I have is the amount of stupidity and prideful ignorance I can tolerate."

"At least I'm trying to learn. You're so wrapped up in your own conceit you can't see anything else. That's the worst kind of ignorance. It's a waste of time to try to show you anything."

"What else could it be when all you offer me is empty words out of an empty mind."

"There's no limit to the cruel things you'll say, is there?" Sibyl asked, unable to completely stifle a sob of hurt. "You're so determined to run this place alone you'll do anything to prove your superiority."

That tiny sob broke the chains of Burch's anger. He didn't need Sibyl's reproof to regret his words. Why couldn't he control his tongue? He never intended to say half the things that came out of his mouth.

"I didn't mean to say that."

"Don't strain yourself to apologize," Sibyl said, rebuffing him. "You've done nothing to make me think you didn't mean it, and I have no more appreciation for empty words than you."

"If you two *must* fight like tomcats all the time," Augusta spoke calmly as she came down the hall, "you could at least decide what to do about the downstairs carpets." They stared at her, silenced by the unexpected severity of her reproof. "Both of you should try to control your tempers. Once harsh words are spoken, they can never be withdrawn." Her kind eyes held more understanding than they knew, but it was her unmistakable unhappiness that made them ashamed of their behavior.

"I shouldn't have said that," Burch repeated, determined to apologize whether Sibyl wanted it or not.

"And I shouldn't have moved your bed without asking you first," Sibyl conceded.

"Now why don't you ask Burch about the money for the Christmas party and the rest of the things we need for the house?" Augusta suggested to Sibyl.

"There's no need to consult Burch about money."

"I thought it might be nice," claimed Augusta with a sigh of resignation.

"I have more than enough for what we need for *our* house," she said with emphasis. "You can begin making the list."

"That may take quite a while, dear."

"Then the sooner we get started, the better. If we keep Lasso waiting too long, he might change his mind."

"Lasso?"

"Mr. Slaughter has kindly offered to escort us to Cheyenne to do our shopping," Sibyl said, catching Burch completely by surprise. "I declined at first, but you're well enough now to be left by yourself for a week or so. Ned can see to your meals."

"There's a woman living up the creek I can have come in. She can't cook as well as you, but it'll be better than Ned."

"Then I guess there's nothing to keep us here."

"How are you going to get there? It's a long way." Sibyl appeared to be more angered than pleased by the question.

"Just enjoy your bachelor days. You don't have to give me a thought for the next week."

"How could I forget you when I can't even recognize my own house. I feel like I'm *in* Virginia."

"You should be pleased to find yourself in an elegantly furnished house, particularly since you didn't have to spend any money or lift a finger to do it."

"I suppose it *is* possible for you two to stand here arguing for the rest of the day, but I see no reason for me to stay and listen," announced Augusta. "It has become quite tiresome." With that she turned on her heel and walked off, completely flabbergasting her niece.

"Do as you wish," Burch growled, and he went into his room, slamming the door behind him.

"Oh, dear," sighed Augusta when Sibyl followed her to her room, "I so hoped you two could learn to get along."

"If you're implying that you hope I'll marry that insufferable egotist, you're going to be greatly disappointed," Sibyl promised. "He gets worse every day."

"There was a time when I thought that would be an ideal solution," her aunt replied wistfully, "but since Burch's injury, I've come to realize that it's a forlorn hope."

"I should think so."

"I never wanted you to be unhappy, to marry a man you found unattractive, one you disliked, or one you thought so full of evil intentions. I could never wish such a fate on anyone, especially not a niece I love so dearly."

"I never said that he was unattractive or that I disliked him," Sibyl countered, feeling an unaccountable need to defend Burch, "and I don't think he's ill-intentioned."

"Forgive me for misinterpreting you," begged Augusta innocently, "but I thought that was the meaning of your words, even if those weren't exactly the ones you used."

"The only thing wrong with him is a lot of outmoded ideas he refuses to give up. I'm sure some girl, if she cares enough to bother, will be able to convince him he's wrong. As rich as he is, I'm sure he can find any number of the silly things willing to try."

"Maybe he'll find one at the Christmas party," her aunt said, nodding her head. "You'll have to make sure we invite plenty of girls for him to choose from. We wouldn't want him to make a poor choice."

"What?" exclaimed Sibyl, thrown out of stride by her aunt's suggestion.

"Lasso tells me that people are coming from over a

hundred miles away to this party, that even the settlers will be here, and they are the ones with the pretty daughters. If we invite several more families, maybe he can find one willing to undertake reforming him."

"I hope he does," Sibyl professed stiffly. "He's getting so old they won't have him if he waits much longer."

"But I don't know what we'll do if he does marry."

"Why should that affect us?"

"You must know that it's bound to be difficult, with three women in the house and only one of them his wife. She will naturally expect to make the decisions."

"Then she will soon learn different," asserted Sibyl. "This is half my house and I'll not hand over the reins to some grasping, insinuating little hussy."

"That's what I meant about it being difficult for us. Naturally Burch will have to take his wife's side whenever there's a disagreement. Since you two already find it so difficult to agree on anything—" Augusta's voice trailed away, leaving the thought unfinished. "I suppose something can be worked out, but I think in the end Burch will buy himself another ranch or expect us to return to Lexington."

Clearly none of these eventualities had ever occurred to Sibyl, and she found them unpleasant and extremely unsettling. She should have realized that it was inevitable Burch would someday bring a wife to Elkhorn, if not her, then someone else. It should have been equally obvious that they could not all continue to live in the house together. Someone was going to have to leave.

"I expect I'd better start on my list if I'm to finish today," Augusta said vaguely and floated off, leaving her niece deep in thought.

Augusta remained a picture of benign concern until the parlor doors closed behind her. Then a complete change came over her, and she tottered to a sofa and dropped into its deep cushions, overcome with muffled laughter. *Augusta Hauxhurst,* she thought to herself, *you ought to be ashamed of yourself for mistreating that poor door so cruelly.* But it was worth it to see the look on Sibyl's face when she realized that Burch could marry someone else. *If she can just keep from losing her temper every time he speaks to her, he'll marry her yet. It's plain as can be that he's very much taken with her, but no man is going to ask a woman to marry him if she argues with every word that comes out of his mouth. I never could make Sibyl understand that being right all the time could be very lonely.* Augusta pulled herself together and began to make the list for the shopping. *A little time apart is just what they need,* she reasoned. *It'll give them both time to cool off and decide that they miss each other.*

In spite of Sibyl's proclaimed indifference, the intensity of the argument with Burch had given her a very nasty shock. Burch's injury had delivered him, virtually helpless, into her control, and she had fooled herself into thinking that they were growing closer together. Now she was forced to admit that they were no nearer understanding each other than they ever had been, that their enormous attraction for each other only complicated things, and that once he got back on his feet things were likely to get even worse. Why did she insist upon his giving in to her, and why did she always think that if he didn't, she had to try to *make* him? If she wanted a man to agree with everything she said, she could marry Jesse. She didn't want a man who would let her run over him, but neither was she a meek female to say yes and amen to his every word. Surely it wasn't asking much for him to assume she could do something more than fix dinner or arrange the furniture.

But did she *really* know as much about running a ranch as Burch? Sure, she could run a farm with stable hands and stock pens and breeding bulls and brood cows, but what did she know about directing ranch hands, managing thousands of wild cows, when to sell to get the best price, how to get the stubborn beasts to market? And what about grass, water, and hay? She knew they had to have plenty of all three to grow fat, but she didn't know how to keep them alive in sub-zero temperatures and week-long blizzards. And Burch did.

She slumped down in her chair. The mental argument was getting her nowhere. She was of two minds about Burch, and perverse enough to argue for both of them. Before long, she wouldn't know what she thought. Unexpectedly, she felt a great desire to cry, to fling herself on her bed and give over to an undignified bout of tears. Just as suddenly, her chin went up. She was not going to give Burch Randall the pleasure of crying over him. She might be besotted and developing the temper of a shrew, but she was not a sniveling weakling.

Burch slammed his door, as angry with himself as with Sibyl. Why, after all this time, did he allow himself to be so infuriated with her? It was his self-control that had caused his uncle to turn over the day-to-day operation of the ranch to him while he was still in his teens, yet Sibyl could unsettle him with no more than a word or a glance. He didn't give a damn about that bed. As a matter of fact, he'd probably like sleeping in it, but instead of accepting it with at least a pretense of pleasure, he had turned it into an excuse to start the same old argument all over again. Why was he so unwilling to meet her halfway? Why didn't he trust her intelligence? Surely he was willing to give her credit for some good intentions.

"Good Lord, I'm becoming as weak and indecisive as a woman." Burch heard his own words, and in a flash of insight recognized the crux of his problem. He *did* think Sibyl was inferior—not to all men, certainly, but to himself. It was true that she didn't know enough to run the ranch by herself, but didn't he also discredit her ability to be able to *learn*? It was disconcerting to think that any woman could run the Elkhorn as well as he could. For years men had said he was one of the best natural-born cattlemen in the West, that he knew more by instinct than the rest of them could

197

learn by hard work. He had been rightly proud of their praise, but maybe it had gone to his head. Maybe he felt *nobody* could ever do *anything* as well as he could. He knew that wasn't so. And if that was the case, wasn't it possible that Sibyl, as well as some others, could learn to do things around the ranch as well as he could?

He had never stinted his praise for her cooking or her household organization. During the weeks he had lain in bed, he discovered that Sibyl saw jobs that needed to be done that had never occurred to him or Aunt Ada. Balaam and Ned were really her employees, not his, and the work they had done with the buildings, the stock pens, the garden, the orchards, and the preparing of food for winter had proved her mettle. If she could accomplish so much in such a short time, how much more would she be able to do five or ten years from now? She obviously wasn't willing to limit herself to choosing wallpaper and deciding what kinds of seeds to order for next year's garden. He might as well realize that she was never going to be a quiet, retiring wife like his aunt, or an uncomplicated, fun-loving companion like Lasso's Mary. She was going to be a dynamic, inquiring, demanding, full-time partner in everything.

She had the intelligence to learn, but he didn't know if she had the ability to compromise, to disagree and yet allow someone else to make the decision without carrying a grudge. His desire for her had continued to grow more intense, but he knew she would never accept their physical relationship without marriage; he hadn't spent weeks lying in bed without figuring that out. Her ownership of half the ranch made their union an even more logical conclusion, a merger of interests as well as convenience.

He didn't hold himself free of blame for the acrimonious turn their arguments had taken, and in the future he intended to make sure that he *did* control his tongue and give a fair hearing to her suggestions. However, he was not going to be swayed by a pretty face and a tempting body, not by a full purse and sumptuous meals, into risking marriage before he was sure that's what he wanted. Nothing was worth that kind of sacrifice.

The trip to Cheyenne was a welcome change. Sibyl sometimes had to grit her teeth to endure Lasso's constant company and boundless cheerfulness. But she didn't care about Lasso, and unless he were annoying her, which seemed to be nearly all the time, she forgot about him. They spent their first night at Lasso's ranch, and she was pleasantly surprised to find that his house was quite comfortable, not nearly so large or pretentious as the Elkhorn, but very sensible and well-furnished. "It lacks any trace of female influence," she remarked to her aunt.

"That can be easily remedied." Sibyl's comment had been offhand, but her aunt's unparalleled inquisitiveness about everything she saw put Sibyl off balance. For a moment she allowed herself to believe that her aunt was actually *interested* in the house, but she agreed with herself that it was an absurd thought and only Augusta's general tolerance enabled her to endure Lasso's showing them everything from the pantry to the corral.

The only time she didn't have to fight to keep from yawning with boredom was when Lasso introduced them to his little girls, two wild things that looked more like range animals than children. They were clearly more at home on a horse than in the house, but their father took great pride in his rambunctious seven-year-old tomboys. Sibyl expected her aunt to cringe at the sight of twin girls in vests, flannel shirts, boots, and hats — miniature cowboys really — but Augusta had a quiet air of contentment about her that Sibyl found baffling.

True, she was a little awed by her surroundings, but she didn't flinch when Lasso shoved the helpless children up to her, saying, "I knew you'd be anxious to meet these critters. I had to give them orders to be off their ponies just so you would know they had legs of their own. Don't see them myself for days at a time."

Sibyl felt uncomfortable, like something important was eluding her, and she was relieved when they resumed their journey.

Cheyenne was fun. It was a bustling town full of more things to buy than Sibyl had ever seen back home. "The railroads bring it in in a hurry, and the cowmen buy it up even faster," Lasso told her one afternoon as they rode down Longhorn Avenue, the road lined with mansions built by absentee cattle barons. "They even have a club house that will knock your eyes out. You didn't expect to find anything like this out here, did you?" Sibyl admitted that she was properly surprised by the luxury and obvious wealth the cattle industry represented.

Augusta had fallen strangely quiet the last several days, and even though Sibyl found herself having to make most of the purchases and discuss them with Lasso, she still managed to get their shopping done within a week. Lasso prophesied that they would have to buy another wagon to carry everything home, but with careful packing all the bolts of cloth, boxes of ornaments, and furniture and hangings were carefully settled into a single wagon when at last they began their return trip. Up until then Sibyl had been able to banish Burch from all but her dreams.

The first night away from the Elkhorn Sibyl had dreamed of making love to Burch. It was the first time in her life she had ever dreamed of such a thing, and she woke with quite a start. However, when she realized it was merely a dream and that every person she had ever known in her life was *not* standing around watching her, she went back to sleep vainly hoping to recapture the threads of her dream. Over the next few nights her dreams increased in scope and intensity until she became so restless and agitated that Augusta was prompted to ask her if she was feeling well.

"I'm fine," Sibyl answered distractedly. She could feel her

skin burn with the heat of embarrassment and was thankful that the dark obscured the crimson flush that covered her face. "I guess I'm just uncomfortable at being away from home."

"The beds aren't very soft. Mine has several very hard lumps in it, but I've never known you to be so fidgety. Are you certain there is nothing bothering you?"

"No, I'm not worried about a thing. You'd better go back to sleep, or you'll have bags under your eyes. And I hate to think what Lasso will have to say about that."

"He would never mention it," replied Augusta comfortably as she drifted back into an untroubled sleep.

But once they turned toward home, Sibyl's problems couldn't be put off any longer; they came crashing down on her, occupying her mind to the exclusion of everything else and changing her dreams from memories of ecstacy to nights of misery.

At first she relived every agonizing moment of their arguments, adding even more devastating remarks that served to drive them further and further apart. Then, as they neared the ranch, her sleep was disturbed by dreams of Burch marrying a dazzling blonde who deferred to him in everything and rode and shot like a professional. Every night she woke up crying when Burch ordered her to pack her furniture and return to Virginia, and for the rest of the night she could do no more than sleep in fits and starts.

The evening air had already turned cold with a threat of unseasonably early snow when the wagon lurched over the rough stones of the rise that brought the Elkhorn into view. Knowing that she was within minutes of seeing Burch again made Sibyl too restive to remain in the wagon, and she finished the trip astride Hospitality. The need to see him, to feel his arms around her, was so great that she felt a strong urge to gallop ahead alone. Yet, when she remembered the bitterness of their arguments, she was reluctant to be the first person to meet him. The misery of that last week before they left for Cheyenne, heightened by the dreams of the last few nights, was still fresh in her mind. Sibyl slowed Hospitality and put the wagon between herself and the house. Somehow it was a protective shield. Against what? She wasn't sure.

Burch had been watching for the wagon for days, but it was Balaam who had come running into the house shouting that Miss Sibyl had come home at last. Burch ordered him back to his chicken pens, an order Balaam derisively ignored, and he hobbled out to the porch before Lasso had time to draw the wagon up to the house. His welcoming smile changed to one of bewilderment and uneasiness when he saw no sign of Sibyl or her horse.

"Where's Sibyl?" he asked, his troubled eyes searching Augusta and Lasso's faces for any sign of tragedy, his voice tight with unacknowledged dread. "Has anything happened to her?"

"Naw," chuckled Lasso, pleased at seeing his friend wriggling on the spit, roasted by the fires of love. "She's just playing peekaboo. Come on out, girl, and stop teasing the poor fella. He's liable to get so upset he'll break the other leg."

"I was just keeping the sun out of my eyes," Sibyl insisted, emerging from behind the wagon, rigid with mortification that her actions would be interpreted as part of a childish game. "It's impossible to ride a horse and carry a parasol," she said, trying to cover her annoyance, "and I refuse to wear a bonnet when it makes me look like a squatters wife."

"If all squatter's wives looked like you, there'd be nothing east of the Mississippi except grass widows and old maids," Lasso said, laughing unnecessarily hard at his own joke.

"I can endure the sun in my eyes," Augusta stated flatly, "but I'll not stand about listening to boyish foolishness until I get freckles across my nose." The men laughed and the incident passed off harmlessly, but the look of anxiety on Burch's face, and the one of relief and happiness that chased it off, banished any doubts Sibyl still had of her welcome at the Elkhorn. The barrier was gone, the deadly poison had been drained away. Once again, the path to a better understanding between them lay open. Sibyl uttered a silent vow that this time she would not open her mouth before she considered the consequences, for she knew now that they were meant to be together. Whatever lay in store for them, no matter how much they differed, they would share it together.

Chapter 17

Sibyl's hands were shaking so badly she almost dropped the last dish Rachel handed her. Her aunt had been gone since noon and the tension between her and Burch had been building to an almost unbearable point.

Lasso had descended upon them before lunch without warning, in a fret over a fever that had both his little girls in bed. In minutes he had talked Augusta into going to the Three Bars "just to take a look at them." Augusta was reluctant to leave Sibyl, but by the time Lasso had praised her courage, her generous nature, and her selfless concern, she would have felt compelled to walk through a blizzard if necessary. Since Lasso had brought the buggy such extreme measures weren't necessary, and Augusta soon departed, looking over her shoulder in anxious concern.

Sibyl knew Burch was just as aware of her as she was of him, and all that stood between them was Rachel, a dour, taciturn woman of middle years who Burch had mysteriously produced to care for him while they were in Cheyenne. Burch said little during dinner, but his eyes followed Sibyl like those of a hungry animal. The longing in his glance was almost tangible, and only his broken leg gave her the courage to remain in the same room after Rachel left, without fear of being consumed by his blatant desire.

There was such a raging conflict within her that she felt weak from the force of it. She knew that she loved Burch and that a part of her longed to feel his touch, his nearness, to luxuriate in the pleasure of being loved and desired. It was so tempting to give up and let someone else be strong for her, make the decisions, and worry about the future, to just melt into his arms and forget ever wanting to run the ranch or prove to him that she needed to depend on no one.

But old habits die hard and she could not really let go, could not completely give up control to anyone. She thought of Kendrick and all the other men she'd known. Was it possible that Burch was different from them? They had made progress toward working out the areas of conflict, so maybe there was hope for them if she could just keep her temper under control. He had treated her so gently this past week that she had begun to believe he might have changed. Even Lasso wasn't so overbearing as he once had been.

"Come sit by the fire," Burch invited her. "You deserve some rest after working so hard." He hopped to the back door and opened it. A freezing blast swept through the room.

"What are you doing? Close that door!"

"It's a surprise I had Ned leave on the steps," he said with a grin, and brandished a bottle of champagne that had been chilling on the back steps. "I thought we deserved a little celebration."

"Where'd you get that?" she asked, getting some glasses.

"It's some of what we ordered for the party. I thought we should test it first, just to make sure it was drinkable."

"Sit back down before you hurt your leg." The splint was off, but Burch had been told to be careful for a few more weeks yet. He lowered himself to a huge bearskin rug in front of the fireplace.

"This is nicer than the stove," he assured her, inviting Sibyl to sit down next to him.

"The fireplace is prettier, but I'm afraid we'll have to hook up the stove again if it gets any colder," she owned, willing to be generous. She watched silently as Burch wrestled with the cork, wise enough at least not to offer to do it for him. The wine was so cold there was no pop and almost no fizz when he poured it.

"You've ruined it," she laughed. "Champagne isn't supposed to have ice crystals in it. It should bubble and tickle your nose."

"Hold it close to you and it'll get warm."

"And give me frostbite on my chest."

"I'll thaw it out," he offered with an uprush of warmth.

"Don't be absurd," she giggled, breathlessly fighting a desire to fling all caution to the winds. "What are we supposed to be celebrating?"

"You."

"Me!" she nearly squeaked, and then had to struggle to get her tumultuous emotions under control. "I thought all you wished to celebrate about me was my departure."

"I stopped wishing that a long time ago."

"When?" she asked, unable to resist.

"When you stepped out of that absurd wagon in the middle of the river and called me a rude, obnoxious cowhand and ordered me to get your wagon out of the river."

"I didn't say anything so awful," protested Sibyl, taking a sip of champagne to hide her pleasure.

"That was one of the nicer things you said. You hadn't had time to get properly warmed up yet." Sibyl looked through her lashes to find that Burch was smiling in a way that caused her senses to sing. She looked back down, watching the last crystal in her champagne dissolve like her crumbling resistance.

"Aunt Augusta tells me all the time that men won't like me if I don't learn to flatter them. I think she's given up hope of my ever learning."

"Men will be drawn to you no matter what you say."

"Why?" she asked, finding that she enjoyed hearing him

say nice things about her, restrained as they were. They were much sweeter to her ears than the extravagant and insincere praise of Moreton Swan.

"Because you're the most beautiful woman in the whole territory, and half the men would let you ride a horse over them just to be able to sit and stare at you."

"I never suspected you were an empty flatterer," she said, fighting off the delicious feeling of warmth that was spreading over her. "I thought cowboys were terribly practical."

"Not at all. If we were, we'd go back East and earn an easy fortune sitting behind some desk instead of risking our hides for ornery steers and spending our nights without a woman. The West is a mighty lonely place, but it makes a man know himself and gives him time to learn what it is he wants."

"Do you know what you want?"

"Yes."

"What?"

"You."

Sibyl's heart thumped painfully. "Now you're flattering me again," she panted, trying to still her quavering voice. "You know you've been trying to get rid of me ever since I got here."

"I've fought with you dozens of times, but have I ever asked you to leave?"

"You asked me *not* to come."

"And haven't I eaten every bite of food you put before me, though all the while I was pining for Sanchez's grub?"

"Beast!" gasped Sibyl with a gurgle of laughter. "If I had only known, I would have told you to eat in the bunkhouse and invited Jesse to share our table." Some of the molten warmth in Burch's eyes turned cold and rigid.

"You would have found his dead body in some eddy in the creek." A glowing desire filled his eyes as he filled her glass. "I wouldn't let Lasso in the house so often if I didn't know he was only interested in your aunt."

"I've been meaning to speak to you about that," she

revealed, sitting up swiftly.

"Your aunt can take care of herself," he said, gently settling her back next to him. "Lasso is completely harmless in spite of the loud noise he makes."

"And I suppose you're going to tell me that you're completely harmless as well."

"I wish I could say otherwise, but I seem to have been defanged and declawed. I'm as helpless as a babe."

"Of all the fibs I've ever heard, that's got to be the biggest. You are the most ornery, determined, and infuriating man alive."

"Does that mean you like me some?" It should have been a joke, but there was so much anxiety to his voice that Sibyl couldn't speak the right words hovering on her lips.

"I suppose I like you well enough. I've never really considered it." She was lying and he knew it.

"Do you think you could love me?"

The words burned their way into Sibyl's brain, making her take too large a swallow of champagne. The coughing gave her a chance to recover her equilibrium, but when she looked into Burch's eyes, they blazed with such feverish longing it suddenly seemed too hot in the room. Part of her wanted to shout "Yes!" and throw herself into his arms. But another part was still distrustful and wanted to seek a refuge from those smoldering eyes.

"I haven't thought of love," she started to say, but the untruth stuck in her throat.

"Are you sure you couldn't?" His hand reached out to touch her shoulder. Sibyl felt a spasm ricochet through her body and all the tension dissipated. She was left limp and helpless.

"Ours is a business arrangement, and we should never cloud business with personal considerations."

"We could turn it over to the lawyers."

"And waste all that money?"

"It wouldn't be nearly as much a waste as your determination to stay away from me."

"I'm not staying away from you."

His hand was caressing her cheek. "Yes, you are," he whispered, sliding closer to her and putting both arms around her. She gulped the last of her champagne.

"I'm not now." With courage bolstered by wine, she snuggled into his arms.

"Isn't this nicer than sitting opposite each other in a parlor and talking about last week's sermon."

"Not even Moreton did that," she giggled. "He couldn't wait to get his hands on me." Burch stiffened perceptibly. "But Aunt Augusta wouldn't leave the room. It used to make him quite angry."

"I can appreciate his feelings," Burch sympathized, allowing his lips to travel along her shoulder.

"You wouldn't if you knew Moreton," she replied, allowing her head to fall back. Burch immediately transferred his attention to the column of her throat. He nibbled her ear and neck until she thought she would boil over.

"Do you love me?" Sibyl asked abruptly, startling him as much by her frightening intensity as by the question itself.

"Yes, I think I've loved you from the very first."

"Are you telling me the truth? You're not just saying it to shut me up?"

"I love you!" Burch groaned and kissed her with such ruthless passion that Sibyl's heart rejoiced in her. She threw her fears and doubts to the winds and returned his embraces with joyous abandon, arching against him, begging for him, yearning for the fulfillment only he could give. Unable to wait a moment longer, she tore at his clothes. It seemed that every button waged an individual battle against her fingers. She lay revealed to Burch's voracious gaze long before she freed his body of the last resisting button.

"What about your leg?" Sibyl managed to ask before succumbing to the maddening pleasure of his tongue on her abdomen.

"I'll show you," Burch said, lowering himself into her welcoming embrace. She rose to meet him and together they raced toward a fulfillment that shook them, enslaved them. At last they had been truly joined, each an inseparable part of the other.

Sibyl opened her eyes. The pale winter light coming through the windows was too weak to chase the shadows away entirely. It could only drive them into the corners of the room where they would slink about like a sulky vanguard, waiting for night to return and reestablish their supremacy.

The sound of soft breathing directed Sibyl's attention to the man lying in peaceful slumber next to her. A smile of utter contentment transfigured her face, a metamorphosis not unlike the rising sun's transformation of morning's dew-moistened landscape. A profound peace filled her and caused her to gaze upon him in wonder. How was it possible that the love of one man, even one so nearly perfect as Burch, could change everything so radically? It seemed as if she were looking at her own life with new eyes, seeing things she had never seen before, seeing sides of issues she never knew existed. And all because of a few tempestuous hours spent in the arms of that insatiable beast.

She smiled again, more like a satisfied cat this time, pleased with herself, content for the first time to be a woman, willing to admit that she *enjoyed* being a woman. On this momentous morning all the slights and restrictions didn't seem very vital. She had no intention of giving in to Burch on every point, but she envisioned a much more satisfactory way of overcoming their differences.

It seemed strange to be in Burch's room, to share his bed as though she belonged there. She looked about the room, aware of the strong masculine feel of it. The absence of lace and frills, the bare dresser tops, the razor and strop next to the bowl and pitcher; the abundance of browns gave the room a rich mellowness that had none of the cloying feeling of pastels or the giddiness of checks and prints. Its strength lay in it stark simplicity, and it was that that made Sibyl feel so deliciously safe.

She snuggled down next to Burch, her bare shoulders chilled by the coldness of the unheated room. Burch barely moved, the muscles in his powerful shoulders remaining soft and supple, the sinews in his huge thighs and legs completely relaxed.

Such a contrast from last night. Then his entire body seemed to grow increasingly more tense, more rock-hard, until he was like marble despite the heat that poured over her like spray from a waterfall. Then his strength, the brutal power of his body, was never more apparent, and Sibyl felt helpless in the face of this annihilating power. He was insatiable. Sibyl had begged, then pleaded with him to stop, too exhausted by her own desire to be able to endure another shattering experience. Yet now, as she felt the warmth radiating from his body to hers, it didn't seem too much at all, and her fingers began to trace tiny arabesques over the surface of his skin. But she didn't get to enjoy the novelty of being the aggressor, regardless of how minor the aggression, for very long. There was a great rustling of bed covers and protesting of springs as Burch woke up, turned over, and wrapped himself about her.

"You smell good," he murmured sleepily, "like roses or summer lilac."

"Make up your mind," she teased. "They're not in the least alike."

"Flowers are all alike."

"Some compliment," she said, punching him lightly. He didn't even open his eyes.

"My aunt used to keep little boxes of dried flowers in all the rooms."

"Sachets."

"I guess so," he said, burying his face in her bosom. "You smell like those, all fresh and outdoorsy. Like springtime."

The pleasant glow spreading all through her wasn't entirely due to the delicious words. Burch's warm breath on her breast and the touch of his tongue on her sensitive skin caused the feelings of last night, waiting just below the surface, to leap to the fore without the least warning. All at once Sibyl found herself trembling in Burch's arms like a frightened maiden, looking forward to what she knew would soon follow, afraid that it would not be as wonderful as she remembered.

"You're soft and warm," he whispered, taunting her nipples with his teeth and tongue.

"Well, you're certainly warm," she said breathlessly, brazenly trailing her hand from his chest to his abdomen, then lower. His response to her touch was electric; his entire body seemed to come alive with pulsating energy, energy that meant to devour her.

"If you keep your hands there, I won't be responsible for myself," he said through strained lips.

"Do you mean this?" she asked, giving him a gentle squeeze. His teeth bit painfully into her aroused breast.

"Gawd almighty woman, let go unless you want me to throw you down and virtually rape you." The brutal force of his words left no doubt in her mind as to their truth.

"I didn't know you could be so sensitive."

"Do you mean like this?" he asked, his jagged breath blurring his words, his fingers finding her and plunging deep within. Sibyl's sharp intake of breath smothered her protest. Burch's exploring fingers, seeking out and finding sensitive spots she didn't know she had, deprived her of speech. Her body arched convulsively, and as his hands continued to plunge within her, driving her to a frenzy, she could only manage an agonized "Stop!"

Burch's hand withdrew partially, but it was enough for her to regain some sense of control, to back away from the feeling that she was going to explode any minute. But both of them had gone too far to hold back for long. Sibyl's agonized writing had brought Burch fully awake and unleashed his craving for her; he didn't need her touch on his member for it to be achingly hard, painfully so. Quickly and without prelude he eased into her, feeling the warmth of her change the pain into longing. Sibyl, too, was beyond the point of needing any encouragement to meet him. She rose, wrapping her body about him, feeling his need, demanding that hers be met. They reached the peak quickly, like a rocket soaring straight up and then bursting in one single, magnificent explosion of color and light. They lay back, panting, in wonder at the power of their combined passion.

"Is it always like this for you?" she asked moments later when the pounding in her temples had stopped.

"How do you mean?"

"I'm not sure. I always thought I wouldn't enjoy making love. I never knew precisely why because no one would talk about it. It was like they were secretly ashamed of it."

"Did your mother tell you that?"

"No. She died when I was ten, but I just supposed that's the way it was. Everyone always spoke of girls who liked boys as shameful creatures. I suppose it was natural to think that no good woman would enjoy what they did with those men."

"But you enjoy it?"

"More every time. And you?"

"I suppose I'm one of the men who gave those girls a bad name. I used them for my pleasure, to relieve a bodily need that periodically became so great I couldn't think about anything else. But with you it's different."

"How?"

"I hardly know how to put it into words. It caught me by surprise." Sibyl smiled pleasurably.

"At first I wanted you because you were the most desirable woman I'd ever seen. Despite your temper and the arguments, the mere thought of your skin, the way your breasts point up, would keep me awake at night. It still does, but it's different now. There's something about being with you that I

213

never felt with any other woman. It's odd because being with you makes me not want to be with another woman."

"You'd better not," she said, sitting up and playfully thumping his chest. Burch pulled her down to him, crushing her warm, soft breasts against chest.

"And what about you, my little chaste miss."

"I know even less than you because I've never been with another man. In fact, I never wanted to be with a man at all. I thought it was degrading, or giving up my right to be thought of as an independent woman."

"I'm surprised you didn't pull a knife on me the first time I touched you."

"I probably would have if I'd had the foresight to bring one. I never had the slightest desire to be touched by Moreton or Kendrick, but from the very first I had to fight against the attraction that kept drawing me to you. I would be so angry with myself I would take it out on you. Then I would go upstairs and think of all the ways I could unsay those words."

"Why didn't you?"

"I know it sounds silly to you, but I had fought so hard all my life to be taken seriously as a capable, competent human, not a pretty female, that I was petrified of giving up an inch of the ground I had gained. It wasn't until I could resist you no longer that I discovered I had grown, not diminished. I feel like I'm a part of you, that together we are more than either of us was alone."

"What a great argument for making love. I'll bet if we posted a copy of it on the walls of every bawdy house in the country, their business would triple."

"You are an obnoxious beast, and I'll never tell you anything again," Sibyl cried, half serious, half laughing. She tried to poke Burch in the side, but he wrestled her down and began to tickle her feet. Sibyl kicked with all her strength, but her protests were barely discernible through shrieks of laughter. Burch's blood was quickly aroused, and

Sibyl could tell from the look in his eye that he was interested in more than feet. But a door was heard to slam downstairs and then sounds coming from the kitchen.

"Rachel!" gasped Sibyl, instantly sobered. "She can't find me rolling around in your bed like an abandoned hussy." She leapt up, grabbing up the pieces of her clothes that she had discarded on the floor the night before.

"Why should you be worried what she'll say?" asked Burch. "It's none of her business."

"That's just the kind of thing a man would say," complained Sibyl bitterly, pulling her dress over her head and wrapping her underwear in a bundle. "Just because nobody cares if you sleep with every female that crosses your path, you think women ought to feel the same way. I haven't got the time to explain it to you now, but I can promise you they don't." She peeped out into the hall to make sure no one would see her, blew Burch a kiss, and scampered down the hall to her own room. Burch lay back, laughing happily.

Breakfast was late. It was an unspoken rule that no matter how much Rachel was allowed to do about the house, Sibyl did the cooking. Balaam and Ned were in the ranch room, directing expectant and wondering glances toward the kitchen long before the smell of ham and coffee promised to relieve the gnawing feeling in their stomachs. Sibyl was sure the only thing that kept Balaam from taking her to task was the fact that Burch wasn't down yet. Not even Balaam expected to be fed before Burch.

"I thought I was going to have to come after you with a lasso," Balaam said when Burch finally put in his appearance looking more than ordinarily spruced up. "An old man like me could starve to death while you stay up there prettifying yourself. You ain't expecting somebody special, are you?" he said, winking at Sibyl, who kept her gaze averted.

"Just thought I'd try and look my best for your hanging," Burch shot back. "You're not worth much, but then it didn't take me very long." Ned's crack of laughter wiped the smile off Balaam's creased face.

"Have your coffee and don't listen to him, Balaam," Sibyl said, "or you're going to get so upset you'll spill it over yourself."

"That's not anger, it's just old age," needled Ned. But this morning Sibyl was neither interested in nor amused by the men's constant banter. Her heart beat a little faster when she noticed the extra care Burch had taken with his dress; she was in more danger of spilling the coffee than Balaam. She didn't eat much, finding herself strangely agitated and compulsive about serving the men and refilling their cups.

"I ain't finished this one yet," Balaam grumbled, so busy planning how to get Ned back that his uncanny ability to notice the very thing one hoped would go unnoticed failed to see that Sibyl was acting unlike herself. Rachel saw it, but then Rachel never said anything.

"I expect I'll be back for lunch," Burch announced casually as he rose from the table.

"Of course you will," added Balaam. "With that leg you'd be a fool to go further than the shed."

"One of these days Ned's going to find your broken and mangled body at the bottom of a canyon," Burch said savagely, "and there's going to be rejoicing throughout half of the territory." Balaam beamed with pleasure.

"Ain't nobody got the best of me yet," he said proudly.

"That's because there ain't no *best* of you to get," said Ned. The two of them went out, happily abusing each other.

"Be careful of your leg," Sibyl said, very conscious of the restraint imposed by Rachel's presence.

"Don't worry. Just think of what I'd miss if I broke it again." His gaze was not shy, and Sibyl found that she was blushing.

"According to the doctor, it would be your whole life," she said gruffly, setting down the plate in her hand because she could not control the tremor. "You really shouldn't go out at

216

all."

"Do you think I should stay?" Sibyl wanted to say yes, but she doubted she could endure the agony of having to act as though nothing had changed in front of Rachel.

"The fresh air will be good for him, miss, and a little exercise won't hurt a man as tough as Mr. Burch."

"You're an admirable woman, Rachel. Take a lesson, Sibyl. Never try to coddle a man."

"I won't," Sibyl replied, stung. "I've never found one who could properly appreciate it." Immediately she wished she could recall those words. The light of challenge flamed in Burch's eyes; there was no way of telling what terrible things he might do when he looked like that. "Of course, I don't know anything about cowboys," she added quickly. "Maybe they're different."

"Backing down?" Burch challenged.

"Of course not. I don't have time for silly games." It was a lame excuse, but her mind was too numb to think of anything better. Mercifully, he left it at that, and a morning spent working with silent, placid Rachel did much to restore her composure, enabling her to face Burch over lunch with a show of outward calm.

The next two days passed blissfully, with the two of them engaged in their separate duties during the day, then joined for unimaginable pleasures at night. Sibyl began to think of the daytime, her work, and Rachel with resentment; they formed a bar to her complete union with Burch. Then on the third morning, Lasso sent over a message that the girls were better and that she could expect Augusta the next day. Now the empty morning hours were invested with new importance; they separated her from the last evening with Burch. Her mind was so thoroughly taken up with Burch that Rachel began to feel concerned about her.

"You feeling all right this morning?" Rachel asked diffidently.

"Why do you ask?" Sibyl replied defensively.

"You aren't acting quite right. It's not good for you to be so pale."

"I guess I'm just worn down from nursing Burch on top of having all this food to put up for the winter."

"I guess that's it," Rachel responded, but she watched Sibyl more closely after that. Sibyl made a determined effort not to betray how completely her thoughts were taken up by Burch.

Being able to get out again had reinvigorated Burch's interest in the ranch, and when Jenkins joined them for lunch the talk soon centered on ranch business. Sibyl's only contribution was to say that she wanted more space for a garden, better pens for the livestock, and a more extensive orchard. Foreseeing an increase in his importance, Balaam tried to involve her in a long discussion on just how many pens they needed, the kinds of trees necessary for pollination, and the varieties that would do best in Wyoming's severe climate, but Sibyl absently agreed to all his suggestions. Her mind was on Burch, and there was no room left for rootstock and cross-pollination. The inner tension was nearly unbearable, but she kept telling herself to wait. They would have the whole evening all to themselves.

But Sibyl's hopes plummeted when Burch came in that evening nearly exhausted after insisting upon riding Silver Birch instead of using the wagon. Again cows dominated they conversation; this time it was the terrible condition of the herds. The more Burch talked about the herds, the more desperate Sibyl became. Her dreams of a wondrous evening spent in his arms receded slowly but steadily. She tried to think of other things, but her thoughts were riveted on his body as never before. Her gaze fastened itself on one powerful forearm, and all her concentration centered on that arm, the swell of muscles as they traveled from wrist to elbow, the supple wrist and the powerful hand that flared out from it. The simple thought of those hands hypnotized her; for three nights they had caused her to experience sensations she had never dreamed were possible. They had brought her body to a new sense of itself and the potential it had for pleasure for both of them. Sibyl felt as though she were on the threshold of a new awareness she had just begun to explore, and Augusta's return meant that their time together was almost at an end. Her body and soul ached to have Burch to herself, to turn his thoughts to her alone, but still he talked on and on about those everlasting cows.

Nothing changed after dinner. The men talked business over coffee while Rachel and Sibyl cleaned up. Sibyl felt like she never wanted to see a cow again; not only had they nearly killed the man she loved so passionately, the continued to keep him from her now that he was well.

"Lasso says that he's bringing Augusta back to us tomorrow," Sibyl blurted out during a pause in the conversation. The news had no effect on anyone except Burch, but the results were all Sibyl had hoped for. Burch was no longer interested in cows, and though Jenkins and Ned continued their discussion, he contributed less and less and glanced more and more frequently in her direction. She met his glance and read in it the same desire that filled her.

"I think I'll go to bed a little early tonight," she said, getting up with a convincing yawn. "There's no need to leave because of me," she protested when the men stood up to go. But she didn't discourage them when Ned and Balaam took themselves off. Rachel went off to do a few final chores in the kitchen, leaving Jenkins still talking to Burch. Sibyl heard the back door close behind Rachel as she mounted the stairs.

The room was icy cold, and Sibyl undressed and climbed into bed quickly. She had barely curled up in a tiny ball in the freezing bed when the back door closed after Jenkins and she heard Burch taking the stairs two at a time. He headed straight for her room. He wasted no time on words; he began taking off his clothes before the door had time to shut. Even in Sibyl's great anxiety to have him next to her, it seemed like only seconds before the bed sank abruptly on one side. The soothing warmth that radiated from his body

219

flowed into hers, relaxing her muscles and enabling her to ignore the cold that enveloped her.

"I didn't expect Jenkins to leave so quickly."

"He didn't want to, but I told him I'd send him to Pennsylvania if he said another word about hay. Jenkins hates trains and easterners above all else."

"I don't care what Jenkins hates," Sibyl murmured, running her hands through the tight, curly hair on Burch's chest and biting playfully at his ear. "I'd much rather talk about what you like." The fingers in the hair began an odyssey toward the sparser hair of his abdomen.

"You don't seem to need any help," Burch said with a shudder, his whole body in the sudden grip of desire. "Let those fingers travel any further south and you'll find out what I like plenty damn quick."

"Are you threatening me?" Sibyl teased, dipping lower into the thickly matted hair between his legs and then making a rapid retreat.

"Yes," grunted Burch, barely able to contain himself. "I'm threatening to devour you in one gulp."

"I don't think you can do that," Sibyl said, letting her fingers dip again until they came into contact with his enflamed manhood.

"I warn you, you're playing with fire," Burch said, tottering on the edge of madness.

"But I'm so cold," Sibyl said, boldly closing her fingers about him. "A fire would keep me warm." With a groan that sounded barely human, Burch pounced upon her, crushing her lips in a searing kiss while roughly spreading her thighs with his legs. His hands sought her breasts, kneading them into painfully sensitive peaks that welcomed the heated caress of his lips. He drove into her, roughly and impatiently. Sibyl rose to meet him, equally impatient to draw him inside her, to have him satisfy a need from so deep within that it seemed she would never be free of its urgency. She clung desperately to him, reveling in his rough strength. With dizzying speed he drove her along the spiral of sensations that lifted her from the earthbound existence and cast her into some radiant sphere, where they alone occupied the swirling, speeding orbit. Then, before she could ready herself, her whole being erupted into a shower of multicolored sparks, and she seemed to disintegrate, to be shattered by the explosion within her.

Chapter 18

"Will it ever stop snowing?" Sibyl asked for the sixth time that morning. The blizzard had been blowing for ten days and it was as if the world outside the house had ceased to exist. "If it doesn't stop soon, nobody will be able to come to the party." But she really wasn't thinking about the Christmas party; she was thinking about Burch, who had left the ranch house two days after Augusta returned from Lasso's.

"I can't expect the boys to keep on risking their lives while I stay here," he explained when, in dismay, Sibyl objected to his intention to join the men on the range.

"But you're not well yet," she pleaded, grasping at any excuse to keep him near her.

His eyes rested on her with a contentment born of four blissful nights spent in her arms. "I'm well enough."

"Are you sure you will be safe?" asked Augusta. "The snow seems to have stopped, at least for now, but the ground is still covered and the drifts make it very treacherous. I wouldn't have risked it myself, but I could not reconcile it with my conscience to leave Sibyl alone any longer."

"I know every foot of this ranch, even under snow, and I

intend to be very careful. It would be terribly unfair to condemn you to a sick room for the third time in three months."

"What do you have to do that somebody else can't do just as well?" Sibyl asked, too upset to consider the implications of her question.

"Are you trying to make me justify my position?" Sibyl blushed vividly and stammered an apology, an occurrence so unprecedented that Augusta was at once astounded and wide-eyed with curiosity as to what could have brought about this incredible change. But there were so many preparations to be made for Burch's departure that Augusta soon forgot her questions. After that they became deeply involved in plans for the Christmas party, and even with Rachel's help there was more than enough to keep them occupied for two weeks.

Then the snow had started, and Balaam thoughtlessly announced that they were in for a *real* blizzard this time. "It's going to be a real bad winter," he said cheerfully. "The boys saw an Arctic owl coming in from Montana, and the Indians say there hasn't been one of them this far south in fifty years." That blithely uttered prediction caused Sibyl to became so jumpy and preoccupied that for a while Augusta was afraid she meant to go looking for Burch herself.

"No sense worrying about Mr. Burch," Balaam said as though he read her thoughts. "They got line cabins all over, and every one of those chaps took enough food outta' here to last a month. I suspect some of them don't mind being snowed in. It beats riding through drifts waist high trying to save cows too stupid to know what's good for them."

"But the cabins aren't very big and they're terribly uncomfortable."

"It don't need much comfort to make it better than a bedroll. After chasing cows in the hot and the cold and the wet and the dry for nigh onto nine months, it's a real pleasure to lay back and not move until the coffee cup's empty."

Sibyl's worry was only partially allayed. Temperatures were falling to ten and twenty degrees below zero, the ground was like iron, and streams froze right down to bedrock. How could any man caught in such a storm survive? She didn't dare think of what the range stock were suffering. Even with the protection of sheds and plenty of feed and water, it was taking all of Ned and Balaam's time to keep the livestock alive. "If it gets any colder, some of them is going to freeze," Balaam remarked pessimistically.

As the days went by, one after another filled with driving snow and continuing silence from the range, Sibyl's face took on a gaunt look and her eyes appeared to sink into their sockets. She spent long moments staring out the window, hoping to see Burch emerge from the swirling snow even though she knew he would be much safer in one of the cabins. Augusta had time to remember her curiosity but decided it was not a good time to probe Sibyl's feelings.

"It's a good thing we had the party to plan," Augusta said as Sibyl sat staring into space over her task. "It would have been very difficult to get through these long days without it."

"It won't do a bit of good if no one can get here. This is the third blizzard already, and Balaam says the worst part of the winter always comes after New Year's."

"Well, there's nothing we can do about that, so it's best not to dwell on it. You can help me make sure I get the spruce boughs spaced evenly. I can't see from here."

Sibyl tried to keep her mind occupied, but their long confinement left them with nothing to do but work on the party, and now their preparations were nearing completion. Rows of cakes, pies, and pastries lined the pantry shelves awaiting the twelve guests who would spend three days and two nights at the Elkhorn. Beds were made, blankets stacked in each corner, and meals planned down to the last dish. With only a few last minute tasks remaining, her mind was prey to constant worry.

But not all her thoughts centered around Burch; part of her mind was given over to probing her own heart. She couldn't come to grips with feelings that were now as ambivalent about love as they earlier had been about Burch. She wanted Burch at her side every minute but would have driven him away if he had not left on his own. She didn't trust him out of her sight but would have entrusted her life to him without hesitation. She was afraid for him and wanted to protect him but knew she couldn't love a man who avoided danger. She didn't want anyone to know she was in love and suffering the anguish of the damned, but she longed to shout to the whole world that it was she, out of all women, that he had chosen.

Would it last? What would she do if it didn't? Could she see him day after day, knowing he would never hold her in his arms again, never drive her wild with his hot kisses and insistent hands? She knew she couldn't. After despairing of love for so long, it was now too precious for her to give up. There could be no going back. That door was closed forever.

On the eleventh day the snow stopped as suddenly as it began, and the temperature shot up to twenty degrees above zero.

"Feels almost like summer," remarked Balaam, delivering some unfrozen eggs. "You might have seen the last of these. I'm surprised they kept at it this long."

"I only need about a dozen more."

"I'll talk to 'em, miss, but I can tell you, *I* wouldn't be laying any eggs if it was up to me." That caused Sibyl to laugh and she felt better than she had in several days.

The sun came out later that afternoon and her spirits

soared. Augusta found her humming over the stove as she prepared dinner.

"That's much more than we can eat, dear," Augusta commented, noting the roast, the pots of vegetables, a pan of hot bread, and a pie waiting to go in the oven.

"I thought some of the men might come in now the weather's cleared."

Balaam soon dashed her hopes. "You won't be seeing a soul for at least two or three days. They've got to get all those cows on their feet before old man North starts sneezing icicles again."

Augusta's heart was wrung by Sibyl's struggle to hide her disappointment, and she hoped that for once Burch would neglect his duties. But he didn't, and by the time early night had fallen, she knew there would be no extra places at the table that evening. She kept up a steady, if somewhat muted, flow of conversation, and if Sibyl didn't answer she went on just as if she had.

The next day was worse, and the dinner was put back in its pots to wait again. On the third night Augusta invited Rachel, Ned, and Balaam to eat with them. Food wouldn't keep forever.

On the fourth day Sibyl said, "I don't think I'll cook tonight unless you want something in particular."

Augusta's heart was wrung, but she decided then and there that Sibyl should not be allowed to sit around feeling sorry for herself.

"That's all right, dear. I'll just fix a few things for myself and the men. You know they don't really like to eat their own cooking, and Rachel's is not very good."

Augusta managed to scorch one dish, spill another, and involve Sibyl in a running discussion about various ways to get the wild taste out of game meat. Feeling guilty about her lack of consideration, Sibyl jerked herself out of her reverie and went into the kitchen.

"You don't have to fumble anymore," she admonished Augusta, taking the pot of ruined beans from her hands. "I promise to come out of my sulks and behave like the mature woman I'm trying to convince Burch I am. He wouldn't be very impressed by my conduct these last few days, would he?"

"It's only natural that you would become a little blue-deviled with all this snow."

"You don't have to try so hard to keep from telling me I've been behaving like an overindulged brat," Sibyl said with a chuckle. "I know it, and I promise I won't do it anymore."

And she was as good as her word. Sibyl fell back into her routine of cooking full meals, and under her energetic prodding they finished the last of the Christmas cooking and cleaning, and put the huge wreath on the front door. It was fortunate that their preparations were complete, for on the seventh day after the blizzard stopped, there was a commotion at the front door and Augusta opened it to find two perfect strangers on her porch.

"I know we're early," announced Emma Stratton, striding into the hall, certain of her welcome, "but I told Auggie if we waited two more days, we were liable to get caught in another of these terrible blizzards and never get here. And I would simple *die* if I missed this party." She looked Augusta over critically and her plucked eyebrows rose. "When did you arrive? A little *too* early, aren't you?" Her near-black eyes were hard and glittering.

"I didn't exactly arrive, I live here," answered Augusta, too thrown by this brazen greeting to make sense.

"What!" Emma's pale skin grew even whiter, heightening the contrast with her brightly colored lips.

The look of shock and disapproval further confused Augusta and absolutely tied her tongue. She stook stock-still, helpless before this energetic amazon, expecting to be swept aside as she took command of the house. A slight diversion was created by the entrance of Emma's brother, a tall, husky man of almost fierce appearance, with the same essentially aristocratic belief in his right to any privilege or property he wanted.

"Well, now, who could you be?" he asked, eyeing Augusta with an appreciation wholly different from that of his sister. "Emma made sure we'd be the first here."

"I'm Augusta Hauxhurst, Burch's aunt," Augusta said in the softest of voices.

"Burch only has one aunt, and she's *dead*," stated Emma, her hard eyes daring Augusta to contradict her.

"I know, and I'm not really his aunt, but Burch says he can't call me Miss Hauxhurst all the time. He insists it's too formal."

"You're much too young to be anybody's aunt," said Auggie Stratton, nearly as taken with Augusta as Lasso had been.

"I never knew anyone bothered to invent a fancy name for his doxy," snapped Emma, "much less allow her to act as hostess to a party of respectable guests." Augusta, only now realizing the role Emma thought she filled Burch's household, became speechless with mortification.

"No need to be so unforgiving, Emma," Auggie said. "It can get pretty lonely out here, and you shouldn't begrudge Burch a few comforts."

"I could care less about his *comforts*, but I won't have this one flung in my face."

"Who is it, Aunt?" called Sibyl, coming through the door at the back of the hall. "I thought I heard you talking to someone."

"My God in heaven, he's got two of them," Emma stammered with an unbelieving gasp, "and they're related."

228

"Damnation, Burch will tell me where he found this pair if I have to break his neck to get it out of him," declared Auggie, acutely envious of any man who could live with two such beautiful women at the same time.

"How do you do?" Sibyl said, coming forward to greet the unexpected arrivals. "You must be the Strattons. I'm Sibyl Cameron, Burch's cousin. I'm so glad you were able to get here despite the snow."

"Spare me," rasped Emma, her voice harsh with contempt and her eyes blatantly insolent. She threw off her cloak, shaking out her long, black hair.

"I beg your pardon?" Sibyl faltered, completely unprepared for such a rude response.

"You can drop this show of gentility. Your *aunt*, or whatever she is, has already explained *what* you are."

"I don't think . . . I mean, it's not quite what it seems. Oh dear, I hardly know what to say. You see, you really don't understand at all," Augusta finished up before her voice failed her entirely. Sibyl looked to her aunt for enlightenment, but the poor lady was utterly devastated.

Sibyl disliked Emma on sight, and her having subjected Augusta to some kind of embarrassment and spoken to her with unexplained rudeness merely supported her instincts. Her eyes grew hard and the smile froze on her lips. "There seems to be some misunderstanding. Burch and the men have still not returned. If there is something I can do . . ."

"You can pack your bags and leave, and take your *aunt* with you. It's an insult to expect Burch's guests to treat you like a decent woman."

Sibyl's eyes blazed in cascade of fury. "You will explain that remark and then apologize to my aunt, or I will see that your bags are thrown out the door and you after them." Sibyl was not as tall or built on such generous lines as Emma, but the larger woman suddenly felt in need of her brother's support.

"Now, ladies there is no call for this throw up."

"I will *not* allow my aunt to be spoken to in such a manner in my own home," stated Sibyl, turning on Auggie with such unabated fury that his fatuous protests were caught in his throat.

"Your home!" exclaimed Emma, unable to contain herself. "Of all the brazen nerve! I can't wait to hear what Burch has to say when he finds his strumpets have been calling the Elkhorn home."

The swiftness of Sibyl's movement caught everyone by surprise. She slapped Emma so hard that she was knocked off balance and would have fallen if her brother had not steadied her. "Ned!" she called toward the back of the house, with a screech that would have caused her mother to blush to the very core of her gentle soul.

"Now you see here, missy . . ."

"No, *you* see here," Sibyl interrupted in a voice tight with suppressed rage. "I *am* Wesley Cameron's niece, and this is my aunt, Augusta Hauxhurst. Since I own half of this ranch, I feel entitled to call it my home. Now you will either apologize to both of us immediately, or you will leave at once."

"How could we know?" mumbled Auggie.

"I don't believe it," Emma snorted, in a towering rage herself, "and I *won't* believe it until I hear the words from Burch's own lips."

"What won't you believe, Emma?" inquired Burch, breezing into the hall not far behind Ned. "Welcome, Auggie. I see you've already met my cousin and her aunt. Whatever caused you to get here so soon?"

"I begged Auggie to come early," Emma purred, turning to Burch without trace of the hard anger of an instant before. "I was afraid we'd get snowed in, and it would break my heart

230

to have to miss your party." She threw her arms around Burch, expecting more than the brotherly peck on the cheek she got.

"Save your compliments for Sibyl and Aunt Augusta. They did everything themselves. What happened to your cheek? It's as red as fire." Emma paled, looking first to Auggie and then to Sibyl for help.

"Yes," cooed Sibyl, "what *did* happen to your cheek?"

"I s—s—stumbled on a r—rotten step and hit it against the post," Emma stammered, embroidering rapidly. "I was just saying I wouldn't believe yóu were so careless as to not have it fixed unless I heard it from your own lips."

"Is one of the steps rotten? I don't remember, but I daresay you're right. But let's not stand here in the hall. Ned, see that the Strattons' bags are taken upstairs. Come on into the front room. You won't believe what Sibyl's done to it since you were here. In fact, you won't recognize a single room in the whole house. Is there a fire?"

"It's already laid. All you have to do is light it." Sibyl directed her answer to Burch, coolly ignoring Emma's presence. "The room won't take more than a few minutes to warm up. You go on with them. I still have a few things to do, and Aunt Augusta will see that Ned puts their bags in the right rooms."

Emma was relieved that Sibyl apparently didn't mean to tell Burch what had really happened, but her displeasure at finding this beautiful woman living at the Elkhorn was nothing compared to her anger at the tender looks that passed between Burch and Sibyl. For the last several years, she had considered Burch her private property, to be picked up when she was ready. She was *ready* now and she had planned, with almost sole ownership of his company for a day and two nights, to arrange it so that their wedding would take place before the spring. It infuriated her to find she had competition. Even a cursory glance convinced Emma she could never rival Sibyl in looks, and she knew that Sibyl's ownership of half the ranch tipped the odds heavily against her. From the hallway alone, she could tell that the house had been transformed. She did not underestimate the value of such comforts to a man; her job was going to be extremely difficult. Fear made her desperate.

"Everyone knows you've run this place for years and years," Emma said, fawning over Burch. "It's sweet of you to give your cousin all the credit, but men like you always get what they want."

Burch tucked Emma's arm in his hand and laughed. "You always did know how to talk up to a man, Emma. My uncle used to tell me if I believed half of what you said, I'd have a head stuffed with cotton."

"Sis always did know how to please a man," agreed her brother, quite willing to help Emma ensnare Burch.

"The only person she has to please for the next few days is herself," said Burch, leading them into the parlor. "Now you make yourself comfortable while I start the fire. Sibyl will bring us some coffee in a few minutes, and in no time at you'll forget it's been snowing for the better part of six weeks."

The door closed behind them and Sibyl stared hard at the barrier, a raging tumult in her mind: outrage at the woman's incredible assumption; anger that she couldn't throw them out; jealousy that she had to fix coffee while Emma sat with Burch. It was almost too much to bear that after waiting so long, she would be denied even a few precious words alone with Burch, denied them by the presence of a predatory strumpet.

"That was not a very good beginning, was it?" remarked Augusta, recovering slightly. "I never thought that our presence here would be the cause of any misunderstanding."

She colored at the memory. "Certainly not of that nature."

"It wouldn't have occurred to anybody else. She only thought of what she would do herself if she had the chance." Augusta found it hard to believe that Sibyl would make such a scathing accusation of anyone, but she could see the hurt and the jealousy, and her heart went out to her.

"I shouldn't think you would be required to see a great deal of her. Lasso is coming over tomorrow and Jesse is due back as well. With the party the next day, you won't have time to give her a thought." Sibyl offered no answer, but Augusta doubted she could do anything to ease her niece's agony. "Maybe you'd better see to the coffee."

"Maybe I'd better. If I make it hot enough, maybe it can melt that block of ice she calls a heart." Sibyl stormed off to the kitchen and Augusta went upstairs to see to the bestowing of the bags. She knew Sibyl well enough to know that the battle lines were drawn. She did not expect to enjoy this party.

Chapter 19

"You should see the goings-on in the bunkhouse, ma'am," Jesse informed Augusta. "You might mistake it for the Laramie Hotel before the spring dance. The boys are washing clothes, shaving, and scrubbing places that only get wet if they fall in the creek. I never knew them to get so excited over any party. It's a good thing the weather is holding, or they'd be offering a month's pay to anyone willing to take their place on the line."

"It has been nice all day," Augusta agreed, torn between wondering which was better for Sibyl: being kept inside and forced to endure the Strattons' company, or knowing that Burch had spent the entire day riding over the ranch with Emma and her brother. "Thank heavens the snow has melted. At least it will make it easier for people to get here."

"Some of the hands are here already. There's plenty of room for them to bunk in with our men," he said, answering Augusta's questioning glance. "There's a year's worth of gossip to catch up on."

Sibyl took no part in the conversation, just as she had taken no part in any since Emma blithely waltzed in and took command of Burch, much as a mother hen would an errant chick. Emma had not left his side for the whole of the previous evening. She had sat next to him at dinner and then pulled him down beside her on the sofa, keeping him there with childhood reminiscences long after everyone else had gone to bed. Augusta had expected Sibyl to make one of her caustic remarks, but she had been uncharacteristically quiet, rarely speaking, and devoting her energies to dinner and seeing that the guests were comfortable.

Emma did not relinquish her hold the next day. She was up before Burch and invaded his bedroom, smiling brightly and teasing him about lying in bed till all hours. "I don't see how you get anything done like that," she say coyly. "You need someone to get you started on your way each day. A man can't be expected to greet the day without a proper beginning." The discovery that Sibyl was up before any of them, preparing a huge breakfast, took the steam out of her engine, but only for a moment.

"I never saw anything like this in my life," observed Auggie, awed at the feast set before them. With heroic determination, he plowed his way through more food than Sibyl though any one man could put away without having to go back to bed to sleep it off. A confidential wink from Burch sent Sibyl's spirits soaring, but Emma saw it and dug in with even greater determination.

"Let's go for a ride," she said with overflowing enthusiasm. "I can't bear to be cooped up for very long. And I haven't seen any of the improvements you've made since last year."

"There's not much to see except for what Sibyl's done around the ranch," said Burch. "I've had all I could do to keep the cows alive this year."

"Isn't that the truth," Auggie added, his mouth full of pancakes and fresh sausage. "I'm afraid we'll find the herds didn't do so well come spring."

"Don't you provide for your cattle through the winter?" inquired Augusta, innocently assuming that everyone did as Burch and Lasso.

"Lord no, ma'am," he said, reaching for the plate of ham. "No sane man ventures out of Cheyenne until spring, but Emma swore she'd bust if we didn't stay long enough to come to this party."

Augusta shut her mouth, aware that she had exposed a vulnerable side of the Strattons.

"Naturally we do all we can for our herds," Emma said, with a glance that would have slain a more stalwart foe than Augusta. "After all, it is the source of our wealth. And I'm so anxious to see what you're doing," she said, turning her heavily penciled eyes to Burch. "Daddy always said no one would know a thing about ranching until they've seen the Elkhorn." Auggie's mouth was too full to defend himself, but Sibyl wasn't sure she could stand any more without getting sick.

"It's a little cool for a ride," Burch pointed out.

"Pooh, what do I care for cold," Emma scoffed. "You must have miss — oh dear, I've forgotten your name again," she claimed apologetically to Sibyl. "I have such a terrible memory."

"It's Cameron, but don't worry about it," replied Sibyl. "I wouldn't want you to be overtaxed while you're here."

Auggie grinned at his sister's discomfiture, but Emma had no time to waste on Sibyl.

"It would be awfully nice if your cousin would pack a lunch for us. Then we wouldn't have to come back so soon, and I could *really* see the ranch."

"It's rather cold for that much riding."

"Fifty dollars says I can stay in the saddle as long as you," Emma challenged Burch gleefully. "Dare you."

"Done!" Burch capitulated, unable to resist a challenge. "But Auggie must be the judge." That didn't suit either brother or sister, but neither objected and Emma and Auggie both rose to go change their clothes.

Burch turned to Sibyl with his disarming smile. "I'm sorry they had to come so early, but at least this will keep them out of your way."

"I don't mind," she lied.

"Don't let Emma get on your nerves," he said, taking her hands in his. "She's a bit bossy, but I've known her since she was ten and she's an old friend."

Sibyl nodded, unable to trust her tongue with even the most commonplace remark.

Burch looked over his shoulder, saw that Augusta's back was turned, and gave Sibyl a swift kiss. "There's a whole lot more I'd like to do," he whispered softly in her ear.

"Well you won't do it now," Sibyl said, reviving magically under his touch. "I dare not imagine what Emma would think."

"I've got all day to learn what Emma thinks," he said with a look of resignation, "and if I know Emma, she won't be shy of telling me. Don't wear yourself out. This party's supposed to be fun for you too." He chucked Sibyl under the chin and left to join the Strattons, to all outward appearances content to be spending his day with Emma.

Sibyl's happiness faded as quickly as it had bloomed. Burch's departure represented a repudiation of her, a preference of Emma's company over hers, and the hurt was almost more than she could hide.

Burch couldn't see that what was perfect solution for him was tearing Sibyl apart. Being with Emma would be easy — there was no desire, no temptation. And he'd get Emma out of Sibyl's hair. He didn't realize how his absence would hurt her, how much she needed his touch, his smile, or any other small tokens of his affection. To him such tiny signs were of no consequence and only made his physical torture more exquisitely painful. Thus, unknowingly, he denied her the very assurances that would have enabled her to ignore Emma's presence.

Lasso's arrival further aggravated the situation by depriving Sibyl of Augusta's company. She had nothing to do for the day and no one to do it with; consequently, she spent her time concentrating on her unhappiness and distorting the little looks and inflections of speech she had witnessed between Emma and Burch. By the time they returned from their ride, she had talked herself into believing they were in love and she was standing in the way of their true happiness.

It was late in the afternoon when they returned. They hurried in, blue from the cold, exhausted from a day in the saddle, and starved for something hot to eat. Emma had also returned with a burning desire to have one of the bulls from the breeding herd Burch had showed them. She didn't despair of getting a cow and one of the calves, but a yearling bull was her immediate objective.

"Wait until you sit down to one of Sibyl's dinners," Lasso said when the spicy smells of roast chicken and frying sausage met them at the door. "You've never tasted anything like it."

"If it's better than breakfast, I can't wait," said Auggie, disappearing to change his clothes. Emma, doing her best to disguise that a day spent in the saddle had made her extremely sore and stiff, smiled sweetly.

"How nice," she said curtly and passed on.

"Did you have a nice day?" asked Augusta, trying to detain Burch at least a moment, for Sibyl's benefit.

"Very pleasant," Burch replied, making her sorry she'd asked. "Auggie is a fool, but Emma is a very sensible woman. She seemed to think very highly of Sibyl's haystacks."

Sibyl hoped that, after being away all day, Burch would linger after Emma had gone. But Burch, unaware that Sibyl wouldn't have cared if they never ate as long as she got him to herself for just a few minutes, hurried away determined to compensate for his absence by a prompt and well-scrubbed appearance at dinner.

At dinner, Emma soon made it clear that she had no intention of crediting Sibyl with the haystacks—or anything else if she could help it.

"I don't think Auggie enjoyed our ride today," she said, sacrificing her brother on the altar of her ambition, "but it was worth it to see what Burch has done in one year. I could have cried with vexation when I saw all those cows placidly eating away at one haystack after another, and just as fat as though they'd had decent grass all summer. I begged Auggie to pay attention to our hayfields, but I couldn't get him to listen to a word I said."

"The men out here do have an unfortunate tendency to think that they have all the answers," commented Sibyl.

"But Burch does," Emma gushed. "I've never seen a man who could come up with so many new ideas. Next I expect to hear he's found a way to double the amount of beef on his steers."

"It won't be all that difficult with the bull in his shed," Auggie observed on cue. "I would give half my herd for two of those bull calves."

"Two of those calves would *make* our herd," Emma remarked pointedly to Burch.

"Then you'd better start sweet-talking Sibyl," Burch suggested. "Her father bred them and they belong to her."

"I'm sure she leaves their management to you," purred Emma.

"You don't know Sibyl very well," Burch replied, banishing Sibyl's scowl with his smile. "She can manage her property without any help from me."

"I tried to give them to the Elkhorn, but Burch wouldn't let me," Sibyl explained with silky politeness.

"Even I've had to come crawling to Sibyl to let me send a few of my cows to that bull," Lasso interposed, not very taken with Emma himself.

"They were her father's life's work," explained Augusta, willing to add her mite.

But Emma was not to be borne down by any such paltry obstacles. "But then he didn't have a *son*, did he? He most certainly meant that they should go to his brother."

"As a matter of fact, he didn't," countered Augusta, showing a combative side no one expected. "Stuart was quite angry with Wesley for deserting the South, and they hadn't spoken for ten years. If he had any suspicion that they would end up in Wyoming, I'm sure he would have given them to the first farmer to show an interest in them."

Sibyl could not repress a smile. "Daddy thought that the West was full of terribly uncivilized ruffians and the sooner the South was separated from them the better."

"Like your grandfather?" Burch said with a wink at Sibyl.

"What a terribly stupid view," remarked Emma, piqued.

"Maybe, but true to his heritage," Burch said.

"That's all beside the point now," said Emma, dismissing a subject that didn't interest her at all. "Those cows are here and Burch is the only one who knows how to make use of them. Of course you'll turn them over to him."

"I probably will," replied Sibyl, spiking her guns quite effectively. "After Lasso's help in recapturing the yearlings, I've decided to give him one of the young bulls for his own use, but the rest are to be used solely to improve the Elkhorn herds."

Auggie knew nothing of the raid on Chalk Canyon and loudly demanded to be told all about it. While Burch recounted the story, Lasso insisted, in loud whispers, on expressing his surprise and appreciation. Emma used the time to reorganize. She had been badly shocked by Burch's quiet acceptance of Sibyl's ownership of the herd. She was finding that he had quite a lot of ties to this intruder and that getting him for herself was going to be harder than she had thought.

"I think we've talked enough about the ranch and cows," she almost sneered. "We don't want to bore your cousins. Tell us about the party. What do you have in store for us?"

"Whatever it is, it can't possibly be what you deserve," Sibyl professed innocently.

"There isn't anything really *planned*," Augusta intervened hurriedly. "We've tried to provide as much food and drink as we could and hope that everyone will enjoy themselves."

"We ought to set up some competitions if the weather holds," suggested Emma. "A party is much more fun when you have a little excitement."

"Sounds like a good idea to me," agreed Jesse. "The boys would love a chance to show off."

"I think it's only fair to make Burch promise not to enter more than one or two," Emma simpered, giving Burch a look that made Sibyl want to claw her eyes out. "It would not be gentlemanly to win all the prizes at your own party."

"But we don't have any prizes," Augusta pointed out.

"Surely you could make some ribbons or sashes or something of that kind. After all, you'll have the whole day to sit inside."

"No, we won't!" The unmistakable ring of challenge sounded in Sibyl's words. "If there are any contests, my aunt and I intend to take part."

"What can you do?" demanded Emma, making no attempt to conceal her sworn.

"We can have a target shoot and horse race for me, and a buggy race for my aunt."

"And she'll win," bragged Lasso, bringing his open palm down on the table hard enough to make the glasses jump. "You ain't seen nothing until you see this little gal with a whip in her hand." Augusta looked as though she'd rather have borne the stigma of being a useless female who sat inside and made ribbons, but with Lasso staking his pride on her, she knew she had no choice, so she smiled bravely and tried to look pleased.

Burch was nearly as surprised as Emma when Sibyl announced that she would enter two contests. "Will you have time? With so many guests arriving and so much to do before tomorrow night, it seems unfair to ask you to do even more." The concern in his voice made Sibyl all the more determined to go through with it.

"There's nothing that Rachel can't do, as long as Ned and Balaam help her. Everything is ready."

"Are you sure you're really up to it? All of the ladies coming have been reared out here," Emma pointed out.

Under her breath, Sibyl used one of the oaths she'd learned from listening to Balaam and Ned. "Fifty dollars says I'll win at least one of the contests." She'd show this brassy hussy she wasn't the only female who could shoot and ride.

"I was just worried that they won't be used to our rough sports," Emma said to Burch in honeyed tones. "I wouldn't want them to feel at a disadvantage." She got up from the table without waiting for Sibyl to rise. "I accept your wager. Come on, Burch, I want you to hear that song I was telling you about."

"You've got to hear it," insisted Auggie, jumping up as well. "It's the rage in Laramie." The men rose from the table, leaving Augusta and Sibyl still seated.

"Aren't you coming?" Burch asked when he saw that Sibyl and Augusta didn't mean to join them.

"No, you go on. We'll join you later," Sibyl said, trying not to show her jealousy.

"You might enjoy it. Emma's going to play her guitar."

"Only one instrument?" Sibyl drawled with feigned surprise, her eyes glinting dangerously. "I expected her to play the violin, the piano, sing both parts, and turn her own pages at the very least."

"I will see to the cleaning up," Augusta volunteered. "You go on and join the others."

"You'll do no such thing," Sibyl said, immediately regretting her outburst. "We'll do it together. Then we can both join Burch and his friends. Don't mind me," she said, turning to Burch. "I'm just a little anxious about the party."

"Are you sure that's all?" he asked, unable to grasp the notion that anyone could be jealous of Emma.

242

"Burch!" called Emma's piercing voice from the parlor. Get your saddlebags in here on the double."

"I'm sure," Sibyl assured him with a weak smile. "Now go to your guests before they come after you."

She would say no more, and feeling unable to plumb the reason for her unhappiness before Emma came to bodily drag him away, Burch followed the others to the front room. Augusta saw the desolate expression on her niece's face and rose to begin clearing the table without comment. With Rachel's help, they soon had everything carried to the kitchen.

"I could not stay here if he married her," Sibyl announced suddenly.

"No, I don't think you could," agreed Augusta, "but Burch is not interested in Emma Stratton as a wife."

"That one's a shrew," added Rachel, who almost never spoke.

"Then she shan't have him," said Sibyl decisively.

243

Chapter 20

The guests had been arriving since before dawn, nearly covering the prairie in front of the Elkhorn with their wagons. Some families had brought tents for sleeping, but most planned to adjourn to the cramped quarters of their wagons for the few hours during the next three days when they were not outside enjoying the spectacular weather, spirited company, and boundless food. The meals for most of the families not staying in the main house issued from communal campfires, generously fueled by scrap lumber from Sibyl's furniture crates, but an inexhaustible supply of barbecued pig, roasted elk, and venison steaks issuing from fires zealously tended by Ned guaranteed that this would be the most memorable of all the Christmas parties ever held at the Elkhorn.

"If I had known we were going to have a competition, I'd have brought my own rifle," complained Sue Ellen Roberts, contemptuously examining the Winchester carbine in her hand. "You can't expect anybody to shoot their best with borrowed firearms."

"You're welcome to all the practice you like," Lasso offered. "We can't start until the rest of the guests arrive."

"It'll take me that long to get used to this *gun*," Sue Ellen sneered disdainfully at one of Burch's finest weapons.

"You don't have to enter the contest," Emma suggested.

"And let you win?" hooted Sue Ellen. "Don't be a fool. This was probably your idea anyway, wanting to show off in front of Burch Randall. Well, this is one contest you won't win." With that, the indignant woman aimed her rifle at a distant post and reduced a small stone that had been placed on top of it to dust.

"You can't get any more accurate than that, strange rifle or no," observed Lasso, leaving Sue Ellen to work out her frustrations in her own way.

The ugly look on Emma's face gave way to a broad smile when she saw Burch heading their way.

"This place is busier than Cheyenne on hanging day," he declared, pointing to the groups of cowboys laying out courses, setting up targets, and preparing their own mounts and equipment for the upcoming contests. "This is going to be the best remembered Christmas party in the territory."

"By the winners, at least," added Lasso dryly. "When do you plan to start?"

"As soon as everybody gets here. I don't want to lose any of the sunlight. You must be living right, Emma. I don't ever remember a Christmas day like this." It was indeed a beautiful day, with an absolutely clear sky. A chinook wind, one of the warm spells so characteristic of Wyoming weather, had followed hard on the heels of the blizzard, and the sun and wind had virtually swept the plains clear of snow. The air was quite brisk, the creeks were running high, and the ground was still a little soggy, but the winter sun was doing its best to make the weather perfect for the day's activities.

Inside the house, Sibyl and Augusta continued to greet their guests and see them settled in their rooms. "Don't you want to practice shooting?" Augusta asked after the last guests had arrived and they had a moment to themselves.

"Do you want to try out your buckboard?"

"Absolutely not!" responded Augusta, becoming agitated. "I can't believe I let you talk me into entering this race."

245

"You know it was as much Lasso's doing as mine."

"He's so proud of teaching me, I couldn't let him down, any more than you could Burch."

"It's not the same at all. I already knew how to ride and shoot a little. Burch can't take the credit or blame for what I do today."

"Then why did you enter the contests, especially two of them?"

Sibyl turned away, as though not wanting to speak at all but determined to choose her words carefully. "I can't let that woman go on taking for granted that just because we were from the East, we're not good for anything except cooking and scrubbing. I doubt she thinks I would even make a good brood cow."

"Sibyl!

"I'm sorry, Aunt, but I can't stand the way everybody acts like I'm helpless and have to be protected and hemmed in and kept from things that might shock me. That's what I came out here to escape. To hear that harpy talk, you'd think I had never stepped out of the house without a parasol, at least one slave, and a freshly raked path to walk on. Do you know she actually had the nerve to tell Burch she felt *sorry* for me? She screwed up her face in that grimace she calls a smile and told him that it must be difficult for people like *me* to understand men like *him*, like we were from a different species."

"What did Burch have to say?"

"What does he ever say to her? Some meaningless nonsense and then he started asking her about what she planned to do in Cheyenne this winter. Which I hope he didn't do intentionally, because the slut invited him to spend the winter in Cheyenne too, telling him how much fun it was and how much he could learn from all the *other* important and successful men that would be there."

"Sibyl! I don't know where you picked up such words, but you've simply got to stop using them even if Miss Stratton deserves them, which I'm sure she does not," admonished her aunt.

"Sorry, Aunt, I get so angry I forget to watch my tongue."

"You have begun to do that quite a lot lately."

The games were a tremendous success. The men joined in with borrowed rifles, horses, or lassos, and everyone displayed the good sportsmanship expected during the Christmas season. Even men of unequaled skill, certain to win their events with ease, were welcomed as competitors by those who had no chance of besting them, but not without a little good-humored ribbing.

"We shouldn't allow Burch in," joked one of his competitors in the target shoot. "If he can pick off an elk halfway from here to Montana, how can he miss anything as big as a bull's eye?" Unfortunately, the women's rifle shoot was not characterized by the same charitable spirit. Sue Ellen Roberts, openly disdainful of her competition, proceeded to put every shot through the center of the target. Most of the other women were delighted to hit the target at all, but there was a grim duel between Emma and Sibyl for second position.

Emma expected to be bested by Sue Ellen, but it never entered her mind that her nearest competition for the runner-up spot would be Sibyl. Both were coming up for their last round at the target, and Emma was only twenty points ahead.

"I should let you go first," Emma said to Sibyl as she took her place at the line. "After all, *you* are the guest."

"In my own home?" queried Sibyl, slightly perplexed.

"I meant in Wyoming." Emma took aim too swiftly and her shot went wide, barely nicking the outside edge of the target. She glanced involuntarily at Sibyl, who continued to smiled sweetly. Emma's next two shots were in the third ring. "Damn," she muttered under her breath. She made herself breathe in slowly and deeply, steadied her aim, and placed the next two shots in the center of the target. She smiled politely to the onlookers but inwardly she raged; that first wild shot had given Sibyl the chance she needed.

Sibyl took her place at the line and paused a few moments to steady her nerves. She was close, but could she do it? She took careful aim and placed the first bullet in the fourth ring. Emma watched intently as Sibyl proceeded to put the next shots in the third and second rings. But that wasn't good enough. She would have to put the last two shots into the bull's eye just to tie. A wide smile of satisfaction spread over Emma's face.

"How's it going?" asked Burch, joining them from the men's rifle shoot that he'd just won.

"Sue Ellen has already won," Sibyl told him.

"I expected that. How're you doing?"

"She's laying third with a chance to tie for second," one of the ladies informed him. "All she has to do is put her last two shots into the center."

Burch didn't need to be told why Sibyl was trying so hard. "Stubborn, hardheaded, and blind," he parroted with a smile warm enough to toast her heart. "Is that enough or do you need egotistical, conceited, and insufferable?"

"That's plenty," she replied, trying not to laugh.

"What *are* you talking about?" demanded Emma.

"Just a little joke," Burch told her. Emma did not like to be kept out of anything involving Burch, and she showed it.

"Take your time and aim carefully," Burch said softly. Sibyl dared not look at him. She was afraid if his eyes looked at her the way his voice sounded, she would be unable to hit the target at all. She forced herself to concentrate, breathe deeply, and squeeze the trigger gently.

"Just barely," called the marker, "but it's a bull's eye."

"Now do it one more time," Burch encouraged her, pride and excitement in his voice. Sibyl's hands were shaking so badly she had to take a few steps away from the line to regain her composure. She couldn't bear to see that warm, admiring look fade from his eyes. She just *had* to hit the center of the target. With great deliberateness she took careful aim, closed her eyes for a tiny prayer, and fired.

"Dead center," called the marker, "and there's a tie for second."

"Good girl, I'm proud of you," Burch congratulated her warmly and gave her a carefully restrained kiss on the lips.

"What about me?" demanded Emma. "I tied her."

"Then you get a kiss too," agreed Burch, giving her a perfunctory peck on the cheek, "and Sue Ellen gets a bear hug." Before the startled woman could escape him, Burch swept her into him arms and kissed her very thoroughly on the mouth to loud applause.

"Let me go, you ruffian," squawked Sue Ellen, swinging her purse at Burch and trying to right her hat at the same time. She was a gruff woman who ruled her husband with an iron hand and frequently stated that she had little use for men, but the crowd suspected that had she been married to someone like Burch Randall, she might have revised her opinion.

Sibyl was very pleased to finish second, but having Emma share in her reward ruined it for her and she spent the time until the buckboard race brooding over the inequity of life that kept a *lady* from punching a *woman* in the nose.

Fortunately, she was able to forget her worries in rooting for Augusta, but her active help wasn't needed. Lasso had taken charge of Augusta, and the poor distracted dear had no chance to listen to any voice but the booming trumpet in her ear.

"Now remember, keep old Sally up to the bit. She's inclined to loaf on you if you give up her a chance, but there's not a better horse in this race. We've been over this ground so many times, you ought to know it like the back of your hand. You'll win it hands down, I know you will." Augusta looked so intent, so acutely miserable that Sibyl would have been willing to give her second if Augusta could

249

win. Sibyl didn't know why her aunt had finally let herself be talked into entering the race, but Augusta never did anything that wasn't important.

The race itself was something of an anticlimax. Augusta got Sally away first and never relinquished the lead. She handled the course like she'd been driving all her life, and in the straightaway held off the closing rush of a raw-boned sorrel driven by a robust young woman with flying red hair and a face covered with freckles.

"There, didn't I tell you ignoramuses she would win!" Lasso shouted to the entire gathering. "Put your money on the quality, they always come through," he exhorted everyone before he bodily plucked the nearly insensate Augusta from the buckboard and kissed her roundly in front of the appreciative spectators. Sibyl, astonished and incensed, started to protest, but Burch's restraining hand stopped her. Lasso put Augusta down, tucked her arm into his, and announced that they were "going inside and have a little something to celebrate."

"Don't stay too long," called Burch. "They'll bring the horses around for the ladies' race any minute now."

Sibyl's euphoria over her aunt's win dissipated quickly, plunging her back to earth with a thud. She had already been told that Emma had the best horse in this corner of the territory and was a sure winner of the race. What of her fifty dollar bet, and her pride?

"The only way she'll lose is if she falls off or the horse falls down," boasted her brother. The nods of agreement from the onlookers convinced Sibyl this was not just brotherly prejudice talking.

"Old Stratton had that horse brought in from the East— Pennsylvania, I think," Burch explained. "It's part Thoroughbred and part Morgan."

"That damned animal cost him a packet, too." Auggie had been drinking steadily since morning, and his wits and speech were not entirely clear.

Sibyl stood quietly while the horses were saddled and the rest of the guests gathered at the start. It was the next to last event of the day and nearly everyone had come to watch. "Worried?" Burch asked.

"A little," she admitted, trying to keep calm.

"You needn't be. Nobody can beat Emma's Lightning."

That's exactly the kind of name she would give her horse, thought Sibyl, incensed. If I only had one of the horses Daddy talked about owning before the war.

"Hospitality is the best of the rest. Just ride him as well as you can and you'll have no trouble finishing second."

"I didn't enter this race to finish second," Sibyl hissed, trying hard not to scream the words at him. "I wanted to win so you would pay attention to somebody besides that unnatural female."

"You make sure you pay attention to that canyon," Burch continued, caught off guard by Sibyl's vehement outburst. "There's still a lot of snow in it and it might be hard to see."

"Not as hard as it is for you to see that hussy is planning to marry you whether you want her or not," Sibyl hissed to Burch in a fierce undertone. "I wouldn't be surprised if she'd already picked out the date."

"She'd better make sure it's not in the middle of hunting season," Burch laughed easily. "I'm not missing a chance for a full elk rack, not even for Emma."

"Good luck, dear," Augusta said, appearing at her side. "Lasso and I will be rooting for you." Sibyl gave her aunt a swift hug and let Burch hoist her into the saddle, his lighthearted laugh still ringing in her ears. He hadn't even bothered to deny it!

"If you should find yourself close to Lightning on the return leg, remember he doesn't have a lot of stamina and tends to get mean when he's tired," Burch told her.

"If he's as good as you say, I won't get within twenty lengths," she said hopelessly and moved up to the starting line.

Emma was already prancing impatiently at the starting line, confident of victory and eager to get the race over so she could use it as another weapon in her assault on Burch. There were six horses entered and it was obvious that Emma's Lightning was the class of the field. His long lean limbs and powerful quarters spoke eloquently of the hot blood that coursed in his veins. The coarse and blocky mounts of the others were outclassed before the starter's gun sounded; only Hospitality could bear comparison to the Eastern bred, and even he could not claim descent from anything more fashionable than swift Indian ponies. Sibyl felt almost sick to her stomach as the starter fired his gun into the clear sky and Emma and Lightning bounded away, leaving the rest like they were standing still.

Emma was taking no chances this time and sent her horse along at a full gallop right from the start. Sibyl couldn't understand her tactics. It was a mile-and-a-half race and even a pure Thoroughbred couldn't keep up that kind of pace for the whole distance. But it looked as though he wouldn't need to, for by the time they had covered half a mile, Emma was over twenty lengths ahead. I'd have to sprout wings and fly over that canyon to win, Sibyl thought to herself.

But even as the thought flashed through her mind, she grasped at it, desperately seeking any possible way to avoid defeat. Was there a way to cross the canyon and avoid the long circle around it? Was there a break in the walls? No. She remembered riding its entire length, and jumping it was the only way across. If she could find the narrowest spot, could Hospitality jump it?

She had been jumping him when Burch wasn't around, but she didn't know his limit. She'd never put him to anything like the canyon. She patted the powerful neck and noted that even after three quarters of a mile his flanks were not wet and he wasn't breathing hard. She looked ahead at Lightning. Maybe he was beginning to run a little rough, she couldn't tell, but there was no sign that he was slowing down. Certainly not enough for her to catch him.

She waited for another furlong, hoping Lightning would show signs of tiring and begin to fight his rider, but the big chestnut continued to stride powerfully, and as the canyon came into view Sibyl knew the choice had been made for her. Lightning was nearly thirty lengths ahead now. Even if he staggered from here to the finish, she couldn't catch him; it had to be the canyon. Refusing to think of the consequences if she miscalculated, Sibyl swung her horse away from the charted course and stood up in the irons. All the contestants were riding astride, a fact that Augusta had deplored, and Sibyl understood that if she were to come through this without a broken neck, she couldn't afford to sit decorously in the saddle like a proper Eastern lady. She knew what she was looking for, the spot where the canyon narrowed to sixteen feet before curving away from the ranch and opening out into the shallow stream they splashed through on the first leg of the race. It was the only spot. She hoped the banks had not been softened by the melting snow. If the ground fell away under Hospitality's feet when they landed, they would suffer nothing worse than a thorough wetting. If it happened as they took off, well, she refused to think of that.

"What's she doing?" Lasso demanded urgently without taking his eyes off Sibyl. "There's no ford on that canyon." Burch's ruddy complexion was like rough chalk.

"Why should she need a ford?" asked Augusta, shocked at the look on Burch's face. "The course goes around the canyon."

"She's going to jump it," Burch said in a bare whisper.

"Jump?" yelped Lasso, his robust bass rising to a shrill tenor. "She'll kill herself."

"Please tell me what you're talking about," begged Augusta. "What is Sibyl going to jump and why should she kill herself?"

"The only way she can beat Emma is to take the short way

back, over that canyon," Lasso explained. Sibyl was now clearly perceived by the crowd to have separated herself from the rest, and a hush fell over the gathering, stilling the merry gossip and overflowing spirits as they realized she was headed straight for the open canyon. What had begun as a harmless competition among friends looking for a little fun had suddenly become a tryst with death, that constant but unacknowledged partner of their everyday existence, and no one misunderstood the seriousness of what Sibyl was about to do.

Snow blurred the outline of the canyon rim, and Sibyl's eyes searched intently for the exact spot she remembered. The other contestants realized what she planned to do and reacted with horror or stunned surprise; Emma, looking back over her shoulder, took a minute to understand before her smile of triumph shattered into an expression of pure rage. She understood only that Sibyl was attempting to steal her certain victory, and she was livid with fury. Her whip cut deeply into Lightning's heaving sides. The temperamental animal was reaching the end of a mile run at top speed, and the pangs of exhaustion stirred his ornery streak; it was badly aggravated by the sting of the whip and the raking of the spurred heels into his frothy sides. He threw up his head and tried to veer off course.

"Faster, you gutless half-breed," screeched Emma, lashing at him even more fiercely. Lightning's neurotic brain lost all interest in the race and centered instead on ridding himself of the human of his back. He had nearly a furlong lead over the rest of the field, but it dwindled swiftly as he sidled, detoured from the course, and tried to savage Emma's legs. Her mounting fury served to feed his opposition, and the two engaged in a fruitless battle of wills.

Meanwhile Sibyl had found the spot she was looking for. She rode up to the rim, pausing long enough to test the ground to satisfy herself it was firm. Then she made a wide circle and rode straight for the canyon. In seconds Hospitality was in full stride; the die was cast, there was no turning back. Sibyl leaned well over his withers, her eyes never leaving the pale tan rim outlined against the light shadows of the far side. A nagging worry that her horse might see the canyon yawning beneath him and try to turn at the last minute was shoved ruthlessly aside. That would end in tragedy; only a heroic jump could mean success.

She was completely unconscious now of the other riders and the hushed spectators. It was only Sibyl and her horse and the yawning canyon rushing at them with sickening quickness. She gripped the reins firmly and felt Hospitality gather himself. He had seen the canyon and was not afraid. She rose in the saddle, doing her best to hold him together as they neared the edge, then lifted him up as he soared into the air.

They seemed to hang in space forever, putting off the inescapable moment when she must learn whether her gamble had been successful. It felt so incredibly easy, so extraordinarily exhilarating to be floating in the air, twelve feet above the rock-strewn streambed below. She wondered how it would feel to crash into the stones, to have her fragile body lie broken in the muddy, ice-cold water. She was only twenty, too young to have her life come to an end.

Hospitality hit the hard-packed earth with a bone-jarring thud, his hind feet landing scant inches from the rim. He gathered his powerful muscles under him and bounded forward, carrying himself and his stunned rider to the finish line a full ten lengths ahead of the embattled Emma.

As though released from a still photograph, the crowd broke into loud shouts and rushed forward to embrace the winner. Death had been cheated once again, and the celebration was theirs as much as Sibyl's.

The release of the terrible tension made Sibyl so dizzy she was barely able to understand what was happening. She slid from the saddle into a pair of powerful arms.

"If you ever do anything like that again, I'll wring your

neck," Burch growled savagely. But he robbed his words of any threat by kissing Sibyl quite passionately. Exultant with her victory and the heavenly feeling of his arms around her, Sibyl kissed him back, heedless of the curious and cheering crowd. "By God, I'm proud of you," he managed to say at last. "That took guts."

"But please don't ever do it again," implored Augusta, ignoring the spectacle of her niece in a public embrace. "I don't think my heart could stand it."

"Damn fool thing to do, of course, but pretty as a picture," added Lasso, reflecting the opinion of most of the bystanders. "It's put Emma Stratton into a proper flame. She looks like a she-wolf at a fresh kill."

The description may have been a bit exaggerated, but it was plain to all Emma was ready to kill *something*. She dismounted from the still-rebellious Lightning and elbowed her way into the knot around Sibyl.

"You cheated!" she shrieked. "You didn't follow the course. I had you by more than twenty-five lengths."

"She's right," agreed Auggie. "Sibyl never would have won if she hadn't jumped that canyon."

"She didn't *win*, I did!" Emma screeched like a snarling beast. "She's got to be disqualified."

"Nothing was said about not jumping the canyon," Lasso pointed out. "We only drew the course around it because we figured you ladies wouldn't want to chance it."

"I wouldn't," agreed one of the contestants who had finally reached the finish line. "There's no power this side of the Devil that could make me put a horse to that ditch. But I don't see any reason why somebody else shouldn't, if they're willing to risk it."

"But it wasn't in the rules," insisted Emma. "I would have jumped it too if I'd thought we could. All it takes is a good horse," she said, sneering at Hospitality.

"She's right," agreed Sibyl, too happy at being in Burch's arms to care about the race. "I *did* leave the course. If you'll cancel our bet, I'll withdraw from the race. Then no one will have to throw me out."

Emma was overjoyed at the success of her protest but mystified to find that no one was particularly anxious to declare her the winner. Certainly no one picked her up in a crushing embrace.

"We'd better start the calf roping, or it'll soon be too dark," someone said.

"You coming?" Burch asked Sibyl.

"I don't think so. I've had enough excitement for one day, and everybody's going to be starved the minute the last calf hits the ground. Aunt and I had the best see that everything's ready."

"I'm competing." He clearly wanted her to be there.

"Well, maybe, but I've got to see about dinner first," Sibyl vacillated, knowing she'd be there whether anyone ate that night or not. Everyone moved off in the direction of the corrals, leaving Emma to savor an uncelebrated victory no one cared she'd won. The hard look of furious hatred made her brother anxious to get out of her way. He knew what his sister was like when she didn't get what she wanted, and he felt sorry for that pretty little Eastern girl.

Chapter 21

The party had been in full swing for more than three hours, and still it didn't show the slightest sign of slowing down. Sibyl had never seen such hard-drinking, hard-playing people in her life and wondered if anyone would be left standing when the dancing began. Even now the fiddles were warming up and the caller was exercising his throat with combinations of "swing your partner" and "do-si-do." The ladies, not exactly teetotalers but imbibing less heavily than the men, were anxiously awaiting this part of the evening. For a lucky few, it had been wonderful to eat food they hadn't worked to prepare and a slice of pure heaven to get up without having to worry about the dishes, pots, or pans, but still the high point of the evening was the dancing and the chance to show off their steps and stockings if their partner could swing them hard enough.

Sibyl's eyes instinctively found Burch, his head showing above all the rest, and her gaze hardened. Since the race, Emma had attached herself to him as though she were a part of him. Even one of the female guests had been moved to comment, "A man's underdrawers don't stick to him as tight as that woman sticks to Burch." Emma was constantly at his side, answering for him, interrupting others to bring Burch's attention back to herself, or simply talking so much everybody gave up trying to get a word in edgewise.

"You'd think she'd have sense enough to know you can't get a man like Burch by trying to corral him."

"Seems more like a bludgeoning if you ask me," remarked another young woman. "But then she probably thinks she's giving him a treat."

The fiddlers began scraping and everyone scrambled to find partners for the first dance. Emma, standing expectantly at Burch's side, was left furious and humiliated before the snickering women when he excused himself.

"The first dance always goes to the hostess. Lasso, get your hands off that woman," Burch called as his friend was about to lead Augusta to the floor. "She's mine. You drag Sibyl out here and we'll exchange for the next dance."

"Surely, with all these other young ladies present, you don't want to be tied to me."

"There's nobody here that's younger than you, *Miss* Hauxhurst, so let's hear no more of that. The way you won that race from start to finish has me completely dazzled."

"Stop that, or you'll have me blushing so Lasso will think you're telling me improper stories."

"You think a lot of his opinion, do you?" Burch asked suddenly serious.

"Yes, I do," Augusta answered simply.

"You won't find a better man," asserted Burch, swinging Augusta off the ground and so ruthlessly through the dance that she came off the floor breathless and was of two minds as to whether to ask Lasso to let her sit out the next one. But after Lasso handed Sibyl over to Burch, he put his arms around Augusta in a way that sent strength surging through her limbs, and she never again thought of sitting down.

"At last," Burch said, leading Sibyl to the floor. "I thought I was never going to get to even speak to you."

"You'd better say everything you want to during this

259

waltz," Sibyl advised him, glancing over her shoulder at the smoldering Emma, who was forcing her embarrassed partner to follow in Burch's wake. "I have the feeling that once she gets hold of you, it'll be impossible to shake Miss Stratton for the rest of the night."

"I like Emma, but it's pretty damned tiring to spend every blessed minute talking to the same person for three days. Even if it is about ranching."

"But I thought you never got your mind off the Elkhorn, that it was the only thing in your life that mattered," she said, her voice a little unsteady. Why was she exposing herself so? Was she so desperate for this man that she had to lay herself open for his insults?

"That may have been true at one time, but not any more. Your Aunt Augusta has shown me there's more to life than a ranch and cows."

"Aunt Augusta!" exclaimed Sibyl, too surprised to keep her voice down.

"Did you want me, dear?" Augusta called, too lost in her own world to be of use to anyone.

"No, she changed her mind," said Burch, and the two of them giggled like little children. Sibyl's spirits skyrocketed so swiftly that she felt dizzy.

"What do you mean by saying Aunt Augusta changed you?" Sibyl asked in a lower voice.

"I saw in her what you would be if you weren't so distrustful of people — men especially, me in particular."

Sibyl stiffened.

"You're both of the same family and background, yet your aunt is at peace with everybody, while you're at war. I can still see you the first morning you fixed breakfast, your hair up, flour all over, humming some tune, and perfectly content with what you were doing. Just like Augusta does all the time. I knew right then that inside that harridan I met at the river was a girl with the spirit and courage of the spitfire, as well as the inner strength and beauty of her aunt. The only problem was to figure out how to find it."

Sibyl made some inarticulate noise that sounded like a sniff and accepted the use of Burch's handkerchief gratefully.

"I didn't even know how to start, and what with you arguing and disputing nearly every word that came out of my mouth, I had all I could do to keep from saying things you'd never forget. But I figured if you didn't learn to trust me, you wouldn't ever trust anybody. And after that first night, I knew if I couldn't have you, I didn't want anybody else. It was sort of a desperate situation for both of us, because you said some things that are pretty hard for a man to swallow."

"I know," admitted Sibyl, wanting so much to dissolve into his arms, "and I was sorry for them, but I couldn't tell you. I was afraid you would think I was weak, and I was determined to make you admit that I was just as good as any man."

"After today, everybody knows you have more courage than nine out of ten men," Burch told her proudly. "Your haystacks proved your brains and this house your domestic skills. What other fields are you set to conquer?"

Sibyl itched to tell him that the only field that mattered was his heart, but she couldn't, not in front of so many people. She wasn't sure she could tell him at all. She was getting used to her vulnerability, but it still scared her.

"I don't think I'll tell you," she said shyly. "Besides, here comes Emma and determination is written all over her."

Burch grimaced slightly. "I know I'm supposed to be nice to my guests, especially old friends, but this one is getting a little tiresome."

"Then dance with the other ladies. They'd love it and I'm sure they can think of something to talk about other than how much fun it would be for everybody if you were to decide to spend the winter in Cheyenne."

"And leave you prey to all these marauding cowboys who have tasted your cooking and seen you ride? That's not taking good care of my belongings."

"I'm not one of your belongings, Burch Randall, and don't you go thinking it."

"Is that a challenge?" he responded with a swift surge of passion.

"No," she said hurriedly, afraid to trust her own response. "Now go ask Sue Ellen to dance before Emma pounces on you."

She didn't get a chance to exchange more than a few words with Burch during the rest of the evening, but he took her advice and danced with every woman and girl in the place, much to their delight and the merriment of the onlookers. He even did a polka with a wizened little grandmother, who retired to her chair breathless, red in the face, and feeling at least a decade younger than she had in years.

"If I was fifty years younger, you young scamp, I'd give that Stratton gal a run for her money."

"If you were fifty years younger, I'd let myself get caught," Burch said, giving her a hearty kiss.

"Fine-looking young man," the old gal was heard to murmur several times during the course of the evening. "He's got a great backside on him, too."

"Grandma," exclaimed her scandalized granddaughter, ineffectually smothering a giggle. "You know you shouldn't talk like that."

"Why not? You don't think they don't discuss us piece by piece, do you? And I'll lay you odds that Stratton gal don't come off very good when compared against that cousin of Burch's. Against either one of them Eastern gals, from what I can see." The young woman finally succeeded in halting her grandparent's embarrassing comments but could hardly wait to whisper them into Emma's ear later in the evening. Emma reply was pungent and not in the least polite.

At two o'clock, the party was still going strong. Augusta and some of the older women had already retired to bed, but the younger women and the men were looking like they would make a night of it. Sibyl had had a long, exhausting day and was tired. The emotional strain of wondering if Burch's affections were being breached by Emma Stratton had taken a terrible toll on her energies, but hardly more than her jump over the canyon. Every time she thought of what might have happened, she started to shake. How could she have done anything so incredibly insane? She pushed it from her mind, only to have it come back. Watching Emma pursue Burch relentlessly throughout the evening had sapped the rest of her energies, even though the looks of resignation Burch cast her over Emma's shoulder did much to support Sibyl's sagging spirits. She would have given anything for one little hug, but anyone could see that if Burch attempted to put his arms around Sibyl, he was going to have to put them around Emma as well.

Sibyl met Burch coming off the dance floor with Emma for at least the tenth time. "I'm going to bed," she told him, fatigue clear in her voice.

"But it's still early," objected Emma.

"There's a lot to be done tomorrow, and I can't afford to sleep late," Sibyl replied caustically, unable to resist a dig.

"I *never* sleep late," declared the indomitable Emma. "Morning is my favorite part of the day."

"Well, it's not mine, but it always seems to come first so there's nothing to be done but face it," said Sibyl, resigned to saying good night to Burch in front of Emma. "Make sure all the fires and lamps are out before you come up," Sibyl reminded Burch.

"How did you ever survive without her?" Emma smirked.

"Not nearly as comfortably as he does now," snapped Sibyl bitterly as she spun on her heel. Try as she might, she could not like Emma Stratton. And she didn't try very hard any more.

Chapter 22

Next morning, Sibyl was in low spirits. Most of her guests were indulging in a rare morning spent in bed, but the mothers of small children were up and Sibyl saw that they had breakfast for their youngsters, who had gone to bed early the previous evening and were now anxious to get out and enjoy what promised to be another beautiful day. She spoke pleasantly to the women and discussed such little things as Melissa's teeth and Joey's boils, but she was conscious of a desire to have all her guests gone from the Elkhorn.

She was tired of tending to everyone's needs and having to ignore her own. She was tired of having to share Burch with strangers and finding nothing left for herself. It didn't help to know that Burch didn't love Emma when it was Emma who was in his arms instead of Sibyl: *She* was tied up all evening slicing cake and seeing that the beer didn't run out; *she* went to bed early, leaving them alone to do heavens only knew what; *she* was forced to trust Burch to resist the temptation Emma was all too ready to toss his way. More than once

Sibyl longed to slap that pouting red mouth and claw at those drooping eyelids until every shred of superiority was erased from Emma's smirking face. Her constant needling was so hard to endure that Sibyl had tried to stay out of her way, but that meant she had stayed away from Burch as well. If it was better for her to see less of Emma, it was much worse to see so little of Burch.

It was no wonder she hadn't slept well and now felt rather headachy, probably from tossing about most of the night. Well, she'd soon have plenty of time to rest because everybody was going home the next day, including Emma, and then the house would be theirs once again. But in the meantime, her headache was getting much worse, and if she had to continue being the smiling hostess for another day and a half, it would be a lot easier if she took one of her powders.

She carried her coffee cup to the kitchen. Every available surface was piled high with anything that could contain food. It would take Rachel the better part of a day to wash everything and put it away. The rest of the house was in much the same state. Sibyl smiled wryly to see the decorations they had worked so hard to put up either pulled down or pulled apart. It was just as well they weren't expecting any more guests till spring. It would take them that long to get the house back in order.

In spite of the disarray, she felt pleased with herself as she mounted the steps to her bedroom. It had been a good party, one it would be hard for her to match next year, but everyone seemed to expect her to try and they were already putting in requests for rooms. It had been a lot of trouble, but it was nice to know that all their hard work had been rewarded. It was even more pleasant to know that Burch had been pleased; he had told her so at least a dozen times during the last three days.

When she reached the top of the landing she could hear

the small noises made by the guests moving about in their rooms. Burch's door was closed. He'd probably stayed up till dawn, she thought as she found her headache powders, and won't get up till noon if I don't wake him. Bother. Her pitcher and water glass were not in her room. Then she remembered she had put them in Emma's room because there hadn't been enough for all the guests. She could use Burch's water and wake him up at the same time. After all, it was really *his* party, and he ought to be up. She opened his door quietly and stuck her head in.

Burch stood across the room with his back to the door, naked to the waist. Emma stood in front him, clad only in a thin negligee, her body pressed against his and her arms wrapped tightly around his neck.

"It feels so good just to be next to you," Emma moaned in a voice husky with passion. "I don't know how I could stand to wait so long."

The headache powder spilled from Sibyl's nerveless hand. For a moment she was unable to think or move; it was too monstrous, too completely horrible to be true. She backed away from the door, a dry sob catching in her throat, and then she raced for her own room. Burch had lied to her! Every word was a pretense, a subterfuge to keep her from seeing the cesspool of lust that corrupted his heart. There, in the very bed where he had held her in his arms and sworn he cared only for her, he had desecrated their love and their home with that tramp.

How could she have been such a fool? Why had she let herself be taken in by this big, brawny cowboy in Levi's? She paced the room, feeling the waves of hysteria and nausea welling up within her, threatening to take her reason and her control. "Aunt Augusta!" she cried, with an agonized moan, and ran to find the only human being who understood her and loved her without reservation.

But Augusta wasn't in her room. The four-poster bed was

neatly made up with the white handmade bedspread's geometric patterns exactly fitted to the rectangular shape of the mattress. Holding back a desire to call for her aunt at the top of her voice, Sibyl hurried downstairs, looking in each room until she entered the small one off the main parlor. She was brought up short by the picture of her aunt, radiantly smiling, seated next to Lasso Slaughter, whose countenance was covered by an equally delirious expression. To Sibyl's utter astonishment, she realized that Lasso had both of her aunt's hands in his, and Augusta was making no attempt to remove them.

"Sibyl, darling," Augusta said without rising, "Lasso has just asked me to marry him and I've accepted. Please wish me happy."

My God, no! Two such horrible disasters couldn't happen in the same minute. It had to be a dream. Maybe she was in Hell. Yet her aunt's image didn't fade and Lasso's voice reached her as effortlessly as ever.

"I'm the happiest man alive. Don't know what I've done to deserve such a prize as Gussie, but I sure aim to see that she doesn't regret it."

Sibyl couldn't move, she couldn't say the words, *any words*, that would congratulate her aunt. She felt bereft, betrayed.

"I'm sure this is no surprise to you, not after you've teased me about Lasso for so long."

Not a surprise! She was stunned, speechless, sick! How could this have happened?

"We've decided against a long engagement. With the girls to care for and the ranch to run, there just isn't time for it.

No, her aunt *had* to wait; she had to give Sibyl time to make her change her mind.

"What your aunt is trying to say is I'm impatient to have her to myself, and she's promised we can be married on New Year's."

"But that's just six days," Sibyl managed to speak at last.

"We'll never manage to get things ready." What am I saying! I've got to stop her before it's too late.

"I knew you'd be happy for me," Augusta said, rising and giving Sibyl a huge hug. She was trembling with excitement, and when she looked into Sibyl's eyes, all of her niece's resistance melted. Augusta's eyes glowed and her small mouth, usually so prim and firm, was relaxed in a smile that betokened complete happiness.

"We decided to ask everybody to stay and celebrate the wedding with us," Lasso told her, nearly bursting with pride. "I want the entire territory to know that I got the best and prettiest little woman in the whole world."

"Lasso, how can you say such a thing with Sibyl standing right in front of you?" asked Augusta, blushing with pleasure.

"Your niece knows I think she's pretty as a spring heifer, but I told her from the first she couldn't hold a candle to you, and she *can't*."

"There's nothing else to do when a man's that foolish over you," said Augusta, fondly looking at her beloved. "If I don't marry him, I don't know what he might do to himself."

"And don't forget the girls," Lasso added.

"I'm not, but I don't want you to think that I'm marrying you because they need a mother."

"I know you're not," Lasso said in a voice completely lacking in heartiness, "and that's the biggest surprise of all."

Sibyl fought to get control of herself. The double blow threatened to destroy her reason. She felt unable to think, to understand, to even *endure* another minute in this horrible house. She mumbled something and turned to leave, to find someplace to be alone before she began to scream in loud, piercing wails. To her unspeakable horror, Burch walked into the room.

"I've been looking everywhere for you three. Why are you hiding here when there's a house full of people wanting to see

269

you?" Burch paused, taking in Sibyl's stricken countenance and the radiant happiness of the couple, and burst into a roar of laughter. "By God, you did it, didn't you, old friend? And she said yes. I can tell by that ridiculous grin on your face."

"Yep, she did," Lasso answered foolishly.

"Now why would you go and throw yourself away on an old hunk like that, Aunt Augusta, when I've been making up to you for months and you wouldn't even give me so much as a good night kiss?"

Augusta blushed rosily and Lasso roared with good humor. Sibyl thought she would scream, but her agony was not to end quickly. Emma Stratton, the brazen, brass-faced whore, came sidling into the parlor like the serpent she was.

"I thought I heard your laugh, Burch. What are you doing in here?"

"Augusta and Lasso have just gotten themselves engaged. When are you getting married?"

"New Year's, and we're inviting everybody to stay and celebrate with us."

"Six more days," exclaimed Emma. "I don't know if I can stand so much fun. The only thing that would make it better would be if there was to be a double wedding," she said meaningfully. "That *would* be something to celebrate."

"I don't think Sibyl could survive more than one at a time," Burch said, turning with sympathy to his beloved. "This party has just about taken the starch out of her as it is. You're looking a little pale this morning."

"I have a headache," Sibyl whispered, wondering what she had ever done to deserve such torment.

"I don't think I ever had a headache," Emma simpered.

"I have some headache powders," offered Augusta, moving toward her niece.

"No, you stay here. I've got some of my own," she said, desperately needing to get away from them, from everyone, until she could come to grips with the dissolution of her whole existence. "I think I'll just lie down for a while. Will you see that everyone is taken care of for me?"

"Of course, dear, but are you sure you wouldn't like for me to come with you?"

"No," she insisted, trying not to shout the word, "there's no need for both of us to be locked away, not on such a day as this." She kissed her aunt and forced herself to speak the hated words. "I'm very happy for you. I've been expecting it for weeks." She finished up with a hiccupped sob.

"Are you sure you're all right?" asked Burch, genuinely worried about her now.

"I'll be fine. I just need a little quiet."

"You poor thing," said Emma with spurious sympathy. "Does that headache make you feel absolutely sick?"

"No, only people can do that." Sibyl realized that she had really upset Augusta now, and she hurried to apologize. "Forget what I said; I'll be all right in a little bit. Now go tell everyone your news and don't give me a thought," she urged and almost ran from the room.

Sibyl moved through the next week like a sleepwalker. A terrible pain, like a heavy weight, pressed down on her chest every waking moment, making it hard for her to breathe, to even move. A great lassitude had overtaken her; some mornings it was almost impossible to get out of bed. Sleepless nights followed days that passed like a dream. But that dream was a nightmare filled with pictures of Emma: Emma in Burch's arms, Emma kissing Burch, Emma running the ranch, Emma taking over everything that was important. The image of Emma grew larger and larger until it towered over Burch, while her own image shrank until it was almost impossible to see her at all.

The reality of her days was hardly different. She spent all of her time with Augusta, cooking endless meals, making preparations for the wedding, and going through the house packing up furniture to be sent in wagons to the Three-Bars. Augusta was too taken up with her own plans to penetrate Sibyl's facade of tired good cheer.

Burch seldom saw her at all; she avoided him as much as she could. When she had to see him, she made sure Augusta or Lasso was with them and then confined her conversation to the practical considerations that concerned the wedding. That wasn't too difficult because Emma rarely allowed the conversation to stray far from herself or weddings, hopefully hers.

It would have been impossible for Burch to be unaware of Sibyl's terrible unhappiness, but he thought it was because of Augusta's decision to marry Lasso. She had to grow accustomed to it sooner or later, he thought, so she might as well begin now. But he didn't understand why she would withdraw from him when he tried to talk to her, or why she would reply with forced gaiety that she was too busy to have time for him just now and sent him off to entertain Emma.

EMMA! That woman had become a curse. She jumped at the opportunity of spending an extra six days at the Elkhorn, even though her brother had to leave.

"You can see to the ranch, Auggie," she had said blithely. "There's no need for me to return as well."

"But you know you never like anything I do."

"Then consider this your chance to prove me wrong," she said, trying to get rid of him quickly. "And don't come back until I send for you," she whispered fiercely when she saw him off.

The weather continued to hold, and Emma and Burch spent most of their days out on the range where the cowboys were doing their best to repair the ravages of the last blizzard. Sibyl had trained herself not to even hear Emma when she gushed, "Seeing Burch run a ranch has been a privilege. I know I've learned more in one week than I've

272

learned in a lifetime."

But to Augusta Sibyl was less reticent.

"I'll bet her eyes haven't left Burch long enough to know whether we're raising cows or kangaroos." But Sibyl's hold on her temper finally snapped when Emma said at least one time too many, "I simply *must* have one of your little bulls."

"Isn't one male enough for you, or must you have every one you see?" That had stopped the conversation cold, and earned her an uncomprehending look from Augusta and an angry glare from Burch.

"I've told you they belong to Sibyl," Burch repeated, weary of Emma and her obsession with Sibyl's bulls.

"You shouldn't have spoken to Emma like that," he said when he at last caught Sibyl alone in her room doing the final handwork on Augusta's wedding dress. "Emma's a pretty robust gal, but her feelings can be hurt."

"I wouldn't worry about her feelings if I were you. I doubt she's heard a single word I've said since she's been here, which seems like a *lifetime.*"

"I know you don't like Emma. . . ."

"No, I don't, but I wouldn't worry about that either. You seem to be making it up to her."

"And what do you mean by that?"

"What could I mean? She hasn't left your side since she got here. I'm surprised she doesn't sleep with you. At least then we could offer her room to the Jeffries, and they wouldn't have to sleep in their wagon."

"As a matter of fact, I like the Jeffries more than I like Emma," he said, tired of Emma's constant presence. "I wish they did have her room."

"Try and convince the Jeffries. You haven't been seen in *their* company for eight days."

"Good Lord, you sound jealous."

"Me!" Sibyl nearly shrieked. "Jealous of that scandalous hussy?"

273

"Don't talk about Emma like that. You don't have to like her . . .

"I *don't*!"

". . . but that's no excuse for calling her names. I've known Emma since we were children and, well, she's almost like my sister." Sibyl tried to achieve a laugh that could indicate the full extent of her scorn, but it sounded more like a hysterical titter.

"You couldn't insult any woman more completely if you tried. I dare you to say that to her face."

"She'd be complimented."

"She'd *say* that was the nicest thing you'd ever said to her, but inside she'd be ready to die and willing to kill any female who'd overheard it."

"You don't understand Emma."

"And you don't understand women. You never have understood me . . ."

"That's the truth!"

". . . and you don't understand Emma Stratton if you don't think being your sister isn't the furthest thing from her mind. And if that *is* what you think, then *you've* got some pretty bizarre ideas about family relations."

"Since you're the expert, maybe you can answer a question for me."

"What?"

"How did a marvelous lady like your aunt end up with a niece like you and," he pursued, ignoring the indignant gasp, "why does she keep on loving a bad-tempered shrew who's never pleased no matter what people do for her."

"What did you ever do to please me?" Sibyl inquired.

"If I weren't a gentleman, I'd tell you."

Sibyl flushed crimson and rose from her seat in a towering rage, uncertain whether she wanted to kill him now, or wait until she found him in Emma's arms and slay them both at the same time.

"If you were a gentleman, you would never even think of making such a reference."

"Why? Are you ashamed of it?"

"I'm ashamed to think that I was so easily taken in; that I could fall, just as dozens of others have no doubt fallen, for a set of powerful thighs and a few sweet promises." Sibyl brushed the spurting tears away from her eyes. "Yes, I'm ashamed to think I was such a fool that I gave you what I proudly denied every other man, even those who asked honorably."

"I never lied to you," Burch spoke softly, reaching out to her. "I do love you."

"Touch me, Burch Randall, and I will scream and scream and *scream* until every man and woman in this place is at that door demanding to know exactly what your intentions are."

"My intentions *were* to talk to you, to try and knock some sense into that hard head of yours, but nothing seems to be able to penetrate that thick hide or that damned snotty-nosed Virginia superiority."

"That's just like a man, especially the variety that grows among the sagebrush, to think that *knocking* some sense into a woman's head is the answer to everything, even clearing his own conscience."

"What is wrong with you?" Burch asked, completely bewildered. "I left here before Christmas after the best four days of my life. I could hardly wait to get back. I even let myself be fooled into thinking you felt the same way."

Sibyl's resistance almost buckled. If she could just believe him; but she couldn't, she had seen the evidence with her own eyes.

"And what do I find waiting for me when I do get back? A virago, clawing at anyone and anything that tries to come near her, a spitfire that denies her own words, her own body."

"Oh, foul," Sibyl cried furiously. "My body can't tell the difference between love that's meant to be shared between

275

two people and the kind that's bought and sold, but my mind can. And I won't settle for that, not if I have to go to my grave a virgin."

"It's a little late for that."

"Beast!" she wailed, then snatched up a small figurine and threw it at him. Burch caught it dexterously.

"Careful, you don't want to break it. It came from Virginia, and everything from Virginia is *priceless*."

"Not quite," retorted Sibyl bitterly. "I seem to have come rather cheaply."

"Don't talk about yourself like that. I won't let you."

"Why should you care? You got what you came for."

"You know that's not true."

"Do I? I can't tell you how ashamed I am to admit I actually *believed* that you loved me, that you wanted me to be your wife."

"We never discussed marriage."

"I *know* that now, but you see I was an innocent fool. I thought when a man said he loved a woman, he also meant that he wanted to marry her. But we're old-fashioned in Virginia, and I guess our ways are outmoded. I suppose I'm outmoded too, but I can't change that now, not that way."

"But I don't want you to change. I love you just as you are, and I do want you to be my wife."

Sibyl thought her heart would break. "A week ago I thought those were the sweetest words any woman could hear. I guess I should be thankful I know better now but, oh God, how I wish I'd never had to learn."

Confused, angry, and completely out of patience, Burch strode across the room and dragged Sibyl roughly out of the chair and into his arms.

"See if this has gone stale after a week." He kissed her with all the fire and passion Sibyl remembered so well. Too desolated to fight and too hungry for even a scrap of his love, Sibyl returned his embrace. "I knew you couldn't deny you wanted me. Your body wouldn't let you. Now why don't you stop this ridiculous nonsense and tell me what's wrong." He was stunned to see her crying almost uncontrollably.

"You'll never understand," she wept. "You've had your way; you got what you wanted. Now go away and leave me alone."

"Good God, woman, I've said I love you and that I want to marry you. What more can you want?"

"Nothing. What more could any woman want? Only tell me how long I get to keep you before I start having to share." The voice was completely cynical, obliterating her utter desolation of spirit, and Burch's temper snapped.

"You are hard to the core, aren't you? Tell me, did *you* mean it when you said you loved me, or were you just after any man willing to make you a woman? Couldn't you find anybody in Virginia with the guts to take on the job?"

The transformation in Sibyl was instantaneous. "Nothing I've ever done has warranted such a low, vile accusation. There are no words adequate to tell you how much I regret what has happened between us. I believed, I hoped, that I had found someone who could understand that I had to be more than a shell, following a man about, doing what he asked, thinking as he told me. My happiness at finding what I had sought for so long is my only possible excuse for behavior whose memory alone causes me an agony of mortification."

"Sibyl, don't let's do this do this to each other. This is no way . . ."

"Sibyl, dear, are you still up?" Augusta was startled to see Burch. "Oh, if I'd known you were here . . ."

"It's all right. He was just asking me about tomorrow. He's done, and I've got just a few more stitches on your dress."

"You poor thing. I had no idea you would have to work so long. I could have worn another dress."

"I wanted to do it, and it'll only take me a few minutes

277

more. See? Isn't it lovely?" She turned back to Burch, but the glassy look told him there was no more to be said. "I think that finishes our business. Good night."

Burch looked like he would say more, but Sibyl's eyes grew harder.

"Please, no more. Nothing can change things now." Burch turned and left, and Sibyl, her heart breaking, turned to her aunt, once more forced to put on a smile to mask the torment that was destroying her.

Chapter 23

The wedding was the most difficult ordeal of Sibyl's short life. She and Burch had not exchanged a word all day, but she didn't need words to sense his presence, didn't need the sound of his voice to know that he was longing to speak to her. The very air around them was charged with unspoken love and unacknowledged longing, unacknowledged on her part at least. Time and time again, she looked up to find him staring at her. Burch's piercing gaze never fell before hers; it would always be Sibyl who finally looked away.

The ceremony itself was held in the ranch room in front of a crackling fire. Burch was the best man and Sibyl, as maid of honor, had to stand listening to the words she had hoped would one day be spoken for them. She choked back bitter tears, knowing that now those words would *never* be spoken for her—with Burch or anyone else. She tried not to let her tears flow freely, but no one except Burch was watching her today; all eyes were on Augusta and Lasso.

At the words "Do you take this man?" Sibyl had to fight to keep from running out of the room. Only knowing what terrible embarrassment it would cause her aunt kept her feet firmly planted, but she dared not look at Burch. That would be too much. None of the guests saw anything wrong when, at the closing words, she flung herself at her aunt, sobbing hysterically, and then transferred her watery embrace to Lasso. After all, weren't you were supposed to cry at weddings?

Only Emma, her eyes and understanding sharpened by jealousy, understood the true meaning of the looks that passed between Burch and Sibyl, and it was like a knife in her belly. But she had no intention of relinquishing her quarry. She might never be able to enjoy Burch's love, but she was determined to marry him, and she saw her chance in Sibyl's rejection. All she needed was an excuse to stay on at the Elkhorn, and she had it in Auggie's failure to return for her.

The next few hours passed in a whirl of activity and an endless round of congratulations, best wishes, and toasts to the happy couple. They had decided against a honeymoon because Lasso's little girls were still not completely recovered from the influenza.

"I don't mind in the least," Augusta told Lasso when he apologized for postponing the trip. "I don't like to travel during the winter, and I'd rather not wait until spring to be married. You'll be even busier then. Besides, I never was comfortable in large resorts or hotels. I'd rather spend the time getting used to my new home and learning how to make you and the girls comfortable."

Burch thought how fortunate his friend was to find such a woman. Some might have been willing to make the sacrifice, but none with such a genuine, cheerful smile. He wondered what Sibyl would have done.

Sibyl accompanied her aunt when she went to change into the dress she would wear on the ride to Lasso's ranch, but Augusta was so excited she could hardly find a buttonhole or hook. "Here, let me," Sibyl said, quickly doing up the buttons.

"You know that I don't want any more of the things here, don't you?" Augusta said to Sibyl.

"There's still a lot that's yours."

"But Lasso's house is already furnished. I really don't have anywhere to put it."

"It's just like you to be giving everything you have to somebody else, but one of these days, when you *do* go on your honeymoon, I'm going to pile it all in a wagon and have Ned take over."

"I wouldn't be able to close the doors," Augusta said, laughing lightheartedly. "No, you keep it. With such a large house, you and Burch won't have any trouble finding a use for it." The smile froze on Sibyl's face, making her look white and tired.

"I hope you'll get some rest after everyone leaves, dear," Augusta urged, concerned at Sibyl's drawn look. "You look worn to the bone."

"Don't worry, I don't plan to come out of my room for days." At least not until Burch leaves the house, she thought.

"I'll come back in a day or two and help you get everything back in order."

"You'll do no such thing," Sibyl stated emphatically. "You'll have your hands full with a new house and family, and I have Rachel to help me, not to mention Ned and Balaam. I ought to come help *you* move in. Never fear," she relented when a slight frown crossed her aunt's brow. "I promise not to intrude on you before the spring thaw."

"That's not it, dear. You *know* Lasso and I would welcome you and Burch at any time. I just realized that I was leaving you here all by yourself, and that's precisely what I came out here to prevent."

"Console yourself that you're only ten miles away instead of two thousand."

"There is that, but your mother would never approve."

"I doubt mother would approve of me under any circumstances," Sibyl professed bitterly.

"You and Burch have been fighting again," Augusta sighed, "and I thought you were getting along at last."

"No more than usual, but he's leaving right after you, so

I'll have weeks of solitude to recover my temper. Now you hurry downstairs before Lasso marches in here and carries you out over his shoulder."

"As if he would."

"That's exactly what he *would* do if he thought anything was going to keep you from him one minute longer than was absolutely necessary."

Augusta turned pink with pleasure. "You know, when I decided to come with you, I never thought to be married myself. It was the furthest thing from my mind that with you so young, beautiful, smart, and rich anyone would even notice me. I hoped so fervently that you could find the kind of happiness I have found with Lasso. I thought that maybe Burch . . ." Her sentence trailed off.

"It looks like I'm the one who shouldn't be thinking of marriage," Sibyl said, trying to keep her feeling of total desolation out of her voice. "And Burch is certainly not the answer to my prayers or my needs, however much he may be chased after by other women."

"I wouldn't place too much importance in that. After all, he didn't get caught," Augusta said, moving briskly to collect her purse and hat. "But he's not going to stay that way forever."

"I know. It's a good thing I didn't sell my house. At least I'll have some place to go back to."

Augusta studied her niece's face closely and did not like what she found. "I don't think you will find Virginia the same as you left it."

Sibyl did not reply and they walked downstairs without another word.

Augusta was immediately engulfed by well-wishers, and except for a kiss and a softly whispered, "May you someday be as happy as I am today," Sibyl was unable to speak to her or even touch her again. Suddenly she felt terribly alone. For the first time in her life, she was without her mother or her aunt. She was on her own.

No sooner had the wedded couple departed than there was a flurry of packing and stowing gear into wagons, bedrolls, and even knapsacks. In less than an hour, Sibyl and Burch found themselves alone with Emma.

"I don't know what has happened to Auggie," she reiterated, rather unconvincingly. "He knows he has to take me to Cheyenne. I'm worried that something may have happened to him."

"Probably lost his way," said Burch, wishing Emma anywhere but the Elkhorn. "Or forgot what day it is."

"Auggie's not dumb," Emma said, with no fraternal feeling, "but it's a fact he can't manage the ranch alone. My husband will have to be an expert rancher. Naturally, he will have a free hand at the T-Bar."

"I hope you don't mind if I leave you to Burch while I see about returning this house to some semblance of order," snapped Sibyl. "As for your *expert rancher*, you'd better hurry and find him before your springtime bloom matures into summer's squash."

"I have to go out on the line this afternoon," Burch told Sibyl, ignoring Emma's indignant gasp. Sibyl didn't answer but just stared at Burch, waiting for him to continue.

"I want to talk with you before I leave."

"Okay, but you'll have to hurry. I have a lot to do." Burch looked so pointedly at Emma she was forced to take the hint.

"Talking secrets? Well, I guess I should see about packing my clothes. But what will I do if Auggie doesn't show up tomorrow?"

"Stay here till he does," said Burch, anxious to get rid of her. But Emma was only too pleased to go; she had gotten what she wanted and could tell from the stony look in Sibyl's eye that their quarrel would not be resolved today.

"May I have my same room?"

"You can have any damned room you want," Burch answered so impatiently that Emma almost laughed to herself.

"It's a shame you're not brother and sister. Then you could have a *real* fight," she said, and walked out.

"I *detest* that female," hissed Sibyl. "I never want to see her again."

"There's nothing wrong with Emma. . . ." Burch began, uninterested.

"I realize you think she's a paragon, but I don't happen to agree with you."

"Why do we always end up talking about Emma?" he demanded in exasperation.

"Probably because you two act more like Siamese twins than old friends. I can't see one without the other."

"I go for weeks without giving her a thought."

"Don't let her hear that; it will break her heart."

"I'm tired of talking about Emma. I want to talk about you."

"Oh, I see, now that Emma's about to leave, you have to look about for someone else and you're ready to fall back on me, is that it?"

"I don't know why you would say such a stupid thing, but no, that's *not* it."

"Now I'm back to being stupid, too. Oh well, I shouldn't have expected my changed status to last very long. But then I'm just a female. Now that the company's gone, I suppose I should go back to cooking and acting like a woman ought."

"I don't know what's wrong with you. I thought you were looking forward to this party, but from the minute the first guest walked in that door, you've been like a snarling wildcat. You weren't anywhere near this bad when you got here."

"There!" she said, pouncing like the wildcat he compared her to. "Now I know how you really feel about me."

"I doubt you know how anybody feels about anything, and that includes yourself. I've never met anybody so full of foul humors, hot temper, and unreasoning fits. Your face and body nearly drive me crazy, but a man would be insane to let

284

himself love you. It'd be safer to fall in love with a lynx."

"Have you any more endearing observations to make?" she asked with freezing politeness. "Don't feel obliged to hurry or leave anything out. The cleaning can wait."

"Don't worry, I won't waste any more time. I thought I could talk some sense into you if I just got you alone, but I've got too much work to do to waste my time when you obviously aren't going to listen to a word I have to say."

"Then don't let me keep you, and please don't feel you have to hurry back to protect me. Ned and Balaam are all I need."

"Your temper is adequate protection against any man ever born," Burch said, stalking from the room.

Sibyl remained standing, listening to his footsteps ascending the stairs. But when she heard Emma's voice calling his name, a shattering sob shook her and she sank into the sofa, crying helplessly.

"Be sure you load these trunks tonight," Sibyl told Ned. "I want to leave at dawn tomorrow."

"Are you sure, miss? Winter is no time to be crossing the prairie."

"It's a damn fool thing to do," insisted Balaam. "You wouldn't get me to do it if you was to order me straight out. I don't like the looks of that sky. We're just as liable to have snow as a clear day."

"All you have to do is load the wagon," ordered Ned, speaking sharply, "and save your advice for those who ask for it."

"Ones as needs it is always the last to ask," prated Balaam, with all the impudence of an old decrepit. "Heading to Laramie in January is just begging for trouble."

"I intend to stop overnight at ranches along the way," Sibyl informed him. "Now stop arguing and get my other trunks. If neither of you wants to go, just say so. I can go by myself."

"I'd take my chances with a blizzard before I'd let you go

alone," Balaam informed her ingeniously. "It's for certain Mr. Burch would break my head if I was to let you jaunter off across the prairie without no one to look after you."

"Don't worry yourself about Mr. Randall. He won't care what happens to me."

"*You* can say that, being as you won't be here to catch it no matter what he does, but I ain't a fool just because I'm old, and I know Mr. Burch is going to be powerful angry when he comes back and finds you ain't here."

"Maybe Miss Stratton's brother will really lose his way, and she'll be here to soften his anger."

"Hmph!" snorted Balaam. "If that's the female that's been following him about like an extra arm, he won't be pleased at all. I can't see why anybody'd want to marry her."

"Marriage is not all that kind of female has to offer," said Sibyl, unable to forget the picture of Burch's muscled shoulders in Emma's embrace. "Besides, not every man's interested in marriage."

"It'd be prison more like, but then there's them that likes that pretty good too. Can't say I ever took to it myself."

"You mean you couldn't find any woman foolish enough to tie herself up to a bag of creaking bones," kidded Ned, who had grown rather fond of the old man.

"Well, it ain't what I meant, but I never was much to look at, not like Mr. Burch or even Mr. Jesse. But then not every woman sets her sights quite so high."

"Nor so low."

"If you're done trying to bait me, Ned Wright, you can pick up your end of this trunk and see if your arms is as powerful as you think your wit is. And don't you think I'm done talking to you, Miss Sibyl, cause I'm not," he informed her, bearing Ned and his end of the trunk away and leaving Sibyl to sink down on the bed, her heart warmed by Balaam's gruff affection.

It had nearly crushed her spirits to pack, but when Burch left the ranch, she knew she couldn't stay. If she had to be alone with him—and now that Augusta wasn't there she most certainly would be alone—she doubted she would have the strength to resist him. She had come close to throwing herself into his arms several times during the last week, but something wouldn't let her. Stubbornness, Augusta would call it. Empty Southern pride would no doubt be Burch's description, but whatever it was, it was just enough to keep her from committing herself to a life of misery.

If she ever once gave in to him—and she knew she would if they were alone for even an hour—she would be trapped with nowhere to go and no excuse for not staying exactly where she was. How could she live with Burch, wondering if he bedded every woman who offered herself to him? With his looks and money, there would be a constant succession of women only too glad to spend a few hours with him, some hoping to entrap him, others just for the pleasure of spending a few hours in the arms of the kind of man most women could only dream about. That would kill her, and if she had to die, then she'd die with dignity.

"Not that it makes any difference in the end," she muttered aloud. "What's dignity after all?" But it *was* something; maybe not much, but it was better than nothing.

She rose with a cheerless demeanor and surveyed the room: Drawers and chests stood open, trunks stood ready to be corded, but she was taking none of the furnishings with her. She supposed she'd have to send for them in the end, but right now she wanted nothing to remind her of Wyoming.

"I brought you some dinner," Rachel said, entering after her gentle knock. "Even you young people have to eat."

"I think I could enjoy a little something," she acknowledged, grateful and a little hungry, "but I've got to finish my packing."

"You eat your dinner, I'll do your packing. Just tell me where you want things." But Rachel didn't need any instructions, and while Sibyl ate she wondered about the tall, rawboned woman who was so silent, such a loyal, hard worker.

"I know it's not my place to interfere, miss, but I don't think it's wise to travel this time of year."

"Balaam has already given me a long list of reasons for not going, but I must."

Rachel seemed to study Sibyl closely, uncomfortably close, Sibyl thought. "Not all reasons seem so good once you've slept on them."

"I've already slept on these, and I expect I'll feel the same way in the morning."

"Don't you think you should wait a little longer?"

"Till when?"

Rachel folded two skirts before she answered. "You and Mr. Randall own this place together. There must be a lot of things to discuss."

"The lawyers can do it just as well." She pushed her plate away.

"Now I've gone and upset you," Rachel apologized.

"No, it was a lovely dinner, but I really wasn't very hungry. It seems like all I've done for days is eat."

"You can't fool me. I served every meal and you're hardly touched a bite. If you get any thinner, the first cold wind will cut right through you."

"I'll be sure to wrap up very tightly."

Rachel picked up the tray but turned back before she reached the door. "It's not so bad only having part of a man's love." Sibyl stared openmouthed, but Rachel picked up the tray and left without saying any more.

"May I come in?" That voice was like a ragged blade across Sibyl's nervous system. Emma entered, without waiting for an invitation. "I couldn't believe it when that old man told me you were leaving."

"So you had to come see for yourself?"

"I think it's the most sensible thing you could do," Emma answered, looking through Sibyl's things like she was shopping. "I never did understand why an Easterner like you would want to come out to Wyoming."

"Did it ever occur to you that *all* the first settlers were Easterners?" Sibyl inquired scathingly.

"You don't have to get insulting," replied Emma, turning away from Sibyl's open trunks with a deprecating sniff. "But you're not like them."

"Oh? How's that?" A girl less self-absorbed would have scented danger, but Emma felt so sure of herself, so close to victory, she was heedless of warning signs.

"They don't give themselves airs, and they have enough sense to leave men's work to the men. You know," she said in a burst of candor, "you don't treat Burch very smart. I know you're a relative and it's not the same as with me, but you sure do put his back up. You'll never get a husband that way, certainly not one as high-spirited and self-assured as Burch."

"And how do you suggest I go about *getting a husband*," Sibyl asked with deceptive cordiality, "one as high-spirited and, uh, self-assured as Burch?"

Emma didn't quite like the look in Sibyl's eye nor the fact that she had risen to her feet. She had the feeling of being circled by a stalking cat, and it was not a pleasant sensation. "You don't have to get so touchy," she said. "I just thought that since you were new out here and not familiar with our ways, you might like a little friendly advice."

"But I would," cooed Sibyl. "Is that how you do it, by being *friendly*?"

"Well, of course you have to be friendly. You don't expect a bear to come back to a honey pot if it bites, do you?"

"What an appropriate phrase. I would never have thought to characterize you as a biting honey pot if you hadn't suggested it, but I do think you've hit the mark."

"Now, wait just a minute," warned Emma, her temper flaring. "I don't know what you're talking about, but I can tell when I'm being insulted."

"It's only a fair exchange, isn't it? Isn't that what you thought I was when you first arrived—a honey pot for Burch to dip into when he liked? Or when he got tired of my aunt?"

"Oh, well, I'm sure I'm sorry for any mistake I made. It was the surprise of finding you here, when I expected to find Burch . . ."

"Alone is the word you're looking for, isn't it?"

"Well, not precisely alone, but I didn't expect to find any other women here."

"So you could be the only honey pot around and lure Burch on until you could slam the door on him."

"I'll have you know that I'm a decent woman."

"A decent *whore*, maybe; a decent woman, never!"

With a scream of rage, Emma launched herself at Sibyl. "I'll teach you to call me a whore," she squalled, trying to grab a handful of Sibyl's abundant hair.

"You don't have to teach me, I already know how," Sibyl responded, dealing Emma a slap across the cheek that caused her to stagger against the bed.

"Bitch!" Emma screamed and lunged at Sibyl again.

"My, my, is that kind of language decent women use out here, or have you confused it with decent whores?" Sibyl deftly sidestepped Emma's bull-like charge and tripped her. Emma fell to the floor with a thundering crash and a torrent of curses.

"I'll kill you for this!" she screeched, scrambling to her feet.

"It's a shame Burch can't see you now. I know he'd be powerfully drawn by your spirit and *self-assurance*." This time Sibyl did not evade Emma's attack and they came together with pulling of hair and rending of clothes.

"Stop!" ordered Rachel, bursting into the room just as Sibyl yanked Emma's head back with a crack that threatened to snap her neck. "Have you gone crazy?"

"I want you out of this house tomorrow," Sibyl said, panting, "with or without your brother."

"This is Burch's house, and I won't leave until he tells me."

"This is my house, too. If you don't leave, I'll have you thrown out."

"Why, you little . . ."

"There'll be no more of that," Rachel said, placing her slight frame between the two women. "You'd best go to your room, Miss Stratton, before anybody sees you."

"I haven't finished with you," Emma threatened, turning her back on Sibyl.

"But I'm finished with you," Sibyl replied, losing much of her fire. "I'm finished with all of this, *forever*."

"What happened?" Ned inquired, entering the room barely seconds after Emma left. "We heard such a crash Balaam was sure you'd knocked over a trunk."

"I weren't such a fool," said Balaam, almost completely out of breath from his hasty return. "I said it *sounded* like Miss Sibyl done knocked over her trunk."

"Miss Stratton slipped on a rug," Sibyl told them, as fruitful as Emma with handy lies. "She turned too quickly and lost her balance."

"If I was to believe everything I heard, I would be an old fool," said Balaam contemptuously.

"You're a dotty old fool," said Ned.

"Old, but no fool," Sibyl admitted with a ghost of a smile. "Could you pretend to believe me?"

"I guess it won't do me no harm," Balaam said, unable to ignore the pleading in Sibyl's eyes.

"No, nor the rest of us," agreed Rachel. "Now Miss Cameron is worn out. I'll finish her packing, and you can load the rest of the trunks in the morning."

"But I thought you said we had to load them tonight?"

"I did, Balaam, but I am awfully tired."

"Good. It's about time you went to sleep and let the rest of us do the same. It's not Christian to be keeping an old man out of his bed at this hour."

"There's nothing Christian about you, you old piece of carrion," said Ned, responding to a look from Rachel and pushing Balaam out the door before him. "I don't know why Mr. Burch didn't feed you to the coyotes long ago."

"Better men than Mr. Burch has tried to do old Balaam a wrong turn and failed," responded the ancient before Ned closed the door behind them. Rachel began to straighten up the room without a word.

"You don't have to do that," Sibyl said, but Rachel didn't stop. Sibyl walked to her dressing table and sat down. The same familiar face stared back at her, but she felt like she was facing a stranger. She couldn't fool herself; she had just had a fight with another woman over a man. She *had* to leave tomorrow. If this was what being in love did to people, if this was how it bent and twisted them, then the sooner she got away from Burch the better. The feeling of being loved, of being held in his arms, of being brought to a peak of exquisite fulfillment was wonderful, but this torment of fear and jealousy was hell. If they had to go together, then she'd just have to do without love. It was impossible to consider going through the rest of her life like this.

Rachel finished straightening the room and started to leave. "It doesn't have to be like this, you know," she said, pausing to look sadly at Sibyl, "not unless you let it."

Chapter 24

The train gathered speed, carrying Sibyl farther and farther away from Burch. She reached out to the figure that grew steadily smaller in the distance, tried to will his horse to run faster, but the train whistle blew furiously, trumpeting its defiance again and again. In desperation, she called out to him, but no sound came from her throat; still the train continued its triumphant shrieking, louder and LOUDER and *LOUDER*! Sibyl woke up with a jolt.

The room was in utter darkness. Frightened, she fumbled with the bedside lamp, found the matches, and stared before her with anxious eyes until the dim light showed packed and corded trunks against the far wall. The tension slowly left her body; she was still at the Elkhorn, in her own room, and in her own bed.

Then what was the harrowing noise that sounded like the shriek of a train whistle? Sibyl threw back the covers; the bitter cold of the room bit at her flesh as though she were naked. She slipped her feet into fur-lined slippers and drew on a thick, servicable robe. Outside the whistling noise rose to a piercing intensity, howling and moaning around the corners of the house. She pulled back the curtains, but even though the clock said the sun should have been up an hour ago, it was so dark outside she couldn't see the bare limbs of the tree that stood less than fifteen feet from her window. All she could make out was a dark, swirling gray mass. That's snow, she realized; it's another blizzard.

She hurried downstairs, but there was no one about. She didn't want Emma to be up, but it was odd that Rachel hadn't come to light the fires. Sibyl decided to start breakfast herself; someone was bound to come in soon. She didn't have long to wait; she had barely poured her coffee when Balaam staggered in, hurtled through the door by a fierce blast of arctic cold and driving snow.

"You're never stepping foot outside this house today, miss, much less going to Laramie," he announced, unable to hide his satisfaction at being proved right. "That snow is blowing harder than any I can remember. No telling now long it'll last." He hurried over to the stove to warm his cold hands.

"Are you sure there's no chance to get through?" Sibyl didn't know why she bothered to ask. Anyone could see that it was impossible to travel in that storm.

"I nearly lost my way between here and the barn. I already put up a rope so's you can hold on. That wind is getting worse, not better. You won't be able to see at all before long."

"Where's Rachel?"

"Probably snowed in at her place."

"Will she be all right by herself?"

"She's used to it, been doing it for years, but you won't be seeing her here at the house for some time."

"And Ned?"

"He's tending to that bull of yours. Old Balaam is okay to take care of pigs and chickens and milk cows," he mimicked, "but I can't be trusted with that precious bull and his harem."

"Is there something wrong?"

"Naw. That fat plug is eating just as fast as he can chew, but I expect he's a mite chilly. It's near twenty below out there now."

"Twenty below *zero*?"

"And going to be colder unless I miss my guess."

"Do we have enough coal?"

"We could survive a storm twice as cold and four times as long as this one is likely to be. It's the cows out on the plains I'm worried about."

"What about the men?" Sibyl asked, unable to keep from thinking of Burch caught in that deadly storm.

"They'll hole up in a cabin somewhere till it blows itself out. They took enough food with them to hold out for a month."

"But we've already had so many blizzards."

"They stocked up real good after New Year's." His hands were warm enough now to allow him to give some thought to his stomach. "Do you have anything here for a man to eat?"

"When didn't she ever?" asked Rachel, entering the kitchen.

"Where'd you come from, woman? Don't try telling me you came through all that snow."

"I slept over," she said, glancing at Sibyl for only the briefest moment.

"Just as well you did," Balaam said, settling down to the plate Sibyl handed him. "At least you'll get something good and hot to eat."

"Ned coming in?" Rachel asked, pouring her coffee.

"Soon as he's through petting that bull."

"Then see that you leave him something to eat," Rachel said, noting the extra food Balaam had seen fit to add to what Sibyl had already given him.

"An old man like me needs lots of fuel to keep warm," he groused, offended.

"An old man like you should be careful to eat past his worth." They continued to swipe at one another, old foes comfortable in their mild antagonism, until Ned came in, hurried along by another blast of wind and powder-dry snow.

"I've never seen anything like it," he announced to Sibyl, "not in all the years I spent on the Sweetwater."

"That couldn't have been too many now, could it?" Balaam badgered, still irked at Rachel's jibes about his age.

"Enough to know that this isn't going to clear up by tomorrow. We're in for it this time."

"And just how long do you suspect that's going to be? You being so experienced an' all."

"Long enough to freeze your worthless bones if Miss Sibyl wasn't too softhearted to know the best way to get rid of an old sucker like you."

"Sucker!" hollered Balaam, turning purple with indignation.

"Leach or tick would have been more to the point, but I was trying not to hurt your feelings."

Sibyl bowed her head to conceal a grin.

"Why, you half-baked cripple, I had broken hundreds of horses before you were dry behind the ears."

"They seem to have broken you up a bit in return," replied Ned nonchalantly, helping himself to something from every pot. "Or maybe you're just coming apart from dry rot."

Balaam rose from his seat, his spare frame shaking with choler, ready to defend himself with words Sibyl wouldn't have found familiar.

"Don't answer him, Balaam," she said, trying not to laugh. "He's just trying to get you to say something thoroughly improper to shock me. Besides, I don't want to have you two bellowing at each other through my breakfast."

"I may not have been raised in no Virginia mansion, but I do know how to behave," said Balaam indignantly.

"If Balaam can't cuss and bellow, he can't talk. He don't know any other way."

"Leave him alone, Ned," said Sibyl. "It's not fair for you to pick on him when he can't answer you back. Are my trunks still in the wagon?"

"Yes, and you'd best not move them if there's any glass or china in them. It's so cold, it'd break with just the slightest jarring."

"Everything I need is still upstairs. Maybe the weather will get better soon."

But as the day wore on, the wind blew even harder and by nightfall the temperature had dropped to thirty below. The snow was beginning to drift badly, threatening to cover fences and fill the deepest canyons. All day Sibyl occupied herself with anything that would help distract her mind and then went to bed right after dinner; she was really tired and the continual shrieking of the wind made her head ache.

But she lay awake for a long time, worry over Burch's well-being steadily eroding her anger at him. She couldn't help feeling guilty for having sent him away with such bitter words ringing in his ears. Her suffering didn't seem so important now; certainly not as important as his safety.

The second day was a repeat of the first, and Sibyl and Rachel went on with their efforts to restore the house to normal. Emma, reluctant to show herself after her skirmish with Sibyl, took advantage of the storm to spend some extra time in bed, but by the middle of the third day she was tired of her own company and finally ventured downstairs from sheer boredom. Neither woman had time to sit and talk to her, so she followed them around, getting in the way and nearly driving Sibyl crazy with her pouting and petulant complaints. She even offered to help with the cleaning.

"That's kind of you, but we don't have much more to do," said Sibyl.

"If I don't find something to do, I'm going to go crazy," Emma whined fretfully. "I've never been caught in a blizzard before."

"What about the blizzards before Christmas?"

"I was in Laramie," laughed Emma, slightly embarrassed but not caring because Burch wasn't around to hear her. "I only left to come to this party."

"But I thought you *loved* staying at the ranch."

"I do, but not all the time."

"How much is 'not all the time'?"

"Not above three or four months of the year, and then not all in one stretch," she said, dispensing with the last of her assumed role. "What is there to *do* on a ranch except hunt and ride? Even the roundup gets boring after a few hours. I don't see how a woman could keep from going crazy in a place like this." Sibyl and Rachel exchanged glances.

"What do you usually do during the winter?"

"I stayed in Cheyenne," confessed Emma. "There are lots of parties and dinners, and loads of people having a good time."

"Don't they have blizzards in Cheyenne?"

"Of course, but the men come for you in sleighs and drive around the streets with lanterns on the sleighs and bells on the horses. It's loads of fun, and when everybody gets too cold, we gather at someone's house, or the Cheyenne Club, and have a party until the storm lets up. Sometimes it goes on for days."

"Don't they ever think about the herds and the men who ride the line?"

"We let our men go after fall roundup and don't hire again until spring. It's a great waste of money to keep them lying up in cabins eating their heads off."

"Burch is out there right now," Sibyl informed her, trying to stem her rising anger at the callousness of this conscience-less fortune hunter, "and our men are with him."

"And it's such a shame, too, when he could be in Cheyenne, or even Chicago, enjoying himself. Those cows can take care of themselves. They always have."

"But the Elkhorn herd doesn't contain much longhorn blood anymore. It's mostly bred from Eastern stock and they need some protecting," said Sibyl, wanting to see the real extent of Emma's ignorance.

"Nearly everybody snickered at Burch's uncle behind his back when he started that, saying he was getting too old. Nobody ever expected Burch to keep it up after he died."

"Which? The beef or the cowboys?"

"Both. Well, maybe not the new stock. Even I can see what a difference that's made, and everybody knows Burch's steers fetch the best prices in Wyoming. When that last check hit town, it made ripples across three states."

So that's why you left Laramie, thought Sibyl, finally understanding why Emma was willing to spend a few weeks on an isolated ranch in the middle of winter.

"Rachel and I still have work to do," said Sibyl, abruptly losing interest in talking to Emma. "You'll have to entertain yourself. There are some books in the sitting room and more upstairs in Burch's room if you want them."

"Burch reads!"

"There's also the piano but not much else, unless you would like to crochet or do some tatting."

"Are you crazy?"

"Well, you could go rub down the horses, but Balaam says they don't like being bothered when it's this cold."

"I wouldn't set foot out that door if they all froze to death."

"Then I suggest the piano. You do play, don't you?"

"Of course," Emma replied pettishly, but from the meaningless strumming that reached Sibyl's and Rachel's ears, they doubted the piano at the T-Bar got much use. Emma continued to shadow them off and on, actually turning her hand to helping Sibyl, but her efforts were so sporadic and she paid so little attention to what she was doing that Sibyl was relieved when they were forced to stop their work in response to Ned's calls from the back of the house. They found him kneeling before the coal stove with a calf in his arms.

"It's nearly frozen to death," he said, settling the weak animal as close to the heat as he thought safe. "It's forty below. Even with the shelter of the sheds, I don't think the calves can stand much more."

"What about the rest of the herd?"

"They're awful weak. It's the wind that's doing the mischief. It's driving so hard it cuts right to the bone." Ned

299

vigorously massaged the calf to get its circulation going, and in a few minutes it raised its head and looked at Sibyl with great big brown eyes.

"I'll tend this one," said Rachel, taking his place beside the calf. "You go look after the others." But in less than fifteen minutes Ned was back with another calf.

"This one was laid down too. If they stay down, they don't get up again," he informed Sibyl.

"How many more are having trouble?"

"Maybe only one, if it doesn't get any colder."

"Then you might as well bring it in now instead of waiting."

Ned returned with Balaam following right behind. "I didn't think to see you take to mothering calves, but then you'll do anything for those fancy beeves, wouldn't you?"

"Button it up, you old, leaky bucket. You have to stay with these calves tonight."

"Me?"

"You don't expect Miss Sibyl to do it, do you?"

"I will," offered Rachel.

"Not on your life. This old windbag has been puffing about how much he could do all week long. Now he'll get his chance to prove it."

Balaam was just winding up for a good jaw when Emma entered the ranch room.

"What is that?" she asked.

"I would have thought that even you could recognize a calf," drawled Sibyl.

"I know *what* it is. I mean what's it doing here?"

"Well, how's anybody to tell you what you want to know when you go asking something else?" demanded Balaam, put out at having a promising argument with Ned interrupted.

"It's here to get warm," Sibyl told Emma, who glowered angrily back at Sibyl.

"How long are they going to stay?"

"Until they're out of danger. They're from *my* herd, and all three are *bull* calves."

Emma was still not happy, but she regarded them with more interest. "Are these the calves Burch and Lasso were carrying on about so?"

"Some of them."

"How many do you have?"

"One bull, fourteen cows and heifers, eighteen yearlings and calves, and every one of the young ones are bulls just like these little fellas," announced Ned promptly, before Sibyl. "Every one is worth his weight in gold."

"They don't look like much to me," said Emma, disappointed. "I thought they'd be bigger at least."

"They will be, just like their pappy."

"You're not meaning to bring that bull in here!" she stammered, truly startled now.

"I will if that's the only way to keep him alive," stated Sibyl.

After that Emma couldn't find much to say, and she soon drifted off to bed.

"You be sure to keep your eye on the rest of the herd," Sibyl told Ned before going off to bed herself. "We can't afford to lose even one of them."

Chapter 25

"I didn't think it was possible, but the storm's worse," Ned told Sibyl when he came in for breakfast the next morning with another calf in his arms. "And the temperature's still dropping. If it doesn't stop, it'll be fifty below by noon."

"What about the herd?"

"I don't think they'll make it," Ned said bluntly. "They're almost dead now. Balaam is prodding them to keep them on their feet and I'm going back now to fetch the last calf."

"This may answer for the calves," said Sibyl doubtfully, "but what are we going to do about the others?" The calves became more active as the heat penetrated their frail bodies and they became aware of pangs of hunger. "We can't haul them back to their mothers every time they have to be fed."

"If they still have mothers," said Ned, dispirited.

"We can't let them die," said Sibyl stubbornly. "How could I face Burch, knowing he and the men saved the cows out on the range, but I couldn't even take care of mine when they had a shed and plenty of food and water?"

"But it's not the food, it's the cold."

"I'm going to have a look at them myself."

"You can't go out in that storm," Ned objected.

"Why not? You and Balaam go back and forth all day."

"I know, but you're a woman."

"You sound like Burch, always thinking women are help-less." But Sibyl sighed in a way that told Ned that sounding like Burch wasn't such a bad thing this morning. "Give me a few minutes to dress."

"Cover everything but your eyes, miss. That wind can freeze the nose right off your face."

Sibyl's attitude bespoke her skepticism, but once out in the driving snow, all doubt vanished. The wind blew with such ferocity she had to hold on to the rope just to keep from falling down or being blown away. It was impossible to see what was in front of her. The familiar arrangement of buildings, corrals, and paths connecting them was com-pletely obliterated by the flying needles that stung her eyes and the incredible cold that hurt her lungs as it bit deeply into the warm tissue. Ned followed behind her, calling encouragement, but his words were ripped away by the shrieking wind. There was no time to listen, anyway; it took all her concentration and energy just to hold on to the rope. After what seemed like an eternity, she felt the wind sud-denly slacken and realized that they had rounded the corner of one of the sheds. At least the cows didn't have to face the icy blast head-on.

But what she saw quickly dashed her hopes. Balaam, his frail frame muffled to the eyes in layer after layer of clothing, moved among the herd, prodding them into constant mo-tion. But it was a losing battle. One cow was already down, and every time Balaam tried to get her to her feet, two more would begin to kneel slowly.

"It's no good, miss," he yelled, near exhaustion himself. "Nothing is going to keep them standing much longer."

"Can't you keep after them?"

"Not without freezing ourselves," Ned told her. "It just doesn't seem that there's any more we can do."

"You can't stand about, miss, or you'll catch your death."

"Where can we talk?" she said, shouting to be heard above the roar of the storm. "I can't leave without trying to do something."

"The bunkhouse," Balaam yelled, gesturing to the long, low building that was used by the hands on the few nights each year they spent at the ranch. They fought their way across the open space, Balaam and Ned holding tightly to Sibyl.

"I'll get a fire started," Balaam said, beginning to throw coal into the big iron stove that stood in the center of the room. "The boys will be plumb frazzled when they find out a lady's been among their belongings," he chuckled.

"This doesn't look much better than those line cabins," said Sibyl, walking about to keep warm and glancing at the hard, narrow bunks pushed against walls thickly plastered with newspaper and catalog pages until they were airtight.

"The boys don't spend above six weeks a year here, so it don't much matter what it's like," said Balaam, pouring out some coal oil and putting a match to it. "What a man can't keep in his bedroll, he don't want."

"This is not helping us decide what to do about the cows," Sibyl reminded them. "We've got to think of something."

"And soon," Ned added unnecessarily.

"There's no room to keep them all up at the house even if we could get them there," Sibyl said, striding up and down the wide aisle between the bunks. "We need a big barn like I had in Virginia."

"Folks out here think barns are a waste of good wood," said Ned. "Especially when they don't keep stock up over the winter."

"The biggest thing we got is the chicken coop," Balaam said, adding his voice to the knell of doom.

"No, it's not," Sibyl announced suddenly. "We've got this bunkhouse, and it's big enough for all the livestock."

"You can't put cows in here!" exclaimed Balaam, scandalized. "The boys will never stand for it."

"We won't tell them," said Sibyl, thinking rapidly.

"You won't have to. They'll know it the minute they put a foot through the doorway."

"That doesn't matter. I can build another bunkhouse, but there's not another herd like this in the world. I want every last animal in here as soon as you can get them on their feet. I'll see to the fire. Now get started." Sibyl knew she need to raise the temperature at least to freezing, but the bunkhouse was huge and just as cold inside as it was outside. She threw more coals into the stove.

If finding a place to house the herd was difficult, getting them moved into it proved to be nearly impossible. Six animals were down and only the most vigorous punishment forced them to their feet. Ned put a rope around each and dragged and pushed the near-dead beasts out into the cutting wind. The cows fought to return to the shelter of the shed, and it took all the men's strength to get them to the bunkhouse.

"They seem determined to stay out there and die," Ned said, panting for breath. "Let's hope they don't lie down and die in here." Sibyl wondered how she was going keep them moving while Ned and Balaam went back for the others, but the new surroundings, protection from the wind, and the heat beginning to come from the stove were enough stimulus to keep the cows from lying down again.

During the next hour, the men worked themselves to near exhaustion, dragging the unwilling heifers into the teeth of the storm and across the short distance to the safety of the bunkhouse. "Don't stop," Sibyl encouraged them. "Remember they're all expecting calves. You're really saving two."

"I can't move," Balaam said, sinking to his knees before the stove after bringing the last heifer. "Not even if the devil was after me."

"Once you get the bull, you can sleep as long as you want."

"No, he can't," Ned corrected her. "There's still the calves to be brought back and food and water hauled in here. No point in saving them from freezing just to let them starve to death."

"I hadn't thought of that," Sibyl said as Balaam groaned loudly. "Can't we leave the calves in the house?"

"We can't feed them as well as their mothers can, and with the heat from their bodies, this bunkhouse will soon be hot enough to make you sweat. We'll probably have to open one of the windows." It seem an incredible idea at first, but the temperature in the bunkhouse was rising quickly, and already Sibyl had discarded some the scarves that had been wrapped tightly about her head.

Balaam went back with Ned to get the bull, complaining all the way that they were driving him to his grave. But when fifteen minutes had passed and there was no sign of them, Sibyl wrapped up again and went to see what was wrong.

For a moment she thought she would have to turn back or lose her way in the swirling, blinding snow. But she caught sight of the shed before panic could overcome her common sense and found Ned and Balaam struggling to make the bull rise. He had lain down to die and had no intention of getting to his feet again.

"We've got to get him up," she said imperatively. "Get a pole and put it under him. We'll lift him to his feet."

"We tried that," Ned said, nearing exhaustion.

"Then try it again. Balaam and I will pull." Ned inserted the pole under the bull, but every time he tried to raise him, the animal simply rolled the other way.

"Balaam, get on the other side." But even though they were able to raise one end of the bull off the ground, Sibyl was too weak to pull the enormous beast to his feet.

"Use a pitchfork," she ordered, just as Rachel, worried by the long absence with no word, rounded the corner of the shed. Rachel took in the situation quickly, pulled a pitchfork out of a hay bale, and jabbed carefully at the bull's tough hide. He didn't move.

"Show him you mean business," shouted Sibyl. Rachel looked uncertain, but she took aim, closed her eyes, and stabbed the tines deep into the still-sensitive flesh of the lethargic bull. With a bellow of pain, the enraged animal lurched to his feet. The men dropped their poles and, taking hold of the rope, pulled him relentlessly out into the snow. Sibyl followed with the pitchfork, giving him a sharp reminder every time he tried to lie down or turn back to the shed.

"At last," Sibyl said with a smile of satisfaction when the bunkhouse door had been closed behind him.

"Now we have to feed them."

"Let them get warm first," Sibyl suggested, thinking that Balaam was not looking very well at all. "They won't starve in the next few hours, and if you drop dead, there won't be anybody to take care of them." Ned started to raise an objection, but the blue color around Balaam's mouth changed his mind.

"Rachel will fix some lunch. It'll be time enough to worry about the calves after you've eaten."

"Where have you been?" demanded a thoroughly frightened Emma. "I was sure you were all dead, and that old woman just staring at me like she couldn't talk."

"We've been moving the herd to the bunkhouse."

"The bunkhouse! Lord, the men will kill you, if Burch doesn't murder you first for filling his house with those dratted calves."

"I don't have anywhere else to put them," Sibyl said, hoping Emma would go away. But Emma had been left with her own company all day and was not about to give up even such an unsatisfactory companion as Sibyl.

"You might have thought of my feelings."

"If it comes to that, they're much more important to me than you are."

"I never expected anybody, especially a fancy lady from Virginia, to put up with crude animals inside the house."

"I think those calves are darling," said Sibyl with a wicked glint in her eyes. "It's you I find crude."

Emma looked as if she were about to attack Sibyl, but Rachel's cold gray eyes changed her mind, and she took refuge in wounded vanity.

"I'm not surprised you're always fighting with Burch," she said spitefully. "No man could get along with you for very long."

"Did he tell you that?" Sibyl asked, suddenly shaking with rage.

"Well, not in so many words," temporized Emma. "But you can tell when a man isn't comfortable around a woman, and poor Burch was positively frantic every time he was around you."

"The day has yet to dawn that'll find Mr. Randall frantic," commented Rachel with a dour expression. "From what I hear tell, the closest he ever came to being excited was when he came upon two elk with sixteen-point racks, and they ran off in opposite directions. He was so bothered over which to shoot first, he nearly missed 'em both."

Emma's rage at being ranked below a pair of elk was so comical Sibyl felt her anger ebb quickly.

"We'll soon have the house back in order, but I'm afraid you're going to have to take care of yourself."

Ned and Balaam came up to the house, but Sibyl didn't call them to the table until she was satisfied that Balaam was looking better. His unusual silence and meekness before Ned's jibes worried her, but before the meal was over he began to rally, and Sibyl saw the old devilish light come back into his eyes.

The calves, reunited with their mothers, soon made themselves at home. The older stock, recovered quickly with the heat, became restless for food and water. It was not a problem to haul the hay from the shed, but the water was frozen solid and snow had to be melted in buckets on the stove. Sibyl tried to push the bull away when he decided he was too thirsty to wait, but he was much too powerful and thrust her aside. When he shoved his nose into the bucket, the folds of loose skin on his neck came into contact with the hot metal of the stove. The smell of burning hair and scorched flesh filled Sibyl's nostrils. With a resentful bellow, the bull backed away and stood shaking his head, trying to rid himself of the pain.

"You're the dumbest, laziest, most stubborn beast I've ever known," Sibyl told him angrily. "You stood in snow up to your belly and you didn't have sense enough to eat some of it. Now you can't wait to stick your nose in a pot of boiling water." She dumped more snow into the bucket. "I've got to melt enough for everybody, so you're going to have to wait your turn."

"You'd better be careful talking to the cows, miss," Balaam warned. "It'll make you crazy as Ned."

Over the next five days, the four of them spent most of their waking hours with the herd. It seemed that it took all of one person's time just to keep enough snow melted for drinking water.

"Now I understand why they're so fat," said Sibyl one afternoon, sinking down in exhaustion. "Even when faced with extinction, all they can think about is eating. I doubt there's enough grass in Wyoming to feed them." The pile of hay was falling rapidly, but Ned assured her that they had enough to last through this storm and several more.

"Buying that hay was the smartest thing anybody around here's done since old Mr. Cameron grabbed this land right out from under the Sioux," Balaam informed her gruffly. Sibyl was too tired to show her pleasure, but she wondered if Burch would feel the same way.

A break in the storm came at the end of the seventh day, but it was only temporary, and in the early evening, the storm blew up with continued violence, routing any hope Sibyl had of being able to return to a normal existence.

There was one advantage: She was rarely forced to endure Emma's company. Not even boredom could cause Emma to hazard going out into the storm, and whenever Sibyl was in the house, Emma was so thankful to have someone to talk to that she managed to put aside her feelings of dislike.

"I don't understand why you have to spend all your time outside when you've got hired hands to tend those cows for you," Emma said fretfully. "Anybody would think you *liked* living among cows."

"There are a lot of things I don't like having to do, but they have to be done nevertheless," Sibyl said, glaring at Emma with clear meaning.

"You don't have to include me in that," Emma said resentfully. "You're not here often enough to know whether I'm alive or dead. Some way to treat a guest. I thought you Virginians were supposed to be so proud of your hospitality."

"We don't like being imposed upon any more than anybody else," Sibyl answered sharply. Emma flounced out of the room at that but returned in less than half an hour.

"Do those men of yours know when this snow is going to stop. It seems like I've been imprisoned here for weeks."

"You ought to know as much as they do. You grew up out here."

"Storms don't matter in Cheyenne."

"I imagine your brother won't be able to come for you right away, even after it clears up, so you might as well make

310

yourself comfortable."

"Oh, my God," she moaned, "I think I shall go mad," and she staggered off to the parlor to attack the piano.

"Sounds like she intends to break it up for kindling," Rachel said after several minutes of fitful banging that bore no relation to any tune Sibyl could remember. "Maybe you should tell her we already have a supply laid in."

"I doubt she'd hear me," replied Sibyl with a grin.

At last, on the twelfth day, the fury of the storm broke; the wind died down to a mere breeze, and the temperatures rose abruptly to only ten degrees below freezing.

"They're getting restless," Ned said of the herd. "It's time to let them out."

"Shouldn't we keep them up one more day?"

"We can take them back if we have to. They know the bunkhouse now and it wouldn't be so hard to drive them in again, but they need to get out. The bull is liable to trample one of the calves before long."

So a little after noon, Sibyl watched as Ned and Balaam freed the herd from its confinement for the first time in ten days. The calves seemed to have forgotten that any world existed outside the bunkhouse, but the older animals remembered their freedom and Sibyl thought they were going to take the door frame off in their haste to get out into the cold, crisp air.

"Just look at that arrogant, sassy brute. He's not the least bit grateful for what we did," Sibyl said as the bull rolled in the snow and cavorted about like a yearling. "He's just like Burch."

The thought of Burch brought back her pain, and she felt all the pleasure in her triumph slip away. Now that the storm was over and the dark sky clearing, there was no reason to put off her departure any longer. Sibyl's spirits plummeted, and it was almost impossible not to cry. She had come to Wyoming seeking something she really didn't expect to find.

Had she not found it, she could have convinced herself it didn't exist.

But she *had* found it, and it was an agony to be forced to give him up altogether. "But not to Emma!" The unintentional words sounded like the last request of a condemned soul.

"What did you say, miss?" Ned asked, preoccupied with the herd.

"Nothing. I was just thinking out loud. How soon do you think we can get through to Laramie?"

"So you still hold to that plan, do you?" he asked, but he had not really expected her to change her mind.

"Only the storm kept me here. Can we leave tomorrow?" Ned looked at the clear sky and the cold but valiant sun.

"Not by wagon. We'll never get through the drifts."

"I know. I meant on horseback." Ned looked hard at Sibyl, but her determination was clear; she would leave if she had to do it alone.

"We'd better leave early. It'll be slow through the canyons and draws, but it'll be better than to wait until everything starts to melt and the ground becomes a sea of mud."

"You can see about sending my things as soon as it's possible to get a wagon through. I'll pack what I need on Dusty."

"Anything more than your toothbrush might kill that useless nag."

Sibyl smiled weakly. "How long before anybody comes in from the range?"

"Can't say. Depends on the herd."

"It doesn't matter. You and Balaam can see to things around here, and Rachel knows the house as well as I do."

"But she don't cook like you do."

"Sometimes I think the only reason you want me to stay is to fix your next meal."

"There's never been anyone like you with a pot, miss, but I

312

guess telling you that ain't going to change your mind."

"No, but it's nice to hear. I never said so, but I thought I'd never see you again after you delivered us to the ranch."

"I did plan to take my money and head for the nearest town, but I'm glad I stayed. You've changed this place a lot, and you're gonna to be missed."

"Thank you," Sibyl said, turning quickly to the house so he couldn't see the tears of sadness she couldn't hold back any longer.

Chapter 26

The scream of the wind had been so incessant for the last six days that Burch was barely conscious of it as he lay in the warm comfort of his bed, putting off the shock of the icy floor to his bare feet. He knew what punishment awaited him outside the cabin door, and he was conscious of a desire to stay right where he was for the rest of the morning. With a rush, like diving into a cold lake, he erupted from the bed and began to put on the many layers of heavy clothing needed to protect him from the sub-zero blasts of arctic wind.

Outside, the wind whipped around the pitifully small trees next to the cabin with terrible force, driving the snow before it like millions of tiny swords. It struck Burch like a body block and sent him stumbling through the drifts toward Silver Birch, who was hobbled in the lee of a bluff with the protection of a thickly grown group of pines at his back. Burch wasted no time on his usual playful antics. He saddled the huge stallion quickly and moved steadily into the teeth of the storm along the floor of the little valley to where it widened out to meet the plain below.

Minutes later it was possible to discern a group of several hundred cows loosely gathered around three large haystacks. Most stood with their backs to the murderous wind, feeding on the hay that Burch had scattered on top of the snow, but two heifers ate directly from the haystack.

Burch dismounted and began to pitchfork the hay to the ground, wondering how long the blizzard would last. It was hard to keep the cows tightly gathered near the haystacks. Their instinct told them to head for the open range, where they would drift before the storm, sometimes for hundreds of miles, not stopping to eat until the storm blew out or they died on their feet. This year, with the range virtually stripped of grass, that would have meant certain death.

Finished with the hay, Burch next took the ax he carried in his saddle scabbard and cut through the thick ice of the small pond backed up behind one of the several dams on Elkhorn Creek. He'd have to check again in a few hours, because some mindless cow always stood in the water until it froze around her and she had to be cut out. But for now, he mounted up quickly and headed back to the cabin.

He warmed his stiff body before the stove, trying to decide what he wanted to eat, but thoughts of Sibyl ruined his concentration and he ate his dinner quickly and without satisfaction. Afterwards, when he tried to decide what to do for the herd, Sibyl kept interrupting his thoughts and he had nothing to show after thirty minutes of fruitless deliberations. In frustration he picked up a book, but his mind kept returning to Sibyl. When he at last turned out the light, he couldn't remember half of what he had read. "This has got to stop," he told himself as he pulled several blankets over him to keep out the numbing cold. "I'll go crazy before I can get back to the ranch." But Sibyl slipped in and out of his uneasy dreams, illusive and yet constantly present, and he woke feeling more tired than when he had gone to sleep.

Next morning the blizzard had eased, and a light snow floated to the ground like airy feathers in a soundless world. Burch decided the best way to keep the unwelcome thoughts and question at bay was to check on the other cabins.

At his first stop, Burch found one of the hands pulling a

steer out of a drift.

"Damned fool won't stay out of that ravine no matter what I do," complained Buck Coker. "This is the third time he's wandered off. Next time I'm going to leave him and have him for dinner when he thaws out next spring."

"Have you heard how anybody else is doing?" asked Burch, giving him a hand.

"About the same as me from what I hear. Damn fool cows acting stupid, but we can handle 'em. When I was cussing so last summer at having to stack all this hay, I never thought I'd be glad to have it," he said, surveying his scattered herd as they ate. "If they don't freeze, they'll be all right come spring."

"Have you seen Jesse?"

"I saw him go by here yesterday," he said, shaking his head. "I didn't think anybody was crazy enough to be out in this storm, but it was Jesse. No mistaking his pinto."

"Which way was he going?"

"That's something else perculiar. He was headed in the direction of Boulder Canyon. We don't have any cows over that way, do we?"

"No. I wonder where he went?"

"Could be over to Blue Mesa. There's more cows there than anywhere else."

"Maybe." Burch visited two more cabins before he reached Blue Mesa a couple of hours before nightfall.

"We ain't seen Jesse since before Christmas," said the two cowhands, struggling to keep nearly a thousand head from starvation. "Wish we had; we sure could use the help." Burch had intended to go on to the next cabin, but by the time he had helped the boys finish up their work, it was too dark.

"Who's in the next cabin?" Burch asked.

"Cody, and fit to be tied he ain't in some snug hotel in Laramie. Don't think you can depend on him staying after the weather breaks."

"It won't matter if he does then," said Burch, preparing to

316

turn in. "Think I'll head on up that way tomorrow."

But he didn't. The more he thought about Jesse and Boulder Canyon, the more certain he was that something didn't fit. The snow picked up again, but instead of turning back, he headed Silver Birch toward the pine-covered ridges that loomed up in the west.

All morning long he climbed under the shelter of the pines. The wind's bitter edge was blunted by their snow-covered boughs, but the falling temperature made the silence under the trees lonely and threatening. Shortly before noon he reached the mouth of the gorge that led into Boulder Canyon. Burch found a trail that was slowly drifting full of snow — a sure sign that a rider had passed through in the last two days. The weather suddenly started to get worse, and Burch hoped the old cabin at the head of the canyon was still standing. He should never have come here, especially not alone.

"What do I care if Jesse comes up here to hide," he said aloud. But still he went on. The canyon narrowed between steep pine-covered walls, a still-flowing stream taking up nearly all of the opening. The signs of a recent traveler along the narrow trail at the stream's edge were unmistakable now. As the canyon opened out abruptly, a familiar shape caught his attention just ahead.

"How the hell did that cow get up here!" he exclaimed, jerking Silver Birch to a halt. The cattle, for there were too many for Burch to count at a glance, were nearly buried by the drifting snow. Burch expected to find them all frozen where they stood, but the canyon walls had provided protection from some of the savagery of the storm and they stared fixedly at him from glazed eyes. It was their captivity that doomed them to certain death.

Cursing any man fool enough to leave his cattle penned and unattended, Burch leaned down and threw the fence rails aside. He drove Silver Birch through, shouting and waving his hat, but the nearly dead cows moved only just enough to crack the surface of the snow. Burch tossed his rope over the nearest horns and literally dragged the traumatized animal out of the drift. As he turned to go back for another, the crusted snow fell from the steer's sides. It wore the Elkhorn brand. With a torrent of curses, Burch knocked the snow from a second steer. It wore the same brand! But who would bring rustled cattle here, risking a chance of discovery, instead of slaughtering them or selling them in Montana?

If he didn't stop asking questions and get them out of the drift, they would soon die. It was already too late for some, he found, when he put his rope over the seventh animal, an old cow. Burch cursed more vehemently and after what seemed like hours of backbreaking work, barely two thirds of the herd—all that were left alive—were drifting down the canyon toward the shelter of the pines.

The cabin was completely bare, but someone had slept there recently and stabled a horse in the lee. Jesse's name kept sounding in Burch's mind, but what possible reason could he have for rustling steers or hiding them here? Burch couldn't find anything to identify the mysterious occupant, so he left. He had to drive the cows to Blue Mesa before nightfall or they would perish; if the storm got much worse, they might *all* perish.

By the time Burch caught up with the herd, the snow was falling so thickly it was hard to see. The cows moved slowly, the stronger ones breaking a path for the others to follow, but they were all too weak to be driven hard. Burch was thankful for the shelter of the pines. For a few, movement warmed their blood and their bodies gave off a healthy steam in the frigid air. Several moved with lowered heads and lagging feet, and on many occasions Silver Birch had to support a wobbly cow with his shoulder. But Burch couldn't abandon them. They were *his* cows and he'd already lost too many.

Burch harried and hurried the animals as the hours

dragged by. When the light grew weaker and the cold more intense, he pushed them even harder. One cow stumbled, and Burch pushed her ruthlessly along. When she stumbled again, he put a rope around her neck and pulled her.

When they at last left the shelter of the pine-covered ridge, the blast of the storm's fury surprised even Burch. The cows staggered dangerously. Some seemed to sense that safety lay ahead, but others were too exhausted to want to do more than lie down and let the darkness sweep over them. On and on they struggled, Burch pushing, pulling, prodding the well-nigh dead animals, forcing them to go on living against their wills. The light was almost gone and still the cabin at Blue Mesa did not come into view. Burch lost precious minutes cleaning the ice balls out of Silver Birch's hooves. His tired eyes probed the gathering darkness about him, but he could find no familiar landmarks in the swirling gloom. How much farther did they have to go? Could he have lost his way? He was going on instinct alone, hoping his sense of direction would not fail him now.

The cows wouldn't hold up much longer. Even now he had two of them in tow, and the strain was beginning to tell on Silver Birch. That mighty stallion had carried him seventy-five miles over difficult terrain, and the ice that still collected in his hooves made each step unbearably painful.

At last Burch was forced to dismount. He tied the reins to his arm and stumbled through the snow, his gallant mount laboring to pull the unwilling cows behind them. Still there was no cabin. He would soon have to make a choice: to stumble on through the night toward certain death, or stop and hope to last until morning. He might be able to survive by killing the largest steer and climbing into the warm carcass, but that wouldn't help Silver Birch or the rest of the herd. Before he had to decide upon one or the other of the grim choices, the faint light from the Blue Mesa cabin penetrated the dark. With his last strength he plowed on through the snow, stumbling at last against the door, too tired to open it.

"Jesus Christ, it's the boss," exclaimed Orvid, pulling Burch into the warmth of the cabin. "We never expected to see you back for days."

"I found the rustled cattle," Burch panted, gratefully accepting a cup of steaming coffee.

Burch remained with the boys for two days until a break in the weather allowed some light through the leaden sky. He saddled up Silver Birch.

"You can't mean to leave yet," objected Orvid.

"I have to get back to my own cabin. My cows may have starved to death while I've been gone."

The trip was extremely taxing. Once Burch nearly lost his way, but before the light disappeared, his own cabin came into view and he stumbled inside, grateful to have defied the elements once more. Immediately after starting the fire, he went back into the nearly inky blackness and fought his way to the herd. Two heifers had taught the rest of them how to tear hay from the stacks, but the lake was frozen solid. He used his last energy to chop enough holes in the ice for the cows to drink, then he staggered back to the cabin and fell on the bed, too tired to eat. He hung his hat on the bedpost, drew the blankets over him, and went to sleep with his boots on.

Only partly awake, Burch lay staring at the ceiling with vacant eyes. He must not have moved all night. He was tempted to turn over and go back to sleep, but his slumbers had not been very restful. All night he lay dreaming about cows and storms and elusive strangers moving among the shadows just out of his reach. The whole while he had the feeling that the shadow was a continuing danger to him, that even now it was circling, waiting.

His dreams of Sibyl were even more troubling. She was moving farther and farther away from him, and the harder

320

he tried to reach her the farther away she moved. Yet all the while she looked beseechingly toward him, pleading for him to come to her, calling out to him to take hold of her outstretched hand. He struggled, but his body felt heavier and heavier, and she moved inexorably away from him until she disappeared from sight. After such dreams it was almost a relief to be awake.

He hadn't thought of much else since New Year's except Sibyl. He'd gone over the whole nine days, almost hour by hour, trying to figure out what had gone wrong, but with no results. He probably shouldn't have spent so much time with Emma, but that hadn't caused Sibyl to say she was ashamed of falling in love with him.

And she couldn't be jealous of Augusta. Even though she might not know it, Sibyl wasn't ready for marriage. But during those idyllic four days, Burch had seen signs that she might be beginning to change her mind. Their nights had been a blazing chain of passionate hours when they could not get enough of each other, but during the day many hours had been spent in companionable silence, Burch cleaning his rifles and getting his gear ready, Sibyl attending to the final preparations for the party. It was these hours of utter contentment, as much as their fiery counterparts, that Burch remembered and looked forward to during the two weeks when he was back out on the range for the first time since his accident.

A great aching filled his chest. He loved Sibyl, simply and utterly. What he felt now was new to him, a quiet content, an unquestioned realization that he wanted to spend the rest of his life with her by his side. He wanted to see her across the table at breakfast, to know she waited for him at the end of a long drive and that the ranch was in her capable hands when he was away. Yes, he was *proud* of what she could do. It didn't matter that she didn't have the quiet ease of Augusta or the worshipful love of Aunt Ada. He was a hardheaded, cross-grained cuss, more likely to take his woman for granted than pamper and spoil her. He *wanted* someone who wouldn't stand for being ignored, someone who could give as good as she got, and Sibyl had already proved she could do that.

But she wasn't all iron and leather, either. The emptiness of his belly reminded him of the food good enough to cause a man to make foolish promises, the bareness of the cabin of the changes she had wrought at the ranch. But all that was unimportant when put next to the chance she had taken in that race, a race she had entered for herself but won for him. He could still recall the cold emptiness that filled him when he realized what she meant to do. But instead of her broken and mangled body being hauled from the muddy bottom, she had galloped up to him, radiantly happy, and laid the laurels of her success at his feet.

And how had he treated her sacrifice? He had spent all his time with his friends, laughing, drinking, showing off, never stopping to realize that she had worked nonstop to insure that *his* party would be a success. He probably deserved her to be angry at him, but all he wanted now was a chance to show her that he loved her more than he ever thought he could love anyone.

Vaguely aware of an uncomfortable ball of covers pressed against his side, Burch shifted position.

The memory of their four days and nights together flooded over him and he became rigid with desire. The smell of her hair, the feel of her skin, the exquisite torture of her body caused the blood to race through his veins and made him squirm uncomfortably. "I've got to stop or it'll drive me crazy," he said out loud. But the hunger would not give him any ease, and he twisted miserably in the bed.

Suddenly he froze, a deathly cold fear sweeping over him in an instant of horrifying realization. The uncomfortable ball was no longer bothering him. It was gradually being reduced in size. *It was moving!* Even through the thick protective cover of his sheepskin coat, he could feel the undulating, twisting, slithering movement. There was a snake in his bed! In one sweeping movement Burch threw off the covers and leapt from the bed. There, in the warm depression of the mattress, was a rattlesnake, coiled and ready to strike. Burch snatched his rifle from against the wall and without regard for the mattress, blasted the venomous creature into bits. He heaved a sigh of relief, letting the awful tension drain from his body. Only then did he become aware of something dangling, writhing, pulling at the thick coat that covered his powerful arms. He looked down into the cold, reptilian eyes of a second snake; its fangs were buried deep in the leather of his coat, and it dangled from his sleeve, unable to free itself. In one swift movement Burch pulled out his knife and severed the snake's head from its body. He collected the remains of the two reptiles and flung them out into the snow. Next he carefully searched the cabin until he was satisfied there were no more snakes, then he sat down on the bed, too weak to stand without shaking.

He had missed death by a hair's-breadth. If he hadn't been too tired to undress the night before, he would now have the venom of at least one snake inside his body. He took off his coat and turned it inside out. Adhering to the thick fur lining where the snake's fangs had penetrated the leather were two drops of liquid. Those two little drops, so small and so clear, represented life and death—*his* life and how close he had come to losing it.

There was no longer a mystery about the cattle or the *accidents* that had happened to him during the past year. He didn't know who or why, but somebody was systematically trying to kill him. Burch cursed himself for being so careless. He had probably passed the man on the way to Boulder Canyon. The man *knew* he would find the cattle, so he had put the two snakes in his cabin, certain that at least one of them would be drawn to the warmth of Burch's body.

Now that his game was exposed, his unknown assailant was going to be more dangerous than ever. But what *was* his game? It couldn't be Jesse because he had nothing to gain,

323

and it couldn't be Ute or Loomis because they were too crazy to do anything systematically. Burch gave up his unprofitable questioning. Whoever was after him was not crazy. They had taken great pains to make his death look like an accident and would probably try again.

But right now Sibyl was the most important thing in the world to him, and as soon as he knew the herd was safe, he was going back to her. After that, he and Jesse would decide what to do about these attempts. Odd, though. If Jesse was on the trail of the man—and his going to Boulder Canyon seemed to indicate that he was—why hadn't he come to Burch with what he'd found? Burch realized that he had let his mind be taken up by so many other things recently that he and Jesse had barely talked for months. That was just one more thing he'd have to do after he saw Sibyl. In the meantime, he had better keep his eyes open. After so many failures, his assailant might be desperate enough to make an open attempt on his life.

Chapter 27

Burch rode swiftly toward the Three Bars and Augusta. He had reached the Elkhorn the night before, almost light-headed with excitement, only to be greeted by Emma melodramatically flinging herself into his arms.

"Where is Sibyl?" he had asked, rudely setting her aside.

"Your precious cousin has gone home to Virginia," Emma answered spitefully, furious over her unequivocal rejection. "The little *lady* couldn't take it out here."

"Of all the lying cats!" exclaimed Balaam. "Miss Sibyl nearly worked herself to the bone keeping her cows from freezing into solid blocks. I didn't notice you offering to heat water or tend the stove."

"It's too bad *you* didn't freeze into a solid block," Emma shouted, turning on him furiously.

"To hell with your cows *and* your solid blocks!" exploded Burch. "Why did she leave?"

"She didn't say nothing to nobody," Balaam said. "Just packed up her things the minute you rode off. Left a letter for me to deliver to her aunt first chance I got."

"Where is it?"

"I done took it."

"Did she leave one for me?"

"Nope," Balaam said with so much callous unconcern

Rachel could have brained him. "Said you'd know. Said it a couple of times, in fact."

"Balaam, I want you to take Miss Stratton home," Burch said with brisk decision. "She can't continue to stay here without a proper chaperon."

"We could fix it so it wouldn't matter," Emma hinted, certain that success was almost within her grasp.

"Touched in the head, that's what she is," Balaam whispered loudly to Rachel, "if she thinks Mr. Burch is gonna settle for side meat when he can have tenderloin." Burch pretended he hadn't heard, but Emma's eyes flashed furiously at the acid-tongued old man.

"I don't know what's happened to Auggie, but I don't feel comfortable leaving you here with no one to protect you."

"Where are you going?" Emma demanded imperatively.

"I'm going to Virginia to bring Sibyl back."

"You mean you're going to *marry* her?" Emma asked, unable to believe it.

"Just as soon as I can."

"Yippee!" shouted Balaam, brandishing his delight in Emma's face.

Lasso was not at home when Burch arrived. "He's taken the girls with him to see what damage has been done to the herd," Augusta explained, looking up from some needlework.

"It's you I wanted to see."

Augusta bit her thread off and folded up her work. "It's about Sibyl, isn't it? You want to know why she left?" Her blue-gray eyes stared at him with soft sadness.

"Didn't you expect I would?"

"I didn't know," she said quietly. "At first I thought you liked her, but lately I decided I must have been wrong."

"Like her!" he parroted, stunned. "I love her."

"Does she know that?"

"Of course she does."

"Did you tell her?"

"Over and over again."

"Most men don't, and we women often go on wondering."

"She had no reason to doubt it," Burch added, thinking of the indescribable pleasure he enjoyed in her arms.

"But she did have doubts," Augusta said. "I saw her becoming more withdrawn, but I was too involved with my own happiness, too blinded by love, to help her when she needed me most." Great tears welled up in her eyes. "When Balaam brought me that letter I almost went after her myself."

"Do you still have the letter?"

Augusta nodded. "I can't think of any reason why you shouldn't see it. She talks as though I knew exactly what she was feeling, what was going on in her mind, but I *didn't* know and I've felt so guilty." She blew her nose and rose to get the letter from a small desk in the corner of the cozy parlor. "She didn't say much. It was almost as though she felt she couldn't confide in me any longer."

Burch almost snatched the letter from Augusta's hand in his haste to read it.

Dear Aunt Augusta,

I am going home, I should have known from the first that coming out here was a mistake, but I never have been able to admit it when I was wrong. I wanted this one last chance so desperately I was willing to try anything. I was too ready to reach out for what I wanted, ready to believe it was what it seemed, but I was just fooling myself. There is no place for me at the Elkhorn and there never can be.

Do you remember asking me what I would do when Burch got married? Well, he probably will soon, and I couldn't stand it. It's ironic that you were the one to find your happiness. Please believe that all my love stays with you. I hope you'll bring Lasso and the girls

327

to visit me someday.

If Burch should ask about me, tell him he will be
hearing from Mr. Clarence soon.

I'll love you always,
Sibyl

"But she still doesn't say anything!" Burch protested. "Do
you know why she left?"

"No, but I can guess," Augusta said deliberately. "I was not
so entirely blinded by my own happiness that I didn't notice
you spent a lot of time with Emma Stratton. If Sibyl believed
that you are on the verge of marrying Emma, she would
never stay in Wyoming."

"Good God! The idea never occurred to me. Emma's like
my sister."

"It's occurred to Emma."

"Maybe," Burch said impatiently, "but it's still the custom
for a man to ask a woman to marry him before his friends
start planning the wedding. Why didn't Sibyl ask me if she
wanted to know?"

"Ask you if you intended to marry another woman?"
Augusta repeated incredulously. "She would never have
dreamed of doing such a thing."

"Why not? Emma would have straight off."

Augusta thought it best to keep her thoughts about Emma
Stratton to herself. "I don't know much about girls in
general," Augusta began, "but I've known Sibyl since she was
born, and she has too much pride to let you see that she loves
you if she has any doubts about your loving her."

"But I've never been in love with Emma."

"Does Sibyl know that? Did you *tell* her you were only
being polite to a guest, or did you leave her to take it on
faith? And what about those terrible arguments?"

"You're the only person I know who *didn't* argue with
Sibyl. She's stubborn, hardheaded, determined to have her

328

way, and absolutely positive that she knows more about everything than any man alive."

"The exact words she used to describe you," Augusta said, unable to repress a tiny smile.

"But she couldn't think I didn't love her. Good Lord, I let her run the place anyway she liked. I never would have done that with Emma and she was *raised* on a ranch."

"Did you ever tell her?"

"I told everybody about her cooking and that the party was all her doing."

"I don't mean that. Men always expect women to be excellent cooks and to give nice parties. Did you tell her about the ranch?"

"I never interfered with anything she did. I didn't need to tell her."

"That's all the more reason."

"Why?"

"After having virtually forced you to leave it to her, she needed to have you tell her that she had done a good job, that you were proud of her."

"I tried to thank her for saving my life a dozen times over, and all she did was shrug it off. How was I to know she wanted to be thanked for a full smokehouse and curtains at the windows?"

"That's not the same thing. Anyone would have tried to save your life."

"Do you mean to tell me that being thankful for butter and eggs and haystacks by the creek is more important than saving my life?"

"It doesn't sound very good when you put it that way," Augusta admitted, "but that's the way Sibyl would see it."

"I will *never* understand women," he announced in disgust, "not if I live to be a thousand years old."

"I don't know that I can explain Sibyl to you, but I'll try. My father was a rich man, something of the proud patriarch, and he spoiled his three daughters terribly. Cornelia

329

grew up before the war believing that life would always be the same. When she saw what the war had done she retreated into a shell. Then she married Stuart and had Sibyl, and we thought she had recovered. But as Sibyl grew older, Cornelia began to depend more and more on her until the child bore more responsibility than any boy her age.

"Things might have turned out even then, but Sibyl, like her father, is extremely intelligent and intolerant of stupidity. When it was made plain to her that everything a man said was to be accepted without question, she rebelled. The result was a lot of ill-natured heckling from the other girls and an intolerable amount of good advice from well-meaning matrons. She responded by taking every opportunity she could to puncture what she saw as pompous conceit and meaningless tradition."

"I imagine she would," grinned Burch.

"But no one could see how terribly she suffered. Sibyl's father, dear man, had absolutely no perception and was exactly the kind of person Sibyl was fighting against. He expected her to be able to make all the decisions when he wasn't there, and then meekly accept his authority on his occasional visits."

"Did she?"

"No, but she could always bring him around gently."

"I never doubted that."

"Stuart was inordinately proud of her, but I don't think he ever admitted, even to himself, that she knew more about the farm than he did. But his pride didn't help Sibyl when she saw her friends marry and assume positions of consequence denied her. Sibyl was always much more beautiful than any of them, and they couldn't help gloating."

"I can't believe no one wanted to marry her."

"Several did, but she didn't want to marry them. She called them little boys playing at being men and drove them from her. I tried to show her her mistake, but she told me she couldn't respect anyone who would buy a pretty pot without knowing whether the cream inside was curdled. And you have to admit that most men never see past Sibyl's face. So when your uncle died, she made up her mind to come out West."

"What for?"

"I don't think she ever thought of that, only what she was hoping to escape. I'm afraid there is very little of Cornelia in Sibyl. She's much more like her grandfather. She will never be able to accept a subordinate position. She might do everything you ever wanted her to do, but she will do it because she wants to, not because you tell her to, no matter how much she loves you." Burch screwed up his face in an expression of great perplexity. "Do you understand what I'm trying to say?" Augusta asked. "I'm not very good at explaining things."

"A little," he said without changing expression.

"Imagine yourself in her shoes and being treated as she has."

"I wouldn't put up with it," Burch said decisively.

"That's just it. *You* could do something about it; Sibyl couldn't. She once told me that coming out here was her last chance to escape."

Burch's expression lightened. "Then why didn't she stay? She got what she wanted."

"It turned out that what she wanted was you, and what she couldn't live without was her self-respect. I imagine it was when she saw she couldn't have them both that she decided to go back."

"But why didn't she say something?"

"Sibyl is a fighter, but she doesn't whine or beg," Augusta said proudly. "Love that is not given freely is not worth the price. It's better to turn your back than try to buy happiness in that manner."

"That's not what I meant," Burch spoke more sharply than he ever had to Augusta, "and you should know it, despite your stiff-necked Southern pride."

"And you should know that you don't rope and brand a wife like you would a cow," Augusta replied severely. "I do not defend Sibyl's conduct during these past months, but you have acted with a lack of perception that I find incredible in one as intelligent as I believe you to be. Both of you laugh at Lasso. Don't deny it, I know you do, but what neither of you sees is that behind the jokes and loud voice he understands how people feel. He senses what's important to me without my ever having to tell him. You and Sibyl are so tied up with your own selves you can't see anything but your *own* wants and needs."

"What should I do?"

"What do you want to do?"

"Shake her until her teeth rattle for being so brainless," Burch said savagely.

"I don't imagine Sibyl could listen very well with her teeth rattling about in her head." Augusta responded dryly, surprising a crack of laughter out of Burch that snapped the mounting tension.

"You'll soon be able to give Lasso back his own," Burch said, bending over to give a surprised Augusta a tender kiss on the cheek. "Thank you."

"Leave your wife alone for one moment, and the neighbors come rustling behind your back," roared Lasso, entering the parlor with the little girls.

Augusta turned pink, but Burch noticed there was no hint of uneasiness between them. Their trust was complete.

"How did you find the herds?" she asked, presenting her cheek for his expected salute.

"Terrible," he replied, abruptly grim. "I hope you won't find yourself married to a pauper come spring."

"I'm sure you and Burch can find a solution between you," she said, rising from the chair. "How about a cup of hot chocolate, girls? Your noses look frozen."

The girls giggled and happily followed Augusta to the kitchen. Burch looked on as Lasso's eyes followed Augusta with obvious contentment.

"I wondered how long it would be before you came hightailing it this way," he said, turning back to his friend.

"I came to ask Augusta if she knew why Sibyl went back to Virginia."

"And did she tell you?"

"Sibyl didn't tell her, but she has some pretty shrewd ideas."

"Augusta always does. And what do you plan to do now?"

"Go after her." Lasso regarded his friend with a fixed stare.

"Do you think that's wise?"

"What do you mean by that?" asked Burch, firing up.

"Exactly what it sounds like," replied Lasso, unmoved. "It didn't seem to me that you two ever got along very well. Too much temper and sharp words between you for my liking."

"I'm not bringing her back for you."

"Who says you're bringing her back?"

"Why the hell do you think I'm going after her?"

"I'm damned if I know, but I do know you're going to have to give her an awfully good reason to change her mind."

"Whose friend are you?" Burch asked angrily. "If I didn't know better, I'd swear you were thinking only of Sibyl."

"I'm thinking of both of you, but I'm thinking of Augusta most of all," Lasso said bluntly. "She thinks the world of you, for which I don't blame her . . ."

"Thanks, but don't try so hard," interrupted Burch.

". . . but she loves her niece. She'll be unhappy with Sibyl back in Virginia, but she'd be downright miserable with her at the Elkhorn and you two carrying on like cock roosters all the time. I don't say I wouldn't like to have Sibyl close by to give Augusta some company, but I don't want it if it's going to mean a constant aggravation to her."

"I want to marry her, you blind fool, not fight with her."

"Are you sure you know the difference, either of you? I always thought you were a sensible man, but from the day that girl arrived, you've acted like a schoolboy suffering his

333

first crush."

Burch rose from his chair in fury. "Then I won't inflict this tawdry tale on you any longer," he said furiously.

"Sit down and stop acting like a lovesick fool," Lasso commanded sternly. "You once told me that if I wasn't willing to accept Augusta like she was, I'd best back off. It was better advice than you knew. I would have married her expecting her to be something she wasn't and never seen the beauty of what she is. You'd better ask yourself the same question. Do you love Sibyl just like she is?"

"Yes," replied Burch miserably after a pause. "More than I suspected."

"You're a fine man, Burch, and one I'm proud to call my friend, but you can be downright stupid when you put your mind to it. Can't you see that Sibyl's no more like Ada than I am? You're one of the lucky ones; you've got two women in one—a comforting companion and a participating partner. You won't get her on any other terms."

"How about some hot coffee and cake?" Augusta asked, setting down a tray loaded with a steaming pot of coffee and slices of fresh stack cake. "You'll need something to keep you warm on your ride back."

For the next half hour nothing was said of the problem that occupied all their minds, but as soon as Augusta took away the cups, Burch asked Lasso, "Will you watch the Elkhorn while I'm gone?"

"Then you are going after her?"

"I always was. I only came here because she didn't leave a letter for me." That was a difficult admission for Burch to make, ever to his closest friend.

"Then you'd best go at once," said Augusta, coming back almost immediately. "The longer you wait, the more difficult it will be to convince her that you love her."

"What should I say to her? I don't mean for you to put words in my mouth," Burch assured them, stung by their incredulous stares. "I didn't say the right things before, and I don't want to make the same mistakes again."

August's eyes softened with understanding. "I don't know what to tell you to say, but I doubt it much matters what words you use. She knows what you're bound to say, in any event. You have to convince her that she has your trust and respect, or she won't come back with you no matter how desperately she wants to."

"I'll bring her back," said Burch. "I don't know how, but I'll do it."

"That's the cricket," said Lasso, wringing Burch's hand.

"I thought you weren't sure."

"Just sure I didn't want a cougar and a lynx sharing a lair next door to me," he grinned.

"Will you give this to Sibyl for me?" Augusta asked, taking a thick envelope from her pocket.

"This must be a dozen pages long," Burch said. "When did you have time to write it?"

Augusta blushed prettily. "I wrote it days ago, I knew you would come."

Chapter 28

Rising from her chair with unladylike abruptness, Sibyl paced the room with short, rapid strides. She moved to the window and jerked back the curtains, but her glazed eyes were focused on something far beyond the wide lawn or the hundred-year-old tulip poplars that gave the house its name. Burch dominated her thoughts and the house merely made it worse.

She had fled to the home of her aunt, Louisa Russell; Louisa had inherited the family home, *the house Uncle Wesley had copied at the Elkhorn*. Sibyl never realized how much the two houses were alike. The three sisters, completely different in personality, had been so alike in their excellent taste that even their furnishings were similar. Several times Sibyl had caught herself half expecting Burch to walk through the door, his guns over his shoulder and another hunting trophy for the already crowded walls. It was almost as though she hadn't left the Elkhorn. All the pressures were still here, all the feelings of futility weighing down her spirits and making her moody and withdrawn.

Sibyl had felt completely drained by the time she reached Virginia, but she was determined not to answer any prying questions. Unexpectedly Aunt Louisa ordered everyone to leave her alone. For almost a week she had kept to her room, as much to escape the family's curious stares as to avoid the haunting memories the familiar rooms evoked. But grief is not fatal in and of itself, and it's impossible for a vibrant young woman to stay in a closed room forever. At last, Sibyl came downstairs.

Louisa never did ask why she had returned. "That's all behind you," she said calmly. "For the present, we need to see about getting you caught up with your old friends. Jessica says everyone is anxious to see you."

"Really, Aunt Louisa, you don't have to look for things for me to do."

"Well, you can't continue to mope about the house," responded a determined voice that bore no resemblance to Sibyl's mother or her Aunt Augusta. "People know you're here, and they will begin to ask questions if they don't see you. You have already caused enough uncomfortable gossip for the family as it is, not that Augusta's marrying a cowboy wasn't the biggest shock of all. I was prepared to learn that you had done something deplorable, but Augusta! I still can't believe it."

"She's extremely happy," Sibyl assured her aunt for the twentieth time. "She has a house of her own, a husband to look after, and two little girls. She's just like you now."

"What's a cowboy like?" her cousin Jessica asked breathlessly.

"I'll thank you not to compare your Uncle Henry to any cowboy," Louisa's frigid tones ruthlessly interrupted her daughter. "Augusta always was a timid girl, so afraid to go about with even the most respectable boys that I was sure she'd end up an old maid. I never dreamed she would disgrace us all by traipsing off to the wilds of wherever it was your Uncle Wesley went and marry the first man she found. It wasn't like she hadn't had her chances here and thrown every one of them away."

"Maybe she didn't love any of those men."

"So it would seem," replied her aunt regally, "but that still

337

doesn't explain why she must go and marry someone from the *territories*!"

"People in Wyoming are just like people anywhere else," Sibyl said wearily.

"So you've assured me, and I hope you may be right, especially if she should decide to visit us."

"You wouldn't turn Aunt Augusta away?" asked Sibyl incredulously.

"No, not even if she had made a *truly* scandalous marriage, but that doesn't mean that I can accept such a catastrophe complacently. Believe me, I shall have a good deal to say to my sister when next I write her."

"I don't think she will care what you say," Sibyl said mutinously. "She's so happy she probably won't ever come back to Virginia again." A sob seemed to catch in Sibyl's throat, but her aunt's inquiring gaze saw only the same set expression she had worn for eight days.

"That's as may be, but whether or not Augusta deigns to visit us has no bearing on your situation," her aunt continued inexorably. "Don't you wish to see your friends?"

"And be forced to listen to them gloat over having a husband and a houseful of anemic children? No, thank you. I had enough of that before."

"Sibyl never had any friends," Jessica, a fledgling sixteen-year-old, said smugly.

"That is a rude and thoughtless remark, young lady. You will apologize to your cousin at once."

Sibyl ignored Jessica's mumbled apology.

"You may want to listen to Bessie Newland brag about her new furniture and their trips to Saratoga Springs, but if I were Jonathan Newland, I'd have to take a headache powder just to go into town with her. And I'd rather have pups than be the mother of that repulsive little Clay."

"Sibyl!" remonstrated her scandalized aunt.

"I'm sorry if I offended you, but I can't stand her snobbery. Bessie is dull, plain, dumpy as a potato, and no

338

more intelligent than a signpost."

Her younger cousin, Priscilla, giggled.

"If that's the way you speak of people you've known all your life, then I'm not surprised you find yourself neglected," her aunt reproved her.

"I haven't said half of what she said about me," retorted Sibyl.

"What do you plan to do?" asked Jessica eagerly.

"I'm not sure yet. I thought I might open the house again or travel abroad."

"That's impossible," decreed her aunt. "You will marry like any other respectable girl. It is out of the question that you should even think of living by yourself, much less traveling abroad without a proper chaperon."

"I survived cowboys, Indians, and a stampede," Sibyl stated a trifle inaccurately. "There's nothing in Virginia to harm me."

"We're not speaking of any possible danger to your person, but of the manner in which a lady is raised and expected to behave," Louisa announced majestically. "Now I've had quite enough of this hiding in your room. I've invited your cousin for dinner, and tomorrow we shall take the carriage out."

"Kendrick?" groaned Sibyl with such a pained grimace that Priscilla giggled again.

"Yes, Kendrick. I've been putting him off, but it's time you faced some company."

"The only way to face Kendrick is by turning your back on him."

"That will be quite enough, Sibyl. Priscilla, you will go to your room until you are able to behave yourself." The uncontrite thirteen-year-old was only too willing to be the first to spread Sibyl's unflattering words.

"And you will oblige me by making no more rude and thoughtless remarks in the presence of your cousins. They are too young to be able to judge them as they should."

"Nothing will come of it, I promise you. I would rather

scrub floors than marry Kendrick."

"I can't understand you at all, Sibyl. Your cousin is a thoroughly respectable man. He has brought his farm back into production and is building up his own law office."

"How mortifying to know there are people in Virginia who think Kendrick could defend a dog against a cat."

"I can see that Wyoming has not improved your manners."

"No, but neither has it made me desperate enough to marry Kendrick."

"You will have the kindness to conceal your attitude while he's here," commanded her aunt, "and when we visit Clara Maynard."

"*Is she coming here?*" exclaimed Sibyl.

"No, we are going there. I've already promised, so there's no getting out of it," her aunt said, anticipating Sibyl's protest. "Everyone will expect to see you sooner or later, and I will *not* have this family continue to be a source of gossip for the whole county if I can possibly prevent it." Louisa paused, apparently uncertain of what to say next. "How much money do you have at your immediate disposal?" she finally asked.

"The ranch made over one hundred and fifty thousand dollars, so my share ought to come to something over fifty thousand after expenses."

"Are you sure you have properly understood the amount?" her aunt asked, astounded. "I had no idea there was so much money to be made in cows."

"Most people don't make that much, but there are some who make a lot more."

"Then you must be married, but with all that money I don't imagine that you would be satisfied with Kendrick."

"No, I don't think I could." Sibyl refrained from telling her aunt that she would not have been satisfied with Kendrick if she had been down to her last penny.

"Well, he's already invited so that can't be helped, but I don't expect anything to come of it."

340

Alone, as she dressed for dinner, Sibyl reluctantly faced the prospect of marriage. There seemed no way out; it was almost as bad as Wyoming. No, nothing could be as bad as seeing Burch married to Emma. The thought of his arms, his lips, his lean hard body, tortured her nightly, but nothing hurt so badly as the memory of Burch, naked to the waist, and Emma's arms about him. Every night she would dream of Burch making love to Emma; then she would wake up, her body shaking and sweat on her brow. The dream persecuted Sibyl and battered at her resistance every day; she couldn't endure it much longer.

She caught sight of her gaunt face as she pinned her mother's pearl broach to her bosom. She couldn't live alone with her memories. She had to drive all remembrance of Burch from her mind, and maybe marriage to some nice anonymous man would help; surely they all weren't as distasteful as Kendrick and Moreton. There would be a house to run and children to raise, and she'd like that. She tried so hard to keep from thinking about Burch and Wyoming, but the powerful shoulders and bushy eyebrows that haunted her sleep would not go away and an anguished "Burch!" escaped her parted lips.

Small spots of red still flamed in Sibyl's cheeks when her aunt followed her to her room, but now she had her anger under control.

"You have done many things I disapproved of," declared Louisa with stately condemnation, "but I never thought to see you display common manners in front of guests."

"I couldn't stand the way Kendrick was talking any longer. He's a stupid, cowardly braggart."

"Kendrick's character has often disappointed his family, but while such shortcomings will be tolerated in a man, they will never be accepted in a woman."

"Why should I have to be so much better than a man just to receive the same respect? At least in Wyoming I wasn't

341

treated like a mindless slave."

"The sooner you forget Wyoming the better. It's no part of your society."

"No. *My* society includes people like Clara Maynard, who gets a husband by sleeping with him and then lying about being pregnant, or Kendrick, who sees nothing wrong with squeezing the very men who were once his family's friends."

"Not everyone is like Clara or Kendrick. I have no doubt there are just as many honest and kind people in Virginia as there are in Wyoming."

"More."

"Possibly, but you won't convince anyone of it by behaving like a savage. They will assume you acquired your manners in Wyoming; they know you didn't learn them here."

"I'm sorry," Sibyl said contritely.

"We will not refer to it again," Louisa relented regally. "Kendrick was at his most provoking tonight, and your drubbing probably did him some good, if anything could do that boy good. Instead, you might as well start thinking about your future. Your cousin can be very helpful when we go to Richmond."

"I don't want to go to Richmond. I'm going to see the house tomorrow," Sibyl said, an overt challenge in her words.

"An agent will see that it is in condition to sell."

"I'm going to keep it. I can't go on living with you."

"Sibyl, I take it as a personal affront that you would want to see that house, and I forbid you to even consider moving there."

"Aunt Louisa, I will go to Richmond with you, or anywhere else you wish to take me, but I cannot stay here."

"You did fall in love with your cousin."

Sibyl turned away without answering.

"I thought so from the start, but I was hoping I was wrong. I told you nothing good would come of running away."

"You're wrong. It was worth the whole trip just to see

Aunt Augusta's face when she married Lasso."

"I will never accustom myself to the fact that my sister would actually *marry* someone with a name like Lasso Slaughter," Louisa moaned.

"You probably won't like Lasso any more than his name. I didn't at first, but you wouldn't believe the difference in Aunt Augusta."

"I suppose I must accept your assurances that Augusta is indeed happy, but that doesn't mean that I wish you to make the same mistake."

"There's no chance of it. My cousin has quite different plans," Sibyl assured her in a bleak voice.

"And so shall you as soon as I can get you to a really good dress shop. There's no point in having cows that can make all that money unless you can spend it on clothes. I think we ought to go to New York as soon as possible. I can't wait for you to show Clara Maynard what a well-chosen dress looks like."

An unexpected wave of bitter anguish gripped Sibyl, and with a rush she threw her arms about her aunt and broke into tears. At last the dam inside her broke, and she began to talk. Out poured all the secrets she had held so tightly in her heart, words tumbling over words in their rush to escape. There was no order or logic to them, but somehow her aunt understood. She offered no words of censorship, only the comfort of knowing someone was there who cared. For the first time in weeks Sibyl felt relaxed and relieved to discover that, in spite of the rigid front, her Aunt Louisa was just as kind and understanding as her younger sister.

Chapter 29

Sibyl hesitated uneasily at the door, then a look of tenacious resolve formed on her face; she took a deep breath, opened the door, and stepped inside. She didn't know why it should take such an effort to enter her old home, but the emotional drain was enormous; just standing in the front hall was like going back in time by tearing out everything that had happened to her in the last six months by the roots. It was much worse than being at Tulip Hall, so excruciatingly painful she wondered if she would ever be able to live here again. The entrance hall, stripped bare of the familiar furnishings, seemed strange, even unfriendly; the parlor, too, looked large and terribly empty. The polished floor's shiny surface denied the softness, the coziness, the easy comfort she remembered. It all seemed to be part of the harsh reality of pain, disappointment, and disillusionment.

She wandered about the house mechanically recording what was needed to make it liveable again, yet all the while thinking of the absent furnishings in their new settings at the Elkhorn, and inseparable from that, Burch. Always, it was Burch. Every empty corner, every missing chair, every disheartening thought contained the germ of some remembrance that would conjure up a memory, some random fragment of those six months, and underscore the bleakness of her future.

Maybe her aunt was right; maybe she couldn't live here again, maybe she should consider selling the house. It contained too many painful links to dreams that had disappointed her, dreams that no longer held out a promise of happiness. Maybe she should leave Lexington altogether and make a totally new life for herself far away from everything that had ever happened to her.

She wandered upstairs and through her old room, searching out the secret corners and remembering the private moments that she had collected over the years. Every one of them had occurred before she met Burch, but now they seemed to exist only through him. Frantically she searched for something to shut out the memories, to ease the hurt, but there was nothing, only the hard, shiny floors emphasizing the emptiness of the house—and her life. With jarring suddenness Sibyl knew that she could never come back; this world was just as closed to her as the Elkhorn.

She drifted into one of the extra bedrooms they had never used, and its strangeness comforted her. Some unused furnishings were stored there, and she sank down on a pile of mattresses by the window and stared thoughtfully through the dusty panes.

She had visited the farm, too. She hadn't expected it to be the same, being owned by someone else and all her father's projects discontinued, but even the barns, with their massive stone foundations supporting two full floors above, seemed to be less imposing than she remembered. She didn't know what she could ever have found to interest her in such a small, predictable property.

Most difficult of all was the visit to her mother's grave. Unsuspecting, she carried the weight of her troubles with her, thinking somehow the burden would be taken from her shoulders. Instead, it weighed even more heavily; there was no answer for her there. Her mother had given in to her grief and let it destroy her. Sibyl couldn't give in, couldn't give up; she had to fight back, to struggle to find some solution for her life. She was alive, vibrant, and determined; she had tasted some of life's sweetness and she wanted more. But how? There were no answers for her in Lexington, not from people who were unable to change, unable to meet the challenges and demands of a new world with honesty and dignity; not from Aunt Louisa who lived by a code Sibyl found repellant.

Only meek, underrated Augusta had the courage to meet the future and accept it. She had a strength none of them had been able to recognize, the courage go forward without denying her past. She was able to take life and love as it was offered to her, and savor its sweetness without longing for the slice someone else had cut away. It made Sibyl ashamed to think she had never seen what Burch and Lasso saw so easily.

"Burch!" The name rose to her lips of its own accord, and she crumpled up with a sob of despair. "I didn't know it could hurt so much to love you. Oh God," she wailed, "why did you let me go? Why aren't you here?"

"I am here."

Sibyl's body turned to stone. She must be going crazy. Now she was hearing things. "Don't be a fool, there's nobody here," she said aloud to calm her racing pulse. "You're letting your imagination get the best of you."

"Just look up," the voice said, echoing through the empty room. Fearfully Sibyl raised her eyes, and through a mist of tears she saw the well-loved features framed in the open doorway. She *must* be dreaming, losing her mind. Maybe she'd fainted. But then the shadowy shape moved toward her, and she heard the sound of his heels on the bare floor, saw the weathered features come into clear focus despite the tears. With a half-smothered shriek she flew up from the window and threw herself into his outstretched arms. His hungry lips found hers, crushing her mouth in a searing kiss that left her breathless. Every bit of the feelings she had so steadfastly refused to acknowledge, all the grinding desire

346

she had staunchly denied, swept her up in a rampaging flood that recognized no restraint; she had no desire for any. She was in the arms of the man she loved, embraced by the body her own body craved, and no one and nothing else in the world mattered.

"Is it really you?" she asked breathlessly, emerging from his embrace.

"Do you have to ask after that welcome?"

"Don't tease me," she begged. "I can't stand it. Just hold me," she implored, unwilling to leave the comforting circle of his arms. Thinking poorly of such a waste of time, Burch applied himself to reassuring her in a manner that soon reduced her bones to mush. But he didn't confine himself to her lips. With his teeth, lips, and tongue he caressed her neck, tantalized her ears, and trailed molten kisses across her shoulders. Sibyl's body, long denied its fulfillment, leapt in response, all of her senses awakened and clamoring for relief.

The smell of him brought memories of the nights they spent in each others arms rushing back, and suddenly it was as though they had been whisked back in time to the blissful days before Christmas, when they were secure in each other's love. Burch's hands traveled over her body, and when she moaned in response, arching her body against his own heated desire, his nimble fingers rapidly unbuttoned the front of her dress to lift out one soft white breast. Sibyl felt as though her whole body would explode when Burch's lips touched her throbbing nipples; she slumped away from him, too weak to stand. Scooping her up, he deposited her on the stack of mattresses.

Sibyl felt like she was floating on a cloud, a cloud of fire that sent flames lapping at every part of her body. Burch had freed the second breast, and the torture of it caused Sibyl to writhe pleasurably, trying to pull his body to hers, her hands trying to open his shirt. She wiggled her body, helping Burch free her from her dress. Then her fumbling fingers joined his to rid him of his restraining garments. There was no slow beginning, no loving tenderness, no lingering caresses. Burch and Sibyl came together without preliminaries, driven by a force that deprived them of reason or control. Burch entered her quickly, driven toward his own release without regard for her. Sibyl, equally oblivious to anything except her own maddening need, strove to satisfy her longing with the same blind haste. The climax came quickly, but it brought no release of the terrible pressure that had been building within them for months.

Almost at once Burch's control reasserted itself, and he began to move slowly, rhythmically, letting his lips and hands caress Sibyl's soft skin, toy with her still-throbbing breasts, hold her lips in long, lingering kisses while his tongue explored her mouth. Gradually, he kindled in her a sense of excitement, a higher level of responsiveness, and a thrill of expectancy. He remembered all the most sensitive places and exploited every one of them until Sibyl was twisting and turning in ecstasy. "Please," she begged of him, but he continued with the same intensity, varying his strokes but never their tempo, until she thought she could stand it no longer.

Sibyl threw herself against him, crying for liberation, demanding relief from the teasing and tantalizing motion. With infinite expertise, Burch was keeping her on the very edge, building the tension, the need for release, but never going far enough to allow her to reach that all-important pinnacle.

"Faster, please go faster," Sibyl begged. Burst after burst of agonizing pleasure swept over her, racking her body from end to end, but never that one magnificent eruption, that one final explosion that would release all the tension, satisfy all the need, achieve all the pleasure that she knew was there. Sibyl could stand it no longer, and she moved on the attack.

Sibyl increased her own tempo without waiting for Burch. She kissed him with all the passion of a tortured soul, nipping at his skin with her teeth until he groaned in protest. Her fingers, those gracefully slim instruments of pleasure, began to explore his body, tickling the rippling muscles of his abdomen, gripping the firm buttocks and drawing them toward her. Before long Burch's body was consumed by the fire she had ignited, and he was no longer able to keep up the steady, torturing tempo. They quickened together, moving toward each other with purpose and urgency. Their breath came in gasps and their bodies grew stiff with the sweet agony that was ready to burst over them like a healing balm. Then at last that ultimate, supreme fulfillment rocked them both at the same instant, fusing them into one entity and cleansing them of the months of waiting and longing.

For a long while afterwards they lay perfectly still, Burch's strong arms holding her tight, wrapped in and warmed by the euphoria of being together again. For a few moments before her ability to think and reason returned, Sibyl thought that this might be enough, that she had magnified the differences and fears that had separated them.

"I still can't believe it," she said in wonder. "It seems like years since I left."

"For me it's like it was yesterday. I can still feel the touch of your skin, smell your hair, hear the soft sound of your breath as you lay sleeping."

"You watched me sleep?"

"I lay for hours with you in my arms, wondering how I was so lucky."

"You must not have slept very much."

"If I had known how little time we had, I wouldn't have slept at all. Why did you leave?"

Sibyl stiffened perceptibly. She knew this was not enough. The warmth was still there, but it was not the sweet, healing warmth of just a few minutes ago. It turned irreversibly into the bitter heat of regret and lost trust. The coldness of the house penetrated Sibyl's joy; she sat up with a slight shiver and began to dress quickly.

"Your aunt deserves an explanation as much as I do," he said, aware of the change in her.

"You went to see Aunt Augusta?"

"As soon as I found you gone. What did you expect me to do, write a letter and then sit back and wait for an answer?"

"I didn't expect you to come, at least not so soon." Sibyl tried to recapture the feeling of elation and failed. Her coolness, the certainty that all intimacy between them was over, communicated itself to Burch and he too began to dress.

"I'd have been here sooner," he said, reaching for his pants, "if it hadn't taken so long to get rid of Emma."

Emma! That hated name seemed to haunt her, to follow her wherever she went, driving the last of the warmth away. Only the coldness and the emptiness of regret remained. Suddenly Sibyl felt as though she couldn't keep from bursting into tears. She ran from the room, fleeing from Burch and the ruin of her dreams. She came to rest in a window seat where she had spent many afternoons as a child. It was here that Burch found her a few minutes later, curled up, staring forlornly out the window. It was a melancholy view; the sun made only a feeble attempt to shine, and the walnut trees stood bare of leaves, unfruitful and unpromising. The whole landscape was wet from the melting snow, a weeping, dripping world outside just as much as inside.

"You do still love me," he said, half question and half statement."

"Yes." To deny it any longer, after what had just happened, would make a wanton out of her. Besides, it felt better to face the truth, bitter as it was. "I suppose I always will." Burch came closer.

"But nothing has changed?"

"No." He sat down next to her, taking her hands in his.

"You know you have to tell me why you left, don't you?" he asked softly. "After coming all the way from Wyoming, you can't turn me away without an explanation."

350

Sibyl did not answer. She couldn't. The overwhelming sense of loss nearly choked her. How could she explain that his tryst with Emma, no matter how fleeting and unimportant in his eyes, had destroyed any chance they had for a future together. She could not love a man who would not be faithful to her. She was giving up too much to share what he offered with another woman. Other women!

"I do hope this man is your cousin." Louisa's regal voice came from the doorway and brought both of them to their feet. The shock of being found virtually in Burch's arms by her aunt reduced Sibyl to stammering incoherence, but Burch turned without haste to find himself being measured by a pair of almost black eyes that gave no hint of the thoughts behind their intense gaze.

"Yes, ma'am, that's who I am, but I don't know you. Should I?"

"I'm Sibyl's aunt, Louisa Russell, Augusta's sister. We don't favor, so don't perjure yourself swearing to a likeness that isn't there."

"No, ma'am," Burch said, smiling in a way that explained a lot to Louisa. "I guess you're wondering how I found Sibyl?"

"Not at all. When I returned home and found that Sibyl was still gone out, I was told that a man had come to the house asking for her. I assumed that you were her cousin and had followed her here."

"Just so, nothing mysterious at all."

"And I suppose you've come to talk with Sibyl about whatever it was that sent her home in such haste. I'll not hide from you that I did not favor Sibyl's going off to live in a territory. Neither will I do anything to stand in your way of convincing her of whatever it is you've come to say. However, this is not the place. If you would like to come to dinner, we would be happy to receive you at seven. We're invited to a ball afterwards. It's Sibyl's first time out, so I'm afraid she can't decline at this late date, but you will be allowed to speak with her when we return."

Burch didn't like being swept up in Louisa's plans, nor did he care for an evening he felt sure was bound to make his task all the more difficult, but he fell in with them without demur. "I wouldn't want to do anything to cause you any trouble."

"I don't know what kind of hospitality Lexington offers its visitors, but I hope you've been able to find suitable accommodations."

"Tolerable."

"Good. Then if you'll excuse us, Sibyl looks as though she could use some rest and quiet. You are not the only difficulty she has to face, so I hope that whatever happens you do not mean to add to them." Burch looked puzzled briefly, then nodded in understanding.

"No, ma'am, I won't add to them."

Louisa looked doubtful of that being possible, but she nearly nodded to Burch. "We'd best be going, Sibyl."

Sibyl looked helplessly at Burch, her eyes full of questions. She didn't want to leave him, but she needed time to think. She had thrown herself into his arms, and for a few seconds nothing else mattered except that he had come after her. But the mention of Emma's name had changed everything; she knew it mattered a lot. She loved Burch more than ever, but she still couldn't go back with him.

"Sibyl," he said softly as she reached the door, "I love you."

"I never expected your cowboy to look so respectable," Louisa commented thoughtfully when the carriage doors had closed behind them. "Jessica is in for quite a surprise, and Kendrick a considerable shock." At Sibyl's questioning gaze Louisa explained, with a ghost of a smile, "I don't blame you. If any man like that had so much as looked at me when I was your age, I would have swooned."

Sibyl couldn't imagine her aunt swooning at any age, but she was grateful for her understanding.

"But don't take that for approval. I still think he's unsuitable."

When Sibyl's cousins learned that a real cowboy was coming to dinner, they fell into a fever of excitement.

"Good Lord, he's not a two-headed monster," Sibyl told them between laughter and vexation. "He's a man just like anybody else."

"Will he wear a big hat and those things on his boots?" demanded Priscilla.

"Will he wear his gun to the table?" asked Jessica.

"He doesn't wear a gun," laughed Sibyl, "and he'll probably wear a suit just like your father."

Young Henry pretended he was too old to be impressed by guns and spurs, but he was dressed and downstairs a half hour earlier than usual. Louisa was completely out of patience with her offspring and threatened them with dire consequences if they stared or spoke so much as a single word out of turn. The atmosphere was so close to that of a sideshow that Sibyl was tempted to pretend to a sudden illness.

Dinner passed off well. Burch arrived dressed in the severe formal style of black wool suit, starched collar, and black tie favored by Louisa and her husband, and quite visibly disappointed young Henry. Jessica was too overcome by his size and good looks to feel the slightest disappointment that he wore neither a gun nor his spurs to the table. And Priscilla, between her older sister and younger brother in age and maturity, couldn't decide which attitude to take and consequently fell into complete silence.

Henry Randall was pleased to discover that Burch was a sensible man, and after spending the better part of the meal discussing the political situation in Washington, the fluctuating market for livestock, and the problems faced by any territory wishing to become a state, he felt they had probably judged all Westerners too severely. No one knew what Louisa thought, for she offered no opinion and no one dared ask her for one.

Sibyl hardly spoke at all. Words and fragments of sentences kept up a steady assault on her mind, conjuring up memories so bittersweet and painful that she would have been hard pressed to answer any question intelligently. It seemed so unreal for them to be sitting here, to all outward appearances like old friends, when powerful undercurrents of emotion were coloring every word and when the force of unuttered thoughts turned their spoken words into shadows, pale, meaningless fillers of time.

Sibyl wasn't surprised at Burch's complete ease, but she was a little hurt that he would virtually ignore her. You should be talking to me, explaining your wretched affair with Emma *to me*, not charming Uncle Henry into accepting you as one of the huge male fraternity. It was unfair for her to be forced to sit at the dinner table, acting as though nothing were wrong, while Burch made a conquest of all her relatives. He was in for a big surprise if he thought her uncle's opinion would carry any weight with her. She had behaved foolishly before, but she wasn't about to make the same mistake again.

Sibyl's mood had not softened by the time they left for the ball. The two younger children remained at home, but Jessica, included in the invitation for the first time, was bursting with excitement. She could barely wait to point Burch out to her equally impressionable friends and whisper a few shocking sentences into their credulous ears.

"I'll introduce you around," Henry Russell offered as they climbed into the ponderous family carriage, "but I wouldn't bother to try to remember any names. There're too many of them, and most are not worth the effort."

"They'll remember yours, and that's enough for tonight," said Louisa. "I trust you realize you can not spend the whole evening dancing with Sibyl," she told him bluntly, fixing him with one of her direct stares. "I have no objection to everyone knowing that you're here and who you are, but I refuse to allow you to do anything that will cause Sibyl to become the subject of gossip and speculation."

"Won't it cause just as much comment if I spend the rest of the time dancing with you and Miss Jessica?" Burch questioned.

Jessica giggled nervously, but Louisa was not shaken easily. "My corns won't stand it, and of course you can't single out Jessica in that way. If you can't stand inaction, you can ask around. I imagine a man of your stamp is used to sizing up women at a glance." In the dark of the carriage she directed an appraising look at Burch. "Living far away from civilization, you must have become quite adept at squeezing the most out of a few days in town." Burch's crack of laughter seemed deafening in the confined space of the carriage.

"Ma'am, you'd make a perfect rancher's wife. Nothing puts you off stride, and nobody hides a thing from you."

"I appreciate the compliment, but I find the same traits are quite useful in Virginia."

"It's a great loss to Wyoming."

"Wyoming already has Augusta, and unless I'm mistaken, you're bent on trying to talk Sibyl into going back as well. I think Wyoming is asking for more than its share of the Hauxhurst family."

Louisa's heavy disapproval did not affect Burch. "You can't blame me for asking. Why should Virginia keep all that loveliness?"

"Because she was born here, this is where her roots are. I don't believe people prosper when they're removed from the only life they understand."

"How do you explain Uncle Wesley's success?"

"Your uncle would have been a success anywhere. He didn't choose Wyoming above any other place; he just had to go *someplace* because he couldn't stay here. Like Sibyl's mama, he had his own solution, and I didn't approve of either one."

"Don't you agree that Sibyl has the same need?"

"What Sibyl needs can be found in anyplace, or nowhere. As yet I'm not convinced that it has been found in Wyoming."

"Whew! You don't mince your words, do you, ma'am?"

"Not when straight talking is needed."

"You needn't talk about me like I'm not here," Sibyl cut in, too irritated to remain silent any longer. "Neither of you can make my decisions for me."

"I've already told you how I feel," her aunt pointed out. "I thought Mr. Randall deserved to be equally well informed."

Fortunately, since Sibyl had become considerably angered by this candid exchange, they had arrived at the assembly hall.

The dancing had already begun when they arrived, and their entrance attracted little attention. A few heads did turn to stare at Burch's imposing figure, but they showed nothing more than the inevitable curiosity at the presence of a new and handsome stranger. "You'd better put your name on Sibyl's dance card right away," advised Louisa. "I expect it will fill up quickly."

"Don't forget yours and Jessica's."

"There'll be time enough for that. I'm not as young as Sibyl, Jessica's not as pretty, and neither of us is nearly as rich. I took Sibyl to visit one of her old friends a few days ago, and that miserable girl managed to worm the amount of the ranch's yearly income out of her. If I know Clara Maynard, she wasted no time in telling every person in town. Once they learn you own the other half of that ranch, they'll be beating a path to both of you."

"The line forms at the cashier's window," Sibyl joked cynically and won a sympathetic grin from Burch.

"It is unfortunate that things should be this way, useless to complain," remarked Louisa.

Before Sibyl could speak any of the thoughts jostling about in her head, the music stopped and people began to move in their direction. It was fortunate that Burch had already chosen his dances, for within seconds their party was surrounded by young men seeking a chance to dance with the beautiful heiress. Many an eager suitor remembered, when the news reached him, that he had always admired Sibyl's beauty and viewed her intelligence and sharp wit as estimable traits that set her off from the average female. Among the crowd of hopefuls, Kendrick Hauxhurst assumed he already occupied the preeminent position. He approached Sibyl with a satisfied smile, certain he would be the first to lead her on to the floor.

"This dance is mine," said Burch, whisking Sibyl right out from under Kendrick's startled nose.

"Who is that?" Kendrick demanded irately of Louisa.

"The cowboy you were so sure was a dishonest, lazy bum," said Louisa, unable to hide her satisfaction at seeing Kendrick's face fall.

"Do you mean *that's* Sibyl's cousin?"

"Yes, that's Burch Randall. He seems quite presentable." She glanced at the awestuck faces about her. "And it seems I'm not the only one to think so."

"A man like that can't work a ranch. Not in all that dirt and grime."

"Dirt washes off," Louisa observed corrosively. "Sibyl's uncle always maintained that Burch was a better rancher than he was. Seems to be quite a marvel, that young man. Not a bad-looking one, either."

There was no need for her to contrast Burch's tall, lean, muscled figure with the soft, slightly stoop-shouldered form of Kendrick. Not even his native prejudice could deny that next to Burch, he came off a poor second.

"But is he educated? Does he—?"

"He doesn't wipe his mouth on his sleeve," Louisa said with satisfaction, "and Henry says he knows more about the things a man ought to know than anybody of his acquaintance. I do not want Sibyl to marry him, but I'd be blind if I didn't know that any woman who finds a man like that is a fool to give him up expecting to find a better one."

Her opinion was shared by just about every other woman present. By the time Burch had danced with Jessica and Louisa, everyone in the hall knew who he was and how much money he was worth, and their curiosity was rampant. Mamas dispatched sons, husbands, brothers, or even casual friends to bring him over and warned a daughter to sit up straight and not show her buck teeth. It was widely believed that Sibyl's capricious nature had caused her to refuse him so, therefore, he was fair game. When such an imposing presence was combined with a large income, it was foolish to balk at his coming from the territories. Why, in no time at all, if married to the right kind of girl, he might be turned into a perfectly respectable husband.

"You don't seem to be enjoying your evening," Burch said to Sibyl during their second dance.

"It's worse than I thought." Sibyl's irritation had been replaced by anger, and Burch could see the familiar signs of battle: her blazing eyes, her erect carriage. "I told Aunt Louisa I didn't want to come. Everyone is staring, just waiting to see what we're going to do. Then they'll spend next week gossiping about it."

"Why do you care?"

"I have to face them every day and live with their dishonesty and hypocritical sympathy. You just see them as somebody you'll dance with and never see again."

"You can escape it by coming back with me."

"Don't start that. Not now, not here."

"Why? What's so awful about telling you that I want you to come back?"

"Not in front of all these people. They're just waiting for me to do something they can disapprove of. They always have and I hate it."

"Then ignore them."

"I can't. This is not Wyoming, where your nearest neighbor is ten miles away and you don't have to see anybody if you don't want to. Everybody's related or has known you from childhood. There are no secrets, no privacy in this kind of community." Her gaze fell on Moreton Swan as the music ended, and her mood turned sour. "There's an example of what I mean. Moreton has brought his mama over. He can't seem to go five steps without her, and I can tell she's already preparing to give me a scolding."

Burch had no trouble picking out the lady in question. She was dressed in unrelieved black, with no ornamentation other than a double strand of pearls knotted and hanging down past her waist. Her hair was pulled back in a tight bun, which might account for the expression of displeasure on her sharp features. Introductions were quickly made.

"I'm relieved to see you've returned to civilized society," said Mrs. Swan in a pinched voice, "though I never understood why you left. So unsuitable for a girl to involve herself with business," she said to Louisa. "Surely your cousin, or your *husband*, could have attended to the details of your inheritance."

"My father taught me to manage my own affairs, and I find I quite like it."

"Moreton will find that unacceptable," she said without so much as looking in her son's direction. "And of course it will be expected that your *relatives* will not presume."

"I'm not the least bit interested in what Moreton finds unacceptable," Sibyl replied with blazing eyes. "And I will undertake to see that any *presumptions* my unfortunate relatives make will not annoy you."

Burch, unmoved by Sibyl's wrath, merely looked amused, but the various expressions of the assembled faces told him no one else shared his casual attitude.

"Mother didn't mean to appear to scold you," Moreton quickly intervened, "though I did wonder at your staying so long."

"I haven't given you the right to wonder at my actions, or your mother to disapprove of them," Sibyl responded tartly.

"If I decide to go out West every year, I shall."

"Moreton's wife can hardly be expected to behave in such an unsuitable manner," stated Mrs. Swan with frigid correctness. "We have a position to uphold, a tradition to maintain."

"I'm confident Moreton's wife will be fully conscious of her responsibilities," interjected Louisa, certain the old woman would provoke Sibyl into a mortifying public scene if not stopped, "but the next dance is forming and Sibyl's partner is waiting for her. Burch, I believe your name is next on my card."

A fresh-faced young man, trembling before the fire in Sibyl's eyes, looked ready to relinquish his claim to her at the first opportunity, but Sibyl turned to him with such a dazzling smile he would have fought tigers for this one dance.

"I expect Sibyl to strike that woman one day," Louisa said to Burch as he guided her skillfully about the floor.

"Does she really believe that Sibyl would marry her son?"

"Yes. *Nothing* will convince her that any girl would decline the honor of being Moreton's wife and heir to the Swan heritage."

"And exactly what's that?"

"An impregnable belief in their absolute superiority to everyone else."

"And especially to Sibyl's presumptuous relatives," Burch said with a burst of laughter that startled everyone in the ballroom.

To Sibyl it was like an electric shock, making every part of her body conscious of his presence. The young man dancing with her felt as though he held lightening in his grasp, and he was unable to take a deep breath until the dance came to an end.

Chapter 30

"Now you two can say what it is you have to say to one another," Louisa announced when they returned home. "I shall be in my room if you want me. Henry?"

"I'm going to bed," her husband stated succinctly. "Anything you have to say to me can wait until the morning."

Sibyl led the way to the front parlor, but she felt trapped when Burch closed the door behind her, reluctant to come to the point; she had made her decision, however, and it was unfair to put off telling Burch any longer.

"Why did you leave?" he asked, without waiting for her to begin.

"You know why," she replied evasively. She still couldn't speak the hated words, confess her humiliation.

"No, I don't. You may have forgotten, but you didn't tell anyone."

"It wasn't anyone else's business."

"Wasn't it mine?"

"If you wanted it to be, but you didn't care."

"What do you mean, I didn't care? Do you think I made love to you just to pass the time of day?"

"Some other men would," she said, looking at the floor.

"I'm not other men," he said harshly. "I made love to you because I couldn't stop myself."

"You never told me that."

"I didn't think I had to. I thought you knew."

"I thought I did, but I was wrong."

"Will you stop talking in riddles? I love you, much more than I ever thought possible."

"Not enough," Sibyl retorted, near tears.

"Enough to listen to you and follow your advice. If you had been at the Elkhorn when I returned, I would have told you that your haystacks were the only thing keeping our herds alive. I've even ordered lumber to build a barn, and Ned and Balaam are already groaning about having to set out dozens of fruit trees. I wouldn't be surprised if Jesse and the boys start to think you're running the Elkhorn, not me."

Sibyl felt no elation, just the oppressive weight of despondency. This would have meant something before Christmas; in fact, she would have been the first to insist that it was the *only* thing that was important. But then Emma arrived, and Sibyl was forced to acknowledge that she was no different from the rest of her sex. It was Burch's desire for Emma, not any feeling of inferiority, that dominated her thoughts and caused the constant pain that weighed on her heart. Why couldn't he see it was jealousy that was killing her?

"There is really no point in our talking any more," she said with great weariness. "There is nothing else to say."

"Hell and damnation," Burch thundered, grabbing her by the shoulders and forcing her to look him in the eye, "you haven't said anything yet. I don't know any more than when I got off that train this morning." It seemed like so long ago instead of just a few hours.

"For God's sake, Burch, stop pretending you're innocent. I can stand knowing you don't love me, but I can't stand this constant lying, this masquerade of not knowing what I'm talking about."

"I don't, goddammit. I haven't understood a thing you've said since I got here. Now that I think back on it, I'm not sure I've understood anything since before Christmas. You were acting peculiar to start with, but all of a sudden you clammed up tighter than a sealed drum, and I haven't been able to get a straight answer out of you since."

"I don't remember your asking for any kind of answer."

"There you go talking in riddles again. If you're still upset because I got angry after the race, I'm sorry, but all I could see was you lying at the bottom of that canyon, your neck broken and your face spattered with mud. It made me crazy; I just couldn't stand the thought of something happening to you." Sibyl struggled to hold back the sobs that were choking her, but it was no use. With an explosive burst, she dropped to the sofa. Burch was at her side in an instant.

"For God's sake, will you tell me what's wrong? I'm nearly crazy with wanting you, yet you keep me at a distance. I've spent days going over everything I've said and done almost back to the moment I met you. I know things were pretty bad at first, but I thought we had gotten past that." He remembered the bliss of holding Sibyl in his arms. "I thought we had gotten past everything."

"So did I," Sibyl cried, abruptly turning on him. "I didn't care about the arguments or your getting mad. None of it mattered, not really, until Emma." She sobbed piteously. "How *could* you, after all you said, after all we had done?"

"What did I *do*?" asked Burch at a loss.

"I thought I had found someone I could depend on, someone I could trust. I was so sure I would never find anybody like you again that I was ready to give up everything for you, to turn my back on my whole family if necessary. Then you had to destroy it all, and for no more than a few moments of lust."

"I'm going to rattle the brains right out of your head if you don't stop talking nonsense, and tell me straight out what's got you tied in knots," Burch roared, nearly ready to strangle her in frustration.

"Emma! What else do you think I'm talking about?"

"What about Emma?" Burch shouted, more confused than ever. "I can't believe you're really jealous of her. She might as well be my sister."

"How dare you compare her to a sister!" Sibyl said, rising to her feet in outrage. "I *saw* you. That's disgusting."

"You know, I thought I was going crazy when I fell in love with you, and now I know it. For weeks nobody's been able to figure out anything you've said, and still I stand here like a fool trying to make sense of the biggest pack of gibberish I ever heard."

"Burch Randall, I saw you with my own eyes."

"*What* did you see with your own eyes? Am I supposed to guess, or are you going to keep me in suspense till spring?"

"I saw her *in your arms*." Burch looked blank. "You were *naked*!"

"Are you sure you're not feverish? Me? With Emma? That's a joke."

"And the laugh's on me. Is that what you were going to say?" asked Sibyl, slapping him as hard as she could. "Get out of this house. You are a liar and a cheat and I never want to see you again."

"I may do just that," thundered Burch, utterly enraged, "but not before you explain just what the hell you're talking about. And don't give me any more of your "you know what I means." You tell me straight out what it was you think you saw, when you saw it, and where."

"I saw you, in your bedroom, on Christmas morning," Sibyl nearly shrieked at him. "She had her arms around your neck and you were kissing her."

Memory came flooding back, and Burch colored despite himself.

"See, you can't deny it," she shouted in miserable triumph. "You know you're a rotten cheat."

"That's not what you saw," Burch said, wondering how to

explain to Sibyl what had happened.

"Do you deny it?" she sobbed. "Do you dare deny that I saw her in your arms?"

"Yes, I do. You saw Emma's arms around me, but you didn't see my arms around her."

"It's the same thing," Sibyl protested, trying to slap him again.

"No, it's not," he retorted, grasping her wrist in a painful grip. "Emma came in my room while I was dressing."

"Do you always entertain women half clothed?" she asked nearly hysterical, "or is it just those you've known since childhood?"

"Will you stop carrying on like a born fool and listen to me?"

"No, I won't ever listen to you again," she sobbed, pounding on his chest with all her might. "I hate you, I *hate* you!" It was impossible to calm her down. After weeks of being held under tight control, her anguish spewed forth like a geyser, becoming more and more uncontrollable. As a last resort, Burch slapped her sharply on the cheek. Sibyl's mouth dropped open and her hand flew to the flaming cheek.

"Now listen to me just one minute before you start shrieking again." Sibyl was infuriated, but she was silent.

"Emma came sneaking into my room, begging me to marry her. I didn't pay her any attention at first, but she started to get hysterical and came at me, saying things like she couldn't live without me and she was saving me from you. I thought she had been in the whiskey and I told her so. That's when she threw herself on me and begged me to save her ranch. I told her I would help Auggie all I could, but I was going to marry you."

Sibyl stared at Burch with vacant eyes.

"She got a little crazy then, going on about you so bad I told her if she didn't stop I was going to have to ask her to

365

leave. Then she broke down and started to cry all over me. I never had a female act like that, and I didn't know what to do. She threw herself on me again and I guess that was when she wrapped her arms around my neck, I don't really remember. Anyway, she kissed me, and that's when I threw her off. I was willing to do what I could to help her recover her spirits, but I wasn't about to let her think all she had to do was cry, and I'd kiss her back to cheerfulness."

Sibyl gaped at Burch, the stinging cheek forgotten. She wanted so desperately to believe him that he would be faithful to her in the face of temptation, but she was afraid. What if he wasn't telling the truth? What if he really did love her but couldn't stay away from other women who made themselves available? She shuddered at the thought of having to endure such a hell. Far better to have nothing than to reach out for something that was always just beyond her grasp. Burch read the doubt in her eyes.

"You don't believe me." It was not a question, just a statement of fact.

Sibyl couldn't answer. She'd never known a man in her life she would have trusted in similar circumstances. How could she trust this man when he didn't conform to any of the codes of behavior she understood?

"There're not many rules in the West," Burch told her, speaking in a solemn voice, "but we have two that no man breaks if he wants to be trusted. We don't turn on our own kind, and we don't lie." He stared hard at Sibyl, and her gaze faltered before his. "I can't prove what I say without dishonoring Emma, and I won't do that. You're going to have to take my word for it. If you can't trust me, it's better I know that now."

"It's not that I don't believe you," Sibyl spoke at last. "I just don't know what to believe."

"I don't see it that way. Either you believe me or you don't. There's no in-between." The love in his eyes had given way to a look of stern, forbidding righteousness.

Sibyl realized that the question at issue was no longer one of love, that the decision was no longer subject to compromise. She had touched Burch in a place where he would not, *could* not give in to her, not even for his own happiness. And it frightened her terribly.

"When my daddy died, Aunt Augusta was the only person I trusted. I can't explain to you how I felt. I've never been able to explain it to anyone here, but I felt desperate to get away from Lexington. I never looked for love, I don't even think I wanted it, certainly not the kind Kendrick offered.

"Then I met you and everything changed. Things went too far, too fast, and before I had time to think, I had given myself to you and plunged heedlessly into love."

"Did you regret it?"

"I never stopped to ask myself that. I was too afraid it wouldn't last. I didn't ask you for promises because I was afraid you wouldn't give them; I didn't confide in anyone because I was afraid they would tell me I was a fool. You see, I never suspected how much I needed to be loved. I'd always pretended I didn't care, but you destroyed my defenses."

"You make me sound like a sneaking thief. I loved you honorably. I want to marry you."

"You didn't at first, and I never forgot that."

"But that was because I didn't know you."

"I thought it didn't make any difference. I did everything I could for you, but I never entirely forgot. Then Emma came and everything fell apart. You seemed to enjoy her company in a way you never enjoyed mine."

"Emma's like one of the boys."

"If you think Emma is the least bit like a boy, then I wonder what you thought of me," she said cuttingly.

"It's not the same."

"How is it different? She's a woman, and she wanted you. I knew it the minute she stepped inside the door."

"I won't go through all that again. I don't want Emma and that's the end of it. I love you and I want to marry you. You're the most important thing in my life, even more important than the Elkhorn. I never thought I would be able to say that, but it comes easy now. The whole time I was following the line I thought of nothing but you, of going back and finding you there, warm and welcoming. I rehearsed what I was going to say dozens of times. I thought of presents to give you, of promises to make, but most of all I thought of you in my arms, inviting and loving. I nearly went crazy when you weren't there.

"And what did I run into? Emma going on about one thing after another, Balaam baiting her, and Rachel sitting silent as a sentinel. It was all I could do to keep from rushing off to Augusta right then and there. You can't imagine what a blow it was to find out she had no more idea than I did why you'd run off. But she said you loved me, and that if I wanted you, I would have to come after you. I did want you, and I did come. Was your aunt right? Do you love me?" The question was simple and direct.

"With all my heart, but I can't go back with you."

"Why?" he asked softly.

"I just can't." She dropped her gaze. "I want to believe you, but I can't."

"Not ever?"

"No," she whispered. There was a long silence that Sibyl didn't dare break. Burch's eyes never left her face, the terrifying intensity of his gaze never relented. Sibyl felt the pressure building within her until she was sure she would shatter into a thousand pieces, but she didn't dare move, didn't dare utter a sound.

"I guess if there's nothing more to say, there are a couple of things we have to settle."

"What?" she asked, barely attending him as she saw her dreams turning to dust all around her.

"Nearly everything in the house is yours. You'll be needing it soon."

"I'll write telling you what I need," she said in a halting voice. "You can keep anything else or send it to Aunt Augusta." Could this really be happening? Was he really going to send everything back?

"Then there's the matter of the herd."

"What do I want with a herd of cows? I don't even have a farm to put them on."

"Then I'll pay you for them," he said, taking out his wallet. "How much are they worth?"

"I don't know," she said vacantly. How could she be thinking of the price of cows when her whole life was coming to pieces. "I don't care what they're worth."

"I must pay you something."

"I don't want your money. Keep them, divide them with Lasso, or give them away if you want. I don't care."

"I won't be held by blackmail," he said in a steely voice he'd never used with her. He walked over to a table and briefly wrote on a piece of paper. "This is a draft on my bank. If it's not enough, I'll pay you more."

"I told you I didn't want your money," Sibyl cried shrilly. She snatched the paper he held out to her and frantically tore it into tiny pieces. "There! That's what I think of your money."

"Either you take it, or I'll ship them to you the minute I get back."

"Why can't I give them to the ranch?" she asked. "It's half mine."

"Because I own the other half." He was inflexible.

"Have the lawyers work it out," she said, too tired to argue any longer. "They can include it in my share of the profits."

"Won't you reconsider?" Sibyl knew he was a proud man. This was her only chance to change her mind; he would *never* ask her again.

She shook her head, unable to speak.

"You'll always be welcome at the Elkhorn. When you visit your aunt, I hope you'll come see us as well." He moved away from her toward the door. She did not dare to look up or let him see the haunted, devastated look in her eyes. She heard the door open. "You could have trusted me," he said softly and closed the door after him.

Sibyl burst into tears.

Chapter 31

It was no use. Sibyl's body was too taut and her mind in too much of a turmoil to sleep. In the hours since Burch had left she had gone over every word, every gesture of their conversation, looking for some reason to believe him, some excuse to change her mind, and every time she reached the same conclusion, only to have her heart rebel and the tears start again. She could not face the thought of never seeing him again. When he was with her, she could be firm and do what she knew was right, but as soon as he was gone, her resolution failed and her heart took over. You love him, it kept saying; don't be a fool, nothing else matters. She tried to reason with herself, but the refrain kept growing louder and more insistent until it was like a drumbeat in her temples. Don't be a fool, you love him. Don't be a fool, you love him! She threw back the covers and got out of bed.

Sibyl paced the floor, so absorbed in her thoughts that she didn't hear her aunt enter the room. Louisa's face had lost some of its formality. She looked anxious and a little troubled.

"Can't sleep?" she asked unnecessarily.

"Not a wink."

"Want to talk?"

"It won't do any good."

"Why don't you try? It can't hurt."

"There's nothing to talk about. I know what I have to do, I just have to learn to accept it. I never thought I'd act like a silly little girl over some smashed dream."

"All of us, even very tough, stubborn, young ladies like you, have our dreams, and it hurts when they die."

"But it's so stupid. I know I made the right decision, but I lie here going over every word I said, and when I reach the same conclusion, I start to cry all over again." At that her tears started. "See? If I keep this up, my eyes will be so swollen everyone will think I'm sick."

"If you keep torturing yourself, you *will* be sick. You've got to get your mind on something else so you can rest. It's going to hurt for a long time, but it will be a lot worse if you give in to it. Do you want me to fix you some warm milk? It'll help you sleep."

"That *would* make me sick," Sibyl said with a watery chuckle. "I detest warm milk."

"How about some tea?"

"No thanks, I think I'll read for a little while. That usually puts me to sleep."

"Okay, but if you plan to sit up for very long, throw a blanket over you. The house is chilled through. There are some extra ones in the trunk."

"I will. And don't worry about me, I'll be all right."

"I know that. I just don't like to see you so unhappy."

"I should be used to that by now," she replied with a bleak smile. "I wasn't very happy before."

"I remember, and I tried to talk to your father several times, but he never had a thought to spare for anything but his dratted books."

"Daddy didn't like people very much. Maybe he had the right idea."

"Hush. I'll have no more of that kind of talk. You get bundled up and get back in bed before you catch cold. Things ae going to be better soon, you'll see."

"Thank you for putting up with me," Sibyl said, giving her aunt a hug. "I don't know what I would have done without you."

"There's no reason for you to be without the support of your family. You've been deserted by both my sisters, so I guess it's up to me to see that you are not alone now." Louisa looked as though she might cry too, but she blinked determinedly and her habitual control reasserted itself. "Try to put it all out of your mind and get some sleep. Good night."

For a long while after Louisa left, Sibyl sat staring vacantly before her. Finally she jerked herself out of her abstraction and went over to an ancient wooden chest with hammered metal straps, which sat in the corner. Fitting the key in the lock, she lifted the heavy lid and the pungent odor of cedar assailed her nostrils. The trunk was only half full. Sibyl lifted out one quilt and then another, but rejected both as too thick and heavy; she passed over several blankets of coarse wool and horsehair because they were too hot and scratchy. Then at the bottom, tucked down in one corner, she found what she wanted — a lacy shawl made of soft lamb's wool. But when she lifted it out of the trunk, a thin volume fell to the floor.

Sibyl started to return the book to the trunk, but the blue marbled covers and calf binding stamped with gold letters caught her attention. She flipped it open and was surprised to find no title page, no printed words at all. Intrigued, she thumbed through several pages and found that all of them were written over in a small but elaborately decorative hand. Turning to the end, she found the last dozen pages free, and she backed up to read the last entry.

March 8th — Celebrated Augusta's second birthday with a party for all her friends. Louisa and Cornelia went to town with their father.

Her grandmother's diary! She wondered if anyone knew

about it. The shawl probably hadn't been unpacked since Mary Ann Gershom Hauxhurst died three years earlier, just six months after the death of her beloved husband. Sibyl had adored her petite English grandmother, so she took the book over to a chair, wrapped the shawl tightly around her shoulders, and settled down to read from the beginning.

Several hours later, more awake than ever, Sibyl closed the book. Her eyes glowed with a strange fire and her body felt like it was being pricked by thousands of tiny needles. She was so excited by what she had read that she couldn't sit still. Jumping up from her chair, she walked briskly about the room, a happy smile of anticipation on her lips. She ran over to the window and looked out. The first gray streaks of dawn were visible over the hills behind the house. In less than an hour it would be light. In less than an hour she would be on her way to find Burch, to tell him that she had changed her mind. She was going back to him and the Elkhorn after all.

Unbelievable relief and a wonderful feeling of contentment spread through her whole being as she climbed into bed. The room was ice cold now, and her chattering teeth distracted her from the problem of how she was going to break the news to her aunt. She doubted Louisa would understand, but it didn't matter now. Her grandmother had explained to her what she couldn't see for herself. Why hadn't she been told of the courage and determination of that tiny English lady who spoiled her so cheerfully when she was a little girl? But for this accidental discovery, she would have let her own fears ruin her chance for happiness.

She could hardly wait to tell Burch, to see his face when she told him about the diary. He would probably still be angry with her, but she never doubted he would forgive her.

Sibyl looked nervously about her as she approached the entrance to the Grand Union Hotel. She dared not think of what Louisa would say when she learned that Sibyl had gone to a hotel by herself, but she could think of no other way to get a message to Burch without letting her aunt know what she meant to do. Louisa was not a harsh mistress, but the servants would never think of keeping anything from her. Why couldn't Henry have been born first instead of Jessica? Boys could go anywhere without being questioned.

Sibyl gathered her courage and walked into the dark interior. It was too early for the porters to be on duty, and as yet there was no one in the lobby. A single clerk sat behind the desk snoring softly, his chair leaned against the wall. The clack of Sibyl's heels on the marble floor caused him to jerk awake, and he stared foolishly at her, rubbing his eyes in disbelief at the sudden appearance of such an astonishing vision.

Advancing with a dignity and outward calm she didn't feel, Sibyl was certain the clerk was wondering what a decent woman was doing in a public hotel at such an early hour. But she need not have worried. He was too bemused to think of anything but the loveliness of the sight before him.

"Excuse me," she said, approaching the desk, "but I wish to send a message to one of your guests. Could you tell me how this is done?" Her voice sounded calm and controlled, but beneath her skirts her knees were shaking badly.

"That depends, miss, on whether the party is up yet."

"I'm sure he is," Sibyl said, wondering why she hadn't thought of that herself. Burch always rose before dawn at the ranch, but there was no reason for him to do so now.

"I'll have to see if William is free to take a message. You can wait in there," the clerk said, indicating a heavily masculine room across the hall from the desk.

"I'd prefer to wait here if you don't mind, and could you please hurry." Sibyl looked around, wondering how soon it would be before someone who knew her aunt and uncle came in and recognized her.

"I'll do my best, miss, but I can't leave the desk, and nobody moves very fast this early." He took a piece of paper from his desk and handed it to Sibyl. "Would you prefer to write your own message?"

"Yes, thank you," Sibyl replied, glad that someone was thinking of all the things she was too upset to think of for herself.

"You'd better use my desk," the clerk said, moving away to allow Sibyl to sit down. She was reluctant to enter his cubicle but realized she couldn't write standing up. She sat down and dipped the pen in ink, but it dried before she could think of what words to use. Uncomfortably aware of the passing time and that the clerk had returned and was standing at her shoulder, she hastily scribbled a few words, blotted the page, and handed him the note.

"Have someone take it as soon as possible," she said, making haste to move out of the cubicle.

"Who is it for?" he asked, indicating that Sibyl had forgotten to put any name on the outside of the note.

"Oh, how stupid of me," she apologized nervously. "It's for Mr. Burch Randall." The clerk's gaze, always alert, became positively intent. Sibyl needed all her courage to keep from slinking away. Given Burch's good looks and general appearance, the clerk was bound to think that any woman coming to a hotel in search of a man of his stamp was no lady. But she had misinterpreted his look.

"Just a minute," he said, consulting a heavy book with large untidy writing over three quarters of one page. He looked up from the book, his eyes so bright Sibyl found herself ready to run away and risk asking her uncle to come. "Mr. Randall left the hotel last night."

"Where did he go? When is he coming back?"

"He's not coming back, he's checked out of his suite. I say, miss, are you all right?" Sibyl had turned pale and staggered as though struck a blow. She reached out to grasp the counter to steady herself. Slowly the room stopped moving and the concerned face of the clerk came back into focus.

"Are you sure it was Mr. Randall and not someone else

who left?"

"Yes, miss, it would be hard to miss one like him. What with every female in the place panting like they had run up three flights of steps, and falling over themselves to see that he had towels and a pitcher of fresh water, I'd have to be blind not to notice him. Mighty generous he was, too."

In the moments of stunned silence that followed, Sibyl was unaware that she held out her hand and the clerk had placed the note in it. Why had Burch left so quickly? She had expected him to wait a few more days, to make at least one more attempt to change her mind. It never occurred to her, even though she knew he would never beg, that he would just turn around and go back home. She left the hotel, her eyes staring blindly ahead, her heart thumping painfully, and her spirits sinking rapidly.

The cold morning air helped to clear her wits, and she walked faster, fearful that someone would see her before she could reach her aunt's house. Why hadn't he waited one more day? She couldn't remember his saying anything about going back home. If he loved her as much as he said, would he have given up so easily? Maybe he had changed his mind and decided that Emma was less trouble than a female who demanded to have her way in everything, one who ran away and had to be chased after.

Thinking of Emma caused her a pang. She finally was able to believe he didn't love her, but no man wants to live alone, and if nothing better offered itself, Burch was bound to make the best of it and settle for what he could get. That thought alone made Sibyl's knees knock.

She was sure Emma would never argue about when to take the steers to market or how to use the hay meadows or whether it was a good idea to buy a windmill. But Emma wouldn't bother about the Elkhorn, either. The corners of the rooms would soon be dusty and cobwebs would hang from every ceiling. Tears in the chair covers would go unnoticed and the dog's paw marks would remain on the polished wood floors for weeks at a time. Worst of all, Burch would sit down to dinners even worse than Sanchez's. Emma had admitted she knew nothing about cooking and was not anxious to learn.

Sibyl's step became more firm, her stride increased in length. She had to go back to the Elkhorn, she had to tell Burch that she loved him and wanted to be his wife. The last thing he told her before he left was that she was always welcome to return if she liked. Well, she wanted to return, she *had* to, but not as a guest.

Chapter 32

Sibyl finished the last of her packing. The sun was up and she guessed the family was sitting down at the breakfast table now. She looked around the room one more time to make sure she hadn't forgotten anything, and suddenly the familiarity made her feel almost like she was back at the Elkhorn. The pit of her stomach was queasy with excitement now that the long period of doubt was over. She felt like she hadn't been really alive during these last weeks, just existing in a state of helpless confusion. Only now could she see how thoroughly that helplessness had affected her, how it had made her indecisive and vacillating. She didn't feel helpless any longer, but she still didn't relish facing her aunt; Louisa was not going to be pleased with her decision.

The younger children had already finished when Sibyl reached the table. Jessica was on the verge of leaving as well but decided to stay when she saw her cousin.

"You almost missed breakfast, but Mama said we were to let you sleep."

"I don't want anything but some coffee," Sibyl said, going to the sideboard for a cup.

"Mama said you didn't sleep well," persisted Jessica, anxious for any tidbit of information Sibyl would let drop.

"I hope it doesn't show. Are my eyes sunken and black?"

"You always look beautiful and you know it," Jessica said enviously. "When is your cousin going to visit us again? I wonder if I should call him my cousin? After all, he is your cousin, and I'm your cousin, so maybe we are all cousins."

"You're not close enough for it to make any difference," Louisa said, entering the room and interrupting the monologue. "Let Sibyl have her breakfast in peace."

"She's not having anything but coffee."

"I imagine she'd enjoy that a lot more without this constant barrage of impertinent questions. You need to talk to Dolly about which dresses you want to take to Richmond. She will need time to get them ready to be packed. There's always too much to do at the last minute to be worrying over whether you forgot your favorite frock."

"I hope you aren't planning to go to Richmond solely on my account," Sibyl said uncomfortably. Her aunt looked at her in mild curiosity and Jessica, thinking that she would hear nothing of more interest, rose to leave.

"Not entirely."

"Good, for I've decided not to go."

Jessica stopped in her tracks, and there was a long pause as her aunt's gaze grew more intent.

Sibyl couldn't endure the scrutiny. "I'm going back to the Elkhorn."

Louisa's stare became positively intimidating. "I've already bought my tickets," Sibyl rushed ahead. "My train leaves at noon."

"You can't be serious," observed her Uncle Henry, looking up from his paper.

"Are you really going to marry your cousin?" Jessica asked, eyes wide in astonishment.

"Yes."

"Why didn't you tell me last night?" demanded Louisa. "When did you tell him?"

Sibyl didn't answer.

"He doesn't know, does he?" asked Louisa in a flat voice.

"No, not yet."

"Good, because you're not going."

"I know what I told you last night, but I've changed my mind, and I know I've done the right thing this time."

"And how's that?" asked her uncle doubtfully.

"I can just feel it. Before I was miserable with any decision I made. I wanted it and didn't want it at the same time. I was angry because of what I lost, unable to appreciate what I had, and upset that anything like this would happen to me."

"I've never heard such gibberish in my life," avowed Henry impatiently.

"What made you change your mind?" Louisa asked with a set, unrelenting expression.

"Grandmother Hauxhurst."

"Grandmother?" exclaimed Jessica. "But she's dead."

"I didn't mean her, I meant her diary."

"Mother never kept a diary," Louisa contradicted her niece categorically.

"Yes, she did. I found it at the bottom of the trunk under the blankets. It was wrapped in a white wool shawl, the one that looks like lace."

Louisa's eyes cleared with memory. "I can't remember that Mother ever used that shawl after Augusta was a little girl."

"She stopped writing in the diary when Augusta was two. That must have been when she hid it in the trunk."

"Bother all that," interrupted Jessica impatiently. "What did it say?"

"Nothing that could have any bearing on this appalling melodrama," stated Louisa crushingly. "My mother was an extremely practical woman."

"But you're wrong," Sibyl insisted.

"Are you implying that I didn't understand my own mother?" demanded Louisa, her wrath beginning to rise.

"I don't think any of us did, including grandfather."

"Young lady, I always did deplore the manner in which

your father thought fit to raise you. You are stubborn, unable to determine when you've gone too far for good taste, and shockingly impulsive. But never, until now, have you been grossly rude."

"But you've never read the diary, or you'd understand."

"*I* do not read the diaries of others," Louisa stated in awful disdain.

"Neither do I," returned Sibyl, her own temper flaring, "but I found it by accident. I didn't even know what it was at first."

"I don't see how that changes the situation."

"It does," Sibyl insisted, "but that's not what I wanted to tell you." Her excitement caused her to forget her anger. "Grandmother started keeping the diary when she met Grandfather. Their whole courtship is there. Her parents disapproved of Grandfather even more than you disapprove of Burch. He was a wild American they didn't trust. Worse still, he was one of those unstable Southern plantation owners who was uncivilized enough to own slaves and was descended from some conscienceless ne'er-do-well who engaged in duels and practiced piracy on the high seas. Grandmother's father was a stolid, prosperous banker and totally against his only daughter marrying an uncouth foreigner."

"I'm quite familiar with the family history, thank you," said Louisa, unplacated, "but I was never aware that my father was ever referred to as an "uncouth foreigner" by anyone."

"Your grandfather said that and a lot more," Sibyl said ruefully. "He forbade Grandmother to see him and even threatened to lock her in her room, or send her to live in the country, if she so much as spoke to him. She was reduced to visiting friends if she wanted to see him. Grandfather was all for having it out with her parents, but Grandmother wouldn't let him."

"I should think not," responded Louisa, horrified.

"But Grandfather loved her and wanted her to come to

Virginia with him. Grandmother didn't know anything about America, and her father told her it was a country filled with savage Indians, filthy slaves, and crude whites. Her friends described the horrors of a sea journey in such terrifying detail she was scared to death to even think of setting foot on a ship. Her father even threatened never to see her again if she married against his wishes."

"Nonsense. Grandfather Gershom brought Grandmother to visit in Virginia twice."

"Grandmother was so confused she hardly knew what to do," Sibyl continued, "but when Grandfather came to tell her it was time for him to return to America, she knew immediately that nothing else mattered if she was with him. She trusted him to take care of her regardless of how strange the country or peculiar its customs."

"I never heard any of that," gushed Jessica, awed.

"Nor anyone else," remarked Louisa crushingly.

"But how does this highly improbably tale affect you?" Uncle Henry wanted to know.

"Don't you see, my problem has been that I was afraid to believe Burch."

"I thought there were other, more serious reservations."

"I used to think so too, but it all came down to believing him. I couldn't say that I trusted him in every other way except this one."

"Admittedly, there is a contradiction there."

"I knew all along that I trusted him, but I was afraid to believe him, afraid that I would be hurt again."

"And now you feel reassured?"

"Yes, because he never hurt me, I hurt myself."

"I do hope your aunt is following your argument, because I feel I'm losing the thread of your reason."

"Just listen," Sibyl entreated impatiently. "Burch never violated my trust, I just thought he did. I saw temptation and assumed that he had succumbed."

"Was there not more evidence than that?" inquired

Louisa, who knew her niece better than her niece thought.

"Yes," Sibyl confessed incurably honest, "but I misunderstood that, too."

"If your understanding has been so consistently at fault, why do you feel compelled to trust it now?" Henry asked with something close to sarcasm.

"I *told* you, I had never met any man I could trust, and I was afraid to trust Burch."

"That seems an unnecessarily rude remark to make in your uncle's presence," remarked Louisa, "not to mention what it says about your father and grandfather."

"You're not trying to understand, either of you. I'm not talking about my family. I'm talking about people like Moreton and Kendrick, even the girls I grew up with like Clara Maynard, who claims to be my best friend but can't wait until my back is turned before she starts spreading gossip about me. I thought Burch was like all those people, but he's not. He's open, frank, and honest. All of the West is like that."

"What makes you say that?"

"They have no past, only the present and future. They are what you see, and they take you at face value, expecting you to do the same with them. There is no effective law, and a man is known by his word; he is loyal to his friends and the outfit which employs him, no matter what."

"You make them sound almost noble," her uncle said impatiently.

"They are, and very gallant, too. I almost didn't see it."

"All this is well and good," interrupted her aunt. "I'm quite glad to hear that these men are honorable and gentlemanly, but that does not change anything. You're not going back."

"Yes, I am," Sibyl said, defiantly facing her aunt. "There's no one who can stop me."

"I can. Henry is your guardian and you're underage."

Sibyl stared blankly at her aunt. "I don't have a guardian. I've always dealt with the lawyers about everything myself."

"Knowing you, we decided it was best that way, but everything had to be countersigned by your uncle."

Unreasoning fury surged through Sibyl's brain. "When do I have control of my own affairs?"

"Not until you're twenty-five."

"Do you mean to tell me that I have to ask your permission for everything I do for the next five years?"

"Legally, yes."

"Did my father know this?"

"Of course. He's responsible for it."

"Damn him!" Sibyl cursed, jumping up from her chair. "Why didn't he have the courage to tell me?"

"Sibyl!" exclaimed Louisa, outraged. "I will *not* have such language in my house, and certainly not from a female."

"Then you should have told my father you would have nothing to do with his infamous scheme. You must have known I would hate it."

"That's why he didn't tell you. He really had no choice. No girl can be left alone."

"I won't have it. I will not be hedged about and ordered around again. That's why I left Virginia in the first place. Why didn't you try to stop me the first time?"

"I almost did, but I was sure you would come back as soon as you saw what the West was really like, and I *thought* Augusta would be there to look after you."

"And instead she slipped her leash and married Lasso. That must have been a surprise."

"Greater than you'll ever know."

"Well, I'll not be the one to return home meekly and sit by the fire, hands in my lap, money safe in the bank, until some *man* comes along to take possession of both."

"You can't leave without my permission," Henry spoke up, "and you don't have it."

"Are you prepared to stop me?"

Henry looked uncertainly at his wife. "I am prepared to cut off your money."

"That won't be enough. I've already paid for my ticket, and I have all I need for the trip. You're going to have to stop me by force, to lock me in my room. Are you prepared for that? If you follow me to the train station, I'll kick and scream until you have me arrested. Only a jail will keep me here." She had spoken so vehemently she was shaking, but no more than her listeners.

"You want to go enough to do all that?" Louisa asked softly.

"That and more. I let my happiness slip out of my hands once. This may be the only chance I have to retrieve it. Please, God, don't let it be too late already."

"You would leave without money and without our approval?"

"I'd leave with nothing more than I stand up in," she declared.

The look of determination Louisa knew so well was firmly fixed to her face. It was clearly no use to appeal to her, and force would only result in a scandal more ugly and terrible in its ramifications than marriage to an unsuitable man.

"Please, Aunt," Sibyl begged, suddenly changed from a raging virago to a pleading child, "don't make me leave you like this. Can't you see that I must go?"

"No, but I see that you are going, and maybe it is best that you do. If you could do the things you say, then you are not fit to live in Virginia. Maybe Wyoming *is* the place for you."

"Please, don't!"

"I have never meant to stand in the way of your happiness, I only wanted to protect you. I have never understood you, but I always loved you."

"And I never understood you. I can't see how you can submit to all this—this tyranny."

"There is no submission. I want to be where I am."

"What a strange family. My mother died to escape, I ran away, and you rise above it all."

"Not at all. These are my people. They're your people

too."

"I guess that's the problem. You see, I never felt like they were my people. I always felt like an outsider, a reject. Maybe everyone who goes to Wyoming feels rejected and is looking for some place to call home." Her temper had cooled and she was feeling sad at leaving her aunt without the prospect of return.

Louisa regarded her steadily for a long time. No one spoke, not even Jessica, who had listened to this whole exchange with her eyes bugging out and her jaw sagging. Finally the silence was broken by Henry.

"I don't know about you, Louisa, but I'll have no part in forcing her to stay here, not for any trust Stuart talked me into taking on."

"No. I wouldn't ask it of you. If she insists on leaving, we have to let her go."

The last of Sibyl's trunks was stowed in the wagon and sent off to the train station. She turned back to the house and one last interview with her aunt. She dreaded it. Louisa had said no more after agreeing that she would not stop Sibyl from returning to Wyoming, but her silence was awful. Her uncle's complaints and Jessica's questions had been easier. Sibyl realized that her aunt's opinion was the only one she cared for. She would not let Louisa's disapproval keep her from going back to Burch, but she didn't want to leave on bad terms. This was her family, and it was important to her that there be no breach.

"Are you really leaving today?" young Henry asked. "Mama said you were."

"Yes, I am."

"Do you need anyone to go along to protect you?"

"Not this time," Sibyl said, smiling despite her anxiety, "but maybe when you're a little older, your mother will let you come for a visit." Sibyl suddenly remembered something. "Would you like to have a keepsake that belonged to a

387

real cowboy?"

"Yes," he said, his face bright with anticipation.

"Come here," Sibyl said as she opened her purse. "You can use this when you go riding, but not here in town." She pulled out a bright red handkerchief with blue polka dots.

"What's it for?" he asked, eyes wide with curiosity.

"It's a handkerchief. No cowboy goes anywhere without one. They use it to keep the dust out of their lungs and the sweat out of their eyes."

"Ugh!" Jessica uttered.

"Don't worry, it's perfectly clean," Sibyl added.

"Can I come visit, too?" begged Priscilla, not the least bit deterred by fears of dust or sweat.

"What would you want to see out there?" asked Jessica with all the disdain she could assume.

"That will be quite enough, children," said Louisa, entering the hall from the back. "Kiss your cousin good-bye. It will probably be some time before you see her again."

"That is, unless you're back within the month," observed her uncle.

Sibyl busied herself kissing her cousins and did not answer. Then suddenly the hall was empty, and she found herself alone with her aunt, having no idea what to say.

"I think you should have this," Louisa said, handing Sibyl a small package, loosely wrapped. Sibyl quickly opened the folded paper to discover her grandmother's diary. "You and she appear to be so much alike it seems only natural that you should keep it. Maybe you can give it to your daughter."

"When she causes me as much trouble as I've caused you?" Sibyl asked, choking.

"You've never been a trouble to me. I worry about you and probably will always do so, but I've never known any woman more capable of taking care of herself. I thought that maybe some day your daughter would have a difficult decision to make. Maybe the diary can help her as it has helped you."

"Thank you," Sibyl said, impulsively throwing her arms about her aunt's unbending neck. "Are you sure you don't want it?"

"No. I'm content with my life and so are my daughters. The Gershom desire for adventure seems to have skipped my branch of the family. Maybe it's just as well, since you and Augusta seem to have such a large share."

"Dear Aunt Louisa, Aunt Augusta is even more conventional than you. No one was shocked more than she when Lasso fell in love with her, and she with him. I don't think she's forgiven herself yet. I'm the only real maverick in the family, the only one to disgrace you."

"You're no disgrace, and you know you're always welcome here. Now you go to your young man. I don't understand how you can throw away your heritage like this, and I utterly deplore the manner in which this whole affair has been conducted, but when all is aid and done, it is not my life, and I don't feel I have a right to dictate what yours should be."

"You're generous."

"No, I'm not. If I could keep you here, I would. I have frequently reproached myself for letting you go in the first place, but there's nothing I can do now except give you my blessing and hope for the best."

"Is there anything you want me to tell Augusta for you?"

For a moment Louisa's eyes grew hard, but then they softened and a reminiscent smile grew in them.

"Wait just a moment," she said, and quickly ascended the stairs. She was back within minutes with another small package. "These were hers, and I want her to have them," Louisa said, opening a small wooden box to reveal a baby's silver cup, spoon, and teething ring. "Maybe she'll have some use for them now."

"I wouldn't dare."

"If you both must marry such hulking men, there's no reason why the family shouldn't realize some benefit from it.

I'm counting on a half-dozen strapping nephews."

"I want all six."

"Don't be greedy." Louisa smiled, but then her expression turned serious. Sibyl had never seen her look so vulnerable. "I love both of you," she said at last, her voice wavering slightly. "Please be careful and don't forget to write me once in a while."

"I mean for you to come visit. I know Aunt Augusta does, too. You can't get rid of us that easily." She smiled through her tears, relieved to see that Louisa had regained her habitual control.

"Maybe I shall, but not if you intend to threaten me with Indians and wild cows. I'm too old to be thrown on a horse and expected to ride to safety."

Chapter 33

Even before the Elkhorn came into view, the muscles across Sibyl's shoulders grew stiff with tension. This was so unlike her first arrival; this time she was almost afraid to reach the worn steps at the back of the house. She had begun her journey confident that Burch would welcome her with open arms; now she wasn't so certain. After all she'd said, after the number of times she had refused his painfully managed entreaties, would he be so forgiving? Would she forgive him if their places were reversed? Sibyl shuddered.

She *hadn't* forgiven him. How could she expect him to do more for her than she had done for him? Beads of sweat broke out on her forehead, and she clasped her hands together to keep them from shaking.

What would she do if he refused to let her stay? It would be impossible to return to Virginia and Aunt Louisa. Sibyl forced these thoughts from her mind. There's no point in worrying about trouble before it gets here, she told herself; besides, it can't be any worse than what I've been through already.

The sight of the great house, massive and quiet in the evening sunlight, silhouetted against the empty sky and the snow-covered hills in the distance, brought a lump to her throat. It didn't remind her of Tulip Hall, not in the least. It was the Elkhorn and it was her home. She *felt* home. She rubbed a few sentimental tears out of her eyes. She hadn't known how much she missed it — the sky and the openness, the marvelous feeling of limitless space. Virginia was the home of her birth, but Wyoming was the home of her spirit and she could never be happy anywhere else.

Nothing had changed; the drifts were still piled deep around the sheds, and the paths churned into thick mud. The wagon wheels made unpleasant sucking noises before coming to a halt in the space between the ranch buildings and the house. The ranch seemed deserted; there was no sign of anyone and even the cattle were out of sight.

"The bunkhouse is the third building down this path," Sibyl informed the taciturn driver. "You'll find someone there to help you unload."

After helping her down he went off, leaving Sibyl to muster the courage to approach the house by herself. She stood on the back stoop for several minutes, striving to find the pluck to turn the knob, until her own sense of the ridiculous came to her rescue. What a silly picture I must make, she thought, standing at my own back door like a naughty child. She opened the door and stepped inside.

Nothing had changed, and somehow she thought it must have. So much had happened to her it seemed impossible that everything else should be just as she left it. The chairs were still pulled up in a tight circle at the far end of the room, and a fire burned invitingly in the grate. She smiled. Burch must be in a mellow mood; he always said wood fires were too great a luxury to indulge in often, especially when the wood had to be hauled from the hills. The smells of cooking caught her attention, and she turned to the kitchen. A quick sampling of several pots informed her Rachel was preparing dinner and the weeks of Sibyl's absence had not improved that good woman's skill. The feeling of self-consciousness began to fade as Sibyl lost herself in doing what she could to render the evening meal more appetizing.

"I never could make it taste like yours." Rachel's calm voice nearly caused Sibyl to drop the pot into the fire. "I was hoping you wouldn't stay away long."

"I couldn't." A great wave of relief swept over Sibyl as the stern face of the older woman broke into one of her rare smiles.

"Do you mean to stay?"

Sibyl didn't reply; how could she when she didn't know the answer herself? Rachel seemed to understand. "Mr. Burch'll be right pleased to have you in the kitchen again. You've ruined him for anything Sanchez or me can fix. If he doesn't stop trying to starve himself, Miss Augusta will take him in, and that wouldn't suit Mr. Lasso at all."

Sibyl was on the verge of asking Rachel about Burch and her aunt when the back door burst open and Balaam blew into the room, eyes dancing and lungs gasping after the first sprint that old body had taken in nearly twenty years.

"Yippee!" he shouted, throwing his hat at the ceiling and doing a dance that resembled someone stomping a rattle-snake to death with bare feet. "I didn't believe that mule-faced windsucker when he wandered in looking for some half-wit to do his work for him, but if you're meaning to stay this time, I'll carry every one of them trunks up the steps by myself."

"I'm staying," Sibyl said, smiling happily. Ned's pleasure at seeing her, when he arrived at the house equally out of breath, made her feel truly welcome.

"If you mean to carry her trunks anywhere before you get some air in your lungs, you'll be under the sod before morning," Rachel scolded Balaam, but without the sharp edge in her voice Sibyl had come to expect. She looked inquisitively at Rachel, but her face was devoid of expression.

"Hush, woman. She didn't come back to hear none of your jaw. It's a pity the one she did come back for ain't here."

"Burch isn't here?" Sibyl asked, even though she knew the

answer already.

"Took Brutus and went hunting," said Balaam. "Least-ways, he took his guns, but he didn't say nothing. He was in such a thundering black rage nobody dared to ask him, either. Came roaring in here like a wagon going downhill, and bit the nose off anybody fool enough to open his mouth. Said his dinner wasn't fit for the hogs and threw it into the snow, damned me for a dried-up crust of something I wouldn't mention in the presence of no lady, and told Ned if he stumbled across him one more time he'd have two gimpy legs. I don't know if he laid his tongue across Rachel, cause I figured the less he saw of my hide the more likely I was to keep it."

"Not everybody is scared of his own shadow," said Rachel.

"And not everybody's got the sense God gave a prairie dog, either. Your skirts may keep you safe, but I ain't got no such protection. Tangling with Burch when he gets himself in a temper may be your idea of fun, but then you're a woman and they don't ever have no sense. Most of them, that is," he added after a swift glance at Sibyl.

"How long did Burch stay?" Sibyl asked, not even hearing Balaam's slip of the tongue.

"Too long to my way of thinking. A big man like Mr. Burch ought not let himself get crazy mad like that. It's not safe for them that has to be around him."

"And he didn't give you any idea how long he was going to be away?"

"I already told you nobody asked him any questions."

"Not everybody," Ned reminded him. "Rachel asked."

"And did he give her any answer except a grunt?" returned the ungallant old coot.

"Not so's you could understand it," replied Ned, grinning. "It sounded a lot like a threat to slay everything with four legs and horns between here and Montana. I didn't offer to go along to keep him company."

"Of course you wouldn't." Balaam said with a wicked

394

gleam in his eye. "Why should you want to leave such soft, warm comfort for the cold, hard ground?"

Sibyl was stunned to see Rachel blush deeply. If it had been any woman other than Rachel, Sibyl would have sworn she was acting like a young girl with her first beau.

"Stow it, you beak-faced buzzard," Ned said darkly, "before I make a half hitch out of that sheep's gut you call a body."

"You'll have to catch me first," responded Balaam undaunted, "and you won't do it, not with that gimpy leg and mooning about like a beardless boy half the day and night."

"I'll break your scrawny neck, and then we'll see how loud you crow." Ned attempted to get his hands on Balaam, but the old man was surprising agile for one so ancient and he danced out of Ned's reach.

"Lover's muscles," Balaam jeered, "soft and spongy from laying in the nest."

With another curse Ned was after him.

"Stop it!" Sibyl's imperious command brought the two tomcats to heel immediately. "I don't know the reason for this incredibly foolish behavior, but I won't have it in my house."

"It's my fault," Rachel said, looking dreadfully uncomfortable. "Balaam is worse than a horsefly in summer, and too wicked to give up teasing Ned."

Sibyl's expression didn't soften.

"Didn't Mr. Burch tell you when he was in Virginia?"

"Tell me what?"

"After we put your trunks on the train in Laramie, Ned and me got married."

Sibyl didn't know why she should feel so weak. She groped for a chair and sat down with something of a plop.

"Good thing you did go to Virginia," Balaam informed her astringently. "You missed all that mooning and carrying on at first. They're just starting to act human most of the time."

Sibyl gathered her wits and pinned a smile on her face. "Naturally I'm very happy for you, but you'll have to forgive my surprise. I had no idea you two even noticed each other."

"Wouldn't have if the pickings hadn't been so slim."

Ned surprised Balaam and got in a sharp rap to the jaw.

"That's enough!" Sibyl shouted. "If you can't stop fighting, you can get out of this house." She sounded so close to hysterics that both men gaped at her in bewilderment.

"That's enough, Ned, leave the old viper alone." Rachel studied Sibyl's face carefully, and she didn't like the wild, cornered look in Sibyl's eyes. "Maybe you would like to rest some, miss. You've had a long journey and you're bound to be tired."

"I'm sorry for raising my voice, but I can't stand this fighting every time you meet," she said with a weak, apologetic smile. "Especially not in the house." The effort she was making to get herself under control was so obvious it was embarrassing.

"I don't need defending, Ned," Rachel said without taking her eyes off Sibyl, "not from an old bag of bones I've known for twenty years."

"You've know each other that long?" Sibyl asked vacantly.

"Nearly. Balaam was old and wrinkled even then."

"You won't win any prizes at the fair yourself."

"No, but I used to be pretty."

"You still are to me," avowed Ned.

"Blind!" exclaimed Balaam, rolling his eyes to the ceiling, "and gimpy into the bargain."

"The driver needs some help with the unloading," Sibyl reminded the men.

"You'll have to pry his eyes off her before he can hear a word," Balaam said of Ned, who was gazing at Rachel adoringly.

"You said you'd carry Miss Cameron's trunks all by yourself," Rachel reminded Balaam. "If you don't hurry up, that driver is going to take his wagon back to Laramie with them trunks still in it."

"I need to talk to Ned anyway," Sibyl added.

"I know what'll happen," muttered Balaam as he shuffled out. "He'll stay here jabbering till everything's done, and then he'll come offering to help. I don't know why love makes people soft in the head as well as the body." He slammed the door behind him.

"Did Mr. Cameron say anything about when he was coming back?" Sibyl asked Ned.

"No."

"Have you seen Jesse?"

"No. Balaam says he's always about during the winter, but I haven't set eyes on him once."

Neither of them saw the expression freeze on Rachel's face.

"I'm going to see my aunt. If Burch returns, send Balaam to get me right away. I've got to see him before he disappears again."

"How long do you plan to stay at Mrs. Slaughter's?"

"I don't know." It sounded strange to hear Augusta called by her married name. "It probably won't be very long. I just want to give her the news from home." Sibyl couldn't tell them that it was impossible for her to sit around the house waiting for Burch to return. She had to do something to escape from her own doubts and self-accusations.

Burch sat staring off into the murky, fathomless distance. He had been doing so, unmoved, for the last hour. Brutus lay stretched out between Burch and the glowing embers of the fire he used to cook his dinner. They were nearly two hundred miles from the Elkhorn, in some of the most beautiful country in North America, but for days he had moved through it unseeing, unmoved by its majesty and grandeur, its unspoiled purity. He had even ignored the elk, bit horn sheep, and bear he had come to hunt. After a week on the trail, he had killed only one large prong-horned antelope to feed himself and his dog.

Everywhere he went, everything that met his gaze reminded him in some way of Sibyl. No, that wasn't true. His thoughts were wholly taken up with Sibyl, and nothing else could enter his mind without being in some way related to her. The blue Montana sky became the sky above her head as she rode across the plains below the Elkhorn; the towering mountains became the barrier of the Blue Ridge that separated their ways of life; and the sparkling streams became the glistening eyes that looked out at the world with such boundless vitality.

For the hundredth time, he cursed the stubborn pride that made him leave Lexington without waiting to see if she would alter her decision. He was a fool, a conceited jackass, to think she would change her mind in one evening just because he had asked her to. It had taken her weeks to decide to leave the Elkhorn; to turn around and go back now was not a step to be taken lightly, especially since Sibyl was endowed with even more stiff-necked pride than he was. She was capable of committing herself totally, but she would give nothing at all unless she was sure his pledge was as unconditional as hers.

Nearly twice a day, he would be on the verge of turning back, but he never did. He had left her, and he would have to wait for her decision. He had given up any right to plead his case on an equal footing when he stormed back to the hotel, brusquely ordered his bill, and stalked off to the train. To go back now would be to beg, and his pride stuck in his throat. He couldn't do that.

But his mind perversely followed the circuitous path it established the first night away from Sibyl and had retraced every night since. No sooner had he accepted the finality of his decision than he began to undermine it. Was he fool enough to think that he was going to be able to forget her? Could Emma, or any other woman, erase from his mind the feeling of her body against his, the softness of her skin, the sweetness of her lips, the sheer ecstasy he found in her embrace? God, these thoughts tortured him every night. He dreamed of her, agonizingly close, maddening lovely, but every time he reached out to touch her, to kiss her, to feel her body join with his, he woke up in a cold sweat and would lie there for hours, more exhausted from the passions that ravaged his reason than from a day in the saddle, too wrought up to sleep.

Walking didn't help; it wasn't wise, either, even with Brutus. He was far from civilization, but not far from Indians still angry at the seizure of their land or grizzly bears drawn by the smell of fresh meat. He had no hankering for his bones to remain undiscovered for the next ten or twenty years. He had a future cut out for himself, one he now realized was irrevocably intertwined with Sibyl. It was surprising how quickly she had become a part of his thinking. It was hard to remember what it was like before she arrived, but it was impossible to think of the future without her.

"You don't know how lucky you are, you heedless devil," he said to his slumbering companion as he stirred the coals. "You love and leave 'em in an hour's time. One game is as good as the next as far as you're concerned. But this is the only hand I get. If I don't play it right, I'm out of the game forever."

Chapter 34

Feeling useless and acutely miserable, Sibyl sat watching her aunt measure the twins for matching dresses. She had been at the Three Bars for nearly a week, but it had taken her less than an hour to see that Lasso and Augusta were cloaked in the aura of happiness she had hoped to find with Burch. It was evident in every word they spoke to each other, the sound of their voices, the softening of the eye, the awareness of the other's presence. In a dozen ways each day they showed that the other was never out of their thoughts.

"Don't you ever do anything for yourself?" she asked peevishly when Augusta returned from taking Lasso his coffee at the corral.

"Far too often," Augusta replied, settling down with her own cup. "Hardly an hour goes by that they aren't thinking of me, looking for ways to give me pleasure, to make me happy. I think they feel guilty for taking me away from you."

Sibyl had to bite her tongue. Of all the unnatural, ungrateful, and selfish nieces, she had to be the worst; but seeing Lasso and Augusta enjoying all the love and happiness she had thrown away was sheer torture. To put a smile on her face and pretend to be happy for her aunt was almost the hardest thing she had ever done. Aunt Louisa should be here; she wouldn't believe half of what she saw with her own eyes, but she would never again ask Sibyl if Augusta were happy. Besotted, Sibyl thought, mindlessly, deliriously, utterly besotted.

"You shouldn't have left Burch without some kind of explanation," Augusta said, choosing her words carefully. "He was naturally quite worried, and I think a little hurt."

"I know, but I had to get away."

"I know you were deeply hurt, too, but it would have been better if you had talked to Burch before going all the way to Virginia."

"I couldn't, not about *her*."

"I've often admired your pride and strength of purpose, dear. It's something I don't have and, goodness me, it's enabled you to do dozens of things I would never dream of attempting, but it seems to me that there are times when a little honest humility would serve you better."

"That's why I came back," Sibyl replied, subdued. "You can't know how hard it was for me to admit I was wrong."

"No, but I can tell it's important to you. Having gone this far, why not go the rest of the way?"

"What do you mean?"

"You still have a chip on your shoulder, something to prove. I have the terrible feeling that if you had any suspicion that Burch so much as looked at another woman since you left, you would turn around and go right back to Virginia."

"And you think I shouldn't?" Sibyl asked, the tension gathering in her body.

"I think you've done enough running away. It's time you stood your ground and faced yourself."

"I didn't run away," Sibyl said, firing up.

"First you ran away from Virginia, and then you ran away from Burch. And now, unless I'm mistaken, you're running away from Virginia again as much as returning to Burch."

"No, but almost," Sibyl admitted, struck.

"What are you going to do if things don't work out this

time? Do you plan to go back to Louisa?"

"I couldn't."

"Where then? You realize, of course, that you can't run away from yourself."

"I do know that, and I don't know what I'll do if Burch won't have me. I haven't let myself think of that."

"I'm glad to know that for once you admit you don't have all the answers. Maybe you'll believe that someone else can know as much as you."

"Did I always act like that?"

"Yes, and you said as much, too. I was so hoping that you would not let it cause you to do anything you regretted."

"I don't know that I do regret it. If I hadn't left Virginia, I would never have met Burch, and if I hadn't fought with him, he would never have admitted that a woman is more than a helpless, pretty ornament."

"Burch never thought that, no matter what he said. He was just not ready for your kind of help."

"I know, but I'm not like his aunt or even like you. I have a terrible temper and I behaved like a shrew. I could never be the kind of wife he was looking for."

"And your jealousy?"

"I'm not proud of that, either, but I have come back. That's as much as saying I was wrong."

"I'm sure that was not easy for you." Augusta looked at her niece, vibrant with life and a passion for involvement, and prayed that she hadn't waited too long. Men had been known to fall out of love just as easily as they fell in love. "Why did you come to see me?"

Sibyl grinned mirthlessly. "It seems to be my fate to be surrounded by besotted lovers while I wait anxiously to see if I'm going to be as fortunate. I ran away from the Elkhorn to escape Ned and Rachel acting like lovebirds; only I get here to find that you and Lasso are even worse."

"I don't know what you mean."

"Oh, don't you? Every time you open your mouth, it's to

402

wonder if you can do something for him or the girls. Is he sure he had enough to eat? Would he like anything special for dinner? And he's as bad as you are. It's disgusting."

Augusta blushed lightly. "Maybe it does seem like that to you, but Lasso has given me so much I worry I can't give him enough in return."

"Don't!" Sibyl protested vehemently with a catch in her throat. "Can't you see it's nothing but stupid jealousy? I'd give my soul to be doing exactly what you're doing, to sit at home, happy and secure in the knowledge that Burch would soon be there, and his love for me would be as deep and unchanging as ever."

Augusta's hand involuntarily went out to Sibyl, but she drew it back quickly.

"That's why I came back. *Because I couldn't do anything else.*" Sibyl struggled to bring her emotions under control while Augusta, unsure of what to say, said nothing.

"I knew I'd been unfair to him. I knew I'd been stubborn and blind and cruel as well. I'll never be able to bear the thought of him with another woman, but the agony of not having him at all was even worse."

"You're not making much sense, dear."

Sibyl pulled herself up with a jerk. "I must be a desperate case. I've never been hysterical in my life, yet here I am as close to having a full-blown fit as anyone can be. You must think me completely stupid."

"Only in love."

"Aunt Louisa thinks I'm crazy."

"Louisa would never understand our men."

"I think she understands our men but not us. According to her we're entirely lacking in discretion and common sense."

"Louisa is admirably suited to the life she leads, but I'm afraid she will never understand us, or we her, so we might as well dismiss her. Do you think you're calm enough to explain yourself now?"

"I hope so. What kind of wife will I make if I go to pieces

whenever something goes wrong?"

Augusta let that pass.

"I never doubted Burch's love until I saw him spending so much time with Emma and so little with me. Then I became hopelessly jealous. I never told you this, but I saw them in the bedroom, with Burch's shirt off and her arms around his neck. I didn't know there was so much pain in the whole world; that must be what it feels like to die. After that, every moment of every day was torture; having to speak to Emma, to smile at her was almost more than I could manage. And Burch went on just like nothing ever happened."

"Why didn't you speak to him?"

"Would you?"

"No," Augusta reluctantly admitted. "I would have gone to my grave rather than let a single word pass my lips."

"I chose to go back to Virginia, to run away as you so rightly put it. I don't know what I thought I would find there, but anything was better than being around Burch and thinking that he loved Emma."

"When he came after me, I didn't want to see him but I had no choice. I tried to keep from telling him what I saw, but he kept after me until I couldn't keep it to myself anymore. He couldn't believe I'd be jealous of Emma; he said she tried to force herself on him, but he told her he was going to marry me."

"Did you believe him?"

"I wanted to, but I was too afraid and I sent him away." She got up and walked over to the window. "I can't tell you how miserable I was. I paced up and down my room, unable to sleep. Then I found Grandmother Gershom's diary."

"I never knew she kept one."

"Neither did Aunt Louisa, but it was about her courtship with Grandfather. It was so much like my own situation that I couldn't help but think I was meant to find it, that it had been lying at the bottom of that trunk for thirty years just waiting for me.

"It made everything fit into place. I couldn't wait to tell Burch, so I went to his hotel as soon as it was light, but he had already left. I followed him, full of confidence and hardly able to wait until I got to the Elkhorn. But now that I'm here all my old doubts are back."

"About Emma?" Augusta asked in dismay.

"No, about whether he'll still want me. And after all I've done, I couldn't blame him if he didn't." She turned quickly. "I don't think I could endure it if he no longer loved me." She was near to breaking down.

"A man doesn't take his gun and go off hunting in the middle of winter if he plans to forget a woman," Augusta pointed out, hoping to restore Sibyl's shaky balance. "There's not much chance of meeting a female with anything less than four feet."

"And you think that with that kind of competition I might win out?" grinned Sibyl, valiantly controlling her unsteady emotions.

"I don't mean any such thing."

"I'd take him in any case."

"Then you ought to be at the Elkhorn when he gets back."

"But no one knows when that will be."

"Then wait. There are enough things there to keep you busy for a little while."

"More like several weeks, or months, as soon as the weather begins to warm up."

"It doesn't matter. The important thing is for you to be there when he returns. If you are, he will probably forget all about this foolishness, and in a short while he may not even remember it. But the longer he waits the more questions he'll have, and the harder it will be to forget the suffering he has endured.

"I don't mean to criticize you, dear, but I think you have forgotten to consider Burch's feelings. You were so taken up with your own unhappiness you had no time to give any thought to what he might be feeling."

"I didn't at first, but I had plenty of time to think about it on the train. That's when I began to worry he might not want me back. I had never looked at my actions from anyone else's point of view. I never thought that anybody else could be feeling the same things I felt."

"You seemed to have learned a lot very quickly. It must have been very painful."

"It was, but it was long overdue," Sibyl said, planting a kiss on Augusta's cheek. "It was nothing more than what you've been trying to teach me all those years when I was too stubborn to listen."

"It's never too late to learn."

"Let's hope not, and now if I'm to take your advice and be waiting at the door like a faithful little woman, I have to get out of here."

"You know you can't leave today, so sit back down. Lasso will see about sending someone with you tomorrow. You would never make it at night in all that snow and ice."

"I don't need anyone to go with me. I came by myself, and I can get back the same way."

"You shouldn't be wandering over these plains alone, not even in the daytime."

"You sound exactly like Aunt Louisa."

"And with a good deal more reason. All you would have to worry about in Virginia would be a broken axle or a hole in the road. That's not to be compared with lawless men and hidden canyons."

"Don't tell Aunt Louisa, or she'll never come to visit us."

"Louisa said she'd come out here!" exclaimed Augusta, gaping at her niece. "Are you sure you heard her right?"

"You know Aunt Louisa *never* says anything she doesn't mean."

"Dear me, what could have possessed her? She disapproves of me so strongly she has not even answered my letter."

"She vows she still loves us both. She just doesn't understand why we must travel to the remote corners of the civilized world to find husbands."

"I can believe that," laughed Augusta ruefully. "She always did think I had no force of character at all."

"Yes, but although she would have expected any kind of atrocious behavior from *me*, she was appalled to learn that *you* had so far forgotten your upbringing as to actually marry someone with the ungentlemanly name of *Lasso*."

"Did she really say that?" asked Augusta, trying to hold back a choke of laughter.

"Almost those very words."

"I can just *hear* her," Augusta said and went into a peal of laughter.

Lasso found them doubled up with laughter, tears running down their cheeks; much better, he thought privately, them the forlorn looks they had exchanged all week. He felt sorry for Sibyl, but he didn't want her upsetting Augusta or making her unhappy.

"You been telling shady stories?"

"We were just laughing at my sister Louisa, something, I'm afraid, that is just as improper," confessed Augusta, "but she does deserve it."

"I shouldn't have made fun of her. She took me in without any questions and was unfailingly kind."

"And why shouldn't she be? You are her niece."

"I caused her a great deal of inconvenience," said Sibyl, drying her eyes, "just as I've caused you a lot of anxiety. You'll be relieved to know I'm leaving tomorrow, Lasso."

He was relieved but careful not to show it.

"Do you have anyone we can send with her?" Augusta asked her husband.

"I told you I don't need anyone."

"I'll go," said Lasso.

"No, you won't," insisted Sibyl, "not after having me on your hands for all this time."

"I might as well. Somebody delivered that damned windmill of yours here."

"My windmill? What's it doing here?"

"The fools left it here when I wasn't around to stop them. I don't know whether they couldn't find the Elkhorn or just didn't want to be bothered to haul that contraption another ten miles, but this'll be as good a time as any to take it over."

"As long as it's not going to inconvenience you."

"Of course, if you could take it yourself, it would save me a heap of trouble."

"Lasso Slaughter, how dare you ask her to carry those heavy crates. Of course you'll go, and if I hear another word, I'll send that blueberry pie I baked for your dinner straight to the bunkhouse."

Being forced to be a witness to loving banter only made Sibyl more anxious to return to the Elkhorn. But as she was packing her clothes, she came upon the small box Louisa had sent Augusta. Sibyl didn't feel like giving it to Augusta right then, but she knew it might be a long time before she got another chance, and she would forget all about it by summer. Augusta and Lasso were sitting companionably by the fire holding hands when she returned.

"I thought you had already gone to bed, dear?"

"I meant to, but I forgot to give you this." She handed Augusta the small box. "Aunt Louisa said it was yours, and now that you were married, you ought to have it." Augusta's puzzled look turned to surprise and then embarrassment as she flushed pink all over.

"What is it?" Lasso asked uneasily.

"Nothing, just my baby cup and spoon. Do you want to see them?"

Lasso, his curiosity disarmed, took the box she handed him, relieved that nothing further had happened to upset his wife, but Sibyl's dogged gaze did not falter.

"It was just a surprise," Augusta explained. "I had no idea they had been preserved."

"That's not enough to cause you to color up like that. It's something else, isn't it?"

"No, it's nothing at all. Seeing them just brought back a lot of old memories."

"Lasso may not know when you're trying to hide something, but I do. You never could tell a lie, not even a very tiny one."

Augusta tried to blunt Sibyl's insistent curiosity, but it was too late; Lasso's attention was caught.

"Why did you give this to your aunt if you thought it might upset her?" he asked accusingly. "She's had too much worry because of you as it is."

"Lasso, it's nothing Sibyl did."

"It seems like one of these lovesick fools is always doing something to throw you in a tizzy. It's enough to make me close my doors to the both of them until they can stop acting like a pair of five-year-olds."

Sibyl flushed angrily at what she felt was an unfair accusation. "I'm just as fond of my aunt as you are, and I'd have thrown that box out the train window if I thought it would upset her."

"If you cared as much for her as you say, you wouldn't be bringing her all your troubles every time you do something stupid or lose your infernal temper."

"Stop, both of you!" Augusta said, coming as close to a shout as was possible for a person of her mild nature. "That's not it at all, and I won't have you fighting, especially over me. I'd have told you before," she said, turning to Lasso, "but it's far too early. I was going to wait until I was certain."

"Certain about what? Don't be so mysterious, Aunt."

But Augusta fumbled for words, unable to find just the right ones to convey such an important message. Suddenly, a blinding flash of intuition struck Sibyl.

"You're going to have a baby! That's it, isn't it?" But Augusta wasn't looking at Sibyl. Her anxious eyes never left Lasso's stunned face.

"Is it true?" he asked in a bare whisper.

"I don't know. I won't be sure for some time yet." She

searched his face anxiously. "You're not upset or angry, are you?"

"Hell no!" he erupted, sweeping Augusta up and kissing her roughly. "I feel like the kid covered with pimples who just got a date with the prettiest girl in town. I'm as happy as a steer in a hay meadow." He swung her around, and then just as abruptly put her down. "You're going to have to start taking care of yourself. You can't go on doing all the work around here."

"There's not a thing wrong with me," said Augusta, breathless and radiant, "and I intend to continue taking care of my family. And that will be easier to do now than later. There's one less to look after."

"I'll have to see about getting someone to help you. I wonder if you'd consider giving up Rachel?" he asked, turning to Sibyl.

"Rachel won't come because she just got married herself," Augusta said, regaining some of her perpetual calm. "Now you stop acting like I'll die of the least effort, or I'll soon be sorry this baby is on the way, if it is on the way, which I really can't be sure of just yet." But Lasso wasn't listening. He was busy counting up on his fingers.

"It oughta show up sometime in late September or the first of October. Damn, right in the middle of roundup. Burch will have to take my steers to market but, hell, I can't ask the man to round them up too. Besides, he's got to come out of those blasted hills first."

Augusta began to chide him gently for worrying about things before they happened, but Lasso paid her no attention and they soon forgot Sibyl's presence in their concern for each other. Unobtrusively, she sought the refuge of her room.

It would be a relief to leave. She didn't know how much longer she could endure the blissful euphoria that surrounded those two. *Why*, she thought bitterly, *must my own unhappiness prevent me from being able to be truly happy for those I*

410

love? I feel like a selfish monster. Maybe I don't deserve happiness.

The glare of the bright sun reflecting off the snow nearly blinded Sibyl, causing her to pull the brim of her hat lower over her eyes. The hard crust crunched under her horse's feet as they broke through to the soft snow underneath. This made traveling slow and more dangerous than usual.

"You should have stayed home," Sibyl told Lasso, who was driving a wagon filled with the crates containing the windmill.

"It's not bad now; just wait a few days. That's the trouble with these warm spells. The sun blazes down for two days and covers the ground with water. Then the temperature drops fifty degrees and you have a crust of ice two inches thick. There's not a cow in Christendom that can break through that to the grass underneath. They'll starve more surely than they would if there was no grass at all."

"You mean a herd is in more danger from ice than a blizzard?"

"Sure. A blizzard just makes it hard to get to the grass; ice makes it impossible."

"If there are such terrible hazards to raising cattle in Wyoming, why do so many try it?"

"Because the land was here for the asking, and the grass is the best in the world. When the winters are reasonable, you can make a fortune."

"And this year?"

"A lot of people are going to find they can make a surer profit in banking. Some of the owners are banks, anyway, or foreigners who buy and sell without ever setting foot on a ranch. They aren't good for Wyoming but they're good for the industry, so we have to put up with them."

"How has the winter affected you?"

"Hard," said Lasso with none of his usual heartiness. "I didn't have but one of your haystacks, and I only put that one up to please Augusta. I suffered a lot less than the

Strattons, but my losses have been heavy."

"Did they lose much?" she asked, trying to make her voice sound flat and casual.

"Auggie doesn't know because they paid off their hands after the fall roundup, but he's not waiting till spring to find out. He and Emma have already gone to Denver to try to sell the whole outfit before anyone can get a head count."

"Where are they going?"

"He says Emma doesn't care as long as it's far away from Wyoming and its iron-willed cowboys." Lasso watched her out of the corner of his eye. "Auggie says it sounds like somebody turned her down, and that doesn't happen to Emma very often." Sibyl's spirits soared, but she rode on in silence.

Lasso couldn't resist an inward smile of satisfaction. He had nothing against Emma; she was a fine woman and lots of fun, but his first loyalty was to this young woman who seemed so necessary to the happiness of the two people he cared about so much. He didn't know what had gotten into Burch, but anybody could see those two were set on having each other. That was okay with him. He liked Sibyl but not all this upset; it worried Augusta, and he wasn't about to let that happen.

And the Strattons *were* selling up, and Emma *was* in Denver, but when she had heard of Sibyl's departure, she made plans to invite herself to the Elkhorn for the summer. If thinking that Emma was heading East would help Sibyl and Burch get things patched up, then Lasso was willing to tell any number of little lies. And as for Emma, well, Emma would have to take care of herself.

"What's this windmill for?" he asked Sibyl when he judged she had been quiet long enough. "It looks like a lot of trouble for nothing."

"It pumps water."

"By itself?"

"The wind drives it."

Lasso's brows furrowed in thought. "You mean you can have all the water you want all summer long just by putting up a windmill?"

"I don't know that it'll do all that, but maybe it will. At least it'll mean we don't have to bring water for the house from the creek."

"Was it expensive?"

"A little."

"Does Burch know you bought it?"

"No."

Lasso thought for a moment. "I know you've had too many people sticking their noses in what's not their business, but if you'll take some advice from me, you'll tell Burch when you do something like this. He might not agree with it, but I can't see him telling you no, not if you go about it in the right way. And it would save you both from some nasty surprises."

"I meant to tell him, but with the blizzards and his not being around most of the time, I just never did."

"Use your own money?"

Sibyl nodded.

"He'll like that even less."

"Do you think I should send it back?"

"No. Burch has some uncomfortable ideas about women, but don't sell him short. He's smart, and he's always looking for better ways to do things. Your uncle came here in the early days when the grass was plentiful and the winters were easy. Everybody made money then, but it's going to take Burch's kind of rancher to survive winters like this one or summers like the last. He won't like it when you think of something before him—he just wasn't raised that way—but he's not one to bite his nose off to spite his face. And he won't hold it against you for knowing a bit more than he does." He looked Sibyl squarely in the eye. "I don't say it wouldn't be a bit easier if his wife wasn't quite so ready to show how much she knew, but they don't come any better than Burch

413

Randall, and he never was one to deny a man his due."

"What are my chances of being that wife?"

"If you have enough sense to use your advantages instead of throwing them in his face, I'd say there isn't a chance in hell of him getting off your hook." There was another slight pause. "I don't think he wants to, either."

Chapter 35

After he had skinned the deer and given Brutus his supper, Burch built his campfire and constructed a spit to roast a haunch of venison for his own dinner, but he didn't pay much attention to the slowly turning meat or the mouth-watering aroma that soon filled the air. For the last two days he could not rid himself of the conviction that he was being followed, and he was worried. There were several Indian hunting parties in the same area, but it wasn't Indians; Brutus knew someone was following them, and he ignored it. *That's* what worried Burch.

Brutus was a big, lumbering mix of several kinds of dog, Great Dane seeming to be the most prominent among them. He had the speed to chase down a wolf and the strength to kill it, and there wasn't a cow or steer on the prairie that would dispute with him. An amazingly ugly dog, he was fiercely loyal and no one doubted his willingness to defend Burch with his last drop of blood. Several times during the day he stopped test the wind, but he did no more than wag his tail and turn back to Burch.

"What is it, boy?" Burch asked Brutus who, sniffing the wind once more after finishing with his own dinner, lay down next to his master and eyed the meat on the spit. "Not one slice! You've already had enough for two of your kind."

Again Brutus stared into the night and whined. "I wish you could talk. Whatever's out there may not bother you, but it's starting to make me real jittery." The venison was soon done and Burch ate his meal in silence. Brutus either forgot what was lurking in the dark, or it went away; when he couldn't coax Burch into feeding him a second time, he dozed peacefully near the fire.

Brutus's unconcern didn't make Burch feel any safer, and when it came time to go to bed, he didn't feel at all comfortable about lying down. He hobbled Silver Birch, who was foraging hungrily on grass uncovered by the melting snow; Montana hadn't suffered as severely from the drought as Wyoming, and Burch didn't want him to wander too far before morning.

"I can't stay up all night," Burch muttered to himself when he couldn't think of any more reasons to put off going to bed, but even as he lay down, he knew he wouldn't be able sleep. A sixth sense warned him that danger was still present, and instinctively he knew he was its intended prey. Brutus still lay by the fire, eyes closed and his great head resting on his paws, but the ears stood erect and the wet black nose seemed to twitch automatically at regular intervals. Burch knew there could be no better guardian of his rest, and he lay down to sleep.

It was Brutus's whine that woke him. The dog was on his feet, staring expectantly into the surrounding darkness. The dying embers cast no light and only the most probing eye could detect the outline of the great beast and the darker human shape nearby. A crack of rifle fire, quickly followed by another, broke the stillness as a spurt of flame showed in the distance. Burch's bedroll, thrown high in the air, was ripped to pieces, the debris Burch had used to stuff it raining to the ground for a radius of twenty yards.

"After him, Brutus!" Burch shouted. "Bring him down." A murderous curse knifed through the dark, and the ground near where Burch lay hidden was torn by scattered shots; then came the sound of horses's hooves in retreat. Brutus needed no extra encouragement and sprang into the inky blackness, heart-stopping growls issuing from his massive throat, cougar-size fangs bared and dripping the saliva of hate. Burch was on his feet, too, and had the hobbles off his horse in seconds. He had recognized Jesse's voice and was determined he wouldn't escape this time.

Somewhere in the distance the rhythmic sound of hooves was broken. Brutus had pulled down a bull once; Burch wondered if he was big enough to pull down a horse. Two more shots, and then the hooves resumed their rhythmic retreat. A cold fear clutched at Burch's stomach. He threw himself on Silver Birch's bare back and kicked him into a gallop. He couldn't hear any sound over the noise of his own mount's galloping hooves, but he didn't need any to know that Jesse would not have ridden away if Brutus had still been on his feet.

Silver Birch sensed he was to follow the path Brutus had taken, and it was not long before they came upon a shape sprawled awkwardly on the prairie. Burch slid from the back of his still-moving mount and knelt down beside his canine friend.

Brutus lay on his side, his eyes half closed with pain and his breath coming in gasps. Burch carefully felt his limbs. They were unbroken, but when he ran his hand across the heaving chest, it came away clammy with warm blood. "The bastard!" cursed Burch. "The bloody, bitching bastard! And you didn't warn me because you thought he was your friend." Burch picked up his dog, nearly staggering under his weight, and started back toward camp. The long walk over nettles, sharp rocks and patches of snow turned his bare feet into a bloody mess, the weight of Brutus nearly ripping the tendons from his bones, but he could not let his friend die in the darkness.

Once settled near the fire and the coals made to dance

with flames, Brutus opened his eyes. They were filled with pain, but not the clouded, dim gaze of death. An attempt to move was quickly abandoned with an agonizing yelp, but Burch began to hope. If the bullet passed through him clean, there was a chance he would pull through. He opened his saddlebags and began to take out various salves and ointments.

"You're not going to like what I'm about to do, old fella; in fact, it's not going to seem the least bit friendly, so if you don't mind I'll just tape these jaws of your shut." Brutus *didn't* like anything that happened to him during the next hour, and Burch would have been in a sad way himself if Brutus could have gotten his jaws open. "That ought to hold you," Burch said at last. He felt his throat close, and he swallowed convulsively several times. "We have a score to settle, old man, but first you've got to hang on."

Sibyl stood back to get a better look at the windmill. A smile broke up the seriousness of her expression as the wheel, not yet attached to a pump, slowly began to turn in the breeze. Three weeks had passed since she had come back from Lasso's, and still Burch had not returned.

She filled the lonely hours with days of hard work and evenings of making plans. She drew up a guide for an extensive orchard and completely reorganized the garden. The farm buildings were reallocated to make their use more efficient, and one of the smaller storage buildings had been turned into a cabin for Rachel and Ned.

"They can't be going back to Rachel's place every night," Sibyl told Balaam when he turned obstinate about the extra work. "The only other thing we could do would be for you to share your cabin with them."

"Well, I ain't going to share with no female, so don't think it," he stated indignantly. With the garden, the cow, the pigs, and the chickens under his jealous care, the crusty old bachelor was an important man at the Elkhorn once again and he was ready to trade upon his advantage.

Another bedroom was newly papered, and Sibyl was only waiting for the weather to warm up before setting the men to whitewashing some of the buildings. She was still trying to decide what color she wanted to paint the house.

"I don't see why you're bothering with paint," said Balaam, his sense of manly pride outraged by her well-organized neatness. "Any man who claps eyes on this ranch painted brighter than a dance hall girl is going to think we're a bunch of sissies," he said, revolted. "I won't be able to hold my head up."

"At least then we won't be forced to look at your ugly face," Ned said, setting Balaam off on a tirade.

"That's enough," Rachel said when she saw Sibyl's brow begin to crease. "You can have my cabin, Balaam. It ought to be plain enough for you."

"It reeks females," Balaam replied contemptuously.

"Better that than sweat and cow dung," Sibyl snapped, out of patience. The long wait was stretching her nerves to the limits. She tried not to show it, but the others were acutely aware that she jumped at the sound of an approaching horse and could be found staring out at the purple hills several times each day.

"You can start sinking the well tomorrow," she told Ned.

"If the weather holds out." The rising wind was blowing banks of dark clouds across the sky. "We might be in for some rain." The wheel whirled faster and faster as the rudder jerked about in the erratic gusts.

"A gully washer," Balaam said.

"The creek and ponds are already full," Ned said with great satisfaction. "With them and this windmill, we'll have more water than we can use come summer."

"If God had wanted water to come shooting up out of the ground, he'd have put a hole there himself," muttered Balaam irritably.

"Don't be such an old fool," Ned told him. "It beats hauling it up from the creek."

"And you won't have to carry water for your garden, either." Sibyl could see that thought hadn't occurred to Balaam.

"You mean there'll be something left over after those greedy cows of his get through filling their bellies?" he asked caustically. He had never accepted the fact that sole responsibility for the prized herd had been given to Ned.

"There ought to be enough for a pig wallow even," Ned taunted.

"You two can abuse each other as much as you like when I'm not around, but if I have to put up with any more of ths now, you'll have to fix your own supper."

The combatants glared at each other but set about their work without any more squabbling.

"You couldn't have found a better way to keep those two peaceful," remarked Rachel as she accompanied Sibyl back to the house. "Ned won't say anything about my cooking and Mr. Randall did his best to swallow it, but the whole time you were gone Balaam never stopped moaning that I was trying to poison him."

"If he said half of what I suspect he said, you should have."

"He's a cross-grained old cuss, but I don't pay any attention to him. Some men just don't like women, and I guess he's one of them."

Chapter 36

Sibyl was almost through setting the table when Jesse walked in unannounced.

"Where have you been?" she asked. "Everybody's been looking for you." She gave him no more than a brief glimpse before going about her work, and she missed the nervous, almost furtive glance he cast about the room. "Have you seen Burch?"

"Not lately," he replied, brightening immediately. "Where is everybody?"

"Rachel has gone to get Ned and Balaam. You're just in time for dinner. When did you last see Burch?"

"Several weeks ago."

"Where?"

"Over the other side of the ridge. He was riding line during the blizzard."

"But that was almost two months ago."

"I guess it was."

"And you haven't seen him since?"

"I haven't had much chance, what with him traipsing off after you and then heading off to Montana. Somebody has to make sure things keep going around here."

Sibyl wondered at the sudden show of hostility; it was

much more than momentary annoyance, and Burch was not one to thoughtlessly anger his employees.

"What you need," Jesse continued, "is a husband to help take care of this place."

"Burch takes care of it just fine."

Jesse was obviously upset about something, and his ire could not be defused so easily. "Don't let him fool you with his show of running about doing nothing. He spends weeks at his hunting, and once he marries Emma Stratton, he won't be here much in between. You can bet your last petticoat that Emma will see to that. No hot, dusty old ranch for Miss Stratton."

Sibyl was dismayed at the sudden weakness in her knees, but forced herself to continue as though his words were not lapping at the foundations of her already shaky confidence.

"Did Burch tell you he was going to marry Miss Stratton?"

"I'm not blind. After the way he acted during Christmas, everybody's got to know his intentions. If his uncle hadn't left half this place to you, he'd have married her long ago."

There was such a strong vein of fierce hatred in Jesse's voice that Sibyl involuntarily looked up in surprise.

"I gather his Virginia trip wasn't any use. You still haven't sold your share of the ranch, have you?"

"I have no intention of selling it to Burch or anyone else."

"Then the sooner you get married, the safer you'll be."

Jesse had never talked or acted this way, and Sibyl didn't understand it. He was gradually becoming more and more enraged until the naked hatred in his eyes almost took her breath away. However, when Rachel returned with Ned and Balaam he seemed to re-collect himself, and sat down to eat without any further outbursts.

Everyone kept questioning Jesse about Burch until he lost his temper and said sharply, "I haven't seen Burch for weeks, and what's more, I didn't want to see him."

"I don't guess he's over-anxious to set eyes on you neither, but that's no call to act uncivil at the table," Balaam shot right back.

Nevertheless, they dropped the subject and asked about the herds instead. A full account of the sometimes heroic efforts of the men captured everyone's interest, and Sibyl never noticed that Rachel didn't contribute a single word to the discussion.

"Your haystacks have been the key to everything," Jesse said generously as he accepted a third cup of coffee. "With all this thawing and freezing, the cows would never have been able to get to the hay if we'd left it uncut."

"Does everyone agree with you?" Sibyl asked.

"It's not a matter of agreement, everyone *knows*. What with paying the boys wages all winter and providing them with plenty to eat, you're about the most popular female this side of the Mississippi."

Later, they all gathered around the fire, the men enjoyed their tobacco and everyone another cup of coffee, while the talk ranged from spring roundup to next year's calves. When the coffee ran out, Rachel got up to fix another pot.

"I think I'll take my cup in," said Sibyl. "I don't want any more."

"I'll take it for you," Jesse offered, jumping up. "I don't want any either."

"Tell Rachel she doesn't need to make more for anybody except Ned and herself," Sibyl told Jesse as he left.

"Miss Cameron says nobody else wants any more coffee," he called out to Rachel, but when he reached her side, he lowered his voice into a fierce whisper. "So you finally got yourself a man?" he said, jerking his head in Ned's direction. "Your standards seem to have fallen a bit. Or are you so old and desperate now you'll settle for anything, even half a man?" His eyes narrowed with barely contained fury; Rachel continued to make the coffee as though she hadn't heard him. "Looks like you'll do anything to keep him, too, much more than you'd do for your own flesh and blood."

Rachel looked Jesse squarely in the face from expressionless eyes. "You wouldn't go with me."

"For six years you acted like Wesley's shadow, leaving me with that sanctimonious bitch, then you show up without warning, expecting me to be delighted to go off with you."

It was an old argument, and Rachel no longer had any energy for it.

"I told you I was sorry."

"Sorry!" The word exploded from him like steam from a pressure cooker. "You shame yourself in front of half the world and all you can find to say to your own son is you're sorry?"

"You've never been willing to hear my side of it."

"I don't take the word of any goddamned slut."

"Are you two talking secrets in there?" Sibyl called out. "Ned's about ready to come get his coffee himself."

"It's almost done," answered Rachel. "It'll just be a minute more."

"That's right," hissed Jesse, "crawl to the poor cripple. Half a man is better than no man, and a woman as worn out and ugly as you ought to be thankful even for that."

Rachel did not even glance at Jesse as she carried the fresh cup of coffee to her husband.

About nine o'clock Balaam stood up and yawned. "I gotta be going. *I* can't spend all day in bed."

"Neither can anybody else, you old crow-bait," said Ned. "Come on Rachel, let's help this antiquated old fidget back to his bed."

"Help me?" sputtered Balaam. "*I* ain't got no gimpy leg; *I* ain't got so many stars in my eyes I can't see what's in front of me. I'm old enough to know better'n to carry on like a beardless fool."

"And you're going to keep on getting older. Not even Satan wants to gather in the likes of you."

"Do they ever stop?" Sibyl asked Rachel, weary of the endless bickering.

"Not so you'd notice it."

"You'd better take Ned off before they really get started."

"I can't leave you by yourself."

"I won't be alone. Jesse's here, and I'm going to bed myself before long."

"It's time you took yourself off too, Jesse." Rachel's eyes never left Sibyl, but she seemed not to see her.

"I'll go in a little bit, after I talk with Miss Cameron about Cody's leaving."

"She shouldn't be up late. She needs her rest too."

"Better not keep your *husband* waiting. It's not all that easy to find a man out here."

"Jesse! exclaimed Sibyl. "What ever made you say something like that?"

"Pay no attention, miss, I learned years ago not to listen to half what these men say. Don't keep her up." The last remark, addressed to Jesse, sounded like a command.

"I guess I shouldn't have said that," Jesse apologized after Rachel had gone, "but she's always acting like everybody's mother."

"Well, I wish you would learn to get along better. There's too much arguing around here." Sibyl could hardly believe those words had come out of *her* mouth; her eyes flew to Jesse's face, but he didn't seem to recognize the irony of her words. "What is this about Cody?" she asked curtly as she sat back down.

"He left the minute the blizzard cleared enough for him to get out. He didn't tell anybody, just left his cows to fend for themselves and headed for Laramie. Didn't even wait for his pay."

"What did Burch do?"

"He was gone after you. I had to take one of the boys from Blue Mesa until I could bring one over from the other side of Wiley's Gap. Now he's too busy hunting to see about getting somebody from Casper to take his place."

"Can't you do it?"

"I could if I wasn't having to ride line and keep tabs on

everybody. You know what?" he said, looking at her as if just struck by an idea. "You ought to take over running this ranch. Everybody knows you're practically doing it now anyway. If it wasn't for you, there might not be any ranch."

"There are still a lot of things I don't know," declared Sibyl. "I can't do all the things Burch does."

"You don't need him. I can help you," Jesse said suggestively.

"He still owns half this ranch," Sibyl replied, beginning to feel uncomfortable, "and legally I can't overrule him."

"You could if you were married. Your husband could take your part. After this winter, the men will listen to you."

"Well, I'm not married, so that doesn't come into it."

"You could marry me. I'd see nobody gave you any back talk."

"What?" barked Sibyl, too stunned to be polite.

"Does it seem so surprising? Surely you know I've admired you from the first."

"I—"

"I've never seen a woman with so much sense, and I'd be proud to have you for my wife."

"I can't," Sibyl said, hardly knowing what to say.

"Why?" demanded Jesse with unloverlike belligerence.

"I like you quite well, but I don't love you."

"You don't have to in the beginning. Liking is a good place to start from."

This isn't happening, Sibyl thought. He has never so much as hinted that he liked me.

"I think it's time for you to go," said Sibyl, rising quickly to find that her legs were unsteady under her. "I'm flattered by your offer, but I really can't consider it."

"Why can't you? Aren't I good enough for you?"

Sibyl was struck with almost physical force by the violent emotion that throbbed in his voice.

"I never thought of it like that, but it wouldn't matter who you were if I love you."

"Is it Burch?"

She stared blankly at him.

"Are you in love with that proud sonofabitch?"

"I didn't say I was in love with anyone," she replied, her temper rising at his crude language and his insistent questioning.

"Then what's wrong with me?" he asked, coming so close to her she could feel his warm breath. "Are you afraid I'm not man enough for you?"

"Get out of here!" she burst out. "I don't allow anyone to speak to me like that. Nor do I accept this kind of interrogation from a hired hand."

"So now I'm a hired hand, am I?" he said, grasping her roughly by the arm. "And hired hands aren't good enough for fancy Miss Cameron from snotty-nosed Virginia."

She slapped him so hard he released her in surprise. "Get out!" she spat, shaking with fury. "You're lucky I don't fire you on the spot."

Jesse's eyes blazed with such intense anger Sibyl was a little afraid of him. "No sniveling female tells me to get out of anywhere," he said, dropping all pretense at politeness. "I've got more right to this place than you."

"I don't want to know how you reached such a preposterous conclusion," Sibyl said with withering contempt, "but this is my house and you're no longer welcome in it. Until Burch returns, you will remain in the bunkhouse."

"You think you've got it all figured out, don't you?" he sneered, fingering his cheek and coming closer to her.

"There's nothing to figure out." He made an attempt to grab her, but Sibyl anticipated him and darted behind the sofa.

"Why are you doing this?" she asked, totally bewildered. "I've never done anything to make you think I'd marry you."

"That's right, I forgot. The Camerons don't marry where they lust, only when they find someone good enough, someone that can advance their position."

"I don't know what you're talking about, but I'm tired of it. I want you out of this house right now."

"You're not going to get rid of me that easily," he said, coming around one end of the sofa, but not before Sibyl had put the huge dining table between them.

"If you touch me again, I'll put a bullet through you."

"You don't have a pistol," he said, advancing along one side of the table, "and there's not a single person to hear you if you scream."

"I don't need help with the likes of you," she scoffed turning the corner quickly and reaching the knives that she kept hanging on the wall next to the cutting block. "This will do just as well."

"No woman has the guts to stick a knife in a man."

"Touch me, and you'll find out." Sibyl was thoroughly enraged. Jesse had had the opportunity to see enough of her temper to feel disinclined to test her determination. He rocked back on his heels, letting his eyes roam appreciatively over her body.

"You're quite a woman, worth a dozen Emma Strattons."

"If you weren't such a swine, I might appreciate your opinion."

Jesse's humor turned instantly. "Nobody calls me a swine."

"Then apologize for your behavior. I might forget about all of this if you keep out of my sight." Jesse made a move toward her but stopped in his tracks when he saw that Sibyl had a pistol in her other hand. "It was in the drawer, under the dish towels," she explained. "Balaam thought I should keep one just in case of an emergency."

"That cursed old weasel."

"But how right he was." Her expression hardened. "I think it would be best if you were to look for a job with another ranch."

"Are you trying to fire me?" Jesse exploded, fury and disbelief ringing in his voice.

"Let's say I'm suggesting you quit."

"You stupid bitch!" he raged. "Burch should have taken the skin off your tail months ago." He reached out toward Sibyl and the pistol in her hand exploded in his face. The bullet sent his hat spinning across the room before it buried itself in the ceiling. Shock and fear sent Jesse reeling backward halfway across the room.

"Touch me, and I'll shoot you dead."

"My God," exclaimed Jesse, "you almost killed me! Have you ever used a gun before?"

"No, but I know how it works. Call me a bitch again, and I'll show you."

"You're crazy."

"I was thinking the same of you. Now why don't you just turn around and get out."

"No goddamned female—" The cocked pistol, aimed straight at his heart, caused him to swallow the rest of his words.

"Don't say another word," Sibyl said, trembling with rage. "I might shoot you just so I won't have to ever set eyes on you again." Jesse's head turned at the sound of the door opening, but Sibyl never took her eyes off him.

"It's time you left," Rachel said calmly, entering the room from the front hall without so much as looking at Sibyl or the gun in her hand. Her inflexible gaze met and held Jesse's eyes. "Miss Cameron needs her sleep, and you can discuss your employment with her when Mr. Randall returns."

Sibyl watched, fascinated. Jesse's blazing eyes seemed to dim slightly and then fall before the cold, impenetrable glare of Rachel. He seemed to wilt, his anger and willpower losing their force.

"Tell Miss Cameron good night, and don't forget to close the door after you."

Jesse wavered indecisively for a moment as his eyes blazed once more, then abruptly he spat a foul curse at both women and stalked from the room.

"I don't know what got into him," Sibyl said, turning to

Rachel, "but I'm glad you came back."

"Probably been out on the range too long," Rachel said, dropping her eyes before Sibyl's thankful smile. "Men get funny when they have no company but their thoughts."

"Well, I don't want anything like that to happen again," Sibyl said, letting her arms fall to her side and the muscles in her body relax. "I've ordered him to stay in the bunkhouse from now on." She put the knife and pistol back in their places. "Now you get back to Ned."

"I'll stay with you tonight."

"There's no need, and I don't want Ned to come looking for you and asking for explanations. The less said the better. You think he'll come back?" she asked when Rachel didn't move.

"No."

"Neither do I, but I'll lock the doors to be on the safe side." She could tell Rachel wasn't reassured. "Don't worry, nothing is going to happen. He was just upset about something, maybe working too hard. I'm sure he'll be all over it tomorrow and probably ready to apologize."

"He hasn't been himself since Wesley," she stumbled and added, "Mr. Cameron died," and then looked as though she wished she hadn't spoken. Sibyl waited for her to continue, but after saying, "If you're sure you're all right," Rachel left.

Sibyl locked the door behind her, thinking that either the strain of waiting was causing her to imagine things or people were acting rather peculiar. Maybe they had all been kept too close this winter. It would be good when spring came, and they were able to go about in the open, like Burch.

But Burch was the one person she fervently wished would give up his open spaces, at least long enough to come home and take her in his arms. Her body ached with longing to feel him close to her, his arms crushing her with his great strength, her lips burning with the heat of his kisses.

When would he come? If he meant to punish her, he had chosen the most effective way. She hadn't slept well since her

430

return, and even Balaam noticed she had lost her bloom. Her nerves were so bad she jumped at the slightest sound, and she had no appetite for more than a few mouthfuls of food. Rachel made it her task to see that Sibyl ate enough, but she was steadily losing weight.

She climbed the stairs listlessly. She would just have to keep on waiting.

She undressed and got into bed. The sheets were cold and rough to her skin, and she curled up in a tight ball. As her body heat began to warm the bed she relaxed, and her thoughts became more indistinct before merging smoothly into her dreams. But she didn't dream for long.

Chapter 37

A sixth sense warning of danger woke her, but not soon enough. The instant she sat up in bed, a large dark shape materialized from the shadows and clamped its hand over her mouth. Sibyl struggled vigorously, but the assailant was too powerful and she couldn't break his hold. She bit into the fleshy part of his hand and had the pleasure of hearing him groan in pain as he released her. She flung back the covers, hoping to reach the gun she kept in the desk across the room. Who was in her room? What did he want? Why hadn't she kept the gun under her pillow like Balaam told her?

With a guttural curse the intruder sprang for her, catching the edge of her gown. The ripping sound was as welcome to her ears as it was unwelcome to his. She stumbled over the chair, threw it aside, and jerked open the drawer, but before she could get her hands on the gun, a powerful hand grasped her by the shoulder and flung her to the floor halfway across the room.

Under the cover of darkness Sibyl rolled away from the lurching shape, scrambled over the bed, and crouched on the far side. As her eyes became more used to the dark, the shape grew more distinct; still she had no idea who he might be or what he wanted. She watched him move about the room looking for her, and ever so quietly her hand closed on the lamp that stood on the table next to her bed. When he came close enough, she rose to her feet and brought it down over his head with a shattering crash. She raced frantically for the pistol, but he was after her almost in the same instant. She wrenched the drawer off its runners, accidentally spilling its contents all over the floor. Frantically she searched for the pistol, but just as her fingers closed around the cold steel of the handle, her arm was struck such an agonizing blow that the muscles were paralyzed and the gun skittered uselessly across the floor.

Forcing herself to ignore the pain, Sibyl plunged after the spinning pistol, but the unknown assailant reached it before she did. "Not this time," said a well-known voice as the butt of the pistol struck her a heavy blow at the base of the skull.

Jesse! thought Sibyl as she fell into an unconscious heap.

Wrapped in a huge oilskin slicker, Sibyl lay motionless in the straw while Jesse hurried to saddle her horse. "I would have been good to you," he said in an accusing voice to her lifeless form. "You are so pretty I would have done anything to please you. But you had to choose Burch instead of me, the cunning bastard. He thought he was going to steal what should be mine, but he was wrong." He led Sibyl's saddled horse over to where her body lay and lifted the lifeless figure in his arms. Her nearness, the warmth of her touch, the smell of her skin, tore at his senses. For a long moment he just stood there, hypnotized by her closeness. "I would have been so good to you," he muttered with pathetic despondency, throwing her across the saddle. It was rather difficult for him to mount with Sibyl draped over the saddle, but at last he had her seated before him. Leading his horse behind, they left the shed at a walk, hoping to make no sound that would betray his presence. He passed through the corral gate and habit made him lean down to close it even though he nearly lost his hold on Sibyl. Muttering curses, he righted Sibyl in the saddle and looked up to find Rachel standing directly in his path.

"I knew you would come back," she said unemotionally. "You never were one to know when to give up."

"Get out of my way."

"Not until you let her down." Rachel looked more closely and realized that Sibyl was not conscious. "What have you done to her?" she asked, anxiety plain in her voice.

"Just a rap on the head when she tried to pull a gun on me."

"May God forgive you," she cried. "Put her down."

"I don't want anybody's forgiveness, especially not yours. You know what I have to do, so get out of my way and let me get on with it." His eyes were wide and gleaming white in the night. "I don't plan to hurt her. I'm going to marry her."

"She'll never marry you. Anyone can see she loves Burch."

The eyes gleamed even whiter. "She'll never marry him. I won't let her. He can't take everything from me."

"It never was yours," she said as though explaining patiently to a child.

"It ought to be. It *will* be," he shouted. Sibyl began to stir in his arms. "Now move! I've got to be going."

"Jesse, no," she pleaded.

"Move!"

"Not until you put her down."

"If you don't move, I'll ride over you."

"Your own mother?"

"My own mother, goddammit! I should have killed you years ago, you rotten *whore*!" Jesse raked his spurs cruelly across Hospitality's sides, and the animal plunged forward. Rachel tried to leap aside but was sent spinning through the air into the snow. Jesse didn't even look back to see if she got up.

The scene that confronted Burch when he walked into the house was not what he expected to find. Rachel lay on the sofa, her head in Ned's lap, having her brow wiped with a damp cloth. Balaam knelt at her side, putting the finishing touches on an enormous bandage that covered her shoulder and held her arm tightly against her side. Three heads turned, three pairs of eyes gaped at him, their owners apparently struck dumb. Burch tossed his gun belt aside and lay the rifle on the table before coming over for a closer look. "What happened here?"

The three looked at each other and then back at him, but no one spoke.

"I thought you could take care of yourselves for a few days, but it looks like I was wrong." He knelt beside Rachel to inspect Balaam's work. "You don't look like you're in very good shape."

"If you had a broken shoulder and collarbone, you wouldn't feel very good either," Balaam said, recovering the use of his ready tongue.

"How come you boys let her get so banged about?"

"Better you should ask what buffalo dung was low enough to ride down a defenseless woman."

"Shut up, you old fool," rasped Ned. From the grim expressions on Ned's and Rachel's faces, Burch gathered there was more wrong than broken bones.

"Did you see Sibyl?" Rachel asked urgently, and instantly Burch's attention was rapt.

"She came back?" Three heads nodded, and unconsciously Burch looked around; at the same instant, he knew he wouldn't see her. "Where is she? What happened?" he demanded, the color fading from his face and the muscles along his jaw becoming rigid. "Tell me!" he thundered when no one answered him.

"Jesse took her," Ned told him.

"What for?"

"We don't know, but some time after midnight, Rachel heard a noise and got up. Jesse had Sibyl on her horse and when Rachel tried to stop him, he ran her down."

"Damn near broke her neck," stuck in Balaam.

"But what did he want with Sibyl?"

Ned and Balaam shook their heads as baffled as Burch.

"Do you know why he took her?" Burch asked Rachel, but she turned away, seeking to avoid his eyes. He was shocked at the anguish and guilt he saw in her face. "You do know, don't you?"

"To make her marry him."

"What?" the three men exclaimed in unison. Rachel closed her eyes, took Ned's hand tightly in hers, and began to speak in halting phrases.

"I met your uncle the day he arrived in Denver. He was too full of rage to be interested in any woman for more than one night, but I fell in love with him and followed him everywhere. He tried to make me stay away, but I wouldn't. He never pretended he loved me, but I would have slept at his door just to be near him. Then he met your aunt and fell in love with her. They married and settled in Wyoming, and I went back to Denver.

"But there was nothing to keep me in Denver, so I came out here. I had a little money and I could earn enough on the land to support myself."

"Did Aunt Ada know?"

"No, but Wesley was never unfaithful to her. Just every once in a while he would come by to make sure I was doing okay." She paused. "I had a son who was raised by my sister, and two years ago he followed me out here. Jesse is my son."

Balaam's head jerked around in Burch's direction, his jaw sagging to expose large gaps in his discolored teeth.

"I didn't want him to stay and I didn't want Wesley to give him a job, but Jesse asked him behind my back, using the fact I was his mother to play on Wesley's sympathies.

"He disliked you from the beginning," she said to Burch. "He saw you as an outsider, but when Wesley left you the ranch, his dislike turned to bitter hatred. It was all my fault for not going back to Denver and taking him with me. I should have seen that he would grow to hate you."

"How could you know how a crazy man's mind works?"

436

asked Balaam.

"That's not it, is it?" asked Burch.

"No, he's not crazy, he's just jealous. Jesse is Wesley Cameron's son, and only child."

"Well, I'll be a horny toad!" exclaimed Balaam.

"Did Uncle know?" Burch asked.

"No. Having Jesse was my idea. He would have felt obligated to take us in, and that would have broken Ada's heart."

"Why did Jesse come here?"

"It was my sister's fault. She's a selfish, spiteful woman, and she never forgave me for what I did. She told Jesse who his father was, that he was a rich man with no children; she built up the notion in Jesse's mind that all he had to do was come out here and Wesley would make him heir to everything he had. It was a terrible jolt to Jesse to find that you were already here, and the apple of your uncle's eye. He never talked to me about it, but I know he thought in time he would supplant you in his father's esteem and then tell him the truth; that's why he worked so hard. He resented you far more than Sibyl."

"She was blood, and I wasn't?"

"Yes. He hoped to divide the two of you, marry her, and somehow wrest control of the ranch from you."

"Why? Sibyl never treated him differently from the other hands."

"He never thought of what Sibyl might want, only that with her he could take from you what was rightfully his. He loves this ranch so much I was afraid at one time he would try to hurt you."

"He tried to *kill* me."

They stared incredulously.

"With a stampede, two rattlesnakes, and last week he tried for the second time with a rifle." Their faces reflected their stupefied horror.

"He shot my dog instead."

"He killed Brutus?" gulped Balaam.

"No, but he came damned close."

"If I'd thought he really would try to harm you, I would have warned you."

"Forget about that now. What about Sibyl?"

"I knew when he showed up last night he meant trouble. All winter I've tried to talk him into going back to my sister's, but he wouldn't listen; he made up his mind he was going to get this ranch. I didn't think he meant Sibyl any harm, so when she insisted I leave her with Jesse, I did. But I couldn't rest, and when I got up to come check on Sibyl, I saw him coming out of the shed with her in the saddle in front of him."

"She went with him?" Burch felt suffocated, unable to breathe.

"She was unconscious. He must have knocked her out," she said, answering his unspoken question.

"The dirty bastard. Do you know where he went?" asked Balaam.

"I know where he is going," Burch said, rising to his feet, "and I'm sure he knows I'll follow him."

"I'll come with you," Balaam offered.

"No, this I have to do alone."

"Be careful," Ned cautioned. "If he's tried to kill you before, he won't stop now."

"I'll be careful." Burch looked at Rachel's agonized countenance, and the anguish in her face melted some of the fury in his heart. "I'll do what I can for him, but I can't let him harm Sibyl."

"I know," she whispered and turned her head away.

Ned held Rachel close and Burch motioned Balaam to follow him out of the room. It would be inhumanly cruel to force Rachel to listen to him make preparations to hunt down her own son.

Sibyl was aware of a terrific pain at the base of her skull, but she couldn't open her eyes. She couldn't understand why she was being bounced up and down so violently; it was making her head ache worse, and she didn't like it. She tried to reach out, to grab on to something to steady her, but she felt confined, her arms pinned to her side and her body firmly anchored to whatever it was that was thrashing about underneath her. She struggled to break the grip of blackness that held her, but she failed and slowly everything slipped away.

Sibyl opened her eyes. Dimly she could make out the light of a fire burning in an open hearth. Her head still ached fiercely, but her suffering became unbearable when she tried to sit up. Thousands of tiny needles of pain exploded behind her eyes and she lay back with a stifled moan. She had no idea where she was or how she had gotten there; she was vaguely aware that someone else was in the cabin with her, but since the person seemed to be no threat, she forgot about it. Unable to just lie there, she started to raise herself into a sitting position; the pain was excruciating, but she forced herself to keep on trying. The squeaking of her bed attracted the attention of the other person.

"It's about time you woke up. I started to think I'd hit you too hard."

"Jesse?" she asked, baffled. "Where am I? What are you doing here?"

"You're bait," he answered with brutal frankness.

"Bait?" she echoed at a loss.

"To draw your precious Burch."

Immediately Sibyl's senses became acute. "Draw Burch where? What for? If you want something, why can't you just tell him?"

"Don't be a fool," he said curtly. "No man walks willingly to his death."

"Death! You mean to kill him?"

"You're damned right. He's escaped for the last time."

439

"But what for? What could he possibly have done to make you want to shoot him?"

"*Kill* him!" Jesse shouted in her face. "I'm going to put a whole clip into his thieving heart."

I've got to think, Sibyl told herself. None of this is making sense. "But why did you bring me here? Where are we, anyway?"

"We're in a cabin way back in the hills. I thought I was the only one who knew about it, but Burch found it and the cattle I hid. He'll know to come here looking for me."

Sibyl was even more confused. "What cattle? What are you talking about?"

"I've been rustling steers out from under his big nose all summer," Jesse disclosed proudly, laughing at his own cleverness. "Neither he nor any of those thick-headed fools that work for him had any idea who was doing it."

"Why?"

"To make Burch look bad, especially since I was going to be the one to find them."

"You actually *stole* cows from the Elkhorn?" Sibyl asked in disbelief.

"They're mine!" he roared.

Sibyl's sense of ownership reared its head, robust and combative. "No they're not," she said, sitting up so quickly an agonizing pain shot through her temples. "They're mine, and I don't allow anybody to steal from me."

"I'm not stealing from anybody."

"I suppose you can explain that."

"I'm going to marry you, and together we can get rid of that interfering, cussing bastard. He tricked my father into leaving half the ranch to him."

"What are you talking about? You know I'll never marry you."

"Wesley Cameron was *my* father, and the Elkhorn should belong to me, not some scum from Kansas City without a drop of Cameron blood."

Sibyl felt like she was losing her grasp on reality. "I don't understand," she said faintly. "Uncle Wesley had no children."

"None whose mother was good enough for him to marry," he said bitterly. "A plain, honest girl was not fit for a fancy Virginian, even though she followed him across three territories while she left her own son to be raised by her sister, a vindictive harpy always breathing hellfire and preaching how I was damned to burn because I was a bastard."

"Rachel," Sibyl said with sudden enlightenment. "Is she your mother?"

"Damn her soul!" cursed Jesse bitterly, looking pitifully vulnerable now that his secret was exposed. He jerked a pot from the fire and ladled some stew into a plate. "Eat this. It's all you're going to get today."

"I'd rather starve," Sibyl said, revolted.

"Suit yourself."

"I'll cook my own dinner."

"There isn't time. Burch can't be far behind us, and I've got to be at the mouth of the canyon before he gets there. You've got to be tied up before I go, so eat now if you're going to eat at all."

Sibyl looked at the lumpy mess on the plate and her stomach heaved. "You might as well go ahead and tie me up now. I couldn't touch a mouthful."

"You're gonna get mighty hungry," Jesse warned as he forced to her lie down and began to wind a rope around Sibyl and the bed.

Why don't you ever *think* before you open your mouth? she berated herself. Why didn't you stall? You might even have been able to talk him into leaving you untied!

"No sense in you trying to scream or get away. There's nobody within twenty miles of this place, and there's nothing between here and the Elkhorn but ice and snow. Besides, you don't know the way back."

Sibyl recognized the truth of this statement and, at the

same time, realized that she had to warn Burch before he walked into Jesse's ambush. She had nothing to gain by antagonizing Jesse or putting him on his guard, so she lay quietly.

"When will you come back?"

"Already sorry you turned down the food?"

"No, I don't like being left alone." That was true, but he didn't have to know she wasn't afraid of him.

"I'll return when I've gotten rid of that cocky bastard." It took him a little while to check his rifle and fill his canteen, but within fifteen minutes he was gone.

Through a small window Sibyl could see the sun beginning to set. I'll wait until it's dark, she thought. Even with the cover of the trees he'd probably see me in the daylight.

Time moved with painful slowness. Sibyl didn't move because she couldn't be sure Jesse wouldn't come back to check on her. He had not tied her hands or feet; she didn't know if it was because they were so far from help, if it was of no consequence if she got away, or if he was testing her and would tie her more securely if she attempted to escape. It didn't matter; either way, she had to escape.

At last she could wait no longer. The ropes held at first, but once she worked them down her body they fell off rather easily. To be considered such a weak and ineffectual foe infuriated her; he would soon lean his mistake. However, she had to find something to eat if she expected to ride for help; she had had no food in twenty-four hours and was feeling a little dizzy. She found some stale bread and canned fruit, but nothing more. In the end she was forced to taste the stew; it wasn't so bad if she didn't look at it. She ate about half a plate, but then her stomach rebelled and she threw the rest into the fire.

Sibyl searched the cabin thoroughly, but Jesse hadn't been so contemptuous of her as to leave any weapons or ammunition behind, or even a jacket. Jesse had also taken the oilskin; the only piece of clothing Sibyl had was her nightgown. It was impossible to consider riding for twenty miles on a freezing night without something to keep her warm; she'd die of pneumonia. There was nothing but a blanket, so Sibyl wrapped it tightly around her shoulders.

The icy ground was torturous to her bare feet, but the chinook winds had cleared great patches in the snow, and if she was careful to walk only on the soft dirt, it was bearable.

But by the time she had saddled Hospitality, her feet were numb, and she was forced to search the cabin again until she found two pairs of socks and a riding crop. She put both pairs of socks on, tucked the crop under her arm, and led Hospitality to the edge of the thin timber that lined the sides of the canyon. The sky was filled with heavy clouds that obscured the moon; maybe she could slip by Jesse in the inky blackness of the pine shadows.

Leading her horse, Sibyl slowly worked her way down the canyon, painstakingly trying to avoid any sound that would warn Jesse of her approach. Her eyes stared into the night, trying to see Jesse or his horse, needing to know where he was hiding but fearful of finding him. Every step of Hospitality's hooves was a potential warning signal, but she had to risk it. She couldn't possibly go for help on foot; her only hope of reaching the Elkhorn was that her horse would instinctively know the way home.

The stream below was rising fast. Its musical rushing around rocks and cascading over falls soothed Sibyl's raw nerves; it also masked the sounds of their movement, but would it be enough? She had almost reached the mouth of the canyon, so maybe she would get through. Then, just as she thought success was within her grasp, a huge shape loomed up out of the dark, causing Sibyl to cry out involuntarily.

"I wondered how long you would wait before you tried to warn your lover," Jesse rasped. Sibyl's smothered shriek only amused him. Recovering quickly, she clambered into the saddle and drove Hospitality forward with cruel lashes across the withers, but Jesse was at the horse's head in seconds and the animal was helplessly caught between opposing wills. Sibyl struck at Jesse in fury, and her crop opened his cheek almost to the bone. With a roar of pain, he pulled her from the saddle and knocked her to the ground.

"If you want to see your lover so much, I'll let you wait for him."

Sibyl stared at him uncomprehendingly.

"With me," he laughed viciously. "You can see him *die*."

He jerked Sibyl to her feet so abruptly she nearly lost the blanket. The first drops of rain began to fall, but Jesse didn't notice. "I'm going to tie you to this tree where you'll have a nice view, but in case you have any idea of warning him, I'm going to gag you." This time Jesse did not take any chances. He bound Sibyl hand and foot to a slim pine, tying the gag so tightly she could hardly breathe.

The rain began to fall much harder, and she was thankful he had tied her in the blanket. It didn't offer much protection and none to her nearly frozen feet, but it was better than nothing.

Burch, she pleaded silently, please don't follow me. Please be so far away you don't know I'm gone. All through the long night she prayed that Burch would not come, but deep within her she knew he would and that his life might depend upon her staying awake. But when he finally did come, she could give him no warning.

Chapter 38

Steam rose from Silver Birch's heated flanks. An icy rain had fallen throughout the night and turned the landscape into a sodden sea of mud. It was almost as though Nature wanted to make up for the yearlong drought in one night. Half an hour before dawn, the rain came down in torrents, pelting Burch mercilessly and soaking through his leather mackintosh; then it slacked off abruptly to a light drizzle. The streams, rising quickly, were already overflowing their banks, threatening to flood any low area. Burch urged his tired mount on. He had at least one more creek to cross and he wanted to reach it before it became impassable.

All during the endless night, Burch had tried not to think of what Jesse might do to Sibyl. Jesse had to be mad; the hate that had been planted and nurtured by his aunt must have escalated out of control when his father left the ranch to Burch. It was improbable that Jesse would harm Sibyl, but in his condition Burch couldn't be sure.

Burch gave his horse a breather when he reached the creek that flowed out of Boulder Canyon; it was already spilling out of its banks and over the low bushes growing along the edge. In the gray dawn, Burch could see the swirling eddies around hidden rocks and the debris, torn loose from the hills above, swirling through the water, each a potentially lethal weapon to anyone crossing the stream.

He was many miles from the Elkhorn, too far to know every foot of this stream. He cast back in his mind to the time two months earlier when he had followed it in the swirling blizzard, but there was nothing in his memory to help him. Then the winds had blurred his vision, and the deep snow had obliterated any sign of the almost-dry streambed. Burch dismounted and walked slowly up the stream, scrutinizing both banks. Soon he found what he was looking for, the worn depression that told of a cattle crossing. The streambed would be free of treacherous holes and boulders unless they had washed down during the night.

Burch remounted and urged his tired horse forward. Silver Birch pranced nervously before the swollen stream; he snorted and shook his head, but under Burch's patient urging, he gingerly entered the swirling torrent. The water that overflowed the banks was shallow and relatively calm, but in the center of the thirty feet of rushing water, Burch could see the major thrust of the rampaging stream. It was impossible to tell how deep it was, but he dared not wait any longer. Even in the short while he spent looking for the crossing, the water had risen to cover several clumps of gorse.

Under his urging, Silver Birch entered the center of the stream and Burch felt him stagger as the force of the current hit him broadside. Burch held his horse up while he gathered his feet solidly under him and once again urged him forward. The water rose until it was halfway up Silver Birch's chest; it shoved the huge horse about like a helpless toy. Burch dared not hurry him for fear that some dislodged rock would cause him to stumble and both of them would be at the mercy of the increasingly violent current.

A sharp crack caused Silver Birch to plunge forward in fright; a double cottonwood tree had split in half. For a moment the doomed tree remained attached to its twin; then with a violent wrench that caused the still-standing tree to

446

shudder, the remaining roots were ripped from the ground and the whole tree hurled into the maw of the angry stream. It was headed straight for Burch.

Burch did not know if his horse could carry them both out of the path of the oncoming tree, but if he dived into the water to relieve his horse of his weight, the current would drag him under. They must perish or survive together. With an earsplitting yell easily heard above the roar of the water, Burch dug his heels into his horse's side and rode furiously toward the shore. Silver Birch's powerful muscles strained against the sandy bottom as his hooves found the opposite bank. Then with a mighty effort, his forelegs pulled his body out of the deep water and the heavily muscled hindquarters sent them surging into the safety of the shallows. An outflung branch raked across his rear, but he charged out of the water, his legs shaking under him. Burch slid out of the saddle.

"I hope it doesn't get any closer than that," he said, knowing how close they had come to death. Silver Birch shook himself, throwing water all over Burch. "I suppose I deserved that, but you're going to have to carry me anyway. I'll never reach that ridge in these boots."

The last clouds gave way before the bright morning sun as Burch rode toward the mouth of the canyon, hugging the base of the ridge so that anyone waiting for him could not see his approach without exposing their own position first. If Jesse planned to ambush him, he was probably waiting where the path became a narrow track at the stream's edge. Burch dismounted and hid his horse in a pine thicket. Then he started to climb the back side of the ridge that formed part of the mouth of the canyon; he was going to come down on Jesse from above.

Over an hour later, after Burch crossed the top of the ridge and stealthily descended the other side, he spotted Jesse crouched at the base of a large tree, his rifle ready, his eyes intently watching the entrance of the canyon. Below him, the swollen stream filled almost the whole width of the canyon; the current lashed out, clawing at trees and rocks, and swallowing large chunks of the yellow earth.

Burch picked his way carefully between the pines. There wasn't much cover, and he tried to keep at least one large tree trunk between him and Jesse in case some sound should betray his presence. Using extreme care, he had come within thirty feet when his eye was caught by the sodden blanket tied to a tree. His curiosity changed to blind fury when he realized that the sagging, rain-soaked body in the blanket was Sibyl. In his wrath, he descended too rapidly and the earth, soaked by too much rain, gave way under his feet, sending him and three tons of dirt hurtling down the hillside toward the rampaging stream.

The avalanche of mud rolled over Jesse, imprisoning him in its slippery grasp at the same time it deposited Burch at Sibyl's feet. He was so horrified by her condition he forgot about Jesse. He dug in his pocket for his knife, swiftly cut the ropes that held her up, and caught her before she slid to the ground. The blanket was soaked through with icy water that drew all the warmth out of her body. Her lips were blue, almost too stiff to move; her eyes opened only slightly, but Burch could see that a fire still glowed deep within them.

"Burch." Her voice was a ragged, hoarse whisper.

Burch threw off the blanket and wrapped her in his own coat. Her limbs were dangerously cold, but she was burning up with fever; he had to get her to a doctor at once. He rose to his feet, intending to wrap her in Jesse's buffalo robe; he was just in time to see Jesse, freed from the mud, point a rifle straight at him. He dove through the air, striking Jesse in the chest as the rifle went off in the air. They tumbled down the hill, coming dangerously close to the edge of the stream.

Jesse found his feet first and scrambled up the hill, trying to reach his rifle, but Burch crawled up behind him, caught him by the ankles, and sent him tumbling down the hill once more. Jesse was on his feet like a cat, springing for Burch's throat with bare hands. Burch could see his eyes, red with fury. A powerful man made more powerful by the mad hatred that drove him, Jesse bore Burch down by the savagery of his attack, but Burch's mighty muscles threw him off. Jesse scooped up two handfuls of the mud beneath his feet and flung it in Burch's face. Unable to see, Burch was almost helpless against Jesse, and the two tumbled down to the edge of the water. Jesse got his hands around Burch's throat, trying to choke him, to push his head under the water. Burch could feel the cold sodden ground beneath his shoulders and then the numbing water as it lapped at his head.

With a wrenching effort, he threw Jesse aside, but before he could clear his eyes of the mud, Jesse struck him from behind with a limb. Dazed, Burch was unable to regain his feet before Jesse raised the limb over his head to deliver a blow that would either break his neck or send him to his death in the swollen stream. But the blow did not fall. Burch cleared his eyes to see Sibyl leaning against a tree, exhausted, and Jesse lying sprawled on the ground where he had fallen after she hit him on the head with a rock.

Burch swept her up in his arms and kissed her passionately.

"If you can kiss me looking like this, you must love me after all," she said, looking adoringly into his eyes.

"I'd take you back in rags."

"I'm near that now." She managed to smile, then a racking cough shook her.

"I've got to get you to a fire. You must get warm." Her sudden gasp of horror caused him to turn just in time to escape having his skull crushed by the stock of Jesse's rifle. Both men lost their footing in the mud, but Jesse was above him and had the advantage. Jesse regained his feet and swung his rifle in a vicious arc. Burch flung himself into the mud to escape the blow. The force of Jesse's swing carried him too far forward; he lost his footing and fell into the stream.

The current grabbed Jesse and swept him out into the center of the stream. Heedless of the danger to himself, Burch plunged in after him, only to find that he, too, was helpless in the raging torrent. Jesse was already beyond his reach, and now Burch was fighting for his own life. He managed to get a precarious hold on a large boulder, but the current was too powerful; his grip was slowly being wrenched loose. In seconds, he would be washed away just like Jesse.

Sibyl watched, paralyzed, until she realized Burch's life depended on her. She struggled to her feet and looked wildly about for some way to save him.

"The rope," Burch called from the water. "Throw me the rope." Sibyl stumbled over to Jesse's horse, untied the rope, and staggered back to the stream's edge. Her hands fumbled and her body shook terribly as she tried to unwind the rope. Painfully slowly, it seemed to her, she got the rope uncoiled.

"Throw it upstream, well above me," Burch directed. She dared not look at him for fear that any second she would see him lose his hold on the rock and be washed away forever. Using all the strength she had, Sibyl whirled the rope above her head, as she had seen the men do so many times, and flung it out into the stream as far as she could. She almost fainted from relief when she saw the rope splash down a full three yards beyond Burch. Almost immediately, the rushing water carried the rope to him.

"Now wrap it around a tree," he said. "Hurry."

That last word, the only time she had ever known him to admit he needed help, drove her to call upon the last of her strength. Images began to blur before her eyes and there was a ringing in her ears, but she stubbornly forced herself to climb the bank to the nearest tree. The pine began to move, to bend and become distorted as she struggled to reach it.

"You can't faint now," she muttered to herself. "He'll die."

On she struggled until she felt rather than saw the tree. She leaned against it and wrapped the rope about the trunk. "Again," she murmured, "again, or it won't hold." But the images blurred completely and she knew no more.

Chapter 39

Sibyl opened her eyes to see the same fire in the same hearth. Could she have dreamed everything? She tried to sit up, but her body wouldn't move. Rolling up on her elbow, she saw a man with his back to her. Jesse, she thought, slumping back on the bed. She tried to remember, tried to concentrate, but her mind refused to hold firmly to any thought except one: Something *was* different. Her eyes roamed about the cabin. It certainly was the same cabin and the same fire. Of course, it was the same man.

But the conviction that this was not the same man was so strong she struggled to prop herself up in the bed. Almost at once she knew that back, knew every part of the body from any angle. She had dreamed of him, longed for him, feared she would never see him again. She could never mistake him for anyone else. "Burch," she called softly.

He turned abruptly, crossing the room in three running strides. A warm, eager smile wreathed his face in a welcome so genuine her eyes went misty, and his beloved image was obscured by a veil of tears.

"Sibyl, my love, I thought you'd never wake."

My love! He had called her his love. Her heart thumped violently in her chest. He did still love her; he did forgive her. Relief, joy, disbelief, and a multitude of other emotions swept over her and she found herself clinging to him, sobbing in his arms.

"It's all right," he said, trying to soothe her.

"I know, that's why I'm crying," she said as she laughed through her tears. "I was so afraid it wouldn't be."

They sat for a long time, talking occasionally but mostly holding tightly to one another. They had waited so long for this moment, had saved up so much to say to each other, yet now all that was important was that they held each other in their arms; as long as their hands could touch, no words were necessary. Someday they would talk, would offer each other explanations, but for now their nearness filled their hearts to overflowing.

"You hungry? he asked at last.

"Starved," she said, starting to get out of bed.

"Don't move, I'm fixing dinner."

"I can't be poisoned now, not after I've waited so long to catch you."

"That's gratitude for you when you've been eating my food for the last three days."

"Three days!" she exclaimed as he brought her a bowl of thick soup from the three-toed pot nestled in the coals.

"You, my girl, have been very sick, and it was only because of my expert care that you are alive at this moment to cast aspersions on my cooking." He noticed her eyes were not laughing. "Don't you remember what happened?"

"Some, but not all."

"Tell me what you can."

"I remember that Jesse left me here when he went to ambush you. I escaped, but I think he was expecting me, and he tied me to a tree while he waited."

"Do you remember anything else?"

"No. Where is Jesse?" she asked, almost afraid of the answer.

"He's dead. I suspected he might try to waylay me, so I came over the top of the ridge."

"I remember now. He hit you with a limb."

"He fell in the creek. I couldn't save him."

"Poor Rachel. You know she's his mother?"

"She told me, and why he kidnapped you."

"But you went after him," she said with sudden recollection. "I remember now I tried to tie the rope around the tree, but I could only get it around once."

"That rope was wound around the tree three times and tied with a double hitch. You could have pulled a horse out with it."

So she hadn't failed him; she had held on long enough.

"I tried so hard, but I wasn't sure . . ."

"I owe you my life." She forgot the soup.

"I guess I owe you *my* life, too."

"Since you owe it to me, can I keep it?"

"Don't ever let me go, no matter how horribly I behave. I'll never tell you how to run the ranch again; I won't even use my money without your permission. I've never been so miserable in my life as when I left you."

"I think your fever is back up again," he said, holding her closely. "You *must* be delirious. I promise I won't hold you to anything you say until you're well enough to know what you're talking about."

Sibyl laughed joyfully and kissed him on the tip of his nose.

"But you said I've been here three days?"

"You were delirious and burning up with fever. I wanted to take you to Augusta, but I didn't dare risk such a long trip, so I brought you here."

"You must be a good doctor. I feel marvelous."

Burch grinned wickedly.

"Don't tell me you did something hideous and I have to be grateful for it."

He grinned even more.

"Tell me right now. I don't trust you the least bit when you wear that indecent smirk of triumph."

"It wasn't anything special. I just fed you lots of hot beef soup."

"And?"

"And held your naked body in my arms for three days." Sibyl flushed.

"You were cold to the marrow," he said more soberly. "I built a big fire and piled every blanket I could find on you, but you were still blue. The only other way I could think of was to use my own body heat."

"And it worked?"

"It warmed us both up. I had a fever almost as bad as yours," he chuckled, his voice husky from the memory.

"And I bet you could hardly wait to tell me about it as soon as I woke up."

"There was one time I thought you might *not* wake up. I waited almost without breathing, praying I would get one more chance to tell you how much I love you and that if you ever run away from me again, I *will* turn you across my knee."

"You're stuck with me. I've burned my bridges in Virginia, and Augusta is expecting a baby, so she won't have time for me any more."

"Would you like a baby?"

"Not this very minute," she said, trying to keep her voice steady. "You'd have to take care of it for me, and the poor thing would never get a change of diapers."

"We can give it to Rachel until it grows up."

"Beast!" she laughed. "It's a good thing I've found out what kind of father you're going to be."

"If we have enough of them, I might learn to do it right. I'll need lots of practice." But the look in his eyes had nothing to do with children, and Sibyl felt dizzy with the emotion that surged through her.

"You get some sleep," Burch said, taking the empty bowl. "I'm not going anywhere." Concern at the way she looked overcame his desire, but it was still a struggle.

Sibyl slept most of the afternoon and woke feeling much stronger. Burch had dinner ready, and she was able to get up and eat at the table, chiding him about the slightly charred crust on the haunch of venison and the lack of a properly balanced table.

"You can serve all the vegetables you like when you get back to the ranch, but if you can find even one single potato hill outside or a jar of anything but dust inside this cabin, you're doing better than I am." Sibyl forbore to tease him, and after dinner she dozed contentedly before the fire while Burch cleaned up. But when he sat down next to her, she came wide awake. There were long stretches of silence in their conversation, but the tension caused by their physical awareness of each other began to grow. They talked of the future and of the past, but the undercurrent was of *now* and it grew stronger with every passing minute.

"I think it's time I tucked you in bed," Burch said at last.

"You're bored with me already and trying to send me off to bed to get rid of me," Sibyl teased to hide her feeling of disappointment. "Do you have a woman hidden outside? I'm afraid she'll be frozen solid if she's been waiting all this time."

"Baggage! I haven't had time for another woman, even if she had been right here next to me," he said, ushering her to bed and beginning to wrap the blankets around her. The tension was almost unbearable, and when he began to make up a bed for himself on the floor Sibyl could stand it no longer.

"Aren't you going to take up your usual position, or don't you care anymore if I stay warm?"

"Do you really want me?"

"After all the trouble you've gone to, it would be a shame if I were to freeze to death now." Burch didn't need to be asked a second time. He shed his clothes quick as a chameleon changes colors and was in the bed almost before Sibyl had time to make room for him. He put his arms about her with extreme care, almost as though he were afraid to touch her.

"Hold me tight," she said, her own voice husky with desire. "I'm not going to break."

But from the powerful embrace that encircled her, she thought she just might. All the restraint, all the rigid control Burch had exercised for days and kept under precarious hold, was discarded. The fear of the last few days, the worry over whether she would live, all found relief in the passionate fever with which he kissed her. He seemed to be reassured by holding her in his arms—feeling her breath on his face, the vibrant warmth coming from her body—and he slowly relaxed. As his anxiety faded, his passions flared and Sibyl felt evidence of his desire against her skin. Her own needs, merely waiting for such a signal, erupted full blown. All the worrying and waiting was over. He was in her arms at last, and no misunderstanding or conflict lay between them. Ahead stretched an unbroken chain of years to spend in contented happiness, free of any shadow of doubt or suspicion to rob them of their sweetness.

Sibyl welcomed Burch as he came to her, at last willing to give up herself, to merge into a unity even more wonderful because of the complete freedom it bestowed on her. She met him, rose to his advance, matched his ardor until they were both consumed by the love they had harbored for so long, waiting for just this moment.

"I think it would be rather nice to have several heirs underfoot," Sibyl said later, turning so she could look deep into Burch's eyes.

"We're not going to die, not ever," he said, holding her close. "You and I will be the oldest couple in the world; our children will have to find their own ranches. Hundreds of years from now we'll still be at the Elkhorn, and people will come from miles around just to stare at us. There'll probably be signs to direct the tourists, and maybe even a special train that comes right up to the front porch."

"What will the signs say?" she asked, abandoning herself

457

to his foolishness.

"Here lives the world's oldest couple. They are so busy being in love they can't find time to die."

Dear Aunt Louisa,

I meant to write you earlier, but things have been so busy it seems I haven't had time to sit down for as much as five minutes. The rains came this year and Burch is expecting a record price for our steers.

Please apologize to everybody for my not having acknowledged all their gifts. I know it was six months ago, but there are so many I just haven't been able to keep up. I didn't know there were so many people in Virginia who remembered me.

All the upset over Jesse has settled down, and hardly anyone speaks of it any more. Poor Rachel has suffered terribly, but Ned never leaves her and we do what we can for her.

I almost forgot. Aunt Augusta was brought to bed of a bouncing boy. He's positively huge, and Lasso's so proud he's about to burst his buttons. Augusta came through the ordeal fit as a fiddle, but Lasso is trying to smother her with kindness. The poor woman says she's going to have to come stay with Burch and me just to be treated like a normal human being again.

The herd is thriving. Burch bred the bull to some of the range cows, but he gave his greatest attention to getting every cow in the herd pregnant. He wants as many young bulls as possible to turn loose on the range in three years. This year's calves are healthy and eight out of the eleven are bulls. We'll be the envy of Wyoming before long.

By the way, I'm expecting a baby myself sometime in the spring. I just hope it doesn't come in the middle of the calving. I don't know how I'll find time for it if it does.

I've got to go. I promise to write more later.

Your loving niece,
Sibyl

"Henry, read this letter!" Louisa demanded, thrusting the folded sheets into her husband's hands. "I can't see anything to do but for me to go to Wyoming this spring."

"What?" exclaimed her startled husband.

"I never would have believed it, not even of Sibyl," declared her outraged aunt, "but I do believe that girl is more concerned about those cows than she is about her own child. Unless I'm there to talk some sense into her head, I wouldn't put it past her to have that baby in a cow brier!"

SEVEN BRIDES:
DAISY

LEIGH GREENWOOD

The state of Texas isn't big enough for Tyler Randolph and his six rough-and-ready brothers. So the rugged loner sets off for New Mexico in search of a lost mine. He is out to find gold in them thar hills, but he strikes the real mother lode when he rescues a feisty and independent beauty from the wilderness. Attacked, shot, and left for dead, Daisy is horrified to wake up in Tyler's cabin. Then a blizzard traps them together, and she is convinced that the mountain man is a fourteen-carat cad— until his unpolished charm claims her love. Before long, Daisy is determined to do some digging of her own to unearth the treasures hidden in Tyler's heart.

___4742-X $6.99/$8.99 CAN

Dorchester Publishing Co., Inc.
P.O. Box 6640
Wayne, PA 19087-8640

Please add $1.75 for shipping and handling for the first book and $.50 for each book thereafter. NY, NYC, and PA residents, please add appropriate sales tax. No cash, stamps, or C.O.D.s. All orders shipped within 6 weeks via postal service book rate. Canadian orders require $2.00 extra postage and must be paid in U.S. dollars through a U.S. banking facility.

Name_____
Address_____
City_____State_____Zip_____
I have enclosed $_____ in payment for the checked book(s).
Payment <u>must</u> accompany all orders. ❑ Please send a free catalog.
CHECK OUT OUR WEBSITE! www.dorchesterpub.com

The Cowboys DREW

LEIGH GREENWOOD

The freedom of the range, the bawling of the longhorns, the lonesome night watch beneath a vast, starry sky—they get into a woman's blood until she knows there is nothing better than the life of a cowgirl . . . except the love of a good man.

As the main attraction for the Wild West show, sharpshooter Drew Townsend has faced her share of audiences. Yet when Cole Benton steps into the ring and challenges her to a shooting contest, she feels as weak-kneed as a newborn calf. It can't be stage fright—she'll hit every target with deadly accuracy—can it be love? Despite her wild attraction to the mysteriously handsome Texan, Drew refuses to believe in romance and all its trappings. But when the cowboy wraps his strong arms around her, she knows that she has truly hit her target—and won herself true love.

___4714-4 $6.99/$8.99 CAN

Dorchester Publishing Co., Inc.
P.O. Box 6640
Wayne, PA 19087-8640

Please add $1.75 for shipping and handling for the first book and $.50 for each book thereafter. NY, NYC, and PA residents, please add appropriate sales tax. No cash, stamps, or C.O.D.s. All orders shipped within 6 weeks via postal service book rate. Canadian orders require $2.00 extra postage and must be paid in U.S. dollars through a U.S. banking facility.

Name _____
Address_____
City_____ State_____ Zip_____
I have enclosed $_____ in payment for the checked book(s).
Payment <u>must</u> accompany all orders. ❏ Please send a free catalog.

The Cowboys

LEIGH GREENWOOD

SEAN

In the West there are only two kinds of women—the wives and mothers and daughters, and the good-time girls. It is said that Pearl Belladonna shows a man the best time ever, but Sean O'Ryan has not come to the gold fields looking for a floozy. He wants gold to buy a ranch, and a virtuous woman to make a wife. The sensual barroom singer might tempt his body with her lush curves, and tease his mind with her bright wit, but she isn't for him. From her red curls to her assumed name, nothing about her seems real until a glimpse into her heart convinces Sean that the lady is, indeed, a pearl beyond price.

___4490-0 $6.99/$8.99 CAN

Dorchester Publishing Co., Inc.
P.O. Box 6640
Wayne, PA 19087-8640

Please add $1.75 for shipping and handling for the first book and $.50 for each book thereafter. NY, NYC, and PA residents, please add appropriate sales tax. No cash, stamps, or C.O.D.s. All orders shipped within 6 weeks via postal service book rate. Canadian orders require $2.00 extra postage and must be paid in U.S. dollars through a U.S. banking facility.

Name_____

Address_____

City_____State_____Zip_____

I have enclosed $_____ in payment for the checked book(s).

Payment <u>must</u> accompany all orders. ❑ Please send a free catalog.

CHECK OUT OUR WEBSITE! www.dorchesterpub.com

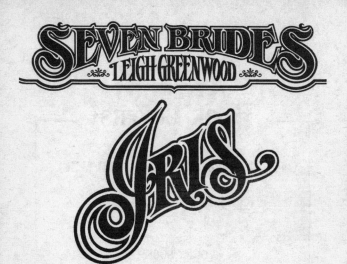

SEVEN BRIDES
LEIGH GREENWOOD

IRIS

Rough and ready as any of the Randolph boys, Monty bristles under his eldest brother's tight rein. All he wants is to light out from Texas for a new beginning. And Iris Richmond has to get her livestock to Wyoming's open ranges before rustlers wipe her out. Monty is heading that way, but the bullheaded wrangler flat out refuses to help her. Never one to take no for an answer, Iris saddles up to coax, rope, and tame the ornery cowboy she's always desired.

___4175-8 $6.99/$8.99 CAN

Dorchester Publishing Co., Inc.
P.O. Box 6640
Wayne, PA 19087-8640

Please add $1.75 for shipping and handling for the first book and $.50 for each book thereafter. NY, NYC, and PA residents, please add appropriate sales tax. No cash, stamps, or C.O.D.s. All orders shipped within 6 weeks via postal service book rate. Canadian orders require $2.00 extra postage and must be paid in U.S. dollars through a U.S. banking facility.

Name_____
Address_____
City_____State_____Zip_____
I have enclosed $_____ in payment for the checked book(s).
Payment <u>must</u> accompany all orders. ❑ Please send a free catalog.

ATTENTION
BOOK LOVERS!

Can't get enough of your favorite **ROMANCE**?

Call **1-800-481-9191** to:

✳ order books,

✳ receive a **FREE** catalog,

✳ join our book clubs to **SAVE 20%!**

Open Mon.-Fri. 10 AM-9 PM EST

Visit **www.dorchesterpub.com**
for special offers and inside
information on the authors you love.

We accept Visa, MasterCard or Discover®.
LEISURE BOOKS ❤ LOVE SPELL

Analytical Methods for Drinking Water

Advances in Sampling and Analysis

Water Quality Measurements Series

Series Editor

Philippe Quevauviller
European Commission, Brussels, Belgium

Published Titles in the Water Quality Measurements Series

Hydrological and Limnological Aspects of Lake Monitoring
Edited by Pertti Heinonen, Giuliano Ziglio and Andre Van der Beken

Quality Assurance for Water Analysis
Authored by Philippe Quevauviller

Detection Methods for Algae, Protozoa and Helminths in Fresh and Drinking Water
Edited by André Van der Beken, Giuliano Ziglio and Franca Palumbo

Analytical Methods for Drinking Water: Advances in Sampling and Analysis
Edited by Philippe Quevauviller and K. Clive Thompson

Forthcoming Titles in the Water Quality Measurements Series

Biological Monitoring of Rivers: Applications and Perspectives
Edited by Giuliano Ziglio, Maurizio Siligardi and Giovanna Flaim

Wastewater Quality Monitoring
Edited by Philippe Quevauviller, Olivier Thomas and André Van der Berken

Analytical Methods for Drinking Water

Advances in Sampling and Analysis

PHILIPPE QUEVAUVILLER
European Commission, Brussels, Belgium

K. CLIVE THOMPSON
ALcontrol Laboratories
South Yorkshire, UK

John Wiley & Sons, Ltd

Copyright © 2006   John Wiley & Sons Ltd, The Atrium, Southern Gate, Chichester,
West Sussex PO19 8SQ, England

Telephone   (+44) 1243 779777

Email (for orders and customer service enquiries): cs-books@wiley.co.uk
Visit our Home Page on www.wileyeurope.com or www.wiley.com

All Rights Reserved. No part of this publication may be reproduced, stored in a retrieval system or
transmitted in any form or by any means, electronic, mechanical, photocopying, recording, scanning or
otherwise, except under the terms of the Copyright, Designs and Patents Act 1988 or under the terms of a
licence issued by the Copyright Licensing Agency Ltd, 90 Tottenham Court Road, London W1T 4LP, UK,
without the permission in writing of the Publisher. Requests to the Publisher should be addressed to the
Permissions Department, John Wiley & Sons Ltd, The Atrium, Southern Gate, Chichester, West Sussex PO19
8SQ, England, or emailed to permreq@wiley.co.uk, or faxed to (+44) 1243 770620.

Designations used by companies to distinguish their products are often claimed as trademarks. All brand names
and product names used in this book are trade names, service marks, trademarks or registered trademarks of
their respective owners. The Publisher is not associated with any product or vendor mentioned in this book.

This publication is designed to provide accurate and authoritative information in regard to the subject matter
covered. It is sold on the understanding that the Publisher is not engaged in rendering professional services. If
professional advice or other expert assistance is required, the services of a competent professional should be
sought.

Other Wiley Editorial Offices

John Wiley & Sons Inc., 111 River Street, Hoboken, NJ 07030, USA

Jossey-Bass, 989 Market Street, San Francisco, CA 94103-1741, USA

Wiley-VCH Verlag GmbH, Boschstr. 12, D-69469 Weinheim, Germany

John Wiley & Sons Australia Ltd, 42 McDougall Street, Milton, Queensland 4064, Australia

John Wiley & Sons (Asia) Pte Ltd, 2 Clementi Loop #02-01, Jin Xing Distripark, Singapore 129809

John Wiley & Sons Canada Ltd, 22 Worcester Road, Etobicoke, Ontario, Canada M9W 1L1

Wiley also publishes its books in a variety of electronic formats. Some content that appears in print may not
be available in electronic books.

Library of Congress Cataloging-in-Publication Data

Quevauviller, Ph.
    Analytical methods for drinking water : advances in sampling and analysis / Philippe Quevauviller,
K. Clive Thompson.
     p. cm.
    Includes bibliographical references and index.
    ISBN-13: 978-0-470-09491-4 (cloth : alk. paper)
    ISBN-10: 0-470-09491-5 (cloth : alk. paper)
    1. Water – Analysis.   2. Drinking water – Analysis.   3. Drinking water – Government policy –
Europe.   4. Drinking water – Government policy – United States.   I. Thompson, K. C.
(Kenneth Clive), 1944–   II. Title.

TD380 .Q48 2006
363 .6′1—dc22   2005010209

British Library Cataloguing in Publication Data

A catalogue record for this book is available from the British Library

ISBN-13: 978-0-470-09491-4 (HB)
ISBN-10: 0-470-094915 (HB)

Typeset in 10.5/12.5pt Times New Roman by TechBooks, New Delhi, India
Printed and bound in Great Britain by TJ International, Padstow, Cornwall
This book is printed on acid-free paper responsibly manufactured from sustainable forestry
in which at least two trees are planted for each one used for paper production.

Dedication

This book is dedicated to the memory of A. L. Wilson (1929–1985).

Antony Leslie (Tony) Wilson was born in Brighton in 1929 and educated at Vardean Grammar School and Kings College, London, where he took an honours degree in chemistry. He worked for eighteen years at the Atomic Energy Research Establishment, Salwick and the Central Electricity Research Laboratories, Leatherhead, before joining the Water Research Association at Medmenham—later to become a constituent laboratory of the Water Research Centre—in 1968. He remained with the Centre until his retirement in 1980, when he held the position of Manager of the Analysis and Instrumentation Division.

His considerable reputation as an analytical chemist was the product of a prodigious capacity for work and the painstaking application of his considerable intellect, not only to the development of a wide range of methods, but also to the fundamental principles of analysis quality control. His work on the latter was especially pioneering and its importance has become very widely recognised.

His approach to the specification and assessment of analytical performance and to the control of analytical errors formed the basis of the standard practices of both the electricity generating and water industries in the U.K. Over the years the former Department of the Environment, in its Harmonised Monitoring Scheme, and the World Health Organization, in its Global Environment's Standing Committee of Analysts have incorporated his ideas on performance characterisation in their published methods.

In 1975 he was awarded the Louis Gordon Memorial Prize for the best paper of the year in the journal *Talanta* (one of a series in which he drew together in a coherent manner the important factors to be considered in characterising the performance of analytical methods).

It is considered very fitting that this book dealing with various aspects of water quality should be dedicated to such an illustrious and dedicated individual.

Contents

Series Preface

Water is a fundamental constituent of life and is essential to a wide range of economic activities. It is also a limited resource, as we are frequently reminded by the tragic effects of drought in certain parts of the world. Even in areas with high precipitation, and in major river basins, overuse and mismanagement of water have created severe constraints on availability. Such problems are widespread and will be made more acute by the accelerating demand on freshwater arising from trends in economic development.

Despite of the fact that water-resource management is essentially a local, river-basin based activity, there are a number of areas of action relevant to all or significant parts of the European Union and for which it is advisable to pool efforts for the purpose of understanding relevant phenomena (e.g. pollution, geochemical studies), developing technical solutions and/or defining management procedures. One of the keys for successful cooperation aimed at studying hydrology, water monitoring, biological activities, etc., is to achieve and ensure good water quality measurements.

Quality measurements are essential for demonstrating the comparability of data obtained worldwide and they form the basis for correct decisions related to management of water resources, monitoring issues, biological quality, etc. Besides the necessary quality control tools developed for various types of physical, chemical and biological measurements, there is a strong need for education and training related to water quality measurements. This need has been recognized by the European Commission, which has funded a series of training courses on this topic that cover aspects such as monitoring and measurement of lake recipients, measurement of heavy metals and organic compounds in drinking and surface water, use of biotic indexes, and methods of analysing algae, protozoa and helminths. In addition, a series of research and development projects have been or are being developed.

This book series will ensure a wide coverage of issues related to water quality measurements, including the topics of the above mentioned courses and the outcome of recent scientific advances. In addition, other aspects related to quality control tools (e.g. certified reference materials for the quality control of water analysis) and monitoring of various types of waters (river, wastewater, groundwater) will also be considered.

This book, *Analytical Methods for Drinking Water: Advances in Sampling and Analysis* is the fourth in the series; it has been written by policymakers and scientific experts in drinking water analytical science and offers the reader an overview of drinking water policies and examples of analytical research directly supporting these policies.

The Series Editor – Philippe Quevauviller

Preface

Drinking water policies and research are intimately linked. It is thanks to the scientific progress made over the last 25 years in identifying and controlling toxic products in drinking water that regulations have developed in such a way that the protection of public health from waterborne diseases has drastically improved. The integration of research outputs into the policy-making progress requires close cooperation among the scientific and policy communities, which is not always straightforward. In the US, drinking water research is an integral part of the US Environmental Protection Agency's base research programme, meaning that research is directly feeding the policy process. In Europe, links have also been established among research and policy development, albeit in a less integrated way. Exchanges between scientific and policy-making communities certainly represent key elements of progress for better environmental protection. In this respect, analytical developments linked to drinking water are at the core of the science-policy debate.

This book reflects this awareness by joining recent analytical developments with policy considerations. The first chapter gives an overview of EU and US drinking water policies, as well as on standardization. Analytical developments are described in depth in Chapter 2, focusing on bromate in drinking water. The third chapter deals with the development of a sampling protocol for determining lead in drinking water, thus mixing analytical development with standardization needs. Finally, Chapter 4 focuses on standardization aspects (pre-normative research) related to materials in contact with drinking water.

This book has been written by experts in the field of drinking water policy and analysis. It does not pretend to give an exhaustive view of drinking water analytical developments, but rather illustrates recent scientific advances in this field, which have contributed to policy development. The gathered information will be of direct use to policymakers, water scientists, researchers and analytical laboratories.

Philippe Quevauviller and K. Clive Thompson

List of Contributors

Jean Baron   CRECEP, 144, 156, av. Paul Vaillant-Couturier, Paris, F-75014, France

A.-Hakim R. Elwaer   Petroleum Research Centre, Chemistry Research Department, PO Box 6431, Tripoli, Libya

Fred S. Hauchman   US Environmental Protection Agency, Office of Research and Development (B105-01), Research Triangle Park, NC 2771, USA

Pierre Hecq   European Commission, Rue de la Loi 200, B-1049, Brussels, Belgium

Adriana Hulsmann   Kiwa Water Research, PO Box 1072, 3430 BB Nieuwegein, The Netherlands

Jennifer L. McLain   Office of Water, US Environmental Protection Agency, 1200 Pennsylvania Avenue, Washington, DC 20460, USA

Cameron W. McLeod   Department of Chemistry, Centre for Analytical Sciences Sheffield University, Sheffield, S3 7HF, UK

Philippe Quevauviller DG Environment (BU9 3/121), European Commission, Rue de la Loi 200, Brussels, B-1049, Belgium

Franz Schmitz   Landesbetrieb Hessisches Landeslabor, Abteilung V Umwelt- und Spurenanalytik, Fachgebiet V 3 Umweltanalytik, Kurfüstenstraße 6, D-65203 Wiesbaden, Germany

Nellie Slaats   Kiwa Water Research, PO Box 1072, 3430 BB Nieuwegein, The Netherlands

K. Clive Thompson   ALcontrol Laboratories, Templeborough House, Mill
                               Close, Rotherham, South Yorkshire, S60 1BZ, UK

Theo Van den Hoven   Kiwa Water Research, PO Box 1072, 3430 BB
                               Nieuwegein, The Netherlands

1
Drinking Water Regulations

Pierre Hecq, Adriana Hulsmann, Fred S. Hauchman, Jennifer L. McLain and **Franz Schmitz**

Analytical Methods for Drinking Water   Edited by P. Quevauviller and K. C. Thompson
© 2006 John Wiley & Sons, Ltd.

> **Disclaimer: The views expressed herein are those of the authors and do not necessarily represent the views of the European Commission nor of the US Environmental Protection Agency policy.**

1.1 EU DIRECTIVE ON DRINKING WATER – PAST, PRESENT AND FUTURE

1.1.1 EU Water Legislation

Water is one of the most comprehensively regulated areas of EU environmental legislation. Early European water policy began in the 1970s with the adoption of political programmes as well as legally binding legislation. As regards programmes, the First Environmental Action Programme covered the period 1973–76. Parallel with political programmes, a first wave of legislation was adopted, starting with the 1975 Surface Water Directive and culminating in the 1980 Drinking Water Directive 80/778/EEC. This initial directive was based upon the scientific and technical state of the art of 25 years ago. Since then both scientific and technological knowledge and the approach to EU legislation has changed. It was therefore necessary not only to adapt the original directive to bring it in line with the current scientific and technical progress, but also to bring it into accordance with the principle of subsidiarity by reducing the number of parameters that member states were obliged to monitor and by focusing on compliance with essential quality and health parameters.

1.1.2 The Drinking Water Directives – Revision Processes

In 1993 the commission organized a European drinking water conference in Brussels to consult all stakeholders in the supply of drinking water about the revision of the

DWD then in force. This resulted, in 1998, in the adoption and entry into force of the current DWD 98/83/EC (OJ L 330, 5.12.98). The 1998 DWD had to be transposed into national legislation 2 years after coming into force, which was at the end of the year 2000, and had to be complied with by the end of 2003 (with some exceptions for critical parameters such as lead and disinfection by products).

In the meantime the commission started preparations for the revision of the new DWD some 5 years after it came into force. This revision process is foreseen in the DWD. Exactly 10 years after the consultation of European stakeholders, the commission started to consult stakeholders on the need for revision of DWD 98/83/EC. This time 25 countries will be involved

1.1.3   Main Aspects of the Drinking Water Directives

Related Community legislation

The first generation of EU water legislation consisted of more or less isolated pieces of legislation, with little or no cross-referencing. The previous DWD 80/778/EEC only makes reference to one piece of EU legislation, namely the Council Directive on the Quality of Surface Water, intended for the abstraction of Drinking Water (75/440/EEC). The current DWD refers to a number of other directives that are related to the original directive or have interactions with that directive:

- the Plant Protection Directive (91/414/EEC) and the Biocides Directive (98/8/EC) both relevant for the pesticides parameter in the Directive and

- the Construction Products Directive (89/106/EEC), relevant for materials and appendages used in the production and distribution of drinking water.

In future revisions of the DWD, attention will be paid to an integrated approach to EU water legislation as the directive has to be brought into line with important developments such as the Water Framework Directive and the European Acceptance Scheme (under development) for materials in contact with drinking water.

Integration of EU water legislation does not only imply compliance with the requirements of various related directives but will also involve harmonization and streamlining of reporting requirements. Reporting requirements will have to address compliance and the state of, and trends in, the quality of aquatic environments.

Principles for drinking water directives

The underling principle for the previous DWD was not specified other than that it had the objective of 'setting standards for human health protection'. The current

DWD aims to protect human health from the adverse effects of contamination of water intended for human consumption by ensuring that it is 'wholesome and clean'. This applies to all water intended for human consumption, as well as to water used in the production and marketing of food, with certain exceptions. Member states are required to monitor the quality of drinking water and to take measures to ensure that it complies with the minimum quality standards. It also lays down a number of requirements for reporting to the commission, and for making information available to the public regarding the quality of drinking water. The directive is based on a number of principles that have been laid down in the Treaty, such as the subsidiarity principle and the precautionary principle. Unlike the early Community legislation, the new Treaty of the European Union states that no Community legislation should go beyond what is necessary to achieve the objectives of the treaty. For drinking water legislation this implies that the high number of parameters in the previous directive has been reduced the better to focus on what are essential and health related parameters in the whole European Union, leaving member states free to add other parameters if they see fit. A HACCP-based directive might reduce the number of parameters even further.

Other principles of the current directive are the precautionary principle, sustainable use of water and water source protection, and of course the political compromise that goes hand in hand with the process of adoption of new legislation by the member states. If future legislation should be based on risk assessment and risk approach, the added value of such an approach should be made clear. Also such an approach should offer at least the same protection level as the current legislation in force. Other basic principles of the directive are the stand-still principle, implying that the implementation of the directive should not result in deterioration of the current level of protection offered in the member states. Also water source protection and sustainable use of water are important aspects of the directive. Also, as in all legislation, compromises are made to accommodate political aspects in the various member states. Future legislation will evidently have to be based on the principles as worded in the treaty, but after careful weighing of advantages and disadvantages of a risk analysis based approach, the principles of such an approach could easily be incorporated into the directive.

Types of water covered by the DWD

The previous DWD covered all water intended for human consumption except for natural mineral waters, medicinal waters, and water used in the food industry not affecting the final product. The current directive covers the same types of waters and has the same exceptions. It also makes it possible for member states to exempt other types of water from the directive, such as hot tap water, second grade water for non-ingestive uses and supplies of less than 10 m^3/day. As yet it is not known if there is a need to change the coverage of the DWD in future revisions of the directive.

Parameters and parametric values

The previous DWD listed more than 62 parameters often together with parametric values such as MACs (maximum allowable concentration), guideline values and minimum levels. Parameters included organoleptic, physico-chemical parameters, undesirable substances, toxic substances, microbiological parameters and minimum requirements for water that had been subject to water conditioning processes to remove hardness. Not all parameters actually had a parametric value in the directive and also no mention was made of the scientific justification for the parameters and the values in the directive. Substances that were used in the preparation of drinking water should remain in the water at values below the parametric value for these substances. One of the main reasons for the revision of the old directive was to restrict the number of parameters to include only essential and health related parameters that are of importance in the many countries of the European Union. It is then left to member states on the basis of the subsidiarity principle to add parameters or to set stricter values as and where necessary but with no breaching the treaty with respect to the rules of fair trade within the EU. The number of parameters is restricted to a total of 48 (microbiological, chemical and indicator) parameters. All parameters that are included in the directive have a parametric value or mention of the fact that water 'should be acceptable to consumers and no abnormal change' should occur. All parametric values are mandatory and guide level values no longer exist in the directive. For future revisions of the DWD discussions could result in new and additional parameters or in even fewer parameters. New parameters might, for example, be endocrine disrupting chemicals, pharmaceuticals, protozoa such as *Giardia* spp. and *Cryptosporidium* spp. or *Legionella* spp. In a risk-analysis based approach it might also be possible that one parameter may have more than one parametric value in various parts of the whole water production and supply process.

Parameters in DWD 98/83/EC

In this DWD a balance is struck between microbiological and chemical risks. Disinfection of drinking water carries the risk of contamination by formation of products that are harmful to human beings, such as trihalomethanes and bromate. However, disinfection reduces the risk of exposure to pathogenic bacteria in the water. Water quality is more than the 48 parameters listed in the current directive. Some parameters that might cause a threat to human health are not yet known. Therefore the DWD has to reinforce the precautionary principle, an important article (Article 4(1)a), which states that water intended for human consumption should be 'wholesome and clean'. Article 10 of the DWD ensures that chemicals used in the preparation of drinking water should not remain in the final product in concentrations higher than absolutely necessary. Another important aspect of Article 10 is the reference to the Construction Products Directive on materials in contact with drinking water during its distribution, in order to avoid an adverse effect on the quality of drinking water by pipe materials, for example.

Basis of parametric values

In setting the parametric values for the various parameters, both short term/acute effects and long term chronic effects have been taken into account as and where appropriate. Basic principles are that the quality of the water should be such that consumers can drink and use water for domestic purposes for a lifetime without the risk of adverse health effects. Also special attention is paid to the protection of vulnerable groups such as children and pregnant women, for instance in setting the values for lead, nitrate and nitrite (babies). WHO guideline values for drinking water, adopted in 1992, were used as a basis for setting parametric values in the DWD, wherever there was a health-based guideline value available. For some parameters a different approach was used, and for others advice was asked of the CSTEE (Scientific Advisory Committee). Parameters in the last category were lead, PAH, pesticides, tri- and tetra-, copper and boron.

Microbiological parameters

The parametric values for the relevant specified microbiological parameters are zero as any positive result indicates the likely presence of pathogenic microorganisms and calls for an immediate response.

Carcinogenic parameters

For genotoxic carcinogens there is normally no threshold below which there is no risk to human health. The WHO applies a criterion for individual carcinogens that implies that there should be no more than one excess cancer in a population of 10^5 resulting from a lifetime's exposure. In the DWD a stricter criterion was used, which implies that there should be no more than one excess cancer in a population of 10^6 resulting from a lifetime's exposure.

Other considerations

A very practical consideration in setting parametric values is the availability of fit-for-purpose analysis methods at the required detection level. For three parameters in the DWD it was, at the time of adoption, not possible to detect the substances at a level that would sufficiently protect human health. For these three parameters, epichlorohydrin, acrylamide and vinyl chloride, a parametric value was adopted that was below the then achievable limit of detection, and for these parameters it was decided to regulate levels in drinking water through product specifications. A second principle for setting parametric values is the availability of treatment methods to ensure that the required removal of the substances could be achieved with the available treatment techniques. Finally, a balance was struck between the risk to human health from the consumption of water not meeting the high standards foreseen in the DWD and the risk from interruption of the water supply (sometimes applying parametric values not as strict as that corresponding to the one in a million criterion).

Sampling and monitoring

The previous DWD 80/778/EEC defines minimum monitoring requirements with a sampling and analysis frequency that is related to the amount of water supplied. A distinction is made between current monitoring, periodic monitoring and occasional monitoring. The current DWD 98/83/EC uses a similar approach where minimum monitoring effort is defined in relation to the amount of water supplied. A regular check of the water quality is defined for some key parameters in so-called check monitoring, and a more comprehensive check of the water quality including all other parameters is carried out with a much lower frequency in so-called audit monitoring. The main difference between both directives is the fact that under the current DWD sampling and monitoring is carried out at the consumer's tap unless it relates to parameters that do not change between the production plant and the tap. Sampling and monitoring under the DWD is, in principle, a check at the last minute and is, in principle, always too late. In the case of water not complying, it has already been supplied to the customer and been consumed. A risk-assessment and risk-management based approach could well cause a major change in sampling and monitoring strategies for drinking water. Moving the place of check and control further back in the production chain from raw water source to tap may be beneficial for some parameters.

Quality control and assurance

Quality control in the 80/778/EEC DWD was restricted to the mention of analytical reference methods. The current DWD goes much further by making ISO/CEN methods compulsory and defining performance criteria for (mostly) chemico-physical parameters. Furthermore, member states need to have some QC/QA system in place in the approved laboratories for drinking water analyses. At the time of adoption of the DWD it was not judged possible to apply an accreditation system for all member states, but it is expected that this will be an additional requirement in the near future.

As future regulation might well be based on risk analysis and approach, the QC/QA system is of vital importance not only to control process performance but also to validate and guarantee the quality of drinking water at the tap.

1.1.4   Revision of the DWD and WHO Guidelines

WHO has adopted the HACCP based approach for drinking water in the so called 'water safety plans'. The European Commission is currently considering whether it would be appropriate to follow this concept in the revision of the DWD.

Issues that will be addressed by the experts in the revision will include such basic questions as how can the underlying principles of the treaty (and the DWD) be maintained and safeguarded in a risk assessment approach:

- subsidiarity principle;
- stand-still principle;
- precautionary principle.

The main question is, of course, how can the same or even higher level of protection of European citizens continue to be guaranteed.

1.1.5   Conclusions

The EU regulation on drinking water has contributed significantly to the supply of safe and wholesome drinking water to European citizens. The current DWD 98/83/EC even improves on that by setting requirements for the quality of drinking water at the consumer's tap. Council directives on drinking water are to a large extent based on WHO guidelines and it is therefore logical that any developments in these guidelines will have to be considered in the revision of the DWD. It is expected that the underlying principles of the current DWD will be further strengthened by a HACCP-like approach. When applied properly and consistently, the added value of a risk-assessment based approach, together with the existing framework of the directive, will be a powerful tool for addressing new and, as yet, partly unknown threats to drinking water such as, for instance, pharmaceuticals, endocrine disrupting chemicals, algal toxins and microorganisms such as *Cryptosporidium*, *Giardia* and viruses. Extending the control of water quality from the final product at the tap to the whole production process will, when accompanied by adequate information to the public, boost the confidence of European consumers in the safety and wholesomeness of their drinking water. Close cooperation between the European Commission and WHO is a prerequisite for achieving this target.

1.2   DRINKING WATER REGULATIONS IN THE UNITED STATES

1.2.1   Introduction

Public water systems in the United States provide high quality drinking water to millions of Americans each day. The application of the multi-barrier concept – that is, selecting and protecting the best available source, using water treatment to control contaminants, and preventing water quality deterioration in the distribution system – has virtually eliminated waterborne diseases of the past such as typhoid and cholera. Nevertheless, some challenges to the safety of the water supply remain. Waterborne disease outbreaks caused by pathogenic microorganisms and toxic chemicals continue to be reported. Contamination of surface and groundwater supplies with various natural and man-made substances may pose either acute or chronic risks if treatment is inadequate. Post-treatment contamination of the distribution system may also pose public health risks. Special groups, such as infants or those with weakened immune systems, may be particularly sensitive to the effects of certain waterborne pathogens and chemicals.

In response to these concerns, the US has enacted strong legislation to ensure the safety of the nation's drinking water supply. The Safe Drinking Water Act (SDWA) authorizes the US Environmental Protection Agency (EPA) to establish national health-based standards that reduce public exposure to microbiological, chemical and radiological contaminants of concern. These federal standards currently apply to approximately 170 000 public water systems throughout the US.[1]

1.2.2   History of the Safe Drinking Water Act

The first national standards for drinking water quality were established by the US Public Health Service in 1914. These standards addressed the bacteriological quality of drinking water and applied only to interstate carriers such as ships and trains. The Public Health Service revised and expanded these standards in 1925, 1946 and 1962, with the latter including regulations for 28 substances. Throughout the 1960s and early 1970s, both the public and Congress became increasingly concerned about the contamination of water supplies by agricultural and industrial chemicals. Surveys indicated that many treatment facilities across the country had major deficiencies. The heightened public awareness about this and other environmental problems led the US government to pass a number of important environmental and public health laws. One of these laws, the Safe Drinking Water Act (SDWA), was passed in 1974 and subsequently amended in 1986 and 1996.

---

[1] Public water systems regulated by EPA may be publicly- or privately-owned, and must serve at least 25 people or 15 service connections for at least 60 days per year. Bottled water is regulated by the US Food and Drug Administration.

1.2.3 Development of Regulations

Overview

The regulatory development process under SDWA begins with an evaluation by EPA of the available science on the health effects and occurrence of a drinking water contaminant. If a contaminant is considered to pose a potential public health risk, EPA conducts a more extensive analysis that involves a detailed review of health effects, occurrence, treatment options, available analytical methods, costs, and benefits. Outside stakeholders, representing groups such as the water industry, environmental and community associations, State regulators and public health organizations, are involved throughout the regulatory development process. EPA then publishes a proposed regulation and solicits public comments. A final regulation is published after considering public comments and any new information that may become available.

Drinking water standards

Each regulated contaminant has a non-enforceable health goal, or maximum contaminant level goal (MCLG), and an enforceable limit, or maximum contaminant level (MCL). An MCLG is established at the level of a contaminant in drinking water for which there is no known or expected health risk. The MCLG is set at zero for microbial pathogens as well as for chemicals that may cause cancer through a nonthreshold mechanism of action. If there is evidence that a carcinogen may exhibit a threshold below which cancer may not occur, the MCLG is set at a level above zero that is considered to pose no risk. For chemicals that are of concern due to the potential for adverse health effects other than cancer, the MCLG is based on the calculation of a reference dose (RfD). The RfD is an estimate of the amount of a chemical that a person can be exposed to on a daily basis that is not anticipated to cause adverse health effects over a person's lifetime. The reference dose is converted into a drinking water exposure level (DWEL) by incorporating default exposure assumptions for body weight (70 kg) and for average daily consumption of drinking water (2 l per day). The DWEL is then used to calculate an MCLG by adjusting it to account for sources of exposure other than drinking water, such as food and air. An MCLG is designed to be protective of sensitive sub-populations that may be at greater risk than the general population (e.g., infants, the elderly, those with compromised immune systems). In addition, an MCLG may be set at levels that are not measurable or quantifiable by currently available analytical methods.

SWDA requires the EPA to promulgate National Primary Drinking Water Regulations (NPDWRs), which specify enforceable maximum contaminant levels (MCLs) or treatment techniques for drinking water contaminants. An MCL is established at a level that is as close to the MCLG as is technically and economically feasible. A treatment technique may be set instead of an MCL if the available analytical methods are not adequate. NPDWRs contain specific criteria and procedures, including requirements for water monitoring, analysis and quality control, to ensure that the drinking water system is in compliance with the MCL. EPA has established MCLs or treatment techniques for a wide range of microorganisms, disinfectants, disinfection byproducts, inorganic and organic chemicals, and radionuclides (EPA, 2004a).

EPA also sets National Secondary Drinking Water Regulations for contaminants that affect the aesthetic (e.g., taste, color or odor), cosmetic (e.g., skin or tooth discoloration) or technical (e.g., corrosivity or scaling) qualities of drinking water. These non-enforceable guidelines include secondary MCLs and recommendations for monitoring (EPA, 2004b).

1.2.4   Highlights of the Safe Drinking Water Act

Implementation of the 1986 Amendments to SDWA led to the development of a number of important rules, including the Total Coliform Rule, the Surface Water Treatment Rule, the Lead and Copper Rule, and regulations for a large number of chemicals of public health concern. All public water systems using surface water sources were required to disinfect and provide specific levels of treatment for microbial pathogens; most systems were required to filter their water. In addition, the 'best available technology' was specified for the treatment of contaminants for which an MCL was established.

The 1996 Amendments greatly enhanced the previous regulatory approach in many respects. In addition to reinforcing the use of sound science in fulfilling the requirements of the Act, a cornerstone of the 1996 Amendments is the fundamental requirement for EPA to use a risk-based standard setting process. The amendments place a strong emphasis on protecting source waters, improving the regulatory process, and conducting research on contaminants of concern. Provisions address the special needs of small water systems, and include requirements for making water quality information available to consumers, conducting health risk reduction benefit analyses, and helping states meet water system infrastructure needs. The EPA is required to develop rules to achieve the goal of providing protection from microbial pathogens while simultaneously ensuring decreasing health risks to the population from disinfection byproducts. A brief discussion of some of the major regulatory and nonregulatory provisions of SDWA is found below.

Regulated contaminants

Six-year review of existing regulations   The EPA is required by the 1996 SDWA Amendments to review each NPDWR at least once every 6 years. Revisions must maintain or increase public health protection. In consultation with stakeholders, the EPA developed a systematic approach for the review of the NPDWRs. This protocol was applied to the Agency's initial Six-Year Review of most of the NPDWRs published prior to the 1996 Amendments. In 2003, EPA published final decisions to not revise 68 chemical NPDWRs and to revise the Total Coliform Rule (TCR). The schedule for reviewing NPDWRs established after 1996 will be based on the respective promulgation dates of these rules (EPA, 2004a, c).

The TCR, published by EPA in 1989, requires all public water systems to monitor for the presence of coliforms (measured as 'total coliforms') in their distribution systems. Coliforms serve as indicators of many enteric pathogens, and are therefore useful in determining the vulnerability of a system to fecal contamination. In reviewing microbial risks with a federal advisory committee, EPA determined that the available data on distribution system risks warranted further analysis. Potential revisions being considered may lead to the establishment of requirements to address the quality of finished water in distribution systems (EPA, 2004d).

Microbial/disinfection byproduct rules   Minimizing the potential health risks associated with exposure to disinfection byproducts (DBPs) without compromising the safety of drinking water from a microbiological perspective poses a major challenge for drinking water providers. In keeping with a phased Microbial/Disinfection Byproduct strategy agreed to by stakeholders and affirmed by the 1996 SDWA Amendments, the EPA has proposed or finalized a number of rules that address both microbial and DBP concerns (EPA, 2004e). The Stage 1 DBP Rule, finalized in 1998, established Maximum Residual Disinfectant Levels (MRDLs) and Goals (MRDLGs) for three disinfectants; MCLGs and MCLs for trihalomethanes, haloacetic acids, chlorite and bromate; and a treatment technique for removal of DBP precursor material. A new Stage 2 DBP Rule, which will be promulgated in 2005, will provide additional public health protection from the potentially harmful effects of DBPs. The proposed rule retains the Stage 1 MCLs but includes revised requirements for collecting monitoring data and calculating compliance. The rule also requires an initial distribution system evaluation that targets the highest risks by identifying compliance sites with the highest DBP occurrence levels in the distribution system.

A series of microbial rules is being developed and implemented concurrently with the DBP rules. The first of these rules, the Interim Enhanced Surface Water Treatment Rule (IESWTR), was finalized in 1998. Key provisions include treatment requirements for *Cryptosporidium* for filtered water systems, tightened turbidity standards, and inclusion of *Cryptosporidium* in the watershed control requirements for unfiltered public water systems. In 2002, EPA finalized the Long-Term 1 Enhanced Surface Water Treatment Rule (LT1ESWTR). This rule extends the provisions of the IESWTR to cover all system sizes, particularly those serving <10 000 individuals. The LT1ESWTR improves control of *Cryptosporidium* in drinking water and addresses risk trade-offs with DBPs. The next generation of surface water treatment rule, the LT2ESWTR, coincides with the proposal and promulgation of the Stage 2 DBP Rule. The LT2ESWTR will strengthen protection against *Cryptosporidium* in the highest risk systems.

The Ground Water Rule (GWR) is a targeted strategy to identify ground water systems at high risk for fecal contamination. The proposed rule establishes a multiple barrier approach to identify and provide corrective measures for public ground water systems at risk of fecal contamination. The GWR will be issued as a final regulation in 2006.

Unregulated contaminants

The 1996 Amendments include a risk-based contaminant selection and decision making process for unregulated contaminants. The EPA must decide whether or not to regulate at least five contaminants every 5 years, based on a consideration of the following three criteria: (i) that the contaminant adversely affects human health; (ii) that it is known or substantially likely to occur in public water systems with a frequency and at levels of public health concern; and (iii) that regulation of the contaminant provides a meaningful opportunity for health risk reduction.

Every 5 years, the EPA is required to develop a list of unregulated microbiological and chemical contaminants that may be regulated by the EPA at some future date (EPA, 2004f). The list, referred to as the Contaminant Candidate List (CCL), was first published by EPA in 1997 and finalized in 1998 after extensive consultation with stakeholders. In establishing the CCL, EPA divided the contaminants into three major categories: (i) a Regulatory Determination Priorities Category, with contaminants that have enough data to determine whether a regulation is necessary; (ii) a Research Priorities Category, which contains contaminants with additional research needs in the areas of health effects, treatment, and/or analytical methods; and (iii) an Occurrence Priorities Category, with contaminants for which additional occurrence data are needed. The 1998 CCL included 50 chemicals and 10 microbial pathogens, most of which were in the Research and Occurrence Priorities Categories.

In 2003, the EPA announced its determination that no regulatory action was appropriate or necessary for nine contaminants on the first CCL. These contaminants included aldrin, dieldrin, hexachlorobutadiene, manganese, metribuzin, naphthalene, sodium, sulfate, and *Acanthamoeba* (for which guidance was developed). A second CCL, issued in 2005 (EPA, 2005), included all the contaminants from the previous CCL for which a regulatory determination was not made. The EPA is developing a more rigorous process for selecting contaminants for future CCLs, using guidance from the National Academy of Sciences (2001) and the National Drinking Water Advisory Council (2004).

National Occurrence Data Base and the Unregulated
Contaminant Monitoring Rule

SDWA has provisions that provide for the collection, organization and sharing of occurrence data on contaminants of potential concern. The National Drinking Water

Contaminant Data Base (NCOD) is a website repository of water sample analytical data on both regulated and unregulated contaminants in public water systems (EPA, 2004g). These data are used to support listing and regulatory determinations on contaminants for which regulations do not currently exist, as well as reviews of existing regulations and monitoring requirements. Under the requirements of the Unregulated Contaminant Monitoring Rule (UCMR), EPA is required to issue a list every 5 years of up to 30 unregulated microbiological, chemical and radiological contaminants for which monitoring is required by water utilities across the country (EPA, 2004h). Depending upon the availability of adequate analytical methods and current contaminant occurrence data, UCMR contaminants may be subjected to the full assessment monitoring, a screening survey, or a pre-screen testing. This rule has important implications for the development of new or improved analytical detection methods for contaminants of potential public health concern.

Prevention approaches

The 1996 amendments include an important new emphasis on preventing contamination problems through source water protection and enhanced water system management. Source water protection is an ongoing process that includes conducting assessments to understand the vulnerabilities of the source to contaminants, monitoring to detect contamination as early as possible, protecting sources using best management practices, and planning for quick response when contamination occurs. The central responsibility for source water assessments, as well as designing and implementing prevention programs, resides with the states. The states also have the responsibility for building the capacity of local water systems to improve system operations and avoid contamination problems.

The national Wellhead Protection Program, established under the 1986 amendments, is a pollution prevention and management program used to protect underground sources of drinking water. States may use the funds from the SDWA-authorized Drinking Water State Revolving Fund to support a mixture of source water-related local assistance activities. Source water protection activities are also supported by other statutory authorities, particularly the Clean Water Act (CWA), the Resource Conservation and Recovery Act (RCRA), the Comprehensive Environmental Response, Compensation and Liability Act (CERCLA) and the Federal Insecticide, Fungicide and Rodenticide Act (FIFRA).

1.2.5 Implementation of Regulations

Once the EPA publishes a final regulation, systems usually have 3 years before they must be in compliance. The states are typically responsible for the implementation and enforcement of standards established by the federal government. The EPA provides oversight, funding and technical assistance to help states administer their programs. Compliance with the standards is determined through the collection, testing and reporting of samples taken from water systems at designated intervals and locations. The use of EPA-approved analytical methods and certified laboratories (EPA, 2004i) is required for compliance monitoring.

In cases of non-compliance, different types of violations may occur: (i) MCL violations; (ii) treatment technique violations; or (iii) monitoring and reporting violations. Varying levels of public notification are required depending on the type of violation, and corrective action must be taken to remedy the situation. EPA works with the states to enforce drinking water standards.

1.2.6   Conclusions

The US has achieved considerable success in ensuring the safety of the public drinking water supply, particularly since SDWA was first passed over 30 years ago. This has been accomplished through the combined efforts of drinking water and health professionals at the federal, state and local levels. Source water protection programs have been implemented, disinfection of public water supplies has become widespread, and regulations to reduce public exposure to a wide range of contaminants have been established. Sensitive analytical detection methods have made it possible to detect a wider range of microbes and chemicals at increasingly lower environmental levels, and improved treatment technologies have become available. In addition, the public has become much more informed and involved in decisions about the safety of their water supply. Effective implementation of SDWA requirements and the cooperation of the drinking water community will continue to be necessary in the coming years in order to meet the challenges posed by new concerns about the quality and quantity of the nation's drinking water supply.

1.3   STANDARDIZATION

1.3.1   Introduction

Legislative directives on the quality of drinking water call for wholesome, clean, and safe water. The European directive, as an example, specifies that the analytical methods used for drinking water should ensure that the results obtained are reliable and comparable (Council Directive 98/83/EC, 1998). Possible risks for the consumer of drinking water from various toxic and health concerns shall be investigated and monitored, e.g. chemical or microbiological contaminants from natural sources or pollutants from material being in contact with drinking water. The result of these investigations is a list of contaminants including an upper limiting value for each of the parameters. Drinking water directives, such as that from the European Union (EU) (Council Directive 98/83/EC, 1998), publish such lists.

1.3.2 Requirements to be Met by Laboratories and Analytical Methods

An effective control of drinking water quality generally is based on data obtained from samples analysed in laboratories.

Regulators, clients, and consumers expect to receive a 'true' result from the laboratory. In order to avoid a semantic discussion about 'what is the true result?', legislators generally define quality requirements to be met by the analytical method and by the laboratory. The minimum requirements to be met by the analytical methods used, according to the European directive (Council Directive 98/83/EC, 1998), shall be capable of measuring concentrations equal to the parametric value with a specified trueness, precision, and limit of detection.

Laboratories shall operate a system of analytical quality control that is subject to checking from time to time by a person who is not under the control of the laboratory and who is approved by the competent authority for that purpose (Council Directive 98/83/EC, 1998). A suitable direction for such a competence check is available (EN/ISO/IEC 17025, 2005). Laboratories qualified for drinking water analyses should fulfill the requirements for an accreditation procedure preferably according to EN/ISO/IEC 17025 (2005).

The laboratories need validated methods for performing a variety of required characteristics, e.g. robust against possible matrix interferences or matrix changes (e.g., hardness), specific and selective for the contaminant of interest, suitable working range, applicable for the control of a maximum contaminant level. Additional desirable characteristics are that the methods should, for example, allow simplified sample preparation, rapid analyses, economical benefits, avoidance of hazardous reagents (e.g., certain solvents), robust apparatus, compatible with the requirements of an analytical quality control (AQC) system.

Approved and validated methods appropriate for drinking water analyses are generally standardized methods. These methods have normally been developed especially for drinking water analyses. During the standardization project the draft standard methods have to go through a validation procedure, including checks for trueness, precision, recovery, and finally an interlaboratory trial before they are published as a standard method.

1.3.3 Standardization in CEN TC 230 Water Analysis and ISO TC 147 Water Quality

General

Standardization is one of the tools used to organize the technical world. Standardization has become an integral component of the economic, social, and legal systems.

International standards from the International Standards Organization (ISO) and European standards (EN) from the European Standardisation Organization (CEN) can remove trade barriers and promote business across national frontiers. Standardization is based on consensus, on scientific findings and on technical progress, and one has to bear in mind the economic consequences (DIN, 1998).

Standardization in CEN and ISO has to be well-founded. Before the work on a new standardization project can start the applicant country has to explain the need and reason for a new standard (see Section 1.3.4 stage 2).

The philosophy of setting standards in CEN and ISO on the one hand and the US Environmental Protection Agency (EPA) on the other hand is different. CEN and ISO prefer documents that do not specify trademarks or equipment produced by a single manufacturer (monopolies), whenever possible (ISO/IEC, 2001) (see Section 1.3.6).

Standard methods (e.g., from ISO, CEN, and EPA) can be adopted as recommendations on a voluntary basis by any laboratory around the world. Governments can decide to incorporate existing standards into their national standards. European standard methods are essential for the national standards politics in Europe: generally, CEN standards shall replace any of the national standard methods within the European member bodies in order to harmonize analytical standard methods (ISO/TC 147, 2003).

Standardization on a European level is the responsibility of CEN. Standardization on an international level is the responsibility of ISO. Today, some 120 national standardization bodies cooperate in activities that aim to stimulate cooperation in the scientific, technical, and economic spheres across national frontiers. Generally, European standards (EN) are based on ISO standards (DIN, 1998).

CEN and ISO standards are elaborated in technical committees (TC) installed for a particular field of action. ISO/TC 147 'Water Quality', founded in 1971, is responsible for the standardization of water analysis methods. The corresponding European committee is CEN/TC 230 'Water Analysis', founded in 1990 (ISO/TC 147, 2003).

Vienna Agreement

Today, CEN and ISO cooperate according to the so-called Vienna Agreement of 1991 in order to save resources and to avoid duplication of work or contradictory standard methods in CEN and ISO. Both organizations agreed on basic principles, for example, on synchronized approval procedures or simultaneous publication. Standardization projects started in ISO can be transferred to CEN, if necessary, and vice versa. The transfer process can be started either by the so-called unique acceptance procedure (UAP, see Section 1.3.5) on a finalized ISO or CEN standard or by the parallel voting procedure (PVP, see Section 1.3.5) on a document qualified for an enquiry process (ISO/CEN, 2001).

Today, most of the standards on water quality are elaborated in ISO/TC 147 before they are transferred to CEN (ISO/TC 147, 2003). Section 1.3.4 describes the procedural steps for the standards elaboration in ISO because they need to meet the requirements for approval in CEN, too.

1.3.4   Development of Standards in ISO/TC 147

General

Today, ISO/TC 147 is subdivided into five subcommittees (SC) working on:

- SC 1 terminology;
- SC 2 physical, chemical, and biochemical methods;
- SC 4 microbiological methods;
- SC 5 biological methods;
- SC 6 sampling.

Each of the subcommittees has set up several working groups (WG). Usually, work items will be allocated to a working group.

National member bodies decide which of the committees they want to support. Member bodies are asked to state their opinion of a distinct field of work by commentaries and by voting on items.

ISO standard methods are developed according to the ISO/IEC Directives, Part 1 (ISO/IEC, 1995). Each of the development stages ends in a decision about whether the project should be continued, postponed, or withdrawn. The ISO Central Secretariat (ISO/CS) in Geneva, Switzerland is responsible for all of the formal aspects (e.g., controlling the standardization process, observance of deadlines for voting processes, distribution of all documents, etc.). The working group is responsible for the technical and editorial work and shall report to the subcommittee (SC) and the technical committee. In ISO/TC 147 Committees and working groups generally meet every 18 months.

Development of standards follows a seven-step procedure (ISO/IEC, 1995). See Table 1.1 for the principles of the ISO standardization process.

Stage 1 – Preliminary

The preliminary stage is applied to a new project. The introduction of a new item requires a simple majority vote of the respective committee member bodies. This stage has no target dates to be considered. The advantage of working without time pressure can be used to prepare a carefully thought out initial draft for the proposal stage.

Table 1.1   Standards development according to ISO/IEC Directives

Stage	Business	Requirements/Comments
1 Preliminary stage	ISO member applies for a new standard proposal	Give purpose and justification for the need of new method
		Approval by a simple majority
2 Proposal stage	Written ballot on a new work item proposal (NP) by members within three months necessary	Approval by a simple majority of member bodies *and* a minimum of five members shall participate actively in the project
3 Preparatory stage	Preparation of a working draft (WD)	Elaboration of a WD for circulation to the members
4 Committee stage	Preparation of a committee draft (CD) and its circulation to all member bodies to comment on it within 3 to 6 months	Consensus, this means a two-thirds majority of member bodies voting on the CD should be in agreement
5 Enquiry stage	Preparation of a Draft International Standard (DIS) and its circulation. Voting period: 5 months. A positive vote may contain minor technical comments	Approval of more than 66.7 % members necessary *and* a maximum of 25 % or fewer disapprovals allowed
6 Approval stage	Preparation of a Final Draft International Standard (FDIS) and its circulation. Voting period: 2 months	Approval of more than 66.7 % members necessary *and* a maximum of 25 % or fewer disapprovals allowed
7 Publication stage	Publication of an ISO standard method	The method is valid for 5 years
Review of a standard	Confirmation of the standard method every 5 years	The method is valid for another 5-year period
Withdrawal of standard	Withdrawal of a standard method, if the standard did not pass Stage 7 successfully or a confirmation at the revision date was not permitted	The method will be deleted from the standards project list

Stage 2 – Proposal

The proposal stage is used for a new standard, and for any amendment and/or revision of an existing standard. A new work item proposal (NP) may be made to the respective committee by, for example, a national body, the secretariat of that technical committee or subcommittee, or an organization in liaison. The applicant has to indicate, among other things, the subject of the proposed item, clarification of the scope and, if necessary, what is excluded, plus specific aims and reasons for a new standard.

Where possible, a draft (e.g., elaborated in the preliminary stage) should be sent out with the new work item proposal, but as a minimum an outline should be attached for the voting procedure. Votes shall be returned within 3 months, and comments on the new proposal are encouraged.

Approval of the new proposal requires a simple majority of the committee members voting on the proposal and at least five member countries willing to participate actively in the project.

Stage 3 – Preparatory

The approved new project will be allocated to a working group. Experts nominated for the participation in the project shall agree on a working group member to act as convenor. The working group prepares a working draft (WD). The working draft should be available within 6 months. The convenor of the working group is responsible for the progress, the editorial work, and the preparation of the working draft according to the target dates.

At the end of this stage the working draft is circulated among the members of the technical committee or subcommittee as a first committee draft (CD).

Stage 4 – Committee

The committee stage is used to circulate the first committee draft to all member bodies for consideration. Votes and comments shall be returned to ISO within 3 months. ISO shall circulate the result of the ballot and a compilation of comments to all member bodies not later than 4 weeks after the closing date for voting. The secretariat shall also indicate its proposal on how to proceed with the project.

Formal approval of the Committee Draft requires a two-thirds majority of the member bodies voting, but ISO sets a high value on the consensus principle.

Following the consensus principle in ISO, every attempt shall be made to resolve all of the negative votes and comments received. That may require the preparation and circulation of a second or subsequent versions of the committee draft until consensus has been reached or a decision to postpone or withdraw the project has been made. When the approval requirements have been met, an enquiry draft can be circulated. Ideally, the period between Stage 4 and Stage 5 should be used to organize and evaluate an interlaboratory trial (see Section 1.3.6). The performance characteristics obtained should be sent out with the proposal for the enquiry draft.

Stage 5 – Enquiry

At the enquiry stage the Draft International Standard (DIS, enquiry draft) shall be available in English and French for circulation to the national member bodies. Votes and comments shall be returned to ISO within 5 months. ISO shall circulate the following documentation:

- result of the ballot;
- compilation of comments received;
- action taken on the comments,

to the national bodies not later than 3 months after the closing date for voting. The secretariat shall also indicate its proposal for proceeding with the project.

Approval of the enquiry draft requires a two-thirds majority of the member bodies voting in favour and a total number of negative votes of not more than 25 % (*Note*: negative votes without a statement about substantial reasons for the disagreement and abstentions are excluded from the total number of votes).

Comments received after the set voting deadline should be considered at the revision phase of the standard method.

The consensus principles remain valid at the enquiry stage, too. When the approval requirements have not met the enquiry draft, comments shall be discussed at a meeting of the committees (TC 147, SC 2) or of the working group, or a revised enquiry draft for voting on it, or a revised committee draft for comments shall be prepared and circulated.

When the approval requirements have been met, the enquiry draft can be forwarded for the preparation as a Final Draft International Standard (FDIS).

Stage 6 – Approval

At the approval stage the Final Draft International Standard (FDIS) shall be distributed within 3 months to all national bodies for a vote within 2 months. All negative votes shall state the technical reasons for disagreement.

Approval requirements for the FDIS are identical to those at the enquiry stage (see above).

If the FDIS fails the approval requirements, the draft shall be referred back to the technical committee or subcommittee and comments shall be discussed at the next meeting. Alternatively a revised enquiry draft for voting on it or a revised committee draft for comments shall be prepared and circulated.

If the FDIS meets the approval requirements, the FDIS can be forwarded to the publication stage.

Stage 7 – Publication

The publication stage ends with the publication of the international standard.

Five-year revision

Standards are valid for 5 years. After that period a decision shall be made to confirm the standard for a further 5 years, to revise it, or to delete it from the working programme.

Withdrawal of standards

Methods shall be deleted from the standards system if they do not pass the approval stage (see above) successfully, or a confirmation after 5 years is refused, or a replacement of an existing standard by a new one takes place.

1.3.5   Special Standards Development Procedures

Some alternative development procedures, within the requirements defined by ISO or CEN, may be applied. Alternative procedures can be beneficial for a standardization organization deciding to adopt an existing document. These alternative procedures offer the following advantages:

* resources can be saved;
* the duplication of work can be avoided;
* the speed of standards elaboration can be increased;
* consensus need to be established only once (ISO/CEN, 2001).

Fast-track procedure

This procedure may be applied if a standard method, developed by another organization is available and appropriate for a ISO standardization project. A standard method submitted directly for approval as an enquiry draft (DIS, Stage 5, see above) starts on the proposal stage (Stage 2 above). After the approval of the project it can be forwarded directly to the enquiry stage (Stage 5 above) without passing through the preparatory stage and committee stage (above), thus speeding up the development process (ISO/IEC, 1995).

Transfer of standard methods according to the Vienna Agreement

The cooperation between ISO and CEN follows the Vienna Agreement (ISO/CEN, 2001), see Section 1.3.3. Standards can be transferred to the other organization either by the unique acceptance procedure (UAP, see section below) or by the parallel voting procedure (PVP, see section below).

Unique acceptance procedure (UAP) The organization (CEN or ISO) that wants to adopt an available standard method from the other organization submits it to its own adoption, voting, and publication procedures. The approved standard to be transferred will be balloted at the enquiry stage of the adopting organization (ISO/DIS or CEN enquiry, respectively). After the positive vote the adopted document can be finalized and published.

The technical content of the publication of the adopted standard should be identical with that of the original publication. Any intended technical alterations or changes shall be discussed and resolved with the secretariat of the developing organization in order to find a satisfactory solution. Ideally, the original standard should be revised according to the PVP (below) if a consensus about the intended changes cannot be reached and the adopting organization decides to insist on the changes. If this is not possible, the amended standard shall include information and reasons for the alteration of the original document (ISO, 2004).

Parallel voting procedure (PVP) This procedure is suitable for transferring projects already started. Once the decision has been made about a CEN or ISO project leadership, the responsible committee drafts a document according to the procedures of the leading organization. The responsible secretariats of CEN and ISO shall ensure the synchronization of the ISO/DIS–CEN enquiry for parallel voting. After a positive vote in CEN and ISO, the adopted document can be finalized and published. Otherwise consultations between CEN and ISO are necessary in order either to resolve the negative votes responsible for the disagreement or to proceed in accordance with the own rules of the respective organization (ISO, 2004).

1.3.6   Drafting of Standards

Besides formal aspects of standardization, analytical standard methods have to follow a general structure with several obligatory technical instructions in the normative body of the standard. The ISO Directives, Part 2 (ISO/IEC, 2001) give advice for the structure of ISO standards. Standard developers can gain supplementary information from a model manuscript (ISO, 1998a). See Table 1.2 for an example of the structure of a EN ISO standard method.

This concept ensures a strict definition of the application range of the standard to be applied. In addition, informative annexes may be presented in order to give further examples and information to the user. The normative part of an analytical standard method in CEN and ISO includes at least the clauses listed below (ISO/IEC, 2001; ISO, 1998). Additional clauses, such as specific definitions or a list of minimum requirements needed, may be added to the standard, if relevant.

Table 1.2 Structure of EN/ISO 15061 (2001). EN/ISO 15061 Water quality – Determination of dissolved bromate: Method by liquid chromatography of ions

Foreword
Introduction
  1 Scope
  2 Normative references
  3 Interferences
  4 Principle
  5 Essential minimum requirements
  6 Reagents
  7 Apparatus
  8 Quality requirements for the separator column
  9 Sampling and sample pretreatment
  10 Procedure
  11 Calculation
  12 Expression of results
  13 Test report
  Annex A (informative) Eluents
  Annex B (informative) Regeneration solutions
  Annex C (informative) Example of column switching technique
  Annex D (informative) Interlaboratory trial
  Annex E (informative) Checked interferences
  Bibliography

Title

The title shall be concise and represent the parameter (sometimes also the analytical technique and matrix, if relevant) treated in the standard (ISO, 1998a). The user of the standard shall be aware that the method is strictly limited to the mentioned sample matrices and any analytical result based on an extension or alteration of the standard method in the user's laboratory cannot refer to the standard method.

Foreword

A foreword shall appear in each standard. It gives the designation and name of the technical committee and subcommittee that prepared the standard (ISO, 1998a).

Introduction

The introduction is an optional element containing commentary about the technical content of the standard or background information (ISO/IEC, 2001).

Scope

The scope specifies briefly the applicability (e.g., parameter to be determined, working range to be applied, appropriate sample matrix types) and the limitation of the method (ISO, 1998a). Limitation means exclusion of any expansion or changes of the standard method (e.g., addition of parameters or sample matrix types not listed).

Normative references

This clause lists a number of other standard methods essential for the application of the standard. Draft International Standards may also be cited in the list. All other documents, for instance any used for the development of the standard, may be listed in an informative bibliography (ISO, 1998a).

Interferences

This section gives information on the technical limitations of the standard method caused by, for example, sample matrix effects (coloured samples can interfere with the photometric detection or element specific spectral interferences (AAS, ICP-OES) or chemical interferences (precipitation reactions, formation of reaction by-products). These details are validated experimentally in laboratories participating actively in the standardization work. The documentation of the interferences may help potential users of a specific standard to decide whether the standard method could be applicable for the requirements of their analytical businesses.

Principle

This clause gives a brief overview of the procedural basis of the analytical method.

Reagents

This clause contains a list of reagents and/or solutions used in the method (ISO/IEC, 2001) including information on the required purity grade as well as concentrations of solutions.

Apparatus

This section defines the analytical system to be used for the determination of the parameters listed in the title of the standard (ISO/IEC, 2001). The suitability of the specified apparatus has also been checked experimentally. Standards developers generally check different technical systems and appropriate alternative equipment, if this exists. Finally, the standards developers (working group members) decide which one of the possible alternative systems shall be part of the normative body of the standard. If applicable, alternative systems can be presented in an informative annex.

CEN and ISO standard developers should not refer to a sole supplier (monopoly situation). Equipment offered by a single manufacturer should not be specified. Where such equipment is not commercially available, detailed specifications for the equipment shall be given in order to enable all users to test comparable apparatus and systems (ISO/IEC, 2001).

Sampling and sample pre-treatment

Generally, this clause refers to an international standard, if such exists. If necessary, specific preconditions and methods of sampling or pre-treatment steps for the preservation of the samples (e.g., filtration, acidification, bottle material, storage conditions) are given.

Procedure

This clause gives advice about all of the procedural elements used for determination of the parameters. This includes the preparation of the test sample, the set-up procedure of the analytical system, the calibration strategy, and the measurement of the sample.

Calculation

This element gives instructions on how to convert a measured value obtained from the parameter of interest into a mass concentration, including the method of calculation (e.g., use of the inverse calibration function, consideration of blank values).

Expression of results

This clause defines the report format of the calculated results (e.g., dimension, number of significant figures).

Test report

The test report contains a minimum of information on the sample (e.g., result, identification data of the sample, applied standard method).

Interlaboratory trial

The presentation of statistical results of data from interlaboratory trials can be handled differently in CEN and ISO. CEN presents these data generally in the normative body of the standard, whereas ISO puts them in the informative annex of the standard. Besides the different philosophies in ISO and CEN on the layout of a standard, the organization and evaluation of an interlaboratory trial is obligatory for the standard developers in CEN and ISO, and the quality of the statistical data from the interlaboratory trial is the final categorical factor in the decision to publish the standard method, to postpone or to withdraw the project from the working list. The criteria for interlaboratory trial data to be met are given in ISO 5725, Part 2 (ISO, 2002).

1.3.7 EU Requirements for Standard Methods

General

Analytical methods used for the control procedures according to the European drinking water directive must be capable of measuring concentrations equal to the parametric value (Council Directive 98/83/EC, 1998). This is a positive requirement and enables laboratories to choose a suitable method among alternatives. The European directive additionally specifies quality requirements concerning trueness, precision, and the limit of detection of the method (see Table 1.3).

The performance characteristics of a method, obtained from an interlaboratory trial (see above), give a first indication of the suitability of an analytical method.

Table 1.3 Parameters with specified performance characteristics

Parameters	Trueness	Precision	Limit of detection
	% of parametric value		
Anions and Oxidizability			
Cl^-, CN^-, $Cr(VI)$, F^-, NO_3^-, NO_2^-, SO_4^{2-}	10	10	10
BrO_3^-	25	25	25
TOC	25	25	10
Elements and Ammonium			
Al, As, B, Cd, Cu, Fe, Mn, Na, Ni, Pb,			
Se, NH_4^+	10	10	10
Hg	20	10	20
Sb	25	25	25
Organic parameters			
1,2-Dichloroethane, tetrachloroethene,	25	25	10
trichloroethene, trihalomethanes (total)			
Benzo(a)pyrene, benzene, pesticides, PAHs	25	25	25

However, it is the duty of the laboratory to validate each of the methods applied for drinking water analyses and to demonstrate the capability of the laboratory to fulfill the required characteristics according to the EU directive (Council Directive 98/83/EC, 1998).

Estimation of trueness and precision The EU directive (Council Directive 98/83/EC, 1998) refers to the definitions for the determination of trueness and precision given in ISO 5725-1 (ISO, 2002). According to this standard, the estimation of the trueness requires 'a large series' of replicate determinations of test samples. But what does 'large series' mean? Neither ISO 5725-1 nor the EU directive resolve this question. The determination of precision also requires a number of replicate determinations of a test sample. Information on a recommended number of replicates is also missing in ISO 5725-1.

A practicable concept is ENV-ISO 13530 (ENV/ISO/TR, 1998). ENV-ISO 13530 is a guide to analytical quality control (AQC). It is applicable to the chemical and physicochemical analysis of waters including drinking water. It describes an AQC concept applicable to analyses carried out frequently or infrequently as well as for complex, time-consuming, procedures producing only few results at a time (e.g., for the determination of complex organic contaminants).

For the estimation of trueness, ENV-ISO 13530 recommends regular participation in external quality procedures such as interlaboratory trials and proficiency schemes for the control of trueness (bias). For internal routine action, the use of control charts, based on the mean, spiking recovery, and analysis of blanks, is recommended. In addition, the standard recommends the use of a mean and/or a range control chart and the execution of a minimum of six replicate determinations of the test sample for the calculation of the standard deviation for the control of the precision.

Limit of detection The EU directive 98/93/EC (see Table 1.3) sets a requirement to be met for the limit of detection (LOD). The determination of the LOD does not follow a standard method. LOD shall be calculated from replicate determinations, either

(a) multiply the within-batch standard deviation of the reproducibility of a natural sample containing a low concentration of the parameter three times, or

(b) multiply the within-batch standard deviation of the reproducibility of a blank solution five times.

Information on a recommended number of replicates is missing in the directive (Council Directive 98/83/EC, 1998).

The LOD represents a qualitative performance data of the method, only. In contrast to the LOD, the Limit of Quantification (LOQ) would represent data valid for carrying out quantitative determinations. For this reason a revised directive (Council Directive 98/83/EC, 1998) should refer to the LOQ. It is intended to define a calculation procedure for LOQ with the publication of the revised ISO 13530 (ENV/ISO/TR, 2004).

As long as the lowest limit of application of the method is significantly lower than the required LOD, additional experiments for the estimation of the LOD do not need to be carried out. This attribute will be the case for the determination of many anions and cations (see later, Tables 1.5 and 1.6).

Examples for the estimation of laboratory internal performance data   ENV-ISO 13530 (ISO/TR, 2003) can be applied to ascertain the laboratory internal values for precision, trueness and LOD according to the EU directive 98/83/EC. The examples in Table 1.4 may give an indication for the internal actions to be applied by the laboratory.

Table 1.4   Example for the estimation of performance characteristics for bromate

Demand for:	Recommended action:
Parametric value 10 μg/l	Execution of a practicable calibration according to ISO 8466-1 (1990) or ISO 8466-2 (2001), e.g. working range 2.5 μg/l to 25 μg/l BrO_3^-
Precision 2.5 μg/l	For frequent determinations: Use the standard deviation of a mean control chart (use of a 10 μg/l BrO_3^- control solution) For infrequent determinations: Calculate the standard deviation from the results of >6 replicate determinations of a 10 μg/l BrO_3^- standard solution *Note*: Whenever available, certified reference materials should be used.
Trueness 2.5 μg/l	*General*: participation in interlaboratory trials, regularly For frequent determinations: Operation of a mean control chart, concentration of the control solution e.g. 10 μg/l BrO_3^- Operation of a recovery control chart, when systematic errors from matrix interferences are expected Measurement of two blank solutions at the beginning and at the end of a batch in order to identify contamination of reagents, of the measurement system and instrumental faults and documentation of the blank values on a blank control chart For infrequent determinations: Measurement of trueness control samples in the lower and upper part of the calibrated working range Replicate measurements of samples Measurement of blanks Measurement of reference material, if available Validity check of the calibration function using material from an independent source
LOD 2.5 μg/l	Inclusion of the LOD value in the calibrated working range (e.g. 2.5 μg/l to 25 μg/l BrO_3^-)

It can be expected that the repertoire of actions recommended in Table 1.4 will be appropriate for the determination of inorganic parameters. For multistage or lengthy procedures that produce only few results at a time, the procedures for infrequent determinations could be carried out. However, this is still problematic for the determination of the performance characteristics for several (ecological important) pesticides where suitable reference materials of appropriate concentration are not available or the LOD requirement are unlikely to be achieved (Council Directive 98/83/EC, 1998).

CEN and ISO standard methods for drinking water analyses

CEN and ISO have already published a number of standard methods suitable for the determination of most of contaminants for the control of the quality of water. For the determination of anions and elements several alternative single and multiple component methods have been approved. For the determination of organic parameters generally multiple-component procedures are available.

Single-component methods are valid for that parameter cited in the scope of the standard, only. Generally, a single-component method requires parameter specific descriptions like sampling procedure, sample preservation and preparation, chemical reaction procedures, and measurement steps. Examples for typical single-component procedures are photometric, electrometric, or atomic absorption spectrometric (AAS) methods. The capital cost for the apparatus is relatively low. However, the obligatory procedural steps may be time consuming and labour intensive.

Multiple component methods are procedures for the determination of more than one parameter at a time. In contrast to single component methods multiple component methods describe a general procedure on sampling, preservation, preparation, and determination for all of the parameters in the scope of the method. Examples for typical multiple component procedures are inductively coupled plasma (ICP-OES or ICP-MS) for element analyses and chromatographic techniques (IC, GC, HPLC). The cost of the apparatus can be very high. However, multiple-component procedures for the determination of inorganic parameters are time saving and labour saving, and offer very high sample throughputs for the laboratories. They are considered to be very cost effective. Multistage procedures like trace level analyses of organic parameters can be time consuming, producing only a few results at a time.

Tables 1.5 to 1.7 present a selection of chemical and indicator parameters with specified requirements according to the EU drinking water directive (Council Directive 98/83/EC, 1998). In Tables 1.5 to 1.7 are listed the parameter, the parameter specific defined maximum contaminant levels, and limits of detection (LOD).

Also listed are recommendations for the application of existing CEN and ISO methods, generally automated multiple-component procedures, suitable for routine analyses with high sample throughput, except for standard methods for the determination of organic parameters which could be time consuming. Nevertheless, any laboratory can choose any alternative method of its choice as long as it is capable of

Table 1.5 Anions and Oxidisability (TOC)

Parameter	Method	Principle[a]	Working range[a] (mg/l)	Parametric value[a] (mg/l)	LOD[a] (mg/l)
Bromate	EN ISO 15061 (2001)	IC	≥0.0005	0.01	0.0025
Chloride	EN ISO 10304-1 (1995)	IC	≥0.1	250	25
Chromium(VI)	ISO/DIS 23913 (2004a)	CFA	≥0.002	0.05	0.005
Cyanide, total	EN/ISO 14403 (2002)	CFA	≥0.01	0.05	0.005
Fluoride	EN ISO 10304-1 (1995)	IC	≥0.1	1.5	0.15
Nitrate	EN ISO 10304-1 (1995)	IC	≥0.1	50	5
Nitrite	EN ISO 10304-1 (1995)	IC	≥0.05	0.5	0.05
Sulfate	EN ISO 10304-1 (1995)	IC	≥0.1	250	25
Total organic carbon (TOC)	EN 1484 (1997a)	Thermic catalytic oxidation	≥1	5	0.5

[a] where:
Parametric value is the required limit according to Council Directive 98/83/EC, 1998.
CFA is continuous flow analyses.
IC is ion chromatography.
LOD is the limit of detection, to be achieved according to Council Directive 98/83/EC, 1998.
Working range is the lowest determinable concentration stated in the method.

Table 1.6 Elements and ammonium

Parameter	Method	Principle[a]	Working range[a] (μg/l)	Parametric value[a] (μg/l)	LOD[a] (μg/l)
Aluminium	EN/ISO 17294-2 (2004)	ICP-MS	≥5	200	20
Ammonium	EN/ISO 14911 (1998)	IC	≥100	500	50
Antimony	EN/ISO 17294-2 (2004)	ICP-MS	≥0.2	5	1.25
Arsenic	EN/ISO 17294-2 (2004)	ICP-MS	≥1	10	1
Boron	EN/ISO 17294-2 (2004)	ICP-MS	≥10	1000	100
Cadmium	EN/ISO 17294-2 (2004)	ICP-MS	≥0.5	5	0.5
Copper	EN/ISO 17294-2 (2004)	ICP-MS	≥2	2000	200
Iron	EN/ISO 11885 (1997b)	ICP-OES	≥20	200	20
Lead	EN/ISO 17294-2 (2004)	ICP-MS	≥0.2	10	1
Mercury	EN 1483 (1997c)	AAS	≥0.1	1	0.1
Nickel	EN/ISO 17294-2 (2004)	ICP-MS	≥1	20	2
Selenium	ISO 9965 (1993)	AAS	≥1	10	1
Sodium	EN/ISO 17294-2 (2004)	ICP-MS	≥10	200 000	20 000

[a] Where:
AAS is atomic absorption spectrometry.
IC is ion chromatography.
ICP is inductively coupled plasma.
LOD is the limit of detection, to be achieved according to Council Directive 98/83/EC, 1998.
MS is mass spectrometry.
OES is optical emission spectrometry.
Parametric value is the required limit according to Council Directive 98/83/EC, 1998.
Working range is the lowest determinable concentration stated in the method.

Table 1.7 Organic parameters

Parameter	Method	Principle[a]	Working range[a]	Parametric value[a]	LOD[a]
Acrylamide	No standard method available in CEN/ISO	To be controlled by product specification		0.1	
Benzene	ISO 11423 (1997a,b)	GC-FID	≥ 1	1	0.25
Benzo(*a*)pyrene	EN/ISO 17993 (2003b)	HPLC-FD	≥ 0.005	0.01	0.0025
1,2-Dichloroethane	EN/ISO 10301 (1997d)	GC-ECD	≥ 5	3	0.3
Epichlorohydrin	EN 14207 (2003a)	GC-MS	≥ 0.1	0.1	
		To be controlled by product specification			
Pesticides[b]	ISO/EN 11369 (1997e)	HPLC-UV	≥ 0.1	0.1	0.025[c]
	EN/ISO 15913 (2003c)	GC-MS	≥ 0.05		
	EN/ISO 6468 (1996)	GC-ECD	≥ 0.01		
Polycyclic aromatic hydrocarbons	EN/ISO 17993 (2003b)	HPLC-FD	≥ 0.005	0.1	0.025
Tetrachloroethene	EN/ISO 10301 (1997d)	GC-ECD	≥ 0.1	10	0.1
Trichloroethene	EN/ISO 10301 (1997d)	GC-ECD	≥ 0.1	10	0.1
Trihalomethanes, total	EN/ISO 10301 (1997d)	GC-ECD		100	10
Vinyl chloride	No standard method available in CEN/ISO	To be controlled by product specification		0.5	

[a] Where:
ECD is electron capture detection.
FD is fluorescence detection.
FID is flame ionization detection.
GC is gas chromatography.
HPLC is high performance liquid chromatography.
LOD is the limit of detection, to be achieved according to Council Directive 98/83/EC, 1998.
MS is mass spectrometry.
Parametric value is the required limit according to Council Directive 98/83/EC, 1998.
UV is ultra violet detection.
Working range is the lowest determinable concentration stated in the method.
[b] Several organic insecticides, herbicides, fungicides, nematocides, acaricides, algicides, rodenticides, slimicides, their relevant metabolites, degradation and reaction products. Only those pesticides which are likely to be present in a given supply need be monitored (Council Directive 98/83/EC, 1998).
[c] The LOD applies to each individual pesticide and may not be achievable for all pesticides at present (Council Directive 98/83/EC, 1998).

meeting the method performance requirements of the EU directive (Council Directive 98/83/EC, 1998). The third column gives information about the analytical principle and the fourth column indicates the lowest concentration determinable cited in the standard method.

Methods for anion analysis   For the determination of anions (except chromate and cyanide), ion chromatographic methods can be applied, because they were developed especially for drinking water analysis. The cited standards and drafts (see Table 1.3) can be used for the control of the parametric value. For chromium determinations now the new ISO 18412 (ISO, 2005) is suitable for the control of the parametric chromium value of 50 µg/l (see Table 1.5), and the required LOD of 5 µg/l could be achieved by the method. The alternative sensitive CFA draft standard method ISO/DIS 23913 (ISO/DIS, 2004) is expected to be published soon. Both methods are applicable for the determination of chromate concentrations ≥2 µg/l and meet the requirements of the EU directive (Council Directive 98/83/EC, 1998). Reference to the CFA method is given due to the economic advantages of the CFA method (high sample through put).

Methods for elemental analyses   For the determination of elements (e.g., lead, cadmium, etc.) the method of ICP-MS (EN Standard, 2004) should be preferred over AAS methods, whenever possible. The ICP-MS determination of iron could be subject to polyatomic interferences so the ICP-OES EN Standard, 1997b method should be applied. For mercury and selenium AAS hydride techniques (EN Standard, 1997c; ISO, 2003b) should be applied due to the higher sensitivity of these techniques compared with the ICP-MS technique (EN Standard, 2004). All of the cited standards (see Table 1.5) can be used for the control of the parametric value.

Methods for organic compounds analyses   The very low parametric values for the organic compounds specified in the European directive 98/83/EC require methods suitable for trace level analyses. There is still demand for the development of new standard methods, because no CEN or ISO standard is currently available for the determination of acrylamide, several pesticides, and vinyl chloride.

HPLC-MS and GC-MS techniques have advantages for the determination of organic contaminants due to their high selectivity and sensitivity. For the determination of pesticides, the user has to apply several standards applicable for selected pesticides.

For the determination of highly volatile halogenated hydrocarbons, the GC-MS technique has not been included explicitly in the principles of EN ISO 10301 (EN/ISO, 1997d), so reference is made to the ECD-technique.

The laboratory shall ensure that it can meet the specified parametric values. This could, however, be a problem for the determination of, for instance, 1,2-dichloroethane and benzo(*a*)pyrene.

Alternative test methods   Due to the relative high parametric values for chloride, iron, nitrate, nitrite, and sulfate, for example (see Tables 1.5 and 1.6), laboratories should consider the application of alternative methods for the measurements. Compared with reference and laboratory standard methods, the so-called 'ready-to-use methods', such as cuvette tests, allow fast and often inexpensive results, as well as needing reduced quantities of reagents and less waste. Provided they give reliable results, these alternative methods could be considered for use in drinking water analysis. ISO 17381 (ISO, 2003c) lists criteria and requirements for the producers and for the users of these tests.

REFERENCES

Council Directive 98/83/EC, 1998. Quality of water intended for human consumption, 3 November 1998, *Official Journal of the European Communities*, Volume 41, 5.12.2998, L 330, 32-54.

DIN, 1998. *A Word about DIN*, Berlin, 1998.

EN Standard, 1995. EN/ISO 10304-1:1995: Water quality – Determination of dissolved fluoride, chloride, nitrite, orthophosphate, bromide, nitrate and sulfate ions, using liquid chromatography of ions, Part 1: Method for water with low contamination (ISO 10304-1:1992) (under revision: ISO/CD 10304:2004-24-11).

EN Standard, 1996. EN/ISO 6468:1996 Water quality – Determination of certain organochlorine insecticides, polychlorinated biphenyls and chlorobenzenes: Gas chromatographic method after liquid–liquid extraction (ISO 6468:1996).

EN Standard, 1997a. EN 1484:1997 Water analysis – Guidelines for the determination of total organic carbon (TOC) and dissolved organic carbon (DOC).

EN Standard, 1997b. EN/ISO 11885:1997 Water quality – Determination of 33 elements by inductively coupled plasma atomic emission spectroscopy (ISO 11885:1996) (under revision).

EN Standard, 1997c. EN 1483:1997 Water quality – Determination of mercury.

EN Standard, 2001. EN/ISO 15061:2001 Water quality – Determination of dissolved bromate – Method by liquid chromatography of ions (ISO 15061:2001).

EN Standard, 2003a. EN 14207:2003 Water quality – Determination of epichlorohydrin.

EN Standard, 2003b. EN/ISO 17993:2003 Water quality – Determination of 15 polycyclic aromatic hydrocarbons (PAH) in water by HPLC with fluorescence detection after liquid–liquid extraction (ISO 17993:2002).

EN Standard, 2003c. EN/ISO 15913:2003 Water quality – Determination of selected phenoxyalkanoic herbicides, including bentazones and hydroxybenzonitriles by gas chromatography and mass spectrometry after solid phase extraction and derivatization (ISO 15913:2000).

Environmental Protection Agency, 2004a. *List of Contaminants and their MCLs*, US Environmental Protection Agency, Washington, DC. http://www.epa.gov/safewater/mcl.html#mcls

Environmental Protection Agency, 2004b. Title 40, Chapter 1, Part 143: *National Secondary Drinking Water Regulations*. US Environmental Protection Agency, Washington, DC. http://www.access.gpo.gov/nara/cfr/waisidx_02/40cfr143_02.html

Environmental Protection Agency, 2004c. *Six-Year Review of Drinking Water Standards*. US Environmental Protection Agency, Washington, DC. http://www.epa.gov/safewater/review.html

Environmental Protection Agency, 2004d. *Total Coliform Rule and Potential Revisions and Distribution System Requirements*. US Environmental Protection Agency, Washington, DC. http://www.epa.gov/safewater/tcr/tcr.html

Environmental Protection Agency, 2004e. *Drinking Water Priority Rulemaking: Microbial and Disinfection Byproduct Rules.* US Environmental Protection Agency, Washington, DC. http://www.epa.gov/safewater/mdbp/mdbp.html

Environmental Protection Agency, 2004f. *Drinking Water Contaminant Candidate List*. US Environmental Protection Agency, Washington, DC. http://www.epa.gov/safewater/ccl/cclfs.html

Environmental Protection Agency, 2004g. *National Contaminant Occurrence Data Base*. US Environmental Protection Agency, Washington, DC. http://www.epa.gov/safewater/data/ncod.html

Environmental Protection Agency, 2004h. *Unregulated Contaminant Monitoring Rule*. US Environmental Protection Agency, Washington, DC. http://www.epa.gov/safewater/ucmr.html

Environmental Protection Agency, 2004i. *Analytical Methods for Drinking Water*. US Environmental Protection Agency, Washington, DC. http://www.epa.gov/safewater/methods/methods.html

Environmental Protection Agency, 2005. *Drinking Water Contaminant Candidate List 2; Final Notice.* US Environmental Protection Agency, Washington, DC. 24 *FR* 9071 www.epa.gov/fedrgster/EPA-WATER/2005/February/Day-24/w3527.html.

International Standards Organization, 1990. Water quality – Calibration and evaluation of analytical methods and estimation of performance characteristics, Part 1: Statistical evaluation of the linear calibration function. ISO 8466-1:1990.

International Standards Organization, 1993. Water quality – Determination of selenium: Atomic absorption spectrometric method (hydride technique). ISO 9965:1993.

International Standards Organization, 1997a. Water quality – Determination of benzene and some derivatives, Part 1: Head-space gas chromatographic method. ISO 11423-1:1997.

International Standards Organization, 1997b. Water quality – Determination of benzene and some derivatives, Part 2: Method using extraction and gas chromatography. ISO 11423-2:1997.

EN Standard, 1997d. Water quality – Determination of highly volatile halogenated hydrocarbons: Gas-chromatographic methods. (EN/ISO 10301:1997).

EN Standard, 1997e. Water quality – Determination of selected plant treatment agents: Method using high performance liquid chromatography with UV detection after solid–liquid extraction. (EN/ISO 11369:1997).

International Standards Organization, 1998a. Model manuscript of a Draft International Standard, Version 1.2.

EN Standard, 1999. Water quality – Determination of dissolved Li^+, Na^+, $NH4^+$, K^+, Mn^{2+}, Ca^{2+}, Mg^{2+}, Sr^{2+} and Ba^{2+} using ion chromatography: Method for water and waste water. (EN/ISO 14911:1999).

International Standards Organization, 2001. Water quality – Calibration and evaluation of analytical methods and estimation of performance characteristics, Part 2: Calibration strategy for non-linear second-order calibration functions. ISO 8466-2:2001.

International Standards Organization, 2002. Accuracy (trueness and precision) of measurement methods and results, Part 2: Basic method for the determination of repeatability and reproducibility of a standard measurement method. ISO 5725-2:1994, corrigendum 1.

EN Standard, 2002. Water quality – Determination of total cyanide and free cyanide by continuous flow analysis. (EN/ISO 14403:2002).

EN Standard, 2004. Application of inductively coupled plasma mass spectrometry (ICP-MS), Part 2: Water quality – Determination of 62 elements. (EN/ISO 17294-2:2004).

International Standards Organization, 2003c. Water quality – Selection and application of ready-to-use test kit methods in water analysis. ISO 17381:2003.

International Standards Organization, 2004. *Guidelines for the Implementation of the Agreement on Technical Co-operation between ISO and CEN* (Vienna Agreement), Fifth edition.

International Standards Organization, CEN, 2001. *Agreement on Technical Co-operation Between ISO and CEN* (Vienna Agreement), Version 3.3.

International Standards Organization/DIS, 2004. Water quality – Determination of chromium(VI) and the sum of chromium(III) and chromium(VI): Method using flow analysis (FIA and CFA) and spectrometric detection. ISO/DIS 23913:2004.

International Standards Organization, 2005. Water quality – Determination of chromium(VI): Photometric method for low contaminated water. ISO/DIS 18412:2005.

International Standards Organization/IEC, 1995. *Directives, Part 1: Procedures for the technical work*, Third edition.

EN Standard, 2005. *General Requirements for the Competence of Testing and Calibration Laboratories* (under revision). (EN/ISO 17025:2005).

International Standards Organization/IEC, 2001. *Directives, Part 2: Rules for the Structure and Drafting of International Standards*, Fourth edition.

International Standards Organization/TC, 2003. Water Quality, *Report of the Secretariat ISO/TC 147*, Document ISO/TC 147 N 575.

EN Standard, 1998. Water quality – Guide to analytical quality control for water analysis water analysis. (EN/ISO/TR 13530:1998) (under revision: ISO/WD 13530).

National Drinking Water Advisory Council, 2004. *Report on the CCL Classification Process to the US Environmental Protection Agency*. National Drinking Water Advisory Council, Washington, DC. http://www.epa.gov/safewater/ndwac/pdfs/report_ccl_ndwac_07-06-04.pdf

National Research Council, 2001. *Classifying Drinking Water Contaminants for Regulatory Consideration*. National Research Council Committee on Drinking Water Contaminants, National Academy Press, Washington, DC.

2
Bromate Determination

A.-Hakim R. Elwaer, Philippe Quevauviller, K. Clive Thompson and Cameron W. McLeod

2.1   INTRODUCTION

The ozonation of water containing bromide generates the formation of several by-products, among which bromate is of particular concern. This substance is regulated by the European Directive on the quality of water intended for human consumption, which has fixed a maximum admissible concentration of 10 µg/L of bromate in drinking water (Council Directive 98/83/EC, 1998). Bromate determination has to be carried out using techniques with detection limits at or below 2.5 µg/L of bromate. This requirement for method sensitivity has highlighted the need for the development of methods that allow the control of the implementation of the regulation (Ingrand *et al.*, 2002).

A wide range of methods exists for determining bromate at the sub-µg/L level to mg/L levels. Most of them have been developed or adapted to meet the objectives of regulations setting up a bromate quality standard, for example in the 1990s the US EPA established a maximum permissible value in the range of 0.1–1 mg/L and analytical methods were first developed to meet this objective. The newly proposed quality standard of 10 µg/L has represented an analytical challenge, which has led to focusing on improvement of the sensitivity within the last few years (Guinamant *et al.*, 2003).

Official methods for bromate determination have been established by regulatory organizations, and one of these methods is ion chromatography with conductivity detection (IC/CD). As an example, the US Environmental Protection Agency (EPA) issued method 300.0 in 1989, which enables a bromate detection limit of 20 µg/L to be achieved (EPA, 1991). This method was, however, faced with interference problems for the analysis of drinking waters containing high levels of chloride (>50 mg/L). This necessitated efforts to improve the sensitivity of the technique, which was achieved either through an improvement in columns technology, enabling a reduction in the detection limit to 1.3 µg/L (EPA, 1997), or to development of sample pre-treatment for removing the main interference (chloride, sulphate and metals), leading to the detection limit being reduced to 0.5 µg/L using the ISO 15061 standard method (ISO, 2000).

Recent work has shown that the sensitivity of bromate analytical methods may be further improved by coupling the separation of bromate by ion chromatography with a specific post-column reaction (Ingrand *et al.*, 2002; Weinberg *et al.*, 2003). Also, inductively coupled plasma mass spectrometry (ICP-MS) linked to ion chromatography or flow injection systems with on-line separation of bromate on alumina microcolumns, enabled detection limits in the range 0.1–0.3 µg/L of bromate to be reached (Elwaer A.R. *et al.*, 1996). Detection limits have been further lowered to 0.05 µg/L by using an ultrasonic nebulizer (Creed *et al.*, 1996) and negative thermal ionization isotope dilution mass spectrometry (NTI-IDMS) (Diemer and Heumann, 1997). Finally, electrospray ion chromatography–tandem mass spectrometry (IC/MS-MS) enabled a detection limit of 0.03 µg/L to be achieved (Diemer and Heumann, 1997; Charles *et al.*, 1996).

From these observations, it could be concluded that these techniques meet legislation requirements. However, they all present complex and sometimes time-consuming procedures, making them prone to error in case of insufficient handling care, and not sufficiently robust for on-site routine monitoring. Cost-effectiveness is another important consideration.

The need for ozone and bromate concentration monitoring in treated water on-site, however, implies that simple, low-cost and robust methods should be available. In this respect, visible spectrophotometry has been shown to be well adapted to on-site determination in comparison with other non-chromatographic methods (Ingrand *et al.*, 2002). However, this technique is not capable of determining bromate at the μg/L level and is therefore not in accordance with European legislation (Ingrand *et al.*, 2002). Progress has been possible through the use of different phenothiazines, which led to detection limits of 0.7 to 2 μg/L (Farrell *et al.*, 1995) or the use of flow injection methods with chlorpromazine, which enabled a detection limit in the same range (0.8 μg/L) to be reached (Gordon *et al.*, 1994). Finally, fluorimetry was identified as being an interesting alternative to spectrophotometry.

Recent progress has been made in connection to the requirements of the Drinking Water Directive, aiming to define IC/CD interference and ways of removing them, and to automate the pre-treatment and injection steps in the framework of a research project funded by the European Commission (Guinamant *et al.*, 2000). This project also included the development of alternative laboratory methods and field methods. This chapter summarizes the main findings of this project on the basis of recent reports (Guinamant *et al.*, 2000; Ingrand *et al.*, 2002).

2.2 ION CHROMATOGRAPHIC METHODS

2.2.1 Identification and Removal of the Main Interferences

Inorganic and organic interferences were investigated with respect to the determination of bromate in natural and drinking waters by an ion chromatographic method (Guinamant *et al.*, 2000; Ingrand *et al.*, 2002). The tested interferences were of two types:

(i) High concentrations of substances that may have an influence on the pre-concentration step and thus have an adverse effect on bromate recovery.

(ii) Presence of compounds that may co-elute with the bromate peak and be detected by the conductivity detector, resulting in a positive interference.

Interference by major inorganic substances present in natural waters in various aqueous matrices were tested using different types of waters (ultrapure water, mineral waters, and filtered river water) which were spiked with 5 and 10 μg/L of bromate. These matrices were additionally spiked with known concentrations of inorganic anions. Pre-treatment cartridges were tested for the elimination of these compounds (Ingrand *et al.*, 2002). Subsequently, various potential organic and (minor) inorganic interferents were spiked to determine possible co-elution with the bromate peak. The studied substances included a range of anionic oxidation by-products such as organic acids, reflecting the fact that bromate is formed during the ozonation of natural waters that also leads to the formation of such by-products. Other products known to be commonly present in ozonated and natural waters were also tested, such as sugars, amino acids, humic and fulvic acids.

Interference during the pre-concentration step

An initial evaluation of the method performance (repeatability, reproducibility) concluded that bromate recoveries (for spiking levels of 5 and 10 µg/L), a result outside the range 90–110 % could be considered as an interference for a given concentration of an interfering substance. In addition, a deviation of more than 5 % in the bromate retention time was also considered to indicate an interference (influencing the peak shape). Examples are decrease in bromate recoveries (in spiked ultrapure water) in the presence of 25 mg/L chloride concentration (decreasing to between 60 and 70 %), while minimal effects were observed for a chloride concentration of 20 mg/L. No significant effects were observed for nitrate levels between 0 and 100 mg/L (as NO_3^-) and sulphate levels up to 200 mg/L (Ingrand *et al.*, 2002). Bicarbonate was shown to influence both the bromate recovery and retention time. The retention time decreased (to 85 %) in the presence of 150 mg/L of HCO_3^-. It was noted that, at a 400 mg/L concentration of HCO_3^-, the recovery rate is still not affected but the retention time decreases to 31 %. At concentrations higher than 450 mg/L HCO_3^-, bromate analysis was considered impossible (Ingrand *et al.*, 2002). A mixture of the four anions mentioned above on 5 and 10 µg/L bromate concentrations indicated interferences at concentrations of 100 mg/L of nitrate, 200 mg/L of sulphate, 10 mg/L of chloride and 50 mg/L of bicarbonate. However, when considered separately these anions did not interfere at these levels.

These experiments demonstrated an important analytical feature, namely that bromate analysis cannot be performed directly for waters containing more than 50 mg/L of bicarbonate and 10 mg/L of chloride (which correspond to levels commonly found in natural waters), and that consequently a pre-treatment step is required. These results were confirmed by the analysis of natural river and mineral waters (Ingrand *et al.*, 2002).

Examples of removal of major inorganic interfering anions

Treatment for removing interfering anions is generally based on the use of cartridges (e.g. DIONEX cartridges). In this context Ingrand *et al.* (2002) tested a range of cartridges for removing interfering anions, such as, for instance, RP C18 cartridges (retaining organic matter), Ag cartridges (retaining halide ions, in particular chloride ions which interfere in bromate analysis), H cartridges (retaining metals and bicarbonate), and Ba cartridges (retaining sulphate). As a result of the tests, and depending on the quality of the water, the combinations of cartridges shown in Table 2.1 were recommended.

Table 2.1 Recommended cartridge combinations to remove major inorganic interfering anions

Combination 1 RP + Ba + Ag + H			Combination 2 RP + Ag + H			Combination 3 Ag + H		
Carbon	>	2 mg/L	Carbon	>	2 mg/L	Carbon	<	2 mg/L
Chloride	>	1 mg/L	Chloride	>	1 mg/L	Chloride	>	1 mg/L
Nitrate	>	100 mg/L	Nitrate	>	100 mg/L	Nitrate	<	100 mg/L
Bicarbonate[a]	>	25 mg/L	Bicarbonate[a]	>	25 mg/L	Bicarbonate[a]	>	25 mg/L
Sulphate[b]	>	100 mg/L	Sulphate	<	100 mg/L	Sulphate	<	100 mg/L

[a] Degassing should be employed for waters containing more than 100 mg HCO_3^-/L in order to eliminate interference in the retention time. Also, as the majority of waters have a higher concentration than this, for practical purposes degassing should be performed systematically.
[b] A single barium cartridge could be used for concentrations up to 1.5 g/L of sulphate, since it does not saturate.

Study of potential organic interference

Organic substances commonly present in natural waters may have strong interfering effects on bromate determinations. Systematic tests were carried out by (Ingrand *et al.* 2002) on effects of 10 mg/L of substances such as sugars, amino acids, urea, low-molecular-weight carboxylic acids likely to be formed through the ozonation process, albumin, humic and fulvic acid, phenol, bisulfite, cyanide, iron and manganese. This level is significantly above the usual concentrations found in waters and the study aimed to test the maximum interference against the background noise, interfering peaks close to the bromate retention time, and bromate recoveries and/or deviations from the baseline. Results of the experiments indicated that none of the compounds tested induced noticeable interfering effects.

2.2.2   Sample Pre-treatment Automation

As mentioned above, the only interfering effects identified on bromate determination were due to the presence of major inorganic anions, and this could be solved by using a proper combination of pre-treatment cartridges. Until recently, this type of pre-treatment had always been manually operated using commercially available disposable ion exchange columns (involving sample injection, elution and separation) followed by detection and quantification using a conductivity detector (see Figure 2.1) or an ultraviolet detector (Guinamant *et al.*, 2000). This manual operation is not without risk of error, and recent developments have enabled to be based this pre-treatment on an automated procedure (Wolfis and Brandt, 1997).

In the above approach, the sample is automatically directed through a single solid phase extraction (SPE) column (containing the same materials as the three manual disposable columns) using an automatic device, which then introduces the collected eluate to the ion chromatographic pre-concentration column where the components are subsequently eluted into the analytical column and separated (Figure 2.2).

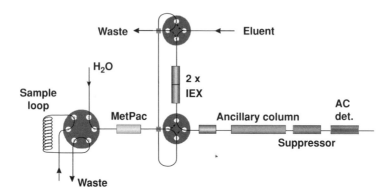

Figure 2.1 Ion chromatographic determination of bromate in water (after Ingrand *et al.*, 2002). Reprinted from Trends in Analytical Chemistry, Vol. 21, No. 1, Ingrand *et al.*, "Determination of bromate . . . ", pp. 1–12, 2002, with permission from Elsevier

Various experiments based on the measurement of calibration curve linearity, recovery assessment for various types of water, reproducibility and detection limits checks, etc., enabled the evaluation of the performance of the automated sample pre-treatment and injection system. The combined pre-treatment and injection of water samples into an ion chromatograph using the automatic SPE improved the overall reliability of the analysis while considerably enhancing the sample throughput (Guinamant *et al.*, 2000; Ingrand *et al.*, 2002). Recently a simple pre-concentration approach was developed using microwave energy for evaporation coupled with ion chromatography for bromate quantitation at 0.1 μg/L detection limits (Liu Y. and Mou S., 2002). Regulatory authorities have been continually validating standard methodologies for trace determination of bromate in waters. The US Environmental Protection Agency has developed a number of standard methods based on the use of

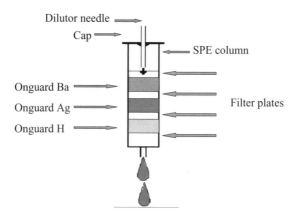

Figure 2.2 Solid phase extraction (SPE) column with three added exchange resins (after Ingrand *et al.*, 2002). Reprinted from Trends in Analytical Chemistry, Vol. 21, No. 1, Ingrand *et al.*, "Determination of bromate . . .", pp. 1–12, 2002, with permission from Elsevier

ion chromatography. These methods were recently reviewed and various parameters evaluated (Hautman *et al.*, 2001).

2.3 ALTERNATIVE LABORATORY METHODS

2.3.1 Ion Chromatography / ICP-MS

Bromate determination may be carried out by coupling an ion chromatographic system to an inductively coupled plasma–mass spectrometry (ICP-MS) system. As shown by (Ingrand *et al.* 2002), this coupling requires an optimization procedure on a multi-element level, for which examples are found in the literature (Guinamant *et al.*, 2000). Experiments demonstrated that interference on the masses of the two bromine isotopes may occur from $^{38}Ar^{40}ArH$ for ^{79}Br and from $^{40}Ar^{40}ArH$ for ^{81}Br (Ingrand *et al.*, 2002). Considering that the natural abundance of ^{38}Ar is only 0.06 % of the natural abundance of ^{40}Ar, the background noise for ^{79}Br is much lower than for ^{81}Br and, consequently, sensitive detection of bromine species by ICP-MS is preferably done via the ^{79}Br isotope. The scheme of the whole experimental set-up for the determination of bromate by IC/ICP-MS is shown in Figure 2.3; additional details on IC and ICP-MS parameters and conditions are given by Ingrand *et al.* (2002). The method has been validated by comparison with a reference IC/CD method (French standard XP T 90-210), using the same criteria as in the automated system. The limit of detection is 0.1 µg/L of bromate without the pre-concentration

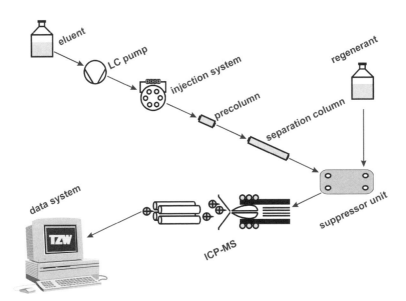

Figure 2.3 Experimental set-up for the IC/ICP-MS coupling (after Ingrand *et al.*, 2002). Reprinted from Trends in Analytical Chemistry, Vol. 21, No. 1, Ingrand *et al.*, "Determination of bromate...", pp. 1–12, 2002, with permission from Elsevier

step. Repeatability and reproducibility of the method are at least comparable to the current IC/CD method. It constitutes a reliable technique and, due to the fact that no sample pre-treatment is necessary, the method is fast, the time for one complete analysis being less than 10 minutes.

2.3.2   Ion Chromatography Spectrophotometry Detection

This method is based on the hyphenation of an ion chromatographic system and a post-column reaction with spectrophotometry detection (IC/CLP). The post-column reaction involves chlorpromazine (CLP) and hydrochloric acid (Gordon *et al.*, 1994). After optimization of the operating conditions (concentration and reagent flow), the first investigations were carried out using a direct injection of samples with neither pre-treatment nor pre-concentration, followed by ion chromatography analysis. This led to a quantification limit of approximately 5 µg/L, which did not meet the requirement of the regulation (Ingrand *et al.*, 2002). An improvement in the detection limit could be achieved by a pre-concentration of the sample. As demonstrated by previous studies, the concentration step suffers from various interference, which requires pre-treatment of the samples prior to the pre-concentration stage. Analytical conditions and typical chromatograms obtained by conductivity (IC/CD) and visible photometric detection after post-column reaction (IC/CLP) are described by Ingrand *et al.* (2002).

The performance of the CLP post-column method was evaluated on three ozonated waters and five final waters (ozonated and then treated with sodium hypochlorite or chlorine dioxide) analysed simultaneously with the reference method (IC/CD) and the CLP post-column method (Table 2.2). The deviations obtained between alternative and reference methods were between 0 and 16%. Highest deviations were observed with the conductivity detector in comparison with the alternative CLP

Table 2.2   Comparison between the reference method and the CLP post-column method in drinking waters, average of three replicates (after Ingrand *et al.*, 2002). Reprinted from Trends in Analytical Chemistry, Vol. 21, No. 1, Ingrand *et al.*, "Determination of bromate . . . ", pp. 1–12, 2002, with permission from Elsevier

Type of water	Concentration of bromate (µg/L)		Deviation (%)
	IC/CD	IC/CLP	
Ozonated water	5.7	5.1	11
Ozonated water	6.9	6.1	12
Ozonated water	7.0	6.7	4
Final water	2.5	2.1	16
Final water	3.7	3.8	3
Final water	12	11	8
Final water	15	14	7
Final water	18	18	0

post-column method (Ingrand *et al.*, 2002). The limit of detection and quantification were respectively 0.2 and 0.3 µg/L, of bromate. The calibration is linear from 0.5 to 20 µg/L, which fulfils the requirements of the latest European regulation.

In another work (Delcomyn, *et al.*, 2001; Weiberg, *et al.*, 2003) ion chromatography was coupled to post-column derivatization prior to UV spectrophotometric detection. In this study 25-mM H_2SO_4 and 0.145-mM $NaNO_2$ were employed to generate *in-situ* nitrous acid, which together with 2-M NaBr generated the tribromide ion in the presence of the eluting oxyhalides detectable at 267 nm. The practical quantitation limit for bromate using this approach is 0.05 µg/L. Earlier, Fuchsin reagent, acidified using HCl, was employed as an IC post-column derivatization reagent for bromate detection at 540 nm (Achilli and Romele, 1999). This method achieved a detection limit of 0.1 µg/L and a working range of 2–50 µg/L of bromate.

Three different post-column reaction methodologies based on ion chromatographic separation have been compared (Echigo *et al.*, 2001). The KI–$(NH_4)_6$ Mo_7O_{24} method, the NaBr–$NaNO_2$ method, and the *o*-dianisidine method showed similar detection limits (0.17, 0.19 and 0.24 µg/L) for bromate analysis with pneumatic reagent delivery systems. With respect to the simplicity of the system, the *o*-dianisidine method is the best option of the three. Also, it is of note that the NaBr–$NaNO_2$ method was considered to be susceptible to interference by matrix ions because of the use of a lower detection wavelength. It was also found that the *o*-dianisidine method can achieve a low µg/L level detection of nitrite with a simpler configuration (i.e., only one post-column reagent) than the KI–$(NH_4)_6Mo_7O_{24}$ method, while the sodium bromide–sodium nitrite method was not sensitive enough for nitrite analysis at the µg/L level. All three methods are compatible with conductivity detection. When used in combination with conductivity detection, this compatibility allows simultaneous analysis of bromate, nitrite, and other common ions in drinking water, such as bromide ions.

2.3.3   Ion Pair Chromatography – Fluorescence Detection

This method consists in the separation of bromate using ion-pair chromatography with post-column reaction and detection with a fluorescence detector (IP/Fluo). The registered signal corresponds to a decrease of fluorescence intensity. The post column reaction involves Carbostyril 124 in acidic conditions (Gahr *et al.*, 1998).

Two parameters were investigated with the aim of improving the reaction: (i) the temperature at which the post-column reaction is carried out (an important factor controlling the chemical reaction), and (ii) the reaction time. Increasing the temperature of the reaction coil from 20 °C to 60 °C significantly improved the efficiency of the post column reaction (Gahr *et al.*, 1998). With respect to the reaction time, the use of a longer reaction coil (15 m rather than 5 m) improved the sensitivity of the method by a factor of 3 (Figure 2.4).

The quantification limit of the method was 1.6 µg/L. This technique has been tested on several ozonated waters or samples after final disinfection with chlorine

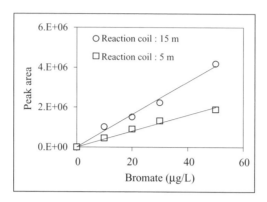

Figure 2.4   Importance of the post-column reaction time on the sensitivity of the fluorescence method (MilliQ water, Carbostyril 5×10^{-7} mol/L, 60 °C). (After Ingrand *et al.*, 2002). Reprinted from Trends in Analytical Chemistry, Vol. 21, No. 1, Ingrand *et al.*, "Determination of bromate . . . ", pp. 1–12, 2002, with permission from Elsevier

or chlorine dioxide, simultaneously with the current IC/CD method (Ingrand *et al.*, 2002). Results obtained from the fluorescence quenching system using Carbostyril 124 were in good agreement with the analyses conducted using IC/CD since the difference between the two techniques did not exceed 1 to 2 µg/L. However, this post-column reaction was affected by chlorite, the major chlorine dioxide by-product. Chlorate, the second largest chlorine dioxide by-product, was not found to interfere.

2.3.4   Flow Injection – ICP-MS

Flow injection (FI) provides a powerful approach to trace element analysis (Valcarcel and Luque de Castro, 1999; Sanz Medel, 1999). FI methodologies are realistic alternatives to ion chromatography and hence offer scope for extending and/or advancing analytical capabilities for bromate determination.

On-line reaction chemistry and traditional laboratory operations, including solid phase extraction, are readily implemented in the flow injection mode and analytical application extends from simple anion/cation determinations to drugs and biomolecules. Ultra-trace determination of bromate in waters has been achieved using a flow injection system having an alumina micro-column interfaced with an ICP-mass spectrometer (Elwaer *et al.*, 1996; Elwaer, 1999), which conferred a high degree of selectivity thanks to (i) the on-line separation/isolation of bromate from bromide and coexisting cations, and (ii) mass selective detection. High sensitivity could be obtained through on-line pre-concentration. Furthermore the alumina microcolumn ICP-MS system eliminated possible molecular ion interference caused by potassium content in the form of $^{40}Ar^{39}K$, thus enhancing the mass-to-charge signal at ^{79}Br. This is due to anionic affinity of the acidic alumina microcolumn, hence the K^+ cation is not retained, as demonstrated in Figure 2.5.

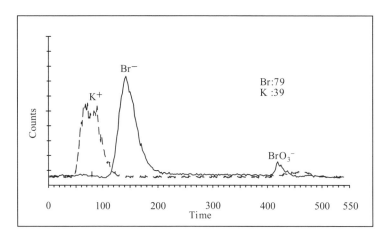

Figure 2.5 Ion time responses (overlays) at m/z 39 and m/z 79 for a spiked mineral water

A flow injection system with a micro-column of strong anion exchanger has been interfaced with an ICP-mass spectrometer via a microconcentric nebulizer to perform on-line separation and trace determination of bromate in drinking waters (Elwaer, 1999; Elwaer *et al.*, 2000). Method development studies examined the effect of sample injection volume, carrier stream flow rate and eluent concentration on system response. Basic performance data for this method were: limit of detection, 0.13 µg/L (500 µL sample injection); analysis time, 5 minutes per sample; precision, 2.6 % RSD (at 5 µg/L).

2.4   FIELD-BASED METHODS

2.4.1   Spectrophotometric Method with Methylene Blue

This method is based on the reaction between bromate and methylene blue in acidic conditions. The first step consists in the optimization of the operating condition (concentration of reagents, reaction time, wavelength, etc.) in order to obtain the best sensitivity (Ingrand *et al.*, 2002).

The robustness of the method has been tested with various matrices: spiked Evian water, ozonated waters and final waters (ozonated and then treated with sodium hypochlorite or chlorine dioxide). The results are compared in Table 2.3 in which matrices A to C naturally contained bromate whereas Evian water was spiked at 5 and 10 µg/L (Ingrand *et al.*, 2002). For Evian water and ozonated waters, concentrations obtained using the field method were in good agreement with the theoretical spiking. However, for final waters treated with sodium hypochlorite or chlorine dioxide, results showed that the disinfection step using sodium hypochlorite is a major source of interference (deviations from 460 to 744 %). Disinfection using chlorine dioxide leads to lower interference (deviation 19 %).

Table 2.3 Determination of bromate in Evian water and in three types of ozonated matrices: comparison between the reference technique (IC/CD) and the methylene blue method (after Ingrand *et al.*, 2002). Reprinted from Trends in Analytical Chemistry, Vol. 21, No. 1, Ingrand *et al.*, "Determination of bromate . . . ", pp. 1–12, 2002, with permission from Elsevier

| | | Concentration in bromate (μg/L) | | Divergence |
| | | IC/CD or | Methylene blue | MB vs IC/CD |
Matrix	Treatment	theoretical spiking	(MB)	(%)
Evian	/	5	4	20
		10	9	10
A	O_3	31	30	3
	$O_3 + ClO^-$	27	151	460
B	O_3	10	12	20
	$O_3 + ClO^-$	18	152	744
C	O_3	23	23	0
	$O_3 + ClO_2$	16	19	19

O_3: Ozonation step.
ClO^-: Disinfection with sodium hypochlorite.
ClO_2: Disinfection with chlorine dioxide.
IC/CD: Ion chromatography with conductivity detection (reference method).

Several methods for removing hypochlorite ions are described in the literature (Gordon *et al.*, 1989; Fletcher and Hemmings, 1985), most of them being based on its oxidizing capacity. Among the tested compounds, only the hydroxylamine hydrochloride pre-treatment was effective in hypochlorite removal. In samples A and B, this pre-treatment suppressed hypochlorite interference. In low mineralized matrices, such as deionized water or sample C (treated with chlorine dioxide), hydroxylamine hydrochloride partially reduced bromate. The use of this agent seemed well adapted for bromate determination using methylene blue (Table 2.4). However, the pre-treatment conditions (concentration and reaction time) needed to be optimized according to the matrix to be analysed (Ingrand *et al.*, 2002).

Table 2.4 Determination of bromate in the presence of hypochlorite ions: evaluation of the hydroxylamine hydrochloride efficiency. Concentrations are in μg/L (after Ingrand *et al.*, 2002). Reprinted from Trends in Analytical Chemistry, Vol. 21, No. 1, Ingrand *et al.*, "Determination of bromate . . . ", pp. 1–12, 2002, with permission from Elsevier

| | | Field method (Methylene Blue 1 mg/L + HCl 2 mol/L) | | | |
| | | Without | Deviation vs | With | Deviation vs |
Matrix	IC/CD	pre-treatment	IC/CD (%)	pre-treatment	IC/CD (%)
DW	25	24	−1	21	−16
+25 μg/L BrO_3^-					
A	27	151	460	32	19
B	18	152	744	22	22
C	16	19	19	15	−6

DW: Deionized water.
IC/CD: Ion chromatography with conductivity detection (reference method).

This method allows determination of bromate at concentration levels from 4 to 50 µg/L, with divergence between results obtained with both IC/CD (reference method) and methylene blue methods lower than 20 %. The high level of interference from hypochlorite ions has been demonstrated but it can be overcome by pre-treating samples with hydroxylamine hydrochloride. Such pre-treatment should be adapted to the matrix analysed on site (Ingrand *et al.*, 2002).

2.4.2   Flow Injection – Spectrophotometric Detection

With reference to bromate determination, there have been few published flow injection (FI) studies. Gordon *et al.* (1994) described a spectrophotometric procedure based on the oxidation of chlorpromazine (CLP). A low limit of quantitation (0.8 µg/L) was realized but the method was susceptible to interference by cations and other co-oxidants.

The flow injection system described by Gordon *et al.* (1994) was suitably adapted by incorporating an alumina micro-column into the manifold, resulting in an on-line pre-concentration/separation and spectrophotometry detection (Elwaer, 1999; Ingrand *et al.*, 2002). The main operational features are described elsewhere (Guinamant *et al.*, 2000; Ingrand *et al.*, 2002). Method development/optimization examined the effect of key flow-injection parameters on system response. Limit of detection was 0.85 µg/L (2mL sample volume, pre-concentration factor: 7) and precision at 10 µg/L was 0.5 % RSD. Of the potential interference tested, (NO_2^- 0.1 mg/L; NO_3^- 50 mg/L; SO_4^{2-} 100 mg/L; Br^- 1 mg/L; ClO_3^- 2 mg/L; Cl^- 100 mg/L; Fe^{3+} 2 mg/L), only nitrite gave a positive response, suggesting that it underwent deposition/elution on the alumina micro-column and oxidized chlorpromazine. Sample pre-treatment with sulphamic acid may be used to remove nitrite interference (Gordon *et al.*, 1994). Further development work and intercomparison with IC and FI/ICP-MS are needed prior to field testing.

2.5   STABILITY OF BROMATE

Previous sections of this chapter discussed the details of newly developed analytical methodologies and strategies for bromate separation and trace quantification. This confirms the current vast interest of the analytical community in bromate determination as a result of ongoing regulatory requirements. The acceptance of such methods depends mainly on the analytical performance as related to accuracy and precision. However, despite all analytical efforts, very little work has been done to investigate the stability of bromate species between sampling and analysis in different water matrices. Studies of bromate stability in water matrices should be carried out before any analytical methodology can be approved.

In this respect the European Commission set up a project on Development of Laboratory and Field Methods for Determination of Bromate in Drinking Water

(Guinamant *et al.*, 2000; Ingrand *et al.*, 2002). This project devised different work packages including stability of bromate in waters, followed by an inter-laboratory comparison exercise to evaluate and validate the developed methods.

Bromate stability was studied in two different dimensions. The first was related to direct evaluation of bromate stability in different water matrices. The second was devoted to stability of bromate species mobilized on activated alumina micro-columns with a view to developing a field sampling methodology from bromate in waters.

2.5.1   Effect of Water Matrix on Bromate Stability

Stability of chemical species during sampling, sample handling, transportation and storage prior to analysis has always been an issue of concern to analytical chemists. Chemical changes of analyte species can be influenced by various parameters including sampling methods, container material, chemical interference, conditions of handling, transportation and storage. Bromate is not considered to be among the naturally occurring brominated compounds and it must therefore be formed as a result of a chemical process. Once formed bromate will maintain its chemical structure unless exposed to a chemical reducing agent. However, water sampling for metals is normally accompanied by nitric acid stabilization which has been confirmed not to affect bromate chemical stability, as will be discussed in the following section (Elwaer *et al.*, 1996).

In this study, the stability of bromate in water samples with different matrix constituents was investigated. Water samples ranged from soft to hard and were spiked with 1 mg/L bromide, 0.5 mg/L chlorite and 0.5 mg/L chlorate. These levels are considered to be higher than those normally observed in waters for these three anionic species. Each sample was also spiked with 2.5, 10 and 25 µg/L of bromate. Furthermore, a 5 µg/L of bromate standard in deionized water was also prepared. Brown glass bottles capped with polypropylene tops and PTFE inserts were used as sample containers. Samples were stored in the dark at 4 °C. Tables 2.5 and 2.6 summarize matrix constituents of each sample, preservation method spike levels and results of analyses. The results clearly demonstrate that for the two high and low total hardness waters tested, samples containing 2.5 to 25 µg/L bromate were stable for at least 20 days and that the addition of 50 mg/L ethylenediamine (EDA) preservative did not affect the results, as illustrated in Table 2.6. The results also confirm that 5 µg/L bromate standard made up in deionized water had the same stability over this period.

The high total hardness stability tests were extended to more than 100 days and bromate results using the FI-ICP-MS method confirmed the stability of bromate over this period. Similarly the presence of 50 mg/L EDA preservative showed no effect on bromate stability. High total hardness water samples were further re-analysed after a period of 100 days and bromate content was found to be stable.

This study concluded that bromate concentrations are stable in hard waters for up to 100 days when stored in brown glass bottles in dark at 4 °C. It was also

Table 2.5 Soft and hard water samples investigated for bromate stability

No.	Sample constituents	Preservation technique	Total hardness (mg/L CaCO$_3$)	Spiked bromate concentration (μg/L)	Analysis schedule (days)
1	Spiked deionized water containing 1 mg/L bromide, 0.5 mg/L chlorite and 0.5 mg/L chlorate (added as KBr, NaClO$_2$ and KClO$_3$)	None	0	5	0, 2, 10, 20
2	Spiked hard water containing 1 mg/L bromide, 0.5 mg/L chlorite and 0.5 mg/L chlorate (added as KBr, NaClO$_2$ and NaClO$_3$)	Addition of 50 mg/L of ethylenedi-amine (EDA)	273 hard water	0, 2.5, 10 and 25	0, 2, 10, 20
3	Spiked hard water containing 1 mg/L bromide, 0.5 mg/L chlorite and 0.5 mg/L chlorate (added as KBr, NaClO$_2$ and KClO$_3$)	None	273 hard water	0, 2.5, 10 and 25	0, 2, 10, 20
4	Spiked soft water containing 1 mg/L bromide, 0.5 mg/L chlorite and 0.5 mg/L chlorate (added as KBr, NaClO$_2$ and NaClO$_3$)	Addition of 50 mg/L of ethylenedi-amine (EDA)	115 soft water	0, 2.5, 10 and 25	0, 2, 10, 20
5	Spiked soft water containing 1 mg/L bromide, 0.5 mg/L chlorite and 0.5 mg/L chlorate (added as KBr, NaClO$_2$ and KClO$_3$)	None	115 soft water	0, 2.5, 10 and 25	0, 2, 10, 20

demonstrated that no preservative was needed to stabilize bromate in the stored water samples.

2.5.2 Stability of Bromate Species Immobilized on Alumina Microcolumns

The previous section addressed the effect of water matrix on bromate stability. This section investigates the possibility of developing an alternative approach to sampling of bromate species in waters by employing columns of a selective packing material. This study was based on the development of an FI system with alumina microcolumns

Table 2.6 Average results of bromate analysis in different waters spiked at 0, 2.5, 10 and 25 μg/L BrO$_3^-$ and analysed at intervals of 0, 2, 10 and 20 days

Sample	Preservation technique	Spike level BrO$_3^-$ (μg/L)	Average bromate over a 20-day period (0, 2, 10 and 20 days) BrO$_3^-$ (μg/L)	RSD (%)
Spiked deionized water containing 1mg/L bromide, 0.5 mg/L chlorite and 0.5 mg/L chlorate (added as KBr, NaClO$_2$ and KClO$_3$)	None	5.00	4.7	16.1
Spiked hard water containing 1 mg/L bromide, 0.5 mg/L chlorite and 0.5 mg/L chlorate (added as KBr, NaClO$_2$ and NaClO$_3$)	Addition of 50 mg/L of ethylenediamine (EDA)	0.0 2.5 10.0 25.0	1.4 2.8 9.8 22.2	61.1 22.9 10.0 6.2
Spiked hard water containing 1 mg/L bromide, 0.5 mg/L chlorite and 0.5 mg/L chlorate (added as KBr, NaClO$_2$ and KClO$_3$)	None	0.0 2.5 10.0 25.0	1.0 3.0 9.2 21.1	— 21.4 10.1 4.6
Spiked soft water containing 1 mg/L bromide, 0.5 mg/L chlorite and 0.5 mg/L chlorate (added as KBr, NaClO$_2$ and NaClO$_3$)	Addition of 50 mg/L of ethylenediamine (EDA)	0.0 2.5 10.0 25.0	— 3.3 10.8 26.8	— 8.6 6.1 16.3
Spiked soft water containing 1 mg/L bromide, 0.5 mg/L chlorite and 0.5 mg/L chlorate (added as KBr, NaClO$_2$ and KClO$_3$)	None	0.0 2.5 10.0 25.0	— 2.9 10.2 25.6	— 13.8 7.3 8.4

interfaced with ICP-MS and used to determine ultra-trace levels of bromate in drinking waters (Elwaer *et al.*, 1996). In this approach, the ion-exchange properties of activated alumina were used to affect the on-line pre-concentration of bromate and rejection of any coexisting bromide (potential interference). As evidenced in the recent literature, including the aforementioned FI–ICP-MS study, micro-column technology is becoming an increasingly important trend in ultra-trace investigations

Table 2.7 Determination of bromate in charged microcolumns. Uncertainties, $\pm s$

Storage time	Bromate concentration	
	$BrO_3^-\ \mu g/L$	RSD (%)
1 hour	5.83 ± 0.22	3.81
1 day	5.76 ± 0.19	3.41
3 days	6.09 ± 0.16	2.56
1 week	6.16 ± 0.16	2.55
2 weeks	6.00 ± 0.22	3.63
3 weeks	6.34 ± 0.06	0.90
4 weeks	5.99 ± 0.31	5.25
8 weeks	6.86 ± 0.13	1.96

(Quevauviller, 1997). Moreover, in Hg and Cr speciation studies (Mena *et al.*, 1995, 1996) analyte-enriched microcolumns have been shown to offer a convenient route to instrument calibration and development as a new reference material (RM) format. With the latter in mind and given the urgent need to validate new methods for the determination of bromate in process and drinking waters, a batch of microcolumns was prepared and analysed over an 8-week period in order to assess bromate stability. Microcolumns of activated alumina ($n = 30$) were charged with bromate standard solution (0.5 ml, 6.0 µg/L) and stored at 4 °C in a light-tight container. Microcolumns were removed at regular time intervals (1 hour, 1 and 3 days and 1, 2, 3, 4 and 8 weeks) and bromate species were eluted and quantified by flow-injection ICP-MS. Analyte recoveries were found to bc quantitative (96–101 %) and reproducible over the 8-week period. These results indicate that for trace level determinations (µg/L) of bromate, a micro-column format may provide a convenient and reliable route for delivery of external calibrants and reference materials. Analytical data for the complete study are summarized in Table 2.7. It is clear from these results that the column-to-column variability is low and that analyte recoveries are essentially quantitative, with good precision (short-term, RSD 0.9–5.3 %; long-term, RSD 3.3 %) for the 8-week period. It is concluded, therefore, that micro-columns of activated alumina provide a useful support for stabilizing bromate and as such provide a simple and convenient means for the delivery of precise quantities of bromate at the trace and ultra-trace level.

2.6 INTERLABORATORY EXCERCISE FOR BROMATE DETERMINATION

Toxicological studies of bromate have provided continuous evidence of its possible carcinogenicity (Kurokawa *et al.*, 1990). As a result a maximum admissible concentration (MAC) of 10 µg/L bromate in drinking waters is recommended by the US EPA (US EPA,1997), the European Commission (Council Directive 98/83) and the WHO (WHO, 1991), this limit has been defined primarily on the basis of the detection

Table 2.8 Bromate concentration in the five samples

| Sample Number | Matrix | Bromate concentration (µg/L) | | | |
		Natural background	Spike level	Total (target) level	Grand mean of all labs
1	Deionized water	0	5.7	5.7	5.38
2	High total hardness borehole water sample	< 0.3	2.7	2.7	2.62
3	Low hardness tapwater	1.1	7.5	8.6	8.70
4	Ozonylated final treated water	Not known	0	?	8.50
5	GAC treated water	~0.3[a]	4.0	4.0[a]	4.14

[a] Values given are mean concentrations in µg/L unless stated otherwise.

capabilities of existing ion chromatographic methodologies rather than on toxicological considerations. The EC recommends detection limits of less than 2.5 µg/L. This has called for the development of more sensitive and/or alternative techniques. A project funded by the Standards, Measurements and Testing Programme of the European Commission, and run jointly with the ISO group, on bromate analysis has enabled the improvement and/or development of methods for the determination of bromate at such concentration levels. Sections 2.2, 2.3 and 2.4 above discussed methods of bromate analysis and their analytical performance. This collaborative work was concluded by the organization of an interlaboratory trial involving 26 European laboratories, which enabled the testing of both a draft ISO standard method and alternative methods.

Five samples were prepared as test materials for the interlaboratory trial, of which the bromate content and matrix composition are given in Tables 2.8 and 2.9 respectively.

Samples 1, 2, 3 and 5 were spiked using a potassium bromate solution. It can be seen that the trial covered the concentration range 2–10 µg/L bromate. The proposed EC limit for bromate is 10 µg/L, thus the lower level of interest for regulatory bromate analysis is about 2.5 µg/L. A result very close to the detection limit of 0.3 µg/L was observed for sample 5, which was a granulated activated-carbon (GAC) treated water. This water had not been treated with ozone and it was felt that it was unlikely to contain bromate; thus a target value of 4.0 rather than 4.3 µg/L was used. The stability of bromate had been tested prior to the interlaboratory study as demonstrated in the previous section. Thirty-three sets of data were generated by 26 laboratories (some laboratories provided results for more than one method). Calibration was either by calibration graph or standard additions. Each participating laboratory received one bottle of each of the above five samples and a calibration solution containing 10 µg/L bromate. This latter solution was prepared from the 1000 mg/L bromate master calibration solution. The laboratories were requested to make a minimum of five replicate determinations on each sample on at least two different days. The

Table 2.9 Sample matrix analysis[a]

Determinand	Sample Number				
	1	2	3	4	5
Conductivity (μS/cm)	<10	567	197	347	202
Calcium (Ca)	<2	81.7	24.4	49.7	37.3
Magnesium (Mg)	<2	19.2	2.05	7.5	1.25
Total hardness ($CaCO_3$)	<5	283	70	155	97.5
Alkalinity (HCO_3)	<10	267	26	79	110
Chloride (Cl)	<10	41	14	21	6.1
Nitrate (NO_3)	<1	7.2	2.9	15.6	<1
Sulphate (SO_4)	<10	44	44	72	4.3
Total organic carbon (C)	<0.3	0.3	2.14	2.2	0.95
Bromide (Br)	<0.010	0.042	0.019	0.036	0.015
Chlorite (ClO_2^-)	<0.010	<0.010	<0.010	<0.010	<0.010
Chlorate (ClO_3^-)	<0.010	<0.010	0.07	<0.010	<0.010
Iron	<0.020	<0.020	0.043	<0.020	<0.020
Aluminium	<0.010	<0.010	0.025	0.059	<0.010
Manganese	<0.005	<0.005	<0.005	0.012	<0.005
Phosphorus (P)	<0.1	<0.1	0.82	<0.1	<0.1

[a] Values given are mean concentrations in mg/L unless stated otherwise.

laboratories were instructed to use their own calibration solutions to calculate their results but also to analyse the provided calibration solution to verify the validity of their calibrants. The results submitted in the interlaboratory study were discussed amongst all participants in a technical meeting. Tables 2.10 and 2.11 summarize the results obtained in the interlaboratory study. The evaluation of data from calibration experiments was performed according to ISO 8466-1 linear calibration function (ISO, 1990) and ISO 8466-2 second-order calibration function (ISO, 2001). Data submitted by the participants in the interlaboratory trial were evaluated according to ISO 5725-2 (ISO, 1994). With the exception of one laboratory, all participating

Table 2.10 Summary of the results of the interlaboratory study (non-ISO methods)

Sample	Number of sets	Mean $\pm s_R$ (μg/L)[a]	RSD_R (%)[a]
1	10	5.61 ± 0.38	6.7
2	9	2.79 ± 0.43	15.2
3	10	8.24 ± 2.42	29.4
4	8	9.45 ± 0.89	9.4
5	12	3.94 ± 0.90	23.0

[a] *Note*: s_R is the reproducibility standard deviation and RSD_R (%) is the reproducibility relative standard deviation.

Table 2.11   Summary of the results of the interlaboratory study (non-ISO methods)

Sample	Number of sets	Mean $\pm s_R$ (μg/L)^a	RSD$_R$ (%)^a
1	17	5.44 ± 0.23	4.1
2	17	2.49 ± 0.50	19.9
3	16	8.26 ± 1.41	17.1
4	15	8.13 ± 1.17	14.3
5	17	3.93 ± 0.64	16.4

^{a} *Note*: s_R is the reproducibility standard deviation and RSD$_R$ (%) is the reproducibility relative standard deviation.

laboratories found results ranging from 9.60 to 10.95 μg/L for the 10 μg/L calibration solution, with a mean of 10.06 μg/L and an interlaboratory standard deviation of 0.30 μg/L (RSD of 3.0 %), which confirmed that the calibration solutions used were of good quality and that possible errors were therefore unlikely to be caused by bias resulting from incorrectly prepared laboratory calibrants.

Calibration functions were calculated according to a linear and a second-order model. Both functions led to RSDs in the same range, except for two laboratories (27 and 29) using non-ISO Carbostyril fluorescence quenching methods (and a linear calibration function). This trial has allowed the introduction of both linear and second order calibration models in the standard ISO/DIS 15061 method (ISO, 2001). The results of some laboratories using non-ISO methods (5, 12, 23 and 27) were not considered to be fit for the purpose because the mean results of at least two of the three spiked samples (samples 2, 3 and 5) led to a recovery lower than 80 % or greater than 120 %, and two of the within laboratory RSDs were greater than 10 % . Data reported from Laboratories 23 (four times), 12 (three times), 5, 25, 26 and 33 (once) were also detected as statistical outliers, following calculations made according to ISO 5725-2 (Table 2.9). (ISO, 1994) The results were considered to be good for this difficult determination. The results obtained using the ISO 15061 IC method (ISO, 2001) indicated that the method is fit for the purpose at the studied levels of bromate concentrations (Table 2.12). However, the results from four laboratories (8, 9, 24 and 31) were not accepted on statistical grounds for the above mentioned reasons. Single statistical outlier results were reported by laboratories 3, 7, 9 and 19. The reproducibility results obtained were used for developing the ISO/DIS 15061 standard (ISO, 2001).

The results obtained for the vast majority of the laboratories carrying out the ISO 15061 IC method were considered to be fit for the purpose. In addition to this method, five alternative methods suitable for trace bromate determinations were also considered, namely on-line IC-ICP-MS, simple on-line column chromatography ICP-MS, IC with chlorpromazine post-column reaction and colorimetric detection, and fluorescence quenching with Carbostyril (with pre-treatment), which are all capable of achieving a bromate detection limit below 1 μg/L. A field method with methylene blue and fluorescence quenching with Carbostyril without sample pre-treatment did not lead to satisfactory results at this level of bromate concentrations.

Table 2.12 Some Bromate results for drinking waters

Sample No.	Sample type/ description	Bromate (μg/L)	Method
1	Non-EC bottled water	26	IC-CD
2	Non-EC bottled water	<0.6	IC-CD
3	Non-EC bottled water	38	IC-CD
4	Non-EC bottled water	<0.6	IC-CD
5	Non-EC bottled water	<0.6	IC-CD
6	Non-EC bottled water	4.9	IC-CD
7	Non-EC bottled water	2.2	IC-CD
8	Non-EC bottled water	<0.6	IC-CD
9	EC bottled water	0.27	FI-ICP-MS
10	EC bottled water	0.21	FI-ICP-MS
11	EC bottled water	0.11	FI-ICP-MS
12	EC bottled water	0.48	FI-ICP-MS
13	EC mineral water	<0.13	FI-ICP-MS
14	EC mineral water	<0.13	FI-ICP-MS
15	EC mineral water	0.85	FI-ICP-MS
16	EC process water	16.0	FI-ICP-MS
17	EC process water	7.4	FI-ICP-MS
18	EC process water	79	FI-ICP-MS
19	Further bottled waters	Mauritius CWM	??
20	Sodium hypochlorite (15%)	1048 mg/L	FI-ICP-MS
21	Water treated with sodium hypochlorite No. 20	15 μg/L	FI-ICP-MS

2.7 TOXICITY, OCCURRENCE AND CURRENT STATUS OF BROMATE IN DRINKING WATERS

Historically bromate has been associated with water treatment as a by-product of such processes as ozonation. However, through the bromate monitoring programmes now in place, evidence has been found that it can also occur in the environment as a result of industrial pollution (e.g., photographic waste) and can affect raw water sources. An example of this has occurred in the UK where levels of bromate have been found in both public and private water sources. The bromate is very stable in the environment and does not readily degrade. Currently the technology and technical expertise for dealing with this type of environmental pollution is in its infancy, and a significant amount of research and development has been undertaken to understand both the technical treatment solutions and the hydrological behaviour mechanisms that could provide long term management options.

The International Agency for Research on Cancer (IARC) and the US Environmental Protection Agency have evaluated the carcinogenicity of bromate in drinking water. Both IARC and US EPA classified this chemical as B2–probable human carcinogen under its current guidelines (US EPA, 1986; IARC, 1990). The cancer weight of evidence classification is based on all routes of exposure. Under its 'Proposed Guidelines for Carcinogen Risk Assessment' (US EPA, 1996), the EPA determined that bromate should be evaluated as a likely human carcinogen by the oral route of exposure.

The US EPA has subsequently published a comprehensive toxicological review of bromate (US EPA, 2001). Studies with rats based on low-dose linear extrapolation, using the time-to-tumour analysis, and using the Monte Carlo analysis to sum the cancer potency estimates for kidney renal tubule tumours, mesotheliomas, and thyroid follicular cell tumours, gave an upper-bound cancer potency estimate for bromate ion of 0.70 per mg/kg day. This potency estimate corresponds to a drinking water unit risk of 2×10^{-5} per µg/L, assuming a daily water consumption of 2 litres/day for a 70-kg adult. Lifetime cancer risks of 10^{-4}, 10^{-5}, and 10^{-6} are associated with bromate concentrations of 5, 0.5, and 0.05 µg/L, respectively. A major source of uncertainty in these estimates is from the interspecies extrapolation of risk from rats to humans.

The acute toxic dose of bromate (expressed as bromate) for a 70-kg individual is estimated at about 3 g (Dreisbach and Robertson, 1987). As a typical person will consume 2 litres of tap water per day, this would correspond to a bromate concentration of 1500 mg/L 'acute concentration'. This is 150 000 times higher than the statutory EC drinking water limit concentration of 10 µg/L (Council Directive, 1998), which can be regarded as a chronic toxicity safe limit.

The important precursor to bromate formation in drinking water is bromide. In the United States, the average bromide concentration in drinking water is estimated to be approximately 100 µg/L (AWWARF, 1997). Only 6.3 µg/L of bromide needs to be quantitatively converted to bromate upon ozonation to exceed the drinking water directive limit of 10 µg/L bromate. Some natural sources of bromine in groundwater are saltwater intrusion and bromide dissolution from sedimentary rocks. Bromate in drinking water is mainly formed from the oxidation of naturally occurring bromide ions. Thus any oxidation process in the presence of a significant concentration of bromide ions can contribute to the formation of bromate (e.g., ozonation of a water containing bromide ions or electrolysis of sodium chloride containing bromide ions in the production of sodium hypochlorite) (Legube *et al.*, 2004). About seven years ago, a sample of sodium hypochlorite that was marketed for water disinfection was submitted to one of the authors (KCT). It contained over 1000 mg/L bromate. Water companies have instituted strict controls over supplied chemicals that are used in water treatment/disinfection processes to ensure absence of significant amounts of bromate and bromide. Table 2.12 gives bromate results for some bottled waters, many of which were found to contain significant levels of bromate. One of the bottled waters listed in Table 2.12 (Sample 3) was previously analysed a few years ago and found to contain 120 µg/L of bromate. All the waters containing bromate were thought to contain bromide derived from seawater intrusion into the ground water aquifer and were subjected to ozonation as a disinfection process. A few years ago, the Coca-Cola soft drinks company, in an attempt to explore the drinking water market, launched a treated bottled water product in the UK under a brand name Dasani. Taste improver calcium chloride containing bromide was added during the treatment process prior to ozonation, thus contributing to bromate formation. Bromate levels as high as 22μg/L were reported in these waters and the product was immediately was removed from the market (*The Guardian*, 2004). The results in Table 2.12 demonstrate the importance of monitoring for bromate in bottled and tap waters whenever ozonation is employed in the water treatment process. Chemicals used in water treatment should also be subjected to bromide and bromate monitoring.

As bromate is stable once generated, attention is being paid to effluents and wastewaters treated by ozonation. Bromide-containing effluents will contribute to the rise of bromate levels in receiving water bodies which are subsequently used as a source for drinking waters. This calls for essential regulation of bromide and bromate in effluents and wastewaters prior to final discharge.

For bromate analysis, ethylenediamine (EDA) is added to the sample in order to convert any hypobromite present into the corresponding bromamines, thus preventing ongoing conversion to bromate. Bromate has been found to be stable in a range of drinking waters over three months using amber glass bottles either with or without EDA (Thompson, 1999).

REFERENCES

Achilli, M. and Romele, L. 1999. *J. Chromatog. A*, **847**, 271–277.

American Water Works Association Research Foundation (1997) Formation and control of brominated ozone by-products. *AWWARF Report* No. 90714.

Charles, L., Pepin, D. and Casetta, B. 1996. *Anal. Chem.*, **68**, 2254.

Council Directive 98/83/EC. 1998. (November 1998), *Official Journal of the European Communities*, **41**, Part 330, 32–54.

Creed, J.T., Magnuson, M.I., Pfaff, J.D. and Brockhoff, C. 1996. *J. Chromatogr. A*, **357**, 74.

Delcomyn, C.A., Weiberg, H.S. and Singer, P.C. 2001. *J. Chromatog. A*, **920**, 213–319.

Diemer, J. and Heumann, K.G. 1997. *Fresenius J. Anal. Chem.*, **357**, 74.

Dreisbach, R. H. and Robertson, W. O. 1987, *Handbook of Poisoning*, Twelfth edition, Appleton and Lange.

Echigo S., Minear R., Yamada H. and Jackson P. 2001. *J. Chromatog. A*, **920**, 205–211.

Elwaer A.E., McLeod C.W., Thompson K.C. and Wiederin D. 1996. *Plasma Source Mass Spectrometry: Developments and Applications*, Royal Society of Chemistry, London, p. 124.

Elwaer A.R. 1999 PhD Thesis, University of Sheffield, UK, Chemistry Department, Elwaer A.R., McLeod C.W. and Thompson K.C. 2000. *Anal. Chem.*, **72**, 5725–5730.

Farrell, S., Joa, J.F. and Pacey, G.E. 1995. *Anal. Chim. Acta*, **313**, 121.

Fletcher I.J. and Hemmings P. 1985. *Analyst*, **110**, 695.

Gahr A., Huber N. and Niessner R. 1998. *Mikrochim. Acta*, **128**, 281.

Gordon, G., Zoshino, K., Themelis, D.G., Wood, D. and Pacey, G.E. 1989. *Anal. Chim. Acta*, **24** 383.

Gordon, G., Bubnis, B., Sweetin, D. and Kuo, C. 1994. *Ozone Sci. Eng.*, **16**, 79.

Guinamant, J.-L., Ingrand, V., Muller, M.C., Noij, Th.H.M., Brandt, A., Bruchet, A., Brosse, C., McLeod, C., Sacher, F., Thompson, K.C., de Swaef, G., Croué, J.P. and Quevauviller, Ph. 2000. Laboratory and field methods for determination of bromate in drinking water, *EUR Report*, EN 19601, European Commission, Brussels, 178, pp.

Hautman, D.P., Munch, D.J., Frebis, C., Wagner, H.P. and Pepich, B.V. 2001. *J. Chromatog. A*, **920**, 221–229.

Ingrand, V., Guinamant, J.-L., Bruchet, A., Brosse, C., Noij, Th.H.M., Brandt, A., Sacher, F., McLeod, C., Elwaer, A.R., Croué, J.P. and Quevauviller, Ph. 2002. Determination of bromate in drinking water: development of laboratory and field methods, *Trends Anal. Chem.*, **21**, 356–365.

International Standards Organization 1990. Water quality – Calibration and evaluation of analytical methods and estimation of performance characteristics, Part 1: Statistical evaluation of the linear calibration function. ISO 8466-1.

International Standards Organization 1994. Accuracy (trueness and precision) of measurement methods and results, Part 2: Basic method for the determination of repeatability and reproducibility of a standard measurement method. ISO 5725-2.

International Standards Organization 2001a. Water quality – Calibration and evaluation of analytical methods and estimation of performance characteristics, Part 2: Calibration strategy for non-linear second-order calibration functions. ISO 8466-2.

International Standards Organization 2001b. Water quality – Determination of dissolved bromate: Method by liquid chromatography of ions. ISO/DIS 15061.

IARC, 1990. *Monographs on the Evaluation of Carcinogenic Risks to Humans*, WHO: Geneva, 1990.

Kurokawa, Y., Maekawa, A. and Takahashi, M. 1990. Toxicity and carcinogenicity of potassium bromate – a new renal carcinogen. *Environ. Health Perspect.* **87**, 309–335.

Legube, B., Parinet, B., Gelinet, K., Berne F. and Croue J. 2004. *Water Research*, **38**, 2185–2195.

Liu, Y., Mou, S. and Heberling S. 2002. *J. Chromatog. A*, **956**, 85–91.

Liu Y. and Mou S. 2004. *Chemosphere*, **55**, 1253–1258.

Quevauviller, P. 1997. EC Workshop on Reference Materials for the Quality Control of Water Analysis, Lisbon, Portugal, June 18–19, 1997.

Mena, M. L. and McLeod, C. W. 1996. *Mikrochim. Acta*, **123**, 103.

Mena, M. L., Morales, A., Cox, A. G., McLeod, C. W. and Quevauviller, P. 1995. *Quim. Anal.*, **14**, 164.

Sanz-Medel, A. (ed.) 1999. *Flow Analysis with Atomic Spectrometric Detectors*, Elsevier.

The Guardian, 2004. March 20.

Thompson, K. C. 1999 Report on the stability of bromate in potable waters and on the interlaboratory trial to test various bromate analysis methods for potable waters. *Contract No SMT4-CT-97-2-2134*, December. (CR258).

US Environmental Protection Agency, 1986. Guidelines for carcinogen risk assessment. Federal Regulation 51(185):33992–34003.

US Environmental Protection Agency, 1991. *EPA Method 300.0*, EPA/600/R93/100.

US Environmental Protection Agency, 1996. Proposed guidelines for carcinogen risk assessment. Federal Regulation 61(79):17960–18011.

US Environmental Protection Agency, 1997. *EPA Method 300.1*, EPA/600/R98/188.

US Environmental Protection Agency, 2001. Toxicological review of bromate, in support of summary information on the integrated risk information system (IRIS), March 2001. CAS No 15541-45-4.

Valcarcel, M. and Luque de Castro, M.D. 1991. *Non-chromatographic Continuous Separation Techniques*, Royal Society of Chemistry, London.

Weinberg, H.S., Delmyn, C.A. and Unnam, V. 2003. *Environ. Sci. Technol.* **37**, 3104–3110.

Wolfis, G. and Brandt, A. 1997. Ontwikkeling van een bepalingsmethode voor bromate in water, SWI 96.213, Nieuwegein.

World Health Organization, 1991. *Revision of the WHO Guidelines for Drinking Water Quality*, WHO, Geneva.

3
Lead Monitoring

Theo van den Hoven and **Nellie Slaats**

Analytical Methods for Drinking Water   Edited by P. Quevauviller and K. C. Thompson
© 2006 John Wiley & Sons, Ltd.

3.1   FACTORS DETERMINING THE LEAD CONCENTRATION IN DRINKING WATER

3.1.1   Sources of Lead in Drinking Water

Lead pipes

Lead pipes are the major source of lead in drinking water. In the past, lead pipes were considered to be a convenient and suitable material for the conveyance of water. Lead is easily formed, cut and jointed, and its flexibility provides resistance to subsidence and frost. The thickness of lead pipe and its resistance to pitting corrosion also made it a desirable and durable material.

In most countries lead pipes are forbidden nowadays and lead pipes are only found in old houses. Lead pipes are encountered almost exclusively in the service pipe and internal plumbing systems.

Plumbing materials

Whilst lead pipes are the main source of high lead concentrations, lead concentrations higher than 10 µg/l can also be observed for properties without any lead pipes. Lead-based solders (for copper plumbing), copper alloys (brasses and bronzes) used mainly for fittings, galvanized steel pipes and uPVC (when stabilized with lead salts) can release lead into drinking water.

Lead based solders (tin/lead solders) contain up to 60 % of lead, which can be released into water through galvanic corrosion. The corrosion rate is increased by high concentrations of chloride and nitrate but is inhibited by sulfate, silicate and orthophosphate. Lead concentrations at the tap depend not only on the corrosion rate but also on the number of leaded joints in the plumbing, the area of solder exposed to water at each joint, and the water usage pattern (Gregory, 1990).

Experiments on the leaching of lead from copper alloy (brasses and bronzes) fittings suggest that lead is prone to be concentrated on the internal surface during machining, leading to the possibility of elevated lead concentrations from new fittings. There is no obvious correlation between the lead content of the alloy (normally between 2.25 % and 5 %) and the tendency for lead to leach.

The zinc lining of galvanized steel pipes can contain up to 1 % lead, whereas steel itself contains much less lead (0.0005 to 0.01 %) (Leroy, 1993). Leaching of lead from galvanized steel depends strongly on the corrosion rate of the material. Zinc lining can be subject to galvanic corrosion, especially in high conductivity waters. This process is also strongly dependent on pH (galvanized steel should not be used for water of a pH under 7.3) and is accelerated by contact with copper materials and high temperatures, as in hot water systems (Wagner, 1992). Orthophosphate and silicate have been demonstrated to be effective at controlling zinc corrosion.

Experience in France shows that lead concentrations from galvanized steel plumbing are normally in the range of <1 to 10 μg/l. However, values between 10 and 25 μg/l can be observed quite frequently. Higher values (up to 100 μg/l or more) are exceptional but only in association with high corrosion of the material, and high iron and zinc concentrations (red waters).

PVC pipes

Unplasticized polyvinyl chloride (uPVC) is a commonly used material for mains and domestic potable water piping. The additives used in uPVC include heat stabilizers to reduce decomposition of the uPVC during manufacture. Stabilizers are often lead salts. It has been shown that leaching of lead can occur, but this seems to be significant only for new uPVC pipes (Packham, 1971; Poels and Dibbets, 1982). In some countries (e.g. France) the application of lead salts as stabilizers is not allowed.

3.1.2 Factors Determining the Lead Concentration in Drinking Water

Lead concentrations at the consumers' tap are mainly determined by the following factors:

- consumer behaviour (e.g. water use pattern, mean inter-use stagnation time);

- water composition (e.g. pH, hardness, orthophosphate (o-PO$_4$) dosing);

- plumbing materials and dimensions.

Consumer behaviour

The *water use pattern* has a major influence on the stagnation time and lead release and thus on lead concentration (e.g. Bailey *et al.*, 1986a). More specifically, the following parameters are of major influence:

- mean inter-use time;
- volume of water drawn;
- flow rate.

Mean inter-use time

WRc performed a detailed study and a statistical assessment of water use in the United Kingdom in relation to the problem of lead monitoring at the consumer's tap (Bailey *et al.*, 1986b). The study covered 100 households in 22 districts in England, Scotland and Wales. The consumption of water, with distinction between potable and non-potable use, and time of use, was recorded for each household during one week. The results of the study are summarized in Table 3.1.

As can be seen in Table 3.1, the mean inter-use stagnation time decreases with increasing numbers of occupants. On average, the inter-use stagnation time is about 30 minutes. This value is in accordance with data observed in independent studies in Germany, France and The Netherlands. The study in France refers to experiments where 30-minute stagnation time samples gave results comparable with composite proportional samples (Randon, 1996). Results from The Netherlands show that composite proportional samples corresponded to 30 minutes' stagnation time in the stagnation curve derived from the lead pipe test (Van den Hoven, 1986). Data from Germany refer to experiments where the average inter-use time has been measured directly, clearly showing the wide spread in mean inter-use stagnation times that can be observed in different households. As lead concentrations rise rapidly in this range of stagnation times, it can be concluded that lead concentrations might vary strongly between households.

Volume of water drawn

The volume of water drawn affects the contact time of the water with plumbing materials and as a result, the amount of metals leaching out of these. In addition, in mixed plumbing systems the volume of water drawn determines which materials affect the

Table 3.1   Inter-use stagnation times for different household sizes (Bailey *et al.*, 1986b)

Household size (persons)	Mean[a] (min)	Standard deviation (min)
1	47	23
2	29	14
3	24	13
4	22	13
5+	18	6

[a] Mean inter-use stagnation time: time between draw for dietetic purposes and the previous draw.

water quality. Therefore, the volume of water drawn affects lead concentrations. On average the volume of water drawn from a tap is 1.2 litres.

Flow rate

Research has shown that the flushing regime for lead pipes has a considerable effect on the lead concentration (Vewin, 1987). If the flow in the pipes is turbulent ($Re >$ 2300) the lead concentration is higher than after flushing with laminar flow. This is probably due to the release of particulate lead. In practice, consumers draw water with an average flow rate of 5 litres/minute, which corresponds to turbulent flow (in pipes of 19 mm diameter, $Re > 5000$).

Water composition

In the case of lead pipes, simple oxidative corrosion of the metal forms a coating of lead carbonate on the inside wall of the pipe. As shown in theoretical and empirical studies, the lead solubility (maximum lead concentration) is a function of water characteristics, mainly pH, alkalinity and temperature, as well as, eventually, orthophosphate concentration (Sheiham and Jackson, 1981; Kuch and Wagner, 1983: Van den Hoven, 1986; Schock, 1989,1990,1994; Wagner, 1992; Leroy, 1993). For a given alkalinity, lead solubility decreases when pH increases. Theoretical lead solubility varies between several mg/l for very soft waters with low pH (alkalinity $<$ 30 mg/l $CaCO_3$ and pH $<$ 6.5) to less than 100 µg/l in waters with alkalinity between 50 and 150 mg/l $CaCO_3$ and pH above 8.

Plumbing dimensions and design

The effect of the dimensions (length and diameter) of lead pipes and other characteristics of domestic plumbing can influence the dissolution of lead:

- the influence of stagnation time on lead concentration varies with pipe diameter. For lead pipes, experimental stagnation curves show that the maximum lead concentration is reached after about 5 to 6 hours for pipes of 10 mm internal diameter but only after several tens of hours for pipes of 50 mm diameter (Kuch and Wagner, 1983). Mass transfer models have been developed for calculating lead concentration for a given stagnation time and equilibrium lead solubility, knowing the lead pipe length and diameter (Kuch and Wagner ,1983; Van den Hoven, 1987);

- the mean inter-use stagnation time is influenced by the configuration of the plumbing system, in particular by the location of the sampling point in the house (relative to other taps, washing machine, toilets, etc.). The situation can be very different between an isolated house and a flat in a collective building;

- when lead is coupled to a dissimilar metal (e.g. copper), galvanic corrosion can occur at a much faster rate, releasing soluble and insoluble corrosion products into the water (Britton and Richards, 1981);

- the environment (room temperature, vibrations, etc.) of lead pipes can also have an impact on lead concentration. Vibrations can be caused by traffic, but also by elevators in apartment buildings or by water hammer in the plumbing system.

3.2   SAMPLING OF LEAD IN DRINKING WATER

3.2.1   Available Sampling Procedures

Sampling of lead in drinking water has to include contributions from all sources and factors influencing the lead concentrations at the tap. Therefore, various sampling techniques with different purposes have been developed and routinely applied. These are listed in the next section.

Tap samples

 (i) *Composite proportional (COMP)*: A consumer operated device is fitted to the drinking-water tap, which splits off a small constant proportion ($\pm 5\%$) of every volume of water drawn for dietetic purposes (during one week);

 (ii) *Fully flushed (FF)*: A sample is taken after prolonged flushing of the tap after flushing at least three plumbing volumes;

 (iii) *Random daytime (RDT)*: During office hours a sampler visits a property at a random time (the choice of the property may also be randomized). A single sample, typically 1 litre, is taken from a drinking water tap without flushing any water from the tap beforehand;

 (iv) *Fixed stagnation time*: After prolonged flushing of the tap, water is allowed to stand in the plumbing system for a defined period after which a sample is taken without flushing the pipe beforehand. A typical fixed stagnation time is 30 minutes (30MS).

 (v) *First draw*: A sample is taken from the drinking water tap in the morning before water has been used anywhere in the house and without flushing the tap beforehand.

Supply area lead level

The lead-pipe test is used to assess the lead level at the consumer's tap. Basically, the lead-pipe test measures the lead concentration in aged lead pipes for selected periods of stagnation. From the stagnation curve the average lead concentration of tap water can be estimated (Van den Hoven, 1987). The lead-pipe test is internationally recognized as being a very useful instrument in determining the effects of remedial actions in decreasing lead solubility in drinking water. In The Netherlands, the government accepts the lead-pipe test for compliance monitoring.

3.2.2 Definition of a 'Representative Sample'

In the Drinking Water Directive 98/83/EC, the parametric value (PV) for lead is 10 µg/l. The parametric value refers to water as it emerges from the customer tap, assessed on the basis of 'representative' monitoring (Note 3). Note 3 is as follows:

> *The values apply to a sample of water intended for human consumption obtained by an adequate sampling method at the tap and taken so as to be representative of a weekly average value ingested by consumers. Where appropriate the sampling and monitoring methods must be applied in a harmonized fashion to be drawn up in accordance with Article 7(4). Member States must take account of the occurrence of peak levels that may cause adverse effects on human health.*

Variations in average weekly lead concentrations at the consumers' tap

The average weekly intake of lead via drinking water is determined by water composition, plumbing system and consumer behaviour. These factors vary considerably, not only between supply zones, properties and individual consumers, but also over time.

The water composition in general varies slowly (seasonally). Although the plumbing system hardly changes over a long period, the influence of vibrations (e.g. by traffic) on the release of lead from service pipes may vary in relatively short periods. These factors determine the pattern of build-up of lead concentration in water inside a lead pipe over time (i.e. the stagnation curve) and the equilibrium lead concentration (saturation or plateau value). Figure 3.1 shows an example of the influence of water characteristics on the stagnation curve.

The water consumption pattern of an individual consumer changes not only seasonally (due to temperature or holidays) but may also vary from day to day, depending, for example, on the number of people at home (including visitors). Furthermore, considerable differences in mean inter-use time between households exist. Therefore, the average weekly intake of lead via drinking water by the individual consumer may vary considerably throughout time. This is illustrated in Figure 3.2, which shows the upper lead stagnation curve of Figure 3.1 between 0 and 90 minutes, being the range of mean inter-use stagnation times typically found.

As shown, a variation of 10 minutes in mean inter-use stagnation time, which is quite normal (Bailey found standard deviations up to 22 minutes, depending on household size), has considerable influence on the average weekly intake of lead via drinking water. Furthermore, this figure shows that by lowering the mean

lead concentration
[μg/l]

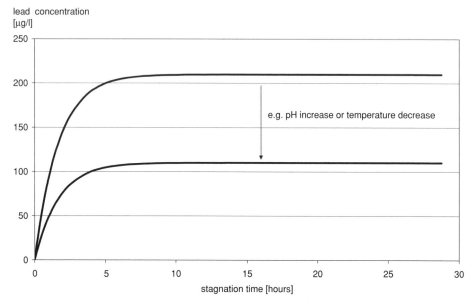

Figure 3.1   Influence of water characteristics on the stagnation curve

lead concentration
[μg/l]

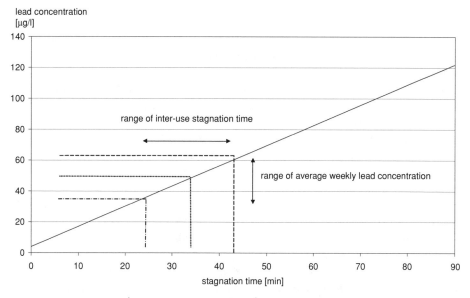

Figure 3.2   Influence of variations in inter-use stagnation time on average weekly lead concentration

lead concentration (µg/l)

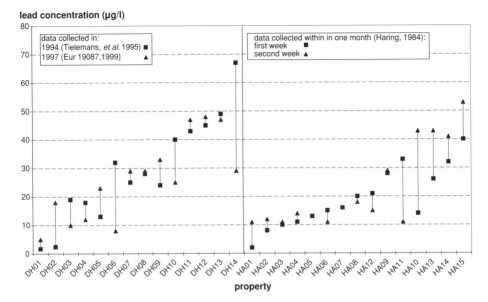

Figure 3.3   Results of duplicate composite proportional samples, showing variations in some properties resulting from variations in consumer behaviour

inter-use stagnation time by flushing before consumption, the average weekly lead concentration can effectively be lowered.

Strong variations in weekly average intake are indeed observed in practice, as can be concluded from two separate studies. One study refers to 15 individual properties (in one supply zone), that were each sampled twice within one month, so the variations in the factors determining the average weekly lead concentration should be small (Haring, 1984). The right hand side of Figure 3.3 gives the results of the first and second composite proportional sample for each property.

The second study refers to 14 individual properties (in one supply zone) that were sampled (composite proportional sampling) in a study in 1994, and were sampled again in the lead monitoring study (Tielemans *et al.*, 1995; EUR19087, 1999). In these properties the plumbing system and household situation were the same and there was no significant change in water quality. The left hand side of Figure 3.3 gives the results of the first and second sample for each property. As can be seen in Figure 3.3, the average weekly concentration of lead in drinking water varies considerably from week to week in some properties, even if two samples are taken one shortly after the other. In about half the properties in each study the concentration is lowest in the first week, in the other half in the second week. This shows that the difference between the two samples in one property cannot be accounted for by water quality change. As the plumbing system remained unchanged, the variation in lead concentration has to be accounted for by variation in consumer behaviour.

Variations of average weekly lead concentrations in a supply zone

At supply zone level, where the water quality may be considered as being approximately uniform, the variation in plumbing systems (both materials and design) and the diversity of household types determines the range of lead levels found at the consumers' tap. In The Netherlands, the average weekly lead concentration, as assessed with composite proportional sampling, was determined in 17 supply zones in the period 1979–1980. In each zone about 50 properties were sampled. Figure 3.4 shows the range of lead concentrations and the median concentration in each of the 17 supply zones. As indicated in this figure, the range of lead concentrations, as determined by proportional sampling, varies widely in some supply zones. For example, in supply zones 4 to 6 the median concentration is well below 10 µg/l, but an individual consumer may still be exposed to an average weekly intake of more than 50 µg/l. On a supply zone level it is therefore necessary to select properties and households representative for that area.

Number of samples

The number of samples needed to get an accurate estimate of the average weekly intake in an area depends on the range of variation of lead levels found in that area and the true level of noncompliance in that area (i.e. the percentage of all properties

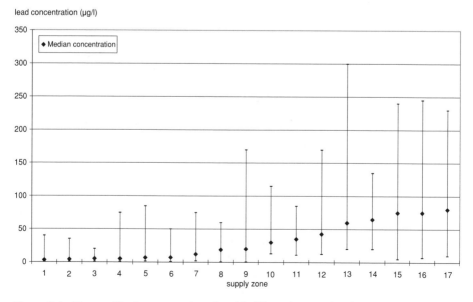

Figure 3.4   Range of lead concentrations found in 17 supply zones in The Netherlands (Haring, 1984)

where lead exceeds the PV). Especially in supply zones with a variation in plumbing systems, the sampling frequency for audit monitoring (DWD98/83/EC, Table B1, Annex II, Common Position) of one sample per year for 50 000 inhabitants is too low to detect the level of excess of the parametric value. If, for instance, the percentage of true noncompliance in an area is 10 %, at least 59 samples from randomly chosen properties are needed to have a 95 % probability of detecting the excess. The number of samples needed increases as the true level of noncompliance decreases (Baggelaar and Van Beek, 1995). The number of samples needed is independent of the size of the supply zone (number of properties) and the sampling procedure used.

Depending on the local situation, the number of samples should be increased, or target monitoring (sampling in properties with lead plumbing or performing lead pipe tests) can be applied in addition to the required audit monitoring. In this way water authorities can take into account the worst case situation (the maximum average weekly intake of lead through drinking water) that might occur in a supply zone.

3.2.3 Representative Sampling at an Individual Consumer's Tap

The composite proportional sample (COMP) procedure is a method that actually aims to collect samples of each draw of water used for dietetic purposes at the monitored tap. This is, therefore, the only procedure that takes into account all variations within one week. Thus, the composite proportional sample should be considered to be the only really representative sample, i.e. representative for the average weekly intake of the consumers sharing the tested tap during the test week.

The composite proportional sample is taken with a consumer operated device fitted to the drinking water tap, which splits off a small constant proportion (≈ 5 %) of every volume of water drawn for dietetic purposes during one week. Figure 3.5 gives a schematic view of a proportional sampling device.

The composite proportional sampling device was developed in the 1970s. In itself, the composite proportional sampling procedure is a long-term test, which is not appropriate for large scale and routine monitoring. Therefore, short-term sampling procedures were developed to give an accurate estimate of the average weekly intake of lead via drinking water, as established with the composite proportional sample.

3.2.4 Lead Analyses in Tap Water

Requirements

With the aim of complying with the parametric value for lead of 10 µg/l, it is important to have satisfactory analytical methods for the detection of lead in drinking water. These methods need to be reviewed on the basis of requirements for the trueness and precision in measuring lead concentrations. Laboratories are allowed to use their

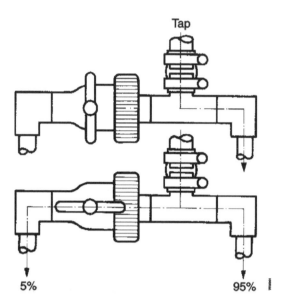

Tap

5%   95%

Figure 3.5 Proportional sampling device. A hose connects the split-off valve and the sample collection bottle, and the discharge of the sample hose should at all times be above water level in the sample bottle, and the air should be able to escape from the sample bottle. In most cases, a 3-litre sample bottle is sufficient for 1 week. A sampler or the consumer has to check that the sample bottle does not overflow and, if necessary, replace the sample bottle with an empty one

own methods, but the results have to be comparable. Table 3.2 gives an overview of the limit, trueness, precision and limit of detection of lead as stated in the DWD.

Sampling and pre-treatment

High variability can be found in the results of lead analyses. This is partly due to limited trueness and precision of analytical methods. Variability in the results of lead analyses also stems from the different pre-treatment methods that are used.

Table 3.2   Required accuracy of lead detection in drinking water

	Limit (μg l^{-1})	Trueness[a] (μg l^{-1})	Precision[b] (μg l^{-1})	LoD[c] (μg l^{-1})	Guideline WHO (μg l^{-1})
Lead Pb	10	1	1	1	10

[a] The closeness of agreement between the average value obtained from a large series of test results and an accepted reference value (ISO 5725-1).
[b] The closeness of agreement between independent test results obtained under stipulated conditions (ISO 5725-1). The precision is computed as the standard deviation.
[c] Limit of detection is either three times within standard deviation of a natural sample containing a low concentration of the compound, or five times the within standard deviation of a blank sample.

Pre-treatment of the sample is especially important if lead particles are present in the sample. To obtain representative results, prescription of representative, reproducible, precise and accurate sampling, pre-treatment and methods of analysis are essential in the sampling procedure.

Analytical techniques

For the determination of lead concentrations in drinking water, the analytical methods are atomic absorption spectrometry – electro-thermal atomization (AAS-ETA or AAS-furnace), inductively coupled plasma with detection by atomic emission spectrometry (ICP-AES) or detection by mass spectrometry (ICP-MS). Laboratories are free to use their own chosen analytical techniques. More attention will be required to achieve the necessary analytical accuracy at the lower limit for lead.

3.3   COMPARISON OF SAMPLING PROCEDURES IN THE FIELD

3.3.1   European Study

The lead sampling procedures described in Section 3.2 were evaluated in a European broad study (EUR19087, 1999). The results of this study are described in this section.

3.3.2   Applied Sampling Procedures

On the basis of the experiences described in Section 3.2, the following sampling procedures were selected for the field experiments:

- composite proportional (COMP) as the reference method;
- 30-minute stagnation time (30MS);
- random daytime (RDT);
- fully flushed (FF).

The 30-minute stagnation time (30MS) was chosen, as it represents the average inter-use stagnation time. Random daytime and fully flushed were added because of their practicality and cost effectiveness. Also, random daytime, when taken during office hours, might be in the range of the average inter-use time. Other sampling methods are very unlikely to give representative results.

For the 30-minute stagnation time procedure, as the internal plumbing system is flushed with three pipe volumes of water before the 30 minutes' stagnation, in a mixed plumbing system (e.g. lead plumbing with copper connection to sampled tap) the water in a 1-litre 30MS sample will have had only limited contact with lead and will therefore have a relatively low lead content. If a larger sample is taken, the lead content will be higher. Therefore, two consecutive 1-litre samples (30MS1, 30MS2) were taken after the stagnation period.

For RDT the best approach seems to be to stay close to the average draw volume, therefore a sample volume of 1 litre was chosen. The sample volume has no effect on the lead content of the FF sample, so a 1-litre sample was chosen.

Although the procedures have already been described in Section 3.2.1, the sampling procedures are clarified below for evaluation in the field test.

Composite proportional (COMP) sample

A consumer-operated device, attached to the tap, collects the composite proportional sample. The composite proportional sampling device is connected to the kitchen tap through a coupling nut or a hose clip. In practice, this might cause problems, as some taps are shaped in a way that makes it very difficult to attach the sampling device (e.g. mixer and spray-type taps). The gap between device and tap should be as short as possible. The device should be connected horizontally.

A hose connects the split-off valve and the sample collection bottle. The hose should go down at least 15 centimetres before bending off horizontally. The discharge from the sample hose should at all times be above the water level in the sample bottle. The air should be able to escape from the sample bottle. In most cases, a 3-litre sample bottle is sufficient for 1 week. A sampler or the consumer has to check that the sample bottle does not overflow and, if necessary, replace the sample bottle with an empty one.

When water for consumption (drinking or cooking) is drawn, the split-off valve should be turned horizontally, thus directing 5 % of the drawn volume to the sample bottle. The valve should be turned vertically when water is drawn for purposes other than consumption (e.g. cleaning, washing hands).

Random daytime sample

The random daytime sample (RDT) has to be taken at a random time during office hours, avoiding the periods of frequent water use (breakfast, lunch and dinner) and the period of overnight stagnation. A professional sampler collects a 1-litre sample, without flushing the tap.

> *NOTE: A sample taken by the consumer cannot be considered a true random daytime sample, as the consumer is likely to take a sample with extreme stagnation time (either a first draw sample or a fully flushed sample).*

Fully flushed sample

The sampler has to estimate the plumbing system volume. The fully flushed (FF) sample is taken after flushing three pipe volumes or 5 minutes (if the plumbing dimensions are not known) at 5 litres/minute. The sampler collects a 1-litre sample.

Thirty minutes' stagnation time

After flushing the system as described before, the water is allowed to stand for 30 minutes. The sampler has to make sure that no water is used from the internal plumbing system during the stagnation period (including alternative taps, toilets and washing machines, as well as the tap that is being sampled). After exactly 30 minutes the first litre (30MS1) and the second litre (30MS2) are drawn.

3.3.3   Characteristics of Test Areas

Test areas have been selected on the basis of:

- water composition (e.g. plumbosolvency, hardness, o-PO$_4$ dosing);
- plumbing materials;
- willingness of water companies and consumers to cooperate.

Although there are numerous different water types to be considered, for the purpose of validation of the protocol the actual lead concentration found in a test area is the most important factor. Three types of area can be distinguished, namely areas with low, medium and high plumbosolvency. A number of properties with comparable water quality (not necessarily the same supply area) is considered as one area. Per area about 30 properties were selected.

With regard to plumbing, the pipe material is the most important factor. Difference is made between lead plumbing and other materials (copper, galvanized steel and plastics). About 50 % of properties selected in each test area should have lead plumbing. Furthermore, the length of the plumbing system will be taken into account. Two categories have been established: less than 20 metres to tap (houses) and more than 30 metres to tap (apartments). Table 3.3 lists the main characteristics of the test areas.

The field tests were performed in eleven areas. The samples from each area were analysed by national laboratories that had proved capable of meeting the demands on analytical capabilities (Section 3.2.4).

Table 3.3   Test-area characteristics

Area	Water composition plumbosolvency	pH range	Remarks
A	low	7.0–7.5	300 mg/l $CaCO_3$ + o-PO_4
B	high	6.9–8.9	200 mg/l $CaCO_3$ upland
C	medium	7.3–7.8	200~250 mg/l $CaCO_3$
D	medium	7.0–8.4	
E	low	7.1–8.9	
F	medium	8.3–8.8	Softened by pellet softening
G	high	7.6–8.4	
H	high	7.1–7.9	
I	medium	8.1–8.4	
J	medium	7.4	
K	low	7.3–8.3	Mix of different water types, partly + o-PO_4

3.3.4   Applied Test Procedures

Figure 3.6 schematically represents the sampling programme performed in each property. As can be seen, the test period in each property was 1 week. On day 0 the composite proportional sampling device was installed, samples were taken (RDT, FF, 30MS1, 30MS2) and the questionnaire was filled out. This questionnaire includes property information (e.g. plumbing type, pipe length, occupants, etc.).

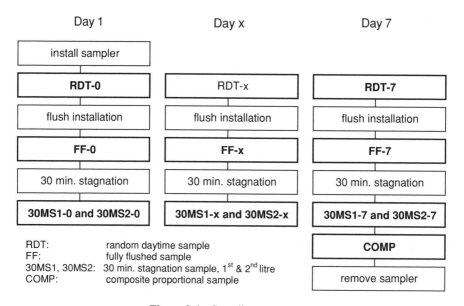

Figure 3.6   Sampling programme

In the middle of the test period (day *x*) samples (RDT, FF, 30MS1, 30MS2) were taken and the sampling device was checked. On day 7 samples were taken (RDT, FF, 30MS1, 30MS2), the COMP sample was collected and the sampling device was removed.

3.3.5 Performance Criteria of Sampling Protocols

Based on the four sample types (RDT, FF, 30MS1 and 30MS2), six sampling procedures were evaluated:

- RDT: random daytime sample;
- FF: fully flushed sample:
- 30MS1: first litre of the 30-minute stagnation sample;
- 30MS2: second litre of the 30-minute stagnation sample;
- 30MSA: the average of first and second litre 30-minute stagnation sample (equals the concentration of a 2-litre, 30-minute stagnation sample);
- av(RDT,FF): the average of the RDT and FF sample taken on the same visit.

The performance of the six procedures is judged on the basis of the following criteria:

- representativeness;
- reproducibility;
- costs, practicality and consumer acceptance.

The sampling methods were evaluated against the composite proportional sample. The composite proportional sample was the only sample type that covered all factors influencing the average weekly intake of the consumer: water quality, plumbing materials, network design and consumer behaviour. As the sample was taken during one week, it was representative for that week only. Results might differ from week to week as a result of changes in water use pattern and water quality. If all factors determining the lead concentration at the tap are constant, the composite proportional sample will give the same result.

By definition, the proportional sampling procedure scores 100 % for the criteria of representativeness and reproducibility. However, this applies only when consumers operate the proportional device correctly. To test whether the consumer has used the device correctly, the volume of the composite proportional sample can be checked. In some test areas the volume of the composite proportional sample was noted and used to calculate the average daily water consumption per person. Figure 3.7 shows the water consumption distribution for these test areas, and Figure 3.8 shows the

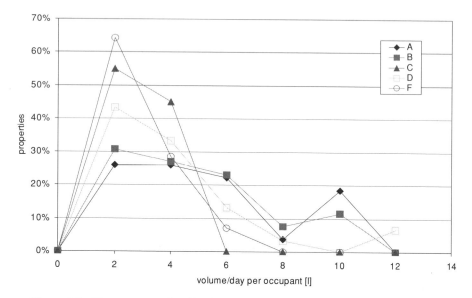

Figure 3.7   Water consumption distribution based on composite proportional sampling

relationship between the mean daily consumption per occupant and the household size.

Figure 3.7 shows that the modal average daily consumption as calculated from the volumes of composite proportional samples was about 2 litres,. This value corresponds with data from other sources. For some households an average daily

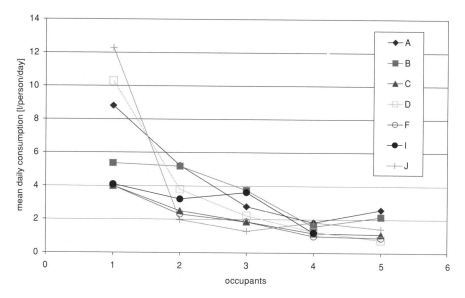

Figure 3.8   Mean daily consumption for different household sizes

consumption of about 10 litres was found. This might be explained by the fact that the occupants were at home during the whole test period. If the occupants had visitors during the test period, this would obviously increase the calculated average daily consumption.

Figure 3.8 shows that the average daily consumption depends on household size. This implies that the average weekly intake of lead by a consumer depends on the number of occupants sharing the same tap.

Both the modal daily consumption per occupant and the dependency on the household size are in accordance with data from other studies. This indicates that, in general, the composite proportional sampling device was operated correctly in the field test. There is some doubt over the apparently high consumption in one-person properties. These high values might stem from real high water use (e.g. tea, visitors, elderly people staying at home all day), but also from improper use of the device. Nevertheless no data have been excluded from the assessment on the basis of this criterion.

3.3.6 Representativeness of the Tested Protocols

The representativeness is judged both on supply area level and for individual properties. Representativeness of the protocols (PROT) is assessed on the basis of the following parameters:

- the relationship between PROT and COMP: both the slope (or x-coefficient) and the correlation coefficient (R^2) of the linear relationship;
- the ratio between PROT and COMP in individual properties;
- the 90 % prediction range of PROT around the parametric value;
- the ability to detect problem properties;
- the average value of tested protocols compared to the average COMP value in a supply zone.

Relationships between results sampling methods

Random daytime sampling (RDT)   Figure 3.9 shows the results of the random daytime samples in all properties, compared to the composite proportional sample. Figure 3.9 indicates that the relationship between RDT and COMP showed considerable variation. In general, RDT seems to overestimate COMP (slope > 1), though for some individual properties RDT underestimates COMP. As a result of the variations the correlation coefficient, R^2, is 0.61.

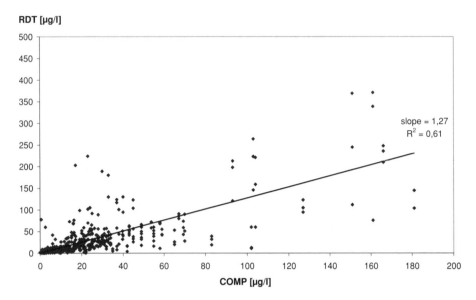

Figure 3.9   Results of RDT sampling in relation to COMP

Fully flushed (FF)   Figure 3.10 shows the FF results, in relation to COMP. As can be seen, the relationship between FF and COMP showed considerable variation. FF generally underestimates COMP. In some cases, however, FF is considerably higher than COMP. This might indicate particle release due to flushing. As a result, R^2 is low: 0.29.

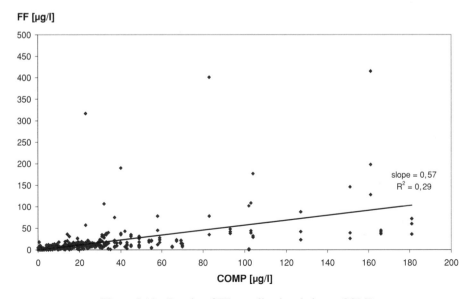

Figure 3.10   Results of FF sampling in relation to COMP

30MS1 [µg/l]

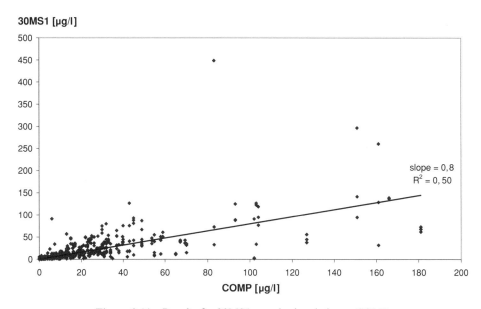

Figure 3.11 Results for 30MS1 samples in relation to COMP

30-Minute stagnation sample: first litre (30MS1) Figure 3.11 shows the results for the 30MS1 sampling procedure. The figure indicates that the relationship between 30MS1 and COMP varied. Generally, 30MS1 somewhat underestimated COMP. The variations resulted in a correlation coefficient, R^2 of 0.5.

30-Minute stagnation sample: second litre (30MS2) Figure 3.12 shows the results of the 30MS2 sampling, versus COMP. This figure indicates that the relationship between 30MS2 and COMP is comparable to the relationship between 30MS1 and COMP: both have a slope of 0.80. The correlation coefficient of 30MS2, however, is somewhat better, 0.56 instead of 0.50 (30MS1).

30-Minute stagnation sample: average of first and second litre (30MSA) Figure 3.13 shows the results of 30MSA sampling, in relation to COMP. The relationship between 30MSA and COMP was about the same as the relationship between the individual samples (30MS1 and 30MS2) and COMP, albeit that R^2 was improved somewhat by averaging 30MS1 and 30MS2. This is a result of averaging-out of extreme values.

Average of random daytime and fully flushed sample (av(RDT,FF)) Figure 3.14 shows the results of av(RDT,FF), in relation to COMP. As shown in the figure, averaging RDT and FF (av(RDT,FF)) resulted, in general, in an underestimation of COMP (slope = 0.92). The correlation of the FF samples to COMP (R2FF = 0.29) influences the correlation coefficient of av(RDT,FF). Consequently, R^2 of av(RDT, FF) is 0.63, which is somewhat less than R^2 of RDT (0.61).

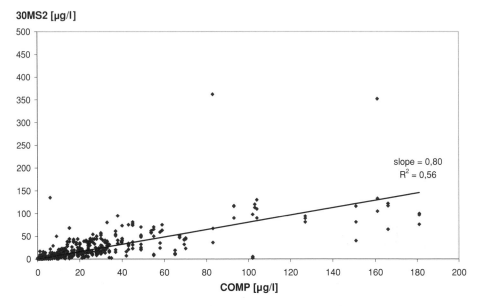

Figure 3.12 Results of 30MS2 sampling in relation to COMP

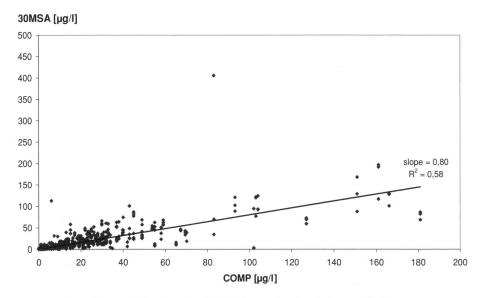

Figure 3.13 Results of 30MSA sampling in relation to COMP

av(RDT,FF) [µg/l]

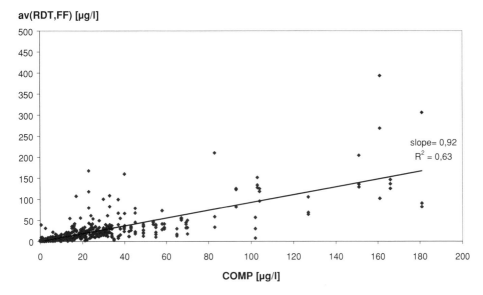

Figure 3.14 Results of av(RDT,FF) in relation to COMP

In summary, all tested sampling procedures show a linear relationship with the composite proportional sample, albeit that the correlation is poor. RDT and the 30-minute stagnation samples, 30MS1, 30MS2 and 30MSA show the best correlation ($R^2 \cong 0.5$–0.6). RDT however, generally seems to overestimate COMP (slope > 1), whereas 30MS somewhat underestimates COMP (slope > 1). FF clearly shows the poorest relationship to COMP: $R^2 = 0.29$ and the slope is 0.57.

Ratio between the tested protocols and the composite proportional sample

The ratio between the result obtained by the tested protocol and the result of the composite proportional sample is another way to express the representativeness of the sampling method. Before showing the results, the approach used is explained:

Ratio between PROT and COMP   Ideally, the ratio between the lead values obtained by the tested protocol (PROT) and the composite proportional sample (COMP) should be unity, or at least constant over a wide concentration range. To determine the variation in the ratio between PROT and COMP, the average ratio is calculated over both the combined test areas (total, all results) and the individual test areas (A–K). The 95 % prediction range of the average ratio is:

$$\text{average} \pm 1.96 \, \frac{\sigma}{\sqrt{n}}$$

where σ = standard deviation of ratio and n = number of samples.

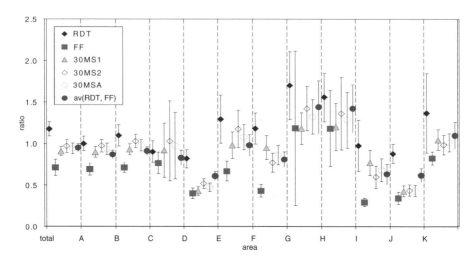

Figure 3.15   95 % prediction range of average ratio between PROT and COMP, for 0<COMP< 200 µg/l

A narrow prediction range indicates that the ratio is fairly constant over the concentration range involved.

Example: The average ratio between RDT and COMP samples of 60 samples taken in an area is 1.24, with a standard deviation of 1.05. With a 95 % probability the true average ratio is in the range of 1.24 ± 0.26.

The 95-% prediction range of the average ratio between the tested protocols and COMP was calculated for all test areas in the ranges 0–200 µg/l, 0–50 µg/l (the former parametric value), 0–25 µg/l (the interim PV) and 0–10 µg/l. The prediction ranges were calculated on the basis of individual samples (i.e. not averaging the three results from each property).

Figure 3.15 shows the 95 % prediction ranges of the average ratios, in the average weekly intake range of 0–200 µg/l (as determined by COMP). It shows that the average ratios between the tested protocols varied between test areas. Furthermore, the width of the prediction range (shown as bars in the figure) varied between areas. Generally however, the width of the prediction range hardly varied between the tested protocols (total, all areas).

The average ratio for RDT was generally higher than 1, whilst the ratio between FF and COMP was generally less than 1. In areas G and H, the average ratio of FF was greater than 1, and the prediction range was relatively wide. This may indicate release of particles during flushing.

The 30MS samples show comparable ratios and prediction ranges, generally somewhat less than 1. In areas D, I and J the average ratio was considerably less than 1 (0.5–0.7).

Figure 3.16 shows the 95 % prediction ranges of the average ratios, in the COMP range of 0–50 µg/l. Generally, the results were comparable to the results for the

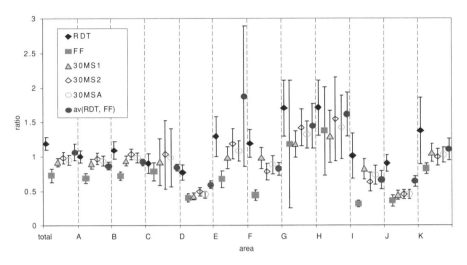

Figure 3.16 95 % prediction range of ratios between PROT and COMP, for 0<COMP<50 µg/l

COMP range of 0–200 µg/l. As the range of 0–50 µg/l included fewer samples, the 95-% prediction ranges for the average ratio were somewhat wider.

Figure 3.17 shows the 95-% prediction ranges of the average ratios, in the COMP range of 0–25 µg/l. As can be seen, the average ratios in the COMP range between 0 and 25 µg/l are comparable to the ratios found in the full range (0–200 µg/l).

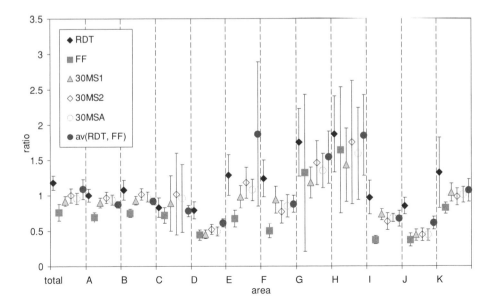

Figure 3.17 95 % prediction range of ratios between PROT and COMP, for 0<COMP<25 µg/l

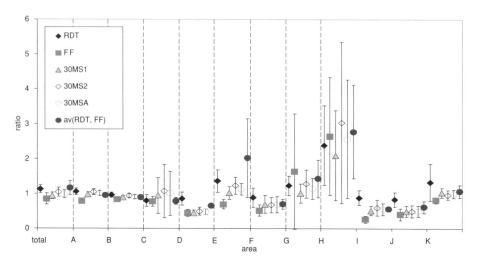

Figure 3.18   95 % prediction range of ratios between PROT and COMP, for 0<COMP<10 µg/l

Finally, Figure 3.18 shows the 95-% prediction ranges of the average ratios, for the COMP range of 0–10 µg/l. The figure indicates that in general, the average ratio between the tested protocols and COMP in the range of 0–10 µg/l is comparable to the average ratio in the full range of concentrations. In some areas, however, the 95-% prediction range seems very wide. This is due to the fact that in these areas only a few properties were found with lead concentrations (in COMP) below 10 µg/l.

Summarizing, assessing the performance of the selected protocol by calculating the ratio between results from the protocols and results from the composite proportional sample shows that RDT, 30MS1, 30MS2 and 30MSA performed best, i.e. the ratios were close to 1 and the 95-% prediction ranges were narrow in most test areas. FF generally underestimates COMP (ratio $\ll$ 1). The average of RDT and FF does not give additional information.

The 90-% prediction range of the tested protocols   The prediction range of a protocol reflects the accuracy of that protocol in predicting the value of the composite proportional sample. Therefore, the 90-% prediction range is applied to assess the representativeness of the tested protocols.

The method applied to determine the 90 % prediction range, can be explained as follows:

The trueness and precision for the prediction of COMP by the tested protocol can be expressed by the 90-% prediction range. In this way the average ratio between the tested protocol and COMP is taken into account, along with the variability or reproducibility of the protocol. The reproducibility is expressed as the relative range.

The 90-% prediction range is calculated as follows:

90-% prediction range =

(PROT/average ratio $\pm$ $^1/_2$ 90 percentile of relative range * PROT)

where average ratio = average ratio between PROT and COMP, and 90 percentile of relative range = 90th percentile of relative range.

Example: The average ratio between RDT and COMP is 1.1, and the 90th-percentile of the relative range is 1.6 for 5 < COMP < 15 μg/l. If RDT is 10 μg/l, the 90 % prediction range for COMP is 9 $\pm$ 8 μg/l.

The 90 % prediction ranges have been calculated for concentrations of the tested protocols around 10, 25 and 50 μg/l. They were calculated on the basis of single samples taken at a property.

Figures 3.19 to 3.21 show the 90 % prediction range of the tested protocols around 10 μg/l, 25 μg/l and 50 μg/l, respectively. These figures include data from all test areas. As shown in Figure 3.19, the 90 % prediction ranges vary between protocols. For example if RDT is 10 μg/l, the range of predicted COMP will be 9 $\pm$ 8 μg/l, with a 90 % probability. The FF and 30MS samples show comparable prediction ranges. The 30MSA sample shows the best prediction range: 10 $\pm$ 4 μg/l.

At around 25 μg/l, the 90 % prediction ranges became much wider. If RDT is 25 μg/l, the range of predicted COMP was 22 $\pm$ 23 μg/l. The 90 % prediction range of FF at this concentration was 33 $\pm$ 14 μg/l. This range was narrower than for RDT,

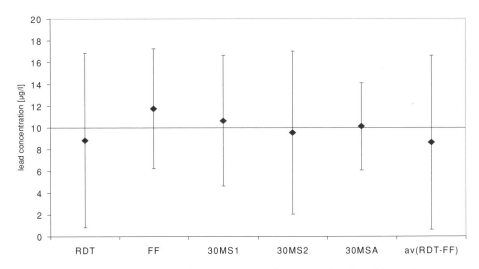

Figure 3.19 90 % prediction range around the parametric value of 10 μg/l

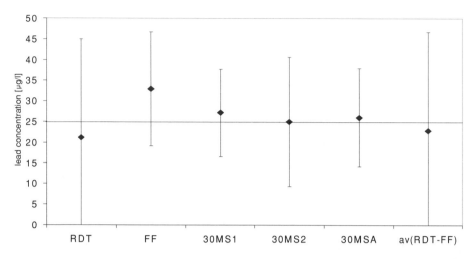

Figure 3.20   90 % prediction range around the interim parametric value of 25 µg/l

on average FF however tends to underestimate COMP. The 30MS samples show the best prediction: between 26 $\pm$ 10 µg/l (30MSA) and 25 $\pm$ 15 µg/l (30MS2).

As Figure 3.21 indicates, all tested protocols showed wide prediction ranges around 50 µg/l. For example if FF was 50 µg/l, the 90 % prediction range of COMP was 73 $\pm$ 74 µg/l. Again 30MSA gave the most narrow prediction interval: 52 $\pm$ 27 µg/l.

Summarizing, 30MSA gives the most accurate reflection of the weekly average concentration, as determined by composite proportional sampling.

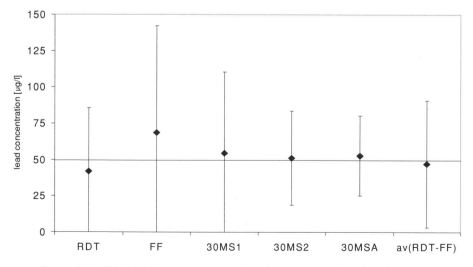

Figure 3.21   90 % prediction range around the former parametric value of 50 µg/l.

3.3.7 Reproducibility of the Tested Protocols

Reproducibility

The reproducibility of the test procedures is expressed as the coefficient of variation, or relative range, of the three samples of one type taken in one property:

$$\text{Relative range} = (\text{max} - \text{min})/\text{mean}$$

Ideally, the relative range is 0 (max = min). The value of the relative range may differ between properties and test areas. Therefore the frequency distribution of relative ranges has to be calculated. The cumulative relative frequency of the relative ranges of the protocols shows the difference in reproducibility of the protocols. The relative range, furthermore, may depend on the lead concentration.

Example: The 90th-percentile of the relative range of PROT is 0.4 in the range of COMP between 5 and 10 μg/l. If the result of PROT is 10 μg/l, we can assume with 90 % probability that PROT is between 8 and 12 μg/l.

Figure 3.22 shows the relative cumulative frequency distribution of the relative range of results of three samples in one property, for all procedures. As shown, the RDT samples exhibit the widest relative range of results. This can be explained by the fact that the stagnation time is not controlled for the RDT sample, whereas stagnation time is controlled for both the FF and 30MS samples. Still, the relative ranges of all procedures seem relatively wide. If, however, we consider the wide ranges of results for composite proportional samples, the reproducibility of FF and

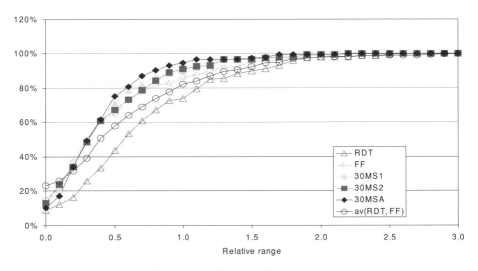

Figure 3.22   Relative range of results of three samples in one property

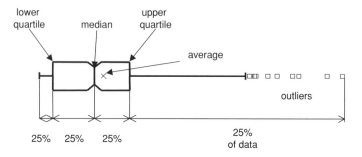

Figure 3.23 Box and whisker plot

30MS is comparable to the reproducibility of the reference procedure (COMP). This can be explained by the fact that FF and 30MS results are not influenced by consumer behaviour.

Box and Whisker plots

Frequency distributions can also be presented in so called 'box and whisker' plots (Figure 3.23). These plots show the relevant characteristics of the frequency distribution: lower quartile, median, upper quartile and outliers.

Example: If the median is 0.4, for 50 % of all samples the relative range is less than 0.4.

Figure 3.24 shows the box and whisker plot of the relative ranges for lead concentrations (as determined by COMP) in the full data range 0–200 µg/l.

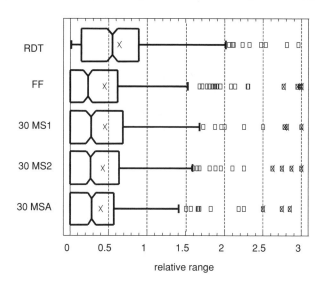

Figure 3.24   Box and whisker plot of the relative range for the full data range (289 properties)

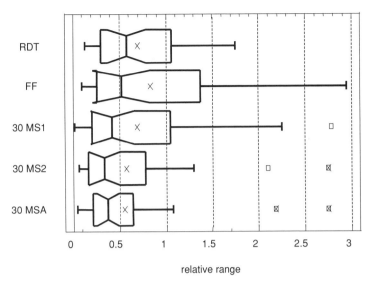

Figure 3.25 Box and whisker plot of the relative range for lead concentrations between 35 and 200 µg/l (32 properties)

As shown in this figure, in all properties RDT shows variation (relative range >0). This is due to the fact that the stagnation time of these samples is variable and not known. In at least 25 % of properties, FF and 30MS samples do not vary across the three sampling days. In this range (0–200 µg/l) the reproducibility of 30MS and FF samples is comparable.

Figure 3.25 shows the box and whisker plot for the concentration range of 35 to 200 µg/l. The range includes 32 properties. The figure shows that the relative ranges of all protocols at high concentration (between 35 and 200 µg/l) are higher than the relative ranges for the full concentration range, i.e. the variability increases with concentration. The outliers of the relative range in the concentration range between 0 and 200 µg/l are accounted for in the relative ranges found in properties with lead concentrations above 35 µg/l.

Figure 3.26 shows the box and whisker plot for the concentration range of 15 to 35 µg/l, around the interim PV of 25 µg/l. This range includes 64 properties. As shown in the figure, the relative ranges of all protocols are less for properties with lead concentrations in the range of 15 to 35 µg/l, than in properties with high lead concentrations. The relative ranges, and therefore the reproducibility, for the FF and 30MS samples are better than for RDT.

Finally, Figure 3.27 shows the box and whisker plot for the concentration range of 5 to 15 µg/l, around the PV of 10 µg/l. This range includes 68 properties. As the figure indicates, in this concentration range the relative ranges of FF and 30MS samples are comparable, albeit that 30MSA samples (the average of 30MS1 and 30MS2) seem to perform somewhat better in terms of reproducibility. Still, the median value

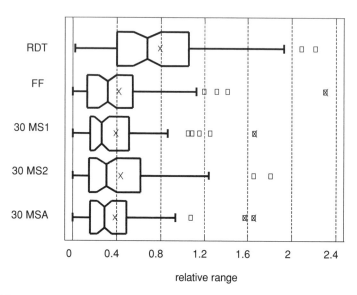

Figure 3.26   Box and whisker plot of the relative range for lead concentrations between 15 and 35 μg/l (64 properties)

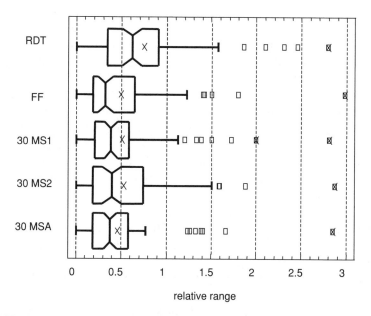

Figure 3.27   Box and whisker plot of the relative range for lead concentrations between 5 and 15 μg/l (68 properties)

for the relative range of these procedures is about 0.4. This means that for 50 % of the tested properties, the results of three samples vary between 8 and 12 µg/l, if the average value is 10 µg/l. In this concentration range, the median relative range of RDT is about 0.6. Consequently, in 50 % of the tested properties the RDT samples vary between 7 and 13 µg/l, at an average RDT of 10 µg/l.

3.3.8 Costs, Practicality and Consumer Acceptance

Costs

Because of the different tariffs in different countries, it is not possible to compare directly the costs of the different protocols. Therefore, Table 3.4 gives a comparison of time needed for taking the samples according to the different procedures, not taking into account travelling time to the consumer. The write-off of the composite proportional sampling device is about 15 Euro per property sampled. The time range is chosen to take into account the probability that a procedure fails (e.g. the composite proportional sample overflows) and the sample has to be taken again. The time for COMP includes consumer information. The times are based on experience from the field tests.

Example of monitoring costs: Under the following assumptions, we can calculate costs for the different monitoring protocols:

- cost for manpower (sampler, including the use of a car): 75 Euro/hour;
- average travel time between properties: 15 minutes;
- analysis costs (including consumables): 30 Euro/sample;
- write-off of sampling device: 15 Euro/property.

Table 3.4 Time required for sampling for different procedures

Procedure	Time needed by sampler	Practicality	Consumer acceptance
COMP	60–75 min[a]	Poor	Poor
RDT	5–10 min	Good	Good
FF	10–15 min	Good	Good
30MS[b]	45–60 min	Moderate	Moderate

[a] At least two visits to one property: one to install the sampling device, one to collect the sample and sampling device.
[b] Two samples need to be analysed.

Using the times given in Table 3.4, this results in the following costs:

- COMP: 158–176 Euro

- RDT: 55–61 Euro

- FF: 61–68 Euro

- 30 MS: 105–124 Euro

This example shows that the differences in monitoring costs are considerable. The composite flow proportional sample, as expected, is the most expensive. For the costs of one COMP sample, three properties can be sampled using RDT! Obviously the 30-minute stagnation time makes 30MS protocols expensive.

Practicality

Practicality covers several aspects of the procedure, such as is the procedure easily applicable, are skilled samplers needed, does the procedure need specific tools, etc. A practical method is easily applied (score: good), an impractical method needs more attention (score: poor).

Consumer acceptance

Consumer acceptance is a very important factor. It might take a lot of time to find enough properties where consumers would be willing to cooperate, if the sampling procedure bothers consumers too much. This is obvious in the case of the composite proportional sample, but consumers might also object to a sampler waiting for 30 minutes in their property to take a stagnation sample.

Table 3.4 summarizes the evaluation of costs (time), practicality and consumer acceptance.

3.3.9 Final Evaluation of Sampling Procedures

According to the Drinking Water Directive, lead monitoring at the tap should be based on 'representative sampling' at the consumer's tap. The lead value determined by a monitoring protocol should be very close to the true average weekly intake. This approach ensures the safety of individual consumers. The sampling method should be 'representative' and accurate.

Five sampling procedures are evaluated on the basis of representativeness (i.e. the accuracy in determining the weekly average intake and the ability to detect problem properties), reproducibility and cost effectiveness, practicality and consumer acceptance.

Random daytime sampling (RDT) is defined as a sample taken at the consumers' tap at a random, unannounced, time during office hours. At a composite COMP lead level of 10 µg/l, the 90% prediction range of RDT is 9 ± 8 µg/l. Nevertheless, in the European study, RDT enables detection of 83% of properties where the lead concentration of the proportional sample exceeds 10 µg/l (problem properties under the Drinking Water Directive). The number of falsely detected properties amounts to 10%. The reproducibility of RDT sampling is poor (the median relative range is 0.6 at lead levels around 10 µg/l). In terms of costs, practicality and consumer acceptance, RDT is the most favourable protocol.

Fully flushed sampling (FF) is defined as a sample taken at the consumers' tap after flushing the plumbing system for at least three pipe volumes. The 90% prediction range of FF at a COMP level of 10 µg/l is 12 ± 6 µg/l. Furthermore FF enables detection of only 45% of problem properties, whereas it results in 4% false positives. FF is very cost effective, practical and acceptable to consumers.

30-Minute stagnation time sampling (30MS) is defined as a sample taken at the consumer's tap after flushing the plumbing system for at least three pipe volumes and allowing the water to stand for 30 minutes. In this study, three types of 30MS sample have been evaluated: the first litre sample (30MS1), the second litre sample (30MS2) and the average of 30MS1 and 30MS2, 30MSA. These procedures perform comparably, although 30MSA shows somewhat better representativeness and reproducibility. The accuracy of 30MSA is the best of the tested protocols. At a COMP lead concentration of 10 µg/l, the range of 30MSA is 10 ± 4 µg/l. The 30MS samples are capable of detecting 76% of problem properties, whereas the amount of false positives is 6%. In terms of cost effectiveness, practicality and consumer acceptance, 30MS scores lowest of the tested protocols, because of the time involved.

The unexpectedly good performance of RDT sampling can be explained by the fact that, in general, it seems to overestimate the average weekly intake, as determined by COMP. Apparently, RDT sampling as defined in this study (samples taken unannounced, during office hours, by a professional sampler) relates to a stagnation time close to or higher than the actual average inter-use stagnation time. The RDT sample contains history of water use at the tap shortly before the sample was taken. Stated otherwise, unlike FF and 30MS, RDT, to some extent accounts for the water consumption pattern of the consumer. In terms of reproducibility 30MS and FF sampling perform best. This can be explained by the fact that both protocols reflect water composition and household installation, but not the variable behaviour of the consumer, which does influence the RDT result. Despite the differences in performance as to representativeness for individual properties, all procedures show the same trend in lead levels found at a distribution area level.

3.3.10   Experience with the Monitoring Protocol in France

Following the outcome of the European project for developing a new protocol for the monitoring of lead in drinking water, field experiments were carried out in France to test and develop practical tools for assessing compliance/noncompliance for lead (Baron, 2001). Experiments were carried out in five supply areas in France, each supply area being a geographical unit supplied by a uniform water quality. In each area a random selection of at least 60 addresses was made. In each property three samples were taken at the kitchen cold water taps using the protocols as described in the European study on lead monitoring and as described before (EUR19087, 1999):

• RDT sample;

• fully flushed sample;

• 30 MS.

No composite proportional sample was taken.

The results from the measurements broadly confirmed the conclusions of the European study. At zone level, RDT or 30MS samples taken in a sufficient number of properties gave almost identical results. RDT is slightly more severe but, above all, it is more practical and acceptable to the consumer.

At individual level (one consumer tap), the French study showed that RDT was not sufficiently reproducible for the assessment of the average concentration based on a single sample. The 30-MS (2l) protocol is more reproducible and representative and is to be preferred in this situation, because with the 30-MS protocol the sampling conditions can be fully controlled by the sampler.

Just as in the European study, FF sampling seemed not to be representative of the average concentration, and only gave an indication of the minimum lead concentration at the tap.

3.4   FIT FOR PURPOSE LEAD MONITORING PROTOCOLS

3.4.1   The Requirements for Sampling and Monitoring Lead in Accordance with the DWD 98/83/EC

Annex I of Council Directive 98/83/EC on the quality of water intended for human consumption has in part B – chemical parameters – entries for the parameters lead (PV of 10 µg/l), copper (PV of 2 mg/l) and nickel (PV of 20 µg/l). There is a note (Note 3) added to the parameters lead, copper and nickel and also a note (Note 4) to the lead parameter. These notes read as follows:

Note 3:

The values apply to a sample of water intended for human consumption obtained by an adequate sampling method at the tap and taken so as to be representative of a weekly average value ingested by consumers. Where appropriate the sampling and monitoring methods must be applied in a harmonised fashion to be drawn up in accordance with Article 7(4). Member States must take account of the occurrence of peak levels that may cause adverse effects on human health.

Note 4:

For water referred to in Article 6(1)(a), (b) and (d), the value must be met at the latest, 15 calendar years after the entry into force of this Directive. The parametric values for lead from five years after the entry into force of this Directive until 15 years after its entry into force is 25 µg/l.

Article 6 specifies the point of compliance:

1. The parametric values set in accordance with Article 5 shall be complied with:
   (a) In the case of water supplied from a distribution network, at the point, within premises or an establishment, at which it emerges from the taps that are normally used for human consumption.

2. In the case of water covered by paragraph 1(a), Member States shall be deemed to have fulfilled their obligations under this Article and under Article 4 and 8(2) where it can be established that non-compliance with the parametric values set in accordance with Article 5 is due to the domestic distribution system or the maintenance thereof except in premises and establishments where water is supplied to the public, such as schools, hospitals and restaurants.

3. Where paragraph 2 applies and there is a risk that water covered by paragraph 1(a) would not comply with the parametric values established in accordance with Article 5, Member States shall nevertheless ensure that:

   (a) appropriate measures are taken to reduce or eliminate the risk of noncompliance with the parametric values, such as advising property owners of any possible remedial action they could take, and/or other measures, such as appropriate treatment techniques, are taken to change the nature or properties of the water before it is supplied so as to reduce or eliminate the risk of the water not complying with the parametric values after supply; and

   (b) the consumers concerned are duly informed and advised of any possible additional remedial action that they should take.

3.4.2   Sampling and Monitoring Strategy

To give more information on the sampling of the metals according to the DWD 98/83/EC, a decision from the commission is under discussion with the member states. The current proposal, which is outlined hereunder, may be modified further to the ongoing negotiations.

Audit monitoring

General requirements   The purpose of audit monitoring is to provide the information necessary to determine whether or not all of the directive's parametric values are being complied with. All parameters set in accordance with Article 5(2) and (3) must be subject to audit monitoring unless it can be established by the competent authorities, for a period of time to be determined by them, that a parameter is not likely to be present in a given supply in concentrations that could risk of a breach of the relevant parametric value.

Monitoring of lead, copper and nickel

Harmonized method: The method to be used for monitoring in supply zones is the method of random sampling during the day (see Note 1, below). Monitoring must be carried out at the supply tap and at frequencies provided for the audit monitoring.

Alternative method: The member states may use the fixed stagnation time sampling method (see Note 2, below), which takes better account of the local or national situation, provided that in the supply zones, it does not lead to fewer breaches of the parametric values than would be the case using the harmonised method.
   Where the alternative method is used, the member states will supply the commission with the appropriate information regarding its implementation (including the stagnation time used) and the justification.

Additional monitoring: In order to increase consumer health protection and improve knowledge about exposure to lead, copper and nickel through drinking water, the member states are urged to increase monitoring and sampling in accordance with the Community guidelines on the monitoring of lead, copper and nickel (see Note 3, below).

Notes:

(1) Random monitoring during the day is defined as taking a sample of water directly from the tap that is usually used for consumption (without taking a sample from, flushing or cleaning the tap before the sample is taken) at a randomly chosen time during the day (during 'normal' working hours).

(2) Monitoring using the fixed stagnation time is defined as emptying and refilling the installation, taking no water from the system for a fixed amount of time and then sampling directly from the tap that is usually used for consumption.

(3) Community guidelines for the monitoring of lead, copper and nickel in accordance with the requirements of Council Directive 98/83/EC on the quality of water intended for human consumption.

3.4.3 Lead Monitoring Purposes

General applications

Monitoring of lead may serve the following applications:

- statutory monitoring in order to check compliance with the Council Directive and national regulations;

- zone assessment;

- assessing/predicting the effect of measures taken to reduce lead in drinking water, such as adjustment of water composition at the treatment facility;

- consumer information on the actual lead intake via drinking water. In case of exceedance of the PV, the monitoring protocol should be able to indicate who is responsible for taking action.

Statutory monitoring   The Drinking Water Directive has the following requirement with respect to representativeness of the monitoring of lead in drinking water:

> The value applies to a sample of water intended for human consumption obtained by an adequate sampling method at the tap and taken so as to be representative of a weekly average value ingested by consumers. Where appropriate the sampling and monitoring methods must be applied in a harmonized fashion to be drawn up in accordance with Article 7(4). Member States must take account of the occurrence of peak levels that may cause adverse effects on human health' (Note 3, part B, Annex I).

On the basis of this study either RDT sampling, as defined in this study, or 30MS are appropriate protocols for statutory monitoring purposes.

Zone assessment   A sufficient number of samples needs to be taken in order to provide statistically valid information on the lead concentrations within a supply zone. The minimum sampling frequencies given in the directive are insufficient in the case of lead. Typically, at least 20 properties should be sampled, whichever sampling method is used. For small supply systems fewer samples may be appropriate, depending on local circumstances.

RDT or 30MS sampling are appropriate for identifying areas that require priority action to reduce lead levels. Previous studies show that the lead pipe test (pipe rigs at the treatment facility) can also be suitable for this purpose.

Assessing/predicting the effect of measures   A distinction should be made between measures taken at the treatment facility and measures taken at specific properties. To evaluate the effect of measures taken at the treatment facility (pH increase, orthophosphate dosing, etc.), both the RDT sampling procedure and the lead pipe test are appropriate. For prediction purposes the lead pipe test is most convenient.

Measures for individual houses consist of lead pipe replacement and flushing before drawing water for consumption. The effect of the first measure can be established using 30-minute stagnation-time sampling and proportional sampling. To assess the effectiveness of flushing, the fully flushed protocol can be applied.

Consumer information   To give the consumer an accurate, and repeatable, value for the average weekly lead concentration, the best approach is 30MS sampling. If, however, the objective is simply to assess compliance or noncompliance, either RDT or 30MS samples can be used. For specific purposes the composite proportional sampling method can be utilized. Identifying causes of observed exceedance of the PV for lead, and thus of responsibility for taking action, should be achieved by 30-minute-stagnation-time samples. After the stagnation period, a number of consecutive 1-litre samples should be taken, corresponding to the dimensions of the service pipes and the house installation.

Special applications

A property where the average weekly lead concentration exceeds the parametric value is considered to be a 'problem property'. The ability of a protocol to detect such properties can be assessed as follows.

The ability to detect problem properties   The *ability of a protocol to detect problem properties* can be expressed as the percentage of 'positives' during the tests. A test is considered positive if both the protocol (PROT) and the reference (COMP) give a value above the parametric value (PV). The *percentage of positives* is the number of properties where both PROT and COMP exceed the PV, divided by the number of properties where COMP exceeds the PV, or:

$$\text{positives [\%]} = (\text{COMP and PROT} > \text{PV})/(\text{COMP} > \text{PV})^* 100\%$$

The protocol should give a realistic estimate of the problems in an area, in order to be used as an effective decision tool. Furthermore the results of the protocol should not

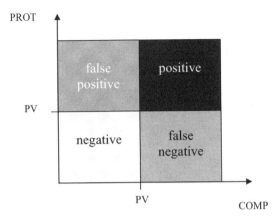

Figure 3.28 Definition of positives and false positives

unnecessarily worry consumers. In other words, the percentage of 'false positives', properties where PROT exceeds the PV, whilst COMP is less than the PV should be low. The *percentage of false positives* is the number of false positives divided by the total number of positives, or:

$$\text{false positives [\%]} = (\text{PROT} >, \text{COMP} < \text{PV})/(\text{PROT} > \text{PV})^*100\,\%$$

Figure 3.28 illustrates the definitions mentioned above.

The *false negative* in Figure 3.28 indicates the percentage of *not detected* problem properties. *Negative* indicates the percentage of properties where the lead concentration is *below* the parametric value. Ideally, the percentage of positives should be 100 % and the percentage of false positives should be close to 0 %.

Figure 3.29 shows the ability of the tested protocols to identify problem properties for the combined test area. All tested protocols are able, to a certain extent, to identify problem properties. The failure to identify a problem property or the false identification of a property as a problem property is likely to be caused by characteristics of the plumbing system.

About 80 % of the properties that are not detected by the protocols have lead service pipes and more than 5 metres of non-lead internal plumbing (copper, galvanized steel or plastic). Also the average weekly lead concentration in these properties is generally low to moderate (10–20 µg/l). In this type of property a large volume of water stands in the household installation. Depending on the design of the installation, the number of users who share the household installation and the service pipe, a volume of water that has stood in the lead service pipe for a longer period reaches the consumers' tap at a given moment. Random daytime sampling has at least a chance of detecting this effect. Fully flushed and 30-minute stagnation-time samples tend to overlook this effect because they are based on a completely flushed system.

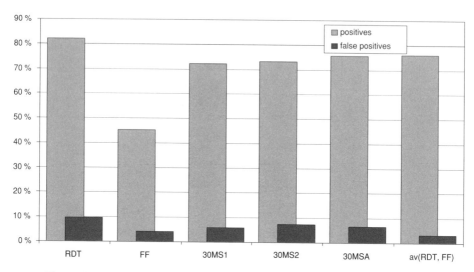

Figure 3.29 Identification of problem properties at a parametric value of 10 µg/l

In this case 30MS sampling would only be able to detect lead concentrations above 10 µg/l by taking a very large sample volume.

Figure 3.30 shows the lead concentration distribution in undetected problem properties for the tested protocols.

On the other hand, properties falsely identified as problem properties have plumbing systems similar to undetected problem properties. Again 80 % of these properties have lead service pipes, and about 20 % have lead plumbing. These properties are

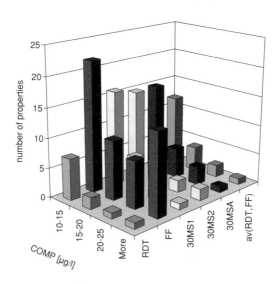

Figure 3.30 Lead concentration distribution in undetected problem properties

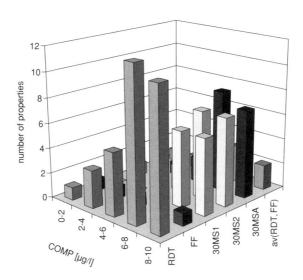

Figure 3.31 Lead concentration distribution in falsely identified problem properties

potential problem properties, and here the consumer behaviour is the dominating factor in determining whether COMP is less than 10 µg/l or not. The lead concentrations of the COMP samples in these properties are generally between 6 and 10 µg/l.

Figure 3.31 shows the lead concentration distribution for properties falsely identified as problem properties.

Approaches for improving detection of problem properties Taking more samples at the same tap (on different visits) can increase the ability of protocols to detect problem properties. This will also unavoidably increase the number of false positives. Therefore, an optimal compromise should be reached between assuring the safety of an individual consumer and the safety of a group of consumers (distribution area).

During the field test three samples of each sample type were taken in each property. Based on three test results we can define two approaches:

- one of three samples exceeds the PV: *positive* if COMP also exceeds the PV, *false positive* if COMP is less than the PV;

- the mean of three samples exceeds the PV: *positive* if COMP also exceeds the PV, *false positive* if COMP is less than the PV.

Figures 3.32 and 3.33 show the results of these approaches for the total test area. These figures show that the percentage of positives is hardly improved by taking three samples at one property, but that the percentage of false positives rises somewhat. Taking three samples in one property increases the sampling costs drastically.

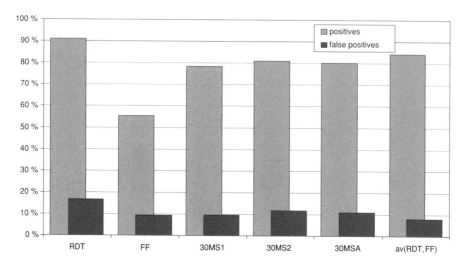

Figure 3.32   Properties detected where at least one of three samples exceeds 10 µg/l

Setting priorities for the intermediate PV   Five years after implementation of the DWD, a transitional period of 10 years starts when the PV for lead in drinking water is set at 25 µg/l. Water companies will take appropriate control measures to lower plumbosolvency. To set priorities, distribution areas will have to be tested. From the results of the field test we can calculate the following:

• the probability that a protocol recognizes a property where lead exceeds 25 µg/l: positive if PROT > 25 µg/l when COMP > 25 µg/l, false positive when PROT > 25 µg/l and COMP < 25 µg/l;

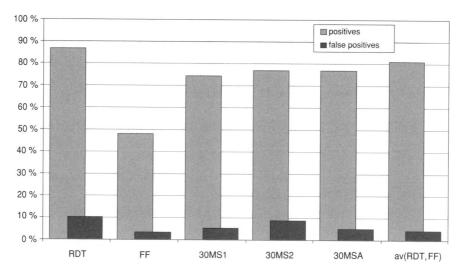

Figure 3.33   Properties detected where the average of three samples exceeds 10 µg/l

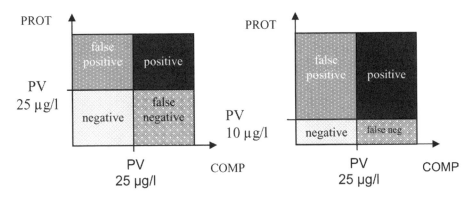

Figure 3.34 Priorities for intermediate PV

- the probability that a protocol recognizes a property where lead in COMP exceeds 25 μg/l, when the PV for PROT is set at 10 μg/l (Figure 3.34).

The results for both approaches, applied to the properties sampled during the field test, are given in Figures 3.35 and 3.36.

These graphs show that for both approaches RDT is more capable of detecting properties with lead exceeding 25 μg/l. The COMP values for the false positives are generally in the range of 10 to 25 μg/l, so lead levels in these properties are in the concentration range where measures will have to be taken in the future (to comply with the PV of 10 μg/l).

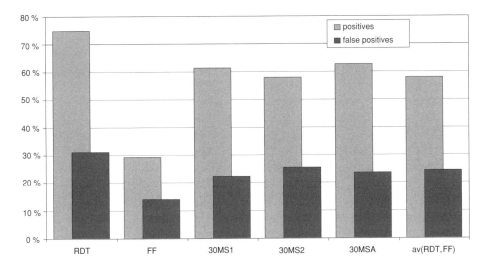

Figure 3.35 Detection of properties with lead > 25μg/l at a PV of 25 μg/l

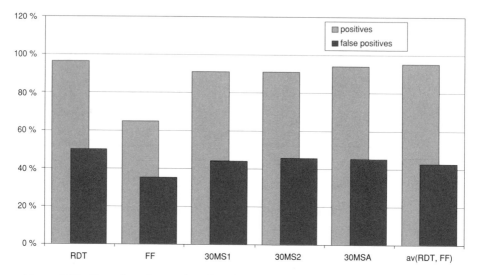

Figure 3.36   Detection of properties where lead > 25µg/l at a PV for protocols of 10 µg/l

Setting priorities for water treatment

When considering measures to decrease the lead content, water companies need to have a representative value for the average lead intake in a supply zone. Figure 3.37 shows the averages of the results for all protocols in all test areas. As shown, RDT and 30MS generally give the best estimate for the average concentration in a test

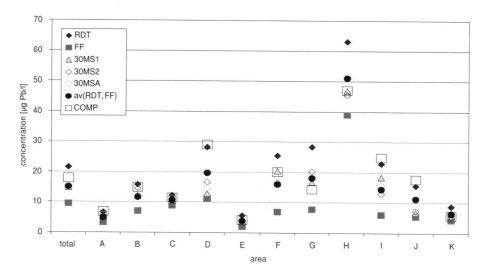

Figure 3.37   Averages of all protocols for all test areas

area. FF however, underestimates the average. In areas D, I and J, only RDT gave a good estimation of the average lead concentration (as determined by COMP). In areas F, G and H the average of RDT substantially exceeded the average of COMP.

3.5   LEAD LEVELS IN DRINKING WATER IN TAP WATER

3.5.1   Overview Lead Levels in Test Areas

The sampling programme as given in Figure 3.6 was carried out in about 230 properties in areas with a water quality as defined in Table 3.3. The lead levels in the test areas measured with the composite proportional sample technique varied from less than the detection limit to about 200 µg/l. The results are summarized in Figure 3.38, which shows the lead concentration distribution for the test areas, and in Table 3.5, which gives the values of composite proportional sampling in all test areas. In about 60 % of the tested lead plumbed properties, the lead concentrations were higher than 10 µg/l. For installations without lead pipes, in 5 % of the properties the lead concentrations were higher than 10 µg/l.

Even though test areas and properties were selected where the lead was expected to be significant (69 % of the tested properties had lead service pipes and/or lead plumbing), only 44 % of the composite proportional samples exceeded the PV of 10 µg/l. About 20 % of all composite proportional samples exceeded the intermediate PV of 25 µg/l and 19 % exceeded the value of 50 µg/l.

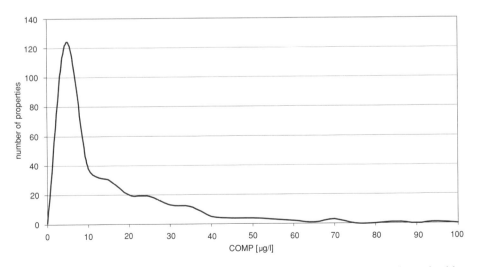

Figure 3.38   Lead concentration distribution throughout combined test area as determined by composite proportional sampling (EUR 19087,1999)

Table 3.5 Values of COMP in test areas

| | | | | Lead concentrations in COMP [µg/l] | | | |
Area	Data	Min.	Max.	Median (50 %)	Upper quartile (75 %)	Lower quartile (25 %)	90 % percentile
Total	289	0	181	7.0	21.0	2.5	38.4
A	27	2	21.6	3.3	8.9	2.0	18.8
B	27	2	53.8	4.7	14.3	2.0	23.1
C	31	1	55	7.0	13.8	2.0	31.2
D	30	1	181	15.5	28.5	8.5	73.4
E	29	0.5	20	3.0	5.0	1.0	9.6
F	29	1	69	16.0	30.5	2.3	45.8
G	25	0.5	45	5.8	20.0	1.9	27.6
H	30	0	166	28.5	58.8	14.3	107.8
I	13	3	55	26.0	34.0	12.0	46.6
J	16	3	65	13.0	22.8	7.0	31.5
K	34	1	33	2.5	5	2.5	12.4

The range of lead concentrations, based on composite proportional sampling, in this study varied from below the detection limit to 181 µg/l. Of the 294 investigated properties, 44 % showed lead levels above 10 µg/l (new PV), and 20 % above 25 µg/l (intermediate PV). Given the relatively high percentage of lead plumbed houses (69 %) in the tested population of properties, these percentages are relatively low. The lead concentrations found in properties without lead pipes vary from below detection limit to 23 µg/l. In only 7 % of these properties does the composite proportional sample exceed 10 µg/l. A high proportion of properties in supply areas with high pH waters and/or orthophosphate dosing showed lead levels below 25 µg/l.

Flushing the tap before use is an effective measure to reduce considerably the lead concentration at the consumer's tap. However, flushing does not guarantee that the lead level will be below 10 µg/l. This study shows that in 50 % of properties where the composite proportional sample exceeded 10 µg/l, the fully flushed sample was less than 10 µg/l. For 70 % of properties where lead exceeded 25 µg/l, the lead concentration after flushing was less than 25 µg/l.

3.5.2 Effect of Water Composition

The effect of water composition cannot be determined clearly from the results in this test, as there is a large variation in plumbing systems and household situations within and between test areas. In the areas where orthophosphate is dosed (A, J and K, partly), the lead levels were significantly lower, but samples from some properties still exceeded the parametric value of 10 µg/l.

The representativeness of the protocols can, at least partly, be explained by the variation in lead concentration ranges between test areas, for example:

- area E : 75 % of data < 5 µg/l, 90 % < 10 µg/l. This explains the poor representativeness;

- area D, F, H, I and J : high concentrations;

- area H and I : very few low concentrations (<10 µg/l);

- area B, C (and G) : same variation ranges and comparable results in representativeness.

3.5.3 Effect of Plumbing Materials

To assess the effect of plumbing materials on the lead concentration as determined by composite proportional sampling, we distinguish the following situations:

- all properties, regardless of installation materials;
- properties with lead service pipes and/or lead plumbing;
- properties with no lead pipes;
- properties without lead, with galvanized steel pipes;
- properties without lead, with copper pipes.

The assessment is carried out on the assumption that the details of the plumbing system were noted correctly by the sampler. In some areas however, it proved extremely difficult to check service pipe and plumbing materials, especially in cases where pipes were hidden behind wall plaster. Figure 3.39 shows the lead concentration frequency for the situations mentioned above.

This figure shows that for installations without lead pipes, the parametric value of 10 µg/l was exceeded in 7 % of these properties. Generally, the intermediate parametric value of 25 µg/l was met in properties without lead pipes. In about 40 % of the tested lead-plumbed properties, the lead concentration complied with the parametric value of 10 µg/l.

3.5.4 Water Consumption

The European study has generated data on daily water consumption throughout Europe. It appears that there are no significant differences in domestic water consumption per person between the tested countries. On average, water consumption amounts to about 2 litres per person per day. The daily water consumption per

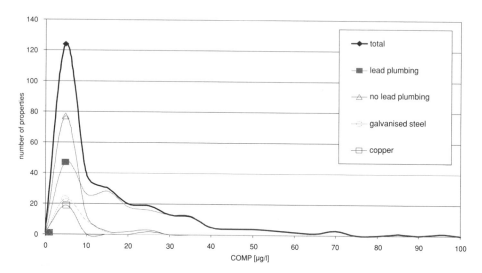

Figure 3.39 Lead concentration frequency for different plumbing systems

occupant decreases with increasing number of occupants from 5–10 litres a day in a one-person household, to 1.5 litres a day in a five-person's household. The high consumption in a one- or two-person household can be explained by the fact that not all water drawn for dietetic purposes is actually consumed, and that these households (in our study) consist mainly of elderly people, who might stay at home all day.

REFERENCES

Baggelaar, P. K. and C. G. E. M. van Beek (1995), Suggestions for the optimisation of large scale ground water quality assessment, *Kiwa report KOA* 95.107 (in Dutch), Nieuwegein, The Netherlands

Bailey, R. J. and P. F. Russel (1981), Predicting drinking water lead levels. *Environmental Technology Letters* **2**, 57–66.

Bailey, R. J., D. Holmes, P. K. Jolly and R. F. Lacey (1986a), Lead concentrations and stagnation time in water drawn through lead domestic pipes, *WRc Report TR 243*.

Bailey, R. J., P. K. Jolly and R. F. Lacey (1986b), Domestic water use patterns, *WRc Report TR 225*.

Baron, J. (2001), Monitoring strategy for lead in drinking water at consumer's tap: field experiments in France, *Water Science Technology: Water Supply* **1**, 193–200.

Britton, A. and W. N. Richards (1981), Factors influencing plumbosolvency in Scotland, *Journal of the Institution of Water Engineers and Scientists* **35**(5), 349–364.

CEC (1980), Council Directive relating to the quality of water intended for human consumption, *Official Journal of the European Communities*, No. L229, 23, 30th August 1980, 11–29 (80/778/EEC).

EUR19087 (1999), Developing a new protocol for the monitoring of lead in drinking water, *Final Report European Commission DGXII*. Project team: Th. J. J. van den Hoven, P. J. Buijs, P. J. Jackson, P. Leroy, J. Baron, A. Boireau, J. Cordonnier, M. H. Marecos do Monte, M. J. Benoliel, I. Wagner.

Gregory, R. (1990), Galvanic corrosion of lead solder in copper pipework, *Journal Institution of Water and Environmental Management*, **4**(2), 112–118.

Haring, B. J. A. (1984), Lead in drinking water, Thesis, University of Amsterdam, The Netherlands.

Kuch, A. and I. Wagner (1983), A mass transfer model to describe lead concentrations in drinking water, *Water Research* **17**(10), 1303–1307.

Leroy, P. (1993), Lead in drinking water – origins, solubility, treatment, *Journal Water SRT – Aqua*, **42**(4), 233–238.

Packham, R. F. (1971), The leaching of toxic stabilisers from unplasticised PVC water pipe: Parts I-III, Water treatment and examination **20**, 108–164.

Poels, C. L. M. and G. Dibbets (1982), The initial migration by lead of unplasticised PVC water pipes, *H2O*, **15** (21), 588–590 (in Dutch).

Randon, G. (1996), Summary of the collective work carrried out by AGHTM concerning the presence of lead in tap water, *AGHTM Congress*, London, May 1996.

Schock, M. R. (1989), Understanding control strategies for lead, *Journal of the American Water Works Association* **81**(7), 88–100.

Schock, M. R. (1990), Causes of temporal variability of lead in domestic plumbing systems, *Environmental Monitoring and Assessment* **15**, 59–82.

Schock, M. R. (1994), Response of lead solubility to dissolved carbonate in drinking water, *Journal of the American Water Works Association* **72**(12), 122–127.

Sheiham I. and P. J. Jackson (1981), The scientific basis for control of lead in drinking water by water treatment, *Journal of the Institution of Water Engineers and Scientists*, **35**(6), 491–515.

Tielemans, M. W. M., J. W. F. Spiering and H. Brink (1995), Pellet softening at the Scheveningen treatment plant (DZH): Significant reduction of the lead and copper content of drinking water, *H2O*, **28** No. 21; 646 (in Dutch).

Vewin (1987), Advice for the approach to the problem of lead in drinking water (in Dutch) VEWIN = the Association for Dutch Water Campanies. It can be located at: VEWIN, P.O. Box 1019, 2280 CA Rijswijk.

Van den Hoven, Th. J. J. (1986), Lead in drinking water, *KIWA-report 96*, Nieuwegein, The Netherlands (in Dutch).

Van den Hoven, Th. J. J. (1987), A new method to determine and control lead levels in tap water, *Aqua* **6**, 315–322.

Wagner, I. (1992), Internal corrosion in domestic drinking water installations, *Journal Water SRT -Aqua*, **41**(4), 219–223.

WHO (1993), *Guidelines for Drinking Water Quality*, second edition, Volume 1, *Recommendations*, World Health Organization, Geneva.

4
Materials in Contact with Drinking Water

Jean Baron*

---

* Chapters 4.2 and 4.3 are based on a co-normative research report (report EUR 19602 EN-2000) carried out by a European Consortium.

Analytical Methods for Drinking Water   Edited by P. Quevauviller and K. C. Thompson
© 2006 John Wiley & Sons, Ltd.

4.1   PARAMETERS USED FOR THE CONTROL OF MATERIALS EFFECTS

The materials used in the construction of drinking water treatment and distribution systems must not affect negatively the quality (organoleptic, toxicological) of the water that is supplied to the consumer.

In order to prevent such negative impact of materials on drinking water quality, it is necessary that all materials and products intended for contact with drinking water can be appropriately assessed and approved before being installed. The European Acceptance Scheme (EAS), which is being developed, will define harmonized rules and principles for such assessment. The range of assessments to be carried out can vary depending on product and material composition characteristics, in particular, it may be different for organic, cementitious or metallic materials.

The formulation of the materials is the first step in the assessment of a product, with reference to lists of accepted substances (positive lists, composition lists) based on toxicological evaluation.

Laboratory testing is usually the second step of the assessment to be carried out, to ensure that after contact with a product drinking water quality will not pose significant risk to health and will comply with the DWD for organoleptic, chemical and bacteriological parameters.

The range of assessment which are or may be necessary is developed in Sections 4.1.1 to 4.1.4 below.

4.1.1   Organoleptic Assessments

The DWD requires that odour, flavour, colour and turbidity of drinking water must be acceptable to the consumer and that no abnormal changes occur.

Odour and flavour

Abnormal odour and/or flavour are an indication of major degradation of water quality. Although bad odours and flavours can be generated by other sources, such as contamination of the drinking water source, experience has shown that materials can readily cause significant problems. Some materials have the capability of leaching into drinking water substances at very low concentrations (often undetectable analytically) that give rise to unacceptable odour and flavour. Testing to ensure that products do not lead to such contamination is a major part of the assessment.

Colour and turbidity

Colour and turbidity of water can also result from migration or interaction between water and materials. Abnormal changes in these parameters are not acceptable to the consumer.

4.1.2 General Hygiene Assessments

Total organic carbon (TOC)

TOC gives an indication of the overall leaching of organic substances from a material. While there is no direct relationship between the organic matter (TOC gives no indication of its composition), and any particular effect on water quality and risk for the consumer, it is necessary to minimize any contribution from materials on this parameter.

Chlorine demand

Interaction between materials and water, or migration of substances, can influence the consumption of chlorine. A chlorine demand test can then be carried out in order to ensure that a material is relatively inert.

4.1.3 Substances that Pose a Risk to Health

Drinking water directive parameters

Chemical parameters, as specified in the DWD, shall be assessed if their presence is indicated during the examination of the formulation of a material.

Positive list substances

Organic substances that have been identified in the formulation of a material have to be measured to ensure that migration limits are not exceeded.

Unsuspected organic substances

An assessment for unsuspected organic substances needs to be carried out in order to reveal the presence of any chemicals in a product that are not indicated by formulation information. Such substances are detected by a procedure based on gas chromatography and mass spectrometry (GCMS).

Composition list substances (metals)

The risk of migration of metallic substances used in the formulation of metallic materials (alloying elements or impurities) must be assessed with regard to their toxicity and also for possible impact on organoleptic quality of drinking water (odour, colour and turbidity).

Cytotoxicity assessment

Migration of substances in water can give rise to cytotoxic effects. A cytotoxicity test can provide an overall assessment of the impact of a material on water quality in addition to chemical analysis. Research has been carried out to develop a harmonized and reliable test procedure. Cytotoxicity testing is part of the assessment in some European countries but it is still unclear as to whether or not it will be part of the European Acceptance Scheme.

4.1.4   Enhancement of Microbial Growth

Tests to assess the potential of materials to enhance microbial growth are used in some European countries. At the European level, research has been carried out and additional research is still necessary to develop a harmonized procedure.

4.2   TEST PROCEDURE FOR METALLIC MATERIALS

4.2.1   Introduction

Background

Materials used for the distribution and treatment of drinking water are not allowed to release substances that affect the quality of the water negatively (toxicological, organoleptic).

The EC Drinking Water Directive is being used as the examination file, although this Directive does not cover all the parameters that are important in the judgement of materials. Hence, the different European countries have regulations and approval schemes for the admittance of products or materials that come into contact with drinking water. Within harmonizing the different approval schemes in Europe, it is the aim of CEN TC164 /WG3 to develop standards for test methods for all materials versus water quality to be used in the assessment of hygienic and toxicological properties.

Metals and alloys are the most common materials in use for domestic installations. To comply with European and national regulations on the quality of water intended for human consumption, it is necessary to take into consideration the interactions between these materials and water.

With the assessment of metallic materials, some problems occur because metallic materials are strongly influenced by water quality and operating conditions. Because water quality and operating conditions are very diverse over Europe, no general conclusions can be drawn about metal release by metallic materials.

From traditionally used materials, such as lead and copper pipes, some relation-ships are known between water quality and metal release. However, little information is available on alloys and new materials coming onto the market. These new materials and alloys must not give problems in complying with regulations.

Scope of the research

The general objective of conormative research was to provide background information in order to produce test methods for metallic materials. Within this scope a short-term test was evaluated and compared with long-term ('rig') tests to determine whether metals can be tested and admitted on the basis of short-term tests.

4.2.2   Metallic Materials

Metallic materials in use in drinking water installations

In Europe only a few types of metallic material are being used in plumbing systems. The regulations in the different member states allowing these materials show some differences; also the percentages of the different materials in drinking water installations show some variations. Metallic materials used in plumbing systems are:

- copper;
- copper alloys, such as brass, gun metal and bronze, which contain up to about 7 % lead, and may also contain a number of additives or impurities (e.g. arsenic, antimony or nickel in gun metal);
- stainless steels, which are alloys of iron that contain at least 12 % chromium, and may contain nickel (Cr-Ni stainless steel) and other elements such as molybdenum;
- galvanized steel. The lining of galvanized steel pipes consists of zinc, which can contain up to 1 % lead. Steel itself contains much less lead (up to 0.01 %);
- lead. Although, in many European countries the use of lead pipes is banned or not recommended, lead pipes are still found in old houses;
- combinations of these materials.

Parameters influencing metal release

Collecting information on metal concentrations at the tap is very complex because the metal release by pipes is strongly influenced by the characteristics of the drinking water, the presence and properties of corrosion layers on metal surfaces, the design of the plumbing system and the flow rate and flow regime of the water through the pipe.

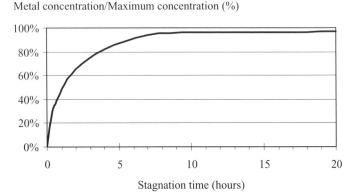

Metal concentration/Maximum concentration (%)

Stagnation time (hours)

Figure 4.1   Typical stagnation curve of a metallic pipe material in contact with drinking water

Water characteristics   For most of the common pure materials such as lead, iron, copper and zinc some relationships have been found between water composition and corrosion and metal migration behaviour (AWWA, 1996; Van den Hoven and van Eekeren, 1988; Wagner, 1992).

In general, in metal drinking water pipes the metal concentration increases rather quickly with time and remains for a time more or less at a constant level, depending on water quality (Van den Hoven and van Eekeren, 1988) (Figure 4.1). From these data it appears that the pH and hydrogen carbonate content in the water play a determining role in the corrosion of these materials. For example, in The Netherlands, rig tests have been performed on a large scale with copper pipes for different water qualities. Models developed on the basis of these results aim to predict copper concentrations at the tap after 24 hours of stagnation time. For instance, for copper pipes the following expression was found in The Netherlands:

$$Cu_{max} \text{ (mg/l)} = 0.52 \text{ TIC (mmol/l)} - 1.37 \text{ pH} + 0.02 \text{ [SO}_4^{2-}\text{] (mg/l)} + 10.2$$

where TIC (Total Inorganic Carbon) stands for the total concentration of carbon dioxide, bicarbonate and carbonate.

This relationship is valid after initial ageing of the material when it is already 'stabilized'. It has been established with slow continuous flow of water.

From the expression for Cu_{max} it can be seen that the copper solubility is strongly dependent on the water quality. For other materials there will be different relationships with water quality. Therefore it is necessary to test the metal release by materials in water of different qualities.

However, very little information is available about the effect of water quality on alloys that are on the market. In the future, new materials can be expected with unknown composition and properties. Additional information is needed on the tendency of other trace metals, like arsenic, cadmium, lead and nickel, often present as impurities or additives in alloys, to contaminate the water. A significant amount of research has been carried out on lead leaching from leaded alloys (Oliphant, 1992). Up until the start of the conormative research, background information was not sufficiently detailed to enable a generalized standard test to be designed.

For materials like stainless steels, the mechanisms are quite different. Corrosion resistance in stainless steels is provided by a passive film that acts as a barrier between the alloy and the water. The passive film is a continuous, non-porous and insoluble film, which, if broken under normal conditions, is self-healing. Due to these characteristics, the uniform corrosion of stainless steels is usually very low and the major risk is pitting corrosion. The pitting corrosion risk of stainless steels is influenced not only by the composition of the alloy and by water quality but also by service conditions, quality of the material and quality of the installation (fitting, soldering conditions, etc.).

Plumbing design   The final metal concentration at the tap is not just determined by water quality. Metal release by metal pipes is also strongly influenced by the type of domestic drinking water installation, such as materials and dimensions (length and diameter). The increase in metal concentration with stagnation time varies with the pipe diameter (Kuch *et al.*, 1983). For instance for lead pipes, calculated and experimental stagnation curves show that 90 % of the maximum lead concentration is reached after 2 hours for pipes of 10-mm internal diameter but more than 24 hours for pipes of 50-mm diameter.

The plumbing design also includes the number and type of fittings or solder used in the installation and various galvanic couplings. Very little information is available on these subjects.

Ageing of metallic surfaces   The corrosion process starts with the chemical reaction between the metal surface and the drinking water and some time is required to develop a corrosion layer with protecting properties on a metal surface. The ageing time of metallic surfaces will differ from one material to the other. For instance, for copper pipes it takes weeks, months, or even years in some cases, depending on the water quality, to develop such a stable film. To get insight into the mechanism of ageing of metallic surfaces, it looks as if it will be necessary to perform (rig) tests over a longer period.

Flow regime   As metal concentrations usually increase with time, it seems obvious that metal concentrations in drinking water might vary strongly during the day because of variations in the stagnation time between use of drinking water. Therefore, tap patterns of consumers seem also to be predominant factors in the metal concentration in drinking water at the tap.

In the tap pattern, the mean inter-use time, the volume of water drawn and flow rate all play a role. The water use pattern depends on the household's size, such as the number and age of occupants but also on habits of water usage of the householders (Bailey *et al.*, 1986).

Table 4.1   Inter-use stagnation times for different household sizes (Bailey *et al.*, 1986)

Household size [persons]	Mean [min]	SD [min]
1	47	23
2	29	14
3	24	13
4	22	13
5+	18	6

Table 4.1 gives a summary of the results of a study of the relationship between mean inter-use time and household size.

These results show clearly the great spread in mean inter-use times that can be observed in different households. As metal concentrations rise rapidly in this range of stagnation times, it can be concluded that metal concentrations might vary widely between households.

Existing test protocols

Until now simplified methods have been available to monitor metal release by metallic pipe materials. In the United Kingdom a sit-and-soak test is available to determine the metal release from drinking water materials. In The Netherlands, copper and lead pipes in combination with water quality are tested in pipe rigs, and in Germany a protocol for testing pipe materials is available (see below).

BS 7766: 1994   The procedure given in the British Standard 7766 has been developed to test those alloys for which no direct data as to their service performance is available. BS 7766 was developed to measure the leaching of lead from brass.

The method consists of taking cylindrical test coupons of specified dimensions and surface finish, and suspending them in a specified volume of a specified test solution representative of a moderately aggressive supply water for a period of 24 hours. The immersions are repeated ten times using fresh test solution. Metals are determined using the extract from the final 24-hour period.

Pipe rig tests in the Netherlands   In The Netherlands in the mid 1980s a pipe rig was developed and used at several pumping stations to measure lead and copper concentrations in the drinking water. The rig consists of three pipes through which water is flowed continuously except when sampling. The flow rate is about 0.05 m/s. The metal concentration in the drinking water is measured after 24-hour stagnation.

For copper, the rig tests are applied at pumping stations where the water has a high copper solubility. For lead, the rigs are placed at the majority of the pumping stations that deliver water to areas with lead pipes. The results from the pipe rig test show a good correlation with metal concentrations at the tap. The Netherlands government has accepted the pipe rig test for compliance monitoring.

Pipe rig tests in Germany (DIN standard)   The German standard DIN 50931-1 went to press at the beginning of 1999. It is the result of intensive mutual interaction between laboratories that are participants in the conormative research project and the German working group, which was establishing a German standard for corrosion tests with drinking water. The exchange of experiences between these two groups resulted in similar testing procedures and protocols. These protocols only differ in nuances.

DIN 50931/1 (1999) describes the design, operation and sampling of a typical plumbing installation for metallic materials testing. In DIN 50931 the last 5 m of a domestic plumbing installation is imitated. In the German Standard DIN 50931, Part 1, an average value calculated from eight samples, which have to be taken after different well-defined stagnation times has been proposed: $1/2$ hour stagnation ($\times 2$), 1 hour ($\times 2$), 2 hours ($\times 1$), 4 hours ($\times 1$), 8 hours ($\times 1$), 16 hours ($\times 1$).

NSF/61 – 1997b test   The ANSI/NSF Standard 61 – 1997b (1997) was approved by the American National Standards Institute in September 1997. This test is a short-time sit-and-soak test procedure developed primarily for the testing of products intended for use in drinking-water installations. The standard includes protocols for testing all types of material, instructions for calculating the product dosages from the measured concentrations after defined exposure times, and criteria for rating of acceptable and unacceptable products.

4.2.3   Experiments Within Conormative Research

Introduction

This paragraph describes the test protocols and experimental results for experiments carried out within the conormative research project.

Sit-and-soak tests have been carried out with BS 7766 standard test water and with laboratory tap waters (composition of waters given in Table 4.3). Pipe rig experiments have been carried out with laboratory tap waters, and four materials have been tested: copper, brass (copper with brass fittings for pipe rigs), galvanized steel, and stainless steel.

Materials used for tests were supplied by manufacturers. The same materials coming from the same batches were supplied to each laboratory.

Investigation of a short-term laboratory procedure for assessing the potential of metals to contaminate potable water

Introduction   The convenience of having a relatively simple, short-term, laboratory procedure to assess the potential of metals to contaminate potable waters, both for the development of new alloys and in determining any limitations on use of established alloys due to water composition, is self evident. The purpose of the investigations undertaken as part of the conormative project was to determine the ease of achieving reproducibility with such tests, and to consider to what extent the quantitative results reflect the levels of contamination achieved in authentic plumbing systems.

Experimental procedure   The experimental procedure used in this part of the project was based on that given in the British Standard BS 7766:1994. This method was used because it is an established procedure with a substantial amount of experimental data and experience behind it, and because it is typical of simple sit-and-soak laboratory procedures.

Details of the method are summarized in Table 4.2. In essence, coupons of the material under test are prepared to defined dimensions and surface finish (the machining is carried out dry, i.e. no lubricating oils, to a surface finish better than 100 μm centre line average, CLA). After a degreasing and washing procedure, the coupons are suspended in the specified test water for 14 days. The test water is changed every 24 hours, except over the two weekend periods, making ten changes altogether. The ambient temperature is controlled throughout the test period at 24 °C. Twenty replicates are run per test and the metal concentrations in the final 24 hour extracts are measured. Five blank samples are run for those days when the concentrations of leachates from the coupons are determined. The blanks are processed in the same way apart from the fact that a test coupon is not suspended in the water. If the blanks show metal levels above the detection limit of the analytical method, the test is void.

Table 4.2   Summary of the laboratory sit-and-soak test procedure (based on BS 7766, 1994)

Test piece	Cylinder
	8 mm diameter × 50 mm long
	1 mm wide 45° chamfer at each end
	2 mm hole 3 mm from one end to suspend sample
Test water	50 mg/l calcium carbonate (dissolved in deionized water)
	50 mg/l sodium chloride
	Total alkalinity = 50 mg/l as $CaCO_3$
	pH 7 ± 0.2 adjusted using CO_2 and filtered air
Test conditions	Each cylinder degreased in methylated spirit and washed in test water
	20 replicates individually suspended in 100 ml test water held at 24°C
	Water changed every 24 hours, except over weekends
	Metal concentrations in test water determined after 14th day (10th change of water)

Experimental programme Initially the materials being used in the pipe rigs, i.e. galvanized steel, stainless steel, copper and brass, were tested by the sit-and-soak procedure. Two sets of tests were carried out, one using the standard test solution given in Table 4.2, and a second using the local water being supplied to the respective pipe rigs in each of the participating laboratories (see Table 4.3). The latter set of tests were carried out in the hope of establishing a correlation between pipe rig results and the laboratory tests.

Because of the difficulty of obtaining a representative surface finish, the original BSI procedure was adapted in the test for galvanized steel. Short sections of pipe, i.d. 21 mm and manufactured to BS 1387: 1985, were cut and the exposed iron and external galvanized surfaces masked using an epoxy paint. The length of pipe cut was calculated to give the same exposed surface area to water volume ratio used in the tests of the other metals, i.e. approximately 13 570 mm^2/l. A short length of glass rod was fixed using an epoxy resin adhesive diametrically across one end of the pipe so that the samples could be suspended above the bottom of their respective beakers during the test.

Because of anticipated difficulties in machining, the stainless steel samples were tested in the form of rectangular bars (50 mm $\times$ 12 mm, thickness = 1.2 mm) rather than cylinders; otherwise the sample geometries were as given in Table 4.2.

When the interest in the procedure progressed to considering interlaboratory reproducibility, a further four sets of tests were carried out using brass samples only. In the last three of these, modifications were introduced into the original procedure; these were:

- the test solution pH adjusted to approx. 8.2;

- the test solution pH adjusted to approx. 8.2 and agitated (using an orbital shaker) during the exposure period;

- the standard test solution, i.e. pH about 7, but the test carried out in an enclosed vessel.

The participating laboratories split into subgroups to carry out these last tests. The reproducibility, both within and between laboratories, was assessed by calculating coefficients of variance and applying a simple *t*-test between means.

Results The results from all these tests are summarized in Table 4.4.

Analysis of reproducibility when using the standard test water: The results for stainless steel were not considered in this part of the programme because the majority of the values for metal leaching were below the analytical detection limits.

A simple *t*-test was carried out on the results between laboratories, and between the results from the same laboratories on the repeat tests, when using the BS test

Table 4.3 Mean composition of laboratory waters supplied to pipe rigs

Laboratory test waters	CRECEP	Kiwa	LHRSP	TZW0	TZW1	TZW2	WRC
Calcium (mg/l)	89.0	72.0	36.0	121.0	60.2	195	13.1
Magnesium (mg/l)	3.2	5.8	6.2	12.0	2.1	24.2	3.7
Sodium (mg/l)	9.2	12.4	16.1	12.6	12.6	12.6	8.8
Potassium (mg/l)	2.3	1.2	2.7	1.8	1.9	1.9	1.5
Bicarbonate (mg HCO_3/l)	223.0	269.1	70.7	328	202.1	435	60.9
Chloride (mg/l)	22.0	9.2	17.0	25.9	17.0	63.8	10.2
Sulphate (mg/l)	25.0	<2.0	66.7	64.0	1.9	146.4	15.4
Nitrate (mg NO_3/l)	21.1	0.62	3.1	31.4	19	34.1	1.7
Phosphate (mg P/l)	—	—	—	—	—	—	0.83
Total hardness (mg $CaCO_3$/l)	236	204	116	351	159	586	48
Total alkalinity (mg $CaCO_3$/l)	183	217	57	269	163.	357	50
pH	7.7	7.7	7.5–8.0	7.2	7.4	7.1	7.5
Total Inorganic Carbon (mg CO_2/l)	169	201	54–50	273	158	374	44
Conductivity (μS/cm)	444	388	310	684	366	1090	—

TZW0 is Karlsruhe tapwater.

TZW1 is Karlsruhe tapwater which has been passed through a nano-filter (filtrate).

TZW2 is the reject water produced when the Karlsruhe tapwater was nano-filtered (concentrate).

Table 4.4 Summary of results of sit-and-soak tests

	Zinc (mg/l)			Lead (µg/l)		
Laboratory	Mean	S.D.	% Covar.	Mean	S.D.	% Covar.
Galvanized steel: BS test water						
CRECEP	2	0.42	21.0	2.65	2	75.5
Kiwa	7.1	3.6	50.1	2.15	1.2	55.8
LHRSP	7.2	2.6	36.6	<10	—	—
TZW	1.71	0.21	12.3	1.00	0.00	2.2
WRc	3.7	0.98	26.5	0.87	0.72	82.8
Galvanized steel: laboratory waters						
CRECEP	1.07	0.39	36.4	5.6	1	17.9
Kiwa	0.80	0.09	11.3	0.78	0.4	51.3
LHRSP	2.08	0.81	39.2	<10	—	—
TZW1	0.94	0.13	13.8	1.7	0.8	47.1
TZW2	1.69	0.19	11.2	3.9	1.3	33.3
WRc	5.13	1.47	28.7	0.94	0.74	78.7

Stainless steel: BS test Water

	Chromium (µg/l)			Nickel (µg/l)			Iron (µg/l)		
	Mean	S.D.	% Covar.	Mean	S.D.	% Covar.	Mean	S.D.	% Covar.
CRECEP	3	0	—	5	2	40	25	6	24
Kiwa	<1	—	—	<1	—	—	<20	—	—
LHRSP	<1	—	—	<1	—	—	<5	—	—
TZW	1	—	—	2.5	0.5	20	10	—	—
WRc	<10	—	—	<10	—	—	4	0	—
Stainless steel: laboratory waters									
CRECEP	<2	—	—	3	2	66.7	33	11	30
Kiwa	<1	—	—	<1	—	—	69	13	18.8
LHRSP	<1	—	—	<1	—	—	4	7	175
TZW1	1.1	0.4	36.4	2.7	0.5	18.5	10	—	—
TZW2	1	—	—	3.9	0.3	7.7	10	—	—
WRc	<10	—	—	<10	—	—	20	3	15

Copper (µg/l)

	BS test water			Laboratory test waters		
	Mean	S.D.	% Covariance	Mean	S.D.	% Covariance
CRECEP	393	80	20.4	390	36	9.3
Kiwa	486	57	11.7	1,485	182	12.3
LHRSP	799	115	14.4	331	80	24.2
TZW	382	54	14.1	—	—	—
TZW1	—	—	—	556	40	7.2
TZW2	—	—	—	912	61	6.7
WRc	254	40	15.7	145	12	8.3

(continued overleaf)

Table 4.4   (*continued*)

	Test number	Zinc (mg/l)			Lead (µg/l)		
		Mean	S.D.	% Covariance	Mean	S.D.	% Covariance
Brass: BS test water							
CRECEP	1	1.47	0.16	11.1	95	23	24.9
	2	1.65	0.15	8.8	80.1	11.85	14.8
	3	1.16	0.13	11	30	7	23
	4	0.69	0.07	11	39	5	13
Kiwa	1	1.14	0.12	10.9	51.7	7.25	14.0
	2	0.82	0.07	8.2	74.5	9.05	12.1
	5	1.98	0.35	18	57	5	9
LHRSP	1	0.32	0.11	35	45.0	7.2	16
	2	0.74	0.13	17	42.5	5.88	13.8
	3	1.23	0.17	14	73	13	18
TZW	1	1.54	0.08	5	34.3	2.51	7.3
	2	1.35	0.06	5	39.4	6.96	17.7
	5	2.93	0.10	4	69	4	6
WRc	1	0.68	0.08	11.5	44.2	10.05	22.7
	2	1.14	0.06	4.8	32.5	6.45	19.8
	3	0.93	0.08	8.5	47	11	23
	4	0.83	0.07	9	49	15	30

Brass: laboratory waters

	Zinc (mg/l)			Lead (µg/l)			Copper (µg/l)		
	Lead (µg/l)								
	Mean	S.D.	% Covariance	Mean	S.D.	% Covariance	Mean	S.D.	% Covariance
CRECEP	0.52	0.1	19.2	33	5	15.2	17	3	17.6
Kiwa	2.34	0.78	33.3	95	33	34.7	186	65	34.9
LHRSP	0.88	0.1	11.4	48	5	10.4	37	9	24.3
TZW1	0.92	0.07	7.6	44	1.7	3.9	35	5.1	14.6
TZW2	2.9	0.28	9.7	73	6.4	8.8	116	8.3	7.2
WRc	0.24	0.25	104.2	8.5	8.4	98.8	—	—	—

Key: Tests 1 and 2 = Standard sit-and-soak procedure based on BS 7766:1994.
     Test 3 = pH of test water increased to about 8.2.
     Test 4 = pH of test water increased to about 8.2 plus agitation during exposure period.
     Test 5 = pH of test water at about 7.0 and coupons exposed in an enclosed vessel.

water. The formula for the *t*-test is as follows:

$$|t| = \frac{(m_1 - m_2).(n_1 + n_2 - 2)}{(\sigma_1^2 - \sigma_2^2)}$$

where $|t| > 2$ for 20 results represents a statistically significant difference;
     $m_1 - m_2$ = difference between the population means of the two sets of data
     σ_x = standard deviation of the *x* data set
     n_x = number of observations in the *x* data set

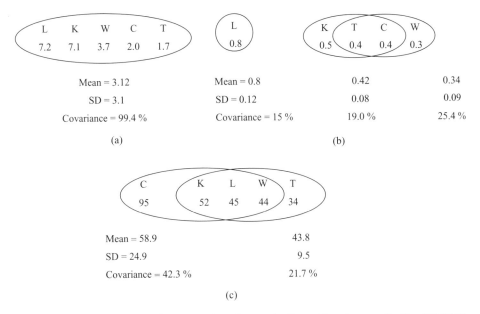

Figure 4.2 Statistically significant groupings (by *t*-test) of inter-laboratory results (C = CRECEP, K = Kiwa, L = LHRSP, T = TZW, W = WRC). (a) *Zn from galvanized (mg/l)*; (b) Cu from copper (mg/l); (c) Pb from brass, Test 1 (mg/l)

The outcome of this analysis is summarized in Figure 4.2 and Table 4.5.

The collective results from the five laboratories for the contamination by Zn from galvanized pipes formed a single group, i.e. there was no statistical difference between the values. However, this was only achieved because the very large scatter between replicates bridged the large difference between means obtained by the different laboratories, see Figure 4.2 (a).

The collective results for Cu contamination from pure copper formed three statistically distinct groups, two overlapping and the highest with LHRSP on its own (Figure 4.2 (b)). The result from LHRSP might be an analytical error on the last

Table 4.5 Statistically significant differences (by *t*-test) between repeat results within the same laboratories for brass tests 1 and 2

Determinand	Statistically significant difference between test results?	
	Pb	Zn
CRECEP	No	No
Kiwa	No	Yes
LHRSP	No	Yes
TZW	No	No
WRc	No	Yes

day's result, a possibility suggested by the much lower values achieved by LHRSP on the earlier days of the test.

The collective results for the contamination of lead from brass obtained from the first set of tests form two overlapping statistical groups (Figure 4.2 (c)). The range of results in the higher statistical group (CRECEP 95 µg/l to WRC 44 µg/l) is wider than that in the lower one (Kiwa 52 µg/l to TZW 34 µg/l). This, and the equivalent results obtained during the development of the original BSI procedure, suggested that it was the CRECEP result that was out of line.

Unfortunately, the lead results from brass in the second set of tests (all laboratories with brass coupons only), where greater care to follow the protocol had been exercised, split into two non-overlapping statistical groups with Kiwa now joining CRECEP in the higher of these. Comparison of the within-laboratory lead results from the two sets of tests showed no statistical difference between them, i.e. each laboratory was able to repeat its results (Table 4.5).

The collective results for the contamination by zinc from brass were even more complicated. The first set of tests produced four distinct statistical groups, two of which were overlapping. WRC and LHRSP both formed statistically distinct groups on their own at the lower end of the range of results. In the repeat experiment, three statistically distinct groups were obtained, none of them overlapping. WRC was still in a group of its own but now this was in the middle of the range.

The within-laboratory comparisons also showed differences with Kiwa, LHRSP and WRC producing statistically distinct sets of results in their repeat tests (Table 4.5).

The collective results for contamination by copper from brass produced two overlapping statistically distinct groups with no obvious candidate for the 'rogue' result. However, all results were very low and would have little practical significance.

Raising the pH of the test solution to its equilibrium value with the atmosphere (Test 3) brought the zinc-from-brass results for the three laboratories concerned into the same statistical population. This was an improvement over any of the previous tests, but the effect was not uniform. Thus, only for CRECEP did raising the pH consistently reduce the zinc contamination level as compared with the previous tests on brass. For LHRSP, the zinc levels were actually increased whereas for WRC the result from test 3 was between those of tests 1 and 2 (see Table 4.4d).

When agitation was introduced (test 4), a statistically significant reduction in the zinc-from-brass level was achieved by CRECEP but not by WRC (see Table 4.4d). However, the two laboratories still remained in the same statistical population (LHRSP did not participate in test 4.)

The results for lead in the same experiments were also not straightforward. The CRECEP and WRC results from test 3 were in the same statistical population with the CRECEP result showing a statistically significant fall from its previous results in tests 1 and 2. However, at the same time the LHRSP result showed a statistically significant rise over its previous tests so that, although it was in the same statistical population as WRC, it was in a different population to that of CRECEP. The introduction of agitation in Test 4 had no statistically significant effect on the lead results for either

Table 4.6 Ranking severity of contamination of metals from brass coupons exposed to the local laboratory waters being supplied to the respective pipe rigs

	CRECEP	Kiwa	LHRSP	TZW1	TZW2	WRc
Lead	5	1	3	4	2	6
Zinc	5	2	4	3	1	6
Copper	5	1	3	4	2	—

1 = highest contamination level, 6 = lowest

CRECEP or WRC. All the lead from brass results for WRC, i.e. from tests 1,2 3 and 4, were in the same statistical population.

Carrying out the extraction process in an enclosed vessel (test 5) to prevent the loss of free CO_2 in the pH 7 test solution, produced a statistically significant increase in the amount of zinc extracted (Table 4.4d). In open beakers, the pH increases (up to about 8) during the 24-hour period because of the loss of free CO_2, whereas this phenomenon does not occur in enclosed vessel where the pH remains lower. As zinc solubility decreases when pH increases, the differences between test 1 (open beakers) and test 5 (enclosed vessel) are consistent with the theory. Unfortunately, the results from the two laboratories concerned, Kiwa and TZW, were not in the same statistical populations. Slight differences in start pH (tolerance in BS 7766 is 7.0 ± 0.2) could explain this difference.

The lead results from the two laboratories were in the same statistical population and for TZW was significantly higher than the corresponding results in tests 1 and 2. The Kiwa lead result in test 5 was only statistically significantly different from their test 2 result (Table 4.4d).

Results with the laboratory pipe rig waters: Because of the different water qualities, it was obviously not possible to study the reproducibility of the results from the tests that used the different laboratory waters being supplied to the respective pipe rigs. However, it was possible to make a few generalizations.

The order of 'severity of contamination' by Zn, Pb and Cu from brass with the different laboratory test waters were approximately the same, for example, the water that is worst for Pb was also worst for Cu and second worst for Zn (Table 4.6).

The order of 'severity of contamination' by Cu from copper and Cu from brass in the different laboratory test waters was also similar although the absolute levels were very different (Table 4.7).

Table 4.7 Comparison of the ranking severity of contamination by copper leached from pure copper and brass coupons exposed to the local laboratory waters being supplied to the respective pipe rigs

	CRECEP	Kiwa	LHRSP	TZW1	TZW2	WRC	Mean (μg/l)
Cu from copper	4	1	5	3	2	6	635
Cu from brass	5	1	3	4	2	—	78

1 = highest contamination level, 6 = lowest

Table 4.8   Materials used in rig experiments

Material tested	Pipe material	Internal diameter (mm)	Fittings	Rig volume (litres)
Copper	Copper, hard drawn	13	None (bent copper)	0.67
Brass[a]	Copper, hard drawn	13	Brass (63.6 % Cu, 1,58 % Pb, O.1 % Sn, 34.7 % Zn)	0.67
Galvanized steel	Galvanized steel (Pr EN 10240)	20	Galvanized steel	1.6
Stainless steel	Stainless steel AISI 304 / 1.4301 (18 % Cr, 9.2 % Ni)	20	Stainless steel AISI 316 / 1.4401 (17 % Cr, 10.6 % Ni, 2.1 % Mo)	1.6

[a] The total inner surface of the brass fittings is 128 cm^2 ± 10 % which represents about 6.5 % of the total inner surface of the test rig.

Reference rig experiments

Experimental procedure   The experimental procedure for pipe rig tests is related to the German standard DIN 50931, Part 1 (see above).

The general philosophy of the test was to simulate an 'average authentic situation' representing operating conditions in a *domestic* plumbing system.

Actually, pipe rigs reproduce the final part of domestic plumbing just before a tap.

Design of rigs: Materials used for rigs and their main characteristics are given in Table 4.8. Figure 4.3 gives a schematic illustration of pipe rig design for each material. For each material, all laboratories received pipes and fittings 'ready to install' from the same manufacturers. For copper rigs, the pipes were prepared (bent) by the manufacturer. For stainless steel, rigs were assembled (press fittings) in all laboratories by a technician appointed by the manufacturer. For galvanized steel and copper with brass fittings, pipes and fittings were delivered to the laboratories, which assembled the rigs by themselves.

Materials were used for experiments without any preconditioning.

Rigs were connected to the laboratory water supply (after water treatment by nanofiltration, at TZW). The test device included equipment (valves, solenoid valves plus programming system, flow meter, sampling valves, etc.) for the adjustment and control of flow regime and for water sampling (Figure 4.4).

The test pipes were installed in a vertical position and were always under pressure.

Flow regime: The flow regime was designed to simulate authentic conditions at a kitchen tap. A total volume of 125 litres was flushed every day with alternate stagnation and flushing periods. Figure 4.5 presents the flow regime for a 24-hour period.

Flushing times were of 1 or 2 minutes at a flow rate of 300 litres per hour, which gives a volume of 5 or 10 litres for each flushing period.

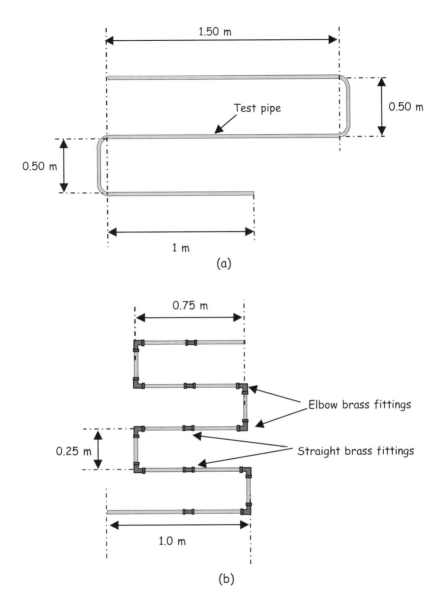

Figure 4.3 Design of test rigs. (a) Pipe materials (copper, galvanized steel, stainless steel); (b) copper pipe with brass fittings

Sampling procedure: Before sampling water for analysis, a small volume of water (approx. 100 ml) was flushed to waste in order to rinse the sampling device and the first few centimetres of the pipe. Then samples of water that had stagnated in contact with the material were taken for analysis. The sampling programme adopted for the first five months of test run was as follows:

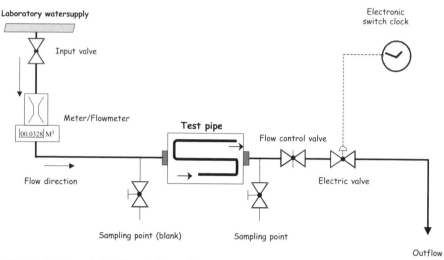

The test pipe is in vertical position and always under pressure

All materials in contact with water before the test pipe must not be metallic

Figure 4.4   Example of test device for pipe rig experiments

Half hour stagnation samples:

• 1st month: samples taken on days 1, 3, 6, 12 and 24.

• Months 2 to 5: Samples were taken each month over five consecutive days. The five samples could then be combined for analysis of an average sample or be analysed separately to calculate the mean concentration.

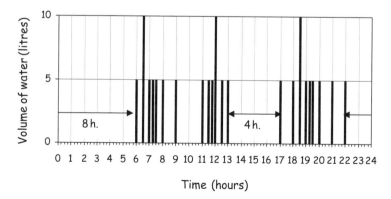

Figure 4.5   Flow regime in pipe rigs for a 24-hour period. Stagnation periods are:15 minutes (6), 30 minutes (9), 1 hour (4), 2 hours (1), 4 hours (1), 8 hours (1) (overnight stagnation)

Stagnation curves:

During months 2 to 5 of the run, stagnation curves for the metals of interest were constructed. This involved taking individual $1/2$, 2, 4 and 8 hour stagnation samples.

The sampling programme was adapted, on behalf of each laboratory, according to observed results and tendencies in contamination by metals. When necessary, test runs were prolonged after the initial 5-month periods and 1 hour and/or 16 hour stagnation samples were taken.

Analysis: pH and metal concentrations were determined in each sample at all stagnation times. Dissolved oxygen was measured for stagnation times of 1 hour or longer (and optionally for $1/2$ hour). Metal concentrations were measured in filtered and non-filtered samples in order to distinguish between soluble and particulate metal.

The list of metals depends on the material:

- Copper: Cu

- Brass: Cu, Zn, Pb

- Galvanized steel: Zn, Pb (and occasionally Cd)

- Stainless steel: Fe, Ni, Cr

Experimental results

Copper: Results for copper are summarized in Table 4.9 and Figure 4.6.

Figure 4.6 presents smoothed 3D plots of copper concentration as a function of stagnation time and operating time for the different test waters. These graphs were calculated from actual data, and they show the main tendencies in the evolution of copper release but 'peaks' were erased by calculation.

(a) Stagnation curves ([Cu] $= f$(stagnation time)). Copper concentration always increase for stagnation time up to 8 hours. CRECEP and TZW performed extra experiments with 16-hour stagnation. For CRECEP and TZW nanofiltration filtrate, Cu concentration still increased between 8 and 16 hours. For TZW tap water and nanofiltration concentrate a maximum was reached between 8 and 16 hours, and concentration generally decreased after 8-hour stagnation. In these cases, the maximum copper concentration was correlated with a minimum dissolved oxygen concentration. In fact, strong oxygen depletion was observed with stagnation time for TZW tap water and nanofiltration concentrate.

Oxygen depletion with stagnation time was also observed with other test waters but not in the same range. High oxygen consumption indicates high corrosion rates and often results in high copper concentrations.

(b) Ageing ([Cu] $= f$(operating time)). The shape of the evolution of copper concentrations with operating time can be described by three types of curve:

Type 1: 'exponential' decrease to a minimum value;

Type 2: increase to a plateau value;

Table 4.9 Copper concentrations in copper rig experiments at different stages. Bold characters: Copper concentration >1 mg/L

Stagnation time	a	CRECEP	KIWA	LHRSP	WRC	TZW Concentrate	TZW Filtrate	TZW Tap
½ hour	Max (*day*)	0.33 (*134*)	**0.82 (*14*)**	0.14 (*24*)	0.39 (*2*)	**4.2 (*819*)**	0.56 (*27*)	**1.5 (*336*)**
	Min (*day*)	0.07 (*263*)	0.15 (*7*)	0.008 (*578*)	0.016 (*5*)	0.56 (*5*)	0.04 (*588*)	0.39 (*5*)
	Mean (*SD*)	0.17 (*0.09*)	0.46 (*0.11*)	0.06 (*0.01*)	0.038	**1.67 (*0.37*)**	0.09 (*0.01*)	**1.3 (*0.1*)**
2 hours	Max (*day*)	0.97 (*75*)	2.3 (*30*)	0.21 (*54*)		**11 (*819*)**	**1.1 (*27*)**	**3.4 (*236*)**
	Min (*day*)	0.22 (*324*)	0.53 (*270*)	0.03 (*578*)		**2.52 (*90*)**	0.08 (*588*)	**2.0 (*5*)**
	Mean (*SD*)	0.42 (*0.18*)	**1.2 (*0.4*)**	0.13 (*0.03*)	0.12	**4.6 (*0.9*)**	0.18 (*0.03*)	**3.2 (*0.3*)**
4 hours	Max (*day*)	**1.55 (*75*)**	**3 (*30*)**	0.39 (*54*)		**13.7 (*792*)**	**1.9 (*5*)**	**8.4 (*139*)**
	Min (*day*)	0.33 (*324*)	0.83 (*90*)	0.034 (*578*)		**3.9 (*69*)**	0.10 (*819*)	**3.25 (*728*)**
	Mean (*SD*)	0.59 (*0.25*)	**1.6 (*0.5*)**	0.2 (*0.06*)	0.17	**7.4 (*1.5*)**	0.24 (*0.04*)	**5.6 (*1.0*)**
8 hours	Max (*day*)	**2.5 (*76*)**	**3.4 (*30*)**	0.5 (*54*)		**17 (*792*)**	**2.7 (*5*)**	**9.3 (*139*)**
	Min (*day*)	0.5 (*364*)	**1.1 (*90*)**	0.05 (*578*)		**7 (*69*)**	0.10 (*819*)	**3.3 (*728*)**
	Mean (*SD*)	0.84 (*0.39*)	**2.1 (*0.7*)**	0.34 (*0.10*)	0.09	**11 (*2*)**	0.34 (*0.07*)	**7.5 (*1.4*)**

[a] Max (*day*) = maximum concentration at given stagnation time (*corresponding operating time*).
Min (*day*) = minimum concentration at given stagnation time (*corresponding operating time*).
Mean (*SD*) = mean concentration for days 100 to 300 (*standard deviation*).

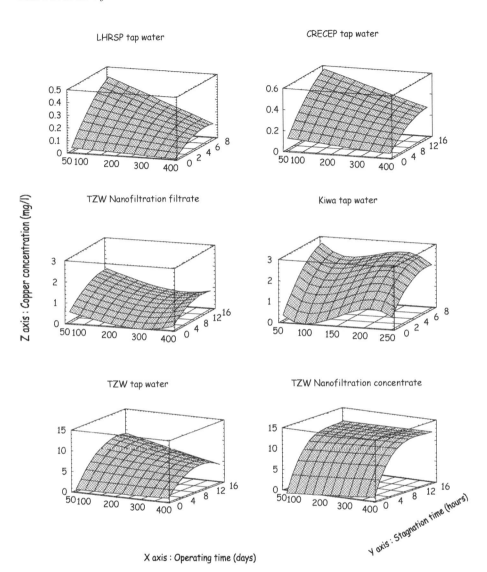

Figure 4.6 Copper rig experiments. Copper concentrations as function of stagnation time and operating time

Type 3: 'peak contamination' after an initial period of low values followed by 'exponential' decrease to a minimum value.

Type 1 or type 3 can describe results from CRECEP, TZW nanofiltration filtrate, WRC, Kiwa and LHRSP. Peak contamination (type 3) appeared in the first weeks in 30-minute stagnation samples (no data exist for longer stagnation times during the first month). After about 2 months' operation, copper concentrations decreased to a minimum with some variation which could be explained (probably) by changes in water quality (pH, temperature, oxygen, etc.).

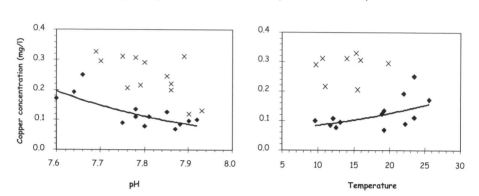

Figure 4.7 Relationship between copper concentration after 30 minutes' stagnation, pH and temperature. Results with CRECEP tap water

The effect of tap water quality is illustrated in Figure 4.7, which shows the relationship between pH and copper or temperature and copper with CRECEP water (values measured during pipe rig experiments). The figure shows that when copper corrosion is 'stabilized' (> 150 days operation), variations in copper concentration may be explained by pH and temperature fluctuations.

For TZW nanofiltration concentrate and tap water, type 2 and type 1 were observed depending on stagnation time (Figure 4.6). For tap water, continuous increase (type 2) was observed for 30 minutes' to 2-hours' stagnation, and (slow) exponential decrease (type 1) was observed for longer stagnation times (4 to 16 hours). For the concentrate, the contamination level increased continuously up to 500 days' operation at any stagnation time and stabilised or started decreasing slowly afterward.

For all waters, large changes in copper concentrations were observed in the first 2 or 3 months of operation. After this initial period, changes were generally slower and more continuous but may be significant over long periods of time.

(c) Copper concentrations – water corrosivity. Table 4.9 gives minimum and maximum copper concentrations at 0.5, 2, 4 and 8 hour stagnation for all laboratories, and the mean concentration between day 100 to 300 (to allow comparisons between the laboratories).

TZW nanofiltration concentrate and tap water appeared to be very corrosive waters for copper with concentrations exceeding 3 mg/l after 2-hours' stagnation. With these waters, contamination by copper quickly increased in the first months of operation and then stabilised or started to decrease.

For other waters, after few weeks' operation, copper concentrations always decreased to a minimum value. In the first weeks of operation the changes were more complex and often started with an initial increase (peak contamination).

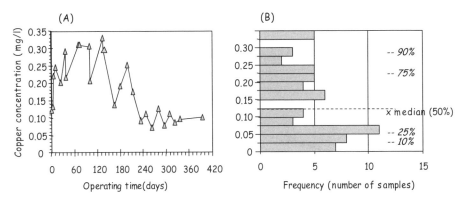

Figure 4.8 Comparison of copper concentrations after a stagnation of ½ hour in CRECEP rig experiments (A) with values observed at consumers' taps (B)

For WRC water (soft water with orthophosphate dosing), initial decrease occured in the very first days of operation and a minimum low level was reached after only 1 or 2 weeks.

In order of decreasing corrosivity, ranking of waters is as follows: TZW concentrate ≫ TZW tap ≫ Kiwa > CRECEP > LHRSP ~ TZW filtrate > WRC.

(d) Comparison of copper rig results with concentrations measured at consumers' taps. In Paris, between June 1997 and June 1999, 63 samples were taken at consumers' taps and copper concentrations were measured. The samples (2 litres) were taken after a fixed fixed stagnation of ½ hour. Figure 4.8 shows a comparison of copper concentrations measured in copper rig experiments after ½ hour of stagnation with values measured at the tap.

The comparison shows that there is good agreement between copper-rig results and actual copper concentrations at the tap. The median value from field experiments (0.125 mg/l) is very close to the range of copper concentrations found in the rig experiments after 'stabilization' (0.07 to 0.13 mg/l).

The scattering of field results can be explained by the variety of situations encountered in actual plumbing systems (diameters and lengths of copper pipes, age, other materials in the plumbing system, etc.). However this comparison indicates that in this case (CRECEP tap water, copper, ½-hour stagnation samples), the pipe-rig experiments are representative of actual contamination levels.

Copper with brass fittings:

(a) Copper. Contamination by copper followed the same general changes as in the copper-rig experiments. Concentration levels were usually the same in both experiments. However, Figure 4.9 shows that copper concentrations were sometimes lower in copper with brass fitting rigs than in copper rigs. This is very

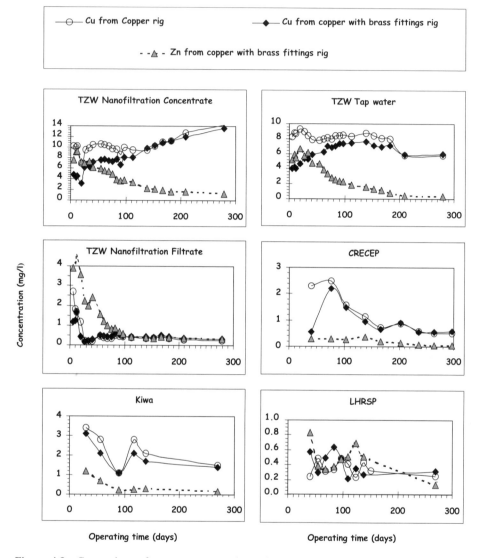

Figure 4.9   Comparison of copper concentrations after 8-hours' stagnation in copper rig and copper with brass fittings rig experiments

clear with the most corrosive waters (TZW filtrate and TZW tap water) in the first months of operation, but it was also observed with other waters. The difference between the two curves was reduced progressively with time until they overlapped almost perfectly. The time period over which differences were observed correlated very well with high zinc concentrations (which, over the same period, exhibited an exponential decrease to a minimum value). This is consistent with other observations that show that zinc can act as a corrosion inhibitor for copper.

The main conclusion from these results is that fitting materials can influence the corrosion rate and behaviour of the pipe materials even if the phenomenon is only temporary (a few days to several months in this case).

(b) Zinc. Results for zinc are summarized in Table 4.10 and Figure 4.10. Zinc is, with copper, a major constituent of brass, and all the results show that zinc is leached in water at significant concentrations with all test waters, where zinc concentrations increased with stagnation times up to 8 hours.

The evolution with operating time followed a type 1 curve (exponential decrease to a minimum value) for all stagnation periods. However, as for copper, variations were observed in the first weeks of operation with, sometimes, peak contamination after an initial period of low values (TZW concentrate, tap water and filtrate, Kiwa).

Very high zinc concentrations (>4 to 9 mg/l) were observed after 8 hours' stagnation with TZW waters (nanofiltration concentrate, filtrate and tap water) but contamination quickly decreased in the first weeks of operation. With other waters, concentrations were lower and did not exceed 1 mg/l even for 8-hours' stagnation. In order of decreasing corrosivity, ranking of waters was as follows: TZW concentrate $\gg$ TZW tap > TZW filtrate > Kiwa $\sim$ LHRSP $\sim$ CRECEP >$\sim$ WRC.

However, it must be noted that after 100 to 200 days, TZW filtrate, Kiwa LHRSP and CRECEP reached 'low' contamination levels in the same concentration range (0.1 to 0.5 mg/l after 8 hours' stagnation) with slow asymptotic decreases there after.

(c) Lead. High lead concentrations (>50 µg/l) were observed with TZW concentrate and TZW tap water in the first days of operation for long stagnation times (>4 hours). Contamination levels quickly decreased in the first days or first week to reach values of less than 10 µg/l in all cases after less than 1 month of operation.

For other test waters the same initial decrease was observed (no data for stagnation over 30 minutes in the first month) in the first weeks of operation. However, initial concentrations did not generally exceed 10 µg/l. After the initial period (10 to 50 days), lead concentrations stabilized at below 5 µg/l and remained at low levels (near analytical detection limits).

For CRECEP, values between 5 and 10 µg/l were observed, but lead was also detected in the blank at the same level. In that case, a small, variable contamination by lead comes from materials before the rigs (a few centimetres of galvanized steel, and brass devices) and cannot be imputed to contamination from brass fittings.

Galvanised steel:

(a) Zinc. Results for zinc are summarized in Table 4.11 and Figure 4.11. With all test waters significant zinc concentrations were detected even after 30 minutes' stagnation and prolonged operating times. Zinc concentrations increased with

Table 4.10 Zinc concentrations in copper with brass fittings rig experiments at different stages

Stagnation time	a	CRECEP	Kiwa	LHRSP	WRC	TZW Concentrate	TZW Filtrate	TZW Tap
1/2 hour	Max (day)	0.12 (1)	0.32 (14)	0.20 (1)	0.2 (1)	1.2 (34)	1.13 (34)	1.04 (34)
	Min (day)	0.01 (296)	0.005 (92)	0.02 (6)	0.03 (86)	0.07 (728)	0.02 (792)	0.04 (244)
	Mean (SD)	0.04 (0.02)	0.01 (0.008)	0.06 (0.03)	0.038	0.15 (0.05)	0.04 (0.01)	0.09 (0.05)
2 hours	Max (day)	0.26 (39)	0.72 (28)	0.30 (40)		2.52 (10)	1.53 (20)	1.74 (55)
	Min (day)	0.01 (394)	0.07 (287)	0.045 (269)		0.12 (279)	0.04 (819)	0.08 (427)
	Mean (SD)	0.06 (0.03)	0.09 (0.03)	0.16 (0.09)	0.25	0.5 (0.2)	0.14 (0.04)	0.28 (0.14)
4 hours	Max (day)	0.47 (39)	1.1 (28)	0.62 (40)		4.83 (20)	2.35 (20)	3.09 (27)
	Min (day)	0.02 (296)	0.11 (287)	0.095 (269)		0.21 (728)	0.05 (755)	0.10 (391)
	Mean (SD)	0.10 (0.08)	0.15 (0.03)	0.28 (0.16)	0.43	1.1 (5)	0.23 (0.03)	0.6 (0.4)
8 hours	Max (day)	0.36 (138)	1.2 (28)	0.83 (40)		9.24 (12)	4.48 (12)	6.71 (20)
	Min (day)	0.04 (325)	0.17 (287)	0.13 (269)		0.34 (728)	0.09 (700)	0.15 (700)
	Mean (SD)	0.16 (0.12)	0.24 (0.06)	0.4 (0.2)	0.40	2.1 (0.9)	0.39 (0.07)	1.1 (0.7)

[a] Max (day) = maximum concentration at given stagnation time (corresponding operating time).
Min (day) = minimum concentration at given stagnation time (corresponding operating time).
Mean (SD) = mean concentration for days 100 to 300 (standard deviation).

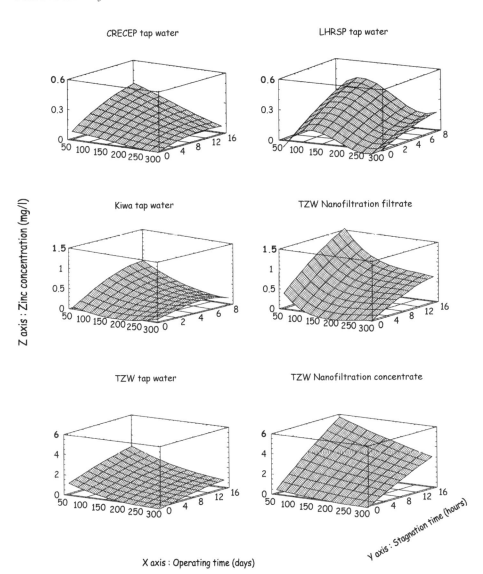

Figure 4.10 Copper with brass fittings rig experiments. Zinc concentrations as function of stagnation time and operating time

stagnation times up to 8 hours in all cases. Experiments carried out with longer stagnation (16 hours: CRECEP, TZW nanofiltration filtrate and concentrate) showed that, generally, the concentration still increased between 8 and 16 hours but tended to stabilize to a plateau or sometimes to decrease slightly (nanofiltration filtrate).

Oxygen depletion was observed in correlation with high zinc concentrations (high corrosion rate), in particular with TZW nanofiltration filtrate and

Table 4.11 Zinc concentrations in galvanized steel rig experiments at different stages

Stagnation time	a	CRECEP	KIWA	LHRSP	WRC	TZW Concentrate	TZW Filtrate
½ hour	Max (*day*)	0.45 (*1*)	0.75 (*1*)	1.0 (*1*)	5.6 (*2*)	4.5 (*336*)	2 (*34*)
	Min (*day*)	0.13 (*363*)	0.47 (*270*)	0.10 (*342*)	0.83 (*5*)	0.77 (*519*)	0.76 (*637*)
	Mean (*SD*)	0.24 (*0.06*)	0.50 (*0.04*)	0.19 (*0.08*)	1.6	2.1 (*0.4*)	1.04 (*0.08*)
2 hours	Max (*day*)	0.95 (*200*)	1.9 (*56*)	0.69 (*54*)		14.3 (*336*)	5.1 (*34*)
	Min (*day*)	0.40 (*296*)	1.2 (*270*)	0.26 (*269*)		2.3 (*519*)	2.2 (*264*)
	Mean (*SD*)	0.58 (*0.18*)	1.6 (*0.4*)	0.41 (*0.10*)	0.67	6.6 (*1.8*)	3.2 (*0.3*)
4 hours	Max (*day*)	1.03 (*75*)	2.9 (*56*)	1.6 (*40*)		19.6 (*336*)	7.8 (*5*)
	Min (*day*)	0.57 (*296*)	1.9 (*270*)	0.35 (*578*)		3.7 (*552*)	3.0 (*364*)
	Mean (*SD*)	0.83 (*0.17*)	2.2 (*0.3*)	0.59 (*0.17*)	3.2	9.7 (*2.1*)	4.7 (*0.5*)
8 hours	Max (*day*)	1.8 (*302*)	3.8 (*56*)	1.6 (*54*)		22.4 (*819*)	8.1 (*27*)
	Min (*day*)	0.88 (*297*)	2.7 (*270*)	0.47 (*342*)		5.1 (*90*)	3.4 (*588*)
	Mean (*SD*)	1.3 (*0.3*)	3.3 (*0.5*)	1.0 (*0.3*)	5.66	14 (*3*)	5.6 (*0.7*)

[a] Max (*day*) = maximum concentration at given stagnation time (*corresponding operating time*).
Min (*day*) = minimum concentration at given stagnation time (*corresponding operating time*).
Mean (*SD*) = mean concentration for days 100 to 300 (*standard deviation*).

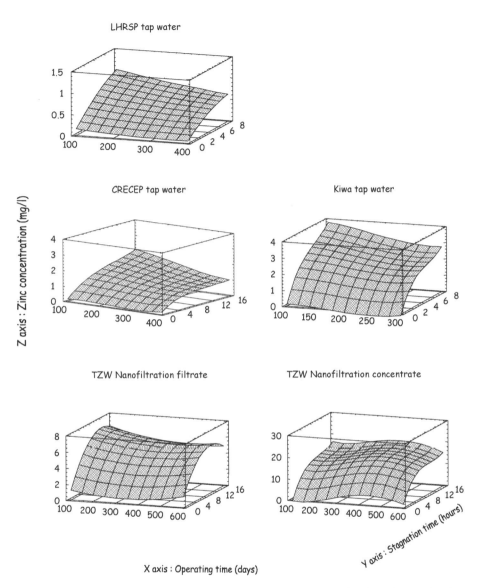

Figure 4.11   Galvanized steel rig experiments. Zinc concentrations as function of stagnation time and operating time

concentrate, where oxygen concentration fell below 1 or 2 mg/l after 8 or 16 hours' stagnation. In the same cases, a slight pH increase could also be observed.

Except with TZW nanofiltration concentrate, zinc concentrations always decreased with operating time, the curves being typically of type 1 (exponential decrease to a minimum value). The maximum levels of contamination occurred

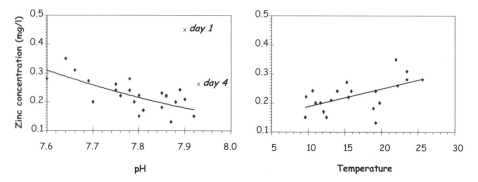

Figure 4.12   Relationship between zinc concentration after 30 minutes' stagnation, pH and temperature. Results with CRECEP tap water

in the first days of operation and were followed by a slow asymptotic decrease with variations, probably due to changes in water quality, over several months.

Figure 4.12 illustrates the relationship between zinc concentration (stagnation of 30 minutes), pH and temperature with CRECEP water. The figure shows that zinc migration was well correlated with pH and temperature, and that small changes in these parameters may significantly affect the contamination level.

The shape of the ageing curves ([Zn] = f(operating time)) was different with TZW nanofiltration concentrate and cannot be described by a simple shape (type 1, 2 or 3). Figure 4.13 shows a comparison between the evolution of zinc concentration (after 8 hours' stagnation) and pH of water. Parallel evolution can be seen: an increase in pH corresponds to a decrease in zinc. Thus, it appears very likely that variations in zinc concentration is due essentially to changes in water quality (pH, but probably also temperature, oxygen or other parameters) and not (only?) to ageing of the material.

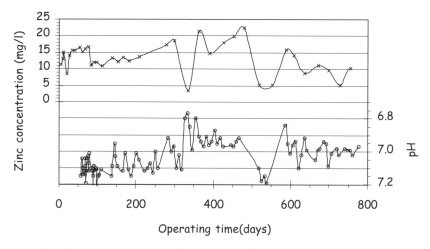

Figure 4.13   Comparison of zinc and pH evolution with operating time for galvanized steel rig with TZW nanofiltration concentrate water

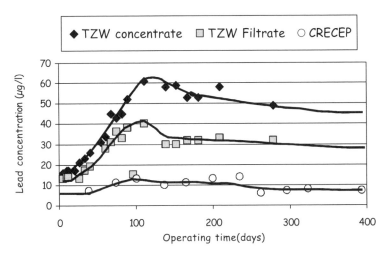

Figure 4.14 Lead concentrations after 8 hours of stagnation as a function of operating time for galvanized Steel rig experiments

In order of decreasing corrosivity, ranking of waters is as follows: TZW concentrate ≫ TZW filtrate ≫ Kiwa > CRECEP > LHRSP.

For WRC, important differences were observed between filtered (dissolved metal) and nonfiltered (total) samples. Particulate metal (total dissolved) represents an important ratio of the total (>50 %). Looking at total metal concentrations up to day 103, WRC should be ranked as TZW filtrate. TZW concentrate and filtrate led to very high zinc concentrations, exceeding 1 mg/l after 30 minutes' stagnation and 5 mg/l after 8 hours (Table 4.11).

(b) Lead. Lead concentrations significantly exceeding 10 μg/l appear only with TZW nanofiltration filtrate and concentrate after 2 hours' stagnation or more.

Values around 10μg/l were also detected with CRECEP water after 8 or 16 hours' stagnation (Figure 4.14).

Results from TZW show that contamination by lead increased continuously in the first months of operation (from day 0 to 100) up to a maximum and then decreased slowly. The maximum level of lead after 8 hours' stagnation was near 60 μg/l for concentrate and 40 μg/l for filtrate during several weeks in both cases. The level of 10 μg/l was frequently exceeded after 1 hour's stagnation. For WRC, even when high (particulate) zinc concentrations were observed, lead remained at low levels (<5 μg/l) and only particulate lead was detected.

These results show that lead is not leached from galvanized steel under the same conditions as is zinc. Migration of lead started only after an initial period of low migration ('induction period') and decreased after a period of high concentration. The induction period was several months with waters of high corrosivity in which high quantities of zinc were leached into the water. With other test waters of lower corrosivity, an increase in lead migration after long operating times cannot be excluded.

Stainless steel: Chromium, nickel and iron have been analysed. For iron, all results were very low and most of them are near detection limits or do not significantly differ from the noise (iron in the test waters). For chromium, all results were below the detection limits of the analytical methods except for one: 25 µg/l after 1 hour's stagnation on day 637. These were both with TZW nanofiltration concentrate.

For nickel, only two results exceeded 10 µg/l: 16 µg/l after 30 minutes' stagnation on day 69, 37 µg/l after 1 hour's stagnation on day 637, both with TZW nanofiltration concentrate. These isolated points cannot be interpreted as real contamination from the material, as all other results were below 5 µg/l.

However, with TZW concentrate, concentrations of between 1 and 5 µg/l were observed, mainly in the first days of operation (with no relation to stagnation time).

4.2.4   Discussion

Achieving reproducibility with a laboratory sit-and-soak test

There are broadly two aspects to determining the reproducibility of a test procedure, which are the ease with which a laboratory can consistently carry out the procedure, and the sensitivity of the results to slight variations in that procedure. Obviously both aspects will be affected to some extent by the clarity of description and comprehensiveness of the test procedure itself.

Certain generalizations can be made about the likely cause of features in sets of results. Thus a large covariance within a single test in a single laboratory would suggest poor experimental control. The converse of this is, of course, when a laboratory consistently produces the same result for repeat tests with low covariance in the data, even where this is significantly different from the result produced by other laboratories for the same test. That laboratory has good experimental control of its procedure.

Consistent differences between laboratories in otherwise low covariance sets of data suggest some systematic difference in the test procedure being carried out in each laboratory. A consistently large covariance found in the same test by most laboratories suggests a result that is intrinsically sensitive to slight variations in the test procedure. It is, of course, possible to get any combination of the above factors.

The covariance values achieved in this project (see Table 4.4), generally indicate good intra-laboratory control of the test procedures. Thus the average covariance figure for the leaching of zinc from brass, from all the tests that used the standard water, whether at pH 7 or 8.2, was 11.3 %. The corresponding figure for the leaching of lead it was 16.8 %.

The covariance within laboratories was highest where the level of metal contamination was either very high or very low, for example a mean of 22.9 % for the leaching of zinc from galvanized steel where the zinc levels where amongst the highest achieved, and a mean of 65.3 % for the leaching of lead from galvanized steel where the results were close to the detection limit of the analytical methods.

Although the reason for the large scatter when metal levels were very low may be easy to understand, the reason for the same effect at high metal concentrations may be open to more than one explanation. The sensitivity of the solubility of zinc corrosion products to solution pH, combined with the open beaker configuration of the test that allows the loss of CO_2 to the atmosphere, are sources of potential variability in the test procedure used. It has been shown also that devices used in the test to cover the beakers and to hold coupons in the test solution influence the diffusion rate of gases (CO_2 and O_2) from the atmosphere to the test solution and vice versa. The tightness of the system or its permeability to gas may vary from one laboratory to the other, and could explain part of the scatter observed between laboratories.

However, bringing the pH of the test solution to equilibrium with the atmosphere, in the brass tests 3 and 4, or carrying out the test with the standard solution in an enclosed vessel as in brass test 5, did not reduce what was admittedly an already low covariance in the results. A second explanation of large scatter could be the (random) presence of particulate matter (e.g. oxides) which is dissolved by the acidification of the test solution after the sample has been removed at the end of the test.

A third possible explanation of large covariance with high contamination levels is that the metal is still not in equilibrium with the test water at the end of the test period. As this often corresponds to a period of rapid change in the level of contamination, the results may be sensitive to the slight variations that inevitably occur from test to test. Prolonging the test period, or the pre-ageing of samples before carrying out the test procedure, may be a way of reducing this effect.

Another consequence of non-equilibrium behaviour is that a short-term test may only provide a snapshot of the interaction between the alloy and water under test. This may mean that for some metals, the test procedure will discriminate poorly between the effect of different waters on the same alloy, the results obtained being more a reflection of the differences in the speed with which an alloy achieves equilibrium with the waters rather than its long term suitability in those waters.

In the present tests, the variability in the results for both zinc and copper from brass are of little practical consequence, given that the values achieved were so far below the maximum acceptable concentration (MAC) for either element. However, for an element where this is not the case, and where the results indicate that the alloy has not reached final equilibrium with the water, it raises questions as to whether the test period should be extended and how long an element should be allowed to exceed its MAC in a test before the use of the alloy in the test water was deemed unacceptable.

The overall conclusion from the test programme is that each laboratory was achieving sufficient experimental control within a test and that the amount of leaching was not hypersensitive to slight deviations from the protocol. The fact that the laboratories as a group could not consistently achieve means within the same statistical population indicated that they were carrying out slightly different tests. This conclusion implies that agreement between laboratories could be reached if sufficient attention were paid to the procedures being carried out in each one and, as a consequence, if the test protocol were to be specified in even greater detail.

Having demonstrated the principle of a laboratory test, the Conormative Group considered it the task of others to develop a specific test protocol. The question remaining for the current project was to consider to what extent a sit-and-soak test represents the situation in authentic plumbing systems and to what extent any deviation is significant.

The extent to which a simple laboratory test can reflect behaviour in an authentic plumbing system

In order to discuss this question it is necessary to consider the potential mechanisms that can control the leaching of metals in contact with potable waters.

Potential mechanisms controlling the leaching of metals and their implications for a test protocol

1. *Rate of corrosion*: The rate at which a metal corrodes obviously provides the ultimate limit on the rate of contamination of the water that comes into contact with it. The corroded material usually changes its physical form through precipitation and/or changes in its oxidation state, etc. No direct attempt was made to measure the corrosion rate in any of the leaching experiments. Where the corrosion rate is the controlling mechanism, dissolved oxygen levels could be a critical factor. Exposing the coupon in an open beaker, where there is the greatest opportunity for oxygen replenishment, could thus represent the worst case for such a situation.

2. *Level of dissolved oxygen in the test water*: Plumbing systems either have no or only restricted access to the atmosphere. Consequently, where water remains static in such systems for extended periods, it is possible to develop low oxygen concentrations. This can occur most frequently in crevices where bulk exchange of water does not occur and oxygen concentrations are maintained by diffusion only. Reduction in dissolved oxygen concentrations may have a beneficial effect where the contamination level is controlled directly by the rate of corrosion. However, low oxygen levels may also destabilize passivating films or lead to the production of a more soluble lower oxidation state of the metal. In this case, exposure in an open beaker would not be the worst case.

   In test 5 of the conormative experiments, the test pieces were exposed in closed vessels to limit the gaseous exchange with the atmosphere (O_2 and CO_2). This limited the replacement of oxygen and so (to some extent) covered this mechanism.

3. *Galvanic interaction with other metallic components*: Galvanic interaction between materials not only increases the rate of corrosion but, by raising the electrochemical potential at which the metal corrodes, may introduce new effects, for example, the development of passivating films or the conversion of a previously protective ion into an aggressive one.

Attempts have been made in the past to examine galvanic interactions by electrically connecting brass coupons to copper electrodes and then testing the combination in accordance with the conventional BSI procedure. Differences in the results from the uncoupled case were found although, because of practical difficulties in maintaining the integrity of the couple and an increased scatter in the data, it was difficult to decide whether or not the differences were significant.

4. *Solubility of corrosion product*: A deposit is usually produced on a metal's surface in neutral waters, which stifles the corrosion reaction; at the same time the deposit dissolves in the water in contact with that surface. Initially the rate of corrosion exceeds the rate of dissolution and the deposit increases in thickness. This increased thickness reduces the corrosion rate further until the latter equals the rate of dissolution and a dynamic equilibrium is achieved. For this point to be reached, the deposit has to have some combination of effectiveness at stifling the corrosion with sufficient mechanical stability to maintain the thickness of the layer required. When this dynamic equilibrium is achieved, the rate of contamination is then, under defined flow conditions, controlled by the solubility of the corrosion product in the water. The standard sit-and-soak procedure used in this project tacitly assumes that this is the major controlling mechanism.

5. *Mechanical stability of corrosion product layer*: Where the corrosion deposit has insufficient mechanical stability to maintain the thickness required to achieve dynamic equilibrium between the corrosion and dissolution rates, particles of the deposit will break off on an intermittent basis producing peaks of contamination. This type of breakdown would only be expected after prolonged ageing (>70 days for brasses) of the test coupon. Determining the difference between the total metal leached into the test solution and its filtered metal content could give an indication of the presence of this problem.

   A corrosion product that broke down relatively infrequently would produce a peak of contamination in what could otherwise be a generally low background level. This might be difficult to detect if the actual period during which metal concentrations were measured was relatively short. However, the less frequent the occurrence the less important it is if the effect is missed.

   The short term nature of the laboratory sit-and-soak test probably means any effect of this nature will be missed by the current test procedure.

6. *Surface finish of the test coupon*: Various manufacturing processes can change the physical form of the metal's initial surface or produce surface films, either of which may influence the characteristics of the corrosion deposit that is developed when in contact with water. These effects may influence or change the mechanism controlling the level of contamination. The standard sit-and-soak test defines a machined surface that will not be representative of a cast surface, for example. In the first set of conormative tests, actual galvanized steel pipe was used to overcome precisely this sort of problem.

7. *Ageing*: Time is required for the film on a metal surface to develop fully. Until this happens, the long term potential of a metal to contaminate the supply will be uncertain. An even more critical effect of ageing is to change the ratio of the elements at the surface of the uncorroded metal. This may result in a delay (induction period) in the contamination of the water by certain of the metal's trace constituents until they have been sufficiently concentrated at the surface.

   The standard sit-and-soak test is, of course, very short. However, if long term ageing was thought to be potentially a significant factor, samples could be preconditioned for whatever length of time was considered appropriate. The conditions could be chosen for practical convenience rather than bearing any particular relation to the final test protocol. Thus, all 20 coupons could be suspended in a 5-litre beaker with the test water flowing through.

8. *Effect of flow regime experienced*: The speed with which a metal's surface comes to equilibrium with a water, and in some cases the characteristics of the corrosion product which is developed, can depend on the flow regime that it has experienced. At present, the standard sit-and-soak test defines static conditions. However, if this mechanism was thought potentially to be significant, different flow regimes could be incorporated into an ageing procedure to cover this.

9. *Aggressivity of the test water*: Different metals, and even different phases of the same alloy, have different vulnerabilities to particular water compositions. The original BSI test water was chosen for its aggressiveness towards lead rich phases. However, it has low aggressiveness to metals that form passivating films, e.g. stainless steel, aluminium, etc.

   In the current project, sit-and-soak tests were carried out using a range of waters. This could be made the standard procedure when testing a metal for general acceptability. The control mechanisms covered by the sit-and-soak test used in this project, and its potential for adaptation, are summarized in Table 4.12.

Table 4.12 Control mechanisms and the sit-and-soak test

Control mechanism	Comments
Solubility	Covered by the current sit-and-soak test
Galvanic interaction	Not covered by the current sit-and-soak test but galvanic test couples have been used in the past
Dissolved oxygen levels	Not covered by current protocol but tests could be carried out in enclosed vessels to (partially) meet this requirement
Surface finish of metal	Not covered by current sit-and-soak test but the difficulty has been met before by using manufactured pipe sections as test pieces; may be practically more difficult with fittings
Ageing	Not covered by current sit-and-soak test but could readily be met by a sample preconditioning stage
Water composition effects	Not covered by current sit-and-soak test but other test waters could and have been used

Pipe-rig results

The main advantage of using a rig procedure is that operating conditions may simulate as closely as possible the authentic situation. Consequently, the mechanism controlling corrosion and water contamination is built into the test apparatus without having to be identified. Disadvantages are the expense, the time involved and the large volume of water needed, which practically implies the use of tap water.

Main outcomes of rig experiments are:

(i) Three distinct behaviours can be identified in the evolution of the level of contamination during the course of the test run:

- Exponential decrease to a minimum value;

- Increase to a maximum value that then either remains constant or which decreases slightly;

- Peak contamination after an initial period of low values (during several weeks or months) followed by a gradual decrease.

    The shape of the curve depends on the material tested and can be different for different metals in an alloy. For a given metal (e.g. copper from copper pipe), the shape can also be different with different test waters and even, for a given test water (e.g. TZW concentrate with copper pipe), it can be different at different stagnation times. Time to reach equilibrium and contamination level also depends on test water characteristics.

(ii) Variations in the characteristics of test water can influence the contamination level. This has been shown for pH and temperature but could be expected also with other parameters (oxygen, alkalinity, sulfate, etc.) if significant variations occur during test operation. Tap water is usually subject to random or seasonal variations (mainly with surface water). Water analyses are then necessary in parallel with metal analyses to avoid misinterpretation of contamination results.

(iii) Tests on pipe rigs with brass fittings show that there is possible influence of the fitting material on the behaviour of the pipe material (reduced contamination by copper due to zinc migration from brass). More generally, this would mean that a material should be tested in authentic situation (fittings with the material(s) they are designed for).

(iv) The use of local tap waters in pipe-rig experiments did not allow the reproducibility of the results between laboratories to be assessed. Slight differences in the test device or test operation could, as for sit-and-soak tests, affect test reproducibility. An accurate definition of test device and test conditions is necessary to reduce this risk. Nevertheless pipe-rig reproducibility will have to be assessed.

Reproducibility within each laboratory can be assessed by comparing copper concentrations from copper rigs and from copper rigs with brass fittings. For all laboratories, copper concentration curves overlap almost perfectly after the initial period where migration of zinc from brass fitting influence (reduce) the migration of copper.

Information from reference rigs is more complete and closer to reality than is information given by a simple sit-and-soak test where only 24-hour stagnation samples are analysed over a short period of time (2 weeks). However, adaptations of sit-and-soak tests could be considered as getting more information on different possible mechanisms (Table 4.13) or to produce stagnation curves. However, static tests cannot cover the influence of flow conditions, which appear also to be an important factor in authentic situations.

Table 4.13   Comparison of the advantages and disadvantages of a sit-and-soak test versus rig tests

Sit-and-soak test		Rig test	
Advantages	Disadvantages	Advantages	Disadvantages
Cheap			Expensive
Short time scale	Does not cover ageing effects	Covers ageing effects	Long time scale
Generally good control of experimental conditions	Experimental conditions may not be authentic and introduce a different control mechanism	Relatively authentic exposure conditions	Poor control of exposure conditions may give problems of reproducibility
Good control of surface finish of coupon	Surface finish may not reflect reality	Authentic surface condition	Poor control of surface finish may introduce variability in the answer
Surface/area volume ratio well controlled	Surface/area volume ratio may not reflect reality	Surface/area volume ratio reflects reality (for a given pipe diameter)	Surface/area volume ratio not well controlled
Small volume of test water required (synthetic or tap water of controlled quality can be used)			Large volume of water required, really has to be on the tap (variation in water quality may introduce scattering of the results)

4.2.5 Conclusions

Because of the variety and specificity of the mechanisms controlling the interaction between water and metallic materials, and as the test water is itself a significant factor in determining the leaching from metals, the procedures used to assess organic materials are not valid for testing metallic materials.

The variety of situations that can occur in authentic plumbing systems cannot be fully represented by any single simple sit-and-soak or pipe-rig test procedure.

The pipe-rig test procedure, carried out in this research can provide the information necessary for the evaluation of potential migration from metallic materials when in contact with potable water.

Conclusions regarding sit-and-soak tests

Experiments carried out with sit-and-soak tests show that it is possible to get reproducible results within laboratories. However, the test has proved to be very sensitive to slight variations in procedure. Further development and improvements in the definition of the procedure will be necessary to achieve reliable inter-laboratory reproducibility.

The sit-and-soak test procedure used in this study, adapted from that in BS 7766, tacitly assumes that the migration of metals in water is governed by the solubility of corrosion products. However, adaptations of the procedure could be possible to cover many of the other potentially controlling mechanisms.

A simple sit-and-soak test procedure (or a set of such tests) can be useful in identifying which controlling mechanisms are operating in a particular situation. However, there appears to be no ready way of correlating the results of such static tests with those contamination levels expected in authentic situations. Consequently sit-and-soak test procedures cannot be reliably used to produce an absolute evaluation of the potential migration from any particular metal.

Conclusions regarding rig tests

A pipe-rig test procedure can simulate an authentic situation and so give a direct quantitative assessment of the potential to contaminate by metals in relation to the particular operating conditions and test water used. Consequently pipe rigs are necessary for the evaluation of potential migrations from metallic materials.

The operating conditions for pipe rigs need to be standardized and their inter-laboratory reproducibility assessed.

The selection of test water(s) is not within the scope of the test protocol itself but should be within the scope of regulation. The research shows that it is not possible to use a single water for all materials to be tested. Test water quality might be chosen according to the material or category of material to be tested, or a range of water qualities might be selected to cover all situations.

The experiments with pipe rigs have shown that pipe fittings can influence the migration of metals from the pipe with which they are used (compare the results from copper rigs with those from copper rigs with brass fittings). The consequence of this is that it is necessary to test the material used to make fittings in authentic situations, that is, connected with the pipe materials for which they are designed.

A comparison of copper concentrations after half-an-hour stagnation in copper rig experiments at CRECEP with field data observed in Paris shows a good agreement in the level of concentrations. Such comparisons would need to be developed in other situations to assess the actual 'representativity' of pipe-rig experiments.

4.3 TEST PROCEDURE FOR CEMENTITIOUS MATERIALS

4.3.1 Introduction

A cement can be defined as a substance that sets and hardens due to chemical reactions that occur upon mixing with water. Cement based materials include two general components:

- the aggregates – these constitute the basic structure of the material, for example sand in the case of cement–mortar lining, sand and gravel in the case of reinforced concrete pipes;
- the binder – responsible for the cohesion and mechanical properties of the material.

Figure 4.15 shows the basic structure of cement-based materials, exemplified by a cement–mortar lining. The binder consists of hydrated cement produced by reacting water with anhydrous cement, which contains calcium silicates and calcium aluminates in various proportions.

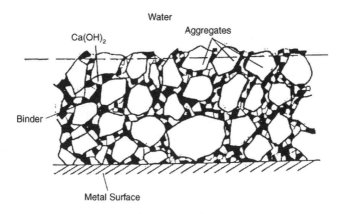

Figure 4.15   Schematic structure of cement-based material

Table 4.14 Typical compositions for some type of cements used for manufacturing pipe)

Parameter	Portland cement	Blast furnace cement	Calcium-aluminate cement
SiO_2 (%)	21	27	3.5
CaO (%)	65	48	38
Free CaO (%)	1.5	0.5	0.5
Al_2O_3 (%)	5	13	36
Fe_2O_3 (%)	2.5	1.5	18
SO_3 (%)	2.5	3.8	0.1
Na_2O (%)	0.3	0.4	0.1
K_2O (%)	0.8	0.8	0.05
MgO (%)	2.0	2.8	0.4
Density (g/cm^3)	3.1	2.9	3.2
Specific surface (cm^2/g)	3870	3850–8450	2750

The basic constituent, the clinker, is obtained from the pyroprocessing of calcareous and argillaceous rock. Portland types of cement include those that are mixtures of clinker and pozzolana, blast furnace slag and fly ash, in a range of combinations. In addition, non-Portland calcium aluminate cements (formerly called high alumina cement or HAC) are manufactured by pyroprocessing bauxite and lime.

Generally, concrete used for water treatment plant pipes, water tanks, and filters is made using (ordinary) Portland cement, whereas cement–mortar linings can be made of different types of cements, such as Portland cements, blast furnace cement or the non-Portland calcium aluminate cement. Each type of cement has a typical composition. Table 4.14 gives the typical composition of the primary cements used for manufacturing pipe.

Structure of the cement matrix in concrete and mortar

During manufacturing of cement-based pipeline products, the silicates and aluminates present in the cement react with water to form products of hydration and, in time, these set to a hard mass. The various solid phases formed come into thermodynamic equilibrium with the interstitial water (pore water), which is rich in calcium, sodium, and potassium hydroxide phases. The presence of these hydroxides raises the pH of the pore water solution to about 13 or 13.5. Table 4.15 gives typical compositions of pore solution for two types of cement: Portland and blast furnace slag cement.

Carbonation of cement based materials in contact with water

Contact of cement based materials with water produces changes in the cement matrix and in the water composition. The interactions between the cement material and

Table 4.15 Typical composition of the pore solution for two types of cement

Parameter	Portland	Blast furnace
pH	13.4	13.2
Calcium (mg Ca/l)	65	37
Magnesium (mg Mg/l)	0.25	0.30
Sodium (mg Na/l)	2 200	1 600
Potassium (mg K/l)	11 500	8 500
Aluminium (mg Al/l)	4.5	25
Sulfate (mg SO$_4$/l)	550	160
Silica (mg SiO$_2$/l)	12	32

the water result from the great surface area of contact between these two phases, especially in the pores. The ions present in the pore water (such as OH^-, Ca^{2+}, Na^+ and K^+) tend to escape into the transported water, which normally contains smaller concentrations of these constituents.

On the other hand, the ions present in the transported water, such as aqueous carbon dioxide and bicarbonate ion, tend to enter into the pore water. The reaction between the hydroxide ions from the pore water and the dissolved aqueous carbon dioxide and bicarbonate ion forms carbonate ion (CO_3^{2-}). As a result, conditions suitable for spontaneous calcium carbonate precipitation may exist in the pores, near the exposed surface. This process is called carbonation. These calcium carbonate deposits can reduce the interaction between transported water and the chemical species in the pores.

Blockage of the pores by carbonation will not occur if a significant proportion of the calcium ions from the calcium hydroxide leaches into the transported water, because the solubility product for calcium carbonate will not be sufficiently exceeded. Then the calcium ions present in the transported water will not contribute to the formation of interstitial calcium carbonate deposits and, consequently, the transported water gains calcium ions. Carbonation can be induced by bringing CO_3^{2-} ions to the pores by dry pretreatment with gaseous CO_2 or a wet pretreatment with water containing a sufficient HCO_3^- concentration. CO_2 and HCO_3^- are converted to CO_3^{2-} in the pores of the material because of the high pH value according to the following reactions:

$$\text{Dry pretreatment: } CO_2 + Ca^{2+} + 2OH^- \Rightarrow CaCO_3(s) + H_2O$$
$$\text{Wet pretreatment: } HCO_3^- + Ca^{2+} + OH^- \Rightarrow CaCO_3(s) + H_2O$$

Influence of water composition

In a calcium carbonate aggressive water, dissolution of the locally precipitated $CaCO_3$ proceeds continuously into the cement based material. The alkaline properties of the cement are inadequate to neutralize the $CaCO_3$-dissolving properties of the water.

If the water in contact with cement is in equilibrium or is oversaturated with respect to calcium carbonate, its deposition leads to blocking of the pores. The calcium carbonate deposit is then stable and the cement material is protected for as long as the transported water remains under these conditions. If the transported water has a low total inorganic carbon (TIC), the deposit may not lead to blocking of the pores, regardless of whether the water transported is oversaturated with $CaCO_3$ or not. In this case the amount of $CaCO_3$ precipitation possible is smaller than the amount of calcium species dissolved.

Effects of cement-based materials on water quality

Contact between water and cement materials can lead to lime (calcium) leaching, which induces a substantial pH increase in the drinking water. The effect on water quality can be seen as:

- an increase in pH. Depending on the buffer capacity of the water, it can be that the pH value rises above the limit value of 9.5. The pH may be as high a 11 to 12 in 'worst-case' conditions (Conroy and Oliphant, 1991);

- an increase in the aluminium content of the drinking water (Conroy and Oliphant, 1991). The different cement types contain different aluminium contents. Some aluminium goes into solution because of the high pH value of the water caused by lime leaching;

- an increase in the potassium content of the drinking water. This is an indicator of a leaching process;

- an increase in hardness of the water.

One of the objectives of the test is to investigate the leaching of mineral micropollutants, such as heavy metals, from cement-based materials. All cements, irrespective of their type, contain small but variable amounts of a range of heavy metals derived from their constituents. These are generally present at trace level.

The behaviour of heavy metals in hydrated cement matrices is not entirely clear. Much research, however, tends to indicate that they are essentially immobilized as insoluble hydroxides within the structure of the hydration products. On the other hand, it is conceivable that under some conditions, they might be 'solved' and transported to the surface through the pore system. The level of increase in the pH of a water and the amount of leaching of other elements which takes place, depends on:

- the TIC and buffer capacity of the transported water;

- the type of cement;

- the contact time between the water and the cement material;

- the pipe diameter.

4.3.2   Technical Background

Preconditioning of test samples

The nature of cement based materials begins to change as soon as they are manufactured and this continuing change cannot easily be controlled or predicted as it is affected by for instance, storage conditions and time of storage. After pipe manufacturing, during storage and transportation, the natural carbonation process takes place and transforms the surface of the mortar lining by $CaCO_3$ deposition into the pores. Also pipes commonly undergo some form of preparation, such as hydraulic tests, disinfecting or rinsing, before they are brought into service. This can lead to changes in the nature of the material. Therefore, in testing cement-based materials, a preconditioning stage may be necessary in order to give each material arriving from the factory a comparable state of carbonation or maturity, including being able to simulate the effects of preparation prior to intended use.

Preconditioning can be a particularly important step in that the validity and reproducibility of the migration test itself might directly depend on the preparation of the test samples.

In the conormative research project, preconditioning with liquid and gaseous carbonation of the cement materials was tested. The preconditioning consists of wet contact with several water types (soft and moderate hardness) or dry contact with CO_2 under several conditions (CO_2-pressure, time). The effect of preconditioning is compared with unpreconditioned cement mortar specimens.

The effect and the results of preconditioning have to be assessed against the following questions:

- Does preconditioning mask/minimize the effects of different ageing times or storage conditions?

- Does preconditioning improve intra- and inter-laboratory reproducibility (with respect to indicative parameters such as pH, aluminium, calcium, potassium, etc.)?

- Does preconditioning improve the relationship with practice?

- Is preconditioning required in order to avoid interference of hydroxyl ions with other parameters to be measured (e.g. taste, aluminium, organic and mineral micropollutants, etc)?

Migration tests

The objective of the research into the migration test was to assess the influence of water characteristics (mainly pH, calcium carbonate aggressiveness and mineral content) on the migration of micropollutants and on the organoleptic quality of water.

The influence of water characteristics on the behaviour of cement-based materials tends to be very significant. Although the dissolution of lime depends on water pH, it is dependent to a greater extent on other factors such as the aggressiveness and mineral content of the water. Some metallic elements or other substances may be leached with aggressive water of low mineral content, while leaching will tend to be reduced in non-aggressive water of medium mineral content.

The test protocol will be the same as the protocol described in the European draft standard of CEN TC164/WG3 for organic materials: test samples (pipes segments) will be filled up with test water for three successive 72-hour periods. The effect of varying the test water characteristics has to be assessed against the following criteria:

- sensitivity of the test method with respect to potential micropollutant leaching;

- reproducibility of test results between and within laboratories (with respect to pH, aluminium, calcium and potassium);

- practicability of water preparation and control;

- migration water should be representative of natural drinking waters or yield representative data, with respect to pH, $CaCO_3$ content (hardness and alkalinity), aggressiveness, silica content and occurrence in different countries.

4.3.3   Effect of Preconditioning and Migration Water

Experimental procedure

The full experimental procedure is summarized below. This full procedure has been applied only for the first mortar tested (ordinary Portland cement). Results from this first set of experiments have allowed some experimental conditions for further tests with blast furnace cement (BFC) and high alumina cement (HAC) mortars to be deleted (see page 165).

Preconditioning: Two categories of method have been used for the preconditioning of cement based materials:

- liquid contact ('wet process'): pipe segments are filled up with the preconditioning water;

- gas contact ('dry process'): pipe segments are filled up with carbon dioxide at a given pressure.

On the basis of existing data, the following different preconditioning conditions were defined:

Reference: no preconditioning. Samples should be stored in the lab until the beginning of migration tests.

Gas contact, CO_2 pressure and exposure duration are as follows: D1: 1 bar CO_2 during 5 days; D2: 2 bar CO_2 during 5 days; D3: 1 bar CO_2 during 1 day; D4: 2 bar CO_2 during 1 day.

Before applying CO_2, samples should be filled up with deionized water for half an hour in order to moisten the cement surface and to allow further carbonation by gas.

Liquid contact, four preconditioning waters should be used with characteristics as follows:

(1) *Wp1*: 20 mg/l $CaCO_3$ of alkalinity and calcium hardness at pH $= 7.0$.

(2) *Wp2*: 200 mg/l $CaCO_3$ of alkalinity and calcium hardness, at equilibrium (pH $\approx$ 7.4);

(3) *Wp3*: Same as Wp2 + 0.25 mmole / l CO_2 (pH $\approx$ 7.2),

(4) *Wp4*: Same as Wp2 + 1.0 mmole / l CO_2 (pH $\approx$ 6.8).

Synthetic waters should be prepared by dissolving calcium chloride and sodium bicarbonate in deionized water and adjusting the pH by bubbling CO_2 and air.

For liquid contact preconditioning, pipe segments should be filled up with water for successive 24-hour periods (72 hours during the weekend).

The initial and minimum preconditioning step consists of five successive contact periods; three times at 24 hours, once at 72 hours and once at 24 hours.

At the end of this procedure, if the pH is below 9.2, migration tests can start. If not, then the same procedure should be applied one more time. At the end of the second week, migration tests should be performed whatever the pH value.

CRECEP, WRC and Kiwa have performed experiments with liquid preconditioning. Kiwa, LHRSP and TZW have performed experiments with gaseous preconditioning. Reference, unpreconditioned, samples have been tested in the five laboratories.

Migration tests: Six test waters have been used with approximately the following characteristics:

Wm1: 200 mg/l of alkalinity and Ca hardness at equilibrium (pH $\approx$ 7.4);

Wm2: same as Wm1 + 0.25 mmol/l CO_2 (pH $\approx$ 7.2);

Wm3: same as Wm 1 + 1.0 mmol/l CO_2 (pH $\approx$ 6.8);

Wm4: 20 mg/l of alkalinity and Ca hardness at equilibrium (pH $\approx$ 8.2);

Wm5: same as Wm4 + 0.25 mmol/l CO_2 (pH $\approx$ 6.6);

Wm6: same as Wm4 + 1.0 mmol/l CO_2 (pH $\approx$ 6.0).

For the first trials, two laboratories (LHRSP and CRECEP) used natural mineral waters (Evian and Volvic) modified by adding hydrochloric acid to reduce alkalinity to 200 and 20 mg/l $CaCO_3$ approximately. The three other labs (Kiwa, TZW and WRC) used synthetic waters prepared by dissolving calcium chloride and sodium bicarbonate in deionized water.

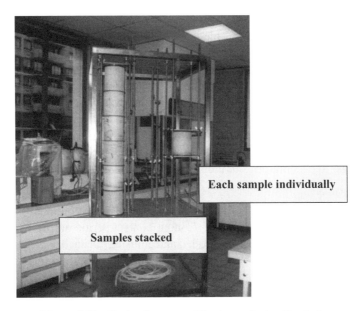

Figure 4.16   Device for preconditioning and migration tests

Test device. For preconditioning, six pipe segments have to be treated with the same water. To ensure good reproducibility, the six pipe segments were stacked in a column to be treated under the same conditions (Figure 4.16). For migration tests, each pipe segment was treated individually (Figure 4.17).

The test devices used are slightly different for each of the five laboratories, but the pipe segments are always set between two stainless steel plates with PTFE gaskets for tightness (Figure 4.17).

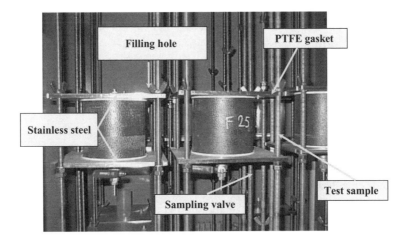

Figure 4.17   Example of device for migration tests

All materials used for the device should be tested to check that they do not contaminate water. A procedural blank in the form of a glass cylinder should be tested in parallel.

Dimension of pipe segments. Samples of materials are taken from actual pipes provided by the manufacturers. Thus the surface/volume ratio (S/V) is fixed by the diameter of the pipe sample. For practical reasons it is easier to handle small samples. Consequently, pipe segments of 150 mm length and 150 mm diameter were used (S/V = 260 cm^2/l). These dimensions allow sufficient cement lining surface and a sufficient volume of water for analysis. Samples were cut in the factory and delivered to each of the five laboratories in the finished form, ready for tests.

Analytical determinations

During preconditioning. pH, aluminium concentration and, optionally, conductivity were determined after each 24- or 72-hour contact period during wet preconditioning. Only CO_2 pressure was controlled and adjusted during dry preconditioning.

During migrations (3 × 72 hours). pH, aluminium concentration and, conductivity were determined after the first and second migration periods. At the end of the third 72-hour period, test waters were sampled for analysis of the following parameters:

pH; total organic carbon;

organoleptic and aesthetic parameters (turbidity, flavour);

mineralization (conductivity, alkalinity, calcium, magnesium, sodium, potassium, chloride, sulphate, nitrate);

mineral micropollutants (aluminium, iron (to check corrosion of cast iron if necessary), chromium and lead).

Materials tested Three materials were tested:

- Ordinary Portland cement (OPC) factory applied using the TATE process (December 1995);

- Blast furnace cement (BFC) factory applied by spinning (July 1996);

- High alumina cement (HAC) factory applied by spinning (April/May 1997)

These materials were chosen because they are representative of what is used in the pipe industry and because they have different compositions:

- Portland cements are calcium-silicate based materials, with less than 2 % free lime;

- Blast furnace cements are mixes of about 30 % OPC and 70 % slag.

- High alumina cements are calcium-aluminate based materials, without free lime.

Tested samples were ductile iron pipe with cement mortar lining, of 150 mm internal diameter.

The full procedure, as described above, was applied for OPC (nine preconditioning conditions and six test waters). After experiments with OPC, some experimental conditions were deleted for tests with HAC and BFC as they did not appear to give additional information. There were dry preconditioning with 1 bar CO_2 (D3 and D4); wet preconditioning with medium mineralized water with added CO_2 (Wp3 and Wp4); and migration waters with 0.25 mmole/l CO_2 (Wm2 and Wm5).

Experimental results

First examination of experimental results has shown that some parameters are good indicators of the behaviour of the materials in contact with water for the purpose of the research: pH, aluminium, calcium and potassium. The evolution of these elements is strongly influenced by the material and by test conditions (preconditioning and test water). Lead and chromium have never been detected at significant levels in any of the experiments carried out for the three materials.

Effect of preconditioning Liquid preconditioning. With a soft (low mineralized) preconditioning water, pH is high (>11 for OPC and BFC) and does not decrease significantly with contact time. At the end of preconditioning, pH was still above 9, even if preconditioning was prolonged for another week (3 × 24 h, 72 h, 24 h). With medium mineralized water, pH was lower (<9 for BFC and HAC) or decreased rapidly below 9 (OPC).

In the first case (soft water) there was no carbonation of the cement, but probably the opposite, an opening of the pores. In the second case, there was effective carbonation ($CaCO_3$ deposit) of the surface, which reduces lime migration in water.

With a soft preconditioning water, the scattering of pH results between the three laboratories seemed to increase with contact time (BFC and HAC), whereas there is good agreement between them for pH and aluminium with medium mineralized water. Aluminium concentration levels were very different for the three materials (HAC > OPC > BFC) but were always in relation to the pH for the individual material.

Effect of preconditioning on migration results. The effects of preconditioning and of migration test water were investigated using multifactor ANOVA (analysis of variance). This statistical tool breaks the variability of data (pH, Al, Ca or K) into contributions due to various factors (preconditioning conditions and CO_2 added in test water).

The analysis showed whether one or both (or neither) factors had a significant effect on the variability and which level of the factor is different from which other. The p value indicates whether the factor has a significant effect on the variability ($p < 0.05$) or not ($p > 0.05$).

Only data obtained with synthetic waters have been considered in these statistics as it appeared that the origin of water (natural or synthetic) had a major effect on the results, in particular for aluminium.

Ordinary Portland Cement. The effect of preconditioning is significant for the four parameters tested (pH, Al, Ca and K) for soft migration waters and for three parameters (pH, Ca and K) with medium mineralized migration waters. All preconditioning, except Wp1 (soft water pH 7) significantly reduced aluminium in soft migration water, but only wet preconditioning using a medium mineralized water (Wp2, Wp3 and Wp4) reduced pH in soft migration water.

All preconditioning significantly reduced pH in medium mineralized migration water with a better efficiency for Wp2, Wp3 and Wp4 (medium mineralized preconditioning water), followed by D1 and D2 (dry preconditioning, 5 days).

Figure 4.18 illustrates the effect of preconditioning on pH.

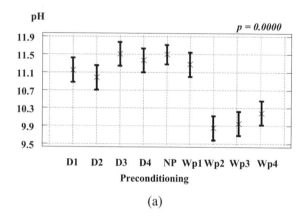

(a)

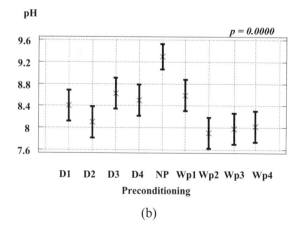

(b)

Figure 4.18 Least square means and 95 % confidence intervals, by preconditioning, for pH after migration using low mineralized water (a) and medium mineralized water (b) for ordinary Portland cement

Calcium migration was increased by Wp1 (soft water preconditioning) for soft migration test water.

For medium mineralized migration water, there was no migration of calcium from the material but, on the contrary, calcium precipitates on the material (initial calcium concentration in migration water is 80 mg/l).

The results for potassium show that the mechanism is different than for other parameters. In fact potassium leaching was decreased in all cases by wet preconditioning. These results indicate that potassium is leached from the cement in contact with water whatever the water characteristics are. The same potassium concentrations were observed with soft and medium mineralized migration waters. (Note that potassium leaching will tend to increase the pH as it is leached from the cement as KOH).

Differences also appeared between preconditioning waters Wp2, Wp3 and Wp4 (medium mineralized water with 0, 0.25 and 1 mmole/l CO_2 added); Wp2 (water at equilibrium) always being the most 'effective' (i.e. differences with unpreconditioned samples are greater). Wp3 and Wp4 were deleted from the following experiments. For dry preconditioning also, differences appear between D1 and D2 (5 days, 1 and 2 bar) and D3 and D4 (1 day, 1 and 2 bar). D3 and D4 were deleted from the following experiments.

Blast Furnace Cement. The effect of preconditioning is significant for pH and aluminium for soft migration water but only for potassium is the case of medium mineralized migration water. However, some effects can be observed for other parameters but they are not statistically significant. General trends are almost identical to OPC, except for pH in soft migration water. In fact, the pH increase was lower with dry preconditioned samples than with wet preconditioned (Wp2).

We can also observe that the material was less reactive than OPC: lower pH, aluminium and potassium concentrations, no significant change of calcium concentration in medium mineralized migration water (initial Ca = 80 mg/l).

High Alumina Cement. No significant effect of preconditioning was detected for the four parameters tested in either migration test water even if some difference appears in the graphs, which indicates the same general trends as for the other materials. pH levels were much lower with this material than with OPC and BFC but aluminium leaching was much more important especially in soft migration water (3 to 8 mg Al /l).

Further experiments however (see Section 4.3.4) show very clearly that preconditioning does in fact have an important and very significant effect. The effect of preconditioning can be 'masked' by the effect of migration test water characteristics (free CO_2 added) which is very important in the case of high alumina cement.

Effect of migration test water characteristics Initially, two main characteristics were expected to have a major influence on reactions of cement-based materials in contact with drinking water, namely the alkalinity of the water (carbonate and hydrogen carbonate contents) and the 'aggressivness' of the water (free CO_2 content).

(the arithmetical sum of alkalinity and free CO_2 contents gives the total inorganic carbon, TIC, of the water).

In fact inorganic carbon contained in water can react with the material to form calcium carbonate ($CaCO_3$) on the surface of the material (carbonation), thus closing the pores of the cement matrix. If TIC is not sufficient for that, no carbonation of the surface occurs and migration of some elements (Ca, K) continues or may be increased. Also if the water is aggressive to calcium carbonate, the deposit is not stabilized and continued migration from the material occurs.

Actually the results from the research confirm these expectations but the origin of the test water (natural or synthetic) also has a very important effect on aluminium migration. This effect has been explained by the presence of silica in natural water (see below).

Effect of test water alkalinity. The effect of alkalinity appears obvious for all materials when comparing results for soft migration water (20 ppm $CaCO_3$) and medium mineralized migration water (200 ppm $CaCO_3$). pH increase and aluminium leaching were far more significant with soft water than with medium mineralized water. Calcium concentration always increased (calcium migration from the cement) in soft waters (initial Ca = 8 mg/l) but it decreased or remained unchanged in medium mineralized water (precipitation of $CaCO_3$ or equilibrium).

On the other hand, potassium leaching is not affected by water alkalinity. Final potassium concentration seems to depend mainly on the contact time (it decreases with time in successive contact periods).

Effect of free CO_2 content of test water (aggressiveness). The effects observed were similar for all materials but are more apparent for high alumina cement. Again, no significant effects were observed on potassium leaching. Looking at pH and aluminium concentration it is seen that final values are lower when test waters (soft or medium mineralized) contain more free CO_2 (more 'aggressive' waters). However, starting pHs were also lower in that case and aluminium concentration depends greatly on pH.

When looking at calcium concentrations the effect of water aggressivness is observed as follows:

- in soft water: calcium leaching is higher with aggressive water (1 mmole/l CO_2);

- in medium mineralized water: calcium concentration decreases (below 80 mg/l) with water at equilibrium, indicating $CaCO_3$ precipitation. It decreases less (OPC), remains stable or sometimes increases (BFC, HAC) with aggressive waters.

It must be noted also that CO_2 addition into test water makes the water less stable (CO_2 tends to escape in contact with atmosphere). Using such water may increase scattering of results.

Comparison of natural and synthetic migration waters, effect of silica. First results obtained with OPC have shown important differences in aluminium concentrations in the results obtained by CRECEP and LHRSP on the one hand, Kiwa, TZW and

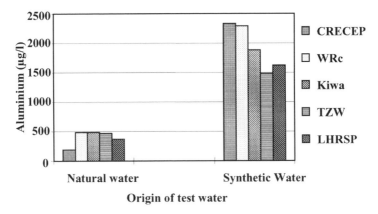

Figure 4.19 Comparison of aluminium concentrations in natural and synthetic, low mineralized migration waters. Results after the third migration, for five laboratories, without preconditioning

WRc on the other. Complementary experiments have been carried out to find out where these differences were coming from (test procedure, laboratories analytical capabilities, test water, etc.).

CRECEP and LHRSP used natural waters because they are more convenient for taste evaluation. Alkalinity of natural waters has been corrected to obtain 20 ppm and 200 ppm $CaCO_3$. The differences were always significant and very large with soft waters, but differences also appeared with medium mineralized waters. Aluminium leaching is lower in natural waters than in synthetic waters.

All laboratories performed experiments on OPC with natural and synthetic waters to ensure that the differences were due to the origin of water. Figure 4.19 shows this actually to be the case, but also that pH is not affected by the origin of the water. The origin of the differences proved to be the silica concentration of natural waters (28.5 mg SiO_2/l in soft water, 13.6 mg SiO_2/l in medium mineralized water).

4.3.4 Reproducibility Tests

In experiments described previously for the three materials, only one sample was tested in each laboratory for each test condition (preconditioning + migration test water). Five replicates in five different laboratories were available for non preconditioned samples and only three replicates for preconditioned samples. Results from the experiments showed that the same tendencies were observed in all laboratories and were generally consistent. However, some differences were also observed and it is difficult to draw conclusions about the reproducibility and repeatability of the test between and within laboratories. To fill this gap, complementary experiments were carried out as described below.

Table 4.16   Characteristics of waters used for experiments

	Preconditioning water	Migration test water
pH	7.4	8.2
Hardness (mg CaCO3/l)	200	20
Alkalinity (mg CaCO3/l)	200	20
Calcium (mg Ca/l)	80	8
Chloride (mg Cl /l)	142	14.2
Sodium (mg Na/l)	92	9.2
Bicarbonates (mg HCO_3/l)	244	24.4

Test procedure

Experiments were performed on HAC mortar samples (applied by spinning on cast iron) in September 1997. Spare samples of the material tested in April/ May 1997 were used for this purpose.

Tests were carried out without preconditioning and with liquid preconditioning in medium mineralized water. Low mineralized synthetic water was used for migration (3×72 hours) in all laboratories. Characteristics of preconditioning and migration test waters are given in Table 4.16.

For both test conditions (with and without preconditioning), each laboratory performed the test on five replicates (at the same time).

Conclusions

Between laboratory reproducibility: All labs observed the same tendencies for all parameters with or without preconditioning. Significant divergences remain between laboratories for most of the parameters tested, and reproducibility was improved by preconditioning.

Within laboratories repeatability: All laboratories obtained comparable repeatability for each parameter, and coefficients of variation were low ($<10\%$) for pH, conductivity and Na. They were higher for Al (20–30 %) Ca (10–20 %) and K (20–50 %). Repeatability was improved or unchanged, depending on the parameter, with preconditioning.

4.3.5   Effect of Preconditioning at Different Ageing Times

One important question about preconditioning is: does it mask / minimize the effects of different ageing times or conditions?

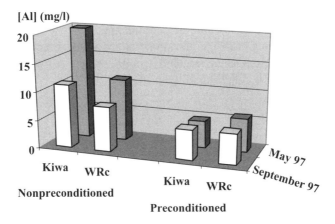

Figure 4.20 Comparison of aluminium concentrations after the third migration in May and September 1997, with and without preconditioning

Figure 4.20 shows aluminium concentrations after the third migration period for the same material (HAC) tested in two laboratories in May 1997 and September 1997 with the same test conditions: liquid preconditioning with medium mineralised water; and low mineralized synthetic migration water at pH 8.

Aluminium concentrations in non-preconditioned samples appeared to be lower in September than in May, and the scattering of results between laboratories was also very important with greater differences in May. For preconditioned samples, differences between the two dates and scattering between laboratories were much lower and all results were in the same range.

These results tend to demonstrate that preconditioning is effective and necessary to minimize the effect of natural uncontrolled ageing, and that liquid preconditioning with medium mineralized water is an efficient means for doing so.

4.3.6 Conclusions

Preconditioning

Preconditioning has a significant effect on the migration behaviour of the material in contact with water. Liquid preconditioning with medium mineralized water and gaseous preconditioning decrease exchanges between the material and water by stabilizing the material.

Liquid preconditioning with low mineralized water increases the exchange between the material and water, and also the range of pH and aluminium concentrations increases during preconditioning. There is no stabilization of the material with such preconditioning water.

Gaseous preconditioning appears to be less practicable and also less representative of the service condition than is liquid preconditioning.

Liquid preconditioning with medium mineralized water at equilibrium proved to be efficient for two important reasons: it improves test reproducibility; and it minimizes the effect of ageing time of the material.

Migration test water

Three parameters; alkalinity, free CO_2 (aggressivity) and silica, were found to have a major influence on the test results:

Soft water was more aggressive to cement-based materials than were medium mineralized waters.. With medium mineralized waters, the surface of the material was quickly carbonated, thus reducing potential exchanges with water.

The addition of CO_2 (aggressive CO_2) to migration test water made it more aggressive, but waters containing free aggressive CO_2 were unstable in contact with the atmosphere. The use of unstable water in the test protocol may result in greater scattering of test results if no precautions are taken to avoid escape of CO_2 during preparation.

The presence of silica in test water has a major effect on aluminium leaching, mainly for soft waters. During their commissioning and service, cement-based materials come into contact with natural waters, which, for most of them, contain dissolved silica.

REFERENCES AND BIBLIOGRAPHY

ANSI/NSF (1997), Standard 61 – 1997b, *Drinking Water System Components – Health Effects*, American National Standards Institute.

AWWA/DVWG-Technologiezentrum Wasser (1996), *Internal Corrosion of Water Distribution Systems*, second edition, AWWA Denver.

Bailey, R.J., Jolly P.K. and Lacey R.F. (1986), Domestic water use patterns, *WRC-report TR 225*.

BS 7766 (1994), *Specification for Assessment of the Potential for Metallic Materials to Affect Adversely the Quality of Water Intended for Human Consumption*, British Standards Institution, London.

Conroy, P.J. and Oliphant, R. (1991), Deterioration of water quality. The effects arising from the use of factory applied cement mortar linings, *WRC Report N DoE* 2723-SW.

DIN (1999), Standard 50931-1 *Corrosion of metals – Corrosion tests with drinking water, Part 1: Testing of change of the composition of drinking water*.

European Commission (2000). Co-normative research on test methods for materials in contact with drinking water, report EUR 19602 EN.

European Consortium (P. Buijs *et al.*) (1998), Developing a new protocol for the monitoring of lead in drinking water, European study.

Franqué, O, Meyer, E. and Sauter, W. (1995), Operation of a test rig to assess the suitability of alloys in different types of water. *Proceedings of International Corrosion Workshop and Seminar*, Internal corrosion in water distribution systems, Chalmers University of Technology, Göteborg.

Kuch, A. (1984), Untersuchungen zum Mechanismus der Aufeisenung in Trinkwasserverteilungssystemen. PhD dissertation, Universität Karlsruhe, Germany.

Kuch, A. and Wagner I. (1983), A mass transfer model to describe lead concentrations in drinking water, *Water Research* **17**, 1303–1307.

Kuch, A., Sontheimer, H. and Wagner, I. (1983), Die Messung der Aufeisenung im Trinkwasser – Ein neues Verfahren zur Beurteilung von Deckschichten in schwarzen Stahlrorhen, *Werkstoffe und Korrosion*, **34**, 107–111.

Meyer, E. (1980). Beeinträchtigung des Trinkwassergüte durch Anlagenteile der Hausinstallation- Bestimmung des Schwermetalleintrags in das Trinkwasser durch Korrosionsvorgänge in metallischen Rohren, *DVGW Schriftenreihe Wasser*, Nr. 23, 113–131.

Meyer, E. (1981), *Gesetzmäßigkeiten des Eintrages von Schwermetallen in Trinkwasser*. Schiftenreihe Verein Wa Bo Lu 52, 9–10, Gustav Fischer Verlag, Stuttgart.

Oliphant, R.J. (1992), Effectiveness of water treatments in preventing contamination from a leaded brass, *Foundation for Water Research Report FR0338.*

Sauter, W. (1995), *Bewertung des Betriebes einer Versuchsanlage zum Vergleich den Metallabgabe von Installationwerkstoffen. Abschlussarbeit im Weiterbildenden Studium Korrosionsschutztechnik*, Märkische Fachhochschule, Iserlohn.

Sauter, W., Meyer E. and Franqué, O. (1996), *Beurteilung von Armaturenwerkstoffen auf ihre Eignung im Trinkwasserbereich*, SHT 61, 10, S 97–100, 105.

Van den Hoven, Th. J.J, and van Eekeren M.W.M. (1988), *Optimal Composition on Drinking Water, Kiwa-report 100*, Nieuwegein.

Van den Hoven, Th. J.J, Baggelaar P.K. and Ekkers G.F. (1990), *Koperafgifte door drinkwaterleidingen, Kiwa-report 111*, Nieuwegein.

Wagner, I. (1992), Internal corrosion in domestic drinking water installations, *Journal Water SRT – Aqua* **41**, 219–223.

Werner, W. (1992), Untersuchungen zum Mechanismus der Flächenkorrosion in Trinkwasserleitungen aus Kupfer, PhD dissertation, Universität Karlsruhe, Germany.

Werner, W. *et al.* (1994), Untersuchungen zur Flächenkorrosion in Trinkwasserleitungen aus Kupfer, *Wasser, Abwasser* **135**, 92–103.

WHO (1998), *Guidelines for Drinking Water Quality*, Second edition, Volume 1, *Recommendations*, World Health Organization, Geneva.

Index

Note: Page numbers in **bold** refer to tables and those in *italics* refer to figures.

Analytical Methods for Drinking Water Edited by P. Quevauviller and K. C. Thompson
© 2006 John Wiley & Sons, Ltd.

With thanks to Geraldine Begley for creation of this index.

RECEIVED

MAR - 7 2006

ENGINEERING LIBRARY